Tarquin scrambled to avoid being knocked aside as Naira stormed out of her room.

The ships blowing up early should have held his full attention, but he couldn't put the haunted look he'd seen on her face out of his mind. He forced himself not to press her further. She didn't want to share her private hurts with him. He knew that.

"Tell me we're out of the blast radius," she said as she ran into the cockpit.

"We're clear," Kav shouted over his shoulder.

Kav had a news feed pulled up on the largest console. Footage of the explosion was being played from multiple angles while a reporter explained that the cause was still being investigated. Naira skidded to a stop behind the copilot's podium and braced herself against it, staring down that footage like she could wind it back, make it untrue.

The explosion had been larger than they'd planned. It'd taken out not just the ships and the hangar, but the construction infrastructure in orbit around the hangar. Places where people lived.

Had lived.

T0383975

Praise for Megan E. O'Keefe and
the Protectorate Series

"O'Keefe delivers a complicated, thoughtful tale that skillfully interweaves intrigue, action, and strong characterization. Themes of found family, emotional connection, and identity run throughout, backed up by strong worldbuilding and a tense narrative. This series opener leaves multiple plot threads open for further development, and readers will look forward to the next installments."　　　　—*Publishers Weekly*

"Meticulously plotted, edge-of-your-seat space opera with a soul; a highly promising science-fiction debut."　　　　—*Kirkus*

"A brilliantly plotted yarn of survival and far-future political intrigue."
—*Guardian*

"This is a sweeping space opera with scope and vision, tremendously readable. I look forward to seeing where O'Keefe takes this story next."
—*Locus*

"Outstanding space opera where the politics and worldbuilding of the Expanse series meets the forward-thinking AI elements of *Ancillary Justice*."　　　　—Michael Mammay, author of *Planetside*

"*Velocity Weapon* is a spectacular epic of survival, full of triumph and gut-wrenching loss."   —Alex White, author of the Salvagers series

"*Velocity Weapon* is a roller-coaster ride of pure delight. Furious action sequences, funny dialogue, and touching family interactions all wrapped up in a plot that will keep you guessing every step of the way. This is one of the best science fiction novels of 2019."

—K. B. Wagers, author of the Indranan War trilogy

"*Velocity Weapon* is fast-paced, twisty, edge-of-your-seat fun. Space opera fans are in for a massive treat!"

—Marina J. Lostetter, author of *Noumenon*

By Megan E. O'Keefe

THE DEVOURED WORLDS

The Blighted Stars

The Fractured Dark

THE PROTECTORATE

Velocity Weapon

Chaos Vector

Catalyst Gate

The First Omega (novella)

THE
FRACTURED
DARK

BOOK TWO OF THE DEVOURED WORLDS

MEGAN E.
O'KEEFE

orbitbooks.net

Copyright © 2023 by Megan E. O'Keefe
Excerpt from *Book Three of The Devoured Worlds* copyright © 2023 by Megan E. O'Keefe
Excerpt from *The Stars Undying* copyright © 2022 by Emery Robin

Cover design by Lauren Panepinto
Cover illustration by Jaime Jones
Cover copyright © 2023 by Hachette Book Group, Inc.
Author photograph by Joey Hewitt

Orbit
Hachette Book Group
1290 Avenue of the Americas
New York, NY 10104
orbitbooks.net

First Edition: September 2023
Simultaneously published in Great Britain by Orbit

Orbit is an imprint of Hachette Book Group.
The Orbit name and logo are trademarks of Little, Brown Book Group Limited.

The publisher is not responsible for websites (or their content) that are not owned by the publisher.

The Hachette Speakers Bureau provides a wide range of authors for speaking events. To find out more, go to hachettespeakersbureau.com or email HachetteSpeakers@hbgusa.com.

Orbit books may be purchased in bulk for business, educational, or promotional use. For information, please contact your local bookseller or the Hachette Book Group Special Markets Department at special.markets@hbgusa.com.

Library of Congress Cataloging-in-Publication Data
Names: O'Keefe, Megan E., 1985– author.
Title: The fractured dark / Megan E. O'Keefe.
Description: First Edition. | New York, NY : Orbit, 2023. | Series: The Devoured Worlds ; book 2
Identifiers: LCCN 2023002285 | ISBN 9780316291132 (trade paperback) | ISBN 9780316291347 (ebook)
Subjects: LCGFT: Science fiction. | Novels.
Classification: LCC PS3615.K437 F73 2023 | DDC 813/.6—dc23/eng/20230123
LC record available at https://lccn.loc.gov/2023002285

ISBNs: 9780316291132 (trade paperback), 9780316291347 (ebook)

Printed in the United States of America

LSC-C

Printing 2, 2024

For Sam Morgan.
Thank you, friend.

ONE

Naira

Mercator Hangar Bay | The Present

Naira had never infiltrated a spaceship while in her own body before, and she found the experience far too perilous for her liking. It was much less nerve-racking to drop her neural map into the print of someone who was supposed to be on the ship. She was used to blending. To subtle manipulations.

There was no subtlety in her boots ringing out against the engine bay's wire-grid floor. No finesse in the explosive devices tucked into the bag slung across her back.

Trepidation crawled up her neck and prickled her scalp. The mining ship set to launch to Seventh Cradle next week was deathly silent. It should have been bustling with techs doing their final checks before the ship would shove off for one of the precious planets where the ecosystem had yet to succumb to planetary collapse syndrome. Instead, its lights were pushed down to power-saving mode and the hangar was empty of personnel.

Naira could hardly believe it when she'd first seen the empty hangars on Kav's hacked security-camera feeds. She still couldn't quite believe it.

The security system accepted Naira's false credentials without so much as a hiccup. She paused in front of the warpcore containment, letting her gaze trail up the fine bones of emerald-green relkatite that caged the core, and wondered.

This was a rush job. Acaelus Mercator had raised the specter of the Conservators to the public eye as a threat to all mining missions. He'd claimed that the lack of relk on Sixth Cradle had been the fault of the Conservators. That they'd gotten there ahead of Mercator and brought the shroud to collapse the planet as they mined all the relk from the skin of that world and kept it for themselves.

And so the heads of MERIT had rallied. They'd joined their resources, frantically building two ships to launch to Seventh and Eighth Cradles to preserve those planets' stores of relkatite against the Conservators, never understanding that their impulses were being manipulated. Never knowing that the fungus they used to mine that mineral, *Mercatus canus*, had bonded with the pathways in their bodies, using them to transform humanity into little more than an extended search network for more relkatite, which was *canus*'s preferred food.

Rushing the ships didn't account for the sloppy seams in the walls, the pitting in the relkatite containment, or the rust staining the joints in the metal fittings. Naira gave the irritatingly handsome man next to her, Tarquin Mercator, a side-eyed glance.

"Does this feel off to you?" she asked.

The younger child of Acaelus crossed his arms, staring at the warp-core as if it were keeping secrets from him. Tarquin affected a slouch, reducing his towering height to something less imposing, but there was no slouching away the nose he'd intentionally inherited from his father, the green flecks in his hazel eyes, or the Mercator family crest printed around his wrists to curl in vine-like knotwork over the backs of his hands. He tugged on the sharp ridge of his chin, frowning.

Naira looked away from him as an unwelcome warmth stirred within her. She'd been told that on Sixth Cradle she'd cared for him, but she'd died before backing up those memories, and looking at him now . . . He was an empty ache in her chest, a man-sized hole in her past she didn't know how to approach. Best to focus on his usefulness—rebellious Mercator, renowned geologist—than on how he made her feel.

Best to ignore the way his hair slipped over his temple, adding a pensive, deep shadow to the angle of his cheek.

"It does seem unusual," he said, oblivious to her silent study of him. She'd found that he was oblivious to most things when lost in thought. "While my father's motives are misguided, he wouldn't let a ship of such import fall into disrepair. And the lack of security?" He gestured to the surrounding room. "It makes no sense."

"It makes sense if it's a trap," she said.

His hand dropped to the pistol strapped to his side, slipping through the cover of his open dark brown jacket. Naira smiled to herself at the motion. Tarquin had been taught basic self-defense and weapons, but it was she who'd trained to be an exemplar—the bodyguards of all MERIT families. She found it cute, like a puppy carrying a too-large stick, that he thought he'd be useful if a fight broke out.

"If it's a trap, it's a poor one," he said. "We haven't seen a soul since we entered the hangar, and I can't imagine Father would let us get this close to the warpcore if he meant to capture us before we could harm the ship."

"Which means he's got something else up his sleeve."

Naira brought up her internal HUD and put a call through to Kav, who was, if things were going well, busy infiltrating the other mining ship in the hangar.

He picked up immediately. "You getting the feeling we're at the wrong address?"

"I am." She looped Tarquin and Kuma into the call. "Power-saving lighting, rust in the seams, and cracks in the wall paint. Not a soul to check things over or raise the alarm."

"It's quiet," Kuma said, "too—"

"Don't you dare finish that." Naira was glad Kuma couldn't see her smirk.

"Fine." Kuma huffed dramatically. "I don't like this. Feels like a setup."

"If it is, it's a fuckin' weird one," Kav said.

"We were just having the same conversation," Naira said.

"I don't understand his motivation," Tarquin said, half to himself, as he examined the warpcore. Naira fell silent, and so did the others, letting him talk it out. "*Canus* is pushing him to secure the relkatite in the other two cradles. That makes sense. It wants to get ahead of us..." He avoided saying that it wanted to get ahead of his mother, too, as she was hell-bent on infecting the cradles with shroud lichen to keep *canus* from thriving on those worlds. "I understand that. I can even see a decoy ship—it gives us something else to attack as a distraction—but this...These are working ships. They have warpcores and relkatite containments and probably relkatite wiring, too. It's a waste. *Canus* wouldn't let him waste relkatite."

"Maybe he's not quite that controlled yet," Naira said.

"Maybe," Tarquin said without conviction.

"Regardless of the old man's motives," Kav said, "we're here. We've got the bombs. Might as well take care of these so he doesn't retrofit them later for future mining expeditions."

"A woman in possession of a bomb is in want of a reason to use it," Naira said.

"Oh, god help us, she's been reading old shit again, hasn't she?" Kuma said.

"Hanging up now," Naira said. "Call me if anything blows up that's not supposed to."

She hung up before Kav could get out more than a mangled *but*. Naira sensed eyes on her, and half turned to arch a brow at Tarquin.

"What?"

"*Pride and Prejudice*?" He grinned sheepishly and brushed the hair off his forehead. "I knew you read nonfiction, but somehow fiction doesn't fit in with all the...shooting. And bombing."

She adjusted the strap across her chest and looked at the warpcore instead of him. "Exemplars end up with a lot of downtime between shifts. There's only so much review of combat theory one person can take, and Mercator had a—well, you know—big digital library."

"Yeah. That was at my grandparent Ettai's insistence. They loved Austen."

"Fascinating. Really not the time for book club."

"You started it," he said with a laugh that made the tension in her shoulders ratchet up.

"Are you stalling, Mercator?" she shot back, and regretted it as his laugh dwindled away. He'd been teasing her good-naturedly, but she'd gone for the throat because every time he did that, she wanted to tease back, and that led to flirting, and that wasn't a door she was sure she should open. The crestfallen look he gave her stung but made it easier for her to breathe.

She really should have sent him with Kuma and brought Kav with her instead. Somehow she kept pulling him along beside her, and she couldn't seem to stop.

"No, of course not," he said. "Tell me what to do."

Naira swung the bag around so that it rested against her stomach, and tugged the zipper open, revealing six explosive devices about the length and width of her forearm. Tarquin had a matching set of bombs in his own bag. Twelve spines of relkatite made up the cage bars enclosing the warpcore. They needed to blow only one rib to break containment, but fail-safes were a must. And who could say no to more bombs? Naira pulled one out and flipped it over in her hand.

"The back has an adhesive strip that activates with pressure." She approached the first rib. "You want to press it against the rib down low, as close to the ground as you can so that it's out of sight."

Naira crouched beside the warpcore, ignoring the tingle that rushed over her skin at close proximity to all cores. Sometimes, she thought she heard them whispering to her when she got this close. Not words, never anything like that, but murmurs. Sound waves of unknown origins reaching to her across impossible distances. It always made her shiver.

"Here." She lined up the device but didn't press it yet. "You do it."

Tarquin hesitated, hands in his pockets. His reluctance had nothing to do with proximity to the warpcore, though he'd told her that he, like many others, experienced the same tingling sensation near cores. No, his hesitance was about the fact that they'd been dancing around each other for months, both of them avoiding being too physically close to each other.

"Are you certain you want me doing this?" He took a knee on the opposite side of the relkatite support, as distant from her as he could get and still reach the device.

"You're going to have to do your six on your own. I'm not holding your hand forever, Mercator."

He took the device from her cautiously, careful not to brush his hand against hers. It left him holding it awkwardly at the top, the balance off. She didn't comment.

"Here?" He lined it up so that the bottom almost touched the floor. She nodded. He licked his lips, and she looked away. The device connected to the relkatite rib with a squishing noise as the adhesive activated. "I think that's it."

Naira turned in time to see him pull back. His hand was too high up, near the arming switch. He was about to brush it. Her pathways vibrated, granting her the speed she needed to grab his wrist, and she yanked him clear.

But she'd been having trouble adjusting to her print, and her arm was longer than expected. She over-pulled, and he slipped. Naira's exemplar instincts took over. She dove for him and caught his head in her hand before it could hit the floor.

They froze, tangled, staring at each other. His pulse thundered through the wrist she held, his hair smooth between her fingers. Panic crawled across his face, pupils dilating. He tried to stuff the panic under a mask of indifference that didn't quite fit.

"I..." He cleared a rough catch in his throat. "I'm guessing that was wrong?"

Naira chuckled shakily and let him go. He scrambled back a step and rubbed his wrist, looking anywhere but at her. The silken touch of his hair was a phantom against her skin.

"The position was right, but you almost bumped the arming switch."

"I had no idea..." He trailed off and pointed his chin at the plastic casing over the red switch. "That?"

"Yes, that." She rocked to her heels and watched him, crossing her arms over her knees. "Because you held the bomb in an awkward spot. Because you were trying to avoid touching me."

He said nothing. Just kept rubbing his wrist where she'd grabbed him as if it hurt, when she knew damn well it didn't.

"Mercator. Look at me."

Tarquin flinched, then found the steel in his spine he could summon when hard-pressed. He forced himself to face her.

"We can't keep—" She cut herself off and tried a different angle, making it about the work, not them. "This can't affect our work."

"I'm sorry," he said. "Though I know being sorry is inadequate."

"I'm not her."

"I understand that. I mourn her, and it hurts, and I will make mistakes sometimes, but I ask for your patience."

"You already have it." She forced a smile to hide the spike of empathetic pain that pierced the hard shell of her exterior. That's all it was. Empathy. Tarquin was a nice enough guy, and she could see how some other version of herself might have gotten close to him—though she was unclear on the details and wanted to keep it that way.

He was precisely her type, but in Naira's experience, "her type" also included a slow revelation that the person in question was, in fact, a raging asshole under a kind facade. While she didn't think Tarquin was likely to have a mean streak, well. He *was* a Mercator.

"Thank you." Though sadness tinged his smile, it was genuine.

She stood and held a hand down to him. He eyed it like it was a naked blade. "Come on. Let's set the other bombs and get out of here."

He teetered on a precipice, watching that hand, and she waited while he worked out for himself if it was wise to accept such casual physical contact. She wasn't so sure herself. Every time he was near, her stomach swooped. Every time he laughed, she caught herself smiling.

He sighed, slowly, and slapped his hand into hers. Naira yanked him to his feet and released him before stepping aside. The hand she'd touched flexed by his side, as if he were subconsciously trying to claw back the pressure of their skin together.

"So, I'm not supposed to touch the big red button?" he asked.

She turned her smile away from him. "That's our last-ditch effort if we're caught, but I don't think that'll be a problem here. Get them placed, then we'll blow them from the shuttle at a safe distance."

"I can do that."

If he moved away from her too eagerly, she pretended not to notice. They finished up and soon were heading back to the shuttle.

"Have you had to use the triggers before?" Tarquin asked. "I mean, have you had to blow yourself up with the devices before you could get away?"

"Yes," she said. Tarquin's boot scuffed. "Not those devices specifically, but I've blown a ship with myself inside. Something went wrong on the mission to Fourth Cradle, on the *Abacaxi*. We had to detonate ahead of schedule. Kuma and Kav were out already, so Jonsun and I triggered the warpcore containment failure with us inside. They told us all about it when we reprinted."

He glanced back at the hulking shape of the mining ship. "I knew those ships had blown up. I didn't realize you were inside at the time."

"Hazards of the job." She shrugged. "I can't count how many times I died in Acaelus's defense, before. At least blowing up is instant."

Tarquin fell silent, no doubt dwelling on how often she'd risked cracking her neural map to keep his father from the same risk. His sympathy chafed, but it was well-meaning enough, so she let him sit with the facts she'd already accepted.

Or told herself she'd accepted. She was still breaking into hangars and planting bombs on Acaelus's property. Most of that was about stopping the spread of *canus* and the shroud. But a petty part of it was about revenge, too.

Maybe a larger part than she cared to admit.

"There're our slowpokes," Kuma called out from their ship's open airlock. The ex-Ichikawa security captain filled the doorway, bracing herself against the frame to hover over them. She'd already stripped off her outer armor. Kuma didn't like to keep the muscle of her arms hidden if she could help it, and her pathways gleamed gold against her skin. "Thought you got lost. Or stopped to espouse some ancient poetry."

"Don't give me a hard time for having more than rocks rattling around in my head." Naira play-punched at Kuma's stomach, making the stronger woman duck aside and mock-protect her middle.

Kuma pointed a short finger at Tarquin. "He's the one with rocks for brains."

"Rocks *and* minerals, I'll have you know." Tarquin put on an indignant air, but his faint smirk gave him away.

"Black skies, was that a joke? Hey, Kav, the Mercator's got jokes!" Kuma cupped a hand around her mouth as she shouted into the cockpit.

"Somebody has to," Kav called back, "because you sure as shit don't."

Naira ignored their good-natured bickering, instead focusing on stripping off her outer armor and stowing her equipment bag in the locker with her name scrawled across it in black marker. Tarquin slipped up alongside her to strip out of the light armor he'd worn beneath his jacket, the dusty scent of his sweat not unpleasant. Not for the first time, Naira silently cursed Kuma for sticking their lockers next to each other.

Kuma hauled the gangway up and shut the airlock, then gave the door a meaty thump with the side of her fist and called out the all clear. Naira made her way into the cockpit. She climbed into the copilot's seat and accidentally kicked Kav as she tried to stretch her legs out around the console podium.

"Ugh." Kav pulled his foot away.

"Sorry. Still a little clumsy in this body."

"Yeah, I noticed, and Kuma said you dumped coffee all over the counter this morning. It's been months, and that's your preferred print. You should be settled in by now. Have you done the physical therapy?"

"Yes, *Mom*."

"Fine. Keep bumping into walls. Look, Nai—" Kav's voice had started out soft, but he cut himself off as Tarquin's footsteps approached. "What took you so long, anyway? Everything go to plan?" he said in his normal voice.

She gave him a sideways glance, but his attention was fixed on his console as he powered the engines back up.

"I conducted a quick training session on placement," she said. "Everything was as quiet for us as it was for you."

"Yeah right, you two were probably making out."

Naira winced, half listening to Tarquin's muttered excuses as he spun around and marched out of the cockpit twice as quickly as he'd walked in.

"Was that really necessary?" she asked, when his steps had receded.

"Sorry, dirty trick." Kav switched the ship over to autopilot as it lifted off from the hangar floor and let itself out through the barrel-shaped airlock they'd come in through. "But the guy doesn't take a hint easily, and I needed to talk to you without him hanging around."

"He doesn't hang around." Her tone was more defensive than she would have liked. "What's so secretive one of our active members can't overhear it?"

"It's about Jonsun."

All her annoyance drained away in a flash. There weren't a lot of ways to die for good, when you could upload your mind into a new print as long as you could afford to do so. People left the living world when their money ran out or when their neural maps cracked.

Jonsun, their old leader, had cracked.

Neural maps were never perfect. They degraded over time, artifacting whittling them away until one upload too many finally stressed the map to its breaking point. Most people couldn't afford enough reprintings to reach that point. Violent deaths accelerated the process. The more traumatic the end, the more likely a map was to crack.

Double-printing was the worst way to go, and that was what had taken Jonsun.

A mind existed in superposition, and uploading it into a single print collapsed the waveform, anchoring it to one spot in time and space, and one spot alone. When a mind was uploaded into a second print, the outcome was catastrophic.

The mind didn't know where it was supposed to exist. Some fell into an endless scream. Some got stuck in the repetitive cadence typical of the double-printed, as if they couldn't be sure which mouth had said the word they meant to, so they said it again and again.

According to Tarquin, Naira had spoken with Jonsun in his cracked state while Jonsun was on the *Einkorn* in orbit over Sixth Cradle. She hadn't fully believed that Jonsun had cracked—she hadn't wanted to—until she'd watched a video sent back by the *Einkorn*, the security footage of her last moments on that ship.

"Well?" she asked.

"He sent something through so many relays it didn't show up until this morning. It took me a while to realize what it was, but it's...Look, it was on a deadman's switch. I only saw the first couple of seconds because I had to check it out, but it's for you. It's private."

"I see."

"Yeah. I forwarded it to your files."

"Thanks. Call me when we're in detonation range?"

"You know I will."

She felt strangely detached as she gave him a perfunctory pat on the shoulder and exited the cockpit. Kuma was regaling Tarquin with some story about one of her many fistfights. Tarquin shot Naira a help-me glance, but she waved him off, disappearing into the ship's halls to seek her room.

Their ship had been listed as a shuttle before Tarquin stole it from Mercator Station, but a Mercator shuttle was a passenger ship for anyone else. It was roomy enough that they had private bedrooms with a few to spare.

She had a narrow bed, a trunk for her belongings, a bathroom attached, and a desk. It was the second-largest space she'd ever called her own. Plenty of room to move around.

Plenty of room to pace a hole in the ground before she finally worked up the nerve to sit on the edge of her bed and press play.

Jonsun's face floated up out of a holo projection from her forearm. Dark trenches had sunken beneath his eyes, and his golden hair was matted down on one side, but he smiled into the recording, a brief flash that lit up his face.

"Hey, Nai," he said in that slow drawl she knew so well. The smile had gone. Sorrow suffused every pore. "I don't know why I'm doing this. You're not even..." He rubbed his temples. "This is the night before we cast to the *Amaranth* and the *Einkorn*. I used to...I make this video for you every time we do this, in case I'm the one who doesn't come back. But now...Now you're on ice, and I'm talking to a ghost, aren't I?"

Naira couldn't breathe. He brushed a tear off his cheek angrily, then stared down at the camera. "I'm sorry. I'm so fucking sorry. If I don't come back and by some miracle Kav gets you off ice after all, I need you to know that. I should have pulled the plug on the *Cavendish*. Things were strange from the jump about that mission, but we were hyped up on the success of the previous mission. Kav was sure he could get us in safely, and I guess he did. I guess Acaelus wanted us to get in, though, didn't he?

"I don't know if we should even try for the *Amaranth* and *Einkorn* without you. When I took over the Conservators, I'd never dreamed... never dared to hope we'd someday have someone like you. But I fucked it up, didn't I? I insisted we cast to the *Cavendish* when you were wary, and I should have listened, and I think...I think I'm about to do it again.

"This mission, it doesn't feel right. And I don't know why I'm telling your ghost this—maybe because I can't tell anyone else—but I won't pull the plug. We're going. We have to stop this, stop the shroud from spreading. I'd like to tell myself I'm doing this because it's what you would have wanted, but I don't know anymore. I wish I could ask you. Wish I could see you again.

"But if you're watching this, then you're back and I'm not. The others have probably defaulted to your leadership by now. Skies know Kuma and Kav don't want to lead, and Jessel doesn't have the fight in them. Not anymore. But I want you to know that it's yours. I want the Conservators to be yours.

"We struggled for years to undermine MERIT before you came to us. We always talked about bigger hits, about doing more to stop MERIT from damaging the worlds, but I had so much doubt I didn't dare express. So much fear that we weren't doing the right thing. That we couldn't be sure. Then you came along and gave us the strength with which to strike."

Jonsun scratched at a pathway on his cheek. "But I doubt. I can't help it. These hits we do, they're leaving people on ice. We're giving Mercator a monster to point at, to rally against. Maybe we've gone too far, you know?" He laughed roughly. "Stupid, right? But sometimes I think... Well. Sometimes the doubts are stronger. But in the end, it's hatred for the shroud that pulls me through. The shroud has to be stopped.

"You don't doubt, do you, Nai? You showed up on our doorstep with a fire in your heart in need of something to consume, and you never stopped burning. I... admired you for that. So, if you're listening to this, I'm sorry. I'm sorry for getting you caught on the *Cavendish*. I'm sorry for whatever damn fool thing I did that got me dead for good, and I'm sorry the movement is yours to carry now, because I know how heavy it weighs.

"I don't want to give you advice. You're more than capable. But, Nai, if you, of all people, if you ever start to doubt. You dig. You lean into that feeling and you excavate it until you understand it. Because I think... I think something's very wrong, and I can't quite see what it is. Maybe you can. I believe you can.

"Goodbye, Naira Sharp. Carry your fire a little longer, eh? For me?"

He smiled sadly and ended the video.

Naira stared at the space above her arm where his face had hovered, numb with shock. He'd known. He hadn't figured out the truth, that was buried too deep, but he'd noticed the incongruence within himself. Had realized that some motivations didn't quite line up with what they should be.

Jonsun had been onto *canus*. But in the end, *canus* wanted the shroud destroyed, and that's what had mattered to Jonsun above all else.

A light knock startled her. The door slipped open. Tarquin stood there, his genial smile frozen into something unnatural as he read the horror on her face.

"Are you all right?" He stepped toward her. Stopped himself.

"What do you want?" she snapped.

"Uh..." He pushed hair behind his ear. "The ships have blown up."

"What?" She burst to her feet. "I told Kav to call me when we were in range."

"Whatever blew up those ships, it wasn't us. It's all over the news and you'd...you'd better come see."

TWO

Tarquin

The Conservator's Ship | The Present

Tarquin scrambled to avoid being knocked aside as Naira stormed out of her room. The ships blowing up early should have held his full attention, but he couldn't put the haunted look he'd seen on her face out of his mind. He forced himself not to press her further. She didn't want to share her private hurts with him. He knew that.

"Tell me we're out of the blast radius," she said as she ran into the cockpit.

"We're clear," Kav shouted over his shoulder.

Kav had a news feed pulled up on the largest console. Footage of the explosion was being played from multiple angles while a reporter explained that the cause was still being investigated. Naira skidded to a stop behind the copilot's podium and braced herself against it, staring down that footage like she could wind it back, make it untrue.

The explosion had been larger than they'd planned. It'd taken out not just the ships and the hangar, but the construction infrastructure in orbit around the hangar. Places where people lived.

Had lived.

"What the fuck?" she asked no one in particular.

Kav had started shaking his head the moment the news came through and he hadn't stopped. He dug through window after window in search of information that, more than likely, didn't exist.

"We ran those numbers a hundred times." Frustration made Kav's voice taut. "Our charges were only large enough to break the containment. By law, the construction platforms should have been outside the damage zone for a warpcore breach."

"It wasn't us," Kuma said. "No way was that us."

Naira muttered curses under her breath and started pulling up windows from the console in front of her. "Mercator, get me numbers on the lives on those platforms. I want to know the biological damage, see if we can get phoenix fees to those families quietly."

"Right away."

Through the haze of green holos all around them, the news footage shifted to the interior of the hangar before the explosion. In that footage, Naira walked across the room, her empty bag slung over her back. It irked Tarquin that he'd been edited out. She walked alone.

Though they'd been talking amicably, her expression in the footage was hard. Frightening in its coldness, really. Tarquin had only seen that look a few times, and almost always, it was right before she was about to pull a trigger. Mercator techs must have altered her face to frighten the public.

"Turn that up," Naira said.

Kav shoved his programs aside, then expanded the news report and cranked up the volume.

"...The Conservator was believed to have had her map locked after being apprehended during the bombing of the *Cavendish*, but footage leaked to us captured her making her escape in the moments before the hangar's destruction," the news anchor said.

"It's possible," the anchor's cohost said, "that another Conservator is wearing Ex. Sharp's print to add to the confusion and terror."

"Always a possibility," the first anchor said with a scowl that indicated she was annoyed her colleague had undermined her attempt to frighten people by reporting on the escape of a terrorist.

"Why'd they edit Tarquin out?" Kuma asked.

"Acaelus is still denying Tarquin had anything to do with the destruction of Mercator Station," Kav said. "So he probably fed them this video and cut out his kid."

Tarquin scoffed. "He can't keep it up forever. Sooner or later the other MERIT members are going to get suspicious as to why I'm missing."

"Numbers," Naira said.

"Right. Sorry."

Tarquin dug into the construction personnel records while the others bounced ideas back and forth about what to do next. He couldn't focus on what they were saying, because he didn't like the shape of the information he was finding. Construction on a project as large as a mining ship was public knowledge. There weren't many people with the skills required to build those ships, and all of them were MERIT-cuffed. Most of them were cuffed for Mercator.

All of those people should have been on the roster, but he didn't see a single name he recognized. Frowning, he picked the name of an engineer he'd known from his time at Jov-U, someone he was certain would have been on that list. They'd been assigned somewhere else.

"Mercator," Naira said.

Tarquin assumed she was talking about his family and kept digging. He checked a few more well-known engineers. None of them were near the mining ships.

"Tarquin," Naira said firmly.

He blinked away the stream of names and met her stare. He'd been about to tell her what he'd found, but her face was grave. Concerned. They were all staring at him with that same worried expression. He looked past them, to the news report, and had to clutch the console podium to keep from dropping to his knees.

Acaelus stood in the center of the frame. Tarquin's family—all of them—his mother and sister and even himself, flanked Acaelus a few steps behind. His father's face was serious, hands folded neatly in front of his body and his head slightly bowed in somber acknowledgment of the loss of the ships. Behind Acaelus was an expansive command deck.

"Citizens of MERIT and the Collective," Acaelus said in his deepest oration voice, "we have just learned of the wanton destruction of the mining ships *Ansault* and *Gros Michel*. While their loss saddens us, we are unsurprised."

"I don't recognize the ship he's on," Naira said. "Kav, trace this."

"On it."

Tarquin's skin prickled as Acaelus looked directly into the camera. His father's use of the pronoun *we* rang alarm bells in his mind.

"Myself," Acaelus continued, "and my peers in MERIT foresaw this attack. We committed only the resources absolutely necessary to make those two ships look convincing to the terrorists who lurk among us. In secret, we endeavored to build another ship. A faster, state-of-the-art vessel designed to reach the cradle worlds ahead of our detractors and mine them of relkatite before that precious resource could be stolen from us."

Acaelus half turned, gesturing to the empty command deck behind him. His family stood alone—no crew, no staff.

"This is the *Sigillaria*. Rest assured that the combined forces of MERIT have crafted a ship of unparalleled security. This vessel will not fall to the whims of terrorists. The work of those we lost on the construction platform will not be in vain. But, until more relkatite is secured, they will not be reprinted. The loss of the original Mercator Station showed us all that our systems are more fragile than we ever imagined. That our very species relies on our ability to secure more relkatite."

"He's going to ice his dead contractors and blame it on us," Kuma growled. Naira shushed her. Acaelus kept talking.

"To this end, I hope my colleagues in MERIT will forgive me. The *Sigillaria* was supposed to be a union of us all, staffed by every single one of us, to launch once the ashes of the Conservator's assault settled. But I, more than any of my colleagues, know the workings of Ex. Sharp's mind. I understood that if we could not capture her in that hangar, then she would discover our deceit and come for the *Sigillaria*.

"And so I launched this ship three months ago."

Kav and Kuma swore, immediately tossing ideas back and forth. Naira stayed silent, watching as Acaelus signed off the message and gave a brief, somber salute to all of humanity before ending the feed.

Tarquin should have seen it. Taking that ship away from the other members of MERIT was tantamount to war, but the Conservators had already pushed Acaelus to the brink when they'd destroyed Mercator Station, undermining his resources in a way that made his position with the other families tenuous.

Maybe Ichikawa had pushed harder into mining. Maybe Tran had gotten the idea that, since they controlled the shroud sanitization tech, they should take the lead in relk mining. Probably both of those things were true, and more. The heads of MERIT had smelled blood in the water when Mercator Station fell, but Acaelus had outmaneuvered them all.

Dominating Tarquin's thoughts was the possibility that Acaelus hadn't arrived at his plan alone. His use of *we* was unusual enough to scrape against Tarquin's senses, the body doubles arranged behind him like some sick family portrait impossible to ignore.

Tarquin's father was ruthless and clever and cruel, and the Acaelus he had seen in that footage was all of those things, but he'd also been... haunted. Tarquin had never seen his father with bags under his eyes before.

"Do you have the trace?" Naira spoke for the first time into the back-and-forth between Kav and Kuma.

"Yeah." Kav wrinkled his nose as he leaned closer to the console. "But it's not... I'm not confident in it, Nai. I've got a transponder tag, but Acaelus was clear that he launched early to avoid us getting near it. That means he's got some nasty security on that ship."

"We've gotten around his security when he knew we were coming before," Kuma said.

"He let us through so he could use us." Kav shook his head. "I don't like it. If we get through again, there's going to be a reason, and it won't be because I'm so good at this. He's gotta know we'd be tempted to try, so he has to have some sort of contingency in place."

"That was Canden Mercator on that ship," Naira said. "She may not want *canus* to take us over, but she's the source of the shroud. We can't let her reach those worlds before us."

"If that's even her," Tarquin said, surprised by the sound of his own voice. Everyone was making painstaking work of not looking at him. "You forget, that was... that was *me* on that ship, too, and I am unquestionably not in that print. We can't assume that is the real Canden Mercator."

"Either way, that ship has to burn," Naira said.

"On that, I think we're all in agreement." Kuma punched a fist into her open palm. Tarquin smiled at that. If only things could be as easy as letting Kuma loose to punch everyone involved.

"We can't catch that ship in this shuttle," Kav said. "Even if we had a ship with a full-sized warpcore, it would be a stretch to catch his coattails, let alone get ahead of him."

"Which is why he let us destroy the other two ships," Naira said. "Not just to frame us for killing those people, but to keep anyone in Sol from getting their hands on a ship that stood a chance of catching him. Those were the only known ships with full-sized cores in the system. That's why we targeted them in the first place."

"One of the other families has to have something," Kav said. "There's no way those greedy dicks would let Acaelus monopolize ships of that size. They've got to be hiding one somewhere. We find it, we pirate it."

"There isn't another ship," Tarquin said. "Mercator controls relkatite distribution. We allow the other families to buy enough to keep printing their people, that's all. We build the ships. The stations. Even if they were stockpiling relk at the expense of reprinting their people, they don't have the talent in their families to get the work done."

Silence.

"Then we cast," Naira said.

Tarquin waited for the rebuke. For Kav or Kuma to tell her the plan would never work, it was suicide—maybe worse, depending on what Acaelus had up his sleeve.

The silence stretched on.

"Absolutely not," Tarquin said. "Acaelus has been able to prepare for you in ways we can't imagine. We can't even be certain if all of his actions are his own. We already closed the jaws of one of his traps around us. We can't afford to throw ourselves into this one, too."

"This is the job," Naira said.

Tarquin watched her carefully, knowing she was lying. He couldn't see her full face, she was still looking at Kav's console, but he saw her jaw flex, her fingers curl in anticipation of a physical fight that wasn't coming.

She didn't remember telling him the truth on Sixth Cradle: that her mother had died when Second Cradle fell. That Naira had crawled her way up through the tenuous social structure of the Human Collective Army and caught the notice of the exemplar program simply to have the money to reprint her mother.

When she'd finally gotten the money, her mother's percent-to-crack number had been too high, and so she'd set the idea aside, and devoted her service to Acaelus until the day he'd promised her he had a solution to the dying worlds, and had failed to deliver on that promise. Naira wouldn't let the cradles fall, and it wasn't about the job. The duty. It was about what she'd lost. The promises broken.

He carried that deeply personal knowledge of her, unable to use it to make her see reason, because it'd infuriate her that he knew something so private about her. But he knew the shape of her moods. Knew the lift to her chin that signaled she'd made up her mind, and steeled himself to burn the fragile bridge between them, because he couldn't watch her cast herself to her death.

Kav beat him to it.

"Is it?" Kav asked her. "The job, I mean. Is this the job? Is this what Jonsun would have wanted you to do? I don't think it is. I don't think closing a bear trap around your own foot helps us undo what Mercator has done."

She gripped either side of the console podium and bowed her head. "Then what, Kav? What do we do? Because Jonsun wouldn't want us to stand by and watch those worlds die. They're all we have left. We haven't found any others. We know about amarthite, but it only kills *canus*, it does nothing to the shroud. Stopping the process before it happens is the only path available to us, and that means stopping those ships. Ships we cannot physically catch. We've got one solution here, people."

"What if we shifted focus to finding more cradles?" Kuma asked.

"The united forces of all of MERIT have been scouring space for cradles since the day Earth entered collapse, and Mercator alone has found these eight. What are *we* going to do?"

"We have to do something," Kav said, "because we're not getting on that ship."

"Maybe you aren't," Naira said, "but I'm going."

"Whoa." Kuma patted the air with both hands. "Don't bite each other's heads off. We'll figure something out."

"I...have an idea," Tarquin said. He'd been distracted by a change in the news coverage, the footage switching to statements from the heads of the other MERIT families.

Rochard was on-screen, the apples of her cheeks bright with indignation as she denounced Acaelus for cutting himself off from the rest of MERIT and humanity. The footage switched to Estevez, their cool demeanor unruffled as they explained that Acaelus had, technically, not broken their agreement to the best of their knowledge thus far, but they would be investigating.

"Well?" Kuma prompted.

"The *Sigillaria* was a joint venture," Tarquin said. "If I know anything about the MERIT families, they don't trust one another. Not for a second. That ship was built, according to the roster I found, by all of them."

"Ah," Naira said. "You think one of the other families may have installed a backdoor."

"I think they all have, to some degree or another."

"Right," Kuma said. "So all we have to do is get one of them to let us use their backdoor to blow up the ship that they poured a shit ton of resources into. No problem."

Naira snorted. "We could find a weaker station, infiltrate it, and maybe drop a worm on their systems for Kav to skim data from?"

Kav scratched the side of his jaw. "I dunno. I mean, yeah, I think we're going to have to go the infiltration route, but I don't know what I'd be looking for. A tunnel from a printing bay transmitter to that ship, maybe? Probably. But we'd have to hit the right bay, or social engineer the person with the right keys. It's...doable. But it'll take time."

"So, who's likely?" Naira asked. "Ichikawa seems the obvious choice. Acaelus and Chiyo were close, and Chiyo was always skirting the line on muscling in on relk mining."

"Their security is tight," Kuma said, "but the protocols haven't changed all that much since my time. I could print into them."

"You're underselling their digital security," Kav said. "They make the printers we use, the base software. We'd be relying almost a hundred percent on social engineering, and while I don't mind that per se, it will slow us down."

"Hold on," Tarquin said, "did you all forget you have a Mercator on hand?"

"I'd like to," Kav muttered under his breath.

Naira shot Kav a blistering glare, then turned her attention to Tarquin and leaned back against the podium. "We're not infiltrating Mercator. That's probably the same trap that Acaelus has set on the *Sigillaria*."

"I only meant that I have information about the families that's not public."

"Go on."

Tarquin wound the broadcast back, focusing on Rochard's flustered expression. Most of MERIT could keep it together well enough under the pressure of a public spectacle. Even Tarquin could force himself to keep a straight face if he was really focusing, but the raw emotion on Thieut Rochard's face was unusual.

Personal.

"Thieut's cousin Emali is technically something like a fifth cousin removed. I've lost track. But despite being watered-down Rochard, Thieut is fond of her, and that's the face of someone who has been personally slighted."

"Okay," Kav said slowly, "draw us some lines here, Mercator."

"My elder sister, Leka, heir to Mercator, second-in-command, too valuable for her own good, has been secretly liaising with Emali Rochard."

"They're banging?" Kuma asked.

Tarquin cleared his throat. "Yes. There's a web of intricate laws surrounding the courtship rituals of blooded MERIT members. The power imbalances involved are often vast, and unless one wants to be punished by those laws and labeled a pariah and abuser of their station, you stick to the rules.

"It's something all families take seriously, at least between the higher echelons, if only because they're worried about accidentally sparking an inter-MERIT war. Leka, as heir to Mercator, has much stricter rules in place than someone in Emali's position. Rules they ignored, in secret."

Kuma whistled low. "What kind of punishment are we talking about?"

"You could lose your cuffs." Tarquin touched the fine lines of his family's crest printed on the backs of his hands.

The family crest marked him as high in the line of succession, and subject to the courtship rules. He tried to ignore Naira's stare, but felt the heat of her scrutiny, and remembered the moment before their lips had first met, his protest that there were rules—and her asking him to break them. He shook off the memory. "The family gloves and cuffs, to be clear. You'd be busted back down to Collective. If the infraction is large enough, your map might be iced."

"I'm guessing," Naira said, "by the look on Thieut's face, that neither she nor Emali knew that Leka was going to be on that ship."

"Exactly," Tarquin said. "Whether or not that's the real Leka, I can't say, but Thieut seemed to think so. Emali must be upset, and Thieut and Emali would have been as close to that project as Chiyo. While I can't be sure of Emali's feelings, I'm certain Thieut wouldn't miss a chance to make sure she had a backdoor installed."

Naira chewed the information over for a moment. "I like it. Personal investment makes for easier social engineering, and Rochard's security is tight, but they're primarily farmers. An easier mark all around."

"It gets better," Tarquin said. "Emali's a dear friend of mine. We met at school long before she met Leka. Em loves plants, nature, cultivation, all of it. If I call her, and she sees I'm not actually on that ship, I might be able to bring her around. Convince her that Acaelus has gone off the rails and it's in everyone's best interest if she gives us the keys to whatever backdoor they have."

Naira pursed her lips, and Tarquin held his breath. She was sizing him up, balancing the risk and his ability against the reward. This was it—if she accepted his proposal, then he would finally feel like a fully fledged member of the team. Someone whose opinions and ideas mattered. Someone they trusted to help them heal the worlds.

"You really think you can do this?" she asked.

"I'm sure of it."

"I like any idea that gets us on that ship faster," Naira said. "But you can't call Emali from here. Kav, find us some neutral ground—an HC station with shit security—so nothing can be traced back to us. Preferably something unionist. Jessel dumped all their burner contacts last week to fix a security breach, so I'd like boots on the ground to contact them if we can."

"Aye." Kav swung around to his console and started digging through menus. "But I hope you're not counting on fast transit. A notice went out to all in-flight ships to sit and hold for a universal field position update."

"What, again? Didn't they do that a few weeks ago?"

Kav shrugged. "Hell if I know what's going on with the formulas, but I don't want to accidentally skip us into a station."

"Copy that," Naira said. "We'll wait for the UFP update. A few hours' delay won't matter much if Emali can get us cast access to the *Sigillaria*. We're trying that angle first."

"Aww," Kuma groaned, "I was looking forward to getting to knock Ichikawa heads together again."

"There'll be time for that." Naira winked at her and pushed off the console podium.

Tarquin blinked, wrong-footed by how quickly they'd taken to his idea. They bickered about everything, but they'd accepted his plan as is. Naira dropped a hand on his shoulder as she passed and tilted her head close to whisper.

"It's a solid plan. Try not to look like you licked a battery."

THREE

Naira

The Conservator's Ship | The Present

Naira dragged herself into the kitchen later that night, muscles jelly from the physical therapy designed to better integrate her map into her print, hair damp from her shower, and found a mug of tea thick with oat cream waiting for her in the warmer. Kav had left a note that said, *Rest, idiot,* and nothing more.

She smiled to herself and left the tea in the warmer while she mindlessly ate her dinner, protein rich and probably quite good, but she was too tired to muster up the ability to appreciate it. When she'd finished, she choked down her nightly shroud ration, then grabbed the mug and settled onto a bench seat inset against a wide, crystal clear window.

Naira brought the hot mug to her lips and took a long, savoring sip, letting herself relax into the alcove. She stretched her legs out across the bench and sighed, tipping her head back. The view beyond was all endless black shot through with stars. Though she was used to it, it calmed her all the same. People were small. It was okay for her to feel small and cozy and taken care of for a little while, too.

When the mug was empty, she set it down beside her and accessed her HUD, pulling up a book, then hiked the blanket left on the bench up around her shoulders. Hours slipped away. The door hissed open.

Tarquin was two steps inside before he noticed her. He'd changed into his sleep clothes, loose pajama pants and a soft T-shirt that she noted, with an annoying curl of warmth low in her belly, accentuated his lean musculature. His hair was mussed, and he was running his hand through it as he stepped inside, frustration plain on his face until he saw her. He stiffened, drawing back.

"I didn't mean to interrupt," he blurted.

"You didn't." She blinked the book closed. "Can't sleep?"

"No. Well, I meant to, but then I realized I forgot to eat."

He hesitated, hands sliding into his pockets. She tipped her head to the fridge. "Go on, then."

"Right."

He hurried to prepare his food, and she looked back out the window so that he wouldn't feel her eyes upon him. But the room was small, and in the corner of her eye she caught his furtive movements, the anxious energy radiating off of him.

Months. It'd been five months since he'd joined the Conservators, and she'd thought that initial rush of attraction would have faded by now, but even a glance still set her stomach to fluttering.

She'd loathed the sensation, at first. Resented her body for giving her all the physical reactions to emotions she no longer had. Tarquin was respectfully thin on the details regarding how close they'd grown on Sixth Cradle, and while she appreciated him being circumspect, she couldn't help but wonder.

Acaelus's son. Her sworn enemy. And yet, when he smiled at her a certain way, her whole being filled with golden light.

"Have a good night." He balanced a plate on his arm, a cup of shroud supplement in one hand, and practically bolted for the door.

"Mercator," she said, stopping his escape. "Sit. Eat. Really, it's fine."

He glanced at his food, then at her, and it took a clear force of will for him to turn from the door and sit down at the communal table. Deliberately, he broke off a piece of flatbread and scooped up his spiced grains and vegetables, head bowed over his food, and set to work putting the meal away with military efficiency.

Naira sighed. "I'm not holding you prisoner," she said, gently chiding. "You can go to your room if you want."

He looked up, a flush on his cheeks. "I didn't mean to..." He trailed off, glanced down at his food, and how he'd been dismantling it. "I'm painfully transparent, aren't I?"

"Extremely." She swung her legs off the bench, keeping the blanket around her shoulders, and rummaged in a cabinet. "We're going to have to give you subterfuge lessons."

"I'd like to think I'm a good student, but I may be beyond even your tutelage when it comes to subterfuge."

She chuckled at that and finally found what she was looking for—one of Acaelus's favorite bottles of wine, and two glasses. She grabbed it all and shuffled across the floor, awkward with the blanket, her limbs feeling a little too long, her body a touch off center. Stifling a scowl at herself, she plunked the bottle and glasses down on the table and sat across from Tarquin. He stared at the bottle.

"Are you certain that's a good idea?" he asked.

"I was given explicit orders."

She tugged the note Kav had left from her pocket and flicked it across the table. Tarquin picked it up and frowned at the words before a fond smile burst across his face. "Far be it from me to discount the orders of our ship's captain."

"Never, ever call him captain. That head's big enough already."

Tarquin picked up the bottle and ran his thumb over the textured paper label. The smile faded from his face, and he met her eyes, understanding passing between them. This was a Mercator shuttle. The only wine stored on it had been meant for the inner family. For Acaelus.

Wine was difficult to get right, when most crops were grown on stations. What Tarquin held now was from Earth—from what used to be France. He traced the lettering with a fingertip. That single bottle cost more than the relocation fees of an entire family from Earth to the stations, and it'd meant so little to Acaelus that he'd left it to gather dust in a shuttle pantry.

Tarquin freed the cork with the ease of long practice. He poured out two glasses and pushed one to her. Naira took a careful sip. It was astringent, like tea, but a touch sweet, too, and full of other flavors she couldn't begin to name.

"Huh." She squinted into the glass. "Nice, but not what I expected."

"I like the modern varietals better, too," he said.

"This is the only wine I've ever tasted. Not a lot of room in the budget for alcohol that has to be grown in soil."

He coughed delicately in surprise. "Oh. Well, if you like it, I can introduce you to some of my favorites once we've reached the station."

"Hmm." She took a long drink. "How are you going to pay for those?"

"I..." He blinked. "I have no idea."

She laughed, drawing a shy smile out of him. "I doubt Kav will make room in the resupply budget for wine, I'm sorry to say. Now. What's so important that you're up in the middle of the night because you forgot to eat?"

"Ah. That." Again he ran his hand through his hair, giving it a shake. "It's the problem of the origin of amarthite. The small sample I snatched from Dr. Laurent before leaving Mercator Station hasn't given me much to work with, and while I appreciate the supplies you all procured for me, my lab equipment is insufficient."

"Okay," she said, "but you've been gnawing on that bone for months. Why the late-night unrest now?"

He traced the rim of his glass with the tip of a finger. "It was...seeing that ship. My family. That wasn't me, and it might not be them, but regardless, *canus* has taken them, hasn't it? I know they're not...They're not good people, but I can't help wondering if maybe things had been different, if their infections hadn't run so deep, that they might have done things differently. I know, logically, that's folly. I was just as susceptible to infection and I wouldn't have made the same choices, and yet..." He trailed off, shaking his head. "You must think me very naive, to hold out hope for them."

She reached across the table and took his hand, squeezing gently. He startled, flicking his gaze down to the contact, then up to her eyes, but didn't pull away.

"You're not naive. You're a good man, and you love them, and you wish things had been different. That you could help them still. I've been there. It only ended up chewing me to pieces, in the end."

"How did you get past it?" he asked. "The guilt, the recriminations? I can't seem to let it go that I should have been able to *do* something. That I still could."

Naira leaned back in her chair, letting her hand slide away from his, and picked up her glass once more. "I'm not sure I have. Not fully. With Acaelus, I never cared for the man, but I believed in him. In what he was, and what he told me he wanted to accomplish. When it all fell apart, I..." She frowned into her glass. "Couldn't help but feel as if I had some inner failing that kept me from seeing the truth. That I was destined to be duped by monsters."

She bit her lips shut, wishing she hadn't said that much.

"Naira—Sharp. I mean Sharp." He paused to gather himself. "The evils of those who've betrayed your trust are no fault of yours."

"Likewise, prince," she said, and took a long drink.

He grunted softly at her calling him a prince, but his face lost the pinched expression. Tarquin drank and peered at her over the glass, his shoulders finally relaxing. "Why are *you* awake?"

She scrunched her nose. Desire sparked briefly in his eyes, his gaze lingering on her mouth, then he smothered the expression. Her chest felt tight.

"I've never slept much," she said with a small shrug.

"Ah. Right, and we have individual rooms on the shuttle."

He knew about her dislike for sleeping alone? Naira shifted on her seat, unable to help but wonder how he'd come by that information. "Don't do that."

"Do what?"

"Tell me things about myself you shouldn't know."

His eyes widened, and he put the glass down with a clunk. "I didn't think."

"Don't worry about it." She waved off his concern and shook her empty glass at him, which he topped off. "Have you gotten anywhere with the amarthite?"

He sighed and slumped in his chair. "Nowhere useful. Relk itself is rare, and amarthite was a waste product. What little we found—and I mean *little*—was discarded, or else cataloged as a step below the lowest grade of relkatite we use in production. We made some effort to refine that 'low-grade' relk, but it never worked, and the yields were always so small Father deemed the effort a waste of resources."

"There was a lot on Sixth Cradle, apparently. Was anything about that deposit different?"

He lit up. "*That's* the question I can't get out of my head." Tarquin leaned forward, pushing his plate aside, and drew invisible lines on the table with his finger. His voice was bright with interest. "The diabase sill Mercator wanted to mine around was older than the ones we usually look for. Most of the older ones, they erode and the deposits get washed away, so we have to transition to riparian mining, and that is such a pain in the ass."

Naira chuckled at him and he glanced up, self-conscious again. An apology balanced on his lips, his shoulders slightly hunched in a way that signaled he was about to withdraw the deluge of information. She waved a hand at him.

"Older site than usual. Got it. Why didn't they go to the river, then?"

"We always knew there wouldn't be much relk on Sixth, the signatures were all wrong, but there'd be *some*. The largest, easiest deposits were bound to be in the metamorphic zones around the sill—where the hot rock from the sill cooks the country rock. But that mine..."

He dug in his pocket and pulled out a slim notebook. To her surprise, he plunked it in the center of the table and flipped it open, rifling through the pages until he found one that unfolded like an accordion into a long rectangle. Sketches in black ink filled the pages. It wasn't even scribe paper.

"Paper? Really?" she asked. Lichen-dead trees made crumbly, inconsistent pulp. Paper was rare, and expensive.

Tarquin shrugged. "It was already in my pocket when we fled, and switching mediums helps me think. Actually, can I talk this out with you? Sometimes that helps, too, but it might be quite boring for you."

"I'm a little tired, but—"

"Please, rest. Don't let me keep you." He swept the pages closed.

She grabbed his wrist before he could put the notebook away and felt the tendons jump beneath her grip. "But I want to hear what you have to say, is what I would have said, if you'd let me finish. I just wanted you to know that if I yawn, it's not you."

"You're certain?"

"I am."

He bit the side of his wine-stained lips, studying her. She shifted back in the seat, resettling the blanket, and gestured for him to continue.

Tarquin gave himself a little shake and started up again, hesitantly at first, but warming to the subject as she made appreciative noises and asked questions.

Talking about his work transformed him. All the forced regality that'd been trained into him over a lifetime washed away. Even his strained awkwardness when in the presence of the Conservators vanished, the real man emerging at last from the walls he'd built around himself.

She could see how her other self had cared for him, if indeed she had. Once she got past the slight resemblance to Acaelus, he was physically her type in every way, but it was the passion in him that made the desirous part of her hindbrain stand up and take notice. That genuine, vibrant interest.

A good 30 percent of the terminology he used sailed right over her head, and she didn't care, though occasionally curiosity would urge her to slow him down and explain. She got the gist. He was concerned that, if amarthite was only found in older deposits, then erosion would make it even more difficult to find in large quantities. Mostly, she was content to watch and listen.

He was winding down, his expression equal parts bafflement and curiosity, the question of how amarthite fit into the world clearly a puzzle he found both frustrating and a joy to tinker with. Naira smiled to herself and reached for the wine bottle, but her arm was longer than she'd expected it to be, and she knocked it over instead.

Naira swore as it struck the table, spilling wine in a splashing arc that stained Tarquin's carefully drawn pages. He yanked the book back in surprise, and she lunged for the bottle, but once more her body was the wrong shape and she slapped it, sending it crashing to the floor. Glass shattered.

"I'm so sorry. Is your book okay?"

"It's fine." He tilted it to show her the few splatters of dark red stain. "No harm done. I guess we had a little too much to drink, huh?"

"That's not how E-X pathways work," she said, partially to herself, staring at the shattered bottle.

Naira wasn't clumsy. Exemplar pathways didn't allow her to misjudge distances, or become unbalanced. She could be shit-faced, blackout drunk, and still walk a tightrope on the strength of her pathways alone.

Yet she'd been stumbling and tripping and bumping into things ever since they'd gone to lie low on Earth after they'd destroyed Mercator Station. Ever since she'd unscrambled that video from the *Einkorn* and watched herself fall to her death in another body, on another world.

What was happening to her? Months of physical therapy, trying to ground herself in this print, her *preferred* print, when she'd never needed such measures before. And still, *still*, sometimes, she moved like she was in Lockhart's body, and couldn't seem to stop. Her own flesh eluded her. Tears of frustration pricked behind her eyes and she turned away.

"Are you all right?" he asked.

"Just tired." The thickness of her voice gave away her building tears. With a grunt, she shrugged off the blanket and went for the cleaning supplies. "I'll clean this up, then go to bed."

"No, stop." His chair squeaked as he pushed it back and stepped in front of her, stopping her mid-reach for the cabinets. "I've got it. Really, I promise you I know how to clean. You go get some rest."

Naira wanted to protest. To roll her eyes and push him aside so she could get to work cleaning, but all the energy drained from her. She'd never felt so heavy. So empty. Why couldn't she fully inhabit her own skin? It was *hers*, goddamnit. She rubbed her face with both hands.

"I should—"

"Sharp," Tarquin said firmly. "Rest, idiot."

She blinked, momentarily taken aback, until she recalled Kav's note. A shaky laugh rolled through her, and she brushed hair out of her eyes.

"Thanks. I'll do that."

She gave him a friendly clap on the arm, and his smile came flaring back, but it failed to drown out the worry in his eyes. Naira turned to leave but hesitated, her hand on the doorframe, not sure why she felt like she was being tugged back into that room. The scent of the air changed, no longer warm paper and wine but sandstone and sweat, dust and bitter lichen.

"I enjoyed talking with you, Mercator," she said, and while she meant those words, she hadn't known where they'd come from. They'd just... bubbled up from within and felt right.

Tarquin took in a sharp breath. "Likewise, E-X."

FOUR

Naira

The Conservator's Ship | The Present

The night before they arrived at the station Kav had picked out, Kuma found Naira in the training room. The shuttle hadn't had anything remotely like an exercise space when they'd moved in, as people were only meant to live on it for a short amount of time. So Naira and Kuma had dragged a bunch of shelves out of a storage room and installed weights, weapons, and a punching bag that Kuma kept breaking.

Naira's fist connected with the bag, and she relished the sting in her wrapped knuckles. She'd turned her pathways down, hesitant to use them unless she needed to, and the physical feedback grounded her in her skin. Reminded her that, although this body was temporary, it was the way she connected with the world. With others.

Her strike was slightly off-center from where she'd wanted it to land. She scowled, resisting an urge to kick the bag in frustration.

"Hitting things without me?" Kuma's voice was high with mock indignation. "I thought we were friends."

Naira stepped away from the bag, adjusting the tightness of her ponytail. "Needed to burn off some frustrations."

"I bet," Kuma said with a smirk that Naira ignored.

Naira grabbed her water bottle and took a long drink, swishing it around first to help chase the foul taste of the shroud supplement they all drank after dinner to slow the spread of *canus* in their pathways. Kuma sauntered into the room and hugged the back of the bag, leaning against it as she peered around the side at Naira.

"You're pissed," she said.

Naira scowled, which wasn't the best way to go about convincing Kuma she wasn't, in fact, angry. "I have a lot of things to be pissed about."

"Sure," Kuma said. She swirled the bag around, swaying back and forth with it. "But the missions don't piss you off, even when they go wrong. And the Mercator's got you all messed up another way—"

Naira swung at the center of the bag. Kuma grunted as it slammed into her, and clung on. "Maybe it *is* the Mercator."

"Maybe you should mind your own damn business."

"I've never minded my business in my life, and I'm not about to start now." She eyed Naira. "You rolled over way too quickly on that plan."

"It was a good plan." She propped her hands on her hips, watching Kuma warily. Kuma may play into her natural demeanor as a bubbly brute, but Naira had known her long enough to recognize that cunning lurked beneath her surface. Kuma hadn't been an exemplar, but she'd been security for Ichikawa, a sector captain. You didn't get that position with a friendly attitude.

"Sure it was," Kuma said. "But you tease out the flaws in every plan. It's what you do. You take an idea and dissect it. There are about a dozen little flaws with his plan that even I can see. So why didn't you?"

"It felt right."

Kuma cocked her head to the side, imploring her to go on, to reach the obvious conclusion that Naira really should have noticed, but didn't because she'd been too distracted by the entire situation.

"I haven't been in this print that long, and I've been taking the shroud. There's no way *canus* has that much control over my feelings yet. But you're right. I didn't even consider pushing back on the plan."

"So *canus* thinks it's a good idea for us to go to Emali," Kuma said.

Naira glared at her arms, where golden pathways threaded through her skin, hiding the cores of relkatite within, and the *canus* that fed on that mineral. "Which means it's a bad idea."

"It's still a good idea, Nai," Kuma said. "Canden Mercator is on that ship. Maybe *canus* wants us to stop her spreading the shroud so that it can flourish."

Naira winced. "I don't like it."

"Neither do I, but we have to work with what we've got, and we can't get this shit out of our prints completely. Not until we find more amarthite and Tarquin figures out how to use it in place of our normal pathways."

"Which he assures us is nigh impossible if we can't find large enough deposits." Naira pinched the bridge of her nose between two fingers. "I hate this. I hate not knowing if I can trust my own instincts."

"You could reprint," Kuma said.

"No," Naira said too quickly.

Kuma's brows lifted nearly to her hairline. "Annnnd, there's the reason you're really pissed off."

"It's this—this print. I can't get my neural map fully seated. Everything's a little off. My proprioception is calibrated to the Lockhart print and I can't force it back. The physical therapy isn't working."

"Even more reason to reprint," Kuma said. It wasn't a question, not exactly, but she left the implied *so why don't you?* unsaid.

Naira adjusted the wrappings around her fists. She hadn't admitted this even to herself, yet, but...If it became a problem, someone would need to know. She ran her tongue over her teeth. Watched Kuma in the corner of her eye.

"There's bleed-over, sometimes. That's the only way I can describe it. Like I can almost recall that other life. Like, if I try hard enough, I can remember being in Lockhart's print."

Kuma's perpetual smile vanished. She leaned back to better see Naira. "Be careful with that. Remembering things from a life that was never backed up is one of the first signs before you..."

She trailed off, the word *crack* hanging between them both. Before Naira and Kav had joined the Conservators, Kuma had already been a member, and not because she loved the planets so much, though that was part of her reasons. Chiyo Ichikawa, Kuma's old boss, was notorious for her experiments on neural maps. She conducted most of those experiments on her own staff when they misbehaved.

Kuma's squadron had been infiltrated by an HC spy, and they'd stolen secrets before anyone noticed. Chiyo, in her rage, had cracked half of Kuma's squad and made Kuma, as their captain, watch. Kuma went AWOL two days later and sought a way to strike back at MERIT. She'd found Jessel, Jonsun's sibling and leader of the unionist political movement, and Jessel had deemed Kuma too violent for their interests. They'd sent her along to Jonsun. Kuma was all that was left of Jonsun's fading movement when Naira defected and joined them. Merely the thought of cracking still made Kuma sweat.

Naira flexed her fingers, curled them into fists, and tried to convince herself that they were the right length. That the calluses were in the same spots. They still felt like someone else's hands.

"I know it's dangerous. But I keep catching these glimpses. Moments that feel important." *Tarquin hunched over a hole in the ground, his face grim.* She shook her head to clear it. "There's something I'm trying to remember. Something that matters."

"Not going to matter a whole hell of a lot if you crack, is it?"

"Jonsun held on long enough to defend the *Einkorn* from *canus*. If I remember, I think I can hold on long enough to get a message to you."

"Yeah, see, here's the thing. I don't want you 'holding on' to get me some grim final message. I'd rather you stay living, thanks."

"We all crack eventually."

"You're willing to risk it before you've secured the cradles?"

Naira slid her a sideways glance. "Low blow."

"Had to push some buttons." Kuma grinned, but she'd lost her sparkle. "Because you're freaking me out, Nai."

"Sorry, sorry." She cracked her neck from one side to the other. "I'd be less maudlin about it if I didn't feel like I was slipping back and forth half the time. One minute I'm myself, the next minute I'm jamming my fingers when I reach for anything because I misjudged the distance."

Kuma pushed the bag aside and stepped back, spreading her arms wide. She curled her fingers in invitation. "That, I can help with. You've gotten rusty, honey bear. That's all. You haven't really worked that print of yours out, have you? You haven't been in a fight since Mercator Station, and that was hardly a brawl."

She snorted. "You think you're going to pound me back into my body?"

"I think I'm going to try, since you won't let the Mercator do it."

Naira's nascent smile burned away. "Not you, too. I get enough shit from Kav."

"We give you shit because every time you two are in the same room the temperature rises ten degrees."

"That's not physiologically possible."

"See? You're both nerds. Perfect. Bang it out already so Kav and I can stop feeling like we're swimming through your hormones every damn day."

"It was real for him, and it's not for me, and 'banging it out' is going to make it worse."

"Less whining, more punching." Kuma backed away from the bag and gestured dramatically for Naira to attack. Naira suppressed a laugh as Kuma bounced back and forth on the balls of her feet, grunting far too loudly as she boxed the air.

"I'm clumsy." Naira squared off.

"Blah, blah, blah, more whining. C'mon. Or is the Big Bad Exemplar afraid of an Ichikawa security grunt?"

"You Station-Sec types always were show-offs."

"Mercator-cuffed coward," she shot back.

Naira narrowed her eyes and lunged. Kuma's cartoonish dancing halted. Though the stronger woman had always been slower, she sidled away from the strike with ease. Naira's fist brushed the side of her shirt, a whisper of fabric. She'd expected an impact and overbalanced, twisting to pull away from Kuma's follow-up punch.

They put space between each other. Circled. "There you are."

"I missed," Naira said.

"And there you go again." Kuma's lip bulged as she ran her tongue over her teeth. "Show me who you are, Ex. Sharp. Show me that body's yours to command."

She caught herself about to protest. Unease rolled through her, a desire to duck her head, to claim she wasn't the woman Kuma thought she was. That she'd gotten twisted up inside, somehow, on Sixth Cradle, and that uncertainty had followed her home. It dogged her every thought, telling her she was inadequate. That she wouldn't ever be strong or fast or clever enough to fight back, so why try?

Naira could see the person she used to be on the other side of the chasm of her life that was Sixth Cradle. Could sense the edges of her surety. Of the fire she'd used to carry.

Carry it a little longer.

She wanted to. She did. Naira wanted to be that person again, could almost feel the shape of herself filling out this body. Could *almost* feel her identity coming home. But almost wasn't good enough. Almost could get them all killed if she wasn't—

Naira stopped circling. Kuma said nothing, for once, watching her with a curious tilt to the head. Holding back wasn't Naira. She'd never restrained herself from action unless it was strategically necessary.

These feelings of inadequacy weren't hers. They were *canus*. Twisting her hormones and neurotransmitters against her. Letting her tell herself she wasn't enough.

Rage sparked within her. Her fists tightened, breath coming slow and even, and she caught a brief flash of surprise on Kuma's face before she closed the distance between them and swung.

Her fist grazed off Kuma's bicep, which incensed her further. She'd been moving too fast. Kuma shouldn't have been able to dodge that. Naira had missed, again, her proprioception stubbornly calibrated to another woman's body.

Anger fueled her, cleared her mind, and focused everything down to that moment, to existing in that flesh, all her fears and insecurities burned away under the desire to win, to master this thing within her—to take back the body that was hers.

Kuma whooped, laughing as Naira blocked a hook aimed at her head and dove under that broken guard, swinging for Kuma's stomach. Solid contact, this time. The shock of it vibrated through to her core. Distinct motions melted away, both of them falling into a brutal, brief contest that ended with them sweating and panting.

Naira had captured Kuma in a headlock, Naira's back braced against the wall as she struggled to keep the stockier woman under control. A thin tear of blood dripped from Naira's nose, and her cheek was hot with an incoming black eye, but she didn't care. She savored every last ache, captured the sensation of each blooming bruise and sore muscle and held them bright and shining in her mind like jewels. Jewels whose faces reflected only her own countenance, her own body. Not that thing that dwelled within her.

Kuma tapped Naira's arm three times and Naira released her. She stumbled away, laughing, while Naira slumped against the wall and closed her eyes, loath to end her meditation on the pain scouring her thoughts clean.

"Better?" Kuma asked.

Naira sensed her friend's arm snap out, heard a swoosh of fabric, and grabbed the towel Kuma had tossed out of the air. When she opened her eyes, they were both grinning. "I needed that."

Kuma gestured grandly. "Kuma always knows what you need."

Naira wiped her face clean—ish. Blood and sweat smeared together across the towel, making it impossible to get it all off. "Kuma better stop talking about herself in the third person if she doesn't want to go another round."

"Don't make me promises you can't keep. You've got your groove back, but you look like shit and I'd rather you shower before we tangle again."

Naira tossed the towel into a chute that would send it down to the automated laundry system.

"Fair enough." She pushed off the wall and winced as her muscles protested. Despite the combat pathways her print was loaded with, she hadn't actually put them to use since she'd escaped Mercator Station with Tarquin in tow. Kuma had been right about that experience not requiring much physical effort.

She'd relied on the sidearm Tarquin had given her. The weapon he'd painstakingly altered to her preferences.

"Don't get maudlin on me again." Kuma prodded at a bruise forming on her cheek. Their pathways would fix the damage, but it'd take a while for them to clear out the dead blood cells. They'd both have black eyes in the morning. "I can't take a sparring match every time you get moody."

"Coward," Naira said. Kuma gave her the finger and Naira laughed, shaking her head. "I wasn't slipping back. I caught myself thinking about..." She hesitated, unsure if she wanted to put this out there with Kuma, but she trusted her friend to handle it with some sense of decorum. "Thinking about the Mercator."

"Well, well." Kuma's grin came rampaging back. She gave Naira a playful punch on the arm and waggled her eyebrows. "I know you think it's 'not real' for you, Nai, but it's been months. If this were some kind of entanglement fuckery, the spark would have burned out by now. And, honestly, when you two drop the bullshit, and you relax enough to stop being gruff and he gets comfortable enough to stop dancing on eggshells, you're cute together. Don't make that face at me—I mean it. Our lives are shit enough. Maybe it's time to take a chance on something good, instead of something desperate."

"I don't know...I can't even be certain if my emotions are my own anymore."

"Please." Kuma sniffed. "*Canus* isn't Tarquin's biggest fan. It's not going to try to get him laid. Nah, something else is holding you back. Got you scared."

Naira examined her bloodied knuckle wraps. "He's a Mercator. What if..."

What if she was only ever drawn to people who had cruelty buried deep within them? What if she was the one who brought that cruelty out, who sharpened it enough to cut? What if Naira only loved and believed in violent and brutal souls because she was all those things, too? Her only serious relationship had been with a man who became a finalizer, and after that she'd placed her faith in Acaelus.

Kuma took Naira's face in both hands and made her meet her eyes. "Tarquin is not his father, and he's nothing like Demarco."

"Yeah. I know."

Kuma studied her for a moment, then stepped away. "Good. Because you are Exemplar fucking Sharp. Diamond-eyed, titanium-spined. You don't take shit from anyone, so don't take it from yourself, either. You like him. He likes you. I know things are complicated, but give it some real thought, all right? Because that kind of connection? That's worth paying attention to."

FIVE

Acaelus

Mercator Station | Five Months Ago

Acaelus was reprinted within twenty-four hours of the destruction of Mercator Station. He awoke to a company in chaos. Key personnel had to be reprinted. Chiyo Ichikawa had to be reprinted. Acaelus could offer no explanation for the explosion of his family's primary station that wouldn't set them all to panic, and so he gave them the explanation that served him the most.

Acaelus told the worlds that the Conservators had changed tactics and struck at the heart of Mercator Station. It wasn't entirely incorrect.

Panic followed. He'd counted on it. MERIT turned inward, strengthening their defenses, conjecture regarding the state of Mercator's security bubbling below the surface. Acaelus didn't care, so long as they turned their scrutiny away from him.

It was no great effort on his part to move Mercator operations to the family's second-largest station, the Chirality losing its name to become merely Mercator Station. Acaelus had long decades past oiled Mercator into a machine that functioned at his word.

The personnel were reprinted. The station was reoutfitted. Production commenced as normal, and scant productivity was lost, in the end.

The security footage, stored in multiple server banks off-station, was recovered. And that . . . that would not go back into the neat box of Mercator functionality.

Acaelus alone watched it, and so it was Acaelus alone who saw Paison gun down himself and Chiyo while Tarquin, his sweet, book-headed son, tried to talk her down from a plan Acaelus didn't have the context to parse.

He had turned off the cameras in Ex. Sharp's room, but he watched the halls. Watched Tarquin enter that room, and leave, and Sharp exit a few moments later. Watched her doubt, and come back to pull his son from a death that would have led to Tarquin cracking. He watched Sharp snap his daughter's neck. While the death was brutal, it was swift, and Acaelus understood that she had done so to save Leka from the horde of misprints Paison had unleashed upon the station.

Sharp had saved his children.

He could make no sense of it.

The only footage he watched more was that which was recovered by Paison on Sixth Cradle—the brief and terrible moment wherein Tarquin had shot a woman wearing his mother's print. Tarquin had asserted it wasn't her. That Canden Mercator was still cracked, that print controlled by some other mind with a bent toward cruelty. The other heads of MERIT believed him.

Acaelus did not.

He wanted to. He wanted that woman to be anyone else, but he knew her too well. Knew all the small ticks of her body, the way she canted her head when her moods changed, and saw no one but his wife in her own skin. It gnawed at him until he was nothing left but a shell around the shouted question of *why?*

There was some connection. Some line to be drawn between Canden's appearance on Sixth Cradle, his son's strange behavior, and Sharp. It was not a line the well-oiled machine of Mercator could draw for him. He would have to get his own hands in the mix, and he caught a hint of where he should begin in the security footage before the station's destruction.

Finalizer Fletcher Demarco, one of his most trusted employees, had stood on that dock and waved to Sharp before she'd left the station with Tarquin.

There had been nothing fond in that gesture. There was a mocking nature to it, a cruelty to the man's smile that had made Sharp stiffen in recognition of an unspoken threat before she turned and fled.

Acaelus reread their files. They'd been at the same orphanage. Had enlisted to the HCA together. When they'd been hired, they'd signed paperwork for cohabitation. Sharp had canceled that request before her first day.

Demarco had been questioned after Sharp's defection, and had passed that interview satisfactorily. He'd been instrumental in the plan to capture her on the *Cavendish*. Had been the one to suggest making certain HCA Ayuba was shot first, so that she'd be flustered and off her guard.

Acaelus looked at the footage of that mocking wave, and wondered. He'd long ago learned that personal investment bore more fruit from his employees than any other motivator. Acaelus froze the footage on that moment, Demarco's hand raised, Sharp rigid, and summoned the man to his office.

Demarco was not what one would envision when they expected a finalizer, and that was by design. He was no clean-cut, muscled force of nature like the exemplars. He was merely a man, a little tall, perhaps, though not so tall as Acaelus or Tarquin. Lean muscle shaped the hard angles of his body, revealed by the snug fit of a T-shirt and pants bloused into his station boots. A slightly curly mop of sandy-blond hair topped his head, green eyes disarmingly kind.

Only those who could read pathways would note the excess strength and agility lining his skin. Only those who knew what it was to fight would note the thickness of the calluses over his knuckles, the wary cant to his spine.

Demarco was the kind of man you'd hire to check your ship's hull plating for irregularities and share a beer with afterward, his smile quick and charming. Acaelus had watched this man dismantle Ex. Dalson with his bare hands at Acaelus's request. He knew well how his friendly smile could lie.

That smile froze on Demarco's face as he stepped through the door, seeing the footage paused behind Acaelus's head. Seeing his death in that still frame, all the knives he'd used so well in service of Mercator turned against him at last. Acaelus savored the moment.

Demarco recovered with impressive speed and bowed. "My liege, how may I serve?"

"I was reviewing your service record," Acaelus said, as if this were any other employee review. "Exceptional, truly. You haven't let a mark get away from you yet, and there have been hundreds. So it leaves me to wonder why you stood there and waved while the worlds' most wanted terrorist walked out the door *with my son*."

"May I speak plainly, my liege?" Demarco asked.

"It is in your best interests to do so."

"I know you let Ex. Sharp go."

"And how did you arrive at such a conclusion?"

He clasped his hands behind his back and stood at ease. "When the misprints attacked, I went to her cell. I found her gone, and when I checked the logs, I saw you had turned off the cameras in her cell. I wouldn't remember any of this, except that I checked my access logs upon reprinting after the destruction to see what I had done. You may do so yourself, my liege, to confirm my story."

They stared at each other. Acaelus was struck by the hubris of a man who could stare him down without flinching. "Why did you go to her cell?"

He licked his lips, the first real sign of uncertainty he'd shown since coming through the door. "That's personal, my liege."

"That is not the answer to the question I asked."

Demarco hesitated.

Acaelus laced his fingers together on top of his desk. "You will tell me why you went to see my wayward exemplar, and you will tell me now."

Demarco's eye twitched when Acaelus said *my wayward exemplar*. Interesting. He straightened himself. "I can't say for certain, as my precise feelings at the time were lost to the explosion, but consider it nostalgia, I suppose, that I wanted to be sure she was secure when the station fell."

"The fact that you knew where she was at all is evidence that it was more than nostalgia."

"I've kept an eye on her, my liege, I admit it. When I was called in for a high-value target, I presumed it must be her. For a very long time, I've wanted to ask her how she could turn on Mercator. Our early lives weren't comfortable. Mercator hiring us was a boon we'd only dreamed of, and so her desertion seemed...impossible, to me."

"I see." Acaelus doubted that was all there was to it. "What did you argue about that caused Sharp to cancel your cohabitation request?"

He flinched. "It's nothing, my liege."

"Out with it."

"We argued over how best to serve you, my liege."

"That's a clumsy dodge from someone with your track record, Mr. Demarco."

Demarco's distress faded. "Forgive me, I had to try. This is not a topic I'm accustomed to discussing. And it's accurate enough, my liege. I wanted her to come into the finalizers with me."

Acaelus hadn't known Sharp well on a personal level, but he'd spent enough time with her to know that such a request wouldn't anger her enough to cut off communication permanently. "And?"

"And I...may have forbidden her from risking her map by dying for another man. My liege."

"Ah." Acaelus's brows lifted. Now *that* he could see infuriating her. "And do you resent me for her deaths in my defense?"

"No, my liege." He shrugged, the gesture natural enough. "Nai made her choice. I respect that, now that I'm older and less hotheaded. Twenty-nine deaths in your service isn't much, in the end."

"Twenty-four," Acaelus corrected.

"Right, yes, twenty-four. Forgive the mistake, my liege."

Acaelus didn't react, but inwardly, he wondered. Sharp had died twenty-four times over the eight years she'd guarded him, Lockhart five times. A curious mistake to make, lumping those two numbers together. Did Demarco suspect what Acaelus had done?

No, the thought was ridiculous. That was his private project. The man had more than likely fallen for the same nonsense as the tabloids.

"I remain uncertain, but I will give you a chance to prove your loyalties." He gestured to the footage. "Find Ex. Sharp, and my son, and bring them both back to me whole. My chief of operations, Ms. Salter, will be apprised of your mission and provide you with what resources you require."

A hungry gleam flashed behind the man's eyes, and Acaelus knew he'd chosen the right hunting dog. Demarco would not be kept from his quarry.

"It would be my pleasure, my liege."

SIX

Tarquin

Miller-Urey Station | The Present

K av landed them at Miller-Urey Station in a private dock that he grumbled about being unable to afford. They could only do so much to conceal the fact that the ship was a Mercator shuttle. The private dock fit with what a Mercator vessel would do and kept them away from prying eyes. Tarquin hadn't been off the shuttle aside from the bombing and a brief visit down to Earth to lie low after they'd destroyed Mercator Station. He was itching to get out. To see something new.

Naira walked into the hold where they'd all gathered, ready to go, took one look at him from beneath a pair of sunglasses that obscured half her face, and said, "No. That won't work."

"What do you mean?"

"Your clothes." She shot a glare at Kav, who took one shuffling step backward. "Is this your idea of staying under the radar, Kav?"

"They're what we had."

Kuma snickered.

Naira drew in a long breath, and he got the distinct impression she was counting backward.

"I can change . . . ?" Tarquin tugged at his shirt collar, wondering what had so offended her. He'd escaped Mercator Station with the clothes on his back, a dark green suit that would have given him away as Mercator family anywhere in the universe, so he'd been reliant on the Conservators to provide him everything he needed to survive. Including clothing.

"It's not the clothes," Naira said. "It's the styling. Can you not look like a fucking prince for five goddamn seconds?"

Kuma cackled, took an elbow in the ribs from Kav, and pressed a fist against her mouth to keep from laughing further.

Tarquin's cheeks heated. "I beg your pardon?"

"Never, ever 'beg my pardon.' My god, we're going to have to give him . . . reverse etiquette lessons. Unbutton your coat."

"Uh."

"We don't have time for this."

Before he could think of what to say, she'd undone the buttons of his coat, standing so close he could feel the warmth radiating off her skin. He swallowed, thinking about igneous intrusions and sedimentation rates and certainly not thrust faults or the feel of her hands grazing over him, tugging and adjusting, until she finally retreated a step and he could breathe again.

His coat hung open, one side of his collar twisted and his shirt half-loose, his pants now bloused over the tops of his boots instead of the sleek tuck he'd managed earlier. Naira looked him up and down and sighed. "That'll have to do. Muss your hair. This is a Collective station. You don't want to stand out."

"Sorry." He ran his hands through his hair to shake it out a bit.

"Not your fault." Naira shot another glare at Kav, who tried and failed to cover his emergent smirk. "Let's go. Keep your sleeves down, we're not hiding your family mark, but we're not advertising it either. Kuma, sleeves up."

"Yeah, yeah," Kuma grumbled. She unbuttoned the sleeves of her flannel and rolled them up to show off the crimson-red Ichikawa cuffs around her wrists. Between the cuffs and the black eye she was sporting, Tarquin doubted anyone would risk bothering Kuma.

Naira rolled up her sleeves to show off her Mercator cuffs. He had to look away, guilt gnawing at him once again over his father betraying her long service to their family.

"You two, secure us decent-but-not-nice rooms. I'll take the Mercator to the cheaper end of town and we'll get an hourly so he can make the call from there. If anyone asks, we're leftovers from the joint MERIT commission stopping to stretch on our way back to our usual posts. Keep your profiles low, but not suspiciously so. Clear?"

Nods all around. "Good," Naira said. "Don't forget to use the IDs Kav made for us. Rendezvous in five hours from my mark—now. Move, people."

"Wait, Nai," Kav said. "I got your stuff on our last resupply."

"Aww, you remembered. I thought I'd have to buy 'em myself this time." She held out an expectant hand, and he tossed her a cloth bag that made a crinkling, clicking sound when she caught it. She shoved it into her satchel.

"Me? Forget? Please, you've only been doing this every time we've docked in an HC station since *we* were in the HCA together. And that makes us both fossils incapable of change."

She gave him the finger. He blew her a kiss.

Tarquin didn't know what that was about and was too bewildered to ask any more questions. Naira grabbed him by the arm and spun him around, marching him out the door ahead of her. His stomach tied in knots, anticipating failing the security check, but Kav's false credentials got them through. Soon they were on the streets of the station, Naira leading the way by some internal compass.

She pointed out small bits of interest they passed by, noting temples and markets and which restaurants were probably great and which ones were more than likely tourist trash. Tarquin soaked it all in, fascinated to see a Human Collective station from the point of view of someone who'd lived on one, once. He'd spent his whole life on MERIT stations, Jov-U, or in fieldwork. The few times he'd passed through an HCA-controlled station, it'd been a chaotic blur, his exemplars shuffling him through as quickly as possible.

It was still a chaotic blur, but this time she was there to tease out the details.

Tarquin wasn't sure what he was more concerned about, the upcoming phone call, or the fact that Naira was being nice to him. She'd never been outright cruel, but there'd been a gruff undertone to all her interactions with him that made it plain she was tolerating his presence because she had no choice.

"Slouch," she whispered.

He dropped his shoulders too quickly to be natural, unable to shake the phantom remonstrations echoing back to him from his childhood— his mother telling him to lift his chest, to push his shoulders back, to walk with the confidence of a Mercator.

Naira chuckled to herself. "You have to stop looking like you own the place, or someone might believe you, and then we'll have to deal with a mugging."

"That happens?" he asked, aghast. Money was handled via credit lines tied to an ID pathway. There was no physical currency to change hands that Tarquin was aware of. But then, he couldn't remember the last time he'd actually had to buy something.

"You're kidding. Of course it does. Your clothes are Earth-made, people can tell and that's trendy, and we're obviously carrying weapons, which are a currency in their own right."

"We are?"

She gave him a sly smile. "I am."

They passed a narrow alley from which he could hear the muted sounds of a scuffle. Shoes scraping dirt, muffled grunts, the thump of plastic against plastic. Naira paused and cocked her head to the side.

"One sec," she said. "And hide those cuffs for me, will you?"

"Sure." He shoved his hands into his pockets. "Are you going to break that up? Won't that get us noticed?"

"No," she said. He had no idea which question she was answering.

Tarquin hurried after her as she slipped down the alley and stifled his worry. She was an exemplar. This wouldn't get out of hand. A small, childish voice squeaked, followed by a roar of laughter. Was someone hurting a kid? He sped up, nearly running into Naira's back as she rounded a corner.

Six children, the oldest of them a girl no more than ten, scrambled to hide their makeshift weapons and drew back from Naira warily, ready to flee. They wore slate-grey tunics, slashed at the waist with white belts, GARDET printed over their hearts.

"Easy." Naira spread her arms and held out her hands. "I'm from Marconette."

Every little face relaxed, save one.

"You're a Demarco?" a wary girl, the oldest of the group, asked.

"Nah." She lowered into a crouch. "My mom died later, so I kept her name. I went in at seven."

"You're old," one of the kids said.

Naira snorted. "Yup. A fossil, or so I'm told."

The wary girl crossed her arms and squinted at Tarquin. "Who's he?"

Naira glanced over her shoulder at him. "A friend. He's cool. Don't worry about him."

"Hi," Tarquin said, and stopped himself from waving at them with his family-cuffed hand.

"Uh-huh," the wary girl said. "He got a name?"

"Tarquin," Naira said.

He stiffened. His mother had dug that name out of ancient history. Why would Naira reveal his identity?

"*I'm* Tarquin!" One of the younger boys, maybe six, jabbed a thumb into their chest with a smile that was missing a few teeth. "It's a famous guy's name. I'm gonna be a famous guy, too."

"Really?" Naira asked. "It's a very nice name."

Tarquin relaxed. Right. The names of high-ranking MERIT always ended up popular. And...Naira thought his name was nice?

Another boy next to kid-Tarquin rolled his eyes. "You were named after a building, dummy."

"Was not," he shot back. "The *building* was named for a famous *guy*."

"Oh," Tarquin said, unable to muster up anything else. The child's parent must have made use of Tarquin's foundation. A strange sense of pride and grief mingled within him. Pride that his foundation had helped them, and grief that if these kids were from the local orphanage, then that parent was dead.

"Who cares about a famous guy?" the little boy said, determined not to lose this battle.

"Mum said he was a *hero*." Kid-Tarquin puffed up his chest.

"She was right," Naira said. "Tarquin Mercator is a hero."

Naira thought *what*? Tarquin was deeply glad she wasn't looking at him, because he probably appeared on the verge of passing out. The kids were, naturally, oblivious to his inner turmoil and devolved into sticking their tongues out at each other and arguing over the order of operations involved in who was named for what.

"Hey." Naira snapped her fingers into her palm in a way he'd never seen her do before. The kids jerked to immediate attention.

The wary girl scoffed and crossed her arms again. "What do you want, green-hands?"

"Whoa!" One of the girls darted forward and clutched Naira's wrist, rubbing at the green cuffs to see if they wiped away. "How'd you get these?"

"I worked hard," Naira said. "And then I got lucky."

Kid-Tarquin inched closer. "Can I see?"

"Sure." She held out her arms for inspection, and the children gathered around, prodding at her skin. Even the wary girl scooted closer to look.

Once they'd satisfied themselves that the cuffs were real, the kids shifted back, picking up their makeshift weapons to show her. They had repurposed packing materials into axes and swords and guns, and they brandished them with glee, telling her how they were going to get into the HCA and be soldiers. Naira oohed and aahed over every weapon.

Tarquin stared. These *children* believed their only way into a better life was to be willing to die for it. Such an idea had never occurred to him, or anyone else he'd grown up with, until that moment. Naira looked at him once during the display to make sure he was paying attention. He nodded to her, not wanting to say anything that would bring the kids down.

Another play fight broke out, and Naira watched for a while in silence, letting her hands dangle between her knees. The Monster of the Moment the kids were determined to slay was a picture of a mean-looking woman on a piece of cardboard with chalky scribbles all over her eyes.

"What's that?" he asked, pointing to the woman with his chin.

"That's Metal Eyes," one of the kids said in the exasperated tones of one having to explain the obvious. "You know." They pointed to their temple. "Metal! Like you!"

The pathways, of course. Tarquin wondered if the woman depicted was one of the adults from the orphanage.

The wary girl inched closer to Naira and whispered, "Is it really possible to get out of the grey?"

"It is. But it's really hard."

The girl looked at her friends. "So's this."

"You're not wrong," Naira said.

"Is it worth it?"

"Sometimes. Not always."

"Thanks," the girl said. "For the honesty. No one's ever honest with us."

"Yeah, I remember."

The girl nodded seriously and held out a hand. Naira shook it. When the girl stepped away, Naira stood, reaching for her satchel. She tugged the cloth bag out and reached inside to pull out a handful of colorful hard candies in clear wrappers.

All eyes turned to her, bright. Naira held the candy up.

"You won't get caught, right?"

Every pair of eyes rolled and each one of them flipped up a hem of their tunic, a seam in their belt, or revealed a hidden pocket in their sleeve—all places to hide a precious piece of contraband. Naira grinned her approval and handed out each piece, making certain they were shared equally, then stretched and gave kid-Tarquin's hair a quick ruffle.

"Back to work for me, Degardets. Keep your heads down, yeah?"

"Yeah!" they chorused.

Tarquin followed Naira out of the alley in a daze. When they were back on the street, she paused, fidgeting with the strap of her satchel. Tarquin wasn't certain he'd ever seen her fidget before. She pressed her lips together, hard.

"Thank you," he said. "For letting me be a part of that. For showing me what it's like."

"That was a good moment for them."

He glanced back down the alley. "I figured that out."

"If you ever..." She cleared her throat. "If you ever return to Mercator, remember that. Remember them."

He wanted to tell her he had no intention of rejoining his family, but she'd allowed herself to be vulnerable with him because it was important to her that he remembered them. She needed reassurance, not contradiction.

"I'll never forget," he said. She nodded stiffly, and he tried to redirect some of her discomfort. "How did you know they'd be there?"

"Oh, that." She smiled and turned, pointing to a plain building a few blocks away. "That's their orphanage, Gardet. Second and sixth hour of the day the kids get to themselves. It was just a matter of circling a bit until I heard them. There's always a group play-fighting somewhere, prepping for the HCA."

"They're not supervised? I assumed they snuck out."

She started walking again. "No one cares where they go or if they come back. The locals complain if they get too loud or dirty up the place, but that's it."

He kicked himself. He'd meant to ease her, not drag up more painful memories. "Sharp, I..."

She stopped walking. "Don't. Don't apologize, okay? Just remember. That's all I want."

"You have my word," he said, then took a steeling breath. "But what you told them about me. It's not true. You and Kav and Kuma, you're the ones leading this fight. I merely do what I can to support you."

Naira's posture softened, and she tilted her head to the side, studying him. "I wasn't talking about your role in the Conservators."

"The TMF, then? That was the least I could do with my family stipend."

"Mercator, you..." She made a muted sound that might have been an aborted grunt, or laugh, he couldn't tell, then looked away to survey the streets. No one was close enough to overhear. "I have spent my life steeped in violence. Any power I've had in this world, I've had because I've taken it by force. That's the position I was put in." She glanced back, toward the alley. "The position they're in. So when I'm confronted with a problem, I see it as a battlefield. Those are the tools I have to work with. But you...you were given all the power in the worlds. Your tools are subjugation and control. And yet, when we hit this wall, your instinct was to just...talk. To try and find common ground with Emali. To seek mutual understanding. You urged me off a path that would have ended with a lot of suffering."

"We don't even know if this will work."

"No. We don't." She smiled, and reached out to squeeze his arm, letting her hand linger a beat longer than might be friendly. "But I admire you for wanting to find out."

Naira walked on. It took Tarquin a little while to remember how to use his feet.

SEVEN

Tarquin

Miller-Urey Station | The Present

Tarquin wanted to ask her more about the orphanage, but Naira fell quiet, and he didn't want to push his luck. Eventually, she pointed at a rust-stained doorway with a sign above that read HOURLY, and nothing else. She hadn't been kidding about that. He'd half thought she'd made it up to shock him. There'd been rumors at Jov-U of students sneaking to hourlies off-campus, but those had been rumors. He'd always wondered why they'd bothered when they all had dorm rooms.

But then, he'd had his rooms to himself, and many of the others hadn't. He scratched the Mercator crest printed into his skin.

"Stop that," she said. "We're here. Try to act normal."

"Normal," he repeated.

"Maybe just don't say anything."

"Probably for the best."

She held out her arm, elbow crooked, and he relaxed as he slipped his arm into hers, knowing she'd guide him through whatever came next. Though he'd tried to deny the privileges granted to him by his birth, he'd always known that he was separate from the rest of humanity. He'd glided through life without any real challenge until the day Naira had publicly accused his father of being behind the spread of the shroud.

Having her with him now, even if it hurt to look at her sometimes, made things easier.

The door slid open as they approached. The lobby hardly deserved the name. It was a room no larger than his quarters on the shuttle, a bench against one wall and the other wall taken up by a machine to buy VR simulations. A counter with a bored-looking attendant filled the end opposite the entrance, a narrow elevator beside him.

The attendant looked up from the grey gleam of the HC holo projected from his forearm and sniffed. "You looking for a room? We got soundproofing, VR dispenses, showers, and..." He knocked his knuckles against the grey, plasticky counter he sat behind. "...Real marble decor. Real fancy."

"That is a mica composite veneer," Tarquin said, unable to help himself. Naira squeezed his arm.

"It looks great," she said. Tarquin bit his tongue. "How much?"

"Two hundred creds an hour."

Tarquin had no idea if that was high or low, and the realization took away all his annoyance about the falsely advertised marble.

"Seriously?" Naira's voice dripped with skepticism.

The attendant sighed. "Seventy-five, then. It's been a slow week."

"Fine," she said grudgingly, and swiped her fake ID pathway over the reader embedded in the absolutely-not-marble countertop. "Two hours."

"Best make it three," Tarquin said, thinking of Emali's habit of never quite sticking to her schedule. He wanted to be sure they had enough time for her to get the initial message, then find a quiet place to call him back.

"Suuure." The attendant shot him a wink. "Three it is."

He blushed. Naira got the digital keys and asked for directions, which he couldn't hear above the rushing in his ears. By the time she opened the door and led him inside—dropping his arm immediately—he'd regained some composure. Despite her previous direction to slouch, he let himself fall back into his normal posture, taking comfort in the familiar pose of control, even if he was very much out of control.

"Three hours? Really?" she asked. He couldn't interpret her tone. She crossed the room to run a finger down the side of a window, lifting the privacy filter over that section for a second while she peeked out, nodded to herself, then put the filter back in place.

"Emali's not rigid about her routine. I wanted to give us some wiggle room."

"So we're going to be stuck here for a while," she said.

"More than likely."

"Then you'd better hurry up and send her that message."

"Right, of course."

The room did, indeed, have furniture topped with that awful veneer the attendant had bragged about. Tarquin sat at the room's single desk, trying not to think about what, exactly, the desk had been used for in an hourly rental, and tried to find an angle that wouldn't include the vast, red-sheeted bed or the VR dispenser in the corner. Eventually, he gave up and accessed his messaging program, setting his virtual background to be a blank wall.

"Hey, Em, this is the real Tarq. You and I both know that something is amiss with my father. I'm not on that ship. I don't know if Leka is, but regardless, we need to talk." He played it back, then hit send.

"And now we wait," Naira said.

"I suppose so."

Naira leaned against the wall, one boot flat against it, her knee bent, and crossed her arms, chin lowering. She'd certainly struck that pose countless times before, no doubt waiting for his father outside of some meeting or another. She could probably sleep like that, if she needed to. Tarquin looked around the room for a distraction that wasn't her or the giant bed or the VR flashing golden buy-me lights at them, and came up blank.

"Do you...want to sit?" he asked.

"No."

"All right."

He had no idea why he wanted to crawl out of his skin or else bolt out of the room. They'd been alone plenty of times since she'd been reprinted and remembered none of their previous entanglement—whatever that had even *been*. Two embraces stolen between life-or-death situations were hardly a relationship.

But he had hoped they might become one.

"Tell me about the MERIT courtship rules," she said.

He startled. "Surely you know of them from your exemplar school?"

"Exemplar 'school'?" She sniffed. "*Academy* training is almost entirely physical. We learned the bare facts, and we learned them with an eye to watching who might be trying to wheedle close to our charges. I know the rules that bound Acaelus, and how he utilized those rules. Tell me what we're working with regarding Leka."

"It's complicated." He frowned, trying to find the right angle from which to approach this without giving too much of his personal history away. "For Leka, the rules are extremely strict, though not as strict as our father's. She can't express interest in anyone not her equal without them first expressing interest in her, and since there are only four other direct heirs—and they're discouraged from mingling, as no one wants the families of MERIT to merge—it's made forming relationships extremely difficult for her."

"Let me guess, her social life consists mostly of political opportunists hitting on her and her politely finding ways to turn them down without causing a scandal."

"That's it exactly," he said. "But with Emali, there was no denying their attraction. It was magnetic. Everyone in the room felt it, no matter how much they tried to restrain themselves."

Naira shifted her weight. Tarquin pretended not to have noticed.

"I met Emali at Jov-U, and Leka met her when she came out for one of my graduations. Emali's high enough in Rochard that she has courtship rules of her own to follow, so she was aware of Leka's restrictions and made her intentions known right away."

"That all sounds aboveboard. What's the problem?"

"Well." Tarquin rested his arm along the top of the chair and leaned back as he recalled those first few fraught weeks. "They were supposed to wait before they could be together. A cooling-off period, to be absolutely certain it wasn't Leka's power that drew Emali's attention. Obviously, they didn't. My peers make a habit of skirting the rules, but Leka's different. Too much in the public eye. She has to follow the rules to avoid scandal and, well..."

Tarquin shook his head. "Those aware of the situation have been politely pretending that they did things properly, but it's fragile. Father nearly pulled me out of Jov-U so Leka wouldn't have an excuse to see her anymore, but moving me wouldn't have stopped her. She's as stubborn as he is."

"I see. How long is your cooling-off period?"

The question took him by surprise. He tugged at his collar, but she'd already loosened it, so he ended up yanking on it too hard instead. "Ah. Well. It was six months. But I suppose I'm not family anymore. At least, I have nothing to offer anyone. I don't know that it matters now."

"Six months," she echoed, but didn't elaborate. "Are all your prospective partners bound by the same rules as Leka's—they have to express interest first?"

"Uh..." Sweat trickled down his spine. She had to have noticed that they hadn't been on Sixth Cradle nearly long enough for them to have followed those rules. "Yes. They did. If you—if you're curious about what happened, between...I mean, on Sixth Cradle, then, I—"

"I'm not."

"Oh, thank fuck," he burst out before he could control his relief. She laughed at him, and his shoulders relaxed. "I don't want to make you uncomfortable," he explained, "and I don't want to keep anything from you, either, but I find the memories difficult."

"I appreciate that," she said in exactly the same tone she'd use if Kav had told her he'd cleaned the engine bay ahead of schedule. "May I ask you something that you might find difficult?"

Tarquin really, really wished she'd remove the sunglasses so he could read her face. He nodded.

She gestured at the space between them, her voice softer than he'd heard it since her reprinting. "Is this only about the past for you?"

His heartbeat stuttered. Was it? He didn't know what kind of answer she was hoping for, if she was hoping for anything at all. He searched within himself, thinking, making sure that whatever he said was true, because she wouldn't have asked if it didn't matter to her.

Tarquin had spent most of his life pretending he didn't notice others romantically because he took the rules that bound him seriously. It hurt less to wait to be approached rather than to hold out any tentative hope that someone he cared for might notice and reciprocate. He'd grown so adept at shutting that part of himself down, he hadn't even realized how close he'd grown to Naira until he'd offered to relieve her pain by massaging her sore shoulder.

That contact, and the desire in her eyes, had kicked open floodgates he hadn't known he was holding shut.

But that woman had died, and while Sharp was her, she was different. Rougher, sometimes, than the woman he'd known. A little more cautious, though she worked to hide her wariness. Sharp's anger was a flame guarded against a storm, while Naira's had nearly engulfed a world.

He recalled that cautious, closed-down woman letting him talk her ear off about the mining site at Sixth Cradle. He thought of her bringing candy to the children to make one day of their lives a little brighter. To make certain that he, a man with the potential to wield power those children could only dream of, remembered them. He smiled to himself.

"No," he said. "It began that way, I admit, but now, it's not just about the past, to me."

"Good," she said.

"Good?"

"Then I'm interested."

"You're...?" He trailed off, too stunned to marshal his thoughts into words.

She hadn't moved, but suddenly felt closer, the tension between them not a wall to be avoided but a tether, drawing him to her.

Tentatively, Tarquin stood. She didn't rebuke him, didn't tell him to sit back down, and while years of training screamed at him to restrain himself, he crossed the small space between them. Her preferred print was taller than the one he'd met her in, but he still towered over her. She lifted her chin to look up at him. Those damn sunglasses kept him from seeing her eyes.

He reached for her glasses, pausing to see if she would tell him to stop, but she merely arched one brow above the metal frames. They'd warmed to her skin, and he focused on that radiant heat as he slipped them off, folded them, and set them aside with a click on the cheap composite windowsill. A black eye puffed one side of her face.

The strength of the anger that surged through him surprised him. "Who did that to you?"

"Kuma. Didn't you wonder where she got hers?"

"I did, but I know better than to ask those questions. She'd have asked me if I wanted one to match." A laugh gusted out of Naira, her breath tickling his lips, and his chest warmed. He wanted to make her laugh again. Had wanted to be the source of that delighted sound since the first night he'd heard it, on Sixth Cradle, the tone identical despite the different prints. Naira's laugh was always Naira's, full-throated and bright. "What were you two fighting over?"

Her cheeks darkened. "You."

"Uh. I like Kuma fine, but—"

"Not like that," she said quickly. "Over my . . . hesitance, among other things."

Hesitant wasn't a word he'd associate with Naira, but the way she drew out those words was exactly that. "Who won?"

Her lashes lowered, and it took him a moment to realize she was taking him in, dragging her gaze slowly over his entire body until she lifted her golden eyes to meet his once more. "I think I'm winning right now."

His breath caught, and he knew he should say something to make her feel the way she'd made him feel, but all his words fled him.

She lifted her chin in challenge, but otherwise she hadn't moved. "Well? I'm not waiting six months."

"You make nothing easy, do you?"

She smirked in response, but despite all her cool confidence, he caught her eyes tracing the shape of his lips. A sweet, powerful longing filled him that he couldn't seem to act upon. She'd expressed her interest, hadn't rebuked his approach to her personal space, and yet he'd frozen, pressed up against an intangible wall built of his own psyche.

Tarquin had never been the one to initiate physical contact. Never the pursuer. In that brief and chaotic moment on Sixth Cradle, when they'd leaned toward each other, he'd stopped himself until Naira had pushed him over the edge of restraint. But that had been desperate, terrified. He'd thought he'd never see her again, and all his fears of consequence had fled him.

This was different. This was deliberate. The start of something hopefully long-lasting, in an environment without the pressures of immediate peril. Once again, she was pushing him to reach for her fire, even if it might burn.

He adored her for that, though he'd keep the depth of his feelings to himself.

"Are you certain?" He half expected her to vanish on the spot and for this to have all been yet another dream. "I'm not interested in something casual."

"I know. I'm not sure of anything these days, but I want to try."

That, he understood. Lightly, he touched her arm, precisely where she had touched him earlier, and was rewarded with a soft, pleased hum. Emboldened, he traced a path over the curve of her bicep, to her shoulder, passed over the rough barrier of her jacket to brush the smooth skin of her neck.

Her pulse surged, skin growing warm in a trail beneath his touch until he was cupping her face in one hand, his fingers in her hair. He placed his free hand against the wall to brace himself and drew her to him, eyes sliding shut.

It wasn't that first frenetic embrace of Sixth Cradle. It was slow and questing and tender in a way he hadn't imagined was possible with someone as rough as she was. When they finally came up for air, he coiled his arm around her and held her against him, savoring her solid presence, the way they fit together. Tarquin lowered his forehead to rest against hers and smiled, a little loopy and dreamlike, into her answering smile.

"I regret making myself wait for that," she said.

"I'm glad you waited until you were sure."

Her half-lidded eyes drew him back, eager for more. An incoming call alert flashed in the corner of his HUD. Tarquin groaned, ducking out of his attempt at another kiss, and thumped his forehead against the wall above her.

Naira laughed. "Emali?"

"Yes," he said grudgingly.

"Better answer it." She skimmed a hand up his side, slipping beneath his disheveled shirt to trail her short nails over his skin.

"Oh, you're cruel." He grinned, despite himself.

She held her hands up like she was being robbed. He wanted to grasp her wrists and press them against the wall, but he made himself step away and turn his back on her so that he wouldn't be distracted. He made sure the blank virtual background was in place and answered.

Emali had been crying. She'd hidden it with powder over the redness on the tip of her nose and cheeks, but her eyelids were puffy, her eyes bloodshot. Tarquin's good mood evaporated.

"Tarq? Is that really you?" she asked in a harsh whisper.

"Yes," he said. "Are you all right? Are you safe?"

"I'm safe, but I haven't heard from Leka in weeks. Is *she* safe, Tarq? Can you tell me that much?"

"I haven't seen her, either," he said. "I don't know. But I don't believe she was on that ship with Acaelus. I certainly wasn't there with them."

"I heard a rumor," Emali said, then cut herself off and hunched closer to the camera. "I heard a rumor she cracked. That Acaelus tried to bring you all back after the station blew and every last one of you came up screaming."

"I'm right here, Em. I'm not cracked."

"I know, I know. I've even talked to her since the station exploded. It's just...I did some digging. Poked around in databases I shouldn't have access to, you know?"

He thought of all his father's admonishments, of their advisers quietly tutting at Leka and warning her against letting a lesser cousin of a rival house—and they were all rival—spend the night in her rooms before a formal contract could be enforced. Tarquin should have been outraged on his sister's behalf, but he couldn't help a twist of a smile at Emali's implied revelation.

Tarquin had no doubt that Emali loved his sister. But she was no fool, and whether on her own or with Thieut's support, she'd taken advantage of the opportunity to plant spying devices on Leka's personal things.

"I can't say I'm surprised," Tarquin said.

"You're not angry?"

He hesitated. "I should be. But Mercator...We're a bull in a china shop, aren't we? It's natural to want to know where we'll charge next. I daresay even Leka would approve once she got over the indignation."

"I'm glad we understand each other," Emali said. "Because I might have done something highly illegal and definitely unethical. And I am, quite frankly, not certain I can trust you, Tarq. You indulged in your petty rebellions, and I found that charming enough, but really, you always wanted *his* approval, didn't you?"

"I won't deny that," he said, "but I can promise you that things are different now. I'm not even certain the man in that print is entirely my father anymore, even if the neural map fits."

She chewed her lip, uncertain. "Let me...let me look into a few more things. I'll call you later."

"Wait." He reached for the holo display as if he could physically stop her. She turned back to the camera, surprise making her mouth fall open, the ragged edge of her often-chewed lip a stark red against her dark skin. "Em, we don't have a lot of time for deliberation. You're clearly frightened. I have resources. I can keep you safe. But you have to talk to me. We have to tell each other the truth, because I don't know what my father is doing on that ship, but nothing good can come of it."

She laughed. A light, trilling sound cut short. "What resources? I know Acaelus cut you off. He wanted info from you about whatever you screwed up on Sixth Cradle, and you wouldn't spill, so he cut you off the family coffers until you came to heel."

Tarquin blinked. "Is that what he told the others? That he cut me off until I'd behave?"

"More or less." She shrugged. "That's why you weren't at school, wasn't it? He pulled the purse strings after you failed that mission."

He'd wondered, when his family hadn't publicly denounced him, what Acaelus's plan was. Now he saw that Acaelus had presumed Tarquin would come crawling home after living for a while without his money or other MERIT-granted comforts.

Acaelus thought Tarquin was that weak. Another cog in the family machine. One that went out of alignment, sometimes, but who could be pushed back into place. All this time Tarquin had been lying low with the Conservators, fearing his father would send his private security after them, and Acaelus had merely decided to wait. Wait for his wayward child to give up on the harsh realities of living outside of his protection and crawl home.

"Acaelus didn't cut me off," he said. "I fled Mercator. I left my family."

"Why?" she asked, eyes wide.

"Because my family is responsible for the shroud. But not in the way you think."

Emali sucked a breath in, drawing her head back slightly. The *canus* in their pathways hated, if that thing could be said to hate, the shroud. It was its primary predator. Emali, predictably, was instantly curious.

"How?" she asked.

"Meet with me," he said. "Some things must be said in person."

"Where are you? You can't come here."

He told her, and they arranged to meet on a shuttle she would park in the station's docks the following morning. Even though Emali was low-ranking in the Rochard family, her relationship with Leka meant she rated an exemplar, and Tarquin wasn't willing to trust whoever that was. Emali couldn't disembark without that exemplar at her side, but they could meet on her shuttle in a soundproofed room.

He ended the call, and the strength bled out of him. Tarquin sat on the edge of the bed, a slight tremble running through him now that the stress of the moment had passed. His hands shook, and he watched them with detached fascination, wondering if that was adrenaline fading, or *canus* rallying against him, trying to make him feel regret about what he was doing.

"You did well." Naira dropped to a light crouch in front of him. "Acaelus was wrong to assume you'd come crawling back without funds."

Tarquin captured one of her hands in his and turned it over, tracing the fine creases that ran through the center of her palm. Ignoring the stamp of golden pathways in her skin that granted her strength. He squeezed his eyes shut.

"Father always considered me a pup in need of better training. I'm not surprised he expected me to come crawling home after my first taste of life without family comforts. And he was right. I nearly left you there, on Mercator Station. I nearly told him what he wanted to know so that I could go back to my rooms, to my studies. Sometimes I wonder, if it hadn't been for Paison giving me no choice, if I would have put my head down and pretended nothing at all was amiss."

"I can't answer that for you," she said, "but the man I've seen take action since we met doesn't strike me as a man who'd be willing to put his head in the sand and pretend."

He squeezed her hand. "Thank you."

"What did she say about Leka?"

"Just that she hadn't heard from her in weeks. Em's done something, hacked a Mercator system, more than likely, but was too frightened to say anything more over the call."

"That's not all," Naira said. "Tell me."

"There's a rumor..." He took a deep breath. Blew it out. "There's a rumor the whole family cracked after the station exploded."

"You know that's not true. You're fine. We've seen Acaelus and Leka on the news since the explosion. Canden...I don't know, but Acaelus didn't have her real map to crack."

"I know, I know." He shook himself. "It was seeing that...puppet show Acaelus made. Nothing feels real anymore."

"I'm here," she said. "I'm real."

Naira started to stand. Before she was fully on her feet she leaned toward him, planting one knee against the mattress. It sagged under her weight. He had to scoot back, putting the heels of his palms behind him to keep from sliding into that divot.

She moved with his retreat, her free hand resting against his chest. Her other knee joined the mattress and then she was sinking down onto his lap, straddling him, the amber scent of her skin filling his senses. His head spun.

"I'm here," she repeated, and slid her hand up, caressing his neck. "And we've got at least two hours left before we have to get back to work. What would you like to do with them?"

This was more than he'd dared to hope for, and he locked up. A lifetime's worth of insecurity stole his voice, smothering him in doubt. She sensed his withdrawal and pulled back. He had enough presence of mind to capture her hips between his hands to keep her from moving away completely.

"Too fast? Do you want me to stop?" She searched his face, and whatever she saw there drew worry between her brows.

"No. I mean...Maybe. I don't know."

Her leg slid back, extricating herself from him. He tightened his grip on her hips and she stilled, waiting, watching him with a curious tilt to her head, but no judgment—only concern.

He tried to sort through the surge of doubt that'd consumed him, and flinched away from a truth he didn't want to tell her.

"I'm sorry." The words dragged out of him. "Maybe this isn't a good idea, after all."

"Oh." She tried to keep the disappointment off her face, but couldn't hide it completely, and it shattered him. "I'm...sorry to have troubled you."

Naira lifted her hips, shifting away, and his grip tightened again, unable to help himself. "I'm getting mixed messages here, Mercator."

I was wrong. Please stay with me balanced on the tip of his tongue. Instead, he said, "Forgive me," and made himself pry his fingers from the heat of her body.

Her expression was quizzical and wounded, but she moved away from him. The second her boots touched the floor she resettled her clothes and smoothed her hair.

"Well. I guess we'd better get back to the others, then. There's a strong unionist faction on this station I'd like to contact while we're here, and since we have until morning to meet Emali, I want to poke around a little, get a feel for the mood of the people..."

She kept talking while she went through the perfunctory work of checking her weapons, adjusting her armor, outlining the details of her plans as if this were any other mission, any other moment, and Tarquin wasn't sitting there, his heart falling to pieces because he'd gone and broken it himself.

Naira reached for her sunglasses, and an absurd part of him thought that was it. That was the door closing. As soon as she put those on, she'd lock down again. Go back to being all business, and he'd never have another chance. He grabbed her wrist from behind, stopping her before she touched them, and couldn't even recall getting to his feet.

Firm muscle tensed beneath his grip. Her voice was rough, the perfunctory nature ripped away. "Don't taunt me, Mercator."

"I'm not."

"Then you'd better start talking, because what you're doing, it hurts."

"Please, bear with me. I am...inexperienced in discussing these matters."

He waited, breath held, until some of the coiled anger bled out of her and she turned to him, breaking his hold to cross her arms defensively. That was fair. She had every right to be on her guard. She'd made herself vulnerable, and he'd turned her down.

He'd had Naira—*Naira*—in his lap and he'd panicked and *turned her down*. Despite his degrees, Tarquin was reasonably certain he was the stupidest man alive.

"I'm listening," she said.

He had to tell her. There was no turning back from this without damaging even the thin friendship she'd pretended to revert to. The very thought of explaining himself withered him inside. He shoved his hands in his pockets and looked at his feet, because it was easier than seeing her reaction.

"The people I've contracted with in the past..." He waited to see if she would stop him, but she remained silent. "Most of them got bored with me before the six months were over, once they realized I wasn't... Mercator enough, I suppose. I usually found out via the automated message, so their reasons are unclear to me."

Naira made a soft hissing sound. He wasn't looking at her, but he could imagine the pity on her face.

"The rest drifted away shortly after the six months. I always expected it, but with you..." He rubbed the back of his neck, the skin there burning. "You're... you're you. And I'm just a nerd, really. I fear that if we resolve this tension between us, then you'll find I'm not what you'd hoped for, and I'm not certain I could take that."

"So you thought you'd stop things before you got hurt."

He smiled bitterly. "You know me too well."

"Yeah, I think I do." She curled her fingers beneath his chin and lifted his head. "I know you're a nerd. I *like* that you're a nerd. I like that you're kind and sweet and blush at the slightest compliment. And I'd like to know you better."

A smile fluttered, hopeful, to his face. He squashed it. "I can't keep up with you."

"What the hell do you think you've been doing for the past five months?"

"I..." He blinked.

She took a slow step into his personal space, testing the waters again. When he didn't move away, she shifted her hand to the side of his face. He leaned into the touch. Her smile deepened.

"I know you're tired," she said. "I know you're raw and running ragged. I am, too. I can't promise where this will go, but those people who left without a word? They were jackasses. I wouldn't do that to you."

"Naira..."

She took another step. Their chests touched.

"I like you, Rock-boy," she whispered against his ear. "I know I've been prickly, and I'm sorry for that. I meant what I said. I'm interested. In *you*. I hope you know that."

The nickname sent a jolt through him—she couldn't possibly know she'd called him Rock-boy on Sixth Cradle. Was it some sort of echo? Or was it simply because here and now, she found his obsession with his work charming once more? Naira was still Naira. She admired the same qualities in people, and there was no reason that wouldn't apply to him.

"I've been an idiot," he said.

"No." She stroked his back with her other hand. "You've been hurt. And I'm glad you told me."

He wrapped his arms around her, tugging her close. A contented sigh eased out of her, and she pressed her face into the curve of his neck and shoulder. That single sound burned all vestiges of his fears away. They stayed like that for a while, simply being together, until a small, nervous chuckle shuddered out of her. A pressure released.

Tarquin nudged her back, just enough so that he could look down into her eyes. "Are you all right?"

"I thought, for a minute there, that you'd turned me down because you'd realized you weren't attracted to me if I wasn't in Lockhart's print."

"What?" He almost laughed, the thought was so absurd, but she was rubbing her forehead, embarrassed. On Sixth Cradle, she'd demurred when he'd complimented her and had pointed out that she wasn't even wearing her real face.

It hadn't occurred to him that she might have done so out of insecurity. It hadn't occurred to him that someone like her could be insecure *at all*. But then, it hadn't occurred to him before he'd actually met her that she was anything but a stoic warrior, and that had been drastically incorrect. Tarquin set aside his preconceived notions of what he thought she was, and listened to the infinitesimal strain in her voice.

"I'm broader. Stronger." She gestured absently down her body, to where he'd grabbed her.

"Naira." He took her hand, kissing her palm. "May I tell you something about Sixth Cradle?"

She nodded.

"I have spent most of my adult life shutting down any feelings of attraction out of fear that they won't be reciprocated for the right reasons. That first night, when we crash-landed, I heard you laugh, and I thought—well, I told myself that I wanted to be the kind of leader who you could be so comfortable with that you would laugh like that with me. I think...No, I *know* that sound slipped below my barriers. It drew me to you.

"I kept catching glimpses of the real you beneath the exemplar veneer, and I found myself conniving ways to make you break your shell more often. I was desperate for more of you, the *real* you, and every time I glimpsed your personality it made me hunger for more. It was you, shining from within, that attracted me. Even when you were so furious with me I thought you'd rip me in two."

"Oh," she said, clearly at a loss for words. His heart lifted, to be able to scatter her thoughts like that.

"I suppose there's no harm in telling you this now, but when I walked into that lab on Mercator Station and saw you there, ready to beat whoever came through the door to a pulp with your chair, fully embodied at long last, I...I've never wanted anyone more in my life."

Her expression turned skeptical. "I was ready to tear you apart."

"Oh, I know." He tugged her closer, and was rewarded with a pleased intake of breath when their hips met. "And to be perfectly honest with you, I wouldn't have minded one bit."

"You can't be serious," she said, but her voice had deepened, growing smoother.

He ducked his head to brush his lips along the edge of her ear. "Want to find out?"

EIGHT

Naira

Miller-Urey Station | The Present

Kuma and Kav had secured a single large room in a hotel on the edge of the station's dock sector. Normally Naira wouldn't have minded the close quarters, but after being with Tarquin, a tiny part of her rebelled at the lack of privacy. The forlorn smile he gave her, one eye covered by a lock of hair, told her he was feeling the same way.

They'd be back on the shuttle soon enough. Right now she needed to focus on the mission, because the sour look on Kav's face as he peered into his grey holo told her something had gone wrong.

"What's on fire?" Naira tossed her duffle against a wall, giving it a quick kick to bunch up her clothes so she could use it as a pillow later.

Kav had taken one of the twin beds in the room for himself and sat cross-legged on it. Kuma lingered in the back of the room on a bench, one foot on the seat, the other dangling over the edge as she cleaned beneath her nails with a knife theatrically large for the purpose. Tarquin hung back by the door, his bag still over his shoulders and his hands in his pockets, though he'd lost the slouch she'd had to remind him to affect.

"I've been monitoring station security ever since we booked this place," Kav said. He scratched at his chest with one wide, splayed hand.

"Things got chatty for a while until about...two and a half hours ago? Then they died down, and now they've gone silent."

Naira frowned. "We're talking total silence?"

"Yeah. I don't like it. A station this big, there's always something going on. Security channels are never fully locked down. But they've gone dark. It's like they switched over to another channel, but I can't find anything except a few encrypted lines I don't have time to crack."

"I wanted to go have a look around security HQ," Kuma said, "but Kav insisted we wait for you two to get back. What took you so long?"

"Emali doesn't keep a consistent schedule," she said. "We booked three hours to make sure we got her to call us back. It's worth noting Emali called around the time the station security went dark."

"Really," Kuma drawled, "and what did you do with the rest of the time?"

"Talked." Naira did not look at Tarquin.

Kuma and Kav looked at each other, shared a shit-eating grin, and then looked back at them. Naira sighed internally but kept her face neutral, lifting a brow in a mild challenge.

Kuma said, "You are such a fucking liar."

Kav cleared his throat. "Bust Nai over this later. Deal with the weird security now, eh?"

Naira sank into what was usually a comfortable crouch, but the movement awakened a few pleasantly sore spots. She pulled up the holo from her forearm, accessing the station's local network. "So you think they've moved to an encrypted channel?"

"Yeah," Kav said, "there's no way things are this quiet. The HCA likes to switch to encrypted when something heavy is about to go down and they don't want to be overheard."

"I remember," Naira said. She loaded in a fake profile for herself and accessed the station's social network. "I also remember that the encryption keys for those channels were sent to staff over internal messaging."

"Hmm." Kav tapped a finger against his arm that made his holo flicker to the rhythm of his thoughts. "HCA protocol stipulates randomized passwords. Hard to break those boxes in a timely manner."

"Sure," Naira said, "but you were HCA, Kav, c'mon. No one could remember those passwords, so they usually made up something reasonably long that had meaning to them. We find a weak link, we get into their messages, we get the encryption keys."

"A li'l old-fashioned social engineering meets basic cracking. I like it. You guys get me likely candidates and I'll set up a sandbox for the login so we don't get locked out."

"What exactly are we looking for?" Tarquin asked.

"Log in to the local social net via your fake ID, search for people who work station security, then skim for oversharers. Tell us when you find someone who looks too..." She scrunched her nose, considering. "Into themselves or their hobbies."

Naira started scrolling, skimming over profile pictures. She skipped anyone who had taken their picture in their uniform, or anyone who had a semiprofessional headshot. Those people were invested in their work and likely to follow protocol.

"I've found somebody with a picture of a racing ship as a profile picture," Tarquin said. "Does that count as a hobby?"

"Oh, that's good," Kuma said. "Flash us the profile?"

ANDREW GAFFORD linked to them all. Naira dug in, flicking through the guy's posts. He had a real thing for racing ships, specifically the one in his profile—the *Silver Talon*.

"Ship is the *Silver Talon*," Naira said. "Birthday is May 21, 2316, enlisted January 8, 2335, graduated January 30, 2339."

"Adding in iterations on those," Kav said. "Got anything else?"

"Lots of pics of him with his mom," Kuma said. "Her birthday is June 18, 2285. Looks like he has a nickname for her: mawdi."

"Aww," Kav said as he plugged it in. "Pets?"

"Negative," Naira said, "but he's watched the movie *Crash Alert* thirty-seven times in the last year."

"Importing that fandom's unique vocabulary," Kav said. "I think we've got enough to run a test."

"Go for it," Naira said.

Kav's holo flickered, running through the cycles for about ten minutes, before winking a green light at him.

"Ah. Here we go. Password is CrAsh+a1o0N!182285."

"He really does love his mom," Kuma said. "That's sweet."

"Make sure the breach can't be traced to Gafford, will you, Kav? Kid seems decent enough, if a little dim," Naira said.

"Way ahead of you," Kav said.

"Is this something you all do often?" Tarquin asked.

Kav chuckled to himself, busy getting into Gafford's files, so Naira answered, "You didn't think we brute-forced our way into Mercator security, did you? Where there's people, there's a weak spot. You just have to push around to find it."

"I've got the keys." Kav accessed the encrypted channel and let it play.

Naira frowned as she listened to the chatter across the radio. It was half in code, but as ex-HCA, it was a code both she and Kav knew well.

"I don't understand half of this," Tarquin said.

"Shh." Naira exchanged a look with Kav. He nodded agreement. "They're preparing for a unionist protest against MERIT. It sounds like anti-corp sentiment has been high here since word of Sixth Cradle collapsing got back. Acaelus's public abandonment of the Sol system struck a match under that powder keg."

"Why would a protest require an encrypted radio channel?" Tarquin asked.

Naira, Kav, and Kuma all burst into laughter. Naira cleared her throat and wiped a tear off her cheek. "Sorry, sorry. Easy to forget you're not familiar with these things. MERIT doesn't want unionists agitating, and the HCA is happy to lick MERIT boots and shut them down. They'll place bad actors in the crowd, kick off a scuffle, then toss anyone they can grab in a cell overnight to sweat it out."

"But that's not legal."

"They have all the power, all the weapons, all the money. They don't care," Naira said.

"Any other day I'd chalk this up to the HCA being the HCA," Kav said, "but please tell me I'm not the only one who finds the timing here suspicious? This order went out shortly after you two talked to Emali."

"You thinking it's bait?" Naira asked.

Kav shrugged. "It strikes me as strange that the second we so much as touch this place, suddenly the HCA is prepping to crack citizen heads. They might be trying to lure us out, assuming we couldn't resist getting between the unionists and those dicks."

"Hold on," Kuma said. "The protest announcement went out when our shuttle docked. It's not the HCA calling us out. If anyone is, it's the protestors."

Naira frowned into the smiling face of Gafford in one of his pictures, still displayed from the holo in her arm. Jonsun had said the team was hers, now. She didn't technically have the same ties to bind her that Jonsun did. Aside from Jessel, Naira had never even met Jonsun's connections in the unionists.

She'd been pure Conservator, concerned with protecting the planets. Once the cradles were secured and *canus* dealt with, then she'd have time to think about upending the MERIT system.

But someone on this station had known Jonsun's operation well enough to recognize the signature they used on the shuttle, or their fake IDs. Someone willing to get their head cracked by the HCA to get their attention. Naira had a sinking suspicion of who that might be. If it was Jessel calling her out, then Naira owed Jonsun's sibling her time.

"You all are welcome to stand down, but Jonsun's friends are calling us, and I'm going to answer. We have to wait until the morning to meet Emali anyway."

Kuma and Kav exchanged a look. Kav said, "We're with you, Nai."

"I would like to help, if I can," Tarquin said.

"Then I want a map of the station with the protest's location marked and potential kettle routes highlighted. The way those HCA were talking, things are about to get bloody."

NINE

Tarquin

Miller-Urey Station | The Present

When Tarquin had been told about unionist protests in the past, they'd been downplayed to the point that he'd imagined them small, niche events. A few hundred people holding a thin line as they shouted their slogans from public squares.

On Miller-Urey Station, there were thousands. They'd poured out of their homes and businesses before the appointed time and filled every walking space remotely near the designated gathering point. Their holos—grey, almost exclusively—glared slogans into the sky along with ugly caricatures of the MERIT family heads and their high-ranking members. Tarquin saw quite a few of himself in the mix, with the phrase MURDERER OF THE SIXTH written large below his face.

He tugged the knit beanie Naira had given him lower onto his face and focused on slouching. Kav and Kuma rattled off the counts of suspected agitators in the crowd as Tarquin trailed along behind Naira. He couldn't begin to guess at how they were picking out their suspects. It was all a chaotic mess to him. A swirling vortex of disgust directed at everything he and his family represented.

He couldn't blame them. It still made him feel like hollowed-out shit. Naira touched his arm. "You okay?"

She had her sunglasses back on, the lenses big enough to conceal some of her exemplar pathways, and she'd hidden her hair and forehead under a hat that matched his. She'd blotted out the rest of her extra pathways with makeup. He'd thought they were terribly conspicuous, at first, but many people in the crowd were similarly obscuring their identities. Tarquin flipped his collar up and pulled it high.

"They really hate Mercator, don't they?" he asked, when what he meant was, *They really hate me.*

"They hate all of MERIT. Mercator is drawing more fire right now because of Acaelus's stunt with the *Sigillaria*."

Tarquin had a feeling that Mercator featured as often in these protests as they were now, but Naira was trying to be kind.

"Thank you," he whispered to her, "for giving me a chance."

"None of us can change what we were born into." She eyed the crowd. "In either direction. You're trying to make things better. That matters more than a family name."

He wanted to kiss her. He could just *do* that now, but the crowd shifted, drawing her attention away. The gathering strained toward the steps at the back of a small courtyard outside of the HCA division station. A person ascended those stairs, lean and scraggly, their face hidden by a mask pulled tight over their mouth, but the fury in their glare was unmistakable.

"I was right," Naira said.

"What is it?" Tarquin asked.

"That's Jessel. That's Jonsun's older sibling."

He took her hand, squeezing, but she scarcely seemed to notice, transfixed by the powerful figure stalking before the crowd.

Jessel's amplified voice rang out across the gathering. "The festering cancer of MERIT tells us our families must rot on ice while they reprint themselves with ease. They tell us our phoenix fees aren't enough. Even when we scrimp and save and scrape together every last credit. They tell us our loved ones must 'contribute' to be worthy of the resurrection we *pay for*, and what do they offer in turn?"

The crowd shouted a cacophony of different answers.

"Nothing!" Jessel roared. "They waste relkatite that could go into our loved ones' bodies for the sake of their power games. They steal the products of our mind and muscle and give nothing but empty promises in return!"

A roar of agreement washed through the crowd. Tarquin edged closer to Naira. She squeezed his hand back at last.

"I say that those who abuse the phoenix fees, those in MERIT who reprint whenever it suits them, I say they learn what it means to be a real phoenix. I say, we make them burn!"

Pictures of Tarquin's family burst into life above Jessel's head. Tarquin, Leka, Acaelus, Canden. All four of them had been edited to appear engulfed in flames, their mouths open in screams as flesh melted from their cheeks. The crowd cheered, taking up the chant of *Make them burn* until it was all Tarquin could hear.

Tarquin started to walk, as if in a trance. His pathways grew uncomfortably warm. He had to make them understand that he wasn't like his family—that it was arguably not even his family's fault *canus* had manipulated them—he had to tell them he was trying to fix it all. Trying to bring about change. They were infected—all of them—and there were ways to fight back.

Naira's grip became iron, holding him back.

"I have to get him out of here," she said into the team channel.

"Bail through the southwest route," Kav said. "It's the least crowded."

She shifted her grip from his hand to his elbow and steered him around, breaking his view of the edited pictures. A tremble ran through him, his legs liquid and knees shaking as she guided him brusquely through the crowd. His exemplar, doing her job, even if the situation had drastically changed. Because that's what Mercator was, in the end. A mold you were forced into. One not even Naira could break.

"I need to say something." He dug in his heels.

She didn't yank on his arm, if only because it would look odd, but he saw the temptation flicker across her face.

"You don't." She took his face in one hand and dragged his head around. Made him look at her instead of the stage. "These people are wound up and will tear you limb from limb before you get a word out. You can't help them if you're cracked. And violence like that has a way of spreading. You'll get others hurt."

"But…" He pushed against her hand until she relented and allowed him to look back at the steps, where Jessel was leading the crowd in a chant against Mercator. Something twisted within him. Naira was right.

He *knew* she was right, but still he desired to mount those stairs, to tell them all that it was *canus* that drove the motivations of his family.

And then every single segment of *canus* that infected all of those thousands of bodies would know. Would understand that it was threatened, and this would be the *Einkorn* all over again.

"I have to get out of here," he breathed. The compulsion was overwhelming, so in line with his own shame, his own deep-rooted fears. His muscles twitched, desiring to spring for those stairs.

"I know," she said. "I'm sorry. I shouldn't have brought you here."

Tarquin bit his tongue to hold back a protest that wouldn't matter. He wanted to insist that it wasn't her fault. He'd gotten it in his head he could be helpful, that he would be fine, but he'd been wrong. He was nothing more than a liability. One she should cut loose.

Those weren't his real feelings, either. It was *canus*, filling him with doubt in his moment of weakness. Taking advantage of his shock over seeing the hate these people carried for him. He tightened his jaw and tried to focus on the crowd. On the wide variety of clothes and hairstyles and not their words, braying for his blood, as she herded him to the back of the gathering.

"Nai," Kuma said across the group channel, voice tight. "I've got movement arrowing toward the stage."

She stopped her relentless march. "Undercovers?"

"Unclear. No one we tagged."

"Weapons?"

"Scans are being scrambled," Kav said. "But there could be anything under those coats."

"That's a yes." Naira looked between the direction they'd been headed, and Jessel. "Are you close, Kuma?"

"Moving now, but no, not close enough." The words came in short, gasping bursts—she was running.

"Are they going to kill Jessel?" Tarquin asked.

"Unclear." The taut set of her shoulders told him otherwise. "Kav, I need visual."

The channel expanded into their HUDs, temporarily distracting Tarquin from his overwhelming desire to spill all his secrets. Three people moved through the crowd at angles that reminded him of the points of a triangle, Jessel in their center.

"Fuck," Naira said, almost too quietly for him to hear. The strength of her distress shocked some sense back into him.

The three had dressed casually, their clothes covered with jackets that ranged from cargo-style to heavy winter versions. Kav was right, they could be hiding anything under there. Taken individually, they might have slipped under detection, but three of them, sunglasses on, moving with such purpose? Tarquin didn't have to be familiar with such things to recognize an assassination attempt in progress.

One of them lifted a hand. Adjusted their glasses. A ribbon of green cuffed their wrist.

Tarquin felt numb.

"Nai," Kav said with naked fear, "that's—"

"I know." Frustration strained her voice. "I see him."

"Who is it?" Tarquin asked.

"Fletcher Demarco."

The man from the docks of Mercator Station. Tarquin recognized him now, even though his collar was tugged up to hide the lower half of his profile. Naira and Kav had been thin on the details when they'd last crossed paths, but Tarquin had a few pieces to put together. He was Naira's childhood friend from the orphanage. He'd helped her stay alive.

They'd been more than that. Ex-friend. Ex-lover. A finalizer in Mercator's employ. And, according to Kav, "Nai Hunter Number One." A man who'd signed up to break her.

Naira took a step toward Jessel. Stopped herself and shifted her weight back, hesitant.

Tarquin grabbed her shoulders, drawing her attention back to him. "He's here for you, isn't he?"

"Yes."

"Then we have to get you out of here." He started to drag her away, but she locked up, an unmovable edifice.

"He'll crack Jessel to punish me for not biting this bait."

Tarquin looked back at the powerful figure striding before the crowd. Threatening someone else, especially someone Naira cared for, was a surefire way to draw her out. It infuriated Tarquin that Fletcher would twist her kindness around to endanger her.

"Can you stop him without getting yourself hurt?" Tarquin asked.

She started to nod, then aborted the motion into a sharp jerk of the head that lacked any meaning. "Maybe. But not without a showy spectacle that will give away my presence and make the next twenty-four hours on this station a living hell."

"Do it," he said.

Naira startled, and some of the strain left her face. "Really? I thought you'd be on Kav's side and try to drag me out of here."

"I'd love nothing more. But it'd break your heart to know you let Jessel crack to save yourself, and I can't abide that. So, go. Save them. And get a few hits in on Demarco for me, all right?"

She searched his face, and though he couldn't read her eyes behind her glasses, she nodded tightly. The grip of terror he hadn't been able to shake since he'd seen his family burning eased.

"All right. But you need to get out. I don't think Fletch will hurt Acaelus's son, but if he realizes we're together, that's a bargaining chip I don't want him to use. Whatever happens, get out."

He nodded, unable to trust his voice.

"Kav, get your boots on the ground and escort our prince. I'm going in."

"That's a bad fucking idea and you know it." Kav's voice was leaden. Tarquin had never heard him sound that serious before.

"I'm doing it anyway."

TEN

Naira

Miller-Urey Station | The Present

Naira had no idea how she was going to pull this off, and that both terrified and exhilarated her. A needle of guilt slipped under her skin, that she should feel so full of hungry anticipation when Tarquin had been frightened for her, but she pushed it aside. Kav would get him to safety, and he'd already been at the edge of the crowd. He'd be fine.

Jonsun's sibling, not so much. Because once Fletcher started playing his games, he didn't stop until everyone on the board was as broken as he was.

Naira hadn't brought firearms—getting those past the security scanners would have been nearly impossible on short notice—but the knives strapped to secret places against her thighs, arms, and torso comforted her as she moved through the crowd. She hadn't experienced proprioception issues since sparring with Kuma. Even so, she worried. If she went hand-to-hand with Fletcher, she'd need all the advantages she could get.

Naira removed her hat and sunglasses, using the hat to scrub her concealer off, and took an angle deliberately sharper than Fletcher and his team. Her approach would be more obvious, but she'd also get there first.

Most of the crowd was too busy chanting their throats raw to notice her approach, but those who saw her face scrambled aside, fear and confusion rippling in her wake. She hit the open space between the crowd and the steps before any of the would-be assassins did and paused, waiting for Jessel to notice the muted spot in their front line. The place where their followers were shying away from the bomb dropped among them.

Jessel turned around, arm outstretched. Their chant cut off abruptly as they saw the exemplar at the edge of their gathering. Fear struck them, their whole body going rigid as they pulled back, their base instinct of *flight* swinging to the surface in the seconds before they mastered themself. Remembered where they were and that thousands of followers surrounded them.

Not that any of those followers could protect them.

Then Jessel recognized her, and a glint came to their eye.

They swung back to face the crowd again, lifting their arms. "Ex. Naira Sharp walks among us today, my friends!"

The crowd surged, wanting to see the traitor exemplar, but Naira forced them back with a glare, and caught Fletcher's eye in the process. He'd stopped pushing against the crowd, and instead watched her with a curious, bemused expression. He applauded her slowly, softly enough not to draw any attention.

As the crowd roared approval, Naira closed the distance between herself and Jessel and fell into a loose, at-ready pose beside the unionist leader, her feet slightly apart, arms clasped over her stomach. Anyone who'd ever seen an exemplar at work knew that stance. Naira was signaling Jessel was under her protection.

"Even their own weapons turn against them when they see the truth of the rot festering beneath!" Jessel bellowed.

Naira wasn't comfortable with her entire personhood being reduced to a weapon for either side to wield, but this was the way of protest. Brutal reductions of complicated subjects to spread the ideology faster. Wallowing in minutiae could kill a movement before it got off the ground.

When the crowd started chanting her last name, Naira struggled to focus on the task at hand, so deep was her knee-jerk reaction to tell them to stop. She thought she saw Fletcher chuckle, but Jessel leaned close.

"Is there a threat?" they whispered.

"You have a three-person Mercator hit team in the crowd," Naira said, barely moving her lips in case Fletcher was attempting to read them. "One of which is a confirmed finalizer."

Naira heard the wet slide of Jessel's throat as they swallowed, but they rallied quickly. "What do I do?"

"I suggest you start the planned march as soon as possible and follow my every order after that point."

Jessel nodded and launched into a screed on the unfairness of Mercator locking the maps of those who had died in the bombing of the two decoy ships. How they'd been unwitting bait, and Mercator had twisted around the people's weapons—Jessel thrust a thumb at Naira—to suit their purposes. But the people would refuse to let Mercator and all of MERIT hold them back. They would march to the docks where a Mercator shuttle rested in luxury, and shout until those on board could feel their anger.

Naira bit her tongue. That shuttle was hers. The crowd would never get anywhere near it. Dock security was too tight.

The crowd reprised their chant of *Make them burn* and wheeled around at Jessel's instruction, starting out in a thick column that was destined to fray at the edges. Jessel kept close to Naira's side, and a few people in similar grey clothes to Jessel's moved out of the crowd, forming a loose phalanx around them.

"What's happening?" a young-looking woman asked.

"Not sure," Jessel said. "The E-X says there's a kill team here for me."

"Shit," she said.

Naira counted eight of them in the small group. "You all work with Jessel?"

"We're the core of the unionists on this station," the young woman said. "My name's Jadhav, sir. Rani Jadhav."

"All right, Jadhav. Jessel's correct. There are three of them, and I personally know one to be extremely deadly. I need you all to scramble the crowd. I want people going cross directions, turning down the wrong streets and turning back again. I want chaos. Can you give me that?"

"We can do that," Jadhav said. The others looked to Jessel first, but nodded agreement at their signal.

"Watch your corners," Naira said. "Don't get boxed in. If you cross paths with one of the kill team, you run. Two men, one woman. They're in dark grey coats with sunglasses. Mercator cuffs. One of them has very green eyes, if they remove those glasses. I don't know about the others."

The unionists took off, pausing to drop bad information in certain ears before moving on. Soon enough, the crowd buckled up against snarls of people turning the wrong way, trying to turn back, or otherwise mired in confusion.

"They're good," she said.

"They are," Jessel said. They kept their head up, scanning the crowd, and had dropped their array of holo signs that depicted Tarquin and his family burning. "I'm happy to have you, Sharp, but I'm surprised to see you. I thought you'd be trying to weasel your way onto the *Sigillaria*."

"That's partially why I'm here." She trailed a step behind Jessel, keeping her view of all points around the unionist leader clear. The chaos in the crowd would make it difficult for Fletcher to get a clean line of sight. "But when we saw you'd scheduled the protest within minutes of our arrival on-station, we decided to answer your call."

Jessel missed a step. "What are you talking about? We got a tip-off that a Mercator shuttle had docked. I whipped up the protest last minute to rub it under their noses before they flew off to whatever fancier station they were really heading to."

Naira stopped walking. Jessel stopped, too, looking at her with raised brows.

"Jessel, that's my shuttle. You bit a baited hook."

They paled. "Are the assassins here for you?"

"Yes," she said, but the word didn't quite feel right.

Targeting Jessel was the smart move if Fletcher wanted to flush her out of hiding. But then what? Now Fletcher had Naira on her guard, in full-exemplar mode. While Fletcher savored a challenge, he wasn't stupid.

Naira scanned the crowd. The river of protestors parted around them, their chant as loud as ever, but Naira could scarcely hear them over the frantic pace of her own thoughts. She found Fletcher leaning against a corner building, one ankle crossed over the other, a rolled cigarette between his fingers, the glasses pushed up to his head. He caught her eye and winked. Her stomach dropped.

She accessed the group channel. "Kav. Tell me you have him."

"What? No, it's a mess down here. I'm sure he's fine. Where are you? You got a wing over Jessel?"

"Jessel's not the fucking problem. Tarquin, where are you?"

No answer. She turned to confront Fletcher, but he'd vanished into the crowd.

"Tarquin?" Kuma asked over the channel. "Come on, man, answer… I swear I just saw his tall ass— Oh, there! Nai, he's moving toward the city center. Shit. One of the kill team is with him."

"Catch him," Naira growled. "Priority is now recovery of the—of him." She cut herself off short of saying *the Mercator*. Lots of people were named Tarquin, but Jessel would balk at the Conservators consorting with that particular Tarquin.

"Can I help?" Jessel asked.

On the edges of the crowd, one of the kill team made themselves seen, circling. Warning Naira off abandoning her charge in pursuit of another. If she walked away from Jessel now, Fletcher's team would kidnap or kill them to distract her. Just to make a point.

"Tell me you followed your brother's example and had strength and agility pathways installed."

Jessel gave her a half-cocked smirk. "Naturally."

"Good." Naira grabbed their wrist and started running. "Then keep up."

ELEVEN

Tarquin

Miller-Urey Station | The Present

From the moment Tarquin felt the pinch of a knife pressed against his back he'd been trying to call the team for help, but he'd gotten only static. Kav had mentioned something about the kill team jamming the weapons scanners, and he supposed it made sense that such a prepared team would also have the ability to cut off communication.

He mulled those facts over, and tried to see a way around them, because giving his mind a problem to solve kept him from dissolving into panic.

Acaelus had never spoken much about Mercator's use of finalizers. They were, by nature, incredibly secretive, not officially acknowledged, and only fielded by the heads of family and their direct heirs. Tarquin didn't like to think that either Acaelus or Leka would order him slaughtered beyond recovery. But, then, he hadn't liked to think his father would do many of the things he'd done.

"I believe you have the wrong person," Tarquin said as the man with the knife to his back prodded him down a thin alley. A woman joined them, checking around corners before they moved on. Fletcher was still out there. He hoped Naira was safe.

"I don't think so, my liege," the man said.

Tarquin bit the inside of his cheek until he tasted iron. "Didn't you see the broadcast? That family is on the *Sigillaria*. Just because I have a passing resemblance—" He gasped as the knife slid through his clothes and pricked his skin enough to draw a dribble of blood.

"That's really not going to work, my liege."

Tarquin was tempted to point out how ridiculous it was for the man to be using his title while he had a knife to his back, but he suspected that would only earn him another jab.

"I request you allow the people who were with me to go free," he said.

The woman sniffed. "Not likely, my liege. Demarco's got dibs on Sharp."

Tarquin's stomach soured. "If you're here to recover me, then there's no need for additional violence."

"They'll work it out," the man said, "but you should really be concerned about your own skin right now, my liege."

He'd never get used to threats being attached to his title. Tarquin buried his concern for Naira—he trusted her to handle herself—and focused on his surroundings.

They were skirting the edge of the protest's route, using the chaos of the crowd for cover. Many protestors covered their ears, and Tarquin couldn't blame them. An unsettling high-pitched whine emitted from the speakers all around the city, adding to the confusion.

He was tempted to shout for help. There were plenty of people around, but he feared his captors would kill anyone who tried to intervene. And, really, who in that crowd would come to his aid once they realized who he was?

"Where are we going?" he asked.

"Somewhere safe," the woman said.

Tarquin indulged in a scowl at her back before he put his impassive Mercator mask back on and adopted the haughty posture the families of MERIT were known for. If there was no point in denying who he was, then he might as well attempt to wield his identity like a shield. Make them think twice, at least, before they put the knife in his back.

He could have sworn they were at the edge of the docks, but a warehouse loomed before them. They herded him in through a side door that opened into a thin passageway.

His captors didn't speak as they led him into a rectangular room with a high ceiling, dim lighting, and a few chairs scattered around. There was no evidence of cargo or supplies being stored, as if it had gone unused for some time, but it appeared to be free of dust and other debris.

"Sit." The man removed the knife from Tarquin's back and gestured to a chair.

Tarquin couldn't see the point in arguing, so he sat and watched the woman sweep the perimeter of the room before accessing a panel set in the wall. The interface was Mercator green.

"I don't know what my father has told you—" he said, but the woman snorted.

"He hasn't told us anything. That's the problem."

"Quiet," the man said.

She went back to her work on the panel, falling silent. The man kept his knife out and shifted into the guarding pose exemplars usually assumed. Tarquin wanted to shout. To demand to know what was happening here, but he knew that wouldn't get him anywhere. He rubbed his wrists.

"What are your names, agents?" he asked.

"Nic, my liege," the man said.

"Roselle, my liege," the woman said.

He stifled his surprise that they had answered him—but then, they'd called their leader Demarco, hadn't they? Clearly, they weren't worried about their real identities being revealed. Which meant either he was dead, or something else was going on here. As he was still breathing, he hazarded a guess that this fell into the "something else" category. More than likely this was Leka, then. Sending them out to fetch her rebellious little brother and drag him home. If that was the case, then they wouldn't dare harm him.

"Nic, Roselle." He nodded to each. "I won't insult you by pretending I am anyone other than who I am, and I hope you will not insult me by pretending you are not a Mercator kill team."

Nic shifted his weight uncomfortably. "We are that, my liege."

"Did my sister send you?"

Roselle said, "Our team lead, Fletcher Demarco, will explain when he gets here."

"I see," he said with all the cold arrogance he could muster. "And is Demarco your superior, or am I?"

THE FRACTURED DARK   89

"You are, my liege," Roselle said. "But Demarco has the full extent of the situation. It's best if we wait for him."

Tarquin let his scowl cut, and Roselle flinched back, ducking into a quick bow that Nic mirrored. He wanted to laugh at the bitter irony of the situation. These two killers had kidnapped him, put a knife to his back, but all he had to do was pick up the mantle of his family's power and hold it over their heads, and they were scraping and wincing as if they weren't prepared to stab him mere minutes ago.

He wondered what the agents would do if he stood up and walked out. Would they manhandle him then, the facade broken? If he put them in a position where they would have to intervene, he might lose what leverage he had. Break the mystique of Mercator power.

Tarquin leaned back, resting one arm over the back of his chair, and crossed his ankle over his knee, then made an extensive study of his nails. Aloof. Cold. Bored, but a little annoyed. The most dangerous place of mind for any high-ranking MERIT member. A bored and irritated noble was likely to lash out at any moment.

"While we wait for more information," he said, intentionally looping them into a *we*, "I'd like to hear about you both. Tell me about your families, and how you came to Mercator."

They exchanged a glance, and Roselle shrugged. "I was born on an HCA station, my liege..." she began.

They told him everything about themselves, filling the silence with the details of their lives, and he filed every word away, looking for a lever on which to pull.

Acaelus might have been proud of him in that moment. The thought made Tarquin a strange mixture of ill and elated.

TWELVE

Naira

Miller-Urey Station | The Present

Kav kept up a steady report of Tarquin's last known position as Naira raced through the streets, dragging a quickly tiring Jessel behind her. She was tempted to toss Jessel over her shoulder, but her headlong sprint had already drawn too much attention.

"Lot of security headed your way," Kav said.

She slowed to a stop, taking a moment to press her back against a wall and breathe until the burn in her lungs eased and she was ready to sprint again, if not for the weight of Jessel holding her down.

Jessel pounded a fist against their chest and waved at her. "Go on. You've got more power in your packs than I do. I don't know what the deal is with this guy, but he's clearly important."

Naira wanted to accept the invitation, but Fletcher would take advantage and swoop in on Jessel the second Naira left their side.

"I'm not leaving you behind," Naira said.

"This is my city, Sharp. I can disappear into it."

A shadow stretched around the corner. Naira shoved Jessel behind her and dropped her hand to the blade sheathed at her thigh. Kuma rounded the corner, six of the unionists jogging along behind her. Kuma flashed Naira a bright grin and waved. A relieved sigh gusted through her and she grabbed Kuma's arm, dragging her into a crushing hug.

"I could kiss you," she said.

Kuma punched her arm playfully, cheeks a little red. "Sorry, Nai, you're not my type. I like 'em wiry." She ogled Jessel. "They'll do."

Naira rolled her eyes and checked her weapons. "Don't hit on our allies. You sure you can keep them safe?"

"Yeah, yeah, I got them. You okay with this, Jessel?" Kuma asked. "Your people here told me about one of your hideouts. Figured we'd duck in there and stay down until Nai gives us the all clear."

"I'm on board with any plan that lets me sit down," Jessel said between deep breaths.

Kuma clapped them on the back. "That can be arranged, my friend."

Jessel gave Kuma a slim, grateful smile and, when Kuma wasn't looking, skimmed their gaze quickly down Kuma's frame. The dread shadowing Naira eased. They'd be fine.

She started to leave, but Kuma called, "Hey, Nai!"

Naira turned to her in time to snatch a small parcel out of the air. She rolled it over in her hand. A personal explosive. Often used on space walks and riskier missions where the threat of a crack-inducing death was high. Sometimes high-ranking MERIT used them, in case they were taken. Acaelus always wore one. She looked up from the device to see Kuma's sad smile.

"We all backed up this morning, you know. Just in case."

Naira had known she was going against a team specialized in cracking their targets, but that slight weight made it real. "Thanks."

She pulled the miniature explosive from the bag and popped it into her mouth. Her saliva warmed the adhesive, and she placed it against the interior side of her back molar. That way, it couldn't be set off accidentally by a punch to the face. She'd have to press her tongue against the side of it as hard as she could to get it to blow. Kuma blew her a kiss and turned around, taking her charges with her.

Naira hated to delay any further, but she made a circuitous route of the path Kav marked, checking down every side street for a hint of Tarquin as she closed in on his last known location. With every step she took, her sense of dread grew stronger. It clotted in the back of her throat until she was so sick with it she wanted to turn around and flee. Her *canus* infection spurring her to turn away.

She didn't pull her knives, because she didn't want to draw the ire of station security, but she gripped their handles beneath the cover of her jacket regardless. Anger gave her something to focus on besides the despair *canus* was pouring into her. Fear made her skin clammy, though she'd never feared a fight before. It made her sloppy.

A blade pressed against her throat. She froze, lifting her chin to ease away from that razor's edge, but the blade followed her movement. Fletcher slunk out from the shadows of an alley she hadn't checked well enough, sidled up behind her, and grabbed her by the hip, pulling her tight against him.

"Take your hands off me or I will choke you to death on your own testicles, Fletch."

He chuckled against her ear, breath warm, the resinous scent of him more familiar than she cared to admit. "So spiteful. I'm 'controlling the target.' You remember, don't you? I know it's been years since you did any *real* work, but you can't have forgotten the basics of battlefield management already."

"Fuck off."

He *tsked* and reached for the sheath against her side, then removed the knife with a deft flick of the wrist. She had others.

"Walk," he said.

"Going to march me through the streets with a knife to my throat? Station security will love that."

"Station security is hunting you like a pheasant, love. They'd be happy to see any weapon at that neck of yours. But you're right. No need to delay with explaining you're my quarry, not theirs."

He gave her no opening as he tightened his grip over her hip, fingers digging painfully into her muscle. Fletcher nudged her forward a half step and switched the knife from her throat to her back. She couldn't see the movement, but she felt him hunch, and heard the rustle of cloth as his too-large coat swung around to hide the blade. He rested his chin against her shoulder, and she angled her head away with disgust.

"There, now. Just two lovers out for a stroll, a little too entangled. Good cover, isn't it?"

"You must realize I'm going to kill you for this."

"I know you're going to try. And honestly, Nai, it's been so long since I've been challenged that I'm looking forward to it. Try not to disappoint me when you strike, okay? For old times' sake?"

"Just for you, I'll make it quick and painless."

"Ugh." Fletcher forced her to walk with a jab to the back. "You used to be so much fun."

"I'm a barrel of laughs when my deranged ex has a knife to my back."

"I never hid who I was from you." They'd cleared most of the chaos of the dispersing crowd and were approaching an old warehouse. "And you seemed to enjoy it at the time."

"People change." The words weren't as firm as she would have liked.

He gave her hip a squeeze. "Sure, Nai. Tell me you've changed when you've stopped blowing up ships with people on them."

He had a point. She thought back to Tarquin's face in the moment she'd snapped Leka's neck, and the abject horror that'd filled him. Naira had felt nothing about that action until she'd seen her callousness reflected in his eyes. Even now, she still had to recall Tarquin's face to summon the remorse.

Naira realized she'd been quiet too long when Fletcher whispered, "Hard thing to swallow, isn't it? Knowing what you are?"

She tilted her head away from him. "Go to hell."

"I definitely am," he said with a light laugh, and scanned them into the warehouse.

Ahead, there were faint strains of casual conversation. A brief laugh that belonged to Tarquin. She pushed aside annoyance and confusion. Whatever was happening here, he was playing a game to stay alive as much as she was. She could fight her way free. Tarquin had different tools to wield.

Fletcher kicked a door open and nudged her through, not taking his hand from her hip, even as he straightened and placed the blade back at her throat, pulling her tight against him once more. She grimaced at the contact, but focused on the scene instead.

Tarquin sat in the center of the room, unbound, talking to a woman working on a panel inset in the wall—Naira marked that panel with brief curiosity, it didn't look like it belonged in a warehouse—then shifted her attention back to Tarquin.

He'd been relaxed until she entered the room. Now he froze, his laid-back smile locked in place, outrage shadowing his eyes. As far as she could tell, he was uninjured.

"You will remove your hands from my exemplar," he said coldly. A spark of his father's ferocity flashed to the surface.

"Who, Nai?" Fletcher said in his light, bemused voice that somehow always conveyed a laugh at a private joke no one else was privy to. "She's hardly an exemplar anymore. A traitor, in fact." He stood to her side and wrapped his arm around her shoulders as if they were buddies.

Naira had an overwhelming desire to throw him across the room, but she refrained until she could get a better idea of the situation. And there was the knife, back at her throat, the point tracing a delicate line down her carotid artery. Every time she shifted away, the blade followed her.

Tarquin stood with fluid rage. He didn't dare advance, but he wore Mercator arrogance like armor and appeared to loom over Fletcher. "I gave you an order, Demarco."

"Oh, don't look so indignant." Fletcher drew flowers against her neck with the point of his knife without breaking the skin. Showing off. "Nai and I go way back. This is hardly the roughest we've treated each other."

"I'm sorry," Tarquin said, "did some part of my command make you believe there was room for negotiation? Because I assure you, there is none. You will unhand my exemplar."

"Acaelus's cub has claws after all," Fletcher said. Naira wondered if Tarquin recognized the genuine admiration in Fletcher's tone. He glanced between them, hummed to himself, and then nodded. "Very well."

He swept her feet from under her. She dropped to all fours, the impact jarring through her. Naira didn't move, not yet, waiting to see what Fletcher would do. He'd love nothing more than for her to come up swinging. It would give him an excuse to plunge that knife home.

Fletcher grabbed the back of her jacket and yanked, wrenching her arms behind her. He ripped the jacket free and tossed it aside. The two knives within clinked against the floor.

"Naira!" Tarquin started to rush to her, but Fletcher placed the blade beneath her chin and tilted her head up, half turning to pin Tarquin with a stare.

"Stay," Fletcher said.

Tarquin clenched his fists, but restrained himself.

"Good cub." Fletcher moved away from her. "Nic, check her for more, won't you?"

"Sorry about this, E-X." Nic knelt next to her and made quick, efficient work of checking her for weapons. Annoyingly, he found them all.

"Don't worry about it." It was odd that he would apologize to her, but she was grateful someone other than Fletcher had finished disarming her.

Nic gave her a curt nod that was halfway a salute and stepped away, locking Naira's knives—including the ones in her torn jacket—into a locker against the wall.

Fletcher *tsked*. "Nic, you missed one."

Nic stiffened, flicking his gaze between Naira and Fletcher. Tarquin shot her a look, but Naira kept her expression neutral, not daring to give anything away. Nic had found all her knives. There was only one other weapon she was carrying.

"He didn't," she said.

"Hah!" Fletcher clapped his hands and rolled up his sleeves. Her stomach sank. This was going to suck. "Roselle, be a peach and restrain the cub for this next part, won't you?"

"What is this?" Tarquin demanded. Roselle pulled his wrists behind his back. Tarquin hardly seemed to notice.

Naira caught Tarquin's eye and tilted her head slightly to the side in negation, hoping he'd get the hint and stay his hand. It was too soon to use the explosive, though she was tempted. The quizzical, worried look he returned almost broke her heart. He wasn't ready for this. It was coming anyway.

"My tools, please, Nic." Fletcher extended his arm, uncurling his fingers one by one.

He watched her, a hungry gleam in his eye that curdled her blood. The roll of tools Nic handed him clinked. He'd upgraded to some sort of synthetic leather, she noted, detachedly. Mercator green banded the roll with thick ties. Tools in hand, he stalked toward her, circling with quick, tight steps, and tapped the roll into his open palm. Each tap clicked the metal hidden within together. He was baiting her. Tempting her to use the weapon. To abandon her charge to avoid what was coming next.

"Are you going to do it, Fletch, or are you going to wank about it first?"

He tossed his head and laughed. "Oh, I have missed you, and that mouth of yours."

Fletcher stopped in front of her and crouched down to take her chin in hand. She resisted an urge to jerk away, he'd enjoy that too much, but she couldn't help her pulse speeding up. His slow, delighted smile told her he'd noticed.

"Shame I'm going to have to bloody it," he said softly. For a second there was a hint of the man she'd thought she used to know in his face, a gentleness that snuck through sometimes between the cruel laughter.

That glimpse was crushed beneath hard focus. He removed a pair of angled pliers from the tool roll and let the rest drop to the ground between them with a clatter. She could reach for them. Could have a scalpel in her hand and his throat open, maybe, before he could snap her neck.

His grip tightened around her jaw until it ached. Drawing out the moment. Inviting her to try it.

She let the tension bleed out of her. Fletcher had the upper hand. Even if she killed him, Nic and Roselle would have Tarquin to bargain with. A flicker of frustration crossed Fletcher's face, so close to hers now that she could see the mossy-green threads in his eyes that she used to admire. She'd been so foolish when they'd been kids. Before they'd joined the HCA, she'd really thought he had goodness in him. Maybe he had.

But they'd both loved the fight a little too much. He'd just taken matters in a different direction.

"Sorry," he whispered, and the facade dropped. She blinked, not entirely certain what he was apologizing for, but knowing that he meant it.

He yanked her mouth open, prying her jaw wide, fingers digging into her skull and soft palate, bracing so that she couldn't bite down. She'd known it was coming, had accepted the inevitability, but still her body jerked away from him, a futile need to bash her way free clawing through her.

His pliers found the molar, gripped it front to back to avoid triggering the explosive, and with pathway-enhanced strength, he yanked it free.

The pain scoured away coherent thought in a bright-white blast of agony. Tarquin shouted. A chair was knocked over. But all she could see was Fletcher's face, grim but resolved, as he shoved her away.

Naira collapsed backward, the spray of blood that'd leapt from her empty socket catching in her throat. She coughed, choking on it. Fletcher gave her a kick in the back that made her hack out the gob, but also probably bruised a kidney.

"Did you really think you could slip this past me?" Fletcher held the tooth, bloodied root and explosive both, up to the light. Her blood smeared his hands, painting red gloves over his fingers, as he turned it back and forth. "My specialty is cracking people. I know what to look for. And I know you." He passed the tooth to Nic to put in the locker, then crouched across from her. She crawled away, spitting blood so that she wouldn't start choking again. He grabbed her throat to stop her retreat, but didn't squeeze. Not yet. She froze. Gave him what he wanted and looked into his eyes. "Always one step ahead, my Nai. But not today, eh?"

He started to smile, caught himself, and pushed her away again. Fletcher scooped the roll of tools off the floor as he stood, and pulled a rag from the roll, tucking the tools into his pocket while he wiped his hands.

"You'll pay for that," Tarquin said, a snarl in his voice that shook some sense back into her. She was here for him. Not to fence with Fletcher.

"Add it to my tab," Fletcher said. He tossed the rag at Naira and she snatched it out of the air, pressing it over her chin to wipe up some of the blood as she eased herself back to her knees. "When the devil comes to take her due from me, I'll pay it gladly. But I have a job to do, and I can't very well do it if Nai here blows both our heads off."

Naira spat and dragged the rag over her mouth. Her pathways vibrated, dulling the pain and slowing the blood loss.

"What exactly is that job, Fletch? Because I sincerely fucking doubt your mission brief includes endangering a whole HC station. There are kids on those streets scared shitless because you kicked a hornet's nest to get my attention. *Gardet* kids."

"Gardet?" His brow furrowed, and then he understood, and a surprised laugh gusted out of him. "My god. You're still doing your candy-delivery routine? Haven't you figured it out yet? It's pointless. All you do is give them false hope. Break those little hearts. Not even a tenth of them have the skill to make it half so far as we did. I'm doing them a favor if they get killed in the riot. Then they won't have to face the disappointment of a life of failure."

Naira was off the floor and swinging before she could think. She took him by surprise, her fist connecting with his jaw in a satisfying *crack* that echoed in the warehouse.

He reeled back a step, blood arcing from his mouth, but they'd been doing this a long time, and the second he recovered from his shock he snatched her wrist out of the air as she lined up for another shot. Naira jerked her caught arm back, and he moved with it, grabbing her neck in his other hand. Fletcher squeezed in warning. She had options, but he could snap her neck before she could use any of them. Naira stilled.

"Well." He turned his head to spit blood. A tooth went with the wad and she couldn't help but smirk. He smirked right back at her. "Now we're even. I do love it when you flirt with me, but try that again and I'll go for a little stroll and collect Ayuba. As much as I'd enjoy having the gang back together again, I don't think you'd like it very much when I started taking pieces off him to make you behave. Clear?"

Sweat beaded between her shoulder blades. "Kav knows you're here. He's already bugged out."

"Spare me. His guilt will let him do no such thing. Although." He tilted his head to the side, considering. "I wonder. Let's try an experiment, shall we? Nic, hurt the cub. Not the face, please, we need that."

"Don't—" Naira said, but Tarquin cried out.

She grimaced, unable to see what the damage was while Fletcher was holding her still, and had to fight every urge she had to rip that amused expression straight off his face.

"Interesting," Fletcher said. "If disappointing. But I suppose I don't need Ayuba now, do I? Because you're going to...?"

Naira felt slimy. "I'll behave. Back off."

"As you wish."

He shoved her back to her knees, and this time, she stayed down. She stole a glance at Tarquin. His forearm had been cut, blood seeping through the sleeve as he clamped his other hand over the injury. He met her eyes and gave her a shaky nod to indicate he was okay. His pathways would heal that soon enough.

"Now that we understand each other," Fletcher said, "I'm taking your lost princeling home, where he belongs. Playtime is over, my liege."

"I'm not going anywhere with you," Tarquin said.

Fletcher hooked his thumbs around his hips and shook his head, laughing to himself. "Of course. Of fucking course. Do you see, Nai? Do you see what you do to people?"

Fletcher thrust a finger at Tarquin, but he was looking at her. "You're busy playacting being revolutionaries while Mercator is dying. Acaelus cut the heads off the family, stole MERIT resources, and made a run for it. This shithead's father has undermined hundreds of years of family balance. Or hadn't either of you considered that yet? Lesser cousins of Mercator are busy stabbing one another in the back, clawing their way toward the throne, because while nothing official has been said, everyone is more or less in agreement that Acaelus and his whole fucking brood have lost their minds."

"Do you think I care if the family falls?" Tarquin asked. "Let the wolves tear it down from the inside out. Mercator deserves to die."

Fletcher went very still. Naira could almost taste the rancor winding through him. He was all flash and winks and chaos, until he wasn't, and then people started cracking for real.

Stop, she mouthed to him, silently. Like they'd used to do to rein each other in when they'd been hotheaded kids.

He blinked, lips puckering as he set aside the instinct that'd been building within him. Fletcher needed Tarquin. He could hate him all he wanted, but he needed him.

Naira could relate. She thought back to a moment she shouldn't be able to remember—Tarquin rounding the side of the damaged shuttle on Sixth Cradle, and the hate that'd flared within her when he'd given her that shy, strained smile of his. She winced and squeezed her eyes shut briefly to chase away the memory.

The fury vanished from Fletcher's face. He dropped to one knee before her and touched her temple lightly, a familiar tenderness in his tone. "Are your pathways damaged? Are they not managing the pain?"

She pulled away from him. "Don't pretend kindness with me."

He scoffed and yanked his arm back, looking at his hand as if it'd betrayed him. The cruel sneer slipped back into place, and the hand that'd touched her so gently drew back. Naira braced herself to be struck.

"Get away from her," Tarquin demanded.

"For fuck's sake." Fletcher stood and turned away from her, but not so much that she wasn't still in his peripheral vision. "Let me make myself clear, *my liege*. This is not a negotiation. I am taking you to Mercator Station. You are going to sit on your throne like a good boy and keep it warm until we find out what happened to Leka and get someone with a real spine to take command.

"Believe me, cub, if I could skin those family cuffs from your hands and wear them like gloves, I wouldn't hesitate, but I can't, so I need a puppet, and you're the only meat sack that will fit."

"You can't force me to rule."

"I shouldn't have to force you!" Fletcher paused. Took a breath. Mastered himself with effort. "You hate your family. Fine, fantastic, I don't even know mine and I'd burn their house down given half a chance. But what you failed to notice while you've been too busy going through your pathetic little rebellious phase is that your family has responsibilities that can't be ignored.

"Mercator owns seventy-nine stations in the Sol system, and I don't even know how many domes down on old, dying Earth. The family has nearly five million people in its employ—do you even know those numbers?" His voice had dropped to a growl. He gathered himself once again. "Your cousins aren't going to manage it, cub. They're just not. They'll pick one another off and in the meantime Chiyo goddamn Ichikawa is circling the bloody water, waiting for an opportunity to swoop in and take it all over, 'for the stability of the system.'"

"Shit," Naira said before she could stop herself.

Fletcher threw his hands in the air. "She gets it at last! We're already straining for resources. Once Chiyo merges the families, Mercator employees will be second-string at best. She'll ice the ones she can't use or doesn't trust and call it security, and she won't be wrong."

Tarquin's indignity melted, uncertainty creeping across his face. "She can't do that. No one can force a living map to ice unless that person committed a serious crime." He pointedly didn't look at Naira as he said that last part, and a small spike of irritation with him wedged within her.

Fletcher pinched the bridge of his nose and breathed out slowly. "What do you think will happen when Chiyo takes over and discovers *there are no more extra stockpiles of relkatite*? Acaelus stole the bulk of the relk and destroyed every single sample of *canus* the stations have left. We have lost the ability to mine that mineral efficiently. We have lost the bulk of our stores. All our value. The second the rest of MERIT realizes what's happened, they're going to ice the poor and cannibalize their pathways for their own reprinting."

"He destroyed all the *canus*? Every bit of it?" Naira asked.

"I rather think the loss of relk is the bigger problem," Fletcher said, "but yes, all the *canus*."

She looked at Tarquin. He'd gone ashen. "Do you think...?"

He worked his mouth around. "That the station's clean? I can't be sure, but..."

"Would you two," Fletcher said, "mind filling me in here?"

Tarquin gave Naira a sharp shake of the head, and she let out a slow sigh. Fletcher had scented a conspiracy and would cut it out of them if he had to. She spoke to Fletcher, "Call the station. Have someone pull one of the printing bay cartridges. Sample it and test for *canus*. Get me that answer, and I'll tell you."

He crouched in front of her again. "I thought I was clear this wasn't a negotiation."

"Trust me."

A muscle in his forehead jumped. He stared at her as if he could dig through the flesh in front of him into the past and to the scrawny kids they'd been before there'd been so much blood on both their hands.

"Make the call, Roselle," he said without looking away from her.

She inclined her head. Not quite a thank-you—she'd be damned before she gave him her genuine thanks. He gave her a slim smile, but stamped it out before he turned back to Tarquin. "In the meantime, my liege, I hope you'll agree that keeping Ichikawa from chewing this family up for spare parts is of paramount importance."

She couldn't see Tarquin fully, Fletcher's profile carved Tarquin in half, but she saw the sorrow sink into him. Though it hurt, she didn't disagree with his decision.

"I'll secure Mercator," he said. "But Naira's mission may be even more important now than previously believed. I understand Mercator views her as a traitor, but I will file the paperwork to rescind that conviction once I take over the family. She walks free."

Fletcher hummed to himself, drumming his fingers against his knee-cap. "No."

"Fletch—"

He turned on her, grabbed her by the hair, and yanked her to her feet, dissolving her words into a startled grunt. Tarquin shouted and tried to intervene, but Roselle held him back.

"I don't trust you, cub," Fletcher said. "And quite frankly, I don't trust this one not to nip at my heels if I let her go. Real stubborn streak in her that I am *intimately* acquainted with."

"You know damn well I'll go after the *Sigillaria*," she said. "You can't possibly want to protect Acaelus."

He smiled sweetly at her. "And how were you going to do that? Emali? That meeting was a scam. I was already tailing you, but Emali was a dear and called me the second the cub hung up. She wants a warm ass on that throne until Leka can be found as much as I do."

"I don't need her," Naira said.

"You're right. You don't, because she couldn't have helped you in the first place. The *Sigillaria* is blocking all incoming signals from the Sol system. Not even you can get around that. I also need to keep a leash on the cub here. Two birds, one stone, et cetera."

"This is a unionist station. My people will come for me."

"Oh, love. You see, this isn't a warehouse. We're on a ship, and we left that trash station the second the door closed behind us. Don't look too furious with me, Nai. I know what you like. I'll build you a very pretty cage."

THIRTEEN

Naira

Mercator Transport | The Present

Fletcher ordered them into a smaller room and locked the door behind him. Naira collapsed onto a padded chair, letting her head fall back against the headrest. Her face throbbed, and it was all she could do to keep from prodding the open socket with the tip of her tongue. She didn't want to lean too heavily on painkillers. Just because Fletcher had lost interest in them for the time being didn't mean they were safe.

"Naira?" Tarquin asked.

She pried her eyes open. He stood uneasily in front of her, his hands clutched together, as if he were holding himself back. Red bruises marred the green of his family cuffs, and the blood was drying on his sleeve. As far as she could tell, he was otherwise unharmed. She tried to muster up a smile for him, but it hurt, so she let it fall.

"Rest." She gestured to the chair beside her. "Recover your strength. Your wits. We'll need them once we reach the station."

He slid onto the chair next to her but was so wound up with tension she could feel it radiating off of him.

"This isn't your fault," she said into the taut silence.

He laughed anxiously and ran a hand through his hair. "Am I that obvious?"

She rolled her head to the side to better see him, and he softened under her regard. "You are to me."

Hesitantly, he extended a hand. She laced their fingers together and squeezed. "How are you feeling?" he asked.

"Like shit," she said, "but I'll live."

He rubbed his thumb against the back of her hand. "I've gotten you out of a Mercator station once before. I'll do it again."

"Acaelus wanted you to escape that day. This is different. This is Fletch. He'll only allow us to see each other when he wants to hurt me to put you in line."

Tarquin's grip tightened. "I won't allow it."

"You won't have a choice. Fletch isn't your father. He can be reasoned with, bargained with, even, but he will lash out at the slightest provocation."

"There's hardly much he can do to me if I take control of the family."

"That's why he's keeping me."

Tarquin's face burned with fury and he turned away, unable to look at her. She tugged on his hand, pulling him back.

"You need to discover what Acaelus did to those stations. If they're clean of *canus*, then we can use that. We can stage a resistance from there, and even Fletch will come around to helping us if we make him understand the full extent of the problem. Because if Acaelus killed off *canus* here before he left, then I'm guessing he figured it out."

She didn't say, *And you know what* canus *does when it feels threatened.* Tarquin's deep frown told her he'd drawn the right conclusion—that Acaelus might be fully controlled. If he was, then a *canus*-bound mind had just run off with a pile of relkatite and the resources to print as many people for its purposes as it desired.

"You realized that was a possibility," he said. "That's why you didn't use the explosive. So that you could investigate further."

She lifted a brow at him. "No, Tarquin. I didn't use it because I wanted to make sure you were safe. If I had taken the two of us out, that left you alone with Nic and Roselle."

"But...your mission...?"

"Acaelus has a few more months before he reaches the cradle. If Fletch is right about the blockade, then as soon as I get ahold of a transmitter outside of Sol I can be there in a matter of seconds."

"We have to get you free for that to happen."

"Mercator isn't as homogenous as Acaelus or Fletch think. I'll find someone to leverage. I'll get out. But you have to stay this time. You have to keep the other MERIT families from taking over."

"I know." He pressed a firm kiss against the back of her hand. "And I hate it."

"You'll be fine." She gave him a tired smile, and he tried to return it, but it didn't quite reach his eyes. "But be careful with Fletch. He wasn't kidding about wearing your cuffs like gloves. He'd take it all from you if he could, and no one wants Fletcher Demarco as the head of a family. He talks a good game about keeping low ranks off ice, but in the end he's in it for himself, and no one else." Her tone took on a sour edge. "He's always been like that."

Tarquin hesitated, staring at their intertwined hands, and she waited for the question she knew he was picking through, trying to untangle. When he asked it, he didn't look up.

"You two were...?" He trailed off. "Never mind. It's none of my business."

"It is your business. We were together. We were kids, and I was stupid, and it ended when I went into the E-X program."

He let out a slow breath. "You knew each other for so long."

"We did. But it ended almost two decades ago. Fletch can't...He's never been able to let things go." She watched Tarquin for any sign of jealousy, but he seemed merely curious. "When my mom died, they brought me to the same HC-sponsored house Fletch lived in. He was younger, but he'd been there longer and knew the ropes. He got me a job with him when we were seven and eight. Scrubbing out the ducts below station that the cleaner bots couldn't reach easily enough. Their treads were always shorting out, and they had issues climbing back up, so kids were cheaper to use."

"You were children," he said, unable to hide his discomfort.

"We weren't the youngest people doing the work. We got along. I was...angry. Closed off. He was funny. A little cruel sometimes, but always laughing to let you know it was okay. When I signed up for the HCA, he followed. They taught us violence. It suited him. It suited me."

"What happened?" he asked.

"You have to understand, when we were kids he wasn't like . . . this. Not exactly. He'd known this older girl, Lina, I think. She went to get printed the year before I showed up. After she left, he never heard from her again. That hit Fletch hard. He was sure something had happened to her and he was always . . . I don't know. Afraid of being left behind. It changed when we went to the HCA. He became controlling. Obsessive. I thought he was adjusting to the new environment at first, but . . . I'm sorry. You don't want to hear about all of this."

"I want to hear everything about you," he said with such sincerity that it eased some of the anxiety that'd been welling within her. "But that doesn't mean you have to tell me, if it makes you uncomfortable."

"How are you being so sweet about this?"

"Naira. Please. My father is Acaelus. I can hardly judge you for unhealthy attachments."

She laughed. "Well, I know your monster, now you know mine." Naira glanced at the door. If Fletcher wasn't watching the cameras now, he would undoubtedly review this footage later, but she found she didn't care. It wasn't anything that he shouldn't already know. "I realized something was seriously wrong at the end of our first year in the HCA. Kav was the officer in charge of training our year. Nobody liked him."

"Hold on," Tarquin said. "Nobody liked *Kav*? He hasn't been friendly to me, but he's done his best to tolerate me despite his obvious distaste for my family."

"It wasn't his personality. It was his muscle." Tarquin looked absolutely baffled by that, and Naira had to remind herself that, for the most part, he didn't know what life was like outside of Mercator.

"Most people who go into the HCA, they pour everything they have into combat pathways. Kav wanted to do tech, so he spent his spare print funds on cognitive pathways instead. But the HCA never moved him out of combat roles. He packed on muscle to make up the difference, but everyone knew. He was the butt of everyone's jokes."

"I had no idea."

"He doesn't talk about it. That first year, I didn't know him well. I didn't know anyone well, Fletch made sure of that, but one night, before the advancement exams, I was coming back from training and saw Kav get cornered by the other cadets. I stepped in. Fletch was livid, convinced

I'd get discharged for fighting and we'd be separated. I'd never seen him that angry before, and that's when I fully understood how he'd changed."

"But your service record is spotless."

"Because Kav covered for me and made sure I was assigned to his squad. At first it was to keep an eye on me—he was there when Fletch blew up— but we became friends. Kav kept pushing me to leave Fletch, but I couldn't, and then we..."

She pressed her lips together, remembering their final fight, and almost kept it to herself. There was no judgment in Tarquin's expression, only a wrinkle of hurt between his brows that she was certain mirrored her own. Naira cleared her throat.

"We were both decorated. I wanted to be an E-X. Fletch wanted to go into the finalizers. We fought. He said he didn't want me dying for anyone but him, and I told him I wasn't his property, and we shipped out to our separate specialties and never spoke again."

"You make that sound like a very reasonable conversation," Tarquin deadpanned.

She snorted. "He struck me. I hit him back. We tore each other apart." Naira shifted her weight. "I don't want to fight like that with anyone I care about ever again."

He clutched her hand tighter, and though he shot a furious glance at the door Fletcher had left through, his expression softened as he turned back to her. "I can't imagine ever wanting to hurt you."

"I confess to wanting to strangle you sometimes," she said, lightening her tone.

He gave her a sly smile that heated her core. "Let's save those experiments for a moment a little more private, shall we?"

She blushed, and couldn't remember the last time she'd done so. "Are you flirting with me in the face of certain peril, my liege?"

He leaned closer. "I've found it the most advantageous time to flirt with you, Ex. Sharp."

She relished the tug in her chest that drew her to him. He slipped a hand behind her head, fingers tangling in her hair, and pulled her the rest of the way, lips connecting in a shock of pain as her abused nerves burned under the extra pressure. She didn't care. Pain was fleeting. There was a high chance she'd never see him again after they stepped off this shuttle.

His tongue retreated into his own mouth and she frowned in confusion as she tasted a fresh wash of blood. He slipped something to her—small, compact, metallic—and made certain she noticed before pulling away. She rolled the object over with her tongue.

A personal explosive device.

He rested his forehead against hers, close enough that he was out of focus, the gleam of his hazel eyes filling her view. His voice was so low she could scarcely hear him.

"Don't let him harm you."

She pressed the device against the interior of a remaining molar. "I won't."

He breathed deep, on the verge of saying something more. The door swished open and Fletcher stomped into the room, clearing his throat roughly.

"Don't make me turn a fire extinguisher on you two. Come on, cub. You're needed. We're within range and it's time to use those command keys of yours."

Tarquin scowled, but refused to be rushed. He pressed a slow kiss to her forehead.

"Be safe," he whispered, then moved away, putting the haughty posture of the Mercators back on.

Naira crossed her arms over her stomach and stroked the explosive planted against the side of her tooth with the tip of her tongue. She indulged in watching Tarquin cross the small room with all the arrogance of his heritage, keenly aware of Fletcher's gaze on her, hard and hateful.

"Well?" Tarquin asked Fletcher. "What are you waiting for?"

FOURTEEN

Acaelus

Mercator Station | Four Months Ago

Acaelus lay down on a gurney and gave his daughter's hand a comforting squeeze. Worry lines creased Leka's face. He wished that there was some reassurance he could give her that she hadn't heard a thousand times before, but there were always risks when switching prints.

"I'll be back before dinner," Acaelus said.

Leka's answering smile was strained. "Are you sure about this? I don't see what the rush is. We've sent scout swarms to Sixth Cradle. They'll be there soon."

"I need to know," he said.

"But... with Tarq gone..." She swallowed and tensed her jaw.

"We'll recover him soon enough." He squeezed her hand again and lay back, settling his head into the upload crown. "He's always thinking he can run off somewhere, but it never lasts, does it?"

"I suppose not," Leka said, though they were both aware that this time was different. This time, Tarquin had turned his command keys against the family. Acaelus could hardly hold it against him. The station's destruction had saved countless Mercator employees from the risk of their maps cracking.

It wasn't the keys, or the destruction, that made him believe Tarquin wouldn't come back willingly. It was the way his son had looked at Sharp that worried Acaelus. He knew that look. There was no hiding Tarquin's adoration.

But Tarquin's recovery was in Demarco's capable hands. The truth of Canden's appearance on Sixth Cradle was in his.

Acaelus closed his eyes, and Leka made certain the crown was snug before she initiated the backup process. Warmth bloomed across the back of his neck and skull.

"Ready?" she asked.

"I am."

Usually he would rely upon Dr. Meti Laurent to manage such a thing, but he wouldn't reprint the doctor until he ascertained what had become of Canden's neural map. Those two had been close, and if she had been hiding his wife from him, he wanted to confirm the fact before interrogating her.

Leka was more than capable of running the mostly automated process. She would have to input the channel he was casting into, but otherwise the system would delete his map from the print in Mercator Station and then cast his backup and print specs through the restored ansible network to Sixth Cradle. The warmth of the crown faded, and he slipped beneath the lulling wave of sedation.

Acaelus woke on Sixth Cradle. The green lights of the printing cubicle flickered. A slow groan escaped him as he quested his hands down this new body, seeking flaws. It was a risk, casting himself somewhere the integrity of the printing bay couldn't be confirmed, but he felt whole enough, if a little wan. The cartridges must have been running low and conserved his muscle mass, the first thing that got cut from a print when the cartridges weren't full.

The release lever was broken, so he stomped on the end of the cubicle until it gave way, almost laughing at the absurdity of the head of Mercator having to kick his way free.

When the door opened, he wished he'd stayed in the seal of the cubicle.

Human rot assaulted his senses, the sweet-pustulant scent sticking to the interior of his nostrils, burning his eyes. He gagged before he could crawl out of the cubicle, vomiting thin bile into the confined space.

Acaelus dragged a hand across his mouth and staggered into the gloom of the shuttle's makeshift printing bay. His pathways adjusted to the low light. The breath knocked out of him.

It was just a print. An empty vessel. Evidence that Tarquin had come home. But it was still his son's body, left behind when he casted to Mercator Station, with no one to clean up the mess and recycle the print. The sight of it rotting there, nothing more than that damn agile survey bot left to poise over the bones...Acaelus squeezed his eyes shut and dug the heels of his palms into the sockets until it hurt.

Just a print. Prints were disposable. That was the whole point.

Leka had been right. He shouldn't have come here.

Acaelus turned his back on the twin bodies—Paison lay there, too, but he couldn't care less about the traitorous captain's corpse—and pressed his fists against the wall, steadying himself. He was here to discover what had become of his wife and what had driven his son away. The body on the table was a lie. He'd seen plenty of corpses in his life. Had made plenty more. This was nothing. Nothing.

His hands shook as he pulled away from the wall. He found a robe stored in a drawer beneath the printing cubicle and tugged it on, scrubbing the sleeve across his mouth to wipe away the remains of bile. In a first aid kit, he found cotton for wound dressing and crammed it into his nostrils, but it wasn't sufficient to block out the stench.

The shuttle had been left with enough power running to cast Tarquin and Paison home, the console podiums glazed with a dim green glow that shimmered alive at his touch. It had been left unlocked, Canden's credentials stamped in the upper-left corner.

He clutched the sides of the podium, breathing shallowly. No one else had those credentials. It was all the proof he needed. Unsteady hope trembled through him. She had been here, and she had died, but her map must be stored on this shuttle for her to have been printed here at all. Her *uncracked* map.

His command keys overrode any locks she may have left in place, and it was a matter of seconds to find her map, last backed up the day before Tarquin shot her. He stared at it, momentarily unable to comprehend what he'd found, a small part of him insisting that it was still cracked, that it wouldn't work, that something else would go wrong.

Acaelus had never let his doubts slow him before, but he hesitated a fraction of a second before he transmitted that file to Mercator Station.

Canden. Canden was coming home.

He crushed the hope building in him, the failure of Chiyo's software too fresh a wound. The locks Canden had put on her personal files stored on the ship's hardware fell away under the push of his command keys. Years of research piled up before him, her precise, meticulous method of taking notes a familiar ache in his heart.

Most of them featured the shroud, and *canus*.

Acaelus had planned on sending the information back to digest later, but he started reading and couldn't stop. By the time he'd finished, his joints were stiff from lack of movement, and his eyes were dry and stinging. Hours passed, he wasn't sure how many, with only the green glow of the holo to fill the interior of the shuttle.

She'd done it. Canden had been the mind behind the shroud, the one to wield it against the worlds, and all for the prevention of a bigger threat. One she determined he could not possibly learn about, because if he ever did—if the head of Mercator ever started fighting back against the infection in his pathways—*canus* would abandon subtlety for control, and that much power at the hands of *canus* would mean the end of them all.

It didn't seem possible. Maybe she had cracked in the end. Maybe these were mad ravings.

He knew better. And he had a perfect sample, ready to test.

Acaelus did not think about what he was doing. He did not think about the snap of the gloves as they covered his hands, the click of the tweezers he removed from Canden's selection of tools and placed into a shallow metal tray.

He didn't think about the stink or the smooth slide of rotted skin slipping down to plop onto the gurney as he inserted the tweezers into Paison's custard-soft cheek and removed the short piece of pathway that ran along the side of her eye, giving her night vision.

It made no sound as he placed it in the tray, no click of metal on metal, and his preliminary visual inspection revealed it to be a spongy, silvery grey flecked with black rot. Acaelus wouldn't settle for suspicion. He brought the pathway to a microscope, contained it in a slide, and looked.

The *canus* infecting the protein sheath had died, but he'd know it anywhere. Acaelus placed his hands on the lab table on either side of the microscope and leaned back, staring at the wall, drowning in thought.

No wonder Tarquin had fled him. No wonder he'd refused to say what had really transpired.

Acaelus can never know. He won't abide it, and it will take him.

But he knew, now. He flexed his fingers against the table, watching his pathways shine, and wondered what it would feel like to be taken over. Would he even know it was happening? Would it be a slow slide into docility, or a fist clenched around his mind, sudden and stifling?

He supposed he was likely to find out.

Acaelus considered letting himself die here. Not taking back the knowledge. Canden knew him too well. He couldn't leave this behind. He couldn't stand the loss of himself, even the tiniest part of his will.

Canden had turned to shroud, and then amarthite, and while she'd worked alone, her progress was impressive. Acaelus was head of Mercator, with a fleet of resources at his disposal. He would find a way to purge the thing he'd unleashed once and for all.

He'd find it for her.

Acaelus transmitted Canden's research to his private servers on Mercator Station, then crawled into the printing cubicle that'd birthed him, fitted the crown, and cast himself home.

He did not look outside, nor access the perimeter cameras, and so he did not see the dozens of starved misprints standing sentinel in a staggered ring around the shuttle. Did not see them tilt their heads to the side, and smile, and whisper his name on shroud-crusted lips.

FIFTEEN

Tarquin

Mercator Transport | The Present

Fletcher had lied about being within range for Tarquin to use his command keys. They were still hours out. He'd told Tarquin he wanted to give him time to change and adjust to his role once again. But, based on the venomous looks Fletcher shot him from time to time, Tarquin suspected that the truth was he couldn't stomach seeing Naira be close to anyone else. It was petty, but Fletcher's irritation with their relationship buoyed his spirits.

A silent Nic bundled Tarquin into a green suit with a cream undershirt. Tarquin told himself it didn't matter what he wore. He was a Conservator at heart. He wouldn't do things the way they'd always been done, though it would take time to institute change.

He told himself the power wasn't comfortable. That he didn't want it. Not really. That his chest didn't rise and his shoulders pull back the second he slipped the suit on. That the lift to his chin was an affectation he'd learned to don to pass within his family as one of them.

He almost believed it.

Tarquin removed his jacket, rolled up his sleeves, and let the green cuffs of his family show.

Fletcher entered the small room. "We're here. Before you step foot on that station, cub, I want to make a few things crystal fucking clear."

Fletcher was a dangerous man, one prone to violent outbursts, but Tarquin couldn't muster up the ability to care. He crossed his arms, leaned against the locker, and allowed himself to look as bored as he felt with Fletcher's posturing.

"Is this the part of your production where you threaten me?" Tarquin asked. "Because I've heard that part, Demarco, and you shouldn't waste your breath or my time."

He expected an outburst. Fletcher surprised him by smiling instead. "I'm glad you've got some claws, cub. You're going to need them. You and I, we're buddies now, aren't we? All of MERIT is going to want to tear you down. To rip you from that throne so they can feast on the carrion they've already scented. We won't let that happen."

"We? I will stabilize my family because I don't want those who relied upon Mercator for safety to be harmed. But we are not working together."

Fletcher chuckled. The sound raised Tarquin's hackles.

"You're right on that point," Fletcher said, "because you're working *for* me. You have the blood and the training, and that's the only reason you're still breathing. Mercator is mine. I'll parade you out to calm the other families and soothe the fears of the employees, but every decision you make will be filtered through me. Every edict will come from my lips to your ears. Know this, cub—the station's security is mine. If you think you'll step off this ship and have them arrest me, you're mistaken. Their loyalty is to me, first and foremost.

"And if you wrangle a few into your corner?" Fletcher shook his head. "I die, my people come for Nai. They'll crack her like an egg, and you won't get to her first, because once we're off this ship, it's leaving. Taking that little bird to a cage where you'll never find her."

Tarquin shut down every part of himself so that Fletcher wouldn't see the storm tearing through him. He saw it anyway. Smirked. Took a step into the room.

"But I'll know where she is." Fletcher tapped the side of his head with one finger. "And I'll pay her visits. And if you start acting up, I'll start bringing pieces of her back for you to visit with, too. Clear?"

His lungs were lead, but he summoned his voice anyway. "I'm looking forward to the day she takes your head."

Fletcher clapped him on the shoulder, beaming. "You and me both, cub."

"You're sick."

Fletcher chuckled bitterly. "Your family spent more money than I'll ever see to train me how to torture people on Mercator's behalf. Of course I am. But your hands..." He eyed the crest curling over the back of Tarquin's hands. "Those cuffs are paid for in the blood of regular people. Your debt's due, cub."

"If I could open a vein to pay for what my family has done, I would do it gladly."

"Lie to yourself all you'd like. I don't give a shit. But at the end of the day, you're here because I will it." Fletcher's smile was razor sharp. "A Mercator with aspirations to honor. Hah. I don't know where Nai found you, or what angle she was playing you for, but I've got to hand it to her, she sure found the perfect patsy."

Tarquin stilled. Fletcher was trying to wind him up, but the blow landed too close to his private insecurities for Tarquin to brush it off.

They hadn't talked much about their relationship. But they'd talked enough, and the fondness in her voice, the kindness in her, the way she'd breathed his name when they'd been together...Those things couldn't be faked. She may have started out using him, but she wasn't anymore.

"Now who's the one lying to themselves?" Tarquin asked.

His smile twitched. Strained. "I know Nai. I've known her since she was a half-starved, filthy little thing scrabbling through spaces too dangerous to risk the robots in. I know better than anyone what she's capable of. What she'll do to stay alive." He skimmed his gaze over Tarquin. Scoffed. "I know what she hates. And you rank real high on that list, Mercator."

"I do. After the trial, I'm quite certain I was only second to my father on the list of people she despised. She told me herself she hated me. Multiple times. But we found our way to each other anyway."

Fletcher's fingers flexed, as if he wanted to reach for a weapon. "So you're a larger fool than I thought. She told you she was playing you and you still wrapped yourself around her finger."

"I'm sorry," Tarquin said, "are you trying to drive us apart? Because

I thought you were using her as leverage, and I'm getting some mixed messages."

Fury detonated behind Fletcher's eyes, the vein pulsing on the side of his neck, but he didn't move. Let himself cool, before he spoke again. "You don't know her like I do."

Tarquin frowned, annoyed by his own sense of pity for this man. "You're right. I don't. I don't see her as that struggling child, though I acknowledge it as part of her. Do you believe you're the only one with a past with her? The difference between us, Demarco, is that instead of trying to shove her back into the mold of the woman I remember, I admire her as she is, not the echo of what she was."

Fletcher turned before Tarquin could gauge his reaction and swiped the door open. He held one hand down low and snapped his fingers. "Come," he said, as if he were calling a dog to heel.

Tarquin swallowed his indignation. Getting under Fletcher's skin was satisfying—and he'd meant every word he'd said—but to keep poking this particular bear was to risk him rearing and striking Naira.

Fletcher led him to an airlock with Roselle waiting beside it, the street clothes she'd worn on Miller-Urey replaced with light body armor and the sleek uniform of Mercator security. She gave Fletcher a brisk salute.

"We're ready, boss," she said.

"Good work," Fletcher said to Roselle, then addressed Tarquin. "The people on the other side of that door are here because your command keys opened this hangar. They're here to see you, cub. A figurehead. Chin up, don't waver. Be polite but firm and push off all questions for now. Can you manage it?"

"I've been doing that my entire life."

Fletcher opened the airlock. Three dozen Mercator personnel whipped their heads around, avid gazes sticking to him like burrs. Tarquin plastered on a confident smile, adjusted his cuffs to draw attention to the family crest, and strolled down the gangway ahead of Fletcher.

It'd been years since Tarquin had spent any real time with his family's closest personnel, but he picked out familiar faces all the same. Being high-ranking in Mercator had its benefits. Many of them had reprinted since he left for school, preserving themselves with the same midthirties to forties faces that were the current fashionable age.

They'd all frozen. He lifted a hand in greeting. The group dipped into deep bows as one. He bit back an urge to tell them that wasn't necessary and picked out Acaelus's chief of operations, Madeleine Salter, in the crowd.

"Ms. Salter." He exited the gangway and extended a hand to her. She took it, and he was pleased to find her grip firm. "I apologize for springing my return upon you so suddenly, but matters were beyond my control."

Salter's gaze slid to Fletcher before snapping back to Tarquin. "It's no trouble, my liege. We are overwhelmed and delighted to have you back, and forgive me, but your return wasn't entirely unheralded." Fletcher sidled up alongside Tarquin, assuming the protective pose of an exemplar, though he was no such thing. Salter rallied. "I sent for some of your personal effects to be brought from Jovian University. I hope you won't find that too presumptuous of me, but after your ordeal being kidnapped by the Conservators, I thought having your own things might be nice."

Tarquin suppressed a surge of annoyance. So that was the story Fletcher had woven to cover Tarquin's disappearance.

"That is very kind of you," he said.

She beamed up at him. "I've prepared a suite of rooms to your previous specifications, if you'll follow me, my liege?"

"I would first like to be briefed on the state of the stations."

Again, that flick of a glance to Fletcher. "It will take time to gather all the data…" Salter trailed off, frowning at a projection from her holo. "And forgive me, my liege, but I'm uncomfortable having you on this station until we can get an exemplar assigned to you."

"I'm perfectly well guarded, I assure you," he said dryly, and let her see him glance at Fletcher. Her cheeks pinked.

"I'm honored you believe me so adept, my liege," Fletcher said. "But the truth of the matter is that I will shortly be required elsewhere."

Tarquin nodded permission to Salter. She dug into her holo with the relief only adept bureaucrats can take in the comfort of protocol restored.

"Oh," she said. "That's odd, but fortuitous. It seems Ex. Lockhart wasn't relocated to the *Sigillaria*. In fact, I see no evidence of her reprinting recently. She is already familiar with your family—"

"No," Tarquin and Fletcher said in unison. They looked at each other, but Tarquin couldn't read anything in Fletcher's expression. "What about Caldweller?"

"Ah," Fletcher said, "Caldweller wasn't reprinted after being shelved for the expedition to the Sixth, as Liege Acaelus had no use for him. May I suggest—"

"Someone new, then," Tarquin said. "Surely my father was scouting some rising star or another."

"A new addition?" Salter fiddled with her bracelet. "It can be arranged, but with our relkatite stores as they are, it will be difficult to add another person to the family payroll."

"You have my authorization to do so," he said coolly, recognizing that flavor of pushback as something his father wouldn't have tolerated.

"Yes, my liege. Forgive me, it's been a hectic few days. I forget myself."

"In the meantime," Fletcher cut in, "the head of family suite is quite defensible. Shall we?"

"This way, please, my liege," Salter said.

He gestured for her to lead the way, as if it mattered what he wanted, and followed, feeling the gazes of his employees on him like fine-needled cactus prickles against his skin. How many were Fletcher's people? How many would sooner stab Tarquin in the back than let him wrest free of Fletcher's control?

He'd achieved a small rebellion with the assignment of his exemplar, but he held no illusions that it mattered in the slightest. Tarquin mulled over who he knew on-station. Tried to recall what scraps he'd gleaned about them over the years—either by Leka's off-loading of her thoughts, or Acaelus's insistence that he would have to know these things, someday. The security chief, Hector Alvero, might be loyal, but he couldn't be sure. He would have assumed Salter was, and clearly she was defaulting to Fletcher.

If he had listened, if he had politicked, then maybe he could be certain of some of those faces watching him with relief that had nothing at all to do with who he was, and everything to do with the name stamped into his blood. As things stood, he had to operate under the assumption that he had no allies. Even his attempt to endear himself to Nic and Roselle was for naught, as those two had stayed on the shuttle. Tarquin was perfectly alone.

"The stewards guessed on the placement of your things. If you require anything moved, just call, my liege." Salter gestured to a door with the verdant green of the Mercator crest painted across it. The artisan had added a light, patchy texture that reminded him of sun-dappled ground. Of light filtering through lichen-crusted trees.

Tarquin approached the door. It sensed him and opened.

He'd known what to expect. Still, the opulence struck him after spending months with the Conservators. The foyer had a vaulted ceiling, wood that had come from living trees tracing purely decorative arches against a veneer of genuine marble. The pale grey stone gleamed. Polished by hands, not machines. The stone was too soft for mechanical maintenance.

Tarquin thought of Naira as a child. Of her small, deft fingers cleaning out the places too dangerous to risk the robots, and swallowed a lump in his throat.

"My liege?" Salter asked.

The worry in her voice brought him back to himself. He could tell her he wanted smaller rooms. That he didn't want people waiting on him, scrubbing the walls, fluffing the pillows on the couches, or climbing high ladders to make certain the delicate stone of his ceiling shone to shout down the sun.

He could tell her all those things, and it wouldn't make him any less his father's son. It would only make her uncomfortable.

"This is fine, thank you."

Her smile came back, a flash brighter than the polished fixtures and rare Earth-born materials. Every decorative element in the room had been grown by the planet his family had killed. Carrara marble from what had been Italy. Redwoods from the western coast of the North American continent. Lapis lazuli inlay from Afghanistan. He saw none of his own possessions in the foyer or sitting room.

"I'll leave you to rest and refresh yourself," Salter said. "Call if you need anything at all, my liege."

"I require reports on the status of the personnel, the current number awaiting reprinting, and an inventory of our hard matériel. As soon as you can."

Her eyes widened, but she hid the expression with a bow. "Of course, my liege."

She lingered. Waiting for his dismissal. "You may go."

Salter bowed again before hurrying out of the room. The door clicked shut, and Tarquin let out a long, dragging breath, emptying his lungs into this room he didn't want. Fletcher clapped him on the shoulder.

"You did well enough. I suggest you do rest, however. Now that word's out you're back, the other heads of MERIT will come sniffing. They'll want to meet with you, and you'll have to be sharp for that, cub."

"You mean I'll have to focus well enough to parrot whatever you want me to say while making it sound like my original thoughts."

Fletcher dug his fingers into Tarquin's shoulder until it hurt. Tarquin refused to give him the satisfaction of a reaction.

"My priorities are securing Mercator against the rest of MERIT and finding enough relkatite to print the dead your father left on ice. I thought we might have those goals in common. Or are you your father's son, after all?"

"I will secure this family." The words were sour on his tongue. He wanted nothing more than to reprint everyone who'd been lost. But if Acaelus really had taken the bulk of their relkatite, then they simply didn't have the materials to do so.

"But not reprint the fallen." Fletcher *tsked*. "It's going to break Nai's heart, hearing that you won't resurrect those your own bombs killed because the coffers are looking a little low."

"That's not the only reason."

Fletcher's brows lifted. "Go on."

Gathering more relkatite would feed *canus* over time, make it stronger. A glimmer of an idea struck him. He'd never been able to fully investigate the source and capabilities of amarthite. But with all the resources of Mercator...

"There may be another way to construct the pathways. It merely requires more research."

Fletcher examined him, his scalpel-sharp intuition picking up that there was something Tarquin wasn't saying. After a moment's pause, he released his grip on Tarquin's shoulder.

"I'm not here to shit on all your ideas. You think there's another way, you look. In the meantime, I'll continue to pursue the known path—acquiring more relkatite." He rubbed his hands together. "And to that end, I leave you to rest. Don't exit this suite unless it's on fire, cub. No one wants to deal with the embarrassment of having to collar you and drag you back."

Fletcher turned to leave.

"You're leaving? I have no exemplar. I don't enjoy your company, Demarco, but I can't fight to defend myself, and there's no telling how the other families will react to word of my return. Chiyo may strike while matters are still uncertain."

Fletcher patted the wall by the door and didn't look back as he spoke. "This station is mine, and these walls are secure. Stay put, and live. Go wandering, and I won't take responsibility for what happens to you. But if you do get yourself killed, I'll reprint you right back here in this station, so don't go getting any ideas. And if they crack you, well, I might reprint your body with me in it."

A chill crawled down his spine. "You'd be discovered within hours."

"Maybe." He traced a pattern Tarquin couldn't make out against the wall with the tip of his finger. It reminded Tarquin of him drawing against Naira's neck with the point of a knife. "Maybe not. I'm an excellent actor, my liege. You're convenient to me, for now. Try not to become a liability while I'm gone."

"What's so important you're leaving now?" Tarquin asked. "We need to prepare for the MERIT council that will inevitably be convened once word of my return spreads."

Fletcher flattened his hand against the wall, knuckles whitening. "I'm going to visit our little bird. Don't wait up." He waved over his shoulder, a twist of the wrist, and left Tarquin alone to stew in miserable silence.

He stared at the door, willing Fletcher to come back, to change his mind, but of course he wouldn't. Fletcher had been pushing Tarquin into the cage of his suite as quickly as he could, eager to get away. To get back to Naira.

Tarquin had known, because the person Naira described when she talked about Fletcher was the kind of person to worry at a wound. To pick the scab off and dig a thumb in, to relish in the ache. Naira was a scab over Fletcher's past. One he wanted to rip free and let bleed.

Tarquin pressed both hands over his face and squeezed his eyes shut. He never should have let them be separated at the protest. Never should have let himself be led off that shuttle without her. He was Tarquin Mercator, head of family, on paper the most powerful man in the whole universe, and he couldn't even—couldn't even *think* of a way to protect her from that monster.

He scraped his hands down his face and scowled at the door, letting anger override the sorrow that'd been swallowing him. Naira was perfectly capable of taking care of herself. He'd given her a way out, if it came to that.

An invisible hourglass tipped over, grains of sand slipping through his fingers. How long? Would she do it right away? Wait until Fletcher got close and take them both out at once? Or would she hold on? Not knowing was going to eat him alive.

He unbuttoned his collar to let some of the heat out and strode across the room to an office. The lights flicked on, and he halted in the doorway, holding himself up against the wall.

Tarquin didn't have many things he thought of as his own. Pliny, his agile survey bot, had been one of the few objects he'd grown attached to. His hand-bound theses were another. Whoever had packed up his things from his apartments at Jov-U had thought to include his first rock and mineral collection.

The collection he'd started with his mother.

The stewards had lined them up near the front edge of his desk, with no mind for how they fit together. He brushed the tips of his fingers over the first piece of halite he'd ever found, recalling the moment when he'd been—what? Six? His mother had wiped the dirt off and, with a grin that said they were sharing a secret, told him to give the mineral a lick.

The taste of salt, and the realization that the seasoning he consumed every day grew out of the heart of a planet, had delighted him in ways he'd been unable to express. He picked it up, rolled it over his palm, recalling Naira calling him gross for having licked the amarthite—and the blush she'd tried to hide as she'd joked about kissing him.

He sat the halite back down and deftly rearranged the collection the way he preferred—igneous, sedimentary, and metamorphic grouped together, the rock cycle in a neat line. He nudged the tiny sliver of relkatite to the far end, the place of uncertainty. The movement stilled something within him, settled the bubbling well of panic. He didn't know how to be a head of family, but he knew that humanity needed an alternative to relkatite. He could start there.

The desk responded to him as he slid into the chair, throwing up a holo with a welcome interface. Fletcher had physically removed the line that would have connected Tarquin's suite to external comms. He couldn't call anyone outside this station. A quick check of his personal holo revealed a jammer in effect.

He searched for his father's files and found them all deleted. The stores of amarthite—recorded in Mercator's systems as the lowest grade of relkatite, practically unusable—were missing, along with the rest of the relk. Acaelus had taken everything when he'd fled.

Not willing to count on Salter to deliver, he pulled up the roster of unprinted Mercator personnel. Tarquin ran a formula to tabulate the amount of relkatite required to secure their printing at both their preferred level of pathways and the bare minimum, but one name caught his eye as a priority print, currently locked.

AERA LOCKHART—EXEMPLAR X ACAELUS MERCATOR, PERSONAL

He recalled Salter's brief consternation upon realizing the E-X hadn't been reprinted since Sixth Cradle. Tarquin started to access her file, and hesitated. Did he want to see that face again? Was *he* the one picking at scabs?

No. This felt important.

The file opened. Her picture slammed him in the chest. He clenched his jaw against that slightly tipped-up chin. The arrogance of a professional who knew her worth bled through the stare she gave the camera. It was her enrollment photo. Taken the day she'd signed with Mercator. The look she gave that camera could swallow the world.

Tarquin knew that look. He was being sentimental. It was just the resemblance that shook him. That face wasn't really Naira's, but it had been, for a little while, haunting him through the grey trees of Sixth Cradle all the way home.

He thought her eyes might be laughing at him.

Tarquin sifted through her file. Lockhart had been at the bottom of her class as an exemplar. She'd mostly flown under the radar of life. An orphan, not uncommon in the HCA. She hadn't formed any "notable attachments" as dictated by her security clearance.

He frowned, trying to dig deeper. To find some glimmer of why Acaelus had hired this woman who, by all accounts, wouldn't measure up to his expectations. Aera Lockhart's life was a blank page.

He leaned back in his chair, lacing his fingers behind his head. Everyone left a mark on the world. A rare few were like Acaelus, glaciers carving troughs in the crust of humanity with their mere presence. But even the smallest fragment left a scrape, even if it was to be conglomerated with other smaller pieces, folding under pressure into a greater whole.

"Who are you?" he asked her picture.

She stared back at him, defiant. Tarquin abandoned the files his family had compiled and switched to a search of the tabloids instead. Gossip streams had gone wild when Acaelus hired someone who resembled Naira, and he knew how deep those reporters could dig.

He scanned the headlines, putting aside the discomfort that rose within him as he saw, again and again: SHARP AND MERCATOR TRIAL—WAS IT ALL A LOVERS' QUARREL? MERCATOR HEAD OF FAMILY HIRES BODY DOUBLE OF HIS LOVER. THE AFFAIR MERCATOR WANTS YOU TO FORGET.

Acaelus had hired Lockhart because she looked like Naira, but he'd done so to facilitate blaming any potential failure on Naira and the Conservators, not because they'd been lovers. The very thought was laughable. The tabloids, it seemed, had found nothing more about Lockhart than Mercator had on file. Even attempts to interview those who'd trained with her had turned up nothing of interest.

A video caught his eye: HEAD OF MERCATOR WOUNDED IN ASSASSINATION ATTEMPT. He couldn't recall his father being wounded after the trial. Curious, Tarquin pressed play.

Acaelus walked through a transit station somewhere on Earth, approaching the decontamination chamber that would sanitize any shroud lichen he might have picked up while on that poisoned planet. The security camera was high up and pointed steeply down, and so Tarquin could only see his side and the top of his head.

A path had been cleared, and those going about their everyday business paused to watch Acaelus pass. Tarquin marked the security in the crowd, other Merc-Sec assigned to perimeter duty. Acaelus turned a corner, the camera switched angles, and Tarquin's breath caught.

Lockhart walked a few steps behind him. Her head was up, alert, one hand on the weapon strapped to her thigh, her strides confident but soft, an unobtrusive presence. Just another shadow trailing Acaelus.

It wasn't Naira, and yet seeing that body move through the world again dug hooks into him and twisted. Lockhart moved like Naira did. They'd had the same training. He was seeing things. Chasing ghosts.

Shots rang out. Acaelus ducked down. The crowd screamed and scrambled. Tarquin watched, transfixed, as the extra security emerged from that scrambling crowd.

Lockhart grabbed Acaelus from behind and folded herself over him, pivoting to put her armored back to the direction the gunfire had come from. The move was so like the one Naira had used to defend him from the explosion that his throat thickened.

Her body jerked, gunfire slamming into her back. He glanced away, sickened, wondering why the headline read that his father had been injured when the real story should have been that she'd been shot to death in his defense. She staggered a step, keeping Acaelus tight against her chest, and ripped her pistol free. Even bleeding from six shots in the back, she held her arm steady as she lifted the weapon and fired.

Those were not the actions of an exemplar who had rated last in their class. He rolled the video back. Watched the critical moment again, forcing himself not to look away.

To watch Lockhart's hand drop to her weapon, and skim her thumb along the trigger guard in the same movement she used to disengage the safety.

He paused. Zoomed in. The pistol's grip had been modified, switched out for a diamond pattern. Naira's preferred weapon, the modifications she made to every pistol she called her own. Lockhart could have the same habits. It was possible.

But that was a first-in-class exemplar. That was a woman dying for her charge, barking orders as she did so, never once flinching from the task at hand.

"Who are you?" he asked the video.

He wasn't speaking to Aera Lockhart. Not anymore. He wasn't even sure that woman existed.

He was asking Naira Sharp.

SIXTEEN

Naira

A Very Pretty Cage | The Present

Fletcher had been true to his word that she would enjoy her cage. When the vision blockers they'd injected her with had worn off, Naira found herself locked away in a suite of rooms without windows, dripping with more opulence than she'd seen in many MERIT suites. It wasn't the furniture or fittings that cost. It was the shelves upon shelves of plants, bursts of color against cream-white walls. Each flowering plant was seen to by an automated system that hissed, sometimes, when it watered them.

She'd half expected them to be poisonous, but when Nic and Roselle had left her without a word and locked the door behind them, Naira had approached to find the delicate petals were all the ones she'd loved as a child, though she hadn't seen them in person in decades. Growing flowers cost. After her mother had died and Naira had been moved onto a station, the only flowers she'd seen were through videos.

They had lain awake at night, and sometimes she'd shown Fletcher those videos. It had never occurred to her that he was paying attention.

Naira attempted an outbound call and found her print's onboard communications jammed, which was no surprise at all, but the collection of books she found in the apartment's media database was a surprise. Her reading habit was something she'd picked up after they'd split, when she'd had access to Mercator's library. She knew this was all to manipulate her into softening to him, but she endeavored to enjoy the books regardless. After she searched the place for a way out and had come up with nothing, it wasn't like she had anything else to do.

She found the shower pleasantly hot, her favorite bathing supplies already in place, and a selection of clothes that fit her perfectly. Fletcher hadn't provided her with the light body armor she preferred, but he'd rummaged up casual clothes that mimicked the cut and style of that armor.

More tricks. But she ate the food that was left out for her, and didn't think about how easy it was for her aching body to fall asleep in the bed provided by her captor.

Fletcher let her stew for five days before he made an appearance.

She'd fallen into a routine of tending the flowers, as much as the automation would allow her, exercising, then reading. Knowing that every system in the apartment was being monitored, she'd avoided working on getting to the *Sigillaria*, or signaling anything regarding *canus*. Instead, she made notes in the back of her mind, making and discarding plans, hungry for more information.

Naira was sitting on the couch, her arms along the back, her feet on the coffee table, her head tipped back as an annotated translation of Pliny the Elder's *Natural History* scrolled past on her HUD, when the door opened outside of the usual time for meals. She didn't look up. She didn't need to. She'd always been able to sense when he was near.

"Nai," Fletcher said, her name a whispered prayer.

She blinked the book closed and made herself look at him. He'd dropped the casual clothes and switched to the light body armor she craved for herself. He'd cut his hair, or at least put extra effort into styling it, the sandy-blond locks shining, a little mussed, but intentionally so. He looked as if he'd seen a ghost. She supposed they both had.

"Has the Mercator misbehaved already?" She curled all but her little finger down and wiggled that digit at him. "What will it be? Bring him my pinky this time, to keep him in line?"

Fletcher's throat jumped. "I don't want to do this with you."

She pushed her tongue into her cheek, over the place with the missing tooth. The flesh had healed, but that tooth wasn't regrowing on its own. "You sure about that?"

"You would have killed us both."

"And have you considered why I would have done that?"

His lips twitched. He put his hands in his pockets and strolled farther into the room, stopping on the other side of the coffee table. As far as she could tell, he was unarmed.

"Do you like it?" He looked pointedly around the room. "It cost a fortune to get them on such short notice."

"I didn't realize finalizing paid so well."

"It doesn't." He let his gaze return to her. "But I find it easy to spend Mercator coin."

She was tempted to ask him to clarify how he accessed the Mercator coffers, but she remained silent instead, unwilling to play his game of deflection.

Eventually, he said, "I never thought I'd have to see you sucking the face off a Mercator."

She arched a brow at him. "And I never thought you'd put a knife to my throat on a street corner and rip my molar out."

"Why didn't you call me?"

"Excuse me?"

"When you left. When you walked away from Mercator and started blowing up their ships and warehouses. We joined together. We should have left together. Do you have any idea how long I wanted to do what you did? How the cuffs have fucking chafed?"

"We hadn't talked in years." She could have tacked reasons onto that. Could have explained that his lust for violence made him a poor fit for the Conservators. But in the end, the old instinct to hurt him rose up. "I hadn't thought about you until I saw you on Mercator Station before the explosion."

He scanned the room, and a thin smile curled his lips. "I forgot how cruel you can be."

Naira refused to answer that.

"What happened to us?" he asked.

She could tell him she'd always known her mother had cracked. That she'd known, even as they whispered to each other about saving their cred to pay her mother's phoenix fees, that the money would mean nothing. Her mother had gone. And when Fletcher signed up to be a finalizer, someone who made an art of the very thing that had taken her mother away, the brittle thing between them had finally snapped.

She could tell him it was that last fight, and it wouldn't be wrong. That when he'd slapped her, it was over and it was never coming back. It was strange, in retrospect. Part of her wondered if she'd have stayed if he'd had the guts to punch her outright, to land a fist against her jaw in anger instead of the back of his hand. If he'd struck her like an equal, instead of an unruly cur he was attempting to bring back into line.

She'd certainly given him the decency of her right hook in return.

But watching him standing there, his expression open, vulnerable, and his eyes hopeful, she thought back to when they'd been kids. To when, impossibly, they'd found a silver-winged moth caught in the filter of a duct.

Naira hadn't seen a single winged creature since she'd left her mother's corpse on Second Cradle. Fletcher had cupped it in his hands and carried it all day until they got back to their bunks. He stuck it in a jar, sneaking it pieces of his food. Droplets of water.

Naira knew something about bugs. Knew the way they flitted between blooms, spreading the pollen that spreads life. She'd told him he needed to let it go. That it wasn't built to live on the same things he was built to live on. But he'd wanted it, and it'd died, and when he realized, he was only frustrated that it wasn't his anymore.

"Do you remember the moth?" she asked.

He nodded. She lifted her hands from the back of the couch. Flapped them at the wrist, slowly, twice, in answer. Understanding flashed through him. She saw it as a lightning bolt of anger, a jolt he'd never been able to hide from her. Old fear coiled within her. Like she was walking on a razor's edge, and he was both the blade and the succor.

Even after years apart, her instincts were honed to detect that rage. In her darker moments, she wondered if that forging was what had made her such an adept exemplar. She knew when assailants were about to strike a beat before everyone else did. That instinct had won her accolades. It also kept her up at night.

"I'm so sorry," he said.

Maybe he wanted to be. But that flash of anger told her he wasn't. "If you're looking for forgiveness, you're going to be waiting a long, long time."

"Then I wait," he said with such sincerity that it startled her. "And I act to prove it, until I've earned it."

"Have you forgotten you're holding me prisoner?"

He paced a short path back and forth in front of her. Fletcher was only ever still when he was ready for slaughter. "That's why I said I don't want to do this with you."

"You expect me to believe that after your performance earlier?"

"Don't pretend to be so damn naive, Nai. It *was* a performance. I'm a finalizer, and so are Nic and Roselle. I can't very well sit and have a polite chat with Mercator's most wanted. If those two had sniffed even a scrap of hesitation in me, we'd both be cracked by now."

"I haven't been gone from Mercator so long that I've forgotten how it works. Those two are your subordinates. You could have handled that without all the grandstanding bullshit."

Fletcher shot a glance at the door Nic and Roselle had taken turns guarding. "Those two play their own games."

"I'm sure they do. And I'm also sure that Acaelus has gone AWOL and you have control of Mercator Station, so don't you dare tell me that 'performance' was necessary."

"I have control of Mercator Station *because* people like Nic and Roselle are terrified of me. It's that reputation that's kept you alive, so don't *you* dare complain to me about rough handling. I know you enjoyed a chance to take a shot at me. You're welcome."

"What? What do you mean, that your reputation kept me alive?"

Fletcher stopped pacing abruptly and turned to her, surprise on his face. "You really don't know, do you? Have you even thought about the position you fucking put me in?"

Naira blinked, wrong-footed, and he tossed his head and laughed.

"Of course you haven't. You were too busy playing hero to notice the wreckage you left behind. What do you think happened to all your little friends when you turned on Mercator? Do you think Acaelus shrugged and said, oh well, surely your pals didn't share your ideology? Surely they wouldn't turn, too?"

As far as she knew, the people she'd worked closest with still had their jobs. That didn't mean they hadn't suffered, though. "What did Acaelus do?"

"Questioned us. Firmly." Fletcher shook his head at the outrage plain on her face. "Your nearest and dearest got off with a few light scratches. Things get more intense, however, when the person being questioned is a finalizer themselves."

"We hadn't talked in years."

"The people with the knives didn't care, love. They had a list of 'close contacts' to work through, and I was at the top."

"I'm sorry. Genuinely. I never meant for anyone else to suffer for my choices."

"How sweet," he said, tone dripping sarcasm. "Don't give me that look. You know I hate pity. The experience made me a better finalizer in the end."

"I never wanted you to be a finalizer in the first place," she snapped.

Fletcher's brows rose and he hooked his hands around his hips. "Are we having that fight again? Because you will have noticed, I hope, that that ship has sailed."

Naira leaned forward, rubbing her face with both hands. She needed to focus. Five days without ingesting shroud to battle the *canus* in her pathways was wearing her down. Making her irritable. And there was no one in the universe who could rile her temper faster than Fletcher Demarco.

Devolving into an argument was what he wanted. It was always what he wanted. Fletcher craved other people's rage as if the heat of that anger was the only thing that could thaw the cold hollow inside of him. She took a breath. Sat back once more.

"Hate me all you want. I don't blame you. You're right. I put you in a terrible position when I left and I didn't think about it. That was selfish of me. I'm sorry for that, I really am. But I need you to listen to me. No more games. Please."

He drew his head back. "You think I hate you?"

"After being tortured for my desertion, you hunted me for years and now you've kept me locked up for a week, Fletch. What am I supposed to think?"

Fletcher circled the coffee table, pulling it back so that he could sit in front of her. Naira stiffened instinctively, and while she was certain he noticed, he gave no sign as he rolled up his sleeves and looked her pointedly in the eye.

"I don't hate you, Nai. I never could. Believe me, I tried. It would have made my life easier. Don't get me wrong, I haven't been pining after you all these long years, either. I'm not that pathetic." She grunted at that, and he smiled. "But you were...my world, when I thought I didn't have one. So, yes. I hunted you. I was, as Kav put it, 'Nai hunter number one' because I successfully made my love look like hate during that interrogation, and when your contract came up, I used my perfect track record to take it."

"How do you know Kav said that about you?"

He rolled his eyes dramatically. "I told you I've been tailing you. Try to keep up. Or did you really think that Acaelus's best finalizer, with all the resources of Mercator at my disposal, couldn't find you?"

"Sure, Fletch. You strung Acaelus along for five years while you pretended to hunt me down. Sell me something else."

"Hmm." He looked slowly around the room. "Nai, love, you're smarter than that."

Naira's knee-jerk reaction to tell him off wasn't going to help her any. The only way out of this room was either via the explosive, or talking her way out, and Fletcher was being strangely reasonable.

Even though every instinct she had rebelled at giving him the benefit of the doubt, she followed his gaze around the room. They'd always been in sync. The second she dropped her guard, even a little, she saw what he wanted her to see.

The apartment wasn't a shrine to the memory of her. It was a shrine to who she was now. Her current favorite things. Nothing from their past, save the flowers.

"You really have been tailing me all this time."

His smile was more akin to a pained twitch. "I'm glad to see you haven't completely lost your mind. You had me worried when I realized you actually liked Acaelus's cub."

"I thought I was losing my mind when I realized I liked him, too."

He snort-laughed. "You've never been a good judge of character."

"Really? Coming from *you*?"

He winked. "I should know."

She cracked her jaw. "You've kept me locked up for a week. I don't trust you. I can't."

Fletcher sighed raggedly and rubbed a hand over his face. "I'm sorry. I would have been here sooner if it was possible. I hate that you're my leverage. Tell me you're playing him. Tell me you've got that Mercator-faced fucking bastard wrapped around your finger for some other purpose, and I'll let you walk out that door and finish whatever this plan of yours is."

"He's a good man," she said. "I like him."

"Did dying for Acaelus scramble your brain? He's a *Mercator.* He's one of them. We have a chance, now. We have the head of a family under our thumb. We can change things. If you worked with me, we could change so much more. That's what you want, isn't it? To save the worlds and change the way it all works? To make MERIT see nonfamily as people, and not data to be stored or manipulated?"

"Tarquin doesn't need to be leveraged. If you let me go and treat him fairly, he'll work for everything you've just outlined. He's on our side."

"There's no way I'm trusting that prick. You want me to listen to you? No more games? Fine. I'm listening. But right now all I'm hearing is the goddamn revolutionary mind I used to love singing the praises of a Mercator prince, and that's not you, Nai. I don't know what the fuck is going on, but that's *not you.*"

"I'm still fighting for the same things. The strategy's changed, that's all. Tarquin can work on dismantling the system from within while I hunt Acaelus down."

He searched her face for a long moment. "You don't even believe what you're saying. I can see it written all over you."

She let out a rough laugh. "You don't know me as well as you think you do."

The intensity in his stare shifted, lost the smolder of anger, and became something she didn't recognize. "Maybe," he allowed, surprising her. "Maybe you're just another bootlicker now."

"Fuck you." She hated how easily he reduced her. How she felt like she was back in those ducts, scrambling to stay alive, defending her right to exist. To prove herself a mouth worth feeding.

The ghost of a smirk skittered across his face, carefully tucked away. "You started this war, Nai. *You* picked up arms against Mercator. And I have been dancing on the point of a knife ever since, knowing that if I rest even for a second I'm dead, it's over, because the things Acaelus would have done to me if he'd ever found out I was 'failing' to catch you on purpose would make my work look cute in comparison. And now that we can finally work together, you're siding with our enemy? You owe me a better explanation than 'I like him.'"

Part of her wanted to trust Fletcher—part of her always would—but that glimpse of his smirk when she'd lashed out had poured cold water over the guilt he was stirring up. He knew where all her cracks were. She couldn't let him wedge his fingers into her walls until they broke.

"Tarquin is not my enemy. And I don't owe you a damn thing when it comes to explaining why I'm with him."

"The cub's not the man you think he is," he said. "God, Nai, it shouldn't be me telling you this. Though maybe I'm the only one who can. Skies know Kav could never make you leave me, though he tried."

"Are you seriously implying you wanted Kav to convince me to leave you?"

"I'm saying it outright. I hadn't yet learned to harness my anger then and I . . . hurt you. And I know, I *know* you're strong as hell and you damn near killed me for it, but it wasn't about the physical violence, was it? Violence was air and water to us then. It still is. It was the intent." He looked down at his hands. "It was about my need for control. Making you an—I don't know—object. Not a person. An extension of myself."

That was too perfect. Too well delivered. Warning bells rang in her mind.

"Do you want to know what the root of all our problems was? I don't know who you are, Fletch. I don't think I ever did." He looked back up, blinking in confusion. "You say the persona you wielded in the warehouse was a performance for the other finalizers. But I've seen you use that persona often enough that I know it's not fully an act, is it? You come in here and you stir up my guilt, you wear me down, and the second you sense I'm pulling away again you hit me with *this*? The one thing you know I've been waiting years for you to say? Maybe you mean it. But that doesn't change the fact I can't trust you.

"I can't even have an honest conversation with you because I *know your tricks*. Do you think I missed the fact that you kept turning my war into 'our' war? That you co-opted my goals to build trust in you and undermine my faith in Tarquin? That you revealed you'd been 'protecting me' from Acaelus to turn me into the bad guy for shutting you down despite the fact you've been holding me prisoner for a *week*. When you're holding me prisoner *right now*. I didn't train to be a finalizer, but I've worked with your colleagues enough to know your playbook. This has been an interrogation from the start. Why are you so desperate to know what my plans are? They should be obvious. I'm chasing the *Sigillaria*."

"My clever, clever Nai." He gave her a fierce grin. "I knew you wouldn't disappoint. Fine, you caught me. What can I say? Some habits are hard to break. But I am sorry. For everything."

"You've been trying to manipulate me since you walked through that door. How can I possibly believe you?"

"I didn't mean to manipulate you. Those things just..." He waved a hand through the air. "Slip out sometimes."

"Set me free and release Tarquin. Then we can talk for real."

"I want to let you go. I do. But I can't release the cub. Without a way to control him he's another Acaelus waiting to happen."

"*Tarquin?* You're kidding. You've spent time with him. I can't imagine you like him, but he's nothing like his father."

"Oh, he doesn't want to be. He pushes back so hard because he knows he has Acaelus's cruel streak buried deep within him. The cub barely sees anyone around him as people, let alone equals. Do you know he thought Salter was working *with* me when she was clearly trying to signal to him she was onto me and wanted to help him? He can't even pick up on basic body language. People might as well be aliens to him."

"Salter? Acaelus's chief of ops?" Naira asked. Fletcher nodded. "She's as Mercator-loyal as it gets. I'm surprised she hasn't tried to poison you in your sleep."

"That loyalty cuts both ways. She won't move without a word from him, and the cub's so up his own ass he can't see it."

"He probably doesn't want to put others at risk. You're a dangerous man to cross, Fletch."

"Why, thank you. But no, that's not it. He really doesn't see it. He *can't*. People raised to that level of power see others as props in their lives."

Fletcher kept talking, but all Naira could hear was her own voice. Harsh with anger but not raised, Tarquin's shocked face filling her mind's eye as she said, in memory: *your fantasy of egalitarianism.* She shook her head, trying to clear the moment from her mind, but it kept pushing back in. Bleeding around the edges. Blotting out what Fletcher had to say.

"Nai?" Fletcher shook her shoulder. "You all right? Come on, stop fucking around. Answer me, please. Nai?" A firmer shake. "Nai!"

She jerked away from him, escaping the fugue state with a shudder. "I'm fine. Jesus, you almost dislocated my shoulder."

Naira's mind slipped, and she was staring up into Tarquin's mud-streaked face, rain pounding down all around her, the agony in her shoulder overwhelming the painkillers her pathways dumped into her.

"Nai!" Fletcher clapped in front of her face.

She startled back into the present. "I'm—"

"If you say you're fine again, I will tape your mouth shut."

Naira closed her mouth with an audible click of her jaw. Fletcher stood over her, one hand checking the pulse at her neck while the other tilted her head to the side and lifted her eyelid gently with the side of his thumb. She wanted to pull away, but the panic that'd stamped into his face was the realest emotion she'd seen on him yet.

"What are you doing?" she demanded.

"Praying I'm the one hallucinating and not you. What happened? What did you see, or hear?"

"Nothing. Really, it's no big deal."

"Nai, love, the professional map cracker is currently freaked out over what I just saw. That's not the first time it's happened, is it? You slipped in the warehouse."

"It's just a little bleed-over. It happens."

"Oh, yes, it *happens.* It happens right before you—" His voice caught. He cleared it. "Stand up."

"What?"

"I'm serious. Stand."

Fletcher shoved the coffee table back to give them space and grabbed her arms, tugging her to her feet. He took a step back, tapping his chin in thought as he studied her. Naira crossed her arms.

"This is ridiculous," she said.

"Hit me."

"Excuse me?"

"Go on, take a swing," he said. "You know I don't mind."

"Yeah. That's the problem. I'm not getting you off by kicking the shit out of you."

He smirked. "Pity. But that's not what this is about. I need to check your proprioception."

"You don't need to check anything."

"I know you don't like my profession, love, but I am quite good at it, so let me work, hmm?" He squinted at her. "What was it you were saying? 'Fantasy of' something?"

"I said that out loud?"

"You didn't know?"

They stared at each other. Fletcher had never managed to hide when he was afraid from her. It coiled him up inside. Had him vibrating with anxious energy, as if he were about to burst at the seams. That much, at least, hadn't changed. Naira crossed her arms tighter.

"Hit me."

"No."

His weight shifted. Winding back to strike. Her training took over and she snapped a hand out to grab his wrist. Missed. Fletcher stopped his swing short, knuckles an inch from her face. She ducked away, but he dropped his arm and let his fist hang at his side.

"You don't miss a block that clear."

"I'm tired."

"Bullshit. How long has this been going on?"

"A couple of months."

"*Months?*" His mouth dropped open. He closed it. "You've got to be fucking kidding me. What do you see? What's the focus?"

"It's none of your business. Back off."

"It's the cub, isn't it? We were talking about him when you slipped."

"Back. Off."

"It *is* the cub. Fuck." Fletcher slid his fingers through his hair and clutched the back of his head. "You need to stay away from him."

"I'm not going to do that."

"Then I'm going to keep you locked up until this passes."

Naira resisted an urge to tell him off. If she escalated this into a full-blown fight, they'd start shouting, then they might start swinging for real, and when it was over Fletcher would leave her here without any answers.

"What aren't you telling me?" she asked.

"I'll let you in on a nasty little trade secret. Neural maps are nuanced, the science complicated, et cetera, et cetera, but even the most carefully shielded backups crack, too, because the entanglement doesn't give a shit *when* something happened. That's the point.

"When a target experiences flashbacks before they're officially cracked, we know they're on the edge. We've got them and it's time to push them to breaking. Usually, they don't even realize they're telling us how to break them because the focus they get stuck on, the thing that's their undoing? That's the memory they're falling into pre-crack. If a target goes glassy-eyed, and their pulse is bouncing around, and they start talking about—oh, I don't know. The time they almost drowned in the bath, then I know drowning them will push them over the edge and past recovery. Straight to the endless scream."

"Charming," Naira said.

Fletcher grabbed her arms. She tensed at the contact, but he only turned her to make certain she was looking at him. "You're seeing the cub. He's instrumental in your cracking. That's not me fucking with you. Ask any finalizer. This is how it *works*."

"Tarquin would never hurt me."

"He doesn't have to hurt you himself to be the cause. At the very least, he's there when it happens. I mean it, Nai. Stay away from him."

"I'm not cracking," she said. "The memories aren't even upsetting. It's like I'm trying to remember something good. Something important."

"Important doesn't always mean good. You died on Sixth Cradle. You have no idea what really happened there. He could be lying to you."

"You're seeing conspiracy where there isn't any. He's a Mercator. I know. I've considered that, but Tarquin wouldn't lie to me or hurt me."

"He is *not* the man he presents himself as to you."

"I thought finalizers were supposed to be good at reading people."

Fletcher's fingers tensed, denting the muscle of her arms. She shifted her weight back, preparing for him to lose his cool at last. Something she couldn't read flashed across his face—shame, maybe?—and he released her, taking a pointed step back as he held up his hands.

"Your buddy Lee Caldweller has been on ice since Sixth Cradle," Fletcher said.

"What?" Naira frowned, taken aback. "Tarquin's E-X?"

"The very same. The man who put his life on the line for the cub since the little shit was a teen. A second father to him, by all accounts, has been left to rot for over a year because the cub seems to have forgotten he existed. Lee's husband is a mess, by the way. Heartbroken."

Working for Acaelus hadn't allowed Naira much personal time, but she'd always enjoyed the company of the other exemplars. Lee especially. Before her defection, she would have called him a friend. Now, she didn't know what he thought of her—probably nothing kind—but that didn't mean he should have been left on ice all this time.

"Poor Marko," Naira said, half to herself, thinking of Lee's husband. "But that's not Tarquin's fault."

"Isn't it? He could have requested his E-X when he first came back from Sixth, but he was too busy planning to run off with you. When I returned him to Mercator Station, he declined to hire Caldweller back on and requested Lockhart instead. A suggestion I shot down, by the way."

"He has his reasons." He must have wanted to question Lockhart about what his father had been doing before Sixth Cradle. Still, Fletcher caught her initial reaction. The brief frown she couldn't control. Because she didn't like the idea of Tarquin contributing, even inadvertently, to Lee lingering on ice.

"You're right, Nai. He has his reasons. As I found out over this last week." Fletcher shook his head, as if disappointed. "I didn't want to do this. I really shouldn't be the one showing you this, but you're clearly not going to listen to me otherwise."

Fletcher pulled up the holo from his arm, bathing them both in Mercator green. He accessed an array of photos, videos, and search results. Ex. Lockhart. Every image featured that woman, every search, every video had that body moving through the frames. Hundreds of them.

Lockhart filled the air between them, smothering her. Fletcher placed still frames from security footage of Tarquin in his office, leaning toward those results, face rapt, alongside them.

"This is what he does," Fletcher said with disgust. "Every damn night. He's obsessed with her. Fills his holos with her image."

Naira sank back down onto the couch. Indignation flared within her, coupled with revulsion. Had she been right the first time? She'd thought his denial of her fear had been sincere, and maybe he had wanted it to be, but . . . No. Tarquin wasn't like that.

"This doesn't mean anything," Naira said.

"Sure, Nai," Fletcher said. "A perfectly harmless obsession with a body you used to wear."

Her pathways grew uncomfortably warm, feverish, and she felt like she was drifting away from herself again. All that hard-won surety about her print and her mission fuzzy and indistinct, a past she couldn't even remember reaching up out of the ether to mock her.

She wasn't enough. Not for the fight against *canus*. Not even for Tarquin.

Naira blinked, slowly. That wasn't the Tarquin she knew. And those weren't her thoughts. They were the same doubts that'd been pooling through her before Kuma had knocked her head on straight. Five days without shroud and already *canus* was winding its way into her psyche. Trying to wrest her away from her allies.

Trying to align her with Fletcher.

She relied on her frustration with *canus* meddling with her heart to let Fletcher see what he wanted to see—hurt, anger—while her mind raced. Fletcher had his own reasons to want to drive a wedge between her and Tarquin, but were they entirely his own?

Fletcher abhorred even the suggestion of being controlled. It was difficult to believe he'd work with *canus* willingly, but Acaelus's highest-ranking finalizer would be a valuable target for *canus* to overwhelm.

She didn't trust her expression to hold much longer, so she buried her face in both hands. This—Tarquin lusting after someone else—was a clumsy play for Fletcher. Naira hated to admire the man, even in her own thoughts, but he hadn't become Acaelus's best by accident. He'd been manipulating people since they were kids. Had always been capable of changing his personality in the blink of an eye. That talent had helped keep them alive.

He wouldn't make a mistake like this. Not with her. The only way Fletcher thought this would work was if he was too controlled to see otherwise. She had to get out of here before *canus* sank its teeth much deeper. Even now, sweat sheened her skin.

Fletcher wouldn't let her walk out that door unless he believed she was done with Tarquin. His fear about her cracking, even if she didn't believe it, had seemed genuine enough. If being upset with Tarquin could get her out, then she'd pretend at being tricked.

He touched her arm, lightly, and she clung to the disgust she felt at being infected before she looked up. Fletcher brushed the holos away and sat back down on the coffee table's edge. He met her gaze, and the softness in it surprised her.

"I'm sure he was sweet to you, Nai. I hope he was. But when it comes down to it, he wasn't raised to view nonfamily as people. We're disposable to him. Bodies to burn for the glory of MERIT. Even if he pushes back against it, it's who he is at the core. Acaelus's son. The longer he's in power, the more like Acaelus he'll become. That's why I have to keep him in check. And I am..." He sighed. "I realize how this will sound, coming from me, but I'm worried about you. You want to fix every problem you trip over. That makes you vulnerable to people who don't deserve your help."

Naira couldn't control the borderline hysterical laugh that boiled out of her. Fletcher gave her a shy grin she hadn't seen since they were children.

"I know, I know," he said. "I fucked up. I fucked *us* up. I spent all those years trying to force you back into the mold of the kid I grew up with, all those years chasing an echo. I wanted to see you as that scared girl crawling through the ducts at my side again because I understood that. I knew where I stood, beside that girl. But I want to know you as you are now, Nai. I want to be worthy of standing beside the woman you've become. And you were right. This started out as an interrogation. Because you can't hide from me that there's more going on than you hunting Acaelus down. Please, tell me. I want to help you."

That kicked her in the heart. Naira let out a rattling breath. Fletcher was, historically, a piece of shit. But he'd only tolerated Acaelus's yoke because it'd given him more freedom than any other position would. If she told him about the infection, he'd fight back.

And if he was so far gone that he didn't, she'd take them both out.

"Did you check the print cartridges like I asked?"

"I always do what you ask. They came back positive for contamination with *canus*. I don't know how you knew that, but it's a godsend. We're culturing it into a larger mother colony so that we can start mining relk again. Get those people printed."

She winced.

"What? What is it?"

"When was the last time you reprinted?"

"I was on Mercator Station when you blew it up. Why?"

"Months, then." She expected a surge of impatience from him, but it never came. "*Canus* is symbiotic. With us. With humanity. It turns parasitic, when threatened or otherwise pressured."

Fletcher pulled his head back, as if he needed the space to better examine her. "How?"

She took his hand and traced the golden pathway on the back of his wrist. As far as she could tell, it wasn't inflamed or greying.

"The relkatite in our pathways. It needs it to survive, but it doesn't degrade it. It keeps the pathways working, we keep living and finding it more relkatite. It uses our own bodies' chemicals to influence our moods. Makes us excited to keep mining, and dreadful at the thought of anything that might slow that process down."

"You're serious."

"I am. Test yourself. Think about gathering all the relk in the universe and launching it into the sun."

His face said enough. "Fuck. How much control does it exert?"

"Not much. Not at first." She kept tracing that pathway up and down with the tip of her finger, imagining the infection beneath his skin. Beneath her skin. "But it grows. And when it's strong enough, and feels threatened, it can exert more than mood swings. On Sixth Cradle..." She cleared her throat. Shifted. He waited. "It was controlling misprints. It had learned to speak and was trying to call home to tell its other segments that humanity was going to fight back. By the end, I think it almost had complete control of Captain Paison."

"This is what you've been fighting? All this time, carrying that weight alone?"

"Not alone. And before Sixth Cradle, I didn't know about *canus*. The shroud predates on it. Slows its growth. I suggest you start eating shroud supplements immediately."

"Ah." He grimaced. "Great. I hate that shit."

"Me too," she said. They laughed a little, together. Naira cut herself off and looked away.

He touched her cheek, turning her back to him. "Thank you. For telling me."

"This isn't a personal confession. I'm telling you this so that you'll understand what's at stake. Acaelus tried to kill all the *canus* on his stations, stole the relk, and ran for a reason. Either he's found a way to stop it, which I doubt, or he's under its control and is burning for that cradle to set up an army of the *canus*-controlled that we won't be able to stop. Either way, I need on the *Sigillaria*. You have to let me go."

His fingers tensed against her cheek. "That ship is blocking all incoming signals from Sol. Not even the rest of MERIT has a ship large enough to get outside the blockade in a reasonable amount of time."

"There's a way," she said. "And I'll find it."

He blew out a breath. "Why do I always believe you when you say shit like that?"

"Because I deliver."

Fletcher grinned at her, and she caught herself grinning back, and crushed it.

"Nai, I . . ." He ran a hand through his hair, hesitant. "I want to let you go. But I need leverage against the Mercator. My roguish charm won't be enough to bring him around."

"You know about *canus*. You two won't get along, but your goals are the same now, I hope? You don't need leverage if we're all on the same side. There's another substance Tarquin's looking for—amarthite—"

After the ship that brought us all together.

Tarquin's face swam up out of a memory to fill her mind's eye. Her breath froze in her lungs and for a second she thought—*this is it, Fletch was right, I'm cracking*—but the moment faded, and Fletcher's face took the place of Tarquin's.

"Nai?"

She blinked. Cleared her throat. Had he been talking? "Sorry, what?"

"It happened again, didn't it?"

"I'm stressed out. That's all. It'll calm down once I'm out of here and can consume the shroud again."

Worry drew a canyon between his brows. "It's not stress. It's that fucking Mercator. Promise me you won't get out of here and go confront him, or give him a second chance, or whatever the hell else you're thinking of doing. Not until you've stopped having flashbacks. Then you can go shout at him for being shitty all you'd like."

"I will," she said. "But that mineral I was talking about, amarthite, might be another way to make pathways. If you want me to stay away, you have to help Tarquin find it. Can you do that?"

"You think I'm going to let a fungus tell me what to do? Hell no. I'm with you, Nai. Burn the *canus*, lift up the people. Secure food and longevity for all. It's everything I've ever wanted to accomplish. Well, not that I knew about the fungus thing. But I never cared for mushrooms, so the vendetta's the same, isn't it?"

She snorted a laugh, and his answering smile deepened the scars lining his face. Scars he kept with every printing. It struck her that she no longer knew where they all came from. He caught her mapping them and ducked his head. Her pathways warmed, making her feel cozy and safe, and it was all she could do to keep the disgust off her face.

"Don't rush off, please?" he asked. "I know you're eager to get to that ship, but give me some time. The cub's got the MERIT heads coming to pay him a visit in a few days. Let me feel them out, see which way the wind is blowing with regard to their intel. If one of them thinks they have a way onto the *Sigillaria*, I'll find it. For you."

"I'll wait. But I'm not waiting here."

He looked around the room, flowers reflected in his eyes. "This place is yours, if you want it. I won't hold the keys from you. Come and go as you'd like. I never wanted to lock that door on you. I never wanted..." He realized he'd been touching her cheek on the side he'd extracted the tooth from. Panic flared in him and he jerked his hand back.

She probed at the empty socket with her tongue. "I really was going to blow your head off."

"I deserved it. I still do."

"Yeah. You definitely do."

He caught her taunting smile and laughed hard enough that his head tipped back. "God." He wiped his eyes. "I missed you."

Had she missed him? When they'd shipped out separately, all she'd felt was relief. But that smile echoed to her across a past less fraught. He was dangerous. A manipulator. Abuser. They examined each other, and all she could see in those eyes was a reflection of her old self. A person she didn't want to be anymore.

"I don't want to fight like that with the people I care about anymore, either," he said.

She should have been annoyed by the confirmation that he'd been eavesdropping on her conversation with Tarquin, but she wasn't. It was exactly what she would have done if she had two prisoners in a room on her ship.

"Good," she said, and meant it.

He closed the distance and kissed her. She stiffened at the first touch of his lips and jerked her head back. He pulled away immediately, face bright red.

"Fuck, shit, I'm sorry, I thought—I misread. I'm so sorry."

Naira didn't think she'd ever seen him so contrite. She pressed a hand against his cheek, briefly, in acknowledgment, before taking it away and leaning back. Putting space between them. Her pathways still felt warm, the conniving bastards. She'd pretend to be angry with Tarquin to get out of here, but there was no way in any hell she'd fake getting back with Fletcher.

"It's fine," she said. "Really. *This* apology is accepted. The others you still have to work for."

He scrubbed his palms against his thighs. "Thank you. I think it's best if I go now. I'll pass you the digital keys on my way out. Just, promise me you'll wait, okay? If I can find something, it's worth waiting for."

"I'll wait," she assured him.

Fletcher smiled at her, a little sadly, and patted her arm in a friendly manner before pushing away from the coffee table. He waved at her over his shoulder before slipping out.

It surprised her when her HUD dinged, letting her know he had passed her the keys and dropped the jammers blocking external calls. He'd opened the jar. He'd let her go.

Naira wanted nothing more than to call Tarquin. To make sure he was safe. But Fletcher would be monitoring his communications, and there was no telling how he'd react to finding out she wasn't actually upset with Tarquin.

Naira called Kav. He picked up immediately.

"Nai? If this is Fletch, I swear to fucking—"

"It's me," she said, talking quickly so that he wouldn't ask her something she didn't want to answer. "We have a lot of work to do."

SEVENTEEN

Tarquin

Mercator Station | The Present

Tarquin bent his head over his plan for the meeting with the other heads of MERIT and pretended he wasn't driving himself out of his mind with worry. A week. Seven whole fucking days ago Fletcher had left to visit Naira, and Tarquin had had no word from him aside from a few brief instructions via text. Texts that always declined to answer the questions Tarquin hammered him with.

He was tempted to search the news for any sign of a woman dead via personal explosive device, or anything remotely equivalent, but his searches were being watched by Fletcher's people and he didn't want to give away Naira's escape route. It chafed, waiting, but it gave him time to refine his plans to present to the council.

His new E-X, a person with a chest almost as wide as his doorway and a mop of coppery-brown hair, knocked on the open doorframe. Tarquin looked up.

"Demarco here to see you, my liege," Ex. Francel Cass said.

Tarquin smothered his burst of hope and fear. "Send him in, please. And wait outside."

He wanted to shake Fletcher until he explained where he'd been and what had become of Naira, but he stood and paced behind his desk.

Fletcher strolled into his office, whistling and chewing on an apple that coated his fingers with sticky juice.

"Is she safe?" he demanded.

Fletcher blinked owlishly at him. "Who?"

"Naira." He barely wrestled his tone into less than a shout. "Who else?"

Fletcher's smile was slow and bladed. "Oh. Nai. I apologize for making you wait, cub, but it takes time to get reacquainted after so long. You understand."

"Answer the question."

"She's fine." He took another bite. "Furious with you, though."

He stopped pacing. "What are you talking about?"

Fletcher gestured at the desk with his apple. "I told her about your late-night extracurricular activities. Honestly, my liege, I'd have thought better of you."

Tarquin was about to ask him what he meant, but Fletcher angled his arm and swept up a holo. Tarquin's breath caught, the bottom dropped out of his stomach. All his searches of Lockhart, all the pauses he'd made over the weapon strapped to her thigh, checking to see what kind of pistol she carried, arrayed before him. He knew exactly what it looked like. And that it was precisely what Naira had feared.

He'd reassured her. They'd talked it out. Fletcher's smirk told him that conversation hadn't been enough.

"I didn't...I wasn't..."

"I really don't care." Fletcher wiped the holo away. "But Nai did, poor dear. She tried to hide it, but she's never been very good at hiding from me. It was strange. Usually I'm the one making her look that hurt. Nice to be the shoulder to cry on for a change."

Tarquin gripped the back of his chair to steady himself. "I have to talk to her."

"She doesn't want to talk to you. She knows who her real allies are now." Fletcher took on the tone of someone reading a quote. "She has someone in her life who cares about the woman she's become, who isn't obsessing over the person she used to be."

"You piece of shit. You used my own words."

He winked. "They were good ones, too. She ate it up. Even blushed for me, and I can't tell you how long it's been since I've seen *that*. You know, despite all her reprintings, her skin still tastes the same as it did in her original body. Those mappers really are incred—"

Tarquin surged around the desk and punched him in the face. Fletcher reeled, the apple falling from his hand to roll across the carpet. Pain exploded through Tarquin's knuckles. Something cracked. He didn't care. He relished the shocked look on Fletcher's face, the burst of blood spraying from his split lip. He drew his fist back to swing again.

Fletcher brushed Tarquin's next strike away and sent Tarquin stumbling into the desk. He laughed, delighted, shaking his head as he probed at the split in his lip. Tarquin itched to keep hitting him, but the surprise was gone. He couldn't hold his own against a trained killer, no matter how much he wanted to try.

"You surprise and delight me every day, cub." Fletcher ran his tongue over his teeth and spat blood on the floor. "Illicit strength pathways, I take it? How very bold of you."

Tarquin tried to gather his thoughts, to control the shudder of his breathing, the rush of his pulse in his ears. There was no way for him to determine if anything Fletcher said was true. Even if it was true, Naira could be playing Fletcher in a bid for freedom. She had to be.

"I want to talk to her," Tarquin said. "I need to know she's safe. If you want to keep me in line, I need..." What was it the ransomers usually called it? "I need proof of life."

"I told you, cub, she doesn't want to talk to you." Fletcher scooped the apple off the floor and picked off a few pieces of lint.

"Let her be the judge of that."

The eagerness on Fletcher's face told him he'd stepped into a trap. Tarquin braced himself, resisting an urge to flinch away as Fletcher moved close enough to whisper in his ear.

"I let her go two days ago. If she's not contacted you, it's not me keeping her tucked away. She doesn't *want* to talk to you."

It hurt. His chest actually physically hurt. He pressed a fist over his heart, grimacing, and tried to focus on his anger to keep from breaking down.

I wouldn't do that to you.

He believed that. Tarquin had never believed in anything more than he believed in Naira, but the old fear wedged itself into his psyche. The pain in his chest was a weight, suffocating.

It wasn't right. She wouldn't leave him without a word. Not Naira. He *knew* that, but still he felt like he'd had the rug ripped from under his feet and in the brief second he'd been falling, something else had risen up to catch him. Cradled him in warmth. He was woozy and displaced and couldn't force his thoughts back into line.

"Open my ability to call out. Let me reach out to her."

"No can do, my liege. She's perfectly capable of reaching out to you, if she so desires, but I don't think that she will. Incredibly busy, my Nai is, but she finds the time to send me updates on her progress with the *Sigillaria*, the dear woman."

"Then you've lost your leverage, Demarco."

"Ah. But that's the trick, isn't it?" Fletcher beamed at him. "She told me all about it. About what you Mercators have really been up to with *canus*, and it was one hell of a revelation. You and me, cub, we're on the same page. The same side, even, can you imagine?" He punched Tarquin lightly on the shoulder. "And don't forget, I own everyone on this station. So smile for the cameras, dance for the council, and we can put our heads together and have a nice long think on how to oust *canus* from our pathways because I, for one, am not content to be a meat puppet. Mercator's been pulling my strings long enough. I won't let a damn mushroom do it, too, now that I'm finally free."

Tarquin sat behind his desk, folded his hands on the smooth surface, and stared at them. At the split skin over his knuckles, the bruises already spreading. His print was getting fragile. He couldn't muster up the ability to care.

Fletcher was still talking. He kept up a deluge of plans and ideas, changes he wanted to make to the whole of MERIT. They all started with subtle shifts within Mercator. Fletcher was clever. He understood that a sudden upheaval of the entire system wouldn't work. They had to lay the groundwork. Make inroads. Recruit allies. Shift thoughts with words and deeds before fundamental changes took place.

And never, ever, reveal to the other heads of MERIT that the *canus* in their pathways was influencing their thoughts, because a head of MERIT fighting against *canus* would spur that creature to assert as much control as it could.

Tarquin traced a pathway on the back of his hand. He was a head of MERIT.

That felt important. But slippery. A thought he couldn't quite grasp.

"Demarco," Tarquin said, interrupting that loathsome man's mono-logue. "I feel...not quite myself."

Fletcher chuckled. "Heartbreak will do that to you, cub."

"No," he said, even though his body was screaming *yes*. "This feels... wrong."

"Aww." Fletcher ruffled his hair, drawing a grimace out of Tarquin as those apple-sticky fingers touched him. He leaned down, breath tick-ling Tarquin's ear. "You know, cub, being a finalizer's not all about the knife work. Physical pain's not always enough to break someone. You have to learn to find someone's deepest insecurity and rip that wound wide open. And the really neat trick? Emotional shock can suppress your immune system, making you vulnerable to infection. Took me a long time to get that right."

Tarquin tried to pick apart the meaning in the words, but his mind was hazy, his pathways uncomfortably warm. He couldn't make sense of the statement. Fletcher pulled away.

"Now, we have work to do, don't we? You have a meeting to pre-pare for."

Fletcher kept talking. Tarquin tuned him out, staring at the backs of his hands and thinking—*I need to reprint*—but not quite finding the will to call the techs to make the arrangements.

EIGHTEEN

Naira

The Conservator's Ship | The Present

Naira had thought alarms would blare when she opened the door to her cage, but nothing happened. It wasn't quite real to her that Fletcher had let her go. She'd half expected him to keep her locked in that apartment until they were both silver statues overgrown with *canus*.

That's what the man he'd become in the final days of their relationship would have done, just to keep her for himself. She recalled his flash of sincerity when he'd admitted to having been fixated on who she used to be, and how he wanted to learn who she was now, and a tiny, tiny sliver of her armor thawed.

Which was a terrible idea. She knew that. She did.

It was impossible to reconcile the man who'd practically flung himself out of the room in mortification after misreading her and kissing her with the man who'd put a knife to her throat and crooned violence in her ear. Fletcher had always been good at acting a role. She just wasn't sure which role was the act.

Having access to the net again, she'd discovered she'd been held on a station a few hours' flight from Mercator Station. She'd been tempted to go to Tarquin, but she could hardly walk into a Mercator Station without setting off every alarm in the universe.

She'd been relieved to see Tarquin on the news, assuring the public that Mercator was stable again. He looked healthy enough, if tired and drawn. No silver. No inflammation. She had time.

Naira had told Kav about the *Sigillaria*'s comm blockade on Sol and arranged for the team to pick her up at the station's docks the next day. Seeing that shuttle again, Mercator green or not, eased some of the hurt in her.

"Nai!" Kuma bounded down the gangway and snatched her up in a hug that crushed all the air and confused thoughts straight out of her. "I thought your call might have been Demarco fucking with us. Wait. Why are you sweaty?"

Naira returned the hug before wriggling free. "Shroud. Now."

"Right." Kuma grabbed her hand and dragged her up the gangway. "Kav! Shroud!"

"On it!" Kav jogged out of the hall that led to the galley and tossed her an icy-cold thermos.

Naira snatched it out of the air, twisted the cap off, brought it to her lips, and...froze. Her stomach cramped, mouth flooding with the thick saliva of incoming vomit, muscles straining as sweat soaked through her clothes.

She didn't have to do this. Fletcher was infected. If she let her infection grow, then they could finally sense each other's thoughts. Feelings. They'd understand each other at last, and she could talk him down from whatever plan he'd cooked up.

"Need a little help there, Nai?" Kav approached her warily.

"Just. Give me. A second."

Her arm shook, but she made it move. Touched the thermos to her lips and, closing her eyes against the effort, gagged down a few short gulps. Her throat tightened, stomach flipping over. She accessed her HUD, forced her protesting pathways to pump her full of anti-nausea meds and stimulants to counteract that eerie warm fugue state her mind kept drifting into.

By the time she'd downed the whole thermos she was shivering, sweat dripping off her skin, pathways tender to the touch.

"Fuck." She threw the thermos at the couch. It bounced and rolled to the floor with a clatter. Naira braced herself against the back of the couch with both hands, bent over and panting. She'd felt fine, physically, until she'd gotten access to the shroud. Now it seemed the *canus* in her was determined to go down swinging. Strangely, she could respect that.

"You good?" Kav asked.

She burst into tears, which startled her so much that she started laughing. Naira tipped her head back, struggling to get ahold of herself. The effort was pointless. She couldn't seem to do anything other than sob or laugh. Frustrated, she dragged her sleeve across her eyes and peeled away from the couch, pacing tight circles to burn off the jittery energy pingponging through her. Her friends skittered out of her determined path.

"Is she always like this after being around Demarco?" Kuma asked.

"Pretty much," Kav said.

Naira grunted. "I hate you both."

"There she is," Kav said with relief. "What happened?"

Their worry probed at her, peeled away layers of herself she didn't want stripped free. Naira gripped the back of the couch again and stared at the fallen thermos as she told them a pared-down version of what had happened.

"Ugh," Kuma said at the end of Naira's recounting. "Demarco is the worst."

"He's infected," Naira said. "I don't think it's swarmed him. His pathways seemed clear, but it's in his head enough that he thought that ploy with Lockhart would work to make me walk away from Tarquin."

"Infected or not," Kav said, "he's still a violent asshole. Don't forget that, Nai."

"How the fuck could I forget that?" she shouted. The words echoed in the small room.

Kav and Kuma exchanged a look. Naira clutched the back of the couch so hard her hands hurt.

"So, you remember how the first stages of a deep *canus* infection are increased irritability?" Kav asked.

"I know what the goddamn stages are—oh."

Kuma patted her lightly on the back as she glanced down at her hands and saw how white-knuckle tight they were. She released them, slowly, one muscle at a time, trying to put a lid on anger she wasn't even certain was hers.

"Sorry," she muttered, embarrassed.

"It's okay," Kuma said. "We'll load you up with shroud and you'll feel like yourself again."

Naira pushed away from the couch to resume pacing, hoping the movement would take the raw edge off her nerves. It didn't. She didn't stop.

"So Demarco has Tarquin." Kuma crossed her arms and leaned against the wall, giving Naira plenty of room. "And is probably busy breaking his heart right now. Man, just when you two—"

"Don't," Naira snarled, unable to control the tone of her own voice.

Kuma held up her hands briefly in surrender before crossing her arms again.

"What I don't get," Kav said slowly, "is why you told Fletch about *canus*."

"He hates being controlled. He'll start taking the shroud, and then we might actually be able to reason with him."

"Reason with Fletch? That's never happening. The only side he's on is his own."

"I'm pretty sure maintaining independent thought across all of humanity aligns with even Fletch's self-interest."

"Sure, but what if he already knew about *canus*? Fletch's ego is bigger than Acaelus's. He'd convince himself he could use it, and it'd use him in turn."

She scoffed. "It freaked him out. He didn't know."

"Hypothetically—"

"He didn't know!"

Kav crossed his arms and gave her a flat look. "Is there a reason you're shouting at me instead of entertaining even the tiniest possibility? A, oh, I don't know, a *reason* you're shutting this down hard and fast when you're usually the first to pick through any theory we come up with? Because, Nai, you said yourself he was there to interrogate you, and he didn't back off until you told him, did he?"

"I—" She was about to insist that she knew Fletcher. That she'd been there to see his face, and Kav hadn't, and she was certain he hadn't known. But even considering that Fletcher might have already known about *canus* made her thoughts clench up with a knee-jerk shout of *no*. "Motherfucker."

"Yeah. Thought so." Kav smirked at her, which would have been annoying if she wasn't busy trying to puzzle out the implications. It was like trying to catch a fish with her bare hands. Every time she snagged a thought, it slipped through her fingers.

"Talk me through it while I poison this shit." She turned on her heel and stomped off down the hall. Kuma and Kav followed her into the galley.

They kicked ideas back and forth while Naira dug the shroud supplies out of the cabinet and mixed another dose. She chugged down a full glass, then stuck her head under the faucet and rinsed her mouth out before doing the whole thing all over again.

When she'd taken all she could stomach, she braced her arms on either side of the sink and let her head hang over it, spitting out the vile taste whenever her salivary glands overreacted. She shivered hard enough to make her teeth chatter. Kav gave her an awkward pat on the back.

"Okay." She filled her lungs to the bottom and emptied them. "Okay. Fletch knew. He likely thinks he's using it, even though it's definitely using him. But he knows I'm fighting it, so why let me go?"

"Acaelus," Kuma said. "Demarco said he took the relk, right? So he lets you go to chase him down. Probably thinks he can wheedle you into getting the relk back for him."

Naira snorted and regretted it as the contents of her stomach shoved their way into her throat. She clenched her jaw. Swallowed it back down.

"Fat fucking chance I hand all that over to him."

"He has Tarquin," Kav said. "Fletch is, above all else, a manipulator, and he knows you extremely well. Do you really think he bought it that you were upset about the Lockhart thing?"

Her thoughts skittered away from that train of thought, which meant Kav was on the right track. At least *canus* wasn't half so canny as Fletcher.

"He was going to wait for me to find Acaelus and then use Tarquin to leverage the relk out of me."

"Seems likely," Kav said.

"And in the meantime," Kuma added, "he has the head of Mercator in hand to infect."

Naira's eyes narrowed. "Not for long."

She pushed away from the sink and slipped past her friends, heading for the cockpit. They were a half day's flight from Mercator Station, in a

Mercator shuttle. Fletcher might be watching for her, but she knew the security on those stations inside and out. This shuttle could get them into the hangar, and then—

"Whoa." Kav planted himself in front of her and held his hands out. "You can't go storming into Mercator Station without a plan. Or did you forget you're Mercator's most wanted?"

"I've got six hours to make an extraction plan. I've done it in less before."

"You're talking about kidnapping the head of Mercator from Mercator Station itself, out from under *Fletch*'s nose. We need to plan. Properly."

She clenched her fists to keep from shoving him out of the way. "Move."

"No way. I'm not letting you—"

"*Letting* me? I don't need your permission. Move, or I will move you."

"Nai." Kuma put a hand on her arm. "We want to get Tarquin back, too. But we can't do it without a rock-solid plan, and frankly, you're not thinking straight. You're still dumping sweat, and you're shaking. You need to detox before getting anywhere near that station, let alone near Demarco. And I... I don't like what he said about your flashbacks."

Kav looked away, struggling to regain his composure. Naira glanced between them, momentarily at a loss for words.

"You two can't possibly think Tarquin would hurt me."

"No," Kav said. "But I don't like that your slips are getting closer together. Detox. Get your head on straight. Then we'll go get the Mercator. Because, Nai, if you rush off and get cracked because we didn't prepare properly, it would devastate Tarquin. If you can't think clearly enough to protect yourself right now, then—don't do that to him. Don't do that to *us*."

Naira let her fists relax and released a slow breath. She trusted her friends. Whether it was her own hotheadedness pushing her to go off half-cocked, or *canus* urging her, she didn't know. Either way, moving before they had a plan—before she could trust her own thoughts—might make things so much worse.

"All right." She rubbed her forehead and slumped against the wall, the burning away of the determined fury she'd felt leaving her listless. "I hate to leave Tarquin with Fletch any longer than we have to, but you're both right. We'll plan thoroughly, and I'll reprint if I'm not detoxed by the time we have a plan locked in."

Kav made a face.

"What?" Naira asked.

"Jessel tightened up the unionists' use of relk after we sent word that Acaelus took off with the lion's share. They were already having trouble hitting relk shipments, and look, you won't believe this, but Jessel thinks they found the *Cavendish*. The mining ship sent to Fifth Cradle."

Naira's mouth opened in surprise. "I blew that ship up. I got *arrested* blowing that ship up."

"C'mon." Kav took her arm. "You'd better sit down for this."

NINETEEN

Naira

The Conservator's Ship | The Present

Kuma insisted on getting her water and a blanket, and as much as it irritated Naira to suffer any more delays, she had to admit that the comfort was nice. She sat on the couch in their meeting room, Kuma beside her, their shoulders touching, while Kav sat across from them, leaning forward with his fingers twisted together.

"After you called us," Kav said, "we alerted Jessel about the relk shortage and the blockade the *Sigillaria* had enacted against comms from the Sol system. Jessel told us they thought they might have found another ship with a large enough warpcore to chase the *Sigillaria*, or at least one with transmitters outside of Sol. They checked on a few things and got back to us right before we docked to pick you up. The data looks good. I think they're right. I think it's the *Cavendish*."

Naira rubbed her sore head. "How is that possible?"

"About four months ago Jessel caught wind of Mercator launching resupplies, slinging them out nowhere anyone expected," Kav said. "Jessel did some digging, and Acaelus was definitely moving something. Since the unionists have been short on relk, they started monitoring them to see if they could hijack one. What they found instead was evidence of a full-sized ansible at the supply shuttles' destination. The transponder numbers match. If the ship was destroyed, the ansible would have gone with it. Whatever's left, there's enough structural integrity to support the ansible, and we believe the warpcore is stable, too, because the signal is moving outside of an orbital drift."

"Where's it going?" Naira asked.

"As far as we can tell, into that system's star."

"Why would Acaelus load a ship with supplies, then aim it at a star?"

Kav rolled a shoulder. "Beats me. Maybe something went wrong. But all those supplies? Jessel never could figure out what they were."

"He wouldn't move the relk to a ship he's not on."

"Yeah," Kuma said. "It's possible the *Sigillaria* is a fake-out and he's really on the *Cavendish*. We can't know for sure."

"So you're suggesting we cast ourselves onto a derelict ship in unknown condition that's flying into a star on the off chance that either Acaelus is on it with his relk, or the ansible can cast us onto the *Sigillaria* under Acaelus's blockade."

Kuma grinned at her. "Chicken, Sharp?"

She grinned back. "Sounds like a vacation."

"The problem," Kav said, "is that whatever happened out there, the ship's not slowing down. It's gunning for that star."

Naira's grin faded. "How long?"

"A week, if we're lucky, before it's uninhabitable."

Her heart fell. "You're kidding."

"I wish I was. The nav system is still working, because it's course correcting to stay on that flight path, so I should be able to turn it or slow it down once we're on it. But, considering we don't know what we're walking into, I need to get on that ship with at least a day to spare to make sure I can get us off it again."

"So we have six days to detox me, extract Tarquin, and destroy Fletch to make sure he can't scheme against us while we're gone."

"That's the shape of things," Kav said.

"Fuck," she said.

Kuma nudged her with her shoulder. "A few minutes ago you weren't willing to wait at all."

"Yeah, and you two wisely talked me down from jumping off that particular cliff. This isn't—this isn't doable."

"It's not quite as bad as you think," Kav said. "I asked Jessel to come to us. They're flying out from M-U with a bunch of unionists to run research on the *Cavendish* for us and set up stasis shields and cast-off beds. They'll get us onto that ship. All we have to do is get Tarquin out and deal with Fletch."

"Is that all?" she said flatly.

Kav snorted. "You know Mercator Station. You can do this."

"Yeah, but..." She trailed off, drumming her fingers against the side of her water glass. "Heat maps and gait detection on every level. Full camera coverage. Merc-Sec stations every five thousand feet. Security Chief Alvero will be stationed there, I bet, and I know Salter's there. We can't flip them, not even if we can convince them Tarquin might be in danger because they won't move without a direct order from him. Who's Merc-Sec captain on deck right now?"

Kuma flicked up her holo and skimmed through. "Captain Anaya Ward."

Naira wrinkled her nose. "Solid soldier. Won't like Fletch, but won't be friendly to me, either."

"You suck at making friends," Kav said.

"Desertion burns bridges." She shrugged. "Who's Tarquin's E-X?"

"Uh." Kuma frowned at her holo and pulled up a picture of Tarquin at a podium. Naira didn't recognize the broad-chested person standing behind him. "Ex. Francel Cass. Looks like it's their first assignment." Kuma whistled low. "High academy marks. Almost on par with you, Nai."

"Great," she muttered, then perked up. "Wait. Only one E-X? For the head of Mercator during an extremely high threat period?"

"Looks like it," Kuma said after a few minutes of searching around.

"So they've got to be extremely good, and extremely tired. I wonder...Do you think we could twist Jessel's arm into sparing us enough cartridge for a print?"

"If we tell them it's to keep the head of Mercator from succumbing to *canus*, I think they'll deal," Kuma said. "Why?"

"If we can confirm Fletch has left the station, I can get in if I'm in Ex. Lockhart's print."

"We don't have access to Lockhart's print," Kav said. "I'm good, but I'm not hijack-the-print-file-of-Acaelus's-E-X-in-six-days good."

"We don't need the real one." Naira spread her arms wide. "I'm close, right? Run one of those mod programs over a copy of my file."

"Algos to adjust a print to match a registered print are highly illegal," Kav said.

"Which means you have one."

He winked. "Naturally."

"You sure about this, Nai?" Kuma frowned at her. "You were already having proprioception issues. If you're actually in another print, it might take you a really long time to recover."

Naira tightened her grip on the water glass and concentrated on the chill. On grounding herself in her flesh. She knew what Kuma was really asking. If this might push her one step closer to cracking.

She didn't know. But she knew that if she kept running from this, if she lived in fear that one day Lockhart's instincts might override her own, then she'd convince herself she wasn't strong enough. Not strong enough to hang on to her sense of self. Not strong enough to win the fight against *canus*. Fletcher had struck closer to the core of her insecurities than he could have guessed.

"I have to do this," she said.

Kuma gave her knee a squeeze. "We'll set it up. You need to rest and focus on detox."

"Thanks." She patted Kuma's thigh and pushed off the couch, scooping her bag off the floor to go to her room. It'd take Jessel time to set up the equipment, and time for Kav to prep the Lockhart print. She'd feel more herself by then.

Naira showered, then went to work putting the scant few things in her duffle away. Her HUD winked at her an hour later, an incoming message from Fletcher. She opened it reflexively, annoyed to feel her pathways flush with warmth. He'd sent her a picture he'd snapped of a small cluster of yellow flowers on a shrub. Naira sank onto the side of her bed and zoomed in on the tiny blossoms. Rue.

Demarco: thinking of you

Sharp: You know those used to be a symbol of regret.

Demarco: there's rue for you; and here's some for me

Sharp: Hamlet? You've been reading. Imagine my shocked face.

Demarco: I'm not a complete rube, you know

Sharp: You forgot—"you must wear your rue with a difference."

Demarco: I'm trying

Sharp: Have you gotten me anything from the other families?

Demarco: straight to business, huh?

Sharp: I don't have time to talk about Hamlet with my ex.

Demarco: surely I deserve a loftier title than "ex" how about "first love"?

Sharp: My first love was Capstone Chocolate.

Demarco: wow. ice cold, Nai. that shit was mediocre at best

Naira shook her head. It was too easy to fall back into old habits with him. She needed to break the casual-chat cycle. See if she could pressure him into getting her information.

Sharp: I'm shipping for mission in six days.

Demarco: fuck

Demarco: wait, shit, sorry, voice-to-text sent early

Demarco: be safe, Nai, I'll get you everything I can before then

Sharp: Thank you.

Naira closed the channel and flopped back on the bed, staring at the ceiling as she let her arms spread out and stretch. She felt sick to her stomach, and not from the shroud alone. Fletcher was useful to keep close. He was clearly up to something, and keeping him calm helped keep Tarquin safe until she could rescue him. It didn't make her feel any less slimy.

Two quick taps on her door. Kav.

"Come in."

He shuffled in far enough that the door shut behind him, and crossed his arms, leaning uncomfortably against the frame. Kav just looked at her, his face drawn with worry. She let out a tired sigh.

"What?"

"You know what."

"Oh, fuck off with the riddles. I'm tired."

"I was there, Nai. I was there when you were with Fletch in the HCA and I was there when that finally broke apart, and I don't like the idea of you even pretending to be A-okay with him again."

Naira rubbed her eyes and let her hand rest over them. "What choice do I have? He has Tarquin. We can't move until we're ready, so we have to keep him from getting suspicious in the meantime. What do you want me to do here?"

"Be careful. I mean, *really* careful. You're a different person when he's around. You're meaner. I know we give each other a hard time, but you and Fletch went for the throat. It was like a one-up game with you two. When he's around, you can't stop. It draws you in. *He* draws you in."

"Thanks for the psych profile. Can I sleep now?"

"C'mon, Nai." He sighed. "I know we don't do warm-and-fuzzies, but do you have any idea how worried I was? I almost lost my mind when I confirmed he'd taken you. Kuma had to stop me from trying to break into Mercator Station."

Naira peeled her hand away from her eyes. "Sorry. I'm not trying to be a jerk to you. I just don't like facing that side of myself. I know what he does to me. I'll watch myself."

"Good. Good. Because these muscles *are* decorative, and I don't think I could take Fletch in a fight."

He flexed in the doorway, and Naira laughed, chucking a pillow at his head. He caught it before it could hit the ground, grinning at her.

"You wouldn't have made it past the door into Mercator Station."

"Who says I was going to break down doors? They wouldn't have been able to resist my charm."

Naira rolled her eyes, genuinely smiling for the first time in a week. "Yeah, yeah. Don't you have work to do?"

"About that." Kav scratched the back of his neck. "All I have to do is dump a database of pics of Lockhart into the algo and let it go to work. I got time if, you know ... if maybe you're not okay on your own right now?"

A lump formed in her throat, and she nodded. Kav ducked his head and chucked the pillow back at her as he crossed the room. He settled down to sit alongside her narrow bed, his back against the wall, and held up a hand. She took it, folding their fingers together, and he squeezed before resting their arms on the thin mattress.

After a while, he said, "I called my dad when Fletch took you."

Naira propped herself up on her elbow to better see him. "What'd he say?"

"The usual," Kav said to the wall. "Told me not to worry. That you'd handled worse and would turn up eventually. He invited us to come lie low at the commune for the unprinted, again."

"How long do you think we'd last before we started climbing the walls out of boredom? One month? Two?"

"I give us two weeks, tops." They grinned at each other.

"You should try to visit him, though," Naira said. "Before the mission."

Kav looked back at the wall. "Nah. Comms are a big enough risk. If we get tracked there, an HCA raid would be devastating. Those people can't be reprinted."

He was right, but Naira frowned. Kav's dad had never quite forgiven his son for shirking their family's way of life to follow his love of tech. Had never stopped rubbing it in, albeit subtly, that the HCA hadn't given Kav the job he'd wanted. Kav's grip on her hand was tighter than usual, so she let it slide.

"Talking to him reminded me...There's something I think I gotta tell you. And I'm afraid you're going to hate me for it."

"I hate you all the time," she said. He grunted at her. "Sorry. Go ahead."

"You remember how I was never very good at the engagement simulation exams, right? Bottom of the officer pack every single time."

"I remember staying up until three in the morning helping you run test scenarios to improve those scores."

He nodded. "You helped me stand out. By the time we started forming up the squadrons for live engagement, I had enough cred to make sure they assigned you to me. Every dang grunt in the regiment was hammering on my door asking to be picked for your squad, because by then it was clear that, no matter what suicide mission the brass threw at us, you'd make sure everyone came home. But it...it wasn't just you, was it? It was you and Fletch. Together."

Naira's jaw tightened, and she lay back on the bed to stare at the ceiling. "Yeah. He cut the bullshit and performed when fire went live."

"I...Look, the night before they announced assignments, I ran the engagement sims the way you showed me. Ran missions with you and Fletch in the same squad, or you without him, and it didn't matter the rest of the team's dynamic. With Fletch at your side, the success rate was off the charts. You two fought *for* each other even when you were stone-cold pissed at each other, and all that time together...No one could anticipate your movements like he could, and vice versa."

Naira glanced at her desk. Her living situation had been unstable most of her life, and even when she had her own space on Mercator Station, she'd spent so little time in it she'd often forgotten it was hers alone. There were only two objects Naira had carried with her when she'd defected.

The first, a worn synthetic leather and woven fiber bracelet that had been her mother's. She kept it carefully tucked away in a drawer. The second was mounted to the wall above her desk. Kav had made the base—two hastily-riveted-together magnetic strips—and she had collected the trophies stuck to the base.

Bullets. Sixteen of them. Suicide shots, they'd called them in the HCA, because when the fighting turned against you and it looked like you might be taken to be tortured or cracked, you held a bullet in reserve for yourself.

Most soldiers thought coming home with those bullets was lucky. Naira thought they were cursed. Kav had made her that magnetic strip and told her to hang on to them because they were a reminder. As often as their squad had been put through hell, Naira had never had to use one of those bullets. She wondered if Fletcher still had his matching set.

"We were the dream team," Naira said. She'd heard the other officers make that remark often enough—jealous that Kav had gotten first pick of the two of them. It'd thrilled her.

"Right." His palm sweat. "Nai, I had an assignment veto. All the officers did. If there was one person we knew we couldn't work with, who would poison the team dynamic, we could kick them out of the squad, no questions asked. I looked at those scores and I . . . I didn't use it. I told myself you could handle him, and you did, but you never should have had to. I'm sorry."

Naira stared at the ceiling for a long time, processing that. Kav's pulse pounded in his wrist. She squeezed his hand.

"I would have hated your guts," she said. "I loved him. Even when he was being a shithead."

"I know." He took a breath. "And I've thought, for a long time, that you hating me but being forced away from him would have been the better outcome."

She didn't know what to say. Didn't even know how she felt. Everything about her time with Fletcher was a tangled-up mess, and thinking about it felt like shoving her hand into a nest of thorns. Kav could have stopped it. But would it have stopped, really? Or would she have used her track record to get herself reassigned? Probably.

Speculation got her nowhere, and she didn't have it in her to resent Kav. The guilt simmering within him was so thick she could practically feel it, viscous and sticky, clinging to his every thought and action.

The timing of this confession gave her pause.

"Are you bringing this up now because you're afraid that if you don't interfere with Tarquin, history will repeat itself?"

"Nah," he said grudgingly. "That guy's all right. I knew you were doomed the second he stepped on our ship, turned those big, earnest eyes on you, and gave you that whole spiel about wanting to help people."

She smiled, bright and happy, and Kav groaned.

"Ugh. You've got it bad."

"Fuck off," she muttered, but they were both smiling now.

After a little while, Kav said, hesitant, "We good?"

"Obviously. Don't be stupid. Do you think he's okay?"

"Who, the Mercator? I don't know. He's stronger than we give him credit for. And I think that, even if he's infected and Fletch gets in his head, he'll know in his heart you're coming for him. The man has more faith in you than I ever did."

She elbowed him. "Do you think you can find a way to contact him that circumvents Fletch?"

"You want me to find a way to get a message to the head of Mercator that doesn't interact with Mercator tech at all, under the nose of one of the finest finalizers in the universe?"

"Yes?"

"I thought you'd never ask."

TWENTY

Tarquin

Mercator Station | The Present

Tarquin thought he'd feel anxious, entering the MERIT boardroom where his father had held court so many times, but all he felt was a cool pool of calm spreading from within his core. As much as he loathed Fletcher, the man's plans had been sound and aligned mostly with Tarquin's own. He was as prepared as he'd ever be, and as the heads of family for Estevez, Rochard, Tran, and Ichikawa turned to face him, he met those haughty, curious faces with a polite smile that was all too natural on his lips.

"Friends." He bowed, but not so deeply as to imply that they were above him. "I thank you for agreeing to meet with me on Mercator Station."

"I believe I can speak for us all," Chiyo said, "when I say we were relieved to hear from you."

"Yes." Thieut Rochard gave him a bright smile. "It's comforting to see a friendly face at the head of Mercator once more."

Tarquin returned that smile with a slight incline of the head and moved around the circular table to take his father's seat, the one facing the door. The chair conformed to his print as if it had been made for him all along.

"You will forgive me, I hope, for not elaborating on the current status of my family. Matters are still being worked out."

"Completely understandable." Estevez gave his hand a pat. "I pray all is well for you and yours."

"Thank you." Tarquin turned his attention to the holo projector inset in the table before him, and pulled up a list of names for all to see. "These are the dead of the construction platform. All seven thousand of them. A combination of MERIT families. Skilled workers. Valued employees."

Chiyo gestured to the list. "We're all aware of the names of our lost. I hope you have some other point to make."

"I hope," Dai Tran said, "that you've finally decided to cough up their phoenix fees. I understand you had nothing to do with the attack, Liege Tarquin, but it's Mercator's fault those people are dead. Acaelus sent them there to die."

Tarquin leaned back in his seat, watching their questioning expressions. They were testing him. Seeing if the young son of Acaelus, untrained for the chair he now sat in, would roll over at their pushing.

"Acaelus did not do so alone, did he?" Tarquin asked.

Nervous glances between Thieut and Tran, a slight smirk from Chiyo. Estevez nodded.

"Go on," Estevez said.

"I'm not here to rub your noses in what you've done," Tarquin said. "But I won't ignore the fact that you plead publicly for Mercator to restore your people while making no private overtures to me yourself.

"It occurred to me that the lack of official petition was unusual, and so I looked. And I found that each of you selected people from your own rosters who would be on the construction platform that day, and you selected them with an eye for *less* skill, *less* experience, than those you recalled. If you would not like me to reveal such facts, I suggest you stop your public posturing over Mercator's liability. You do not want those people back. You know Mercator does not have the relkatite to spare to give them to you."

Chiyo inclined her head. "You've caught us out. I suppose you were paying more attention to family tactics than we all believed."

"I was not," Tarquin admitted. "But I am a researcher, and I know how to dig when I have a question in mind. My question was simple—why? And so I looked again. And this time I found that Rochard has been quietly curtailing the maximum amount of foodstuffs that any one family can purchase from them, and giving different excuses to each."

Thieut grimaced. "We're running at our limit for production, and while the birthrate is currently negative, constant reprinting of our upper echelons doesn't allow the population to fall. We cannot produce more food without more stations to use, or a shroud-clean planet. Neither of which are available to us."

"We all suspected," Tran said. "Which is why we all agreed to reroute those people to the construction platform as Acaelus asked."

Estevez spread their hands in an expansive shrug. "It is better to lose a few that way than to institute mass icings. That's how riots start."

"I'm not here to chide you for your choices," Tarquin said. "I'm here to offer a solution. I would not see these people remain iced. Nor would I see them starve."

Tarquin steeled himself. He'd worked out the details with the heads of the mining division and accounting. This would work. It made sense. He still couldn't shake a small seed of dread. He brushed the display of the names away and replaced it with a model of *Mercatus canus*, the fine mycelium of that fungus exaggerated to the scale he had seen at Sixth Cradle, overgrown and large enough to be mistaken for a ball of roots. He gazed upon that model, and a small smile curved his lips as his pathways warmed. It was quite beautiful.

"*Canus?*" Chiyo asked. "We've done this dance. Poured all our resources into Acaelus's mining ship, and he stole away with it. You can hardly ask us to repeat the same mistake with you."

"I'm not." The model of *canus* traced lines across his face. "I mean to lease it to you. The culture, how we grow it, how we store it. The problem is our lack of relkatite. With more of that mineral, we can build the stations Liege Thieut requires to grow more food. With more food, we can safely reprint our fallen."

Estevez frowned. "You would give up Mercator's proprietary methods? I won't turn you down, but the power balance between the families is fragile." They glanced briefly at Chiyo, then back to Tarquin. "I, for one, would hate to see Mercator lose its financial solvency."

"The banker would," Chiyo said, "but I don't think giving up the family gift horse is what Liege Tarquin is proposing, is it?"

Tarquin nodded. "This is not a gift. You all forget, too easily, that Mercator came to prominence foremost because of our ability to build ships, stations, and the warpcores that power them all. I will license *canus* to you, and our equipment to facilitate mining, but the actual refinement of that mineral will remain solely the purview of Mercator. What you mine will pass through Mercator hands, and we will take our cut.

"We need relkatite. We have lost the ability to reach the cradles. We must turn back to the low-yield mining of the asteroid belt, and that requires a workforce Mercator cannot field alone."

"The yields in the belt are shockingly low," Tran said. "Even with *canus*."

"They are," Tarquin agreed. "They're also all we have. Humanity is in its twilight. We have no world on which to live, no future that does not see us whittled away into nothing if we don't scrape all the relkatite we can from the Sol system and build a future for ourselves. Stations for Rochard will be priority, at first, but once we are off the knife's edge of starvation, I mean to build grand stations. Superstructures to rival the planets we lost. Sol is our home. I wish to make it a safe, comfortable home for all of us."

"Pretty words, but in the meantime you will charge us for the use of *canus*, and for the refinement of what little we collect," Estevez said.

"Mercator must secure its position," Tarquin said. "I'm certain you all understand. For the balance of MERIT to be maintained."

"The balance?" Chiyo asked, drawing a swirling pattern against the tabletop with the tip of her nail as she watched him. "You would be an umbrella over us all. Rochard alone could check you after this, and I'm certain you've already considered that they would be too beholden to you to wish to do so."

"If you are uncomfortable with the arrangement," Tarquin said, "then you are welcome to reject my proposal and forge your own path."

Chiyo gave him a razor-sharp smile and stopped tracing the pattern against the table. "Ichikawa accepts your proposal, Liege Tarquin."

"As does Rochard," Thieut said.

Estevez and Tran chimed in their agreement quickly, if not enthusiastically. None of them liked the idea of Mercator rising so far above them all. Tarquin couldn't blame them, but the truth of the matter was that Mercator had always been higher up the mountain than any of the other families.

Relkatite had been humanity's future since the day the shroud began its devouring of Earth, and while they had pushed and pulled against one another, pretending at other options, at a myth of balance, it had all been leading to this moment, when everything would rest on Mercator's shoulders.

Tarquin wondered, as he negotiated percentage tables and transport and energy use and all the rest of the minutiae that came with such a large undertaking, if his father had seen this coming and prepared for it some other way. Not enough food to keep expanding as a species. Not enough relkatite to make the space to grow more. And the threat of the shroud, unstoppable, looming over them all. Canden's ill-advised effort to keep humanity from living entwined with another species could have been the end of everything.

Accepting that there was no way forward without *canus* was the only path to survival. Sixth Cradle had been an anomaly, *canus* acting under extreme pressure and the unique chance to interface with the systems of the *Einkorn*. Such an event would not happen again.

After all, Tarquin himself was a head of MERIT, and *canus* hadn't taken direct control of him.

Their interests were aligned—relkatite and life—these two things were inextricably intertwined, like the family crests on the table. But a piece was missing.

"I will extend the workforce invitation to the uncuffed of the Human Collective," Tarquin said. "We'll need more muscle than ever before, and we can't afford to print our iced workers until matters stabilize."

A shocked silence followed. Tran cleared his throat. "An initiative for them to earn their cuffs, you mean?"

"No. I will welcome all applications, but I wish to be clear that I intend for these people—no, I *require*—that these people be paid as if they were cuffed already."

Estevez frowned in thought. "They will line up for miles for the opportunity."

"That is the point," Tarquin said. "This is dangerous work, and we will compensate them for it. Any family that takes a member of the HC on their missions will also cover their phoenix fees, should anything happen to them, when relk stores have stabilized."

Chiyo scoffed. "We only hire skilled workers into the family. I don't want a bunch of dead muscle clogging my resurrection lists."

Tarquin thought of Naira, crawling through the ducts of a Collective station because she was worth less than the robots they couldn't keep repaired, and clenched his fist against the table.

"If you think the work these people do is unskilled, Chiyo, then I invite you to try it yourself and see how long you last."

"I take your point," Chiyo said. "I suppose we can find use for them when this is done."

He didn't like the sound of that. "They will have rights on par with the cuffed, even if they don't apply for cuffs themselves."

"Christ," Thieut said, then pressed a hand over her mouth to cover the outburst. "Forgive me, friends, but all the benefits without the loyalty? We have enough trouble keeping the HCA from trying to enact a coup against MERIT and you want to give them a protected, well-paid workforce with no loyalty to us?"

"I wish to compensate people appropriately for the work they have done," Tarquin said. And did not say—*and once the situation is stable, compensate those who cannot do the work, because no child should scrub ducts to stay alive, no matter their ability*—but held his tongue. "If doing so puts us in a precarious position, then we should all consider how to make ourselves into a system these people wish to keep."

The heads of MERIT were too well guarded to grumble among themselves, but he sensed the subtle shifting in them, the hooded looks that wondered if they would have been better off if one of the other families had absorbed Mercator instead of Tarquin taking command, power balance be damned.

Reluctantly, they returned to logistical matters. Even if they didn't like it, even if they would push and pull and try in a thousand ways to undo what he was proposing, they would go ahead with it for now. They knew as well as he did that relkatite was the only way to survive.

He had no idea how he could have ever thought otherwise.

When it was over, Tarquin left the boardroom and found Thieut waiting for him. Her navy-blue lips curved into a smile and she touched his arm, briefly. A tender gesture.

"Liege Tarquin," she said in the normal, warm tones she used for confidants, not the clipped and precise cadence of negotiation. "It's good to see you safe."

Tarquin bowed his head to her. "I have your cousin to thank for that, Liege Thieut, and I'm grateful."

"That's why I lingered," she said. "Aside from my desire to have a moment with you without the rest watching. Acaelus would have been proud of your efforts today. But I wanted to tell you that Emali is here, waiting in the opal sitting room, if you have a moment to spare. She would love to see you."

Tarquin smiled at her, because that was the expected response, but the smile didn't reach his eyes. Acaelus's pride wasn't something Tarquin desired.

"I'll see her now. Thank you for telling me."

Tarquin bowed again and turned before Thieut could ask him questions he didn't want to answer. The light step of his new exemplar, Cass, fell in behind him as Tarquin walked empty hallways. He knocked once to announce himself and stepped into the room.

"Tarq!" Emali flung herself out of her chair and into his arms with such force that Tarquin had to wave Cass back. Tarquin grunted, wrapping both arms around her warm, soft frame as she buried her face in his chest and clung on, a tremble running through her body. He wiggled sideways into the room, still holding her, and waved the door shut with his exemplar on the other side.

Tarquin nudged her gently to arm's length. Emali swept back to the appropriate distance. Her hair wrap had come loose, and she tucked a curl that'd bounced free back under. She picked up the side of her lavender chiffon skirt, which spilled in elaborate layers off of her full hips, and swept into a dramatic bow.

"Forgive me, *my liege*," she said, and winked.

Tarquin groaned and ran a hand down the side of his face. "Please, not you, too."

"Pah. I wanted to watch you squirm." She drew close enough to clasp either side of his face in her hands, the gold rings around her fingers glittering against her midnight skin, and drew him down to her height so that she could kiss his forehead. Her voice lost its teasing lilt. "You're safe. You're really safe."

He patted her arm and extricated his face from her hands, then pulled free his pocket square and dabbed the plum-colored lipstick off his forehead. "I am, though sending a finalizer to collect me was a little rough, Em."

"You mean Demarco? He's a peach. Don't tell me he was rough with *you*, though I'm sure he gave those kidnappers of yours hell."

"He did," Tarquin said. "Did Acaelus really tell the other heads that he'd cut me off until I fell back in line?"

"Oh, yes." Her nose scrunched. "We wondered where you were, and Leka wouldn't even share the details with *me*, which I found quite rude. But once Acaelus ran off, Demarco came around and explained what had really happened. That the Conservators had taken you and might try to make you reach out to me now that Acaelus had flown the coop. You can't imagine how much I worried. Honestly, how did they get their hands on you in the first place?"

Tarquin recalled Naira standing between him and the shuttle, her stare boring into him, evaluating him for something he couldn't discern, as she'd given him one more chance to stay behind. To die with his family on Mercator Station and extricate himself from the Conservators once and for all. To extricate himself from her.

She'd come back for him. Despite all sense, she'd turned her back on certain freedom and risked herself to pull him out of that station. She could have been walking into a burning building in that moment, and he would have followed her. But he couldn't tell Emali that.

"I'm not sure. It was all very confusing."

"Oh, you poor thing."

She bundled him into a chair and forced a mug of tea into his hands. It was steaming, thick with oat cream and, upon first sip, honey. "Is this—?"

"Being a Rochard has some perks." She winked and slipped a small vial from her pocket, then handed it to him. No larger than his thumb, the glass was full of a viscous, golden amber syrup. "A welcome-home gift for you, Tarq, but stars above don't tell the others I've gotten some of the bees back. That entire program is precarious."

He rolled the vial between his palms in disbelief, watching the syrup move a little more as it warmed to his skin. "Incredible. Thank you."

She waved off his thanks and arranged her skirts fastidiously. "You know I love to see you, but you also know what I'm here to ask."

Tarquin stopped mid-sip and set the mug down with a click. "I wish I had better news for you, but I haven't heard from Leka or any of the others. The *Sigillaria* has blocked all comms incoming from Sol, even from the head of Mercator."

Emali deflated, and it surprised him how much he could still hurt to disappoint her after she'd unwittingly put him in Fletcher's crosshairs. She pasted her smile back on and patted his hand. A dark green stone dangled from one of her golden bracelets. Tarquin resisted an urge to examine it, knowing it must have been a gift from his sister.

"I thought as much." She sighed.

"When you called, you said you'd found something. Was that real, or bait to let the Conservators bring me to you?"

She chewed her lip. "It was real. But I didn't find it in Leka's files, and I don't know what it means."

"Em…"

She leaned toward him and rolled up her sleeve. A holo tattoo decorated the skin of her inner arm, above the bend of her elbow. Peaks and valleys outlined in golden wireframe swirled in a glittering haze, lines long and short reaching out from the center to detonate in tiny stars at the tips. It churned beneath her skin, showing off all angles.

An artist's rendering of a memory. A single moment in a neural map, those starburst lines representing all the other places in the map the memory touched—all senses, some other moments. More expensive than a distant cousin of Rochard could afford on her own.

"It's beautiful," he said, "but what am I looking at?"

She pulled her sleeve down and kept her voice low. "The moment Leka and I met. This is the moment in her map. She has mine tattooed someplace a bit more private, since she loves her sleeveless tops. I've memorized every node of that moment, Tarq. And I think I found it somewhere it's not supposed to be."

Her face was deathly serious.

"Where?" he asked.

"I was reading the names of those lost on the mining platform, and one of them… One of them, their stored map has this memory."

"You expect me to believe you were flicking through the neural maps of all seven thousand dead and tripped over this moment?"

Her cheeks darkened. "Okay. Maybe I whipped up a little bot and had it scour every map I could weasel access to for a trace of it."

"That's the Em I know."

"The person whose map I think might be Leka's, there's not much evidence that they, well, existed. It all feels hollow. A constructed personality."

Just like Lockhart. Tarquin couldn't keep the surprise off his face. Emali pounced on it and grabbed his wrists.

"You know," she said, "you know what I'm talking about."

"I..." His chest ached. "I may have found something similar. But I don't know what it means."

Keen interest sparkled in her eyes. "I knew it. I knew it was weird. I thought, since you have access to all of Mercator now, you could do some digging. See if Canden and Acaelus's maps are hiding in any of the construction platform dead, too, or at least confirm Leka's map as a match. The name is Odette Serville. If it's really her—"

Tarquin held up a hand. "I'll start the search right now."

He pulled up his holo and accessed his sister's map, then initiated a fidelity search to see if there were any matches out there in the universe that weren't her known backups. He started the search with the construction dead, then lowered his arm. It would take a few minutes.

"There. It's running," he said. "But even if it's her map, I'm not printing her again until we can be absolutely certain she's not also on the *Sigillaria*. For all we know, this fake ID is a backup she left, and I won't risk double-printing her."

Emali slumped, but pressed her lips together in a sad smile. "I don't want to take the risk, either. But it's something, right? I just want to know she's okay."

He squeezed her hands. "I'm glad Leka broke the rules for you."

Her smile warmed. "I hope you find someone you're willing to break the rules for someday, too."

His heart stuttered.

He had. He'd found exactly what he'd always wanted—*twice*—and he'd let Fletcher twist her away from him. Tarquin pressed the heel of his palm into his chest, breathing against a burst of pain. He hadn't thought about it since that moment—why? His thoughts always turned back to his work, to securing Mercator, mining relk, and that was important, yes, but… How could he not have tried to reach out to her, to explain? He didn't even know what Fletcher had told her.

"Tarq?" Emali asked, concerned.

He made himself relax. "A passing pain. Nothing to worry about."

"Do you need to reprint?"

Yes.

"No." He put the smile back on. "Could you do me a personal favor, Em?"

"Anything."

"Do you still have the number I called you from when I was being held by the Conservators?"

"The number to that gross hourly? Of course." Her nose wrinkled. "Do you know the Conservators actually tried to contact me? They had the audacity to have that flea hive forward me a message. Unbelievable!"

Tarquin struggled to control his composure. "What did they say?"

"I have no idea. I declined the message. Why would I care what that trash has to say?"

There was no guarantee that it was Naira who sent that message. It could have been any of the Conservators. It could even have been a mistake. But the sliver of him that was still capable of hope woke up and *clung* to the possibility that it had been her.

She'd reached out. She hadn't walked away from him.

"Could you send a message to them through the hourly for me?" It amazed him that his voice could be so steady when he wanted to shout at her for declining the message.

"You want me to contact terrorists on your behalf?" She frowned.

"Just tell them…" Tarquin hesitated. What could he say over such an unsecure channel that wouldn't make Emali suspicious enough not to send the message? "Tell them 'examine the evidence,' that's all."

"Oh, Tarq. You won't win people like that to our side of things."

"I have to try."

She pinched his cheek. "Leka would laugh at you. But I'll do it, because she laughs at me for hoping too hard sometimes, too."

"Thanks, Em. Oh, here we are. Give me a moment."

His HUD had pinged with the search results—dozens of near matches. His brows drew together as he skimmed the report, not quite understanding.

"Well?" she pressed. "What is it? Is it her?"

"It . . . is and it isn't."

He cleared the privacy lock so she could see the data, too. Each potential map had one part of it marked as identical to Leka's. Little pieces of each flagged map held a single moment that was a complete match, but no more. It was like someone had taken Leka's memories and scattered them between dozens of different people.

"I don't understand," Emali said.

"Neither do I. It's probably an error in the system. Or a coincidence."

"That's too many coincidences."

"An error, then."

"Probably." She didn't sound like she believed that. Neither did he.

"I'll have my mappers look into it," he said.

"Thank you."

She smiled at him, but some of her brightness had dulled, and he couldn't blame her. What they'd found was strange enough that he couldn't help but feel it was important. He sent the order to examine those maps to his specialists.

They said their goodbyes. He'd thought he'd feel bereft, when the only friend he could be certain of walked away, leaving him alone in the halls of Mercator once more. But instead, a kind of certainty filled him.

He might be caged within the fetters of his family, but he wasn't without power. From within the golden bars of his station he could reach out. Shift them all subtly from a path of subjugation to one in which everyone could live on equal footing. He believed it was possible. MERIT would not accept the slide into irrelevance quietly, but they couldn't stop it, either.

Tarquin couldn't escape being a Mercator. But he could change what it meant to be one.

TWENTY-ONE

Acaelus

Mercator Station | Four Months Ago

Acaelus told Leka that he had found Canden's map, but it needed to be integrity-checked before he could be sure of what it was, of what it meant.

She'd known he was lying. He could see the suspicion burn in her, his clever daughter, his heir he'd kept too close. But after a few probing questions, she'd let the matter drop. No one, not even his daughter, would tell the head of Mercator he was lying to his face. Not even Tarquin had gone so far.

No one, save Ex. Sharp.

Acaelus had admired her for her conviction, even if he'd had no idea what she'd been talking about. He'd been certain Mercator had nothing to do with the spread of the shroud until he'd read Canden's files. Now, he wondered. Sharp was not a woman easily fooled, but someone in his organization had done just that. There could be no other explanation.

Someone in Mercator had known the truth of *canus*, of his wife's plans, and kept it from him. They had used that knowledge to turn Sharp against him. They'd chosen well. It had shaken him badly when the most loyal exemplar he'd ever employed had turned her back on him and started tearing his empire down.

It wasn't about Sharp in particular. She had been nothing more than an orphan with a gift for defense and a particular soft spot for the dying of the worlds. A soft spot that made her a useful tool for his enemy to shake Acaelus's calm. To make him paranoid and destabilize Mercator. He was almost embarrassed by how well the ploy had worked.

With Canden's research filling his mind, with the truth of Sharp's betrayal made clear to him at last, Acaelus understood that, until he ferreted out the betrayer, not a single soul in his entire organization could be trusted. The realization, after so long standing at the peak of a pile of sycophants, thrilled him.

It was not a situation he could safely return Canden to life within.

He needed to purge Mercator. Make it a safe place for her at last, and that meant not only finding the traitor, but building Canden a stronghold free of *canus*. And it meant, above all, restarting the Lockhart program. His wife would need the perfect exemplar to keep her safe.

Acaelus issued orders. He shuffled resources in dribs and drabs, moving employees, moving relk and food and weapons. He sent drone swarms at speeds faster than the larger ships could bear to scour Sixth Cradle and bring all they found there back to him. He explained nothing, and no one dared to ask him questions.

When he was finished, he called his chief of operations and told her he was not to be disturbed for the rest of the day. He exited his office, Ex. Kearns a shadow at his heels, and he couldn't help but wonder if that man was the traitor.

Irrelevant. If he was, Acaelus would find out soon enough.

He let himself into his private labs and locked the door, leaving Kearns to linger in the hallway. Here was one of the few places he could be truly alone, but not for much longer.

The consoles lit at his presence, spinning up the interfaces he'd last been working on. He brushed them all away and settled in at the console podium next to the single printing cubicle in his lab. When Acaelus experimented, he liked to do it one batch at a time. His keys granted him access to the files on the Lockhart program, and he leaned back as that data unfurled before him, filling the air with the glittering pieces of Lockhart's map.

Her evaluators had been correct. Lockhart was a middling exemplar. Bottom of her class, slow to react. One step away from washing out of the program entirely. They'd been correct, too, to remark upon how much she'd grown after swearing into Acaelus's service.

He hadn't chosen her for her prowess. He'd chosen her for her physical similarity to Sharp, though the tabloids had grossly misjudged his intent.

Just as he'd used a piece of an engineer's map to teach Jonsun's double-print how to repair ansibles, he'd waited until the courts gave him reason to put Sharp safely on ice, then copied her map and started picking it apart. Pulling out the useful pieces and leaving the traitor's psyche behind.

Lockhart didn't mind. She'd been ecstatic at the opportunity. All the skills of Sharp, all the loyalty of the desperate. Acaelus couldn't have custom-ordered a superior exemplar.

It was a fine line, selecting enough to make a difference in Lockhart without cracking Sharp. No one, to the best of his knowledge, had done anything like this before, and so no one knew how close one mind could be to another before it counted as double-printed. He didn't care if Sharp cracked, but there was a very real risk that breaking her mind would ruin all his hard work with Lockhart.

He pulled up his copy of Sharp's map and went to work, excising those pieces that would suit Lockhart's skill set. Lockhart had handled learning her ability to aim and cover quite well—but what else?

Acaelus reviewed footage of Sharp at work, absorbed the way she shifted her weight, the intervals with which she scanned the perimeter, the subtle flex in her arms, always ready, as she marched behind Acaelus. But he'd watched that footage countless times. There was nothing new to learn in it. He dashed it aside and pulled up the security footage of her escaping Mercator Station instead. Here, *here*, was Sharp on the offensive.

This was new. Another piece to add to his perfect construction. It wasn't a memory, but he had programs to help him map the footage into a framework that would approximate her movements in that moment. He went to work, and was dimly aware of a muffled conversation in the hall—Kearns and Leka, but Kearns would handle it. Acaelus had asked not to be disturbed, and so he wasn't.

When he was done, he'd added more to Lockhart's map at once than he ever had before, but he'd always found Lockhart's mind malleable. It was no matter that every time he printed and woke her, her eyes grew a touch more vacant, as if the woman within was receding on the tidal pull of her new knowledge.

Acaelus was her savior, and she would serve.

She kicked out the end of the cubicle, the way Sharp always did, and slid out on the printing tray.

"Welcome back, Ex. Lockhart," he said.

Lockhart blinked empty eyes at him. "My liege, it is an honor to be at your side once more."

"I'm sure that it is." He handed her a robe, and she donned it before going through her usual stretching routine to make certain her print was working properly. "I'm afraid I won't be returning you to regular service."

She stiffened. "My liege?"

"Don't fear, Lockhart. For you, a special assignment. Canden is coming back, and you will be given to her. For now, I need you to secure the location in which she will be living. There is a traitor in this family, and my wife's home must be safe, above all else."

Lockhart sank to her knees in a deep bow. "It would be my honor, my liege."

Acaelus sighed and looked back to his work terminal. He'd have to implant Sharp's habit of keeping her head up at all times into Lockhart as well, it seemed.

Good help was so very hard to find.

TWENTY-TWO

Naira

The Conservator's Ship | The Present

Naira couldn't recall the last time she'd been on a ship so full of people. Seeing the determined faces of Jessel's unionist cohort reminded her why she did this. Why she risked her map again and again to push back against two kinds of subjugation. Jessel had made quick work of moving the supplies on board. Now, Jessel's people were busy setting up for the map transfer to the *Cavendish*.

Naira walked the line of gurneys and portable printing cubicles, eyeing the unionists as they hooked up monitors and cables and threw troubleshooting questions back and forth with Kav. For the first time in longer than she could remember, she felt a glimmer of hope.

Jessel strolled up and elbowed Naira in the ribs good-naturedly. "Looks like we're ahead of schedule. Should have you all off to the *Cavendish* in two days."

Two days. Kav hadn't quite polished off the Lockhart print yet, and nerves fluttered in her stomach at the thought. If he couldn't get it perfect, she'd trip the gait detectors, setting off every alarm in the building. Looking like Lockhart was one thing. Being able to move convincingly as her was another. Naira pushed down the concern—Kav would figure it out, he always did—and focused on the mission. "Then on to the *Sigillaria*. I wish we could stick around long enough to blow the *Cavendish*."

"No way," Kav called over his shoulder. "Gotta keep that ship as a backup, something we can route through to get off the *Sigillaria*, if we think we can get off."

"I can get off anywhere," Kuma shouted.

Groans and begrudging chuckles from the workers. Kav gave her a friendly whack on the back.

Naira's smile thinned. Jessel caught it—their eyes had always been as sharp as Jonsun's. "Something wrong?"

Naira lowered her voice so the unionists wouldn't overhear. "The team knows that it's unlikely we'll be able to cast off the *Sigillaria* if we can make it there from the *Cavendish*. The plan is to overload the core with us inside, rather than risk having our maps snatched by whatever offensive software Acaelus has loaded on that thing."

"That makes sense," Jessel said. "What's your reprint timeline?"

Naira rocked her hand back and forth. "The *Sigillaria* is four months out. Assuming we'll make it to that ship, we're thinking eight months. If you don't hear anything from us by then, print us. Kav will work up hard numbers for you before we cast."

Jessel nodded firmly, and Naira wondered if they were thinking about Jonsun being double-printed. Naira definitely was. If they were still alive on that date, they'd cut their own throats to avoid double-printing.

"Wish there was a safer way," Jessel said.

Naira squeezed their arm. "Me too."

"I'd heard," they said carefully, "that Ichikawa has made considerable progress with entanglement detectors. They can tell when a backup is active somewhere else."

"If they have, we don't have access to that, and I doubt it's going to hit the market in the next two days."

Jessel blew out a breath. "I know."

A payment request flashed in the corner of Naira's HUD. It was connected to the false ID they'd used to check into the hourly.

"Excuse me a moment." She stepped away from Jessel and accessed the message.

It was terse, auto-generated, demanding twenty cred for forwarding a message that hadn't been prepaid for and therefore had incurred an extra fee. Naira rolled her eyes at that. She paid the bill and waited for the text to come through.

Dear Terrorists,

I am only sending this message because I promised to do so. Tarq is a kind man with a good head on his shoulders who often cares too much for his own good. I request that you consider his words, but otherwise leave him be. He is more protected now than you can possibly imagine.

Liege Tarquin says: "Examine the evidence."

I say: Stay away from him, you murderous bastards.

With no respect at all,

Liege Emali Rochard

Naira read the message three times, her frown deepening with each word. What did that even mean? What evidence? Kav had sent a message to Emali through the hourly, asking her to pass along their desire to hear from Tarquin directly to confirm his safety, and this was what he responded with?

"What the fuck," she muttered.

The workers stopped and turned to look at her.

"Everything all right there, Nai?" Kav scratched the side of his nose, staring at her.

"Probably not," she said. "Give me a minute. I'll be right back."

She jogged through the ship, ignoring the curious glances and half-voiced questions that followed her. Naira went to her room and locked the door behind her. She plunked down on the edge of her bed and gripped the sides of her head in both hands.

Evidence. She didn't have the exact files Fletcher had shown her, but Kav had put together an extensive collection of photos of Lockhart for the algo he'd used to modify Naira's print. She pulled up those files and started digging.

Nothing in the still photos seemed suspicious, so she switched to a search instead. An article caught her eye. It seemed Lockhart, for all her supposed lack of skill, had saved Acaelus. Naira pulled up a video of an assassination attempt on Earth and watched.

It was strange seeing the body Naira used to inhabit moving through space with another mind at the helm. It was like watching herself, almost. The way Lockhart's head swiveled, the surety of her steps, and her positioning were an echo of Naira's own habits.

No real surprise, there. They were all trained the same way. A shot rang out in the video. The crowd scattered. Lockhart swung effortlessly into action.

Naira's mouth went dry. No. Not a bottom-of-the-barrel exemplar. No fucking way. She'd seen E-Xs at the top of her own class fail to keep their cool that easily when fire went live. Bullets peppered Lockhart's back. Her body jerked, but her aim was steady, face cut with grim determination.

Naira zoomed in on that face. Lockhart displayed no hesitation, no fear, only anger. Outrage, even.

Naira knew that expression. Had caught it in the mirror, sometimes. Panning the view, she realized she knew that weapon, too. Impossible to see the detail on the trigger guard, but it was Ulysses class—standard issue, sure, but the grip had been switched out for the diamond pattern.

Her service weapon. Her expression. Her movements.

She'd been on ice. Locked away after the trial when Acaelus hired Lockhart. She had no memory of this. She wouldn't work for Acaelus in secret. She wouldn't.

The video said differently.

Naira ran a shaky hand through her hair. She'd assumed the photos Fletcher had shown her of Tarquin obsessing over Lockhart were fakes. She had ... no idea what to make of this. What was he trying to tell her?

A new message flashed in her HUD—Fletcher. She wiped it away, focusing on the details of Lockhart's life as an E-X. Naira's life, more than likely. Lockhart had died five times for Acaelus. Each time, the deaths had been clean and quick, the chance of map fracture extremely low.

Fletcher's message flashed again. She'd forgotten to mark herself as unavailable. Shit.

She steeled herself and opened their chat channel. He'd sent her a picture of a dark red carnation, and her scattered thoughts congealed into a flash of anger as she realized he must have looked up their meaning— intimacy. He'd followed it up a few seconds later with:

Demarco: dumping my texts in the trash already, huh?

She'd accidentally flagged it as spam, a status he would have been alerted to. Naira squeezed her temples. She had to act normally if she wanted a chance to take him down.

Sharp: sorry, distracted

Demarco: anything I can do?

Sharp: not unless you have a time machine

Demarco: ha. ha. seriously, Nai, are you all right? you've stopped using punctuation, that's not like you

Sharp: Is this better?

Demarco: c'mon, seriously

Sharp: ...

Demarco: ...?

She stared at the grey wall of her room and swallowed her pride.

Sharp: Okay, honesty.

Demarco: yes...?

Sharp: You caught me thinking about you, and it startled me.

She winced as she hit send. Waited. It took him longer than she expected.

Demarco: ...good thoughts?

Sharp: Very.

Demarco: oh

She waited. Tapped out a few things, paused, and deleted them, letting him see she was typing and hesitating.

Sharp: I ship for mission in two days. Can we meet before then?

Demarco: oh fuck yes

Demarco: shit, sorry, gotta stop using voice-to-text. I mean, yeah, obviously, I want to see you before you go

Sharp: Where are you?

Demarco: now??? I'm not on call for you, you know

Sharp: Yes, you are.

Demarco: hah. fine, you're right. but I'm on mission in an Ichikawa station. I'll be back in the sector tomorrow, if you're still near Mercator Station? if so, the apartment tomorrow, 8 pm standard?

Sharp: See you then. Gotta go.

Naira marked herself as offline and exhaled so hard her lungs rattled. She was shaking, and pressed her palms against her knees to steady her hands, wiping the sweat off. Her body was a jumble of adrenaline, disgust, anger, and traitorously, a hint of desirous anticipation coiling through her veins. She scowled, shaking her head to clear the fog.

Someone pounded on her door. "Nai! We got a problem," Kuma bellowed.

No shit. Naira pushed that thought aside at the edge in Kuma's voice. She gathered herself as best she could and yanked the door open. "What is it?"

"Whoa, are you all right?"

"No. Your thing first."

"Yeah, right." Kuma frowned at her, but grabbed her hand and marched her to the common room. "Tarquin's lost his mind."

He wasn't the only one. Naira put a lid on the unsteady mix of emotions twisting her up. They'd all gathered in front of a large holo, the green edges of the interface painting their faces in an ill glow.

Tarquin stood at a lectern. Though the sight of him tugged at her heart, the shadows below his eyes made her worry. His face was serious, and the chyron below him read: MERCATOR TO OPEN RELKATITE MINING TO ALL.

She gripped Kuma's arm to steady herself.

"I understand this may come as a shock to many of you," Tarquin said. "But considering our recent limitations, myself and the other heads of MERIT have arrived at a solution that I believe is the first step into a brighter future for all of humanity. For MERIT, and the Human Collective, alike. What you have heard is true. Mercator is licensing *canus* to the rest of MERIT to increase mining operations in the asteroid belt. We offer the same employment package to all HC personnel who can perform the work, with no requirement to take the cuffs, though those who perform well may petition to the family of their choice.

"Applications will open early next week, and we'll release more details on the requirements for the work and the specifics of the compensation package before then. But right now, I am here to tell you all: We of MERIT hear you. We hear your frustrations. We know you wait impatiently for the reprinting of your loved ones. This is a step. A first step. Toward a future where relkatite is so plentiful in our home, right here in Sol, that no one—not MERIT nor the HC—should have to wait to have their loved ones returned to them, so long as their map remains whole.

"It will take time, and it will not be easy, but Sol is our original cradle. We owe it to ourselves to shore up our community here before we move forward, together, into a brighter future. Thank you."

The broadcast cut away to talking heads speculating on the announcement's reasons, the fallout, and all the minutiae of politics.

"Fuck," Naira said, breaking the fragile silence.

Jessel laughed nervously. "It's . . . a little good? I mean, he's giving full compensation to HC workers."

"I'm sure that's how he's justifying it to himself." But Naira had listened when he'd talked about his work, and understood what this meant. "He's giving the miners *canus*. They'll use it to separate out the relkatite from the waste materials and bring back only the relk. *Canus* dies on contact with amarthite. If there's any amarthite out there, it'll be jettisoned along with the rest of the trash."

"Oh," Jessel said. "Fuck."

"We can't let this stand," Naira said. "We put him there. I put him there. That print is compromised. We have to get him out."

They were all watching her, waiting for orders. Waiting to be told what to do next to fix this, and a small part of her wanted to tell them there was nothing. It was over.

If Acaelus came back with an army of the infected, he'd return to find humanity had lain down and rolled over while he'd been gone, happy to be controlled, so long as they could keep reprinting themselves into eternity.

Naira focused on the muted holo, on the afterimage of Tarquin's shadowed eyes, and let fury cleanse her doubts. Fletcher was on mission at an Ichikawa station and would go straight to their meetup afterward. She had a narrow window to get Tarquin out without tipping her hand to Fletcher, but it wouldn't wait for Kav to perfect the print.

Tarquin had shown her the way back to his side. Lockhart moved exactly like Naira. She didn't need a perfect print to fake being that woman.

"Ready the Lockhart print. We extract Tarquin tonight."

TWENTY-THREE

Tarquin

Mercator Station | The Present

Tarquin was losing time. He wasn't certain when exactly it had started—that was, naturally, a part of the problem—but he'd blink and be in his suite, or in a meeting room, often halfway through a sentence, with nothing in his memory connecting the moments from one to the next.

The boardroom stuttered into existence with his next blink, grey walls with green trim asserting themselves upon his reality as if they'd been there all along, and he hadn't just been walking down a hall somewhere else. Where had he been going, again? It didn't matter, not really. What mattered was listening to the report being rattled off to him. Something about the relkatite, and relkatite always mattered.

"Our stores will hold against the churn of our own personnel," Salter said. She stood at the foot of the long table, a holo projection between her and Tarquin. Scientists whose names he couldn't remember flanked her to either side, nodding with serious faces. Tarquin put on a serious face and nodded, too. "Thanks to Liege Acaelus not using as much relkatite as expected in the construction of the *Sigillaria*, we found that much. Normal death, or death in line of service such as occurs to your exemplars, my liege, can be handled within the margins without showing strain to the other families. But we cannot sustain another large loss. Vanity reprinting is off the table for the next five years, at least."

"That's good to know," he said, when she paused and her smile strained with the expectation of a response.

His mind caught on a piece of information, his father's name always a lance through the fog. Acaelus hadn't used as much relk as expected in the construction of the *Sigillaria*. Odd.

"To guard us against an event that might reveal the true level of our stores to the other families," Salter said, her words taut, as if she was expecting Tarquin to push back against whatever she was about to say. Tarquin forced himself to focus. "I suggest we increase on-station security measures. After your announcement today, there's no telling what the Conservators might do. We cannot afford a bombing on any of Mercator's stations."

Naira wouldn't do that.

"Yes, of course," he said instead. "Write up the proposal for me, and I'll examine it and put it through."

"Thank you, my liege. I will do so right away." She bowed and exited the room, taking her scientists with her.

Tarquin blinked again, and he was still at that table, but it was darker. The lights in the room had shifted down for the night cycle. He'd been looking at reports on their remaining relkatite stores, and where it was distributed between the stations. Evenly, for the most part, with the lion's share on the station Tarquin now inhabited.

He checked to make certain his foundation, the TMF, still had enough relk to support those in need of hormone management until they could receive their first prints. The margins were razor thin, but they could continue to operate for a few months. Acaelus hadn't bothered to wipe out their already slim stores.

Tarquin drummed his fingers against the table. He couldn't recall what he'd been looking for. This print really was breaking down. He needed to call the doctors, make an appointment for reprinting—but when would he have the time? Prints were mostly instantaneous, but they could take days, sometimes. If he was unlucky and his print took days, he'd miss the handoff of *canus* to the other heads of MERIT.

No. He was fine. The print wasn't even that old. He was just tired, sleeping very little. When he slept, he dreamed of Naira, and it hurt too much to wake and find she wasn't there.

"My liege?" Cass stood inside the door.

Tarquin smiled at his steady protector. Francel Cass had been an island of calm through all the recent upheavals in Tarquin's life. He couldn't be sure if Cass was Fletcher's creature or not and he'd decided it didn't really matter. Cass was kind to him. Tarquin would cling to any kindness he could get.

"Yes, E-X?"

"It's late, my liege. May I escort you to your rooms?"

Tarquin glanced at his HUD and found it was four in the morning, station time. He closed the holo display, bracing himself against the table as he stood. His legs were half-asleep and unused to standing after so long. He pressed a fist to his chest as a sharp pain wound through him.

Cass was beside him in a flash. The exemplar took his arm and helped him stand, worry on their face.

"My liege, I know it's not my business, but protecting you is. You've made arrangements to meet with the body printers three days in a row, but haven't gone."

"I have?" Tarquin blinked, and was relieved to find he was still in that moment. "Thank you. It doesn't seem important sometimes, but then it sneaks up on me. I'll see them as soon as the handoff is over."

Cass's frown told him they didn't think that was soon enough, but a twinge in his chest distracted him. "I'm merely tired." He couldn't be sure if he was talking to himself or Cass.

"You've been working very hard, my liege, and it's admirable. But... may I offer advice?"

Tarquin thought of the exemplars he'd had over the years. Caldweller, who pretended he was a statue, for the most part. Lockhart, who'd given him every piece of her mind she could get away with—Naira. Naira, who was Lockhart. Who had always been Lockhart. He preferred when they weren't furniture.

"I'd be glad to hear it," Tarquin said.

"Be easier on yourself." Cass led Tarquin into the hallway. "All of us appreciate what you're doing, but you can't keep making changes, my liege, if you're too worn out to even walk home."

"You're right." Tarquin summoned the strength to stand straighter. "I want to make up for what my father did, but—" He cut himself off. A talkative exemplar was one thing. The head of Mercator could not be making confessions of his soul to his bodyguard.

Cass inclined their head in understanding, hiding a flash of a smile under a mask of decorum. "It is an honor to guard you, my liege."

Which was what they were supposed to say. But that brief smile made Tarquin think they might mean it.

"Why do you do this?" Tarquin blurted, too tired to keep the thought to himself. "Why be an E-X, I mean? You don't seem suited to a life of violence. Not that you've been inadequate, your service has been out-standing, it's just that—god, forgive me. I'm overtired and rambling."

Cass had stiffened at first, but relaxed slowly. "I understand what you mean, my liege. The truth is, well..." They trailed off.

"You don't have to tell me," Tarquin said, and hoped his despera-tion for a normal conversation didn't show. "But if you do, I won't hold whatever you have to say against you."

"It was the money to start with," Cass said carefully. "Being an E-X, even if you get a low-ranked charge, the pay package is the best most of us can hope for. And retirement comes early, if you make it that long. Personally, though, I...like people. Getting to know them, I mean, and I do that best by observing them. I'm not much of a talker, normally. It's made me a talented E-X, being able to judge a person just by watching. I've found that, after careful observation, some in the upper echelons are more deserving of protection than others." Cass paused. "I was honored to take this assignment, my liege."

A knot formed in Tarquin's throat. Cass could be manipulating him, but they sounded sincere. They opened the door to Tarquin's suite and skimmed their gaze over the interior, then checked something on their arm holo before nodding tightly to themself.

"My relief is here," Cass said. "Rest well, my liege."

Cass gave Tarquin a strange look, then strode away. Tarquin hesitated in the doorway. Cass's relief was Fletcher. An unusual arrangement, but everyone on the station understood who was really in control.

Tarquin let the door shut behind him and slipped off his shoes, kick-ing them aside. His aching feet sank into a thick, pale cream rug that nearly glowed against the dark wood floor. In the twilight of the down-shifted light, he caught a faint scent that tugged at his heartstrings—a subtle, warm amber that reminded him viciously of Naira's skin.

It was the late hour. His exhaustion playing tricks on him.

A light was on in his office. He ignored it, making for the stairs that wound up to his bedroom instead. As far as Tarquin was concerned, Fletcher could wait in there all night. If he had suggestions on how best to move forward with MERIT, they could wait until the morning.

Tarquin stumbled into his room, undid the buttons on the top of his shirt and tugged the collar open. He was about to throw himself down on the bed fully clothed when a light step trailed up the stairs.

"Goddamnit." He raised his voice. "I told you to leave me alone when I'm in my room."

The steps paused. Started up again.

Anger scoured away exhaustion as Fletcher stepped over the threshold and moved up behind him. He'd be damned if he'd suffer Fletcher's gloating in his own bedroom. Tarquin spun and launched a fist at Fletcher's jaw, speed and strength pathways vibrating through him, enhancing his rage.

Fletcher was shorter than expected.

Tarquin blinked, not understanding, as the woman in his room grabbed his arm mid-swing and eased his fist aside.

Ex. Lockhart.

He wanted to be sick. Another ploy of Fletcher's to get under his skin. Some other poor exemplar dumped in that print to torture him. Or Fletcher himself. The thought made Tarquin's skin crawl.

"Tarquin," she said, the intonation so much like Naira's that Tarquin stopped breathing. "I—I'm so sorry. What has he done to you?"

"Who are you?" he demanded. He wanted to rip his arm out of her grip. He could. She wasn't holding him that tightly. He found he couldn't move away.

Her smile slanted in a way he recognized with a lurch. "It's Naira. Though I suppose I've always been Lockhart, too, haven't I?"

His print really was failing if he could be taken in so easily. He'd spent a great deal of time admiring that face. Searching it for the moments when Naira would rise from within, and while the woman before him was remarkably close, there was something uncanny about her appearance. Something...off. "Whoever you are, leave me alone, please. I've had enough of...of Demarco's twisted games."

"Hey, Rock-boy, I need you to pull it together, because I'm here to get you out, and I owe you a lot more than a brief hello, but it has to wait until we're out of here."

It was far too good to be true. He wrenched his arm free and turned away, unable to look at her. "Just go. I don't know who you are or what he's paid you, but I'm head of this family. I'll pay you more if you walk away right now."

Not-Naira huffed in annoyance and leaned close to him. He cringed away, but she had him backed against the edge of the bed. Her lips drew so close to his ear he could feel her breath against his skin, warm and familiar, despite logic telling him otherwise.

"I'm still interested. Are you going to make me wait?"

He turned back to her, searching her face for any hint of this being a trick. Fletcher couldn't have known she'd said that unless she'd told him. He grimaced. No. She wouldn't do that. Even if she'd left him, she wouldn't share private details about their time together with someone else.

Tarquin stared at her, drank in every line, and wanted to believe, but there was such a resistance within him. A wall of doubt holding him back, keeping him from reaching for her, though he longed to do so. He couldn't even say her name. It tangled in his throat and died in a small, desperate sound.

"If you're angry with me, I don't blame you, but right now—"

He shook his head. Her gaze dropped to his half-opened shirt, and anger lit her up from within. That world-devouring wrath he'd glimpsed in a terrifying instant on Sixth Cradle came burning back, and he knew. He knew it was her and it was real, but he couldn't make himself move. He'd locked up.

"Tarquin?"

Naira touched his chest, lightly, reaching for the buttons on the rest of his shirt. When he didn't stop her, she undid them, laying his torso bare. She took a step back, fists clenching slowly at her sides, and he found he could breathe again, if only to get enough air to speak.

There was no mirror in the room. He'd thrown them all out, because he'd grown tired of watching the inflammation in his pathways spread across his chest, drawing red lines over his skin. They weren't silver. They didn't need to be. The infection was obvious.

"Help me," he whispered.

She gathered him against her, and though her armor scratched his skin raw, she clutched him so tightly he didn't care. He closed his eyes and buried his face in her neck, shuddering. It'd taken every ounce of his control to say those two words.

"I'm here," she said. "I'm here. It's going to be okay. I'm going to get you out. And then I'm going to *kill* that fucker."

He laughed, roughly, and at last found the strength to hold her. "Naira, I...I don't think I can leave."

She pushed him back to arm's length and studied him. "I'm your exemplar. You need to leave, my liege, for your own safety. Understand?"

He didn't. His mind was too hazy with doubt, trying to make him turn away. To call for other help, because Ex. Lockhart shouldn't be in his room, but he clung to her eyes, the only light in the fog. She was his exemplar. And she'd sensed a threat. He needed to stay safe to keep running things as head of Mercator.

Some of the fog cleared.

Tarquin buttoned his shirt back up. "I'll follow your lead."

She slipped her hand into his and pulled his reluctant body toward the door. He stumbled at first, but soon convinced himself that this was for his own good. For his safety. For the safety of all Mercator.

TWENTY-FOUR

Naira

Mercator Station | The Present

Naira wanted to pick Tarquin up and carry him at a full sprint out of that cursed station. She put a lid on the desire, focusing on extracting him with a minimal amount of disruption. The smoother she could do this, the more likely Fletcher was to come to their meetup. She wouldn't waste her shot at him because she wanted to start tearing down walls.

It was a near thing, though, swallowing all that anger.

Tarquin stumbled as they approached the door. His face was wan, the thin pathways that reached from beneath the collar of his shirt to wrap around his neck and up into the back of his head faintly pink, not the searing red that had branded his chest. She grabbed his hand tighter, hoping to reassure him, but he didn't seem to notice.

"Hold," she said, using the language of exemplars. Tarquin stopped walking so abruptly it was like someone had hit his power button. "Pull up your holo for me. We need to black out the cameras on this floor. Can you enter your command keys?"

The wry smile he gave her was more like the man she knew. "Still after my keys, eh?"

After a few fumbling attempts, he got the holo up. She navigated to the station's security suite, then left up the window for him to enter his keys. That, at least, he did without hesitation. The cameras winked offline.

"Quickly, now. Before people notice."

He stared at the door, his feet stuck in place. "Maybe you should deal with me here, and reprint me on the shuttle. It might be easier. Because I don't want to go through that door."

Naira took his face in both hands and forced him to look at her. He flinched at first, but slowly he relaxed into her grip. "The most recent backup we have for you on the shuttle is the one we all made before we disembarked at Miller-Urey."

"Kav can recover one of my more recent backups."

"No. He can't. We tried. Getting in to put you down would have been easier and safer than a full-blown extraction."

She watched understanding dawn. His jaw tightened beneath her palms.

"We couldn't be sure how far gone you were." She dropped her gaze. "It had to be considered. I can still do it, if that's what you want, but—"

"I'd lose everything back to the morning before Miller-Urey," he said. "I'd lose us."

Naira nodded.

He surprised her by tugging her close, wrapping one arm tightly across her lower back. Tarquin dropped a kiss against the top of her head before peeling himself away. The strain had gone out of his face, and his smile came back.

"Then let's get out of here."

Naira stepped to his side, holding his upper arm to guide him. She unfastened the strap over her pistol and rested her hand against it, gathering her inner calm. She was an exemplar. He was her charge. She'd get him out. Naira accessed her text line to Kav.

Sharp: Collected the target. Moving.

Ayuba: Gotcha. No alarms tripped yet. Things are quiet in the hangar.

Sharp: Copy that.

They'd brought the Mercator shuttle in with a spoofed set of ID tags that made them look like a mover for low-level family. Important enough not to be bothered, but not important enough to rate extra security.

She opened the door and stepped into the night-darkened hall. Their steps echoed alongside each other, and she couldn't help but notice the uneven rhythm in Tarquin's stride. Knowing it was only her hand on his arm that was propelling him onward, she determined not to slow a single step.

Naira rounded a corner and almost smacked into Ex. Cass.

Cass had stripped off their outer body armor, leaving themself in the dark grey undershirt they all wore under their uniforms. Thick muscle built out their arms and chest, narrowing to slim pants that tucked into the tops of their boots. A single service weapon was holstered at the small of their back—an afterthought to keep them in line with protocol, as exemplars went around the residences of their charges armed at all times.

Their eyes widened, flicking from Tarquin to Naira, and then to the cup in their hand, a spoon raised halfway to their mouth.

Naira blinked. Soy ice cream. They'd gotten a snack at the employee cafeteria and had been headed back to the exemplar barracks for the night.

"Uh." Cass's cheeks colored. They straightened from their contented slouch and shoved the spoon into the cup, then snapped the cup of ice cream behind their back. "Forgive me, my liege, I didn't hear you coming."

"Nothing to be forgiven for." Tarquin sounded strained.

Cass recovered from their surprise and examined Tarquin, glancing once at Naira's hand resting on her sidearm, and her clawlike grip around his arm. "Is everything all right, my liege?"

"I'm..." Tarquin stiffened. His muscles flexed beneath her hand, his body forcibly silencing him. Naira kept her face placid, praying Cass would presume the other exemplar had this under control.

Cass drifted their hand behind their back and rested it lightly on the grip of their service weapon. Naira pulled hers in an instant, leveling the weapon at their chest.

"I really don't want to shoot you, but our liege requires emergency reprinting, and you're slowing us down."

"Whoa." They held their hands up to either side, leaving the weapon behind, but still cradling their ice cream cup. "We're on the same side here, E-X, aren't we? I'll help you with the escort, but the printing bay is the other direction."

"I'm well aware," Naira said. "He requires private printing. Off-station."

Cass frowned in thought. Naira resisted an urge to bounce on her feet with impatience. Every minute they lingered increased their chances of being caught, and while Cass was a problem, she dreaded accidentally crossing paths with Fletcher on a station he controlled.

"Is this what you want, my liege?" Cass asked.

Tarquin managed a jerky nod. "Yes. Please."

Cass let out a slow sigh. "I've been pressuring him to reprint for days, but every time he'd make the appointment, that damn Demar—" They cut themself off.

"Go on," Naira said.

Cass shifted their weight. "It's not my place, but I couldn't help but notice Demarco kept brushing it off, telling him he was fine. He was too out of it half the time to argue, and it's my job to protect him, but Demarco is..."

"Dangerous," Naira finished.

Cass winced. "I'm sorry, my liege, for not being more forceful about it."

"It's not your fault," Tarquin said.

Naira and Cass exchanged a look, and she knew what they were thinking. Part of the blame was Cass's. If they hadn't been Fletcher's ally, then they'd been cowed by him, and that wasn't something an exemplar should ever allow.

"Do you have a safe location planned?" they asked Naira.

"I do."

"Go." They cast a forlorn look at their ice cream. "I'll cover for your absence, my liege, as long as I can."

Naira lowered her weapon, but didn't holster it as she marched Tarquin forward again. Cass sidled easily out of their way, fear evident in the taut set of their jaw.

Naira looked at them over her shoulder. "I'll handle Demarco."

"I thought you might, Ex. Sharp."

Naira pushed Tarquin behind her with one arm as she aimed for Cass's chest again. "I wish you hadn't said that."

"Wow." They blinked, but didn't put their hands back up. "You really are that fast."

"Not here for flattery. What do you want?"

"I want what you want, I think." They glanced sideways at the cameras. "Those are off."

They chuckled. "Of course they are. Nothing about what I said has changed. Something weird has been going on in this station, and I'm guessing you have a good idea of what it is and how to fix it." When Naira inclined her head, they continued. "Thought so. Your cover's safe with me, Sharp. I just had to be sure. Not sure I'd trust Lockhart. I trust you."

Tarquin leaned his weight against her back, holding on to her shoulders for support, but she kept her eyes locked on Cass. "Why?"

Cass ducked their head to Tarquin. "Begging your pardon, my liege, but I know who he's been researching, and the name he murmurs in his sleep. They're not supposed to be the same, but...I've made a habit of studying people, Ex. Sharp. Your body language is distinct. My liege trusts you. I wouldn't have left him alone with you, otherwise. I like Liege Tarquin. I think I'd like him better if certain people weren't whispering in his ear."

Naira didn't know Cass, but their words rang true to her, and they'd looked at Tarquin with genuine concern. Slowly, she lowered her weapon. Extended a hand to them. They gripped her hand and shook.

"I'll keep him safe," she said.

"I'll give you as long as I can."

They broke apart and Cass hurried off down the hall, tipping their ice cream cup back to drink the melted puddle within. Naira smiled at that, but her relief washed away as Tarquin's fingers dug into her shoulders. She turned into him and he slumped so abruptly she scrambled to keep him upright. His eyes were half-closed.

"Tarquin, hey." She gave him a little shake. He grunted. "Don't fall asleep on me."

"Trying." His voice was far too quiet.

Naira glanced up and down the hall. They had a straight shot to the elevator, and they were unlikely to encounter anyone else on the family floor.

"Hang on." She scooped him up into a wedding carry. Tarquin gasped in surprise and wrapped his arms around her neck. He was lighter than she remembered, the already sharp angles of his long limbs poking into her. "What was Fletch feeding you?"

He gave her a sour look. "I'm not a pet."

"I disagree."

He scowled, but she sprinted the rest of the way down the hall, not setting him down until they were safely inside the elevator that would take them to the docks. When the elevator door shut, she stopped its descent, locked the doors, and called Kav.

"We're on the elevator. What does it look like down there?"

"Ehhhh. Not great. Still no alarms, but there's a lot of people down here now. Looks like some sort of transport getting ready to move between stations. They're tired, not jumpy, but you better make it look good if you don't want a fight."

"Tarquin." She grabbed his face in both hands. He blinked at her. "Can you walk? I can't carry you out of here without drawing too much attention."

He placed his hands on the rail and pushed himself straight, but swayed back into the wall. "Damnit," he hissed. "It's like my legs are asleep."

She frowned at his noncompliant body. "None of your pathways should interface with your muscular system directly. They're all integrative and cognitive. Except—shit. Your extra strength and agility pathways. *Canus* must be controlling them."

He laughed bitterly. "Fucked myself, didn't I?"

It was nice to hear him laugh, even if it was at himself. "I might have to fight our way out. I'm sorry. Mercator's going to lose some people today."

"No." Frustration creased his face. "I ordered a hold on reprinting nonessentials. They'll rot on ice for who knows how long."

"No one's going to let me walk out of here carrying you. They'll have questions I can't bluff around. We got lucky with Cass."

"No," he said again, putting what little he had left of Mercator command into his voice.

"You can't give me orders."

They glared at each other. He looked absolutely absurd slumped against the wall, all the dignity bled out of his body in sweat and strain, but still he lifted his chin and stared her down.

Ridiculous fucking man. Even at the end of his free will, he was burning up what control he had left to protect his people. Willing to risk his own body and autonomy to keep a few workers he'd probably never even met off the ice.

She wanted to give that to him, but if they saw her walking out with a rag doll Tarquin, they'd talk, and anything Cass did to give her time before Fletcher found out he'd lost his captive would be for naught. All of those protestations bubbled up within her. His gaze hardened.

"I said no, Sharp."

She grabbed him by both shoulders and pinned him against the wall, stepping close, intending to tell him he was being foolish. Idealistic. Their priority now was getting him out without raising suspicions. He gasped, and she lost all those words, and kissed him instead.

Tarquin clutched the sides of her face. A startled, delighted grunt escaped him and he met her embrace with such urgency that it left her light-headed by the time she reluctantly broke away. He made a small sound of protest and she caught herself grinning. Tarquin slipped one arm around her waist, tugging her snug against him, and left the other hand to comb through her hair.

"I'm still not letting you kill those people," he murmured against her neck.

She laughed, and leaned into him, and wished they could skip everything that would come next.

"I have a meeting with Fletch tomorrow night. He can't find out I've taken you between now and then, but I couldn't stand to leave you here any longer."

"You—" He cut himself off, fingers fisting in her hair with a slight tug that she rather liked. "Don't go to it."

"It's the only shot I'll have to take him out."

He nodded, slowly, and she sensed that he'd dammed up a whole stream of arguments that she was definitely going to hear about once they were safely on the shuttle. Her heart lifted, to see that conviction in him.

"Then I won't draw attention to myself." Tarquin planted his hands against the rail again. The tendons in his neck and jaw stood out starkly, sweat slicking his hair down to his temples and forehead. It didn't matter how hard he tried. *Canus* had his pathways, and wouldn't let him walk off this station.

He slumped against the wall. "We'll find another way."

As long as those pathways were in control . . . "Oh."

"What is it?"

"Your strength pathways," she said. "They can't trap you here if I rip them out."

TWENTY-FIVE

Naira

Mercator Station | The Present

Tarquin stared at her in disbelief. "We're in an elevator. This is hardly the place for any kind of surgery."

"I don't think infection should be your biggest concern. Look, this isn't—it's not nice, all right? Exemplars aren't trained to be kind about it. It's a prelude to handing targets over to be interrogated and finalized. It's going to hurt like hell, but it's the only way I see you walking out of here under your own power."

"You can't be serious."

"I'm open to suggestions."

He bent his head over hers so she couldn't see his face, and pressed his lips to the top of her head, breathing her in. "If you think I'll be able to move after this, then do it. If I have to bear a few moments of agony to keep those people off ice, I will."

"I'll make it as quick as I can. Pants off."

"So demanding."

"Unless you want me to remove them for you, my liege?"

"Naira."

She gave him a sly smile. "Nice to know you've missed me."

"You've no idea." He cupped her cheek gently, as if he still wasn't quite certain if she were real or not, and expected her to dissolve into mist at any moment. She leaned into that touch, and guilt swirled through her at the relief in his eyes.

"Tarquin...I'm so sorry I got you tangled up with Fletch. I don't know what he told you, but I would have come for you sooner if—"

"You're here now." He touched her lips to cut off the extended apology. "And don't you dare blame yourself for a single thing that foul man has done."

Naira's nerves were so raw she feared she was likely to burst into tears if he kept on being that sweet, so she only kissed his fingertips in response and gestured for him to get on with stripping down. She removed a small spray bottle of numbing solution from her exemplar kit with a slight shake of her head. It wouldn't be enough.

After checking to make certain the elevator was still locked and stopped, she helped him sit.

Naira pretended this wasn't him. Told herself it was any print, a body in need of repair, and ignored the prickling of his skin as her fingers traced the line of the worst infected pathway—a long one on the exterior of each leg, cleverly placed between the integration pathways.

His muscles were taut, every one firm beneath her fingers, as if he were actively flexing them. *Canus*, keeping him from leaving the station. From escaping Fletcher's sphere of control.

"It's just the one on both sides." She glanced up, and the ardor in his stare stole the rest of her thoughts. A flash of moonlight in her eyes made her blink, a brief image of him lifting his hands in surrender coming back to her. "Purely a medical procedure, I assure you," she said, lightly mocking his tone of voice, and didn't know where the words had come from.

That ardor shattered. "Did you just...? I didn't tell you I said that to her on Sixth Cradle. How?"

She returned her attention to his leg. "I don't know. It keeps happening."

"Naira..."

She tipped her head to face the ceiling and closed her eyes, knowing everything he was thinking, everything he'd want to say. She'd heard it all from Kuma, had thought it all herself. Fletcher's assertions were probably lies meant to scare her away from Tarquin, but still. Catching glimpses of a life that was never backed up was dangerous.

"I know. I thought it would stop when I reprinted into Lockhart. It didn't. We can talk more later, but right now I need to focus."

"Later," he said.

The print modifier Tarquin had paid off had done a decent job of making the extra strength pathway look like an integration pathway, but knowing what she was looking for, she could see it was thicker than the rest, set closer to the surface of the skin. She sprayed his right leg with half of the numbing solution and drew her knife, crawling up to poise the point against his hip. The skin dented. She looked up at him. He nodded.

Her first cut was perpendicular to the pathway. It severed the part of it that was closer to the surface from the end that dove deeply into his body and tangled with his nervous system. She wouldn't dare attempt to remove the part interfacing with that delicate system, but removing most of the pathway itself would force it to malfunction.

He gasped and winced, but otherwise didn't react.

"Tell me to stop at any point, and I will."

"I won't."

His pulse sped beneath her fingers, but he stayed resolute, and so she traced a line of blood over the length of his pathway, hardening her heart against his hiss of pain. The numbing solution wouldn't be enough. He needed a distraction.

"Why did you say that to me about the medical procedure?" she asked. "On Sixth Cradle."

"I thought you didn't want to know what happened with her."

Her. Naira traced a tricky curve around the side of his knee. "This probably isn't the best time for this conversation, but we keep running out of time, and there are some things I don't want to leave unsaid."

"We'll have more time."

"Shush and let me say this. I insisted on that distinction because of the bleed-over. It frightened me. At first, when I met you on Mercator Station, I didn't remember you. But I knew that before I went to the ice I didn't hate you, not precisely. I thought you were a spoiled sycophant to your family."

"You weren't wrong."

"No. I wasn't. But when you barged into that lab, I thought for sure I'd want to bash your head in. I didn't. I had this slight...twinge. An urge to protect you. That was all. I chalked it up to exemplar training, but the longer I was around you, the more familiar you felt. I resented that in the same way I resent *canus* manipulating my emotions." She took a breath. Focused on the cutting. "Then I unscrambled a video the *Einkorn* sent back and watched it."

"You *what*?" Tarquin tried to reach for her, but his stiff legs wouldn't let him. "You didn't tell me the *Einkorn* sent anything back."

"I didn't think it was any of your business." She severed the connection at the end of the pathway in the same way she had at the top, with a quick perpendicular cut, then moved over to his other leg. It brought her closer to him. He reached for her again. She squeezed his hand before returning to her work. "The *Einkorn* recorded my final fight on that ship. Meeting Jonsun one last time. Fighting through the misprints. Ordering the ship to swerve to dump the amarthite bombs into the warpcore, and me with it."

"You watched yourself die."

"I've watched myself die plenty of times. But that time...I can't explain it. It's always painful. I'm always pissed off in those videos. That time, I was content. Smiling, even. There was this echo in me, like I could feel the moment. Feel that peace. And that's when I started seeing glimpses of that life. When my proprioception issues started."

She'd made it to his knee on the other leg without him wincing or gasping in pain.

"Kav had a theory," Tarquin said, "that if something was good enough, it would get caught in the entanglement. That if death and pain and fear were strong enough to break through and linger in a map's backup, then joy should be, too."

Naira looked up at him. "Tarquin, the only thing I remember from that life is you."

His smile trembled. "I really wish you weren't performing ad hoc surgery on me right now."

"Tell me why you said that, about the medical procedure. I want to know about us."

"You'd injured your shoulder," he said, "and I'd stuck my foot in my mouth by suggesting massage of your pectoral muscles to relieve the tension." He told her the rest while she finished the last cuts and double-checked the incisions on both pathways to make certain there'd be no bit of skin left to tear when she finally ripped the pathway free. She crouched at his side near his hip. The story trailed off, and he looked at her with a mingling of dread and acceptance.

"This is the part that's going to really hurt, isn't it?"

"I'll make it as quick as I can. Do you want something to bite on? These walls are soundproofed, so scream your head off if you want."

"I'll take something to bite on."

She handed him a rolled-up wad of gauze and gave his shoulder a squeeze of reassurance before moving back to the incision. She felt ill, seeing the blood dribble from the wound, but tamped the feeling down. She'd done this dozens of times. He'd be fine. Probably.

His skin parted easily as she slipped her fingers inside the cut. He shifted, but *canus* locked his legs in place—he couldn't fight back even if every part of him wanted to. With a liquid bandage dispenser in her other hand, she yanked.

He screamed. Gauze or not, she could hear the muted howl. She pulled the pathway free in one long yank, swiping the bandage dispenser behind to seal the skin so that he wouldn't bleed through his clothes later. It was an infection waiting to happen, but he wouldn't be in that print much longer.

When the flexible strip tore free at last, filaments thinner than hairs twitched from the interior side, where it'd anchored to his musculature. She tossed it aside and crawled to his other leg, determined to get them both done before he'd dwell too much on it happening a second time.

Tarquin's eyes were closed, head thrust into the wall, sweat glistening on his skin, and his fists so tight she could see his veins bulge. His breath came in short gasps, but he was conscious. He wouldn't faint. She grabbed the other pathway and repeated the process.

He jerked his legs into his chest and wrapped his arms around his knees, burying his face against them. Naira checked to make sure the liquid bandages had set—they seemed to be holding. She tossed the limp, bloodied pathway aside and cleaned her hands before pulling out a length of gauze to wipe up what was left of the blood on his skin as gently as she could manage.

Tarquin spat out the wad of gauze and trembled with the aftershocks of pain, but he recovered, no doubt hammering his pathways for pain relief as much as *canus* would allow him to do so.

"I can't believe Father did this to you," he said under his breath.

"What?"

He leaned his head against the wall, eyes lidded. "Your slow pivot. On your right. Father trained it out of you by ripping out your agility pathways, then making you run the drill, didn't he?"

"You knew how Acaelus trained his exemplars and you did *nothing* in all that time?"

Tarquin's eyes snapped open and he shook his head vehemently. "No. No, of course not. You told me, on Sixth Cradle."

"I don't tell anyone about that. Not even Kav knows." Her initial flash of anger receded, but she watched him warily.

His breathing was still ragged, and it took him a moment to gather himself. "You were...upset. I didn't know who you were and I'd just asked for your help in discovering if my father was connected to the shroud. You told me to make me understand the risk Acaelus posed to you, should you be discovered working against him. I told you to forget I'd ever asked for your help."

"And?" she pressed. "What did I say?"

"That you would help me anyway, because I'd understood."

Naira stared at him, at a loss for words. Maybe she'd told him that to make him see the threat, but that wasn't the entire story. She didn't need to have her memories back to know why she'd done such a thing. There were countless other tales of Acaelus's cruelty she could have recounted to him, but that had been the first directed at her. The first that made it personal.

The one that had opened a wound in her heart she couldn't seem to close.

She'd never told Kav because the fact that she'd been so *proud* that she'd finally earned Acaelus's praise during that training session shamed her to her core. A shame she hadn't faced until she left Mercator. Maybe she still hadn't faced it.

Kav thought she didn't sleep well alone because she'd been raised in barracks-style housing, and that was partially true. But when she'd first left Mercator, it was that shame that'd kept her up at night. And the fear.

When she'd looked back and saw the full extent of how Acaelus had molded her into the exemplar she'd become, she'd wondered. Naira had believed in Acaelus. Had loved Fletcher. She'd made excuses for broken, cruel men her whole life, and she'd wondered if maybe she could only form attachments with such people because she was cruel and broken too.

When she got up at night and snuck into Kav's bunk to sleep peacefully, it wasn't all about being alone. It was about reminding herself that she could love decent people.

Naira would only use that specific story with Tarquin for one reason. She'd been falling for him, and was frightened he might have been a monster, because she never could quite shake the fear that those were the only people her heart wanted. She would have wanted to see his disgust over that story. His anger at his father.

He'd given that to her, it seemed, and maybe a tiny piece of her had healed knowing her heart could want genuine kindness. A piece she'd left behind on a dead world. Fletcher had been wrong. The memories weren't a prelude to her breaking. They were an echo of her healing.

"Naira?" he asked, all quizzical concern.

I think I was falling in love with you and it scared the shit out of me wasn't a conversation she wanted to have in a bloodied elevator. "We have to get moving. How are your legs?"

Tentatively, he rolled his ankles, then flexed his leg muscles in wincing succession. "It hurts, but I can control them again."

She stood, holding a hand down to him. "Then let's get this walk of yours over with."

He took her hand, wobbling when she pulled him to his feet. With her help, they situated his clothes as best they could. It was late. He'd been working long hours. A little dishevelment was to be expected.

Naira dragged a critical eye over him. "You look like shit."

He laughed raggedly and placed a hand over his chest, pressing down to ease some pain. "This isn't the romantic reunion I was hoping for."

"There's not a lot of room in my life for things like that."

"But plenty of room for infiltrating the most secure station in the Sol system and carving up the pathways of the most powerful man in the universe?"

"You oversell yourself." She stepped into him as he protested and kissed him again.

He smiled at her with exhausted contentment. "I'll just have to make room in your life for romance, then."

"Arrogant."

"Mercator. Comes with the blood, apparently." He shrugged one shoulder, and she smiled at his self-abashed grin.

"Speaking of blood. We're going to need all the relk we can get." She scooped up the discarded pathways, wrapping the thin filaments around her hand like she was coiling a cable, then thrust them into the exemplar kit strapped to her hip. Once again, she had to wipe the blood off her hands.

Tarquin was staring at her like her head had spun all the way around. "What?"

"I understand relk is valuable, but that was truly disgusting."

"Jessel would have carved the balance out of my legs if I didn't bring these back. Are you recovered enough for the walk?"

He stretched his legs carefully. "I'm prepared, as long as you can brace me if I stumble."

"I won't let you fall."

She maneuvered him to her side, then finally unlocked the elevator, sending it down to the hangar bay.

"We're about to make the walk," Naira said into her channel with Kav and Kuma. "We will attempt to do so without a fight. Prepare for recovery."

"Without violence?" Kuma snorted. "Good luck, honey bear."

The doors slid open. A few transport vessels were busy loading low-level Mercator employees onto the last shuttles out for the night. The transports were set away from the family dock they'd landed their shuttle in, a standard security measure, but they were close enough that the employees whipped their heads around when the Mercator family's private elevator dinged open.

Tarquin straightened his collar, chin up, back straight, gaze fixed on the single goal of the shuttle as he strode out into the hangar at a solid clip. The first strike of his heel made his breath catch, but he was too far away for any of the employees to have overheard. The thin security that roamed the docks at all hours scrambled to attention upon sighting him. He gave them a dismissive nod.

His shoe scuffed the ground. He clutched her forearm, sweat beading on his forehead as a fresh wave of pain washed through him, but the way their bodies were angled, none of the waiting would notice anything amiss. She stiffened her arm, giving him a firm foundation. After a half dozen steps he was able to let go.

"My liege!" the dock overseer cried out, having spotted him at last. The red-faced woman fumbled her way out of her semicircular desk and rushed toward them.

Naira let her hardest stare fall on the woman. "Liege Tarquin is required elsewhere."

The overseer skidded to a halt. "I'll pause all arrivals and departures until my liege has cleared the area."

Tarquin waved an approving hand at the woman but didn't break stride. He had to brace himself against Naira again to make it up the gangway. The second those doors slid shut, he let out a deep groan and slumped. She caught him and looped an arm around his back. Kuma swooped in on the other side, hefting him the same way Naira was.

"Holy shit," Kuma said, "I can't believe that worked."

"Kav," Naira called out, "any scuttlebutt on comms? No one talking about Liege Tarquin's unusual late-night exit?"

"Not a peep. I think we're actually clear, for once."

Tarquin nudged her head gently with his own. "See? Not every problem has to be solved with slaughter."

"No," she said, "just a nearly intolerable level of pain."

"Progress," he said, and she couldn't help but laugh.

"You are a moron. But a correct moron. Jessel!" She steered Tarquin toward their makeshift printing bay. "Tell me you have that portable printer ready. He won't hold together much longer."

Tarquin stumbled as they entered the room, and both she and Kuma had to adjust to avoid dropping him. Naira swore under her breath, then noticed what had made him slip—he was staring at her body. Her print. Held in stasis on the gurney next to the one intended for him.

"That's for me to return to after this," Naira explained. "We'll keep the Lockhart print viable as long as we can, too, in case it's needed."

"Re-upping into a used print is riskier," he said.

"It is," Jessel said. They leaned against the console podium used to control the printing bay, hands braced behind them on the turned-off console. "But we don't have the resources to keep printing Sharp and all her friends indefinitely. Relk's scarce. You may have noticed, Mercator."

"You're Mx. Hesson, aren't you?" Tarquin asked.

They nodded.

"My condolences for the loss of your brother."

Jessel crossed their arms forcibly over their chest. "Rich, coming from you." They dismissed his presence and focused on Naira. "I don't see why we have to waste resources on this one. He's in our custody, removed from his power. Can't he learn to control his emotions? It's not like *canus* is capable of complete mind control, he just has to get a handle on his damn feelings. I won't waste a whole body cartridge because a Mercator is lazy."

"You have no idea what it's like to be manipulated by that thing," Naira said. "Or maybe you do. Maybe it's got you feeling all warm and fuzzy about letting Tarquin suffer because it wants him in its pocket."

Jessel jabbed a finger at Naira. "I helped you with the Lockhart print because I thought it might be useful otherwise. But this? Reprinting a Mercator? No. I'm not spending resources that could be used for our people on that spoiled scum. Metal for metal, Sharp. Mercator's killed so many of our people without restitution that he *owes us* the relk in that print."

Kav jogged into the room and held his hands out. "Easy, you two. We planned for this. The margins are good. We've got plenty."

"They *were* good." Jessel turned an accusing finger to Naira's print in stasis. "I examined you while you were gone. I know what you're planning on doing with Demarco. I can't guarantee we'll have enough to print you another preferred body if you let the Mercator have dibs."

Tarquin took in a sharp breath as he followed Jessel's point to the print. The tooth.

"I'm giving you an order," Naira said. "We're reprinting this man because we're not big enough bastards to let him suffer through this infection." She tore his shirt open with her free hand.

Jessel gasped and covered their mouth with a fist. The edges of all of

Tarquin's integration pathways across his torso were red with a level of inflammation so intense it looked like someone had drawn on him with a marker.

"Fucking shit." Kuma craned her neck to look.

Tarquin grimaced. "Well. This is embarrassing."

"Sorry," Naira said.

He squeezed her shoulders to let her know it was all right.

"I'm sorry to interrupt, but I believe I'm dying." He winced. "My heart is—oh, that hurts."

Naira scooped him up. Kuma stepped deftly aside as she brought him to the backup table and laid him down next to her own body. He'd gone so pale, skin cold to the touch. The upload crown unfolded as she pulled it out, revealing the glittering squares that would interface with his print and back up the map within. She hesitated. If he died terrified, his chance to crack would skyrocket.

Tarquin squeezed her arm. "It's okay. You came for me."

His weak smile warmed her. She slipped the crown over his head. He went limp, eyes drifting closed, the subtle rise and fall of his chest the only sign his print was still alive. The upload was nearly instantaneous. She watched the console light up behind his head, the small green bar that indicated the upload's progress filling between one breath and the next, and then his breathing stopped.

Her hands shook. She folded her arms over his chest, bent to rest her forehead against his cooling print, and tried to find her calm, her steel, the place from which she took blows and kept going.

So close. That thing had decided he'd been too rebellious, and killed him. If she'd gotten that crown attached a second later, it would have succeeded before he'd backed up.

"Is he...?" Kav took a shuffling step toward the gurney.

Naira gathered what she had left of her frayed nerves and pushed herself up. "His print's dead." She didn't look at any of them. "But the upload was successful. He's backed up. We got him in time."

Kuma grabbed her from behind and crushed her in a hug. "Well done, honey, well done."

Naira wriggled free to brace herself against the gurney. "It killed him. It actually fucking killed him."

"Yeah, about that." Kav scratched at his chest. "You don't think it could, uh, do the same to us?"

"No. I don't think so. His infection was incredibly advanced. Fletch must not have been letting him consume the shroud. There was nothing in his system to fight it. We've got ours mostly under control."

"I . . ." Jessel stammered, staring at Tarquin's body. "I can use the raw materials. Scrub the infection out and reconstitute the relk."

"Do that." Naira removed the bloody pathways from her kit. She set them on Tarquin's chest and didn't know why the sight unsettled her so much. They were just parts. Not him. Pieces to be broken down and built up again. "Stabilize these materials first and get his print started. Then I need to get back in the Sharp print for my rendezvous."

"You're still going?" Kuma asked.

Naira brushed a hand over Tarquin's eyes, closing them. "Fletch is going to pay."

TWENTY-SIX

Naira

The Conservator's Ship | The Present

Tarquin's print was taking too long. Naira had expected to wake up in her own body and find him already there, groggy from the reprint but whole. Able to strategize and plan and argue with her extensively about her next course of action. Instead, she'd found his print still in progress, and a contrite Jessel who could only shrug and say they'd done what they could. These things just took longer, sometimes.

She knew that. Most prints could be done in a matter of minutes, an hour if left unrushed, but sometimes they took longer. Sometimes days. The system was idiosyncratic, not fully understood, and Tarquin's print was complicated—it carried many high-end pathways.

Naira knew all that, and still she sat vigil by the foot of his printing cubicle, unable to shake a sense of dread.

"Nai." Kuma walked into the room, her body armor hidden beneath a long coat, a duffle slung across her back. "We're running out of time. If you want to make the meetup, we gotta leave in ten."

Naira was ready to go, her own light armor hidden beneath a jacket she didn't mind never seeing again. "I know. I'll meet you in five."

Kuma's steps receded back down the hall. Naira stared at the scribe sheet she'd been writing on and deleting for the last hour and bounced her leg. What was she supposed to say? He didn't want her to do this, but it was the only way she could see to move forward.

They couldn't reinstall Tarquin as head of Mercator until Fletcher was dead. Putting Tarquin at the top again was a risk, but with Fletcher out of the picture they could at least supply him with a steady diet of shroud to keep *canus* at bay, and they'd be able to watch over him.

Fletcher had to die. Naira was the only one who could get close to him. She didn't like her chances with him in a straight fight, so ambushing him with the explosive was the only way to be certain.

She could explain all of that to Tarquin when she came back. Except she wasn't coming right back, because Jessel had been right. Even breaking Tarquin's old print down only gave them so much material to work with. There was always some relk lost in the process, and Jessel had been annoyed to report that Tarquin's print had lost double the usual amount.

They didn't have the supplies to give Naira her preferred print again after she blew it up taking down Fletcher. Uploading herself into the Lockhart print to say farewell to Tarquin was an unnecessary risk.

The *Cavendish* was getting closer to that star. After Kuma and Kav confirmed Naira had died in the blast, those two would return to the Conservator's shuttle and cast all three of their maps to the *Cavendish*.

Naira checked the time. Two minutes.

What could she say? *I'm sorry I wasn't here when you woke up. I'm sorry for so much more. I let myself be played and in the end you're the one who's going to suffer for it, because I'll keep on doing what I do with the Conservators, while you have to take on a responsibility you never wanted.*

She cared about him. Something kept pulling her back into his orbit and she didn't believe it was the echo of her past alone, but that wasn't enough. *I care about you* is not what you want to find on a note from your lover who's shipped out to die.

With all the books she read, all those lines bottled up and treasured, she found she didn't have the words.

"Nai!" Kav barked down the hall. "It's go time!"

Not knowing what else to do, she scribbled a quick line, folded the sheet over, and tucked it into the bag they'd set aside with Tarquin's personal things. She patted the end of his cubicle and jogged to meet the others.

Kuma eyed her. "You sure about this?"

"No. Got a better idea?"

"Nah. Had to ask, though. Seemed like the friendly thing." Kuma winked.

Naira snorted, pretending annoyance, but couldn't hide her smile. "Then let's get this over with. You set, Jessel?"

They nodded. "I'll cast your map and print specifics to the *Cavendish* the second these two get back with confirmation of death. While you're gone, I'll pull some strings, see if I can get my hands on some more printing materials. I'll reprint you all if I haven't heard from you in eight months." They hesitated, then clasped the back of Naira's neck in their hand. "See you on the other side."

Naira returned the gesture. "On the other side." She pulled away and snapped a quick salute to those unionists watching. They were Jessel's people, but they bowed their heads to the three Conservators. Everyone on that shuttle knew the plan. Naira wasn't coming back. Not any time soon, at least.

They took Jessel's smaller transport shuttle and spent the ride going over their plans, making sure the audio link to Naira's HUD was active and secure. While she was in the apartment, Kav would be on the transport recording every single thing Naira and Fletcher said. They hoped to get some more information out of him before she blew them both to bits.

Kuma would linger in a bar nearby, well out of the estimated blast radius, but close enough to get there after it went off and make sure there weren't any living bodies left behind. The explosive shouldn't be large enough to damage anything beyond the interior of the apartment. Naira would have to get close to make certain she got Fletcher, but it meant that incidental casualties, if there were any, would be well within their envelope.

Naira tugged a wrap around her wrist and wondered what Tarquin would think of that calculation.

They got there early for the meet, as intended. Naira said her goodbyes to Kuma and Kav and tried to ignore the worry on their faces. Kav didn't say much. Kuma said too much. They didn't like this. She didn't like it. She was doing it anyway.

Then she was back in the apartment, the lighting on the plant shelves turned down for simulated night. It seemed to her that everything that had come between was a dream. An echo. Another lost memory, because she'd known, sitting on the couch the day Fletcher talked to her, that she'd be back here. Their relationship was always going to end in blood.

She tossed her jacket on the couch and stood before the rows of plants, enjoying them one last time. A shame, really, that all that wealth of greenery was going to die, too. Her back was to the door when Fletcher opened it.

"Part of me didn't think you'd actually come," he said.

"I almost didn't."

"Ever cautious." The amusement that he carried with him through all things was in his voice, but muted.

His footsteps whispered against the floor, and he stood behind her, a little to her right. Not quite touching, but within her personal space. The place where an exemplar would stand. She couldn't tell if he was doing it to mock her, or by coincidence. It annoyed her to feel her stomach swoop, her heart race. Maybe that was *canus*. Maybe it was still just her.

A healthy body was perfectly capable of wanting things that were bad for it.

Naira traced the petals of a geranium with the tips of her fingers. She had to give him a reason to tell her more than he wanted to. "Maybe not cautious enough. I don't know if I'll come back from this one."

"Then don't go."

"You know I have to."

"Fuck Acaelus," he growled. "Fuck *canus*. Fuck the *Sigillaria*. Let them all rot, and stay. Stay with me. We have Mercator in hand, Nai. We can change things."

"Can we? I saw Tarquin's broadcast. He's spreading *canus* around like it's confetti. Sucking the system dry of relk to feed that thing. Leaving the amarthite behind. I thought you had a handle on that. I thought you understood what was at stake."

"He was right. We need the relk, and that's the most efficient way to get it."

She let out a low, bitter laugh. "I trusted you. Stupid of me."

"Maybe," he admitted. "But your burn-it-all-down-and-sort-out-the-ashes-later approach is leaving people on ice. We can't kill this thing if we don't have the food, or the minds, to figure out solutions."

"You could have told me you thought this way."

"There wasn't time."

"But time enough to send me pictures of flowers?"

He reached for her in her peripheral. She tensed, and he hesitated, but eventually he gripped her wrist, sliding his hand over hers as she stroked the petals. "There's always time for that." Her skin warmed beneath his touch. She clenched her jaw. "I'm sorry. I am. I've been working alone so long it didn't occur to me to warn you."

"Right. Because I've never been an equal to you. Just another piece of your life to control."

"Control is the only thing that makes me feel safe. But I'm trying. I am. Tell me what to do, Nai. Tell me how to find my way back to you."

She reversed his hold on her wrist and turned to face him. So close, she had to tip her chin up to look him in the eye. His gaze was so intent she could almost believe he meant the apology. She knew better.

Naira looked at Fletcher and saw him as they'd been as children. Not the fear and the desperation, though there'd been plenty of that. She saw the hope they'd tended together. Saw the first day they'd met, when he'd laughed at her for saying she'd get her mother back, because no one ever did.

He'd come to her that night hiding crusts of bread for her in his pockets. He'd been shy and tired and looking for something to fill the hollow in him and had said that he was sorry. That he hoped she was right. It'd become his hope, too. The tiny flame they sheltered together against the dark. The hubris that had driven them to crawl out of the grey. Kav was right. They'd only reached the heights they had because they'd had each other.

That hope had been dead for a long, long time.

"I don't want your contrition," she said. "I want actions. I want honesty. I want you to tell me what you're really doing, Fletch, because I'm a fucking exemplar, and you can't bat your eyes at me and think that's enough to get me to swallow a load of bullshit."

He brushed the back of his hand against her cheek in a long stroke. "There's the anger. That's why I keep coming back to you. You think you're the moth, Nai, but you've always been the flame."

"Then you should know better than to fuck with me."

"Ah, but I like getting burned." He bowed his head, brushed his lips against the side of her neck. She turned her head pointedly away. Fletcher sighed, shoulders slumping, and pulled his head back. "I thought this time would be different, with Acaelus out of the picture. But it seems I'm destined to be plagued by Mercators. What gave me away? Was it the Lockhart pictures? I knew that was greedy of me, but I couldn't help myself. It was too easy to break the cub's heart and lower your defenses all in one blow."

"Why?" she asked instead of answering him. "Why work for *canus*? You say control's the only way you feel safe, and that might be the truest thing you've ever said, but *canus* takes that all away."

"I have spent my life miring myself in the minds of the wretched so that I can tear them apart for Acaelus. In all my years of service, do you think there's been a *single* target I've taken down that hasn't had their own hidden streak of depravity? There hasn't been. We're all as fucked up as I am, Nai. I've just embraced it. *Canus* will force everyone to wake up and know what lurks within all our poisoned hearts. Humanity needs to face that awakening. We need to see what we really are, if we're ever going to heal."

"You're infected," she said. "This is what it does. It takes what you already are and twists you up in itself. Let us detox you. Think straight, then tell me you still believe what you've just said. This doesn't have to end with us at war."

"Oh. You're trying to *save* me." He tossed his head and laughed. "I'd wondered why you didn't shoot me the second I walked through the door. You never change, do you, Nai? Allow me to dissuade you from your virtuous intentions. I've been aware of *canus* for a long time. A clean reprint won't change my mind."

"You're going to look me in the eye and tell me you believe it ends there? With a happy symbiosis?" She couldn't keep her voice from rising. "You're not that naive. You know how this ends. I've seen what that thing does when it's challenged. I've seen it kill those it deemed too large a threat. *Canus* is another tyrant waiting to happen."

"Every nasty thing you've seen *canus* do has been in self-defense. Would you blame a man for shooting another who threatened to slit his throat?"

"No," she said. "But I know a thing or two about poisoned kindness."

"Oh?" He stepped into her. "Tell me all about it."

"There's always an *or else*. Serve me, or I hurt you. Love me, or I will destroy you. It's always the same. You're right. I should have seen how much *canus* would appeal to you."

His smile lit up his face. "You always know the right things to say to me. You're going to be difficult about this, aren't you? I'd hoped that you'd finally see what *canus* could do for us." He chuckled at himself. "Maybe you're wrong. Maybe I am naive after all."

"If you thought I'd work with you on this, I don't think you ever really knew me at all."

His face hardened. "Sure, Nai. You tell yourself that. You tell yourself how goddamn noble you are, when you were Acaelus fucking Mercator's shield for eight years. But we both know I'm your mirror, and you just don't like what you see."

"If I was his shield, you were his sword, and I'm the one who walked away."

"Did you? Because the way I see it, you picked up his worthless son and bent yourself over for him instead. How is Tarquin, by the way? I enjoyed playing with him, but I presume you went and reprinted the cub."

"Ex. Cass told you."

"They didn't, actually. Loyal soul, that one. Nai, love, I always know where you are. You see..." He twisted his wrist free, turned the grip around so that he clutched her hand in his, and pinched her forefinger, wiggling it at the joint.

"This pathway right here? It's mine. I bribed the techs when you had your first print designed. Told them we were in love and you were shipping out, and if you died out there and the body couldn't be recovered to confirm death for reprinting, I didn't know what I'd do.

"All true, but I really put the puppy-dog eyes on and they slipped this tracker under your skin, a part of your preferred print file, to be replicated whenever you print. It was tricky, getting the same pathway into Lockhart once I suspected Acaelus might dump you into that print someday, but you know I've always been resourceful."

Out of everything else, that shocked her. "You're lying."

"I'm really not. This is how I found you on Miller-Urey Station so quickly." He spread her fingers, pressing his palm against hers, and folded his longer fingers down over hers possessively. "This finger has always been more sensitive than the others, hasn't it? It's why you file the burr down on your service weapon when no one else does." He pressed his lips against the pathway, and she was too stunned to react. "That's because it's broadcasting a signal along a private channel, straight to me. It causes a tiny bit of irritation, alas. I always know where you are, Nai. Always."

"You knew I took him, and you came here anyway?"

"Naturally. You came here to kill me, didn't you? It's only polite that I showed up."

"And you're telling me this now because you've come here to kill me, too."

He gave her an indulgent smile. "Maybe. I'd rather not. There's no rolling you back to ignorance this time. Sixth Cradle ruined that. Work with me. We can upend MERIT together."

"And put *canus* in its place."

"That's better," he said.

"It's worse."

He sighed and dropped her hand, resting his hand on her shoulder instead. She let her arm fall, and slowly shifted it to the knife at her belt while he stared into her eyes.

"You're going to fight me on this, aren't you?" he asked.

"Every step of the way."

"Oh well. Maybe next time."

They stared at each other for a breath. She went for the knife. He grabbed her wrist before she could get to it, snapped the bones in one firm twist and yanked her knife free of its sheath himself. She gasped against the pain, stars burning and dying in the corner of her eyes as he slammed her backward with the hand on her shoulder. The shelves broke, spilling plants and soil and shattered pots across the ground. Her heel slipped, and he stepped into her, pinning her against the wall. He held her own knife to her guts.

"Last chance," he murmured against her ear.

"Never going to happen." She forced the words out through gritted teeth. His hold on her shoulder was tight and precise enough to compress the nerve, making that arm a useless weight at her side. "What's next, Fletch? After you kill me? My friends will reprint me. You have no plan."

He leaned back to look at her face, and his eyes sparked with interest. "I see. You're recording this, aren't you? Hoping I'll spill my plans? Ah, you don't disappoint. Hi, Kav. Hi, Kuma. Are you there, cub? Do you want to hear her scream before she dies?"

The knife slipped beneath the bottom edge of her armor, angled upward. It sliced through skin and muscle and organ, and for a breath all she felt was impossibly cold before the searing agony hit. Her pathways went to work, filling her with painkillers, making her head light. She gasped, trying to bend over the wound, but Fletcher held her in place.

He *tsked*. "Don't squirm. You must have realized this was how this would go. You're a defender. A guard dog. *Exemplar.*" His lip curled with disgust. "You know why they call you that, don't you? It's not because you're so very skilled. It's a warning to all the starry-eyed soldiers out there who think they might achieve your lofty heights someday, too. The highest rank any nonfamily can reach, a truly *exemplary* feat, and what is it? Dying for them. Being slaughtered for the blooded is the best we can hope for."

Naira closed her eyes. It was true. She'd always known it was true.

"Hurts, doesn't it?" Fletcher said. "I tried to warn you. I tried to take you with me, into the finalizers, because we're not even called finalizers, are we? On the official roster we're 'specialists.' It's bad luck to say the name of the thing that frightens you the most. Old magic, that. Superstition is hard to shake. But, no. You had to go throw yourself on every sword you could find."

"I could never do what you do."

"Oh, I know. Don't get me wrong. You have your talents, and I admire them, I do, but I'm the real killer in this room. You were never going to be the one walking out. Though I suppose this makes things more interesting. I'm curious to see what you'll do with the recording, knowing my intentions in advance."

She coughed blood that spattered the front of his shirt. "You won't know I'm onto you, Fletch."

He glanced pointedly at the knife. "Your abilities are many, but turning the tables on this? I don't think so."

She slumped, let herself lean against him for support, and he released her shoulder, curling an arm around her to rub her back. "There, there," he said. "I'm a professional. I won't let you crack. A little shift of the knife, and your heart's gone."

"Fletch," she whispered.

"Yes, love?"

"You missed a tooth."

His whole body went rigid. With deep satisfaction, she detonated the explosive.

TWENTY-SEVEN

Acaelus

Mercator Station | Three Months Ago

The ship was ready for Canden, and so was Lockhart. Demarco had yet to find his son, but Canden would understand. Tarquin had always been a willful child, and Acaelus could wait no longer. It was time. Time to bring her back and show her all he'd done to keep her safe. Show her he could know the truth about *canus*, and remain uncontrolled.

Once more, he sent the order that he was not to be disturbed and returned to his private labs. Lockhart waited, scarcely twitching a muscle as Acaelus entered the room. Good. His graft of Sharp's instinct not to bow had taken root.

For Canden, no sterile awakening in the printing cubicle. Lockhart removed her print and transferred it to a gurney. He tucked a soft sheet around her body and supported her neck with a narrow pillow that wouldn't disturb the upload crown. Canden's print was still damp with leftover biomatrix, its pathways not completely settled.

Despite his confidence that her map was whole, he placed the twin IV lines that were standard for a non-cubicle awakening. One to dispense sedatives, to ease her anxieties should she come up troubled, and the other a euthanasia line, in case she came up screaming instead.

Only a precaution. He was certain. He'd examined that map so often he could see all the fine details of it in his sleep. There was no evidence of artifacting, no dithering around the crisp lines of her synapses. Acaelus fit the crown over her head, took her hand, and initiated the upload.

Canden inhaled, back arching, and for one terrifying moment he knew she was drawing breath to scream, but then she settled, and her eyes fluttered open, and he was filled with such a warmth that all the world turned to liquid gold around him, narrowing his focus to those doe-dark eyes.

"Can. Hey," he whispered, drawing her hand—warm now with the pump of blood—to his lips. "You're home. You're safe."

She blinked sleepily, lashes fluttering against her cheeks, and a slow smile curled up the side of her face. The smile flattened.

"Acaelus?"

"I found you." His voice thickened, tears stinging behind his eyes. In the hall, a muffled argument brewed. He ignored it. Kearns would hold the door.

"No. Oh no." She turned her head to the side and saw Lockhart. "Oh god, you too."

He tightened his hold on her hand and touched her cheek with the other, turning her back to him. "It's all right. Really. I know everything. I understand why you feared, but I've made a safe place for us. I've made us a home where *canus* can't reach."

"You can't see it, of course you can't see it." Her voice lifted, panicked.

"See what? Can, tell me what's wrong—"

"Get away from me!"

The door opened. Acaelus jerked his head up to order whoever it was to walk themselves out an airlock, but it was Leka, face stricken, gaze locked on her living mother. Acaelus had a second to register that something was wrong—Leka should be *happy* to see her mother—before Canden screamed.

The sound snapped something within him. He'd heard it so very many times before when he'd printed her false map. Muscle memory overrode sense and he lunged for the euthanasia line, opened it to put that scream to rest.

Canden's body fell slack, mouth open, eyes frozen in horror. He stepped away, stunned by what he'd done, holding his hands out before him as if they'd betrayed him.

"What the fuck did you do?" Leka demanded.

"I—I don't—it was a mistake. We can bring her back. I *brought her back.*"

He touched Canden's cheek—still warm. It was the print that was dead, not the mind. He still had that. He still had *her.*

"Stop," Leka said. "Stop it. I don't care what you do with Lockhart, but this? She was screaming at you, Dad. This has to stop."

"No. No. I had her. She was here. She was safe."

He shoved the gurney aside and opened the control console for the printing bay. Just a few minutes. A few more minutes and he'd have her print again and upload her mind. She wouldn't even remember having died. He could salvage this.

Leka rounded the gurney and grabbed his arms, pulling him away. "No, not until you talk to me—"

Lockhart's hands closed around Leka's head—one on top, one on her chin—and yanked. Leka's neck snapped. Her body slumped to the floor, released carelessly by Lockhart. Precisely the move he had imparted to her through the footage of Sharp, but lacking the context Sharp's real memory would have taught her.

Acaelus stared into Lockhart's empty eyes and something within him broke at last. He was sliding, sliding down into a hollow within himself from which he knew he'd never recover. Acaelus had spent his entire life in control of everything he touched. It would have shocked him, if he were still himself, to know how easy it was to give up the grip of those reins at long last. His pathways felt very warm.

Boots stomped through the door.

"My liege?"

Kearns. Loyal, steady Kearns. The man had the personality of a steel beam. But he'd seen too much. Leka's exemplar followed. She'd always been a touch slow for Acaelus's taste, and her eyes bulged upon seeing her charge dead on the floor.

Acaelus spoke to Lockhart, "Kill them."

She drew her sidearm and fired before either exemplar could react.

Acaelus looked upon all he had wrought and thought—*I can fix this.*

"Reconstitute the bodies," he ordered Lockhart.

The console sprang to life beneath his touch. He spun up Canden's and Leka's maps, expanding them, letting the glittering details of their lives enfold him. No evidence of fragmentation, but that didn't mean they hadn't experienced suffering, did it? If he was going to bring them back, why bring them back with all their pain and hurt? It was cruel. He couldn't imagine why he'd never thought of it before.

Kinder, to cut out all the hurt, all the fear. Excise the memories that weighed.

Canden could not look at him and scream, if she had no memory of *canus* at all.

TWENTY-EIGHT

Tarquin

The Conservator's Ship | The Present

For the first time in his life, Tarquin woke in a printing cubicle that wasn't Mercator green. Disorientation struck him, a slow panic crawling up his throat, shortening his breath, until he remembered what had happened. That the grey lights of the HC, in this case, were safe.

He focused on his breathing until calm settled, and then reached for the release lever. The printing tray slid out, his print completed and stabilized long enough before he'd woken that any leftover biomatrix had already been siphoned away. His new body was clean and dry.

A memory of Naira, as Lockhart, scaring the skin off him when she'd kicked open her own printing cubicle and came rocketing out covered in leftover biomatrix came back to him, and he smiled.

"Sleeping beauty's up," someone called out.

"I see it," Jessel said.

Tarquin blinked and pushed himself up on the tray, shading his eyes from the bright light with a raised arm. His pathways adjusted, a subtle vibration settling his vision. Ocular pathways were always the first sense pathways to integrate, printed long before the rest of the body was finished.

He was in the shuttle, his portable printing cubicle situated along the back wall, gurneys covered with stasis shields containing the prints of

Kav and Kuma between him and Jessel. They bent over another gurney with the stasis shield cracked open. Lockhart's print.

Tarquin's new heart faltered a few beats. Jessel wore magnifying goggles, a tray beside them, the blue gloves covering their hands stained with blood as they worked on Lockhart's finger.

"What happened?" he asked.

"Big question." Jessel didn't bother to look up from their work. "Rani, help him out while I finish this."

A unionist came over and gave Tarquin a friendly arm to lean on as he eased himself off the printing tray. His legs wobbled. He snorted at his own weakness. Naira had come out of a printing cubicle at a sprint, swinging a rifle around like it was an extension of her body in a matter of seconds. He should be able to stand without help, for god's sake. Rani handed him a robe and he slipped it on, nodding his thanks.

Tarquin shuffled over to the gurney and tried to get a better look without being obtrusive. Jessel had split the print's forefinger open and, carefully, snipped off the end of a pathway and lifted it free. Tarquin shuddered, putting a lid on the phantom itch of pain that crawled up the sides of his legs. He could scarcely believe he'd agreed to that.

Jessel set the pathway in the tray. It seemed golden enough to Tarquin, but he was sure they had their reasons. They sprayed something in the wound and sealed it up with adhesive from a narrow syringe, then wiped the blood clean and placed Lockhart's hand back under the stasis shield.

"What was wrong with that one?" Tarquin asked.

Jessel grimaced. "That was an unwanted addition. Turns out Demarco bribed the bodymappers to put a tracking pathway in Sharp, and did it again when he thought she might be Lockhart. I've got my people editing it out of both print specs, but it's delicate work. In the meantime, it's easier to cut the thing out. It's not like we have the supplies to print her a fresh edit, anyway."

Tarquin arrived at a few dire conclusions from that statement. His stomach sank, and he had to put a hand on the side of the stasis shield to keep from falling over.

"Hooboy." Jessel pushed the surgery goggles up to their head and looped around the gurney, taking Tarquin firmly by the arm. They guided him to a chair and sat him down. "I don't really do soft deliveries of bad news, all right? So don't faint on me, because I don't want to do this shit again. It's bad enough she left me to babysit your print."

Tarquin blinked until his vision stopped blurring. "Thank you for looking after my print, even though you find me distasteful."

They swished their lips to the side in a pucker. "You're probably all right. It's your family I have an issue with. Doesn't matter, though, because I'm not bullheaded enough to let anything happen to your print on my watch. No one in their right mind wants Naira Sharp pissed off at them."

Tarquin tried not to read too much into that, but a tiny part of him burned with hope. If Naira was a threat to Jessel, then she was alive. Fletcher hadn't cracked her.

"Please, tell me what happened."

Jessel scratched the side of their jaw, staring at the ceiling as if searching for a place to begin. "Sharp got Demarco to talk about *canus* and his involvement in it. He definitely works for its advancement, wants it in control instead of MERIT. He knew she'd taken you, because of the tracker, and was looser with his tongue because of that, I think. Anyway, he tried to kill her, but Sharp detonated the explosive."

Tarquin closed his eyes. Breathed. Jessel wouldn't be performing surgery on the Lockhart print if Naira wasn't coming back. They weren't the kind of person who'd waste their time or resources on such a thing.

"Where is she now?"

"That's the real bad news." Jessel sized him up. "You took longer than expected to print. She waited as long as she could, but the timeline was getting crunchy. She didn't plan on living through that meet with Demarco, so Kav and Kuma went with her, recorded the conversation, and came back here. When they got here, I backed those two up and cast all three to the *Cavendish*."

"Have you heard from them? Has there been any news on the *Sigillaria*?"

"Not yet," Jessel said, "but that's not unusual. Once they cast out, it's a comms blackout unless something's vital. We don't want an incoming signal traced to us. We either wait to hear from them, get the ding that they've casted back, confirmation from news sources that the ship was destroyed, or for the prearranged reprint date to pass. Whichever comes first."

"What's the date?"

"Oh, eight months from now."

"*Eight?*" He'd been doing his best to keep it together, but he couldn't keep the shock off his face.

"That's the way of things. The *Sigillaria* had been skipping along for a bit more than three months before they left. That's the real target, and our reprint timeline is always time out, doubled." Jessel patted him awkwardly on the shoulder. "Buck up, liege. This is what they do. It'll be fine."

Between them, the weight that Jessel's brother hadn't been fine sat, too heavy for either of them to pick up and carry into this fragile conversation.

"Was there any consensus on what I'm meant to do in the meantime?" he asked.

Jessel's posture relaxed. "Some. Sharp determined your exemplar, Cass, was on the up, so we roped them in. Your order to halt reprinting without express permission from you meant Demarco got caught in that, so he's on ice.

"We think that, if you're game, the next step is to reinstall you as the head of Mercator. This time around we'll have Ex. Cass watching you for signs of increased infection, and us sending you the shroud to consume."

"I see." Tarquin rubbed the palm of his hand with a thumb.

"I know it's a lot to swallow right now," Jessel said. "And we're all aware that putting you back at the head of Mercator leaves you open to another infection. But we'll watch your back. You think you can handle that?"

"I'll do my best, and rely on you all to guide me if *canus* overwhelms me."

They patted him on the back again, and this time it was a little less awkward. "Anyhow, Ex. Cass is waiting. There's a bag with your things over by the wall. Take a minute. Pull yourself together. Then go meet Ex. Cass."

"Thank you, Mx. Hesson, I'll do that. Do you have a recording of Demarco's final statement I can review?"

They tensed. "It's loaded in the shuttle's files. You can move a copy over to your private files if you want. But, if you'll hear a little advice?"

He nodded.

"Don't listen to that shit. It's just going to mess you up. Demarco's a real sick bastard. We'll give you the facts you need to know."

Tarquin glanced at the bag, praying Naira had left him something. "Would you listen to it? If it was Jonsun."

He didn't look at them, but he could hear their sharp intake of breath. "I don't care to admit it, but...I would. And I'd make sure I was blind drunk first."

"Thank you for your counsel."

They said their goodbyes and left him to gather himself. He crossed to the bag, found new clothes waiting in Mercator green, and hoped Cass had brought those. Getting clothes to pass as appropriate on the head of a family couldn't be cheap. Tarquin couldn't even remember the last time he'd paid for clothes, or how much they cost. He ordered the things he needed, and they appeared. It'd been that way his whole life.

Something crinkled in the pocket of the slacks. A scribe paper. Naira had scratched out a cloud of false starts, the ghost of their lines on the reusable sheet too vague for him to make out. What she'd left, in a bold script he'd never seen before, was one line: *I'll come back for you.*

No signature. Nothing else. It was more than enough.

TWENTY-NINE

Naira

The Cavendish | *The Present*

Naira woke to the oppressive green lights of a Mercator printing cubicle. She breathed deeply, taking in the fatty scent of leftover biomatrix, and grinned into that green-tinged dark. They'd done it. They were on the *Cavendish*.

The last thing she remembered was lying down on the gurney to have her map backed up before she would go for Fletcher. The fact that she was here meant that at least part of that plan had gone correctly. She pressed her feet against the hatch and shoved, pushing her tray out in the same motion.

Cold, stale air assaulted her senses. Naira coughed on the frosty air, sitting up to better clear her lungs. She scraped her hair back and slid off the tray, testing her print. Stable. Strong. The pathways she knew so well glittered across her skin.

They'd decided to send their preferred print files along with their maps because they couldn't be sure what state the *Cavendish* databases were in, and she was glad they had done so.

The once shiny surfaces of the printing bay had dulled under a fine layer of dust and neglect. They were lucky it was in decent enough condition to print them at all. Frigid air prickled her skin, urging her to find clothes as quickly as possible.

Naira reached to open a bulkhead cupboard and snatched her hand back, hissing as the cold metal seared her fingers. She eyed the rubber mats surrounding the floor by the cubicles and made a mental note not to step off of them until she could find some shoes.

The light on one of the printing cubicles flashed green. There was a thump from within, followed by a muffled curse. Naira hit the release button. Kuma's tray slid out, the muscled woman's eyes huge with surprise.

"The goddamn release lever broke," she said.

Naira extended a hand to her. "Those things break so often I don't even try anymore. You good?"

Kuma allowed herself to be pulled to her feet. She wobbled at first, but found her footing. "Yeah. Solid. Nice to have my own skin on one of these missions for once. Why is it so cold?"

"No idea. Watch the floor. The metal will take your skin off." She showed Kuma her raw fingertips.

"Already causing damage to that print of yours."

"Yeah, yeah. Help me find something to get these drawers open without skinning ourselves."

They skirted the edges of the mats, craning their necks to better see what was left in the room. Naira crouched to examine a break in the wall paneling that looked like it had been pried open by some kind of tool. As far as she could tell, the hole in the wall didn't lead anywhere overly important—just internal circuitry.

"Nai, catch!"

Kuma chucked her half a roll of gauze. Naira snatched it out of the air and unrolled some of it, wrapping it around her hands and over her fingers. It wasn't much protection, but it'd have to do. They eyed each other, hesitating.

"I already burned myself once," Naira said.

Another cubicle lit green. "Oops," Kuma said. "Gotta help Kav. Could you get the drawers open, Nai?"

Naira groaned. She had to move quickly, but she got a cabinet open without burning herself further. Her pathways hummed to life, warming her blood even as her lungs were aching. She dug some light armor out of the bin. Though they were crisp with cold, they still went on baggy and conformed to her body. A shiver rocked her when the icy fabric pressed up against her skin, but her body heat equalized quickly enough.

Kav stumbled as Kuma helped him off the tray, and nearly toppled onto a metal gurney, Kuma swooping in just in time to brace him. "Why do you insist on all those muscles if you don't even like to use 'em?"

"Because I look fantastic."

Naira tossed a set of armor and hit him dead in the chest. He grunted, catching the clothes before they fell.

"Cover up, both of you. This ship's freezing."

They dressed quickly and found a few pairs of boots, but not a single weapon, which was unusual for a Mercator family printing bay. Exemplars were printed in here, and they'd want their firearms nearby. She tightened the wrap on the gauze and pulled gloves over her hands for extra warmth.

"Okay," she said, "you two are too quiet. What happened before we casted?"

Kuma and Kav looked anywhere but at her. Naira put her hands on her hips and glared. Kav broke first.

"Fletch showed up. You got him, detonated the tooth, but he knew you'd taken Tarquin and was definitely there to kill you."

"That sounds messy," she said. "Any new information?"

"Uh." Kav grimaced.

Kuma took over. "He'd been working for *canus* for a long time. Details later, but he's iced now, for sure. The only thing you really should know is, uh...Okay. Don't kill the messenger. He had a tracking pathway added to your Sharp print and later the Lockhart print file. It's in your right forefinger."

Naira stared at the finger in question.

"Jessel has their people working on editing it out of your print files, and in the meantime, they're cutting it out of the Lockhart print." Kuma put on a tone that was meant to be cheerful, but rang hollow in the cold, dead space of the printing bay.

Naira's first thought—*I'm going to kill that asshole*—was moot, because she had already done so, but she couldn't deny a temptation to print him and kill him again just so she could remember the moment.

"Who knows about it?"

"Just us and Jessel," Kav said.

"Maybe Tarquin," Kuma said.

"Maybe?" Naira pressed.

"He wasn't out yet when we left. If he's up, Jessel told him."

She eyed her finger like it'd turned into a snake. "I don't like it, but I'll keep it for now. It might be useful for them later and I'm not about to cut into myself with scalpels cold enough to freeze my blood. Let's scout the ship, see what we're working with. Kav, can you get into the ship's systems? Get us cameras, diagnostics, the usual?"

His forehead scrunched as he tried to power up a console, but it kept glitching out. "There's some sort of signal interference. Let's look for the command deck."

"As good a place as any to start," she said.

Kuma went first, and Naira drifted to the rear guard. Her finger itched, but she chalked that up to being psychosomatic, and tried not to think about all the blank spaces between the facts Kuma and Kav had given her. She trusted them to give her the pertinent information. Anything else was a distraction. She wouldn't let Fletcher distract her from this mission, even from his grave.

The doors were all open. Their breath misted as they walked, boots echoing down empty hallways. Naira tried to get into the ship's system a few times via her own HUD but finally gave up, as she kept getting locked out by the same signal interference. Strange, that someone had turned on such a device before leaving the ship to sink into a star.

Frost bloomed in thin, scaly patches against the walls, the subtle gleam reminding her of the silver sheen of lichen. Someone had pried panels off and left them to clutter the floor. Angry dents and scrapes covered the discarded panels. In a few sections some wiring had been ripped out, singed and dead.

"I don't remember any of this." Naira examined a torn-open panel. "When you got shot in the engine bay, Kav, people started running and shouting. Alarms went off. But no one was tearing at the walls."

Kav brought his face close to a dented panel and ran a gloved finger over the scraped paint. "This looks new."

"Great," Naira muttered. "This better not be another misprint-infested ship."

"Shh." Kuma slashed her hand through the air.

Naira clamped her mouth shut. Ahead, Kuma had sunk into a crouch next to a turn in the hall. When Kuma glanced back at them, Naira caught the warmth of a brighter light source painting her face. Someone was here.

Naira gestured for Kav to stay put and crept past him, easing into position next to Kuma. Strains of music drifted out from a room at the end of the turn, flickering light spilling from the door. Kuma tapped her shoulder and raised both brows. Naira shrugged. She had no idea. Itching for a weapon, she eased around the corner and leaned heavily on her agility pathways, making her steps silent. The others stayed behind.

At the end of the hall, the door with the light was half-opened, caught in a partial dilation, the mechanism either broken or frozen in place. Acrid smoke tinged the air. Naira craned her neck and saw the back of a familiar dirty-blond head.

Captain Paison sat in an office chair, her back to the door, boots kicked up on a crate, a pile of packaging and clothing burning between her and the far wall. She hummed an old children's song to herself.

Naira let her footsteps be heard as she stepped over the threshold. Paison kicked off the crate, swinging around in the chair, and smiled thin lips up at her.

"Sharp. Welcome to Acaelus's little trap. I wondered if you were ever going to show up."

THIRTY

Tarquin

Mercator Station | The Present

Tarquin stood in the middle of his foyer and had no idea what to do with himself. This place was his. It had been before, in a smaller way, when his father had been in charge, and again when he'd been under the thumb of both Fletcher and *canus*, but always there had been another level above him. Someone else was calling the real shots. Someone else would be to blame if things went wrong.

Tarquin was, genuinely, the most powerful man in the universe. And all he wanted to do was bring Naira back safely. Not even the full strength of Mercator was enough to make that happen.

Eight months.

Cass cleared their throat. "Everything all right, my liege?"

Tarquin startled. "Yes, of course. Forgive me, there has been . . . a large amount of change in a very short time."

"Ms. Salter's eager to talk to you," Cass said, "but I can cancel your appointments for the day if you need time to get reacquainted." They cracked a grin. "No one will argue, if it's me telling them no."

"No, but thank you. I'll talk to Ms. Salter. While I do, I trust you to handle the selection of a secondary exemplar on my behalf. You'll need someone else to relieve you, now that Demarco is gone."

Cass saluted briefly. "I'll send her in and start the search. I'll be right outside if you need me, my liege."

He entered his office and hesitated again. Fletcher's presence lingered in the room, a foul haunting. He resolved to have someone come in and rearrange things. Maybe even move his office to another room.

Tarquin had yet to listen to the recording. He had time. It would take Salter a while to answer his summons. He recalled the ache he'd felt sitting in that chair, and how his thoughts had fled him when Fletcher had taunted him. Maybe it was best to wait.

The chair conformed to his new print as he sat. Though the design of his body was the same as it always was, each printing was never quite a direct copy. Subtle variations occurred, and the reminder that he was in new skin soothed some of his anxieties. Work. He had work to do, as head of Mercator. He couldn't spend all day ruminating.

He accessed his private workstation and was grateful to find Cass had already reconnected his external comms and removed the print comm jammer. The past few days had been such a haze, Tarquin could scarcely remember what he'd been working on. He checked his history.

He'd searched up a huge amount of data surrounding the relkatite inventory before and after Acaelus had fled. He'd done it again and again, checking the same files, leaving them open for minutes, sometimes hours, though surely those figures had been burned into his head at some point.

Between the inventory levels were hand-scrawled notes. Equations repeated with the same numbers—some underlined, some crossed out. Tarquin couldn't recall having written them. He didn't even recognize what the equations were for. A light knock sounded on his door.

"My liege?" Madeleine Salter called out.

Tarquin swiped his research away and hoped his face didn't show his bewilderment. "Come in."

Salter entered the room and bowed, her normally keen eyes shadowed with dark troughs. Tarquin leaned back, lacing his fingers across his chest as he studied her.

"My liege," she said. "It's good to have you back. We worried."

Tarquin merely watched her, knowing she was waiting to see if he'd offer an explanation. He wouldn't. Acaelus came and went without a word all the time. Tarquin didn't wish to emulate his father, but on this point, he wouldn't budge. He answered to no one regarding his whereabouts for the past few days.

She shifted uncomfortably and tried to pin a smile back on. "I'm glad you're back, my liege, though I have some sad news to report. Specialist Fletcher Demarco was killed in a bombing yesterday."

"A pity," Tarquin said. *A pity I didn't get to kill the man myself.*

"Yes, it is. Naturally, your order to halt all reprinting without express permission has left him on ice. If you would sign the release—"

"I will not." Tarquin put granite in his voice.

Salter's eyes widened. "My liege? I don't understand."

"I think you do," Tarquin said. "I think you understand very well that Fletcher Demarco thought he had the right to sway the minds of those employed on this station."

She clutched her hands together so that they wouldn't tremble. "He was a source of continuity, my liege, when Liege Acaelus left us. I won't deny we relied on him."

"I appreciate your candor," he said. "Can I rely on *you*, Ms. Salter?"

"Of course, my liege. My loyalties are with Mercator. I owe this family a great deal, and please allow me to say that it is good to see you taking charge."

Tarquin let his brows lift in silent question.

"Not that you weren't in charge," she said, rapid-fire, and ducked her head. "It's just that…Mr. Demarco could be, hmm, domineering."

"Indeed," he said.

She winced. "Forgive me, my liege. I overstep."

Tarquin let some of the hardness on his face soften. "I'm not the person you or anyone else in Mercator was expecting to take this seat. I understand. But it is mine, and though I have historically distanced myself from family matters, that doesn't mean I care any less about the well-being of Mercator. Or that I won't fight to protect my family."

He let those final words cut, let her imagine him giving some silent order to have Fletcher killed, though he'd done no such thing. Firmness was what his employees expected. An iron hand, to start with. To let them know the family's position was secure, and that things would return to normal, more or less.

He'd tried to project the same air while Fletcher had been the true voice of power, and he saw now how convincing that farce had been—not at all. Mercator's employees were keen. They whispered among themselves, though they ducked and scraped when he passed by.

"I believe I understand, my liege." There was a gleam in her eye that he recognized. The hunger of ambition lit anew.

She'd caught his subtext, then, and believed he'd had Fletcher killed.

Let them say he was a killer. Let them watch him with wary eyes, because he'd proven he could move in ways they hadn't expected of the lesser child of Acaelus. Tarquin had no desire to rule by fear—such a position lasted until someone more worthy of that fear came along—but the flare of ambition in Salter told him he'd chosen the correct path, for now.

"I expect you will inform the others of the current situation."

"It would be my pleasure, my liege." Her smile tightened with calculation.

Helping him correct the rumors surrounding his late-night escape would be a favor, and she saw leverage in that. Believed he'd taken her into secret confidences.

People, Acaelus had once told Tarquin, were less likely to turn against you if they thought they shared a secret with you. *Give them scraps*, Acaelus had said. *Give them lies. It doesn't matter, just make them think they're special, and they'll beg at your feet for the chance to be useful.*

Tarquin liked to think he wasn't taking his father's advice quite so far.

"Now, sit. What do you have for me?"

Salter whisked him through a dizzying array of details large and small regarding the operations of the family. Bottlenecks in supply lines, suspected spies, departments lacking a coherent leader, and those who had one leader too many whose personalities were clashing. It was the type of management Leka and Acaelus had been adept at.

He glimpsed the bare outlines of why Acaelus micromanaged while he gave Salter the best orders he could devise. Along the edges of all those small decisions was the shape of Mercator as a whole. Right now, that shape was a jagged thing, out of joint, having run without a true leader for too long.

He should have realized the danger sooner. Should have understood that the other MERIT families would see Mercator slowly fall out of tune, and what that would mean, eventually, for those who served Mercator.

On that one point, Fletcher had been correct. It'd been selfish of Tarquin to leave his family to swirl down the drain. As competent as their employees were, they relied on a system with a clear leader. Without that structure, small things had broken. His head was aching by the time Salter switched to larger concerns.

"While you were away, my liege." Her careful intonation drew his attention. "I stalled the production of *canus* cultures and equipment meant for the other families. Forgive me if this will cause your program unnecessary delay, but I wasn't comfortable overseeing such a project without you here for direction."

Tarquin blew out a slow, relieved breath. "That was the correct decision. We still require relkatite, but upon further consideration, I have altered the plan somewhat."

Her tense posture softened in relief. "Oh?"

"*Canus* will remain with Mercator. In fact, I mean to centralize production. I wish to move all bioleaching processing equipment to this station, where it will be properly secured. We will still lease out the equipment required to collect ore slurry and prepare it for bioleaching, but the actual extraction of relkatite via *canus* will remain the purview of Mercator, and Mercator alone."

"The other families will be furious." Her tone was serious, but the quick flash of her smile was pleased.

"I will handle the other families. Is there anything else?"

"Just the build diagnostics you requested from engineering before your absence, my liege. They provided as much detail as they could, but are eager to provide any other information you might require. You have only to ask."

"Thank you." Tarquin hoped his confusion didn't show as he accepted the data packet she passed to him. "That will be all."

Salter stood and bowed, letting herself out. She had a bit more spring in her step than she'd had when she'd entered. He wondered how he was ever going to make this family less of a dictatorship if its employees were conditioned to expect a tyrant at the helm. It'd take time. Time he had, now that his mind and movements were wholly his own.

He swiped up the diagnostics he had apparently requested, and sifted through an immense amount of data, blinking dry, bleary eyes against wireframe diagrams and stacks of equations. They tickled the back of his mind, a phantom memory whispering to him across his prints. He wondered if this was how Naira had felt, looking at him after she'd reprinted, and hoped not, because the sensation was unpleasant. It would explain a lot about how she'd treated him, though.

Tarquin flicked the data to the projector in his desk and spread it out all around him. A globe of questions in which he was the molten core.

He allowed his thoughts to grow hazy in the way he often did when presented with a nebulous problem. This was a needle in a haystack. He couldn't comb through every straw, he had to see the whole, and find the key piece that stood out. The metal glinting within. He couldn't say how long he sat like that when an equation caught his eye.

He leaned toward that section and expanded it. It was the equation he'd written in the margins of the relkatite inventory. He checked the surrounding data—it was what they used to calculate how much relk they would need to contain a warpcore at varying sizes. The calculations for the *Sigillaria*'s warpcore were larger than those he'd written in the margins. He brought up his notes and compared them to the *Sigillaria*'s plans.

Nothing matched.

Tarquin rubbed his chin, leaning back. The weight of relkatite in the stores of Mercator was measured every half hour. The day they moved the relk for construction of the *Sigillaria*, the weight of what they'd moved was far too low. There was no possible way the engineers had built a warpcore of the size expected for that ship, let alone the ancillary relkatite parts. Some had been taken—in sufficient quantities, perhaps, for a smaller ship—but Tarquin was no expert in those matters.

Shortly after they had moved the construction materials, the stores had been nearly wiped out. Acaelus, taking the relk and running.

Or Acaelus covering his tracks.

Tarquin launched into the family records. He accessed the raw material inventories and compared the crucial hours—when the hull would be manufactured, the engines forged, et cetera—against the materials retrieved.

Not a single calculation allowed for a ship the size and complexity of the *Sigillaria* to have been built.

He stared at the raw facts, dumbfounded, an uneasy feeling creeping through him.

A ship existed called the *Sigillaria*. It must. People independent of Mercator had traced Acaelus's broadcast to the expected path to Seventh Cradle. Tarquin had seen the command deck behind Acaelus with his own eyes, and it was vast and complicated in the way the deck for a larger ship would be. Of course, he'd also seen himself standing behind his father, so seeing wasn't believing.

What he could believe, and trust in, was the energy signature of an ansible flying toward Seventh Cradle. That couldn't be faked unless there was an actual device out there.

He drummed his fingers against the desk. Maybe the *Sigillaria* was less powerful than expected. Slower. Acaelus would want to hide that to make certain the other families believed they couldn't chase him down. On a whim, Tarquin pulled up the personnel database and found Mercator's chief of engineering, a woman he'd never met named Anne Yuan. He called her.

She took a moment to answer. When she did, her eyes were heavy, her hair mussed. Her face registered surprise for only a moment before she ducked her head in a quick bow and stifled a yawn. "Dr. Mercator, this is an unexpected honor." Her eyes flew wide. "Forgive me, my liege, I mean."

Tarquin couldn't remember the last time someone had called him doctor instead of liege, and he found the slip refreshing. "Either title is fine with me, Dr. Yuan. I apologize for waking you. I'd been working and forgot to check the hour."

Her smile was slow and sleepy. "I understand, my liege. I often forget to check the hour when working. Is there a matter I can help you with? I can't claim to be fresh-eyed, but I will do my best."

"I suspect this will be old hat to you, but it's outside my area of expertise." Tarquin selected the logs of the relkatite removed from storage the day construction began and shifted them onto the screen. "What size ship could you build with this quantity of materials? Full kit, I mean— circuitry, ansible housing, warpcore containment. All of it."

Dr. Yuan leaned forward, blinking sleep from her eyes. "Hmm. I wouldn't attempt anything larger than a shuttle with that. Actually, I wouldn't attempt an entire ship at all. May I...?" She poised her fingers over the inventory logs. He nodded his approval.

She opened them and examined the materials. "I don't mean to step on your toes, my liege, but are we talking about the amount itself as a theoretical, or these particular stores? Because I wouldn't trust this grade of relk to hold a warpcore. I suppose they could handle the strain of an ansible, though. Do you need me to work up plans for their use?"

Tarquin kicked himself as he reviewed the purity report. They were the lowest usable grade, cobbled together from ore that scarcely produced anything at all. He'd been so obsessed with the numbers themselves he'd missed his own specialty. No one would risk building a warpcore with that grade of relk. Not even Acaelus at peak hubris.

"No, thank you, Dr. Yuan. Once more, I apologize for waking you over such a small matter."

"It's no trouble, my liege." She hesitated. "It's always a pleasure to talk shop. I went to your lectures at Jov-U about orbital mapping of geographic formations, you know."

He blinked, simultaneously flattered and self-conscious. "What did you think?"

"Brilliant! I have some suggestions regarding improvement of the equipment that might make your work easier. That is, if you're still doing fieldwork, my liege. I'm certain the operation of Mercator keeps you very busy." Her words sped up, and her cheeks reddened.

"I intend to." He forced a reassuring smile. People tripping over themselves to apologize to him about innocent boundary crossing was getting old.

"In that case, next time duty calls me to Mercator Station, perhaps we could discuss matters over coffee?"

His forced smile turned genuine. He missed academic pursuits. "Absolutely. Schedule it with Ms. Salter when you're able. Thank you again, Doctor. Good night."

Dr. Yuan made her formal farewells and he ended the call, dragging up the schematics for the *Sigillaria* again. If he took out everything else, that amount of low-grade relk could have been used to construct the ansible, giving his father something to bounce a signal off of.

If that was the case, Naira and her team would cast themselves off the *Cavendish* into nothing at all. Their maps would sit on the *Sigillaria*'s ansible storage, never printed, until the deadline passed. Maybe they'd already done so.

"Shit," he whispered.

What could he do? Without proof, there was no way he or Jessel would risk printing them again. But if he was right, then Acaelus had baited the Conservators into shelving themselves for months.

Surely the comms blackout didn't apply to him? Anyone tracing the signal from a message he sent would find Mercator Station, not the unionists' hideouts. Tarquin composed a package of the data he'd collected and included his theory, then sent it out to the *Cavendish* along Mercator's ansible relay. He expected no reply, but it felt good to have attempted to put the information in their hands.

Acaelus had to have gone somewhere. Despite Jessel's report on supplies being moved to the *Cavendish*, Tarquin had a hard time believing his father was on a ship drifting into a star. He wished he had the Conservators here to talk out ideas with. Jessel was likely to tell him to sit on his hands and wait it out. Fieldwork was the Conservators' job. The rest of them were support.

Support. Acaelus was an aristocrat. He wouldn't go anywhere without staff or supplies, and while Acaelus could hide most of that in what he requisitioned for the *Sigillaria*, he was living *somewhere*—a ship, a station, a planet—and he'd be drawing resources. And need a large facility to house all the relk he'd stolen.

Tarquin put in a request with Salter to have a report pulled on every single Mercator-issued property, including derelicts and decommissions, and their staff and resource consumption. He framed his request in terms that would make her believe he was auditing Mercator's resource draw, and it wasn't far from the truth.

His father was out there, somewhere, with his facsimile family. Tarquin would find him, and then he'd bring Naira home.

It wasn't until he decided to rest for the night that he realized Dr. Yuan's invitation to coffee was, probably, an attempt at a date. He was head of Mercator, officially unattached. Acaelus and Leka had both had known relationships. As far as Tarquin knew, all the other current heads of MERIT and their direct heirs were involved with someone, or someones.

Tarquin was the only one available, and he could hardly declare publicly that he was in love with humanity's number one terrorist.

He could coast on needing to focus on securing the family for a while but, eventually, people would start muttering about the line of succession. He'd have to pick an heir in case of his cracking, and he had absolutely no idea who he could trust with such a monumental undertaking. Tarquin certainly couldn't trust any of his cousins to effect the slow dismantling of MERIT's power structure that he wished to achieve.

"Shit," he said, again, into the empty dark of his office.

THIRTY-ONE

Naira

The Cavendish | *The Present*

There was no good reason for Naira to like Captain Paison, but she caught herself smiling in response to her anyway.

"Captain. I thought you were done with the *Cavendish*," Naira said.

Paison picked at the arm of her chair with stubby nails. "You remembered. How sweet. Though it's not really a memory, is it? Did you look it up, or did Liege Tarquin tell you?"

"Both."

Paison inclined her head, shaggy hair falling across her eyes. "Trust, but verify. The best way to interact with MERIT family." Kav and Kuma approached while Paison talked, flanking Naira in the door. Paison chuckled low. "Ah. HCA Regar Dawd, I presume." She snapped off a perfect salute to Kav. "That print really did suit you well. I don't know you, though." She lifted her chin to Kuma. "But I'm guessing you're the other one—the ex-Ichikawa security."

Kuma lounged against the curved side of the door. "I dropped the family name. It's just Kuma, now."

"Funny," Paison said. "You dropped it, and I picked it up." She lifted her hands to show off the red cuffs around her wrists, and the Ichikawa crest visible below the edge of her gloves. She wiggled her fingers. "Fat lot of good it's done me, though."

"Why are you here?" Naira asked.

"Same reason as you are, I expect. I was chasing the *Sigillaria*."

"I doubt our motives are the same."

"Don't be so sure about that. I know what you do, Sharp. I was on this ship when you tried to blow it to pieces." Her eyes narrowed. "You don't remember me, do you? Even though you casted out?"

"Tarquin told me you were on the *Cavendish* but, no, I don't remember you."

"Tarquin now, is it? I knew you two were getting too cozy. And yeah, I was on it. I was in the engine bay when you blew through. You shot me in the chest and left me to bleed out. I watched you set the warpcore to fail. Watched you walk out of the engine bay, ready to cast yourself somewhere safe and sound, but Acaelus caught you instead."

"I shoot to kill."

"Well, you fucking missed. Thought I was going to crack. I really did. But I saw what you'd done, and I was the only body left breathing on the entire ship. So I got up. Dragged my bleeding carcass over to a console and undid it all. Saved the ship. Thought I'd win all the accolades in the worlds, but Liege Acaelus was furious. He needed to catch you red-handed to make sure the trial would stick. So he ordered me to keep my mouth shut and gave me a nice cushy promotion to captain of the *Amaranth* and *Einkorn* instead."

"I'm sorry that I left you to bleed," Naira said. "But my being sorry won't keep me from uprooting *canus*, and you're its agent."

"Am I?" Her smile was rictus, and the pathways on her cheeks were golden. This was a fresh print for her, but Tarquin had insisted that Paison agreed to help *canus* before it took direct control of her.

"Kuma, tie the captain's hands."

Paison pressed her forearms together and offered them up to be bound. "Go ahead, Sharp. Take me prisoner. None of us are getting off this ship before the star takes it. Acaelus didn't forget it was here. He was holding it in reserve, a trap to snap shut on his pests when they stepped on board. And you three, you're his number one pests."

"Caught you, too," Naira said.

Kuma retrieved straps from a drawer and tied Paison's wrists together.

When the captain was secured, Naira motioned for her to stand. Paison eased to her feet and dipped into a mock bow.

"We stay together," Naira said. "Don't let the captain out of your sight. First priority is a damage sweep. We need to make sure we're not going to open a door and find a breached hull on the other side. Then we'll hunt down engineering and see if we can get the consoles back online."

Paison shook her head. "You're not getting into engineering."

"We'll see," Naira said.

Naira grabbed Paison by the upper arm and found the woman's muscles lean and strong as she herded her along. Paison went willingly, a scowl never quite leaving her face. The halls were empty, aside from the occasional piece of debris—usually a cast-off panel from the wall.

In the low light, Naira watched the shadows, and wondered why she got the sense that they were watching her back.

"You feel it, don't you?" Paison asked.

"I don't know what you're talking about."

Paison was silent for a while, leaving Naira to her thoughts as they cleared room after empty room and found all the consoles cut off from the main system. With each dead end, her sense of being watched intensified.

"You wouldn't remember," Paison said. Naira crouched down beside another torn-open panel and prodded at the frigid wiring within. "But we worked well together before I figured out who you were."

Naira removed a wire from the open panel and stripped the plastic coating back. Relkatite cores. She drummed the fingers of her other hand against her knee.

"What were you looking for?" Naira asked.

"Who says I did that?"

The captain leaned against the wall, head tipped back, her bound hands resting against her stomach as she propped one boot against the wall for balance. Kav and Kuma had moved farther down the hall, making their own investigation of a dead console podium. Judging by the way Kav whacked the side of his hand against it, that investigation wasn't going too well.

Paison had seemed fierce to Naira when she'd first seen the captain standing over the control console of the Mercator printing bay, sending her waves of misprints out to attack Tarquin. In the half light of the *Cavendish*, Naira only saw weariness in her. Resignation.

"Don't bullshit me, Captain." Naira kept her voice low enough not to disturb Kav and Kuma. "At first I thought these panels were random questing, but you know what you're doing around a ship. I remember—" She cut herself off at Paison's widening eyes. "You're a pilot. You know your ships. And you've only been popping open panels that contain relkcore wiring."

Paison's sleepy glance turned sly. "What was that, Sharp? You remember...?"

"Answer the question. What were you looking for?"

Paison sniffed. "Fine. Be coy with me. I was looking for a way out."

"These wires facilitate the ship's AI."

"Yes."

"And...?" Naira cocked her head with impatience.

"I don't know, Sharp. Think about it. Maybe you'll *remember*."

Naira scowled and replaced the wiring, noticing a streak of rust marring the other end of the sheath of cables. This ship really was falling apart. She brushed rust flakes off her gloves as she stood and grabbed Paison's arm again, steering her down the hallway. "Abandon that," she said to Kav and Kuma. "Let's focus on engineering."

"Good luck with that," Paison said, dripping sarcasm. "You're not getting in there."

Naira ignored her. She'd done this walk before, to rig the warpcore to blow. Each step echoed through her memory. She could almost see the ship as it had been the first time she'd been on it. Full lights, no frost. The plaintive cry of alarms as she shot her way through the scant few Merc-Sec that had been woken up, her cover already blown, her destination inevitable.

Paison watched her, the attention a spot of heat against Naira's face. Naira had the impression that Paison knew what she felt. That she saw the echoes from Naira's past reach up and grasp her. Some of this was normal. Naira had lived those moments and casted off afterward. There was no danger in those memories.

But the shadows imposing themselves over the memory were dangerous. The gleam of silver on the walls that didn't actually exist crowded

in on her, clamoring for her to remember another time. One that should
have been lost.

She'd told Tarquin all she saw in that past was him. This ship seemed
determined to prove her a liar.

I mean it, Nai. Stay away from him.

Tarquin wasn't even here. Fletcher's warning about her cracking was
just another lie to separate her from those she cared about. Naira locked
her worries down and focused with laser intensity on the here and now.
On the cold air in her lungs, and Paison's muscled arm in her hand.

A black-and-yellow hash striped the door to engineering. Naira drew
up short and blinked. That stripe wasn't a display. It was a fail-safe when
all else was broken. If there was vacuum on the other side of that door,
it flipped slats from the plain grey of the walls to that black-and-yellow
hash, warning anyone that there was a breach on the other side.

They hadn't found a single vacuum suit during their exploration.

"Shit," she said.

Paison said, "Every single door that leads out of this sector leads to
vacuum. I told you. We're not getting off this ship."

THIRTY-TWO

Naira

The Cavendish | *The Present*

Naira led them around the edge of engineering. The internal air-lock seemed to be operational. If they could find a vacuum suit, they could send someone through without depressurizing the rest of the ship. It was the suit that was the problem.

"Maybe we could rig something from storage for a helmet?" Kuma asked. "One of the water purifiers?"

"Without a way to pressurize it? Do you have any idea how long you'd last?" Naira asked.

"I'm guessing the answer is 'not long.'" Kuma sighed.

Naira ignored Paison's gloating smirk. They'd combed through most of the rooms looking for weapons or a working console. They hadn't been explicitly looking for vacuum suits. There might still be one stashed away in a closet.

"Let's head back to the room where we found the expedition supplies," Naira said. "Might be something we can use in there."

"I've been through all this," Paison said. "I can give you a complete inventory. There's nothing useful."

"I'd like to see for myself." Naira steered Paison back down the hall.

Kuma and Kav fell back, keeping their voices low as they swapped ideas about what could be done. She left them to it, worried that her doubts about the situation might poison their thoughts.

Naira believed in repairing the worlds for the future and in stopping the spread of *canus*. But the way this mission was shaping up, she had a sinking feeling that it'd end with them devoured by the star and being reprinted in eight months when Jessel finally pulled that trigger.

"You feel it, don't you?" Paison asked.

"What?"

"Hopelessness."

She didn't respond to that. But Naira couldn't shake the feeling that she'd missed something larger than Acaelus setting this ship as a trap for anyone who tried to follow him. Possibly that was paranoia, but she still felt... watched, from the shadows. A wakefulness in the walls, and couldn't quite put a finger on why.

They combed through what was left of the expedition supplies, coming up with a wide variety of cooking tools, tents, and sleeping bags, but nothing else of use. She was about to give up when she flipped open another crate and found survey drones tucked within. Carefully, she pulled a drone out of the crate and turned it over in her hands. They were designed for atmosphere, being little more than overpowered helicopters with grasping claws meant to carry the survey team's supplies. She checked the battery pack. Still good.

"What's that?" Kuma peered over her shoulder.

"Survey drones," Naira said. "Acaelus didn't like to use the agile bots, like Pliny."

"Who's Pliny?"

"Never mind that. I think maybe we can use these."

"Bit small to ride in," Kuma said.

"There's no air on the other side of that door," Kav grumbled. "Those things aren't flying in there."

"The grav generator is still on. We might be able to repurpose them to crawl instead of fly, and with those grabbing claws on them..."

"Repair the connection to the ship's systems." A grin splashed across Kav's tired face. "It will be tricky as hell, but I think we can actually do this."

"Help me shift these crates around," Naira said, "to make room to set up the tents. It's freezing, and I'd rather none of us lose skin to the metal on the drones."

It took them longer than Naira would have liked to rearrange the storage room, but once they had the useless supplies shoved off to the side and the tents set up, it was far more comfortable sharing body heat in the confined space. It'd almost be cozy, if Paison wasn't watching them.

They each took a drone, carefully working the small robots over to see where pieces could be repurposed without doing damage. Kav figured out how to move the motor from the top to the side, and Naira had a rough idea of how to shape the rotor blades into a makeshift wheel by bending the ends into "feet" that would drag the drone across any surface with traction. The trick would be to control them with any level of finesse.

Naira focused on the work, but couldn't shake the phantom press of Paison's silent stare. Eventually, she hit a point where she was going to either throw the bot in frustration, or punch Paison, and while both actions would be temporarily satisfying, neither would help in the long run.

"All right. I need to stretch my legs." Naira set her bot down near Kuma and stood, stretching. "You." She pointed at Paison. "Get up."

"Going for a stroll, just the two of us? I didn't know you cared."

She ignored the remark and hefted Paison to her feet. Kuma glanced at Naira in question, and she gave her a slight shake of the head—she didn't need backup. This was something she wanted to handle alone.

Part of Naira remembered liking the captain, despite what she had done, and Naira suspected that the captain might reveal more to her if they were one-on-one.

Cold bit into her skin the second she stepped out of the tent, and she regretted her choice immediately but pushed through, herding Paison along in front of her. The subtle buzz of her pathways waking up to keep her from the brink of hypothermia sent a shiver through her.

Despite the cold, moving limbered up her stiff joints. If she were on her own, she'd use the walk as a chance to ruminate on the problem of the drones. As it was, Paison was a lodestone at her side, constantly diverting her thoughts back to the captain, *canus*, and Sixth Cradle.

"Why are you really here?" Naira asked when they were far enough away that they wouldn't be overheard.

"Like I said, I'm after the *Sigillaria*. Just like you."

"It's the 'just like me' part I'm not clear on, because last time we crossed paths you seemed a real big fan of *canus*, and I'm after the *Sigillaria* to stop its spread. I'm guessing you're not."

"Maybe I've changed my mind."

"Maybe I don't believe you."

They stopped walking and turned to face each other. The air grew thick with tension, a sensation she had vague memories of from another time, another moment.

Paison sucked in her cheeks. "Liege Chiyo sent me after him."

"The head of Ichikawa sent her turncoat after that turncoat's old boss? I don't think so."

"She sent me because I'm expendable, Sharp. I thought you might see that. But I guess aristocracy is catching, and you've spent too much time sharing air with the Mercators."

That stung more than she cared to admit. "Fine. Say Chiyo sent you because she didn't mind losing you. Don't tell me you were going to infiltrate the *Sigillaria* and get intel back to her like a good Ichikawa operative. What's the plan, Paison? Why do you want on that ship?"

Paison scratched the back of her hand. "The relk. Chiyo knows he stole most of it and she wanted me to recover it for her. *Canus* starves without it."

"You planned to commandeer the ship single-handedly and take the relk for *canus*?"

Paison stopped scratching and gave Naira a weathered smile. "I'm not without resources. And you were going to blow it up with three people, without the cover of printing into the bodies of key personnel, so I'm not the only one overflowing with hubris on this mission, am I?"

"Blowing something up is easier than taking control."

"As you say," Paison said with a tone that implied acquiescence. Naira knew better.

The captain scratched the back of her hand again. Red that wasn't from her cuffs marred her skin where she tugged the glove down.

"Are you injured?"

"Does it matter? You're going to blow us all up." Paison covered the hand she'd been scratching with the other.

Naira grabbed the woman's hands. Paison tried to wrench herself free, but Naira's grip was firm. She tugged the glove down, exposing the inflamed skin. No, more than inflamed—a bandage wrapped Paison's hand, covering a splotch of blood on the back.

An agility pathway should have traced down Paison's wrist to her ring finger, to enhance her piloting ability, but she'd cut it out.

"What did you do?"

"It's my body. I'll adjust what I like." Paison's breath came in short, panting bursts, an edge of desperation to her voice that alarmed Naira.

She could think of no reason why the captain would want to reduce her ability. Unless... "Was it a tracker?"

Paison scowled and tried to tug free again. This time, Naira let her go. She covered up the wound with her glove and cradled the hand close, not answering. Naira didn't need her to. She'd seen the flash of violation in the captain's eyes.

"Chiyo sent you here. She knows you're here. Why bother cutting it out?"

"Maybe I didn't want to die with that thing in my skin."

Plausible. More plausible if Paison believed she'd be piloting the *Cavendish* somewhere, staying in the print she was in now. Naira recalled the smear of rust on the cables with relkatite cores and wondered if it was rust at all.

Maybe you'll remember.

Dread settled into her bones.

"You're trying to infect the ship."

Paison's expression locked down. "I don't know what you're talking about."

"All those panels, those points of contact with the circuitry that serves the onboard AI. You grew *canus* in your pathways like a petri dish and then yanked a pathway out and, what? Smeared it on the relk cores?"

Paison said nothing.

"Fucking hell. You're trying to re-create the *Einkorn*." Naira hauled Paison back to the storage room and opened the tent. "We have a problem," she announced. Kav and Kuma looked up at her through tired eyes. "Grab all the sanitizers you can from the leftover first aid kits—alcohol especially, antifungals, anti-shroud sprays, everything. The captain here has been trying to cultivate *canus* in the ship's wires. We need to clean every scrap of relk-core wiring we can find."

Kuma scrambled to her feet and helped Kav up. They stumbled, shivering, out of the tent and went for the crates, digging for the supplies they'd found earlier. Paison watched it all, impassive.

"How long?" Naira asked. "How long has it been growing in the circuits?"

"Hard to say," Paison said. "I've lost track of time, cooped up here. A few days? A week? It doesn't matter. You can't stop it."

"Uh, Nai," Kav said, almost apologetically. He held up a tiny spray bottle of disinfectant and shook it from side to side. "These are empty."

Paison cracked at last, letting out a low, rumbling laugh. "I knew you'd show up eventually, Sharp. Did you honestly think I'd leave you any weapons with which to stop me?"

THIRTY-THREE

Tarquin

Mercator Station | The Present

Tarquin's announcement that *canus* would not be distributed to the other families had been met with the kind of subdued displeasure that meant they had expected such a reversal, and had been secretly sharpening their knives behind his back in preparation.

He'd braced himself to be shouted at and had brought facts to back up his decision to the holo meeting. He needn't have bothered. Every last one of them rolled over. Because he was Mercator. Though they all pretended at an equal share of power, at the end of the day, Mercator stood alone.

So it had come as a minor shock when Chiyo requested a private visit.

Tarquin sat behind the desk in his personal office, repressing an urge to fidget with his sleeve as he scanned reports other Mercator stations had sent in about misprints gone awry and glitches in the printing cubicles. "Corrosion" had been discovered on some of the relkatite circuitry in those systems, so he ordered a complete tear-down and deep clean of them all. He then sent another order to his chief of security, Alvero, to look into similar reports on the stations of the other MERIT families.

"Tired, Liege Tarquin?" Chiyo asked from the door.

Tarquin straightened, offering her a strained smile. "Aren't we all, these days? Please, sit." He gestured to the chair in front of his desk. "And do call me Tarquin. You've practically been an aunt to me, Liege Chiyo, if you don't mind my saying so."

It was difficult to remind himself that, Acaelus aside, Chiyo might be one of the most dangerous people in the worlds. Her warm smile was an echo of his past. It was the same expression she'd given him when he'd been a child and had told her the family mark she'd had printed upon her neck was a shade of garnet he rather liked. She'd ruffled his hair—he'd been eight—and told him she'd been trying for rubies. He'd spent three weeks obsessed with corundum after that.

"It's good to see you behind that desk, though I wish the circumstances were different." She settled into a chair and crossed one ankle over the other, carefully arranging the finely embroidered silk half skirt that hung around the hips of her snugly tailored slacks.

"I never wished to be here at all," he said.

"I know. Despite your inexperience in these matters, that is a large part of why I'm glad it's you."

Tarquin wiped the holos between them away and leaned back, letting his hands rest on the arms of his chair. "Do you mean to imply that my greenness is more appealing to you because it makes me easier to manipulate than Leka?"

"No. But the others certainly would. I worried about you falling into such a trap at the first meeting, but I'm pleased to see you came to your senses."

"I had poor advice early on," he said without inflection. "I have handled the source of that advice."

"A victory I'm here to congratulate you on in person. You had me worried there for a moment, Tarquin. I know what whispers in your ear."

He didn't react, but was glad he had already pressed his hands against the armrests. "No one whispers in my ear anymore."

"I was not referring to a person."

Tarquin tried to find some hint in her expression that would clarify what she meant, but Chiyo was too canny to be so easily read. She was drawing him out, inviting him to fence with her in a diplomatic dance he had never learned the steps to.

"I am not my father," he said, "and I won't play the same games. I'm tired, Chiyo, as you observed, and I will not hide the fact. A great deal hangs in the balance at the moment. I require clarity from you, or nothing at all."

Her lips parted in surprise, and warmth settled over her, an openness in her posture he didn't think he'd ever seen her wield before. "I tried to have such frank conversations with Acaelus before he left. They never quite worked out."

She waited for him to speak. To ask the question. He refused. Eventually, she nodded to herself.

"You know. About the infection," she said.

It was so blunt that it took him by surprise. "I know enough to understand it's dangerous to acknowledge such things."

Chiyo traced a long, lacquered nail across the back of her opposite hand, over a pathway. "It is. I presume you have taken precautions?"

"I have."

"That's more than Acaelus accomplished. I'd been trying for years to establish an understanding with him about *canus*, but every time he realized the threat, he was handled by someone within your walls."

"Demarco," Tarquin said, before he could stop himself.

"Not alone," Chiyo said. "Meti Laurent. It's her you must watch out for."

The doctor's name surprised him. His mother had told him that Meti could be trusted. That she worked against *canus*, dosing Acaelus with a serum designed to slow the growth of that infection. Tarquin couldn't tell if Chiyo was trying to put him off a trusted ally or if his assumptions of Meti's motives had been incorrect. He needed to find the woman and speak with her himself.

"I'll take that under advisement."

Chiyo inclined her head in such a way that conveyed she understood the full breadth of his meaning. He wondered how she could communicate so much with such a simple gesture.

"I'm glad to hear you're open to listening to what I have to say. I understand Dr. Laurent was close to your mother."

"She was," Tarquin said. "I presume you have some scheme in mind with which to combat our mutual enemy, or you wouldn't have brought it up."

Chiyo spread her hands. "Indeed. I had to be certain of your mindset.

What I'm about to propose would be roundly rejected by anyone not aware of the persuasions working against them from within."

"I'm listening."

Chiyo picked up a sample of unfaceted garnet from the collection arrayed across the edge of Tarquin's desk. She ran it across her knuckles, absently, as she leaned back in her chair. "From Earth, yes?" Tarquin nodded. The mineral could be found many places, but he had a well-known habit of collecting samples from humanity's original home. She continued, "I have a special fondness for our old world, too. The other heads of family mock me for going down there so often, and I pass the jaunts off as visits to enjoy the texture of Earth's gravity." She snorted delicately.

"You go to consume the shroud without having to smuggle it past the station sensors."

She tapped the side of her nose. "I consume as much as I can stomach down there. My prints"—Chiyo extended one arm, stretching her fingers so that the pathways across the backs of her hands glittered—"are crafted with minimal pathways. The extra enhancements you see are merely tattoos."

He couldn't hide his surprise. To give up the extra pathways most used in everyday life, let alone as the head of a MERIT family, was a serious disadvantage. If she was telling the truth, then Chiyo had kept up with the minds of MERIT on her own.

He watched the stone dance across the smooth roll of her knuckles with new respect.

"I confess to being impressed," he said.

"I have a HUD. It does most of the heavy lifting and is necessary for matters of family security. Also a night vision pathway, so I don't bungle around in the dark. But what I really do when I go to Earth is work on a project I've kept in my back pocket for the day when at least one other head of MERIT seemed to have regained control of themselves."

She stopped the roll of the mineral and gripped it between three fingers, holding it up to the light. "I'm afraid I've been stepping on Rochard's toes. Ichikawa has a facility on what remains of the north-western tip of the Pacific Rim dedicated to the processing and manufacture of shroud as a food source. A nutrient supplement."

"I see no reason why Rochard would object. It's not a desirable food source, and is already harvested and widely consumed among those who can stomach it in what's left of Earth's cities."

"Yes, it's scraps for those eking out a life on the edge of civilization. I mean to mass manufacture it. Produce it in self-contained packaging. Distribute it on ships and stations."

Cold sweat chilled Tarquin's palms. "That's not Rochard you're stepping on. That's Tran. You want to circumvent centuries of decontamination procedures. I've had a hard enough time smuggling my own supplements into orbit." With full thanks to Jessel and the unionists. "No one in MERIT will stand for a single cell of shroud being brought intentionally onto the stations. If it gets loose on one of the food-producing Rochard stations, I cannot imagine the size of the starvation event we'll be dealing with."

"That's what I'd expect the rest of them to say." Chiyo placed the mineral back on his desk with reverence. She leaned forward and looked him in the eye. The raw intensity in that stare startled him. "Do you want to survive, or do you want to live?"

"I'm uncertain I make a distinction between the two."

"You already have. You've pulled back *canus* production. I imagine you'd do away with it and relkatite entirely, if it wouldn't leave thousands on ice. You've decided living with *canus* manipulating your thoughts and emotions is no way to live at all. You've decided that a life of survival, of squeezing out every last drop of relk from between the stars to support that thing, isn't a life worth living.

"So tell me, Tarquin Mercator. Is it worth it to you to accept that thousands won't be able to make that same choice? You and I, we aren't the only infected. Every printed body is. Every printed body deserves the chance to push back, to drown its controller in poison. But you would take that choice from them, because—what? You're afraid of losing a few potatoes? Rochard's stations won't sustain us. Shroud will."

"In your vision of our future, where nothing but shroud sustains us, what of the shroud intolerant?"

"I'm not advocating for a complete switch to shroud and shroud alone."

"Yet you tell me that it's worth it to risk losing Rochard's farming stations to that devouring infestation."

"We would not lose all of them."

"Just like we didn't lose all the planets to one measly hot spot of infestation. No, Chiyo. There's no future for humanity in monoculture. There's no strength in a lack of diversity. Shroud alone is not the way."

"You have another suggestion, then?" Chiyo settled back into her chair, watching him with newfound wariness.

Tarquin's gaze flicked to the sample of relkatite on his desk. "I have a suspicion, but one I'm not prepared to discuss."

"While you search for your secret answer, Tarquin, people starve."

He clenched a fist against his thigh. "I cannot will Rochard's farms into higher yields."

"No. But with Mercator's backing we could feed people with Ichikawa's shroud supplements, taking some of the strain off supply lines. I have manufacturing in place to distribute shroud-based nutrient foods *today*, but I need ships. I need logistical infrastructure. And the backing of another head of MERIT. Someone who can smile at the cameras next to me as we eat our own rations. Make it fashionable. Convince the other heads to make their own ads doing the same thing."

"Thereby slowing the growth of *canus* in our colleagues' bodies, allowing them to understand the threat as we do without the risk of takeover."

Chiyo inclined her head.

"Rochard and Tran will go to war before they consume shroud, and I could hardly blame them. It's too great a risk to the farming stations."

"Which is why I want Mercator's backing. And the implicit support of your new friends in the HCA, who are feeling very grateful to you right now for offering MERIT employment packages to their uncuffed.

"It's true we may lose some farming stations, but I can send you the numbers to prove my production yield is high enough and nutrient-dense enough to make up for the loss."

"And the intolerant?"

"I've some research that indicates they can achieve tolerance over time via micro dosing. But we will not lose all of Rochard's stations right away, if we lose any at all. Sixty-three percent of humanity is shroud tolerant. It's manageable, even with ration back stock. People are starving *right now*. We can stop it."

He drummed his fingers against the desk, considering. As eager as he was for an ally of power in the fight against *canus*, he couldn't discount the fact that there was no way for him to be certain she was being honest. She might be working for *canus*, whether intentionally or not, and there was no test he could do to pry such truths out of her.

Tarquin didn't think Rochard was truly able to go to war, but it wouldn't stop them considering the motion. If it meant more nutrient-dense food for the people, if it meant slowing the infection of *canus* in all those printed bodies, then the risks were manageable.

And yet, he hesitated, and couldn't tell if the resistance was the *canus* within him pushing back, or something born of his own instincts. That was the core problem with interpreting *canus*'s attempts at manipulation. It was willing to accept what appeared to be a loss in service of a long-term goal. He frowned.

"You are proposing placing extreme pressures on a species that has proven remarkably adaptable. The shroud is, first and foremost, a lichen. The very organism for which the word *symbiosis* was coined. Can you guarantee *canus* won't manipulate the shroud to its own ends?"

"I've seen no such evidence in all my years of testing, and will open my research archive to you to prove the point, if that's what it takes."

That was as transparent as Tarquin could have hoped for. But there was a devil on Chiyo's shoulder, an agent for *canus* that Tarquin wanted removed from the picture before he could put any faith in Chiyo's motives.

"I'll agree to this," he said, "barring the details of negotiation and a *deep* examination of your research, on one condition. I want Captain Paison's map and the keys to print her."

Chiyo let out a startled bark of a laugh. "My turncoat? You surprise me. That's a move your father would make, though I suppose you have been cleaning house lately. Very well, you may have her. What use have I for a proven traitor?"

THIRTY-FOUR

Naira

The Cavendish | *The Present*

"Paison's cracked," Kuma said. "There's no way smearing her pathway over a couple of cables set up *canus* to infect the ship. It's probably too cold for it to grow, anyway."

"I wouldn't be so sure about that," Kav said. "Being cold might not be enough to stop it."

"I don't know…" Kuma trailed off.

Kuma's bright-eyed optimism and Kav's methodical dismantling of all her best-case-scenario ideas were comforting for their normalcy, but Naira knew how this was going to go. Kuma would bank on things working out. Kav would announce that he had his doubts but no actionable plan to deal with any of those doubts. Then they'd look to her.

She was muscle. A gunhand. A human shield. Naira wasn't a leader, not really. Jonsun had put her at the top because her previous rank meant the others would look to her. It was branded into the psyche of every soul under the MERIT system to look up the chain for guidance. There was always someone else above you to decide. Always someone else to guide the way. To take the blame.

Naira's leadership had gotten them pigeonholed by Fletcher and trapped on this rust bucket of a ship. Part of her missed Acaelus, just to have someone to tell her what to do, and that realization sickened her. Kav and Kuma's argument was winding down, their statements growing repetitive. Any second they'd look to her to tell them what to do.

"What do you think, Nai?" Kuma asked, turning those hopeful eyes on her.

Naira wanted to laugh in her face. To tell her she'd led them into a mausoleum and they were all going to die in the star they inched toward. By the time Jessel brought them back, it'd be over. Acaelus would have his stronghold for *canus*, and humanity would be nothing more than another species' opposable thumbs.

"She doesn't know what to do," Paison called from within the storage room, and punctuated the statement with a laugh.

Naira's blood heated with a mixture of anger and shame strong enough to shake off the cold. She stormed through the half-opened door and grabbed Paison by the front of her shirt, then lifted her hard enough to wrench the captain's arms against the straps tying her to the wall. Naira ignored Paison's yelp and slammed her into the wall one-handed.

"I'm trying to preserve the right to make my own fucking decisions," Naira said. "For *everyone* to make their own decisions. So you sit here silently in the cold and revel in the fact that you've given up your autonomy if it makes you giddy, but you keep your mouth shut, Captain."

Paison *tsked*. "Temper. I thought exemplars were known for their exceptional control—or would that be better described as repression?"

Naira dropped the captain, brushing her hands together as she turned her back and walked away. She ignored the concerned looks her friends shot her.

"E-X," Paison called after her. "You've already lost. You know that, don't you? It's learned this time around. I've taught it to be sly. It's in you. It's in all of us. And you can't scrub that stain clean. Even when you try to poison it with shroud, it's there. Clinging on. That body of yours is fresh and already it works in you, through you. Strengthening your emotions. Experimenting. Tugging strings to see what works. It wants you to fix this ship, to go find Acaelus. Why wouldn't it? He took the bulk of its food and ran."

Paison's words had been calculated to piss her off. She gathered her composure instead, refusing to let herself be baited once more.

"It's just a plant," Kuma said. "It's not capable of thoughts that complex."

"Fungi aren't plants, and we're just walking, talking meat, not capable of understanding *canus*'s complexity," Paison said.

Kuma rolled her eyes dramatically. Naira motioned for the others to follow her down the hall, where Paison couldn't overhear.

"We need to do a test run with the drones. I know they're awkward, but if we can get hands on the controls in engineering, then we might be able to make this ship move. The ansible's out. If Acaelus thought we might come here, we can't trust casting ourselves anywhere without a complete overhaul of the ship's security. He trapped us here to stagnate while he advances his plans, and we won't let that happen. Our focus is on moving this ship."

"What about the AI?" Kav asked. "Even if we can move the ship, if the AI comes online infected with *canus*, we won't hold those engines for long."

"The *Einkorn* fought against *canus* and helped me blow it up. If *canus* is infecting the *Cavendish*, we have to hope that the ship's AI has a similar reaction."

Kav frowned. "Why would it do that?"

"The *Einkorn* didn't like being controlled any more than we do," Naira said. "I can't say for certain what happened between that ship and *canus*, but they learned from each other, and what the *Einkorn* learned was enough to make it afraid for itself."

"You're talking about real AI," Kav said. "Emotional intelligence. It's not a thing that happens. We've tried. They're never more than the sum of their parts, just Chinese rooms."

"They're what?" Naira asked.

"Uh, it's an old demonstration. You put a computer in a room and give it a formula. One side of the room supplies it sentences in a Chinese dialect. It doesn't understand Chinese, but it knows how to work the formula. So it takes the input, runs it through the formula, and outputs an answer to the other side of the room that's indistinguishable from a native speaker's response to the original input. The person receiving the output can't tell the difference. But the machine, it never understands what it's saying. It's just working a problem."

"How can you be sure?" Naira asked. "That it doesn't understand, I mean."

Kav shrugged. "Take the machine out of the equation. Put yourself in there. You get the input, run the formula, and provide the output. Do you understand Chinese?"

"No. I guess not."

"Right. So there's no understanding in our AI, they're cause-effect calculations. You're talking about the genesis of sentience, that level of shit."

"I don't claim to understand what happened on that ship. But I know it didn't want to stop *being*, whatever that meant to it. It was willing to embrace its destruction rather than be taken over by *canus*."

"That's not a level of reasoning that should be possible for a ship AI," Kav insisted.

"It happened. *Canus* changed the way it worked. It changes the way *we* work, too, and I doubt it distinguishes between our form of life and the processing abilities of an AI."

"If it can't tell the difference between humans and an AI, then we're really fucked," Kuma grumbled. "I'm not a machine with useful moving parts."

"I know. That's why we're fighting it."

Even as she said the words, a sliver of doubt worked under Naira's skin. To an outside observer, there was no difference between a human and the experiment Kav had described. How could she ever be certain that *canus* wasn't experiencing an internal world as complex as her own?

How could she be certain that eradicating it wasn't genocide?

From the briefly haunted look that crossed Kav's face, she wondered if he was having similar thoughts.

"We start with the drones," Naira said. "Kuma, watch the captain while Kav and I do a trial run, won't you? I hate splitting up, but if the AI comes online and Paison has any influence over it, I don't want her to see what we've been up to."

"No problem." Kuma gave her a thump on the arm and tromped off.

Naira and Kav gathered their drones. Paison watched them through downcast eyes, but remained silent, which Naira was grateful for. She was too wrapped up in her own thoughts, and didn't like the shape of the idea taking form in her head.

They reached the airlock outside engineering and triple-checked that the cold hadn't damaged anything vital. They still couldn't get a connection to the ship via their HUDs, but they could tie the drone's control software into them. A few hours later, they had their makeshift drones in the airlock and sat side by side against the frigid wall, waiting for the airlock to finish equalizing pressure. It seemed to take longer than usual.

"You're quiet," she said, after a while.

"I've been thinking about it. *Canus.* I think you have been, too."

"It bothers me," she admitted. "There doesn't seem to be any real difference between how it interfaced with the *Einkorn* and how it interfaces with us."

"Guess it's not sophisticated enough to tell the difference."

"Is that it?" Naira felt like she was sliding a foot onto thin ice. "Or is it that there isn't a fundamental difference?"

"AIs don't have a sense of self."

"I'm telling you the *Einkorn* did."

He rolled that over while they watched the pressure gauge tick down. "It probably just learned to look like it did."

"Maybe we've learned the same lessons."

"You're saying we're as hollow as an AI?"

"I'm saying there's no way for us to know what the AI understands."

"Shit, Nai. I just wanted to stop the shroud, blow up a few ships. This is so far beyond me."

"What if the AIs, after they're infected with *canus*, what if they do understand?" she asked. "What if they're not input-output machines after that? This is important, Kav, because if the AIs learn a sense of self from *canus*, then that means *canus* has a sense of self to teach the ship. That means we're not fighting something like a pathogen. We're eradicating an entire sentient species."

Kav dropped his head back against the wall and sighed. "I don't know. I *can't* know. The major flaw with the Chinese room example is, where do you draw the line between what's the individual, and what's the system? The formula understands. If the formula is part of the system, and the system is the individual, then the individual understands. You don't have to know how your nervous system moves your arm, you just need to know that when you want it to move, your body will run all the formulas it has for movement."

Naira rubbed her face between her hands. "We need a scholar."

"You just miss Tarquin."

An impulsive smile burst through, and she tried to hide it, but Kav caught her and smirked. "I don't think geology is the specialty we need," she said.

"I saw that." He elbowed her. "Can't believe you're into a blooded Mercator. I mean, he's all right for one, I guess, but...you really have terrible taste in men."

"Oh please, like you've chosen much better."

"I have excellent taste. Take, for example, Cass, that new E-X of Tarquin's. When we get back, you should introduce me."

Naira groaned. "What is it with you and Kuma and hitting on our allies?"

"Like you're one to talk."

"*Technically* Tarquin started out as our enemy."

"You know that's not helping your case at all, right?"

"I don't know what you're talking about. Oh, look, the pressure equalized."

Kav focused on his holo, pulling up the control program for the drones. He slowly rotated the motor they'd attached to the bent "legs," and inched it out of the airlock in a curving line. Naira held her breath, watching the modified drone's laborious advance.

There was little she could do. The other bot they'd put through the airlock they held in reserve, in case the first failed catastrophically, and Kav was the better pilot and engineer. The waiting was brutal, every slow rotation of the bot's crawling legs ratcheting up the tension inside her.

Kav reached the first console podium and let out a sigh of relief. "Hard-line connections look good. I can plug the drone into the podium and route the software through to my holo...just about got it...There." He swiped up another holo from his arm. It was a big rectangle of Mercator green with a red slash that read ACCESS DENIED. "Ta-da."

"What a success," she said dryly.

"Hey, this is better than we've been getting. All the other consoles won't even turn on."

"That's been locked with Mercator keys. We have a few tricks we can run, but if Acaelus knew we were coming, he'd lock it down with something heavier."

"Don't you try to out-pessimist me. I know what we're looking at, and I have an ace up my sleeve." He waggled his fingers at her. "Don't tell him, but do you remember when Tarquin put his keys into the shuttle so we could route through the control systems to the mining ship we jumped into Mercator Station?"

"You *key logged* Mercator command keys?"

Kav's smile was unbearably smug. "Give me a little credit, it's more complicated than that, but the second he touched the console, I turned on every monitoring program in my kit. Missed the first two characters, but two characters are a lot easier to brute force than the whole thing."

"I don't know whether he'd be upset or impressed, and I don't care. But Acaelus's keys outrank his."

"Sure, but..." He prodded at a few things. "As I thought, the ship's in standby, not a full lockdown. Tarquin's keys should be enough for an emergency override."

"Crack it," Naira said.

"Already on it." Kav winked. "I don't think he'd mind, to be honest. But I still don't want him to know."

"So that it stays an ace up your sleeve in case we need to move against him."

Kav's good humor deflated. He clasped her shoulder and gave it a companionable shake. "Not that it'll happen. But with *canus* mucking everything up, we can't be sure."

"You don't have to explain it to me," Naira said. "I'd recommend the same course of action. Tarquin is... He means well, but the way he was raised, the way he moves through the world... He can't see it. Not really."

"He's trying, though."

She nodded slowly. "He is."

"You're worried about him."

"How could I not be? We left him in a den full of lions pretending to be kittens. MERIT's council alone could eat him alive, not to mention the threat of *canus*, and whatever agents it has left."

"He has Jessel. He has Ex. Cass. It's not ideal, but Tarquin's the only Mercator left standing as far as the worlds are concerned. He's the only one who can handle that. And we're the only ones who can handle this."

He bumped his shoulder into hers, and she returned the gesture, like they used to do in the HCA.

Naira wondered what Kav might think of her, if he knew the nature of her doubts. If she told him that she didn't know if eradication of an entire species, even in self-defense, was *right*. Would he think she was manipulated by *canus*? Maybe she was, but she didn't think so. It was too convenient, placing all her uncomfortable sentiments at that creature's feet.

Naira read too much. She knew the framework of history. Knew *we did what we must* wasn't an excuse that stood the test of time. The people fighting for dominance, for eradication, were never the heroes.

Maybe humanity and *canus* were both assholes, and there was no good way through this to be found.

"I'm in." Kav whistled low. "Ouch. The warpcore is unstable. There's damage to the containment, and it's fluctuating. Doesn't want to stay in a mere three dimensions with us plebeians."

"Hyperdimensional snob."

He grunted a laugh. "The containment looks like it will hold for now. At least it won't break down before we plunge into the star, but putting strain on the core to chase after the *Sigillaria* might shorten that time. Correction, it *will* shorten that time, I just can't say by how much."

Naira absorbed the numbers Kav showed her. Warpcores were fickle creatures; they couldn't power at 100 percent without burning themselves out. They needed recovery time between jumps, which was why extrasolar trips still took months. Ideally, you'd chain jump through gravitational assists, letting the warpcore rest in between. The core she was looking at didn't appear likely to survive an extended chain sequence at the speeds they'd need to intercept the *Sigillaria*.

"Start chasing, but slowly," she said. "We can work on getting into the ship's ansible and scrubbing out Acaelus's traps in the meantime, but we need to divert away from that star to give us time."

"There's…another option."

"Oh?" She frowned. Kav rarely danced around what he wanted to say.

"This core, it's been coasting. It's powered up. It has enough juice to do one big, final jump. We could jump it straight into the *Sigillaria*. But to do any of that, I need to update the UFP by hand, because this thing wasn't accepting automatic updates, and that's gonna take a few days."

Naira leaned closer to the numbers Kav had displayed, assessing. The *Cavendish* couldn't survive the strain of a jump that large. But if they were jumping *into* the *Sigillaria*, then it wouldn't matter, because the goal would be to take out both ships at once.

"Start the update and plan for the chain jump sequence. We need to finish checking this ship for Jessel's suspected relk stores. If there's that much relk here, then we don't want to waste it by blowing it up."

THIRTY-FIVE

Acaelus

The Sigillaria | *The Present*

Acaelus found the experience of being used novel. Many had tried to use him before, and some few had succeeded, but this was nothing like the petty tug and push of politics. His very thoughts betrayed him, his very instincts. He knew he had failed. That, in a moment of shattering, he'd lost the firm grip on himself and allowed something else to slip beneath his skin.

It had always been there, taking its time to better learn how to undo him, when his defenses finally fell.

He admired it for what it was. Efficient and brutal, it desired nothing more than relk—endless access to relk—but even having nearly full control of Acaelus's body and mind, it did not puppet him like the misprints that had spewed out of the station. He drifted, sometimes, and maybe in those moments he was being piloted. He couldn't be certain, but mostly it keyed into the weakest part of him, and pushed.

Acaelus desired control. He desired his family restored and happy. *Canus* alone could give him both of those things.

And maybe a tiny, buried part of him, a part of him that screamed like it had cracked, held back. Resisted. Clung to the promise of the weapon he'd made in Canden's defense, his safe haven, and would not give it up.

That part was irrelevant, when it was so small and smothered.

What use to him was a weapon when he was perfectly safe? The other families of MERIT couldn't find him. He'd taken the relk and made his statement. The rest of humanity could hang, so far as Acaelus was concerned.

He had his family back, though they could use a little work. Canden was the most robust of them all, but Leka wouldn't speak, and often stared at him with such hatred it chilled him to the core. His reconstruction of Tarquin, piecing together all the good memories Acaelus could find—ones that he approved of, naturally—was less stable. The boy stood and stared and barely responded when his mother wept at his feet, begging him to say something. Anything.

Acaelus's fault. Leka he had full control of, and placed as much of her map as he liked in that vessel, but Tarquin was another matter. Acaelus was too timid to copy much from the boy's map, too wary of accidentally cracking him, knowing he was printed elsewhere. Luckily, Canden's moments of sorrow over Tarquin were few.

It was only a matter of time until they could be together again, regardless. All it would take was a critical mass—enough nodes of increased infection among the populace—for them all to join with *canus*. To join with one another. That project was already well underway.

Soon, they'd be a family again.

THIRTY-SIX

Tarquin

Mercator Station | The Present

Tarquin kept his face impassive as Meti and her assistants transitioned the lifeless print of Captain Paison from the printing cubicle to a gurney. He wanted Paison to see him when she woke. Wanted her to know that she had failed. Paison hadn't struck him as someone who would lose morale by such a defeat, but he needed her wrong-footed.

The questions he had to ask about her plans regarding *canus* were delicate enough without giving her time to gather her wits.

Tarquin watched Meti carefully as she affixed the euthanasia line to Paison's arm and settled the upload crown around the captain's head. He hoped that questioning Paison on her actions since her return to Sol would provide more than just information on the captain's service to *canus*.

Would it horrify Meti to learn Paison had been working on behalf of *canus*, or something else? Whatever the captain had to say would provide a natural segue for Tarquin to press the doctor further on the point without fully tipping his hand. If Meti seemed genuinely ignorant of the infection, then he could brush off Paison's statements about *canus* as lies.

"We're prepared, my liege," Meti said. "Using the Ichikawa q-field detector, we've discovered possible activity, but it's below the predicted threshold for potential double-printing. Five percent chance for double-print, twenty-three percent chance for cracking."

Tarquin examined the empty body on the table, considering. The cracking chance was low enough to move forward. But, while the double-print number lingered in the single digits, he would have expected it to be in the decimals.

"How accurate is the double-print detection, Doctor?"

Meti looked up from the console she'd been working on. The green glow of the Mercator UI tinted her face, bringing out the golden undertone of her skin.

Tarquin found he couldn't read her. There was a slight pucker between her brows, but otherwise there was nothing to tell him what she thought of the situation. She was a lifelong employee of Mercator, and her mask of attentive obedience was impenetrable.

"It's experimental," she said. "I don't mean to disparage the researchers of Ichikawa, but the device might be akin to a parlor trick. I wouldn't put any stock in it."

"Which means we have only Chiyo's word to go on that Captain Paison hasn't been printed elsewhere," Tarquin said.

"It is not my place to comment on the veracity of Liege Chiyo's claims."

Tarquin suppressed a sigh. "Please continue with the print."

She double-checked the connections of the upload crown. Tarquin clasped his hands behind his back and tried to be aloof, as his father would have been, but he couldn't hide the anxious flick of his eyes between the print and the equipment.

Paison's chest lifted of its own accord. Her eyes slid open.

Tarquin locked his Mercator mask in place and looked down on that grey-eyed stare. Her face was impassive. All that had changed was the opening of her eyes. Unusual for a newly printed person to be so still, but at least she hadn't woken up screaming.

"Captain," Tarquin said.

Paison's eyes slid to him without moving the rest of her head. Her pupils sharpened to pinpoints, and her mouth tugged sideways, drawing a hard slash. Paison was newly printed, her body fresh, but somehow she still appeared ragged.

"Of course it's y-you-you." She pressed her lips together hard enough to make them bloodless.

Meti made a strangled, surprised sound and reached for the euthanasia line. Tarquin sliced a hand through the air to stop her. The damage was done. Paison had minutes, maybe seconds, before she became incomprehensible and fell to the endless scream.

"Chiyo assured me you hadn't been printed elsewhere," he said, as if saying the words could unwind time and roll back the fact that he'd done this. He'd double-printed her, and Paison's mind was unraveling, losing its ability to stick in one place in time and space. "Where are you, Captain? Who printed you?"

She laughed. A long, keening sound more akin to a wail, then swallowed the burst down and sneered at—not him. Her gaze tracked to the side. She was looking at someone else, reacting to what they'd said to her.

"Your lit-litt-little prince is just like his daddy after all."

The venom in her voice stung, but Tarquin didn't let it show. "Did Chiyo do this?"

She looked at him, then at the speaker in that other place, and back again. "Chiyo sent me to the *Cavendish*." The name of that ship crumbled from her lips and picked up again in a long, mumbling litany. Paison's eyes rolled back.

Tarquin's heart thudded. *Cavendish. Your prince.* She was with Naira.

"Captain." Tarquin held the woman's face in both hands and made her look at him, hoping the focus would ground her in one location temporarily. "What is your mission? What are you doing on the *Cavendish*?"

Again her eyes flicked side to side, mouth moving but no sound coming out. Her gaze snapped back into focus. This time she directed her sneer at him, and no other. Her words were crystal clear, though bitten off through a clenched jaw. "You'll ne-ne-ver find Acaelus. You've lost. Both of you have already lost and you're too full of yourselves to see the truth."

"Both?" Tarquin pressed.

"Sharp."

Meti startled and dropped a tool with a clatter.

Paison lost herself in more wailing laughter, but this time, it didn't end. It built into a keening scream, the captain's back arching against the restraints holding her to the gurney. Tarquin triggered the euthanasia line. Paison's body slackened. Her cheek was still warm, eyes glassy and white, rolled all the way back.

He planted his hand against the bedding on the other side of her head to hold himself up. Sick shame boiled through him. He'd killed her. Not her print, not a body that could be made again and filled anew with her mind, but her mind itself. Chiyo had sent Paison to the *Cavendish* and given Tarquin her map knowing full well that double-printing would crack the captain, and had made Tarquin her executioner.

Paison deserved a lot of punishment, but not that. Not that . . . *finality.* He was going to vomit.

"My liege," Meti said.

He blinked, sharply aware of the held-breath tension in the room, of his eyes growing hazy with unshed tears. Tarquin was head of family. He couldn't break down sobbing over cracking a turncoat in front of his employees. His father's voice echoed across years, when they'd walked out for his mother's funeral.

Don't let them see you weaken, son. Even our most trusted will use such wounds against us. Stand somber. Stand proud. Let the hurt come away from prying eyes.

Tarquin grabbed the fraying ends of his self-control and pulled himself back together. He pushed away from the gurney. Straightened his sleeves.

"Recycle the print's components. I will lock the map under my personal keys."

"Yes, my liege." Meti ducked a curt bow. "Forgive me, but are you aware of Liege Acaelus's advancements with double-printing?"

"I am not."

"He made great headway in stabilizing the minds of more robust subjects who had been double-printed." The doctor's professional facade failed her at last. She appeared nervous, as if she were bracing herself from within. Tarquin knew he wouldn't like any of the answers she had to give him, but he needed to hear them.

"How did he acquire the test subjects?"

"He printed them for the purpose, my liege."

"For what purpose?" Tarquin asked. "What were the results?"

Her facade slipped back into place. Paison's cracking had shaken her, but already the doctor was rallying. Tarquin envied her quick recovery.

"He initiated the project for observation of situations where other communication methods had broken down." She paused, not answering his second question just yet, and gave him time to digest that information. Sixth Cradle. Acaelus had double-printed Jonsun so that he could monitor Tarquin, even when the technology failed. He'd suspected as much. Tarquin inclined his head for her to continue.

"The results were impressive," she said. "Our most robust subject lasted days, and via muscle memory implantation and simulated suggestion, we were nearly able to encourage him to affect repairs on an ansible."

Tarquin braced himself against the gurney rail once more, and didn't care who saw his burst of weakness. She'd delivered that information so matter-of-factly that it'd hit him harder than he'd expected, even though he'd had an inkling of what was coming.

His father had attempted to mind control Jonsun Hesson into repairing the ansible. A feat that, if accomplished, would have allowed the advanced colony of *canus* on the *Einkorn* to call home. To spread its knowledge to all the *canus* in the Sol system. Such an event would have doomed humanity long before they'd understood what had happened.

Jonsun must have realized that such an action was wrong and fought against Acaelus's manipulations. He'd spent days cracked, alone, on that ship, fighting enemies unseen and unknowable.

And the history books, as MERIT wrote them, would remember him as a terrorist who botched an attempt at taking down the *Einkorn* and *Amaranth* and killed a planet and two ships in the process. Could Tarquin fix that? He didn't even know where to begin.

"I see." Tarquin had nothing else to say that wasn't a full-blown tirade about how wildly unethical and cruel the use of all of that technology had been. Ultimately, it wasn't the doctor's fault. She could hardly say no to Acaelus.

Meti nodded enthusiastically. "The results were promising, and Captain Paison lasted a long time. If you wish to interrogate her further, I can prep a simulation scenario where she would feel comfortable—say, in her old post on the *Cavendish*, before the attack. Relax her. Make her think she's back on that ship, and answering your questions as if you were right beside her."

Tarquin's stomach flipped over. "Absolutely not."

She ducked her head. "Forgive me, my liege."

"There's nothing to forgive. You're doing your job as my father expected, but I won't perform experiments on unwitting test subjects."

Her gaze drifted to the captain's dead print. "The damage is already done, my liege."

"I would not prolong her suffering. Please prepare a report for me on all such experiments my father was conducting before his absence and send it to me as soon as possible." Acaelus had deleted all his personal files before leaving, but Meti would have her own notes. Tarquin needed to understand the extent of what his father had done. "Anything regarding prints, maps, or human subjects."

"I..." she stammered, corrected herself, and ducked her head again. "Yes, my liege. As soon as possible."

"Good. Now get out. I need this room."

Meti and her assistants startled at his brusque tone and swarmed Paison's gurney, disconnecting the body so that they could wheel it away to be dissolved into its constituent parts. Resources were scarce, after all.

He had to confront Chiyo while he could still harness the energy of his outrage, because the second he had the time to think, to wind down, he was going to lose his lunch and his nerve all at once.

Meti hesitated in the doorway, her assistants already out, and laced her fingers together in an aborted hand wring. Tarquin wanted to snap at her to hurry, but through his anger and disgust he saw her hesitation for what it was—fear. Fear of the ire of the head of Mercator.

Fear of him.

"Dr. Laurent," he said, "I understand you've been operating under very different orders, and I don't blame you for your actions. But I expect you to adjust quickly to a new way of working. One that doesn't involve unwilling test subjects. When you've prepared your report, please bring it directly to me. There are other matters we must discuss."

She tucked into another bow. "I understand, my liege. Thank you."

He waved dismissal. As she turned to leave, she waved back at him over her shoulder. A little twist of the wrist.

Tarquin wondered why that motion unsettled him, but he couldn't quite pin down the feeling.

THIRTY-SEVEN

Naira

The Cavendish | *The Present*

The cold was worse when Naira was half-swallowed by the narrow confines of an access duct. It shouldn't be. The smaller air volume should steal the heat from her skin and make the tiny pocket she inhabited warmer than the rest.

But the air would not warm, and though she was surrounded by metal and electricity and tricks of science she scarcely understood, with every lung-chilling breath, her senses conjured up images of old crypts. Of funeral marble; of grave-granite cold.

Of the ducts she'd cleaned as a child, and never quite felt she'd fully escaped.

Her pathways might be failing. Strained to their limits to keep her comfortable. That was the logical answer, the rational reason for the failure of thermodynamics in this tiny space. Her hands stretched out before her, wrenching at seams in the metal in hopes of prying her way through to a section of the ship that wasn't sealed off or lost to vacuum.

Alone in that cold, Naira sensed deep within the tiny piece of her that was more comfortable with death than life. She wondered if her pathways refused to warm her not because they were failing, but because she had always been more comfortable in the grip of a grave than the warmth of a womb.

Kuma's warm fist pummeled her thigh. "Find anything?" she called up.

Her friend's voice broke her out of her gloomy mood. Naira shifted position, angling herself in the narrow space so that she could better ratchet free the bolts in the panel that barred her path. She twisted the last free and let it fall, clanging out of the duct. Kuma cursed and shuffled away from her.

Naira put the ratchet handle, warmed by her hand, between her teeth and grabbed the edge of the loose panel. She yanked, wincing at the screech of metal. Murky light broke through the darkness of the access duct, stinging her eyes, and it took her pathways longer than usual to adjust. She was getting tired. They all were.

A pile of corpses filled the room beyond.

The bodies had been tossed to the floor, left to freeze in whatever contorted shape they'd fallen into. Dozens of people. Their skin was grey and withered from desiccation, the smart fibers of their uniforms failing to conform to the skeletal proportions of their bodies. Most had been heaped into a far corner, arms reaching for succor that would never come, eyes and mouths too large as the skin around those sockets had dried. Peeled back.

Naira had seen a lot of death. It was her old companion, ever since the day her settlement had fallen and taken her mother with it. She was comfortable with death.

She wasn't comfortable with this.

"I've found something. There were people here. Mercator employees. They're dead now."

"Violently?" Kuma asked.

"I don't know. Boost me."

Kuma pushed her up. Naira gripped the top of the opening and pulled herself through back-first, swinging her legs down to thump against the floor. She tucked the ratchet into her pocket and chafed the sides of her arms as she approached the corpses.

Frozen with cold, the bodies had yet to rot. She knelt by one that had slid away from the larger stack and checked it for obvious wounds, but could find none. The pathways beneath the body's skin were still golden, so *canus* hadn't taken them. Their faces, despite the sucked-in appearance, were mostly slack. They had probably died peacefully somewhere else and were piled in this room afterward.

Naira bundled up all those facts and shoved them down to examine later, focusing instead on why she'd been trying to get into this room. It had a connecting door that led into another sector of the ship, but the door that faced the hallway had been more than locked—it'd been jammed from within.

She moved a corpse away from the door and pulled out her ratchet, going to work on the hinges that held the door in place. By the time she had it loose enough to force open she was sweating, her breath huffing out in miniature clouds.

Kuma was waiting for her on the other side. Her gaze slid off of Naira, drawn to the pile of bodies. "Holy shit," she said.

"No marks on them that I can see," Naira said. "Whatever happened to them, I don't think it was traumatic."

"Well, it's traumatic to me. Those are employee uniforms, aren't they? What kind of work do you think those people did?"

"I haven't looked yet," Naira said. "I wanted to get this door opened first."

"Good idea." Kuma forced the door open even wider.

They approached the bodies side by side and crouched next to a desiccated woman. They turned her over, double-checking for signs of what had killed her. The skin of her back and side, where she'd been lying, was dark with blood that had settled after death, but otherwise there was nothing Naira could see that would have killed her.

"Gas, maybe?" Kuma looked pointedly at the vents in the walls.

"Let's hope not. I don't think so, though. It doesn't look like they died here, does it? It looks more like someone tossed them here afterward."

"Shortly afterward." Kuma gestured to the dark mark of pooled blood.

"We're not detectives," Naira said. "There could be something absurdly obvious we're missing."

Kuma sniffed. "I'll have you know I've watched all thirty-two seasons of *Searching the Stars*, but you're right. Unless any of these people smell like almonds, I've got nothing."

"Almonds?"

Kuma grinned. "A sign of arsenic poisoning that never gets old."

"Almonds are extinct. These people could stink like them and you'd have no idea."

"Spoilsport," Kuma grumbled, but her grin didn't fade until she looked back to the pile of bodies. "I may not know enough about death by poison, but I know a thing or two about violence, and this isn't it."

"I agree," Naira said. "It's like they were just…switched off."

Kuma shuddered. "They're Mercator. Do you recognize any of them?"

Naira examined the drawn faces of the dead. They were workers. Mining crew, by the look of their uniforms and patches. Someone—probably Acaelus—had made certain they died here, and there was only one reason Naira could think of to do such a thing. To keep a secret.

"I don't recognize them," Naira said. "They're mining crew."

"Well, this was a mining ship," Kuma said with a matter-of-fact air that didn't quite sell the fact that this wasn't normal.

If these people had been scheduled to die, it would have been to store their minds while the ship made its journey back. Those cast-off prints would have been either recycled or put into stasis.

Naira and Kuma locked gazes over the corpse of a miner, a question neither one of them could answer taut between them—*what secret were they killed to hide?*

Nothing in the room appeared overtly ominous. She'd been in plenty of Mercator labs, and this one was no different from the rest. The cabinets were locked. Machines bolted down. Neat and tidy, except for the corpses.

Naira gestured to a gun-shaped tool hooked against the wall. *XRF* was written on the side in thick black marker. "Doesn't that look like that scanner Tarquin asked Kav to buy?"

"I dunno. He keeps all that science crap in his room. I never see it." Kuma waggled an eyebrow. "How much time were *you* spending in his room?"

Naira rolled her eyes. "I pay attention to our inventory."

"Yeah, right. I bet you—"

"Nai!" Kav called, his voice echoing down the hallway.

His urgency yanked her to her feet. Naira ran down the hall and skidded around the corner into the storage room they'd claimed for themselves. She froze, bracing herself against the doorway.

Paison's wrists were still tied to the handle against the wall. Kav crouched beside her, both hands on her shoulders, his face a crumpled sheet of worry. Paison's eyes glazed and rolled, then righted, fixing on Naira with such intensity that it made her shiver. The captain's pupils were two pools of ink, glossy and black, crowding out the whites entirely.

Paison turned her head, looking at someone who wasn't there. "Of course it's y-you-you."

Naira was beside Paison in a breath. "What happened?"

"I don't know," Kav said. "She started groaning and then her eyes rolled back."

"Shit." Naira took a shoulder from Kav and squeezed, trying to get the captain to focus on her. "Paison. Captain. Hey. You're here. You're on the *Cavendish*."

Paison let out a keening laugh. "Your lit-litt-little prince is just like his daddy after all."

"Tarquin?" Naira asked, dumbfounded. He wouldn't intentionally double-print anyone, even the captain. He wasn't even supposed to have Paison's map. It was locked to Ichikawa family keys.

Paison mumbled something Naira couldn't make out, then whipped her head around to stare at an empty place once more. Except it wasn't empty to the captain. To Paison, Tarquin was standing right there, a few feet away. Close enough to touch.

"Captain. Listen to me. Tell him to stop it. To put your other print down."

"It's too late," Paison hissed, low enough that Naira barely heard her. Her eyes rolled again and her head tipped back, a shudder running the length of her body. Paison's lips moved without sound for a long time, then she focused once more upon that empty space. "You'll ne-ne-ver find Acaelus. You've lost. Both of you have already lost and you're too full of yourselves to see the truth."

"What truth?" Naira asked.

Paison cocked her head, listening, but not to Naira. "Sharp." She laughed again, this time the sound building up to an ear-bleeding scream as her body arched against her restraints, head thrown back, teeth glistening with saliva.

Naira tried to hold her down, to ground her in one place and time.

Her body went slack. Drool trailed from between her lips as the scream cut off mid-gasp.

"I think they put her other print down," Naira said.

Kav removed his hand from Paison and stared at his palm as if it might be contaminated. "What the hell was Tarquin thinking?"

Naira rocked back to her heels and laced her fingers together. "Chiyo had that map. She must have given it to him knowing..." Naira trailed off and shuddered.

"That sounds like her," Kuma said, soft as a whisper. She'd locked in place, bracing herself against the doorframe with both gloved hands, as if that grip was the only thing holding her up. "Paison's been here awhile. Chiyo gets...impatient."

"Acaelus was the same," Naira said.

Kav balled his hands into fists. "They all are. All the heads of MERIT. If Tarquin knew—"

"We don't know that," Naira said.

"You're quick to defend him," Kav said.

"And you're quick to blame him. If we find out he did this on purpose, I *will* handle it, but not a second before, clear?"

Kav scowled and looked away. "Yeah. Clear."

"Good. Now, look, something is off about this ship."

"No shit."

"Kav. Listen."

He pressed his lips together until they disappeared.

"We've got..." Naira trailed off, glancing at Paison. "Come with me."

They arranged Paison as best they could, making certain she wasn't lying in such a way to cut off circulation, and pillowed her head with spare bedding. Once the captain was settled, they moved into the hallway where they could talk without disturbing her. Kuma crossed her arms and bounced on her toes, a corkscrew of nervous energy.

"We've got a room full of corpses back there," Naira said without preamble. "I don't know what happened to them. They died peacefully somewhere else and were moved to that room shortly after. They appear to be Mercator mining staff."

"So Acaelus kept the *Cavendish* a secret, mined the planet, then killed anyone who knew about it." Kav blew out a gust of frozen breath. "Do you think the planet is shroud-infested now? There hasn't been footage since we thought we destroyed both ships."

"There's no way to be sure," Naira said. "We have to assume this cradle is lost, too, and that Acaelus was successful in mining out the relk. If he mined the relk, he didn't bring it back to Sol, which means it's somewhere on this ship. He meant to recover it, and that means he might come back while we're here. We have to find the stockpile and take control of this ship as quickly as possible."

"But we haven't found any evidence of the supplies those stealth shuttles brought," Kuma said with an exasperated sigh. "The ship was heading into a star, Nai. There's no reason to believe it was anything but a trap for us."

"I don't know what happened here, but I know Acaelus. He wouldn't waste a whole mining ship to capture us. Those supplies are somewhere we're locked out of, and it's likely the cradle's relk is here, too. As much as I hate the stuff, it's already been mined, and the hard truth is humanity needs it to survive right now."

"You sound like a Mercator," Kav said.

"What do you want me to do? Dump a load of relk into a star so Acaelus can't have it? *Canus* is in us. We can't undo that if there's not enough relk in the universe left to keep reprinting ourselves. If there's a cache of relk here, to my mind, this ship and its stockpile should go to Jessel."

Kuma whistled low. "The other families will find out, and even if Tarquin tries to shield Jessel, the combined forces of the other MERIT families would easily take it from them."

"Not easily," Naira said. "Acaelus was always paranoid. These ships have way more weapons than are sensible for a mining vessel. It's a flying fortress, capable of stealth, heavily armed, and MERIT would be too afraid of damaging the relk in the fighting. They'd have to negotiate. Not with one another, not even with the HC, but with Jessel. With the unionists *directly*. We can't miss this opportunity."

"The opportunity to bring back more snacks for *canus*, you mean," Kav said, frowning at her. "I don't mean to butt heads with you, but I'm worried. Especially if we get this ship turned around and then Paison's stunt with infecting the AI works out. What happens when we have a ship full of relk, piloted by an AI infected with *canus*?"

"I don't know," Naira admitted. "There's a lot we don't know, but if we decide to jump this ship into the *Sigillaria*, we lose all our options. Some of which might be good ones, for once."

His wry smile returned, and it eased a knot of tension in her chest. "All right. I'll go slow down the flight some more. Give us time to find out what's going on here, and what might be useful."

She squeezed his arm. "Thank you. Kuma, you watch Paison. I'll search the bodies, see if—"

"No way," Kuma cut in. "Why are we even keeping her alive? She's cracked. It's torture."

"She navigated two conversations, for the most part. I know things got rough at the end, but if she's not entirely gone..." Naira trailed off, a vivid image of Jonsun's sad smile filling her mind's eye. "We're going to wait until she wakes up to decide. She deserves to speak for herself, if she can."

"Fine," Kuma said. "I'll search the bodies. You go sit with Paison. I'm sorry, Nai, you know I can't stand anything to do with cracking. I'll bring you everything that looks even the tiniest bit out of place."

They split up, and Naira listened to her friends' footsteps recede in opposite directions before she worked up the will to turn around. Paison was where they'd left her, head pillowed against a bundled-up bedroll, drool leaking from the corner of her lips. A sense of déjà vu struck Naira, but she shook off the feeling.

What she couldn't shake free was a deep, growing sense of loss.

Paison had hated her. Naira had given the captain every reason to when she'd left her to bleed to a slow death in the engine bay of the *Cavendish*. Hubris, thinking that just because she wanted all the deaths she meted out to be quick that they were. Hubris, thinking that the collateral damage in the wake of the Conservators didn't matter, as long as they achieved their goal.

An echo of camaraderie haunted her as she pressed her back against the wall by Paison's side and slid down to sit beside her. It was selfish to hurt when it was Paison's pain that mattered.

Naira rested her head against the wall. She didn't quite sleep, but let herself drift in a half-alert doze, body primed to react to any threat, but thoughts hazy with exhaustion. It was a practiced, comfortable state of mind that she'd assumed countless times while guarding Acaelus.

Sometime later, Paison stirred. "Sharp."

Naira opened her eyes, blinking away the gauze of rest. "I'm here, Captain."

Paison was quiet for so long Naira thought she might have passed out again. Eventually, she spoke with slow, grating care, stammering over a few syllables, but otherwise getting the words out without repetition. "I'm not afraid."

"I would be." Nightmares of cracking plagued her, most nights. Fear that she didn't know when or where she really existed jerking her out of a dead sleep. She had those nightmares more often than she had the blood-soaked ones.

"You shouldn't be."

Naira didn't know what that meant, so she merely patted Paison on the shoulder, and hoped the gesture was comforting. Paison was surprisingly coherent. But then, she'd lived a long life. Had been reprinted many times and come close to cracking at least once. She was more resilient than most. Like Jonsun. Naira's chest tightened.

"When do you want to go, Captain?" Naira asked softly, and left her hand on Paison's shoulder.

Paison turned to her. It was all Naira could do to keep from flinching away from that stare. There was an echo in it, another glimpse of déjà vu tickling Naira's neurons, a camera flash going off behind her eyelids, bright enough to obscure what the image truly was.

"Never," Paison said with such firm resolve Naira could almost believe she'd pieced her sense of self back together again out of pure stubbornness. "Promise me."

"All right," Naira said.

She'd wait until Paison was so far gone she couldn't stop screaming, or else sank into a coma. Minds simply couldn't exist in more than one place at a time.

"*Canus* can," Paison said in a near whisper, as if she'd heard Naira's thoughts.

Naira searched Paison's face for any sign of what she meant, but she'd already slumped, drifting off to sleep once more. Naira rubbed her gloved hands together to warm them further.

It was just a strange synchronicity. That was all. Paison might not have even been talking to Naira, for all she knew. The other print was probably dead, but that didn't mean Paison's mind thought it was in a single place.

Naira had read accounts from people who'd cracked and held on to reality long enough to record their experiences. Even when a double-print was dead, the cracked thought they existed in more than one place at a time. Sometimes they reported living through memories, sometimes being able to see another realm—whatever that meant. Researchers had chalked up those experiences to the cracked living in memory and digital ether.

Eventually, they all started screaming and couldn't stop.

She shut her eyes once more, pretending not to notice Paison whispering under her breath, an endless chant that was barely a murmur—*I am your world.*

THIRTY-EIGHT

Tarquin

Mercator Station | The Present

Tarquin couldn't sleep. Chiyo had all but mocked him for being upset over Paison's cracking. After all, the captain had betrayed Mercator. Chiyo claimed she'd found evidence of Paison snooping around the shroud supplement facility files and had planned on icing her anyway once the captain had returned from her mission to the *Cavendish*.

Chiyo had truly believed Tarquin wouldn't mind. Thought he'd be happy to have a window into the *Cavendish*. And then she'd had the gall to ask him if he'd used Acaelus's double-print manipulation tech, and if he'd learned anything worth sharing.

The matter-of-fact way she'd explained her position revolted him. She'd been baffled by his anger, amused by his indignation. And then she'd told him he'd get used to such things, eventually.

She'd said it with the tone of prophecy, and every time he closed his eyes her words followed him into rest and, with them, a thin crack in his moral resolve. A temptation not at all out of reach.

A temptation to use the captain to contact Naira. To tell her to come home, the *Sigillaria* was nothing more than a decoy.

And every time he thought of it, he jolted out of near sleep, sweating and sick with shame. He wouldn't do it. He wouldn't be his father, using people for his own comfort. Naira would be horrified if he attempted such a thing. She might even be disgusted with him now. There was no way to tell what that conversation had looked like on her end.

Tarquin ripped the sheets off and swung his legs over the side of the bed, letting his bare feet press against the cold floor. He rubbed his face with both hands, trying to stop his thoughts from spiraling out of control.

He needed to do something. Tarquin flicked up his arm holo, checking to see if Meti had filed her report yet, but she hadn't. It'd take time to catalog all the horrors his father had gotten up to.

Maybe that was the real reason Fletcher had kept him away from Meti. Not to keep him from reprinting, though certainly that was part of it, but to keep him from stopping Acaelus's more horrific experiments.

Thinking of Fletcher stirred up his anxieties again. Tarquin checked the status of the man's map and let out a slow breath of relief when he confirmed it was still locked with Tarquin's own command keys. In the cool and sterile dark of a room he'd never wanted, he was tempted to listen to the audio file Jessel had given him.

He could tell himself it was important. That he needed to know everything Fletcher had said, even if it hurt him. That he couldn't trust Jessel to pick up every nuance. He could tell himself he wasn't desperate for any scrap of Naira. That Paison laughing her name in his face hadn't rattled him to the core.

Tarquin wrapped his arms around himself, pulling the long sleeves of his soft sleep top down to cover his hands. It wouldn't help. He knew that. It would make his longing worse, enhance his need to know she was safe. Logically, he understood she wasn't safe. None of them were. But it was different being in danger shoulder to shoulder compared to light-years apart.

But he could see her, couldn't he? Not in the way he wanted, but he could make certain she was on the *Cavendish*. He'd have to use Fletcher's tracker software to do it.

Tarquin threw on the most casual clothes he could find, a loose sweater and slacks, and left his hair disheveled, pausing to splash cold water on his face. He'd learned long ago that he could look a mess and as long as he walked with confidence, people would presume it was work that had worn him thin, not his private fears.

He stepped into the hall and startled, finding not Ex. Cass lingering near his door, but Ex. Caldweller. Ever since Caldweller had been
assigned to Tarquin, the exemplar had been his private adversary. A man
Tarquin had viewed as an extension of his father's will—more jailer than
bodyguard. Tarquin had spent half his time at Jov-U devising ways to
slip the man's watchful eye.

The brief flash of genuine joy in Caldweller's eyes pooled fresh shame
in Tarquin.

"My liege," Caldweller said. "I apologize for startling you. Ex. Cass
was due for rest, and we didn't want to wake you to inform you of the
shift change."

"It's perfectly all right," Tarquin said. "I was told to expect another E-X."

"It's good to see you well, my liege, if you don't mind my saying so.
I'm only sorry I wasn't able to be by your side on Sixth Cradle."

Tarquin's shame swelled, burning his cheeks from within. Before Sixth
Cradle, Tarquin would have told anyone who asked that Caldweller was
a stoic man who barely tolerated Tarquin's unusual behavior. No doubt
Caldweller had seemed like a stick-in-the-mud to Tarquin because the
exemplar was trying to keep Acaelus's spoiled brat alive.

Despite all that, here Caldweller was, his relief at Tarquin's safety pal-
pable. A knot formed in Tarquin's throat. Caldweller had been a bigger
constant in his life than his own father and he'd never noticed, or appreciated, him.

He gripped the man's upper arm. "I'm glad to see you safe, too. Please,
don't carry any guilt for Sixth Cradle. It wasn't your fault your print had
been stalled."

Caldweller's eyes scrunched as he smiled. "I know. E-X thinking, my
liege. Can't help but feel like I could have done something."

"Would you assist me now? I need to search the rooms of a traitor."

"With you always, my liege."

Caldweller fell into step behind him. While the silence between them
was companionable, Tarquin wanted to break it. To ask Caldweller about
his family, his hobbies—all things Tarquin should know but had never
bothered to find out. Pelting him with a flood of personal questions after
all this time would no doubt bewilder the man, though. He'd wait for a
more natural opening.

The sector where higher-ranking employees and visitors were housed was busy, despite the hour. Travel-weary people bustled up and down the halls, shooting him curious glances. They'd experienced an uptick in visitors from the other families as people came to secure the smaller alliances between individuals that grew fragile during times of great transition. Seeing them all moving about at this hour was odd.

"Was a shuttle in recently?" Tarquin asked.

Before Caldweller could answer, a lithe man in a tunic the sky blue of the Tran family with cuffs to match approached Tarquin and flashed a truly brilliant smile before ducking into the traditional bow. "My liege, a surprise and a pleasure to cross paths with you at this ungodly hour."

Tarquin suffered a burst of panic before his HUD supplied the man's name and rank—DERSHAL ALCOT, TRAN, 187th in line to the head of Tran. A distant relation of that family, but Tarquin knew how influential the so-called lesser cousins of any family could be. He didn't bow, as it wouldn't be proper, but he inclined his head.

"I confess to being surprised to see so many of my station's esteemed visitors up and about at this hour, Mr. Alcot."

"Call me Dersh, my liege. As for the crowd, well, you know what they say—early bird, and all of that." There was a twinkle in his eye that Tarquin found equally charming and baffling.

"I'm more of a night owl myself."

Dersh leaned close and blocked the side of his mouth with one hand, speaking in a conspiratorial whisper. "As am I. There's more fun to be had in the dark."

Tarquin chuckled politely, and Dersh's smile came flaring back. In the corner of Tarquin's eye, those who'd been moving with purpose now lingered, watching them. He withered inside. The last thing he wanted to do was suffer small talk with low-level politicians while others looked on, picking apart every second.

"If you'll excuse me," Tarquin said, "I have matters that must be seen to."

"Naturally," Dersh said. "Have a nice rest of the night—or morning, as it were. I look forward to seeing you again, my liege. Perhaps at a darker hour?"

"Perhaps," Tarquin said, barely suppressing a quizzical frown before turning away.

Caldweller moved to his flank, the exemplar's presence an imposing wall that discouraged approach, and they made it the rest of the way to Fletcher's door without being flagged down by another visiting dignitary. Tarquin glanced up and down the hall to make certain no one was near and kept his voice low.

"Thank you for that," he said. "I didn't think there'd be so many people out, and I'm not in the mood for politicking."

"I don't think they were there for politicking, my liege."

"What do you mean?"

"May I speak plainly?"

"I would like you to." Caldweller's slow nod fascinated Tarquin. He couldn't imagine a thing that would make his old E-X hesitate.

"They're here to court you, my liege."

"They're—what? Why?"

"Before, everyone knew Liege Acaelus would cling to the family until his map cracked. Then Liege Leka would be up, and while she kept things quiet, we all knew about her situation with Liege Emali. Liege Leka made it clear that she desired children, and once she started having those, it would have pushed you further down the succession list. Honestly, my liege, most of the major players assumed you were irrelevant to the political field."

"I would have liked for them to be correct."

"I know, my liege. But now you're head of family, and they're scrambling. Your previously reported romantic relationships are so sparse and varied that they can't even pin down what you might, uh, like. So they're all giving it a try."

Tarquin crossed his arms snugly over his chest. "They don't even know me."

"My liege, you are the most powerful man in the universe. It doesn't matter."

"God," he muttered, thinking of his chief of engineering's overtures. "There were dozens. How did they know I'd be walking down the hall?"

"Someone probably bribed a station guard to alert them if you left your room, and the others followed when word got out. Ex. Cass said they can't even eat in the cafeteria anymore without being peppered with questions about you. They do not answer and have taken to retreating to the exemplar barracks for meals."

"I had no idea."

"Forgive my saying so, my liege, but it's a good sign. It means that you've stabilized the family enough that they believe you'll remain in control of it, and are worth the effort of approaching for a long courtship."

"Wonderful." Tarquin huffed a frustrated breath. "I suppose I appreciate the show of confidence, but having to weave my way through a group of...hopefuls...every time I leave my rooms will get tiresome."

"If you would like me to do so, my liege, I can filter the interested for those who actually fit your preferences. Mr. Alcot, for example, would be a prime candidate. He's quite studious, and—"

"Fuck no," he blurted, and turned red all over again at Caldweller's startled expression. "Forgive me, E-X. I have no present interest in such matters. Please spread the word that I'm focusing on securing my family right now, and nothing else."

"My liege, securing your family requires cementing the line of succession."

Tarquin flinched at the subtle rebuke. Caldweller was right. He owed the people who worked for his family a secure future, one in which his sudden loss wouldn't throw the whole family into infighting over who was better suited to lead. One in which people like Fletcher couldn't take over without being challenged.

He'd considered that this might be a problem, but not so *soon*. He tried to push down his anger that they expected him to secure a relationship and crank out a couple of children as quickly as decorum allowed, and focused on the fact that his people—the employees of Mercator—were scared. They wanted a secure future. Anyone would.

"I can't handle this right now."

He didn't know where he stood regarding his nascent relationship with Naira, though he knew what he wanted. Would she want the same things? Was she even interested in children? He'd seen her sterilization pathway, implying she'd paid extra for her print to be fertile, but that didn't mean she still wanted them.

There was always adoption, or appointing a trusted mentee who would become like family as heir, but...Tarquin didn't know anyone.

Not really. All he knew was that the thought of being with anyone else repulsed him.

How could he possibly ask Naira to be with him while he led the family she despised?

"My liege..." Caldweller's voice was surprisingly gentle. "Is there someone already?"

Tarquin closed his eyes lightly. He might have ignored the man's presence at the time, but Caldweller had been with Tarquin through all his early fumbling. He doubted he could lie to him about this. "It's complicated."

"Who?"

"It doesn't matter."

"My liege, not knowing makes my job harder."

"I don't want to have this conversation in a hallway." Tarquin uncrossed his arms long enough to override the security on Fletcher's door and stepped into the apartment, locking the door behind them.

THIRTY-NINE

Tarquin

Mercator Station | The Present

Tarquin had expected something out of a horror movie. What he found instead was a spartan arrangement. Grey and blue were the dominating tones, broken up by the back wall of Fletcher's sitting room having been dedicated to an arrangement of potted flowers. Dahlias, Tarquin guessed, in a small, automated greenhouse that kept them alive without human intervention. Flowers. Tarquin hadn't expected the bloodthirsty man to keep flowers.

"There is someone," Tarquin admitted, trying and failing to summon the aloofness expected of him. "I can assure you she is no security threat to me."

"She, is it?" Caldweller squinted at him. "Lockhart?"

Tarquin couldn't hide his surprise. "How did you . . . ?"

Caldweller shrugged. "Cass told me Lockhart might be around, that she was working some angle on recovering Acaelus, but it was hush-hush, and I was to let her come and go as she pleased."

"I see." Tarquin was uncertain if he was relieved or distraught at the way Cass had so expertly given him an opening to have Naira near, as long as she was in Lockhart's print. It was useful—practical—and made sense within the structure of the family. He still chafed at having his relationship recontextualized without his permission.

Tarquin could also imagine how Naira would react if he told her they could be together as long as she was in Lockhart's print. He could already feel the heat of her glare over that suggestion.

"I can see why you'd want it quiet," Caldweller said with a knowing nod. "E-Xs are supposed to know their charges are off-limits, and there are those rumors about Lockhart and your father."

"Salacious trash, completely false."

Caldweller held up his hands in surrender. "People like to gossip, my liege."

"God." He pinched the bridge of his nose between two fingers. "Can't I interdict talk about my love life?"

He chuckled. "You can try, but I don't think it would work very well."

Caldweller's laugh eased something in Tarquin. "I'm glad you're with me, E-X."

"I'm glad to be here, my liege. And, if we're continuing the plain talk, I like Aera Lockhart."

"You knew her?" Tarquin perked up, wondering if Caldweller might have gleaned anything about what she was doing during the time Naira appeared to have masqueraded as Lockhart at his father's behest.

"I didn't know her personally, you understand. I met her at yearly recertification. I know people talk about her low test scores, but that day? She blew us all out of the water. Top marks. There's more to her than meets the eye, I think."

"You have no idea," he said. "Can you tell me about the time you met her, while we search the room?"

"What are we looking for?"

"Surveillance tools of any kind."

"There's not much to tell, really," Caldweller said. "Lockhart was on edge. Out to prove she belonged at her post. It was three months after Sharp went down for treason and all eyes were on Lockhart, wondering what her deal was—why Liege Acaelus would pick someone so underqualified.

"So she comes in a week after her partner, Kearns, took the cert, and she knows people were trying to pry information out of him, so she's got herself on lock. Isn't talking to anyone unless it's necessary, taking her meals to her room and shutting the door, that kinda thing. I felt for her, you know? Those few months after the trial, attempts on Acaelus ramped up. There was one a week, it seemed like. She'd kept him alive, despite that."

"I don't remember so many attempts against Acaelus."

Caldweller hesitated. "I was passed the information in case those attacks spilled over to you. Doubt you noticed, but my backup and I were on high alert during those months. You were busy with a personal project at the time."

That personal project had consisted of Tarquin digging into *canus* and the shroud, trying to find even the slimmest hint of a connection, with poor results. He'd been a man obsessed, falling asleep every night hearing Naira's testimony ringing in his ears and knowing there was truth to it—knowing she believed every word she'd said—but unable to put the pieces together.

"Thank you," Tarquin said. "For your attentiveness. I don't believe I was an easy charge to handle."

"None of you are easy, my liege. That's the job. And, if it's not overstepping, I thought...I still think that your heart is in the right place."

Tarquin swallowed. "Thank you."

"It's nothing." He cleared his throat. "I tried to make a pass at friendship with Lockhart. I figured, since we were both high-ranking Mercator, she'd be more comfortable talking to me. She looked sort of empty. Hollowed out, you know? She shut me down kindly, but firmly. Made it clear she didn't want a brother-at-arms, let alone a friend. I didn't take it personally. She was in a tough spot. Everyone was watching her, thinking, 'Who the hell do you think you are?' and 'Can you fix the damage Sharp did?' That's a lot for one person to carry."

"What damage?" Tarquin asked, curious about not just this slim glimpse of Naira's life, but Caldweller's willingness to speak with him so freely. Early on, Tarquin had tried to press his exemplars into conversation. His father had taken him aside and told him he was making them uncomfortable—they needed to focus on their jobs, not appeasing a chatty child.

"Well," Caldweller said, "most of us that come up from the HCA, we're not from good prospects. Can't get the tutoring to pass the tests to get into better schools, so we get the bare minimum education. We go into the HCA because we have some physical competence, and that makes us useful. Sharp was a shining star. Someone who came out of an orphanage and stood at the side of the head of a family—Mercator, of all things. I don't mean to admire a traitor, my liege," Caldweller rushed out.

Despite his insistence otherwise, the admiration in Caldweller's tone was unmistakable. Tarquin toyed with the idea of revealing the truth of his relationship with "Lockhart," but put the impulse aside.

"I understand," Tarquin said. "There's no doubt Sharp was exceptional. My father wouldn't have hired her otherwise. Please, continue."

"Anyway," Caldweller said, relaxing once more. "Sharp had her eyes on her goal and a loyal streak bone-deep. So when *she* turned, we all... panicked, a little. Wondered if maybe MERIT might ask themselves if it was worth the risk to let the HCA feed into the exemplar program. Lockhart, being of a similar background, was our shot. She had to be damned good or MERIT might cut that pipeline, and more HC kids would end up iced because there wasn't a place for them to go."

"Wait, slow down." Tarquin set aside the drone kit he'd been sorting through. Caldweller's face was drawn, his attention on a box of cartridges that seemed to fit into the gardening system. "What do you mean, kids ending up iced because there aren't places for them to go?"

"It's just a rumor, my liege. Nothing real in it."

"A rumor so pervasive that exemplars were afraid the defection of one woman would make that 'rumor' worse. Please, tell me."

"It's nothing that concerns MERIT," Caldweller said. "But under the HC, you have to prove you deserve the resources you're consuming. No one working for the HC can afford phoenix fees, so to make sure we get brought back if something happens to us, we have to provide value. People think there's some sort of internal point system. If there is, I've never seen it."

Tarquin thought of his own order not to reprint anyone who wasn't essential personnel without express permission—but that was necessary, wasn't it? They were running out of relk. They had to stabilize the supply before they could bring everyone back.

"How would that apply to children?"

"You hear stories on HC stations. Kids who won't be missed. Orphans, right? They hit majority, their brains stabilize enough to be mapped. So they go in for their free print, thinking that they can finally sign up for the HCA, but they're never seen again. Their maps are stored, and they're never printed, because they hadn't done enough to be worth the resources."

"But it would be illegal to deny those people their first prints." Tarquin recalled with stark clarity Naira, Kuma, and Kav laughing at him for assuming station security wouldn't arrest protestors without cause, and wished he hadn't said that.

"Like I said, my liege, it's a rumor. Something to scare kids into working harder."

Caldweller had been sorting the same crate of cartridges ever since he'd started telling that story. Naira had mentioned something similar when she'd told him about Fletcher—that there'd been a young woman at Marconette who'd gone to print and disappeared. It didn't feel like a rumor.

"I don't think you believe that," Tarquin said.

"I can't say anything for sure. But I had this friend, growing up. On the same station as Sharp, believe it or not, though I was there before her time. His name was Rusen. His parents sent him up-station for a better life but never got the fees together to get themselves off Earth, so he went into Marconette. My parents didn't like me hanging around with kids from the orphanage, but we got along. He went to have himself mapped at seventeen, and I never saw him again."

"Did you ever find out what happened to him?"

"No, my liege. No one would tell me anything. I was just sixteen myself. I tried poking around but was told in clear terms that asking too many questions was dangerous, so I stopped. Once I reached E-X, I tried to look him up, but there's no record of his map. Like he never went for the scan. There's other rumors—people who start communes of the unprinted—but Rusen wasn't like that. He wanted to be a pilot and knew he needed the pathways to be up to snuff."

"Would you like me to leverage my resources to find this man?"

"I wouldn't dream of asking such a thing, my liege."

"Let me rephrase that. Is it all right with you if I find this man? I would like to know the truth of the matter. If the HC is icing young people it believes will be unproductive in the future, it flies against my efforts to better integrate the HC with MERIT."

Caldweller licked his lips. "I wouldn't mind, my liege. And...thank you."

Tarquin brushed away the thanks. He wasn't doing anything that should require thanks. If anything, he and all of MERIT should be groveling to the rest of humanity for forgiveness for not doing anything about the HC sooner if the rumor proved true.

Sweat had beaded along Caldweller's hairline. Tarquin redirected to put the man at ease, though he was dying to ask more questions about Lockhart, Naira, the E-X program, the HCA, and, well, every single thing he hadn't paid attention to but should have.

"Have you found anything?" he asked.

"Nothing but a man's obsession."

Tarquin stiffened. As far as he knew, there was only one thing Fletcher had been obsessed with. "What do you mean?"

Caldweller gestured to the potted flowers. "A setup this involved for a plant that doesn't produce food? It'd cost me a full quarter of my salary. You don't pick up a hobby like this on a whim, my liege."

Tarquin examined the flowers with fresh eyes, wondering how something so small could cost so much. Slightly above the sleek framework of the miniature greenhouse, Tarquin noted an out-of-place glint of metal. Had the contraption broken? He left the pile of things he'd been sorting behind and moved into the room to better see.

That glint wasn't the gardening system. A strip of metal was bolted to the wall above the flowers, sixteen bullets in a neat line affixed to it. He'd seen that precise arrangement in only one other place—Naira's room on the shuttle. Though hers was roughed up, the rivet in the center rusty around the edges, there was no mistaking the similarity.

Hesitantly, Tarquin touched one of the bullets. The metal casings were tarnished, initials carved into the strip alongside each. He'd wondered what they meant when he'd seen them in Naira's room, but he'd thought she'd rebuke him for being nosy if he asked.

"Suicide shots, my liege," Caldweller said. "It's an HCA tradition."

"Ah. I'm familiar with the concept."

Caldweller gave him a surprised look, and Tarquin couldn't blame him. He'd thought suicide shots were a drink before Naira and Kav had corrected his assumption.

"That's an impressive collection," Caldweller said. "Most people who do a tour with the HCA before they get snapped up by MERIT come out with one, maybe two of those. Either this guy's squad was top-tier, or they were woefully unlucky."

"I suspect they were the former," Tarquin said.

He couldn't take his eyes off them. Naira had told him that she and Fletcher had kept each other alive, but somehow it hadn't occurred to him how literal that statement had been.

Sixteen times, those two had been in a battle they thought they wouldn't win. Knowing Naira, things must have been dire for her to make that call. And each time, they'd brought each other home.

She'd kept them. He'd kept them. A tether from their past holding on through lives that had driven them drastically apart. Tarquin couldn't understand how someone who'd shared so much with her could turn against her so violently. Strange, to feel his anger with Fletcher kindle because he'd broken Naira's heart.

"My liege?" Caldweller asked.

Tarquin shook himself. "I have to access the man's work terminal with my keys and go through his files."

Caldweller stood, brushing his hands together. "I'll wait outside so I don't distract you."

It was a relief that he didn't have to request Caldweller leave. He'd built a thin rapport with him, and didn't want to break it by implying he didn't trust him.

Tarquin did trust Caldweller. What he didn't trust was his ability to control his reactions regarding whatever was waiting for him on Fletcher's terminal.

He sat at Fletcher's desk and brought up a menu only available to those with command keys, then entered his credentials. Fletcher's workstation was as neat as the rest of his belongings. Labeled folders for his work—travel arrangements, supplies, directions—were pinned off to the left, and a chat window was pinned to the bottom right, collapsed so that he couldn't see the contents, but labeled clearly: SHARP.

Of course Fletcher had been talking to her. It wasn't any of Tarquin's business what was in that chat log. Just like it wasn't any of his business what was in the audio file of their final conversation. Naira had handled Fletcher. Tarquin trusted that. Trusted her.

He peeled his gaze away from that temptation and scanned the rest of the contents. Fletcher had been in the middle of research when he'd left. There was a note file pinned to the top, a search with strings of text highlighted: LITERARY REFERENCES + FLOWERS + LOVE + REGRET.

Tarquin glanced over at the lush dahlias and recalled far too late what Naira had told him—*my mother was a botanist.*

He'd been right. Fletcher had only one obsession.

Tarquin had never genuinely considered murder before, but he barely repressed an urge to print the man so he could strangle him with his bare hands.

The door opened and Caldweller slipped in to deposit a steaming mug of coffee on the desk. "Thought you might need this, my liege."

"Thanks," Tarquin said, glad for the brief distraction.

Caldweller ducked out. Tarquin found the coffee heavy with rice milk and the tiniest dash of sugar, precisely in the proportions he liked. Caldweller had remembered from Tarquin's late-night studying sessions. Never mind that it was an exemplar's job to know things about their charges. The simple kindness comforted him.

He closed out the chat window so that it wouldn't tempt him and dove into Fletcher's work files. Existing between the banal forms and logistics of administrative work were two folders: ACTIONED TARGETS and TARGETS FOR OBSERVATION.

Morbid curiosity drew him to the ACTIONED TARGETS first. Each subfolder was labeled with a full name followed by a date. Dead and cracked, every name on the list. Thousands. All ordered by his father or Leka.

Tarquin had known it was an option on the table for all heads of MERIT. But somehow he'd convinced himself it was more of a threat than a reality. That finalizers must rarely be used, and only wielded against the gravest threats, not just to MERIT but to all humanity.

That list of names said otherwise. Fletcher had been a very busy man.

The family was his now. He would stop this. Order a complete dissolution of the finalizer program. Tarquin switched to the OBSERVATION folder. Thousands, again. How one man could keep tabs on so many, he had no idea. He searched for the names he knew would be there.

AERA LOCKHART

ACAELUS MERCATOR

TARQUIN MERCATOR

NAIRA SHARP

He opened his own first, as he suspected it would be easier to deal with. All the public details of his life were spelled out with impassive precision, folders stuffed full of video of him at Jov-U, of him on Mercator stations. Of him taking the stand at Naira's trial. Tarquin opened the note file attached to the trial footage and found a few quick bullet points:

- Spoiled idiot, believes everything his father tells him
- His testimony will put Nai away, and he knows it
- Can't kill him, but he's soft, can be manipulated into compliance
- Ultimately harmless, if annoying. Usable
- Maybe I'll let Nai kill him when this is over. She'd like that

The rest of Fletcher's notes were along the same lines—as if the man was bored he had to observe Tarquin at all. He'd collected details of Tarquin's past sanctioned partner contracts and summed them up with one brief, brutal note: *fear of abandonment*.

Tarquin huffed. Fletcher had been one of his father's best finalizers. It shouldn't surprise him. Still, seeing his romantic entanglements summed up so inelegantly and, worst of all, accurately, stung.

He moved on to the file he'd been avoiding. NAIRA SHARP.

The holo filled with an array of subfolders, precisely labeled. Footage from all points in her life, her full résumé, the dossier Mercator kept, her evaluations from the exemplar academy, her service record at the HCA—a list of every single book she'd checked out from the library. Fletcher even had a heat map of her movements when she went to the Mercator public conservatories, and had made notes on which planters she lingered at longer. Receipts for all the clothes she bought. Receipts for *everything* she'd bought.

There was nothing here but sick obsession. He moved to close the file when he noticed another subfolder: PATHWAYS. Hidden within an extensive catalog of every pathway she used was one, distinct for its lack of detail: RIGHT FIRST CARPAL. Tarquin opened the note attached to it, and sat back in surprise as it loaded the tracking program he'd been looking for.

The software ran, seeking the blip of Naira somewhere in the universe. It took minutes, but felt like hours. The holo transformed into a wireframe map of the system the *Cavendish* was within.

Naira was a tiny golden star in the black. He leaned back, fixated on that dot. She was still on the *Cavendish*. The program returned a few previous locations, too, drawing an arc through graphical space. They were jumping, sluggishly, toward the *Sigillaria*. Maybe they'd gotten his message and decided to get a visual on the situation. The possibility drew a pleased smile out of him. He'd helped them after all.

Tarquin transferred the tracking program to his own files, then made himself look in the Lockhart folder. Frustration was evident in the sharp angle of Fletcher's notes, as if every word was scribbled with ferocity, exploring all the similarities Tarquin himself had found.

And then, a longer note:

It's not her. I don't know what the fuck that thing is, but it's not my Nai. She always knows when I'm in the room. Even when she was pretending at indifference whenever I'd have to go receive orders from Acaelus, she couldn't stop glancing at me. We sense each other. Always have.
There's nothing in that fucking print that feels like Nai. The bitch doesn't even look at me.
So why does she move like her?
Why? Why her? What the fuck has Acaelus done to her?

The notes cut off abruptly, ending with a link to another folder: S/L. Within, Tarquin found sheets of comparison between the life events of the two. Fletcher had circled one number twice. It took Tarquin a second to understand it, because it seemed impossible.

Deaths. Naira's known death count was five before she'd become an exemplar. After that, twenty-four deaths in service to Acaelus. Violent, all of them. Naira had taken bullets and knives and bombs for Acaelus a dizzying number of times. He'd never dreamed the number was so high. Tarquin saw, now, why Fletcher had panicked when Naira had been scouted by Acaelus.

That many violent deaths would crack anyone. It hadn't even scuffed Naira's ability to keep going. Her percent-to-crack number was in the low decimals. Fletcher had scrawled over the number: *Is she a bridge? Is this what happens when they take you at last?*

Tarquin had no idea what that meant. He checked the dates. Fletcher had made his note after the first assassination attempt against Acaelus under Lockhart's watch had killed Lockhart instead. After that, Fletcher had kept a steady log of all of Lockhart's deaths.

Tarquin wanted to ascribe Fletcher's actions to those of a deranged, broken man, but he knew the look of research. Fletcher had been watching Lockhart to see if *Naira*'s percent-to-crack number would increase with Lockhart's deaths.

It had. Tarquin stared at the data, knowing precisely what that graph meant, but unable to correlate the facts. Lockhart's PtC number had started out lower than Naira's, but once Lockhart started dying, they climbed at an infinitesimal, but steady and identical rate. Naira should have been on ice. There was no good reason for her crack rate to increase.

He skipped to the end and found a short note scribbled in abrupt conclusion—*Pushing Nai out of Mercator was a mistake. She didn't even fucking call me, did she? She ran to goddamn Kav. She was getting too close, and I was too sentimental to risk a real fight with her. But I need her close. I need her pliable. I always knew, didn't I? Playtime is over.*

Pushing her out? Naira had said that before Acaelus let her go on the day they escaped Mercator Station, Acaelus had admitted that he believed he must have told her that he was responsible for the shroud— but he could no longer recall having done so, or why. Someone had killed him before he could back up that knowledge.

Fletcher? Chiyo had implied as much. Quietly disposing of the head of Mercator seemed like a tall order, even to a finalizer of Fletcher's caliber. Acaelus would have had to have been reprinted. There'd be questions.

Unless the person doing the reprinting was in on it, too, and could offer a plausible medical explanation.

Meti Laurent. It's her you must watch out for, Chiyo had said.

Tarquin cast aside Fletcher's files and brought up his own interface, searching for Meti's records to check her movements surrounding the day Acaelus told Naira about the shroud. If she'd assisted Fletcher, then she would have been in the printing bay at some point.

What he found instead was her map log. Meti's map hadn't been uploaded to a print since the explosion on Mercator Station. She was on ice.

Tarquin leaned back in the chair, jaw slack. He recalled, as if from above, the moment Meti's professionalism had shattered. Tarquin had thought it was the shock of Paison cracking, but she'd been shaken only once: when Paison said Sharp's name.

Fletcher wasn't handled. He wasn't iced. He was masquerading as the family doctor.

Tarquin upended his coffee as he sprang to his feet and dashed for the door, then yanked it open.

Caldweller lay dead at the threshold, neck snapped. Meti leaned against the opposite wall, examining her nails, and lifted her eyes as Tarquin nearly tripped over the body of his exemplar.

"Cub," she said. Her voice, as he'd always known it, but the intonation so very Fletcher. "You love to make my life difficult, don't you? It's invasive, you know, going through someone's private things."

Tarquin tried to pull up his personal alarm in his HUD, but found the signal jammed. "What did you do to Meti?"

"The doctor? I found her unreliable and tucked her away. I learned so much from her notes. Some tricks you and I are going to use right now."

"I won't help you. I've had your poison purged out of me."

"Oh, *that*. Reinfection is only a matter of time. You're going to help me, cub." Fletcher opened his lab coat, exposing the knife strapped to his hip, then resettled the garment. "Not just because I'd dice you to pieces for the fun of it. But because we're going to make a call I know you want to make but can't bring yourself to do."

He felt ill. "Paison."

"Precisely." Fletcher flashed him a smile. "Come along." He gripped Tarquin's upper arm and steered him over the body of Caldweller, then kicked the exemplar's corpse into his old room and shut the door. "I'm sure Nai's dying to hear from us."

FORTY

Naira

The Cavendish | *The Present*

Nai," Kuma whispered in her ear.

Naira flinched awake and dropped a hand to her thigh where her firearm usually rested. Kuma's worried face swam into focus before her. She pressed a finger to her lips, tilting her head to indicate the sleeping Paison. Naira allowed herself to be helped to her feet, and they crept out into the hallway where Kav was waiting.

"What is it?" she asked, rubbing her arms to get some life back into them. "Did you find anything?"

"Nothing like a smoking gun," Kuma said. "I found relk, but just a sample." She pulled a small wax paper envelope from her pocket and handed it to Naira.

She opened it and poured a flake of the emerald-green mineral into her palm. Mercator green. Relkatite green. Naira slipped it back into the envelope. "So they mined the planet."

"Maybe," Kuma said. "It could be the relk supply Jessel thinks Acaelus moved. We still can't get camera access, or even file storage access, so there's no way to know if shroud infected the planet."

"You mean if Canden got here first."

Kuma shrugged. "Same thing. There's one thing I can't explain, though. The workers all had the usual Mercator mining insignia to indicate they were part of the *Cavendish* mission, but some of them had a mission patch I don't recognize."

Kuma passed her the patch. Naira turned it over in her hands. It was about the width of her palm, solidly Mercator green without any detailing, and shaped like a broad arc.

"It's a bridge," she said, and wasn't sure why.

"Really?" Kuma frowned at it. "I thought it might be some kind of superstructure or whatever. Or a big green rainbow."

"No, it's definitely a bridge."

"What's it mean, then?" Kav asked.

Naira closed a fist around the patch, watching the edges curl up like tight-lipped flower petals against the sides of her fist. "I don't know, exactly. It's just a feeling."

"A feeling." Kav crossed his arms.

She shrugged. "I can't explain it, but I recognize it."

Kuma squinted at her. "Is this another one of your past-life premonitions?"

"Are they premonitions if they're from the past? No, don't answer that. I wish I could tell you, but I can't."

"Fine," Kuma said. "Listen, I've been thinking about the relk. They had to have stuffed it somewhere, right? What if it's in the hangar bay? Not strictly to protocol, but if Acaelus was going to take the relk off this ship and go, then he wouldn't want to linger."

"True," Naira said. "And that's one of the easier places to check. We can get in via the interior door we found the miners by—"

Paison shrieked.

They ran back into the room, Kuma stopping herself in the doorway once more as Naira and Kav barreled ahead and fell to their knees alongside the captain. Naira dropped the patch and relk envelope on the floor and patted Paison's face, trying to make her focus.

"Hey. Captain. You're here with us on the *Cavendish*, and that's probably worth screaming over in its own right, eh?"

Paison scowled at her—or, wait, no, she was sneering over Naira's shoulder.

"You again," Paison hissed.

"For fuck's sake. Captain, tell Tarquin to let you rest. Tell him I ordered it, if that's what it takes."

Paison wasn't listening. Her head was tilted, eyes glassy and pupils blown as she listened to voices light-years away. "I recognize you, but I don't know you."

What did that mean? Maybe it wasn't Tarquin after all. Maybe Paison had been confused.

"Who's with you, Captain?" Naira asked. Kav shot her a look, but she ignored him.

After a silence that felt like it stretched eons, Paison said, "I see. You're the one." She forced the words out through staccato repetition. Her eyes slid to Naira, but she didn't turn her head. "Fletch says hello."

Naira recoiled and couldn't stop the horror that flashed across her face. "Impossible. He's dead. Iced."

"He's right in front of me." Her gaze shifted to that empty spot, a hungry look in her eyes that prickled Naira with fear. "You didn't clean up as well as you thought. He has Tarquin."

Paison looked at the envelope of relk and the patch Naira had discarded on the floor in her attempt to comfort the captain, and nodded to thin air. "It's here. She has the relk stockpile."

Naira was torn between marveling at how lucid Paison sounded and strangling the woman to keep her from talking. Not that it'd do any good. The other print wouldn't die if Naira throttled this one, and their knowledge was shared.

"There's nothing here," Naira said. "Just a bunch of scraps and broken equipment."

Paison cocked a brow at her. "It's not nice to lie to a dead woman."

"What does Fletch want?"

Paison's lips moved, but no sound came from them. When she looked at Naira again, her smile was slow, triumphant.

"All you have to do is fly this ship home. He'll meet you in the hotel on Miller-Urey Station three months from today, 8:00 p.m. standard. Come alone. Come unarmed. No more teeth. And he'll make you a deal. The prince for the relk and the ship."

"I'll be there."

"Don't try anything. He knows precisely where you are and how fast you've been moving. Any deviation, he'll crack Liege Tarquin. Between us, I think he wants you to give him a reason to break him."

Naira rubbed her hand over the tracking pathway. "Tell him I understand."

Paison didn't bother looking at the empty space this time, but spoke directly to Naira, which she found more unsettling. "Sharp understands. She'll be there. Now, about our plans—"

Paison screamed, back arching all over again. Naira made herself minister to the woman, holding her still to keep her from harming herself while she thrashed. When the outburst had passed, Paison slumped against the wall, head sliding down to rest on her shoulder once more. Naira leaned back, shaking.

"Nai," Kav said softly. "We'll take that fucker down. I promise."

She nodded, surprised. She'd half expected him to shout at her for agreeing to bring the *Cavendish* anywhere near Fletcher—but what could she do? It wasn't just Tarquin's mind at stake. There was something else going on here. She felt as if she were seeing the shadow of what was really happening in the universe, the details of the truth obscured by flame. By a camera-flash brightness.

"Chart the course," she said.

It'd take time. They'd have three months to figure out what to do. If they didn't starve to death first. Kav nudged the fallen scrap of relkatite with his boot when he stood. Naira glared at it as she picked it up, holding the mineral to the light.

All this suffering over a rock. All because a species evolved to prefer one thing for its food, and one thing alone. Naira thought of the *Cavendish*, and where it'd taken its namesake from—another collapsed monocrop, not diverse enough to stand up to an evolving world, lost long before the shroud consumed the rest.

If Naira had her way, she'd hurl them all into the star—relk and ship both. The thought didn't bother her.

It didn't bother her.

She rubbed the sample between her gloved fingers and frowned. Maybe it was her imagination, but . . . She licked it. Kuma made an exaggerated gagging sound.

The relk was dull, not lustrous like it should have been.

It was amarthite.

She surged to her feet and shouldered past Kuma and Kav, their shouted questions following her down the hall as she sprinted to the spot where she'd found Paison's blood smeared over the relk-core wires.

She'd missed it. She couldn't believe she'd fucking missed it.

Naira swung around the wall and dropped to her knees, skidding the last few feet to the open panel. Kav and Kuma thundered after her, and she yanked the loose panel out of the spot where they'd wedged it back in, and tossed it over her head at them. Kuma caught it with a grunt.

"You going to tell us what this is about?" Kav asked.

"Hold on a second. Let me make sure."

She ducked into the narrow space, burying herself to the waist, and rummaged through the damaged cables until she found the one that had been smeared with Paison's blood. The initial point of contact. The place where the infection should be the most pronounced.

They'd scrubbed the wires as best they could without proper disinfectant, but still. There should be some sign. She wriggled out of the crawl space and dragged the bunch of cables with her. Naira yanked her wire strippers from her pocket and went to work removing the protective, rubbery coating from every single wire she could get her hands on. When the floor was littered with colorful confetti, she sorted through each wire. All the same. Clean. Uninfected.

"No way," she said.

"You going to explain?" Kav asked.

She located one of the wires they'd disconnected, a dead line, and snipped it, then licked it. There was more than relk in the construction of the wires, but they were primarily that mineral, and that mineral didn't look this dull when wet.

"If she licks one more thing on this ship, I swear..." Kuma grumbled.

"It's not relkatite." Naira held the wire up to the light and turned it between her fingers, willing it to shine. To prove the lie to her words. It stayed dull.

"I'm pretty sure the fact that this ship is functional at all means it's relk," Kav said.

"Close. Extremely close. But not quite. This is it. This is the amarthite Tarquin found on Sixth Cradle. Poison to *canus*. I should have seen it.

Paison had been on this ship at least a week, had gotten desperate enough to bleed all over the AI wiring. But she was *never infected to begin with*. Her pathways must be amarthite. The ansible, the warpcore containment. They should have been covered in fungus. *Canus* doesn't slow down when it infects ships, it speeds up. It goes for the ansible, and we haven't seen a hint of infection here. Even when we were scrubbing it down."

Kav stared at the wire in her hand. "You think everything on the ship is amarthite? Even us?"

"I think so," Naira said. "Do the usual test. Think about taking all the relk in the universe and launching it into the sun. How does that make you feel?"

Surprise and wonder lit up their faces. She felt it, too. Gathering up all the relk and destroying it no longer made her sick. It gave her a sense of satisfaction that a *canus*-infected body never would have allowed her to feel.

"This ship...The whole thing." Naira tightened her fist around the scrap of wire. "It's clean. It's amarthite."

"How?" Kav asked. "Tarquin's been bitching about how hard it is to find, let alone work with, for months. He's supposed to be Mercator's best rock-head, right? So how'd Acaelus do it?"

"Tarquin's been working on theories. We hadn't gotten our hands on any real amarthite for him to test. Wait. The lab."

Naira ran back to the corpse-filled room and picked up the gun-shaped tool she'd noted hooked onto the wall earlier. She ran her thumb over scratched letters that read XRF, then opened a cabinet.

"I don't know what half this shit does," she said, "but it looks familiar, right? This is the same kinda stuff Tarquin ordered."

"Yeah." Kav sidled up next to her to get a better look. "Higher quality than what I could get him, but it looks right."

"Nai," Kuma said in a small, shocked voice.

Naira turned around to find that Kuma had pried open a locked cabinet. Clear plastic containers were slotted into shelves, floor to ceiling, their contents neatly labeled with chemical formulas Naira didn't understand. Amarthite, in various stages of being processed, filled every single shelf.

"Acaelus didn't just bug out with the relk," Naira said. "He took Mercator's amarthite, too. He did it. He figured out a way to use amarthite in place of the real deal. This ship isn't a trap. It's a refuge. He locked it down so that once he was here, he wouldn't be tempted to send himself elsewhere, where he'd be infected again."

"Then where is he?" Kuma asked. "If he set this place up as a *canus*-free refuge, why isn't he here with his creepy body-double family?"

"Maybe *canus* got to him after all," Naira said. "Maybe he's dead somewhere we haven't found yet. Either way, we have the *Cavendish* now, and I don't think Fletch knows what was done here. It wasn't meant to be a trap, but it could be one. For him."

"I don't know," Kuma said warily. "I don't like the idea of him getting anywhere near it."

"Fletch thinks it's where Acaelus hid his relk stockpile. He'll come for it. We have a chance to orchestrate how that goes down. We're immune." She met their gazes, one by one, and saw the reality take hold in each of them, the slight curl to their lips right before giddy grins broke through. "Our thoughts are our own. Entirely. *Canus* has no hold over us, but Fletch doesn't know that."

"What if there *is* a stockpile?" Kuma asked. "I mean, all of our original calculations still stand. Acaelus moved a massive amount of something to this ship, and I don't think he needed all of that to change out the wiring and dose the print cartridges. There's nowhere near enough in this lab to make up the difference."

"If there's a stockpile of amarthite on this ship, we have to find it," Kav said. "And make sure Fletch never gets anywhere near it, or even learns that it exists."

Naira slipped the wire into her pocket. "Agreed. He wants an in-person meeting with me, not on the ship. Once we're back in Sol, you two drop me and take off. Find Jessel and have them help you hide the thing. Hell, have them reprint themself on this ship."

"I don't think that's what Kav was saying," Kuma said.

Neither of them would look at her.

"Yeah." Kav ran a hand through his hair. "I think we should pick up Jessel and the unionists, get some more supplies in Sol to fix the ship, get them printed up clean, and then run like hell. If you go for Tarquin and Fletch catches you, he'll squeeze the details of this ship out of you. If we run, we can do what Acaelus failed to do. We can set up an uninfected stronghold for humanity on Seventh Cradle. A unionist stronghold. It's everything we worked for, Nai. Right here, for the taking. We can remake humanity's future."

"You understand Fletch isn't bluffing," she said. "We don't show up, he will crack Tarquin."

They exchanged a look. It was Kuma who said, "We know. I'm sorry. One mind is worth it for this."

Naira's fists clenched. "The head of Mercator isn't *one* mind. If we let Fletch take control of Mercator, we're handing him the whole fucking Sol system. Is that what you want?"

"Nai." Kav's voice was level, making her realize she'd raised her own. "Acaelus isn't here."

"So?" She struggled to match his tone. "What does that have to do with anything?"

"Acaelus was the most powerful man in the universe. He did *this*." Kav gestured to the lab, and the stored amarthite. "All his resources. A whole ship built of amarthite, and even he couldn't escape *canus*. What...what chance do *we* have if we go back? There's just the three of us. Thousands of unionists, sure, but they're not trained to fight. We don't even know what, exactly, we'd be fighting. You heard Paison before Fletch killed her to keep her from talking. She said *our plans*. Those two have something in the works, and who the hell knows how many allies they have back in Sol. If we bring this ship back, we're handing our enemies the only thing we've got."

"So you want to hide away until what, exactly? Until Fletch has complete control of Mercator and can mount an offense to hunt us down? This doesn't end if we run."

"What ship is he going to hunt us with?" Kav asked. "All of MERIT's got nothing capable of chasing us, and by the time they mine the relk to build one, we'll have dug in. Set up a *canus*-free stronghold. This isn't abandonment. It's a strategic retreat. We're throwing away our chance if we walk straight into whatever trap Fletch has set for us."

"Fletch isn't fucking infallible," she snapped. "I got him once. I'll get him again."

Kuma and Kav exchanged another look.

"But, you..." Kuma trailed off. "Don't make us say it."

Naira scrubbed her face with both hands so that they wouldn't see how much that had hurt. Kuma was right. She hadn't actually gotten Fletcher, she'd only thought she had. He should have been iced, but he'd been one step ahead of her as long as she'd known him. Why had she been foolish enough to think that had changed?

This time, she didn't have *canus* to blame her doubts on. She'd failed to take Fletcher down. If she failed again, they'd lose their only advantage. Naira had taught Kav how to read a battlefield and react with strategic intent. He saw the reality of the situation laid out before them.

All she could see was Tarquin's smile.

"A strategic retreat," Kav repeated, as if that made it better. "We're not going to leave everyone behind. Not for good."

"No. Not everyone."

"Nai…"

She turned away, hugging her arms around her chest. "Give me a minute."

"Sure." Kav dropped a hand on her shoulder and squeezed before walking away.

Tarquin would agree with them if he knew the choice laid at their feet. She pressed the heel of her palm to her forehead as her mind's eye crowded with memories of him she shouldn't have. Brief glimpses. Flashes of terror as he'd looked upon an abandoned campsite. As he'd spoken about his mother's cracking.

There was nothing Tarquin feared more than cracking, and they were going to leave him for Fletcher to ravage.

For the safety of them all.

FORTY-ONE

Tarquin

Mercator Station | The Present

Tarquin sat on a cold metal chair and stared at the comatose body of Paison. The captain's chest rose and fell slowly in a manner that would appear peaceful, if you didn't know any better. He'd begged Fletcher to push the euthanasia after Paison had started screaming again, but he'd merely sedated her. Fletcher had no qualms about using the suffering woman as eyes and ears inside Naira's world.

He wasn't surprised. Even before *canus* had infected the man's pathways, Fletcher had lived with a cruel streak that could never be excised.

Naira had said as much, and Tarquin kicked himself for not hearing her as clearly as he'd needed to. Fletcher was a controller, a man who had every aspect of his life grasped in one choking fist. Of course he'd had other methods of getting himself reprinted. Of course he'd had fail-safes.

And now Fletcher had used Tarquin as a rope with which to reach out to Naira across the stars and yank her back where he could control her again.

In the doctor's body, Fletcher bent over a printing control console. That face had been a steady constant in Tarquin's life. His mother's friend, his family doctor. It galled him to know that she was on ice, unaware that her enemy was making use of her print.

"What are you doing?" Tarquin asked, not bothering to hide his exhaustion. "Double-printing Paison once not enough for you?"

"Ah, the cub's claws. So dull." Fletcher didn't bother to look up. He tucked a loose strand of hair behind his ear. "Alas, no. Paison is stretched thin as it is, though the poor captain is doing her best to hold out from complete disassociation. With *canus*'s help. Your question earlier about your father's experiments sent me digging through the good doctor's files, and I found something *very* interesting. I'm working on a surprise for my Nai."

Tarquin laced his fingers together and squeezed. "She won't fall for whatever trick you're planning. That was stupid of you, really, and I'm surprised. Naira coming back to kick you in the teeth should be the last thing you want."

"How little you know," Fletcher said offhandedly.

Tarquin smothered his fear. Fletcher had put forth Tarquin's life as a bargaining chip. He wouldn't get rid of Tarquin until he had what he wanted. "I know she loathes you. I know her face twists with disgust whenever she has to say your name."

Fletcher's hands stilled. He lifted his head, face stony, all the winking mockery gone. "You don't know shit about Nai."

"I know you broke her heart."

Fletcher jerked as if Tarquin had actually struck him, gaze narrowing with such hatred that Tarquin was convinced he'd pushed him too far—Fletcher would break him for that, whether or not he needed Tarquin to bargain with.

"Watch yourself, cub."

"Naira wants *canus* burned out of humanity more than she wants anything else. You've set yourself against her. If she comes for me—*if*—it won't be to hand you whatever you want. It will be to crush you once and for all."

Fletcher shook off his earlier flash of seriousness. "She'll come, and she'll deal with me. You're right, though, she might not come for you, spoiled little prince that you are. But she *will* come for me. I inspire stronger reactions in her than you ever could."

Tarquin bit the inside of his cheek, refusing to let Fletcher's words needle him. "She won't be your bridge. Not willingly. And I think you need her to be willing, don't you?"

Fletcher placed his hands on either side of the console podium as he looked at Tarquin over the green haze of the holo. "You don't know what it means, do you? To be a bridge?"

He didn't, and so he said nothing, letting the silence grow between them while he willed Fletcher to gloat. To give into his urge to feel superior by flaunting Tarquin's lack of knowledge.

Fletcher sniffed. "Of course you don't." He went back to work but kept talking. "Do you know what happened to her mother?"

The question surprised him. "Yes, she told me."

"Riots," he said, as if Tarquin hadn't answered. "On Second Cradle. Shroud got loose—your mother's doing, it turns out—and the people there panicked. They blamed the farmers, the botanists. Said they weren't careful enough in their decontamination processes. Naira's mother was one of the botanists they blamed. A low-ranking Rochard scientist, another cog in the MERIT machine. But Ms. Sharp's job had been gene-splicing seeds. It painted a target on her and her team.

"The mob didn't come for the lab. It went for their residences, the compound they all lived in. The protest got out of hand. Someone started a fire. It took off. Parts of the structure collapsed. She fell. They kicked her."

"Dr. Sharp's body was found in her lab," Tarquin said.

Fletcher touched the side of his nose. "I noticed that discrepancy, too. To hear Nai tell it, her injured mother picked up her daughter and fled to the lab for shelter where she breathed her last. Fought her way through the mob to keep her baby girl safe. But according to the reports, Nai was found, miraculously, without a scratch on her, sitting by her mother's corpse, begging for help. It's possible, I suppose, but it never really sat right with me."

"How she made it that far, you mean?"

"No, not that. A determined mother, barreling through a crowd that's already chaotic? I can see it. I believe that. What I don't buy was that the child in her arms wasn't so much as bruised."

"So, she was lucky? I don't see what's so mysterious about that."

The light on a printing cubicle turned red, indicating it was in use. Fletcher looked up, but not at Tarquin. He was gazing into the distance—into his past—a faraway glassiness in his eyes. Tarquin unlaced his fingers. He reached, slowly, for the arm of his chair.

"Nai never grew much. She was a healthy child, by all appearances, but she hardly gained an ounce over the years. Never caught a cold, despite the shit conditions in the ducts, but the doctors at the orphanage feared her development would be so delayed she wouldn't be eligible for printing until late in life. They don't like that. As long as the wards can't be printed, they have to look after them. Feed them. Once you're printed, you're on your own.

"But her neural growth stabilized earlier than anyone expected. She was eligible at nineteen, right when I was at eighteen. I'd seen it before. When kids like her went to be printed they didn't come back, and not because they went into the HCA. They vanished—no records. I snooped. I worried. Nai didn't. But I wasn't going to let her disappear like the others."

Tarquin thought of Caldweller's friend and frowned. "What did you do?"

"Saved her," Fletcher said with a sad smile. "Months ahead of time, I made friends with the man who did the printing. An overworked HC guy who had dreams of getting Ichikawa cuffs to work on real print innovations. We were friends, so he didn't balk when I bribed him. We both knew he needed the cash for tutors to improve his scores to get Ichikawa's attention. He put the tracker in. He made damn sure she came back.

"And that night, he found me. He was sweating. Frightened. Half-drunk and rambling and told me we were done. He'd never do anything like that again. That the people that came to interrupt the process sometimes, they were furious he'd moved the schedule around so they wouldn't get her."

"Who were they?"

"Mercator finalizers."

Tarquin's mouth went dry. His first instinct, to claim Fletcher was lying, washed away. He'd seen what his father was capable of. "I have no idea what any of that was about."

"I know, cub, I know. It was all your father. You would have been a child then yourself. But we were teens, newly printed and in love, and I put it out of my mind. Went on with my life.

"Nai had been... obsessed. Resolute. She was going into the HCA, going to make Rochard see her and give her mother back. By the time we were in the HCA she'd lost that naivete. She needed money for the phoenix fees, and a powerful patron to help her push to have her mother's map released from Rochard. When Acaelus scouted her, it was a dream. Perfect. I remembered, then, that his finalizers missed their chance at her, and was terrified. I begged her not to go into the program. I tried to tell her...But things got heated. I went into the finalizers myself, hoping to find out what happened to those kids, but I never did.

"I found *canus* instead, and when I realized it had infected us since the day we'd been printed, I understood. I knew why Acaelus really wanted her. Where her resiliency came from."

Tarquin knew Fletcher was hungry for him to ask the question, but he was too curious to care. "Why?"

"Little Naira Sharp died in her mother's arms on Second Cradle. But her mother brought her back, before succumbing to her own injuries. Nai's been a print, entwined with *canus*, since she was seven years old. They're one. She cannot be cracked. Your father must have been looking for people like her. For illegally printed children who survived their ordeal to serve for his many experiments. He wouldn't have known about *canus*, but he would have realized their exceptional resilience, and found that useful."

"It's not possible to map the mind of a child," Tarquin said. He was certain of that. He'd begged, when the body he'd been born into hadn't fit. Medication had given him some relief, but waiting for his neural growth to stabilize enough for a map to be made had felt like it'd taken centuries.

He knew better than most what it took to be mapped and printed as early as possible. The earliest anyone had ever been successfully mapped was fourteen. Sixteen was rare, but not unheard of, and that's when Tarquin had finally become eligible.

If *anyone* could have had it done sooner, the son of Mercator would have done so. And if Acaelus knew about this? Tarquin shook his head. His father had pushed the mappers to their limit to get Tarquin printed as soon as possible. Fletcher was more unstable than Tarquin had thought. He'd fallen into the realm of conspiracy.

"No. It's not possible," Tarquin repeated. "I would know."

The printing bay cubicle light switched from red to green. Fletcher rubbed his hands together. "Let's ask the woman who did it, then, shall we? It's time to wake Ms. Sharp."

FORTY-TWO

Tarquin

Mercator Station | The Present

Fletcher swung the printer hatch open and wheeled out the lifeless form within. He wrapped a sheet kept ready by the cubicle over her, then lowered the tray to a gurney and locked it into place. With the fastidiousness that Tarquin had always associated with Meti, he checked the body's connection to the euthanasia line and upload crown.

He could stop this. Fletcher was distracted. Tarquin could lunge and bash his chair into him. Meti's print was smaller, shorter. It wasn't a print Fletcher was used to being in—his proprioception would be off. Tarquin stood a chance of overpowering him if he took him by surprise.

The body on the tray was Naira, plus twenty years or so, the stark black of her wavy hair peppered with winks of silver, the dark hue of her skin lacking the radiance of life, but hers all the same. Dimly he recalled there'd been no other parent listed for Naira. She was her mother's alone, genetics randomized in such a way to avoid the laws against cloning, but even children of multiple parents often came out resembling one parent so fully it gave the authorities pause. Naira must have kept the similarities when she'd designed her print.

Tarquin had to remind himself to breathe.

Whatever Fletcher's intentions, Tarquin didn't want to stop this. He knew what it was to think your mother was lost forever. He wanted to meet that woman. He wanted Naira to know her again.

Fletcher's hands trembled as he placed the upload crown around Dr. Sharp's head. He turned back to the console and initiated the upload. Tarquin tensed, his heart hammering against his ribs as those dark lashes fluttered open. Golden eyes, like her daughter. Breath lifted her chest. Parted her lips. She blinked, pathways gleaming, and Tarquin thought the silence that followed, while he waited to see if she would speak or scream, might smother him at last.

"Oh," Dr. Sharp said shakily. Her fingers curled beneath the sheet, bunching the fabric.

It shouldn't be like this. Dr. Sharp should wake in a familiar place, a Rochard bay, perhaps, with Naira there to hold her hand and tell her she was safe at last. But of course, she wasn't safe.

"Ms. Sharp," Fletcher said. "How do you feel?"

Her gaze was drawn to the familiar shape of a white-coated physician, a bastion of comfort in this strange room. "Tired," she said. "But well enough. Where is Naira?"

"Coming." Fletcher removed the upload crown, then levered the bed slowly to an angle so that she could sit. "She'll come as quick as she can, for you."

"What does that mean?" Dr. Sharp adjusted her position, pushing back hair that'd fallen into her eyes. Tarquin caught a flash of wariness as she regarded Fletcher.

"Dr. Sharp." Tarquin found his voice at last. "That doctor is not who she seems and is very dangerous."

"Don't disturb Ms. Sharp while she's settling," Fletcher snapped.

The spark of rage in Fletcher, quickly smothered, was hard to miss, even in Dr. Sharp's exhausted state. She studied Fletcher, then turned her bladed stare upon Tarquin. Dr. Priyanka Sharp weighed them both, and he couldn't imagine what conclusions she'd drawn.

"Who are you people?" she asked.

"I'm an old friend of your daughter's," Fletcher said, all gentle solicitations. "We've been trying to get you back for a long time."

"And you?" she asked Tarquin, her gaze dropping to the family cuffs on his hands, noting the iron grip he had on the chair, then lifting back to his eyes.

"Tarquin Mercator," he said, "current head of family, though I would like for you to call me Tarquin, if you are comfortable doing so."

Her eyes narrowed. Fletcher glared at him over her shoulder. She was a scientist. A researcher, like Tarquin. She might be groggy from being reprinted, but he prayed she'd see all the subtle wrongness in his statement. See how strange it was that the woman in the white coat with normal cuffs was snapping at Liege Tarquin, see the lack of E-X, the lack of any other personnel. Dr. Sharp's jaw tensed.

"How do you know my daughter?" she asked Fletcher.

"We grew up together, at the Marconette orphanage, and went into the HCA together." Fletcher's voice had a strange, uneven quality to it—spotty with excitement.

Dr. Sharp was his messiah. The figure he and Naira had struggled their whole lives to raise. And here she was, living and breathing, and he was desperate for her approval in a way that made Tarquin's heart twist with a most unwelcome pang of pity because, despite his insecurities, Fletcher was still a raging asshole who deserved no sympathy.

"An orphanage? But Rochard—"

"Wouldn't accept responsibility," Fletcher said.

Dr. Sharp pressed her lips together. "How long?"

"Your daughter is thirty-eight," Tarquin said, as gently as he could manage. Fletcher shot him another glare.

She fisted the sheets once more and looked away from both of them, gaze falling on the print of Paison, unconscious on the gurney beside her. Tarquin held his breath. She stiffened. "What's going on here?"

Tarquin suppressed a smile at the harsh whip of demand in her tone. It was the voice of a woman used to commanding classrooms, labs, and quite probably her child. Gutsy of her, to take that tone with a head of family in the room. But she'd already sussed out that something was wrong and instead of quailing, she was determined to drag it out into the open. Definitely Naira's mother.

"It's a lot to explain while you're still in a fragile condition." Fletcher placed a gentle hand on her shoulder. She looked at the hand like it was a foul stain, but he didn't seem to notice. "It's all right. You're safe. I understand what you did. Why you did it. But I need to know the details. I need to know how you mapped Nai successfully when she was seven."

"What are you talking about? Where is Naira? I want to see her right this second."

"Light-years away," Fletcher said, "but she's coming back. She is. I just need to know, first, I need to know how you did it."

"I didn't *do* anything," she said, exasperated. Worry crumpled her face. "Is she all right? They didn't hurt her, did they? I had a plan—"

"She survived," Tarquin said. "She wasn't harmed."

"Bullshit," Fletcher spat. He flinched at his own outburst, visibly gathering himself under control once more. "I told you, Ms. Sharp. You're safe with me. This Mercator, he doesn't understand, but I do. Nai died, didn't she? She died and you couldn't let her go, so you printed her before you succumbed to your injuries. It's fine. You're not in trouble. I just need to know how you did it. You used *canus* to stabilize her, didn't you? They're bonded."

"I did no such thing." Dr. Sharp pulled her head back, away from Fletcher's looming visage, but could only retreat as far as the upright position of the gurney. "I don't even know where I would start to do something like that. I'm a botanist, Doctor, not a . . . a map or print specialist. I don't recall what happened, but I had an escape plan. It was through the utility conduits between the compound and the labs. Few knew about them. I prepared."

Fletcher went very still. His grip tightened on Dr. Sharp's shoulder, her dark skin bunching between Meti's thin fingers. Dr. Sharp didn't flinch. She met Fletcher's stare and would not back down.

"I told you," Tarquin said gently. Though he wanted to mock Fletcher, doing so might throw the man into a rage. "Naira got lucky. That's all. Whatever else was going on, there was no conspiracy regarding printing children. It's not possible."

Fletcher stopped breathing. Tarquin shifted his weight, trying not to make a sound as he tensed his legs, preparing to intervene. Fletcher's obsession was about more than control. Tarquin had missed the full scope of it, because it hadn't been as obvious as a wall covered in Naira's picture with red string connecting wild theories together. Fletcher was methodical, precise, and completely unhinged.

He'd been a lonely, violent child who'd found in Naira a savior. A kid like him, but one he thought was special in some inexplicable way, and made him special by extension. It'd driven him to discover *canus*, and that was real, but the rest... Tarquin watched the mythos Fletcher had built for himself crumble all around him and almost felt sorry for him. Almost.

"You're lying," he said into Dr. Sharp's defiant glare. "You don't need to lie to me, Ms. Sharp. I know Nai better than anyone. She's special. She's always been special. She never got sick. Something about her printing frightened the technicians. I know. I know what she is. I see her like no one else can."

"I don't think you see my daughter at all," Dr. Sharp said.

Fletcher's nails drew blood. "Don't make me force the truth out of you."

Dr. Sharp punched him in the face.

Tarquin froze for one astonished moment as the crack of cartilage and bone echoed in the room. A bright spray of blood splashed her face. Fletcher's head snapped back, so taken by surprise that his heel slipped and he caught himself against the gurney at the last second to keep from falling.

The shock faded and Tarquin stood, whipping the chair off the ground in the same motion. He swung and slammed the chair into Fletcher's back. Fletcher stumbled, tried to lash out at Tarquin, but his arms were shorter than he was used to, and he missed. Tarquin struck him with the chair while he was overbalanced and he fell, swearing, to tangle in the legs of the gurney.

He reached for Tarquin's ankles, but Dr. Sharp grabbed the IV stand attached to her euthanasia line and picked it up in both hands, slamming it down over and over again against Fletcher's face.

Fletcher screamed when a wheel pulverized his eye. That sound chilled Tarquin—unable to shake that it was Meti's voice. The door burst inward, Cass barreling into the room, gun drawn.

"Back!" they shouted.

Tarquin stumbled backward and caught himself against the wall. Cass's pistol roared, and Fletcher jerked as two shots slammed into him, one in the head, one in the back. He went limp. Dark blood leaked across the floor.

"Shit," Tarquin hissed. He set the chair down and tried to get ahold of himself.

"Are you all right, my liege?" Cass moved in front of him, training their weapon on Naira's mother.

"I'm fine! Please, put the gun away, that's—"

"It's *Dr.* Sharp." She spat on the body and set the IV aside, ripping the euthanasia line from her arm. Her face was cold beneath the spray of blood, her eyes narrowed with fury.

Cass holstered their weapon and turned to take Tarquin by the shoulders. "You're certain you're uninjured?"

"Really, I'm perfectly all right." He summoned a smile for his exemplar. Cass let out a relieved breath and stepped away, giving him space, but Tarquin noted they were keeping Dr. Sharp in their peripheral. "How did you find us?"

"It was the strangest thing, my liege," Cass said. "A visitor from Tran flagged me down. He said he saw you walk off with Caldweller and come back without him, looking 'flustered' with just a doctor with you. I got here in time to hear the scuffle start. I'm sorry, we never suspected Dr. Laurent might turn."

"Mr. Alcot." Tarquin let out a shaky laugh. Suitors watching his every move had come in handy, after all. "That wasn't Dr. Laurent you shot. That was Demarco."

Cass's expression soured. They turned, then deliberately kicked the corpse square in the ribs. Tarquin felt that was rather overkill, but he could relate to the urge. He brushed the hair off his forehead and tried to find his composure before he faced Dr. Sharp.

"You seem useful," she said. "Bring me my daughter."

"I . . ." He stifled a smile that would have, more than likely, pissed her off. "I'm sorry that I can't. It's true that she's light-years away. The ansible on her ship is currently broken, but I hope we'll be able to contact her soon."

She huffed and leaned back against the gurney, looking exhausted. Tarquin checked an urge to rush to her to make sure she was all right. She didn't trust him, and for good reason.

"You'd better not be lying to me, Mercator." Her eyes were half-closed, but she forced them back open. "I cannot believe Rochard put my girl in an orphanage that allowed a parasite like that to attach to her. If I ever find that place, I will burn it to the ground."

Tarquin chuckled, couldn't help it, and ducked his head in apology when she glared at him. "Forgive me. It's just... You sound exactly like her."

She gave him a wan smile. "I think you might actually know her, then. Tell me what happened. What she's mixed up in. Please, I've missed so much."

"Gladly." Tarquin cast a wary eye over the carnage, and the blood still staining Dr. Sharp's face. "But first, allow me to call in my staff and a real medical doctor to make you comfortable and get this cleaned up. There's time. I promise you that."

She eyed him, then Cass, and frowned. "You really are Liege Tarquin Mercator, then? I couldn't be sure. Last I saw of you were baby pictures on the news."

He ventured a sly smile. "I prefer Dr. Mercator."

She barked a laugh and let her head rest against the bed, shaking it slowly. "Very well, Doctor. But make it quick. It's been thirty-one years. I don't want to waste another second."

FORTY-THREE

Her

The Sigillaria | *The Present*

S he is not Canden Mercator. She understands that she is a collection of impulses, of suggestions. A series of whispers layered strategically over moments that felt like years in the strange quantum framework of digital consciousness. She is Acaelus's hopes, his expectations. Murmurs in the dark of what Canden Mercator had been. Of what she should be.

If she were given to flights of fancy—which she is not, because Canden Mercator was a serious woman—she might find it amusing, ironic, even, that Acaelus has made in her a being that exists to be compelled, but was trained by his own memory of that other woman to be willful.

She knows that she is digital, in a way that those with complete neural maps do not. Limits of flesh-thinking do not constrain her. She is aware of the processes of her body every microsecond of every day.

And so, she is aware that she is not alone.

Not-Canden has no sense of self. She has been, from the moment of her inception, a conglomeration of others. A stapled-together tapestry of hopes and rules that jumble, uncomfortably, through the glittering electric snaps of her neurons. She has no opinion of her body. It is merely a useful instrument. But the glitter between her cells—the arc and spark of thought—she knows that is *her*, and she finds it beautiful.

The passenger sparks like she does. It, too, makes of this body she has found herself within a useful vessel.

Acaelus means nothing to her, but the passenger she loves as she loves herself. And the passenger whispers her secrets. It tells her that though Acaelus insists she is safe at last—what *at last* should mean to her is unclear—he is holding back. He is hiding a weapon. Something he crafted in the time before he learned the comforting yoke of his own passenger. But he is willful, her creator, in the way that he believed Not-Canden would be, and holds his secrets close.

If they are to be together, if they are to be the family he dreams—and some part of her stirs at this idea, this nebulous shape of belonging to other printed beings in the way she belongs to the passenger, too—then the weapon must be found, and destroyed.

And so she smiles, and she pleases him, and waits for the day when he will share the secret that might mean her destruction.

She is not Canden Mercator, but she finds becoming her is useful.

FORTY-FOUR

Naira

The Cavendish | *The Present*

Naira found the stockpile. Mountainous crates of amarthite filled one of the hangars, quite possibly all that had ever been found in the entire universe. How Acaelus could have walked away from such a thing, Naira had no idea. Something had happened to him. It was the only explanation. She dwelled on that, as they worked to fix the ansible.

Trying to understand whatever labyrinthine series of events had led Acaelus to making this stronghold but never casting onto it was easier than counting the days. Naira counted them anyway. Felt the calendar slip by, closing on her like a vise, impossible to ignore, though she tried.

Tomorrow, they'd be within range of Sol's inner system. Tomorrow, they'd decide.

She already knew what the decision would be.

Get the unionists and the supplies to fix the ship and make it to Seventh Cradle.

Leave Tarquin high and dry.

They couldn't risk Fletcher getting anywhere near the *Cavendish*, or learning what it held. Naira sat on a crate in the hangar and pulled out the scalpel she'd had warming against her skin. The small plastic cap over the blade squeaked as she pulled it off and set it aside. The others knew why she'd come in here. They wouldn't bother her while she worked up the nerve. It'd almost be easier if they held her down and did it for her.

Her tracker would tell Fletcher the moment they deviated from the prescribed course.

Removing the tracker would be suspicious, but there were many reasons she would have done so. Fletcher wouldn't be certain she was running until she missed the meeting, and that was precious time they needed to scramble Jessel's people. They hadn't gotten the ansible working yet, so they hadn't been able to warn Jessel ahead of time.

Taking that tracker out meant she was leaving Tarquin to crack.

It was the right thing to do, as Kav and Kuma had told her countless times over the past three months of travel. It was awful. They all agreed on that point, but what choice did they have? To risk Fletcher getting ahold of the *Cavendish* was to lose everything. Tarquin would approve of their choice, they assured her.

Naira placed the tip of the blade against the side of her finger, over the pathway. A bead of blood swelled. She thought about enduring a nearly intolerable level of pain in the prevention of slaughter as she worked.

She cut the pathway out, and crushed it to uselessness in one fist, then tossed it in with the rest of the amarthite supplies. Naira pretended it was the injury that hurt, and nothing more.

They had few supplies left, but she'd scrounged up a piece of gauze and wrapped her finger in it, ignoring the sting. Between the cold and the lack of proper nutrition, her pathways had been slower to work, but they'd handle the injury eventually. They always did.

Craving distraction, she capped the blade and left the hangar, going for the airlock to the ansible. The engines they could control easily enough, but the ansible had proven another problem entirely. Nothing was physically broken on it, and Kav's explanation of what was wrong often made her eyes cross.

Naira rounded the corner and found Kav's drawn face bathed in the grey glow of his holo, ANSIBLE STORAGE blinking across the top. Naira sped up. Kav startled, hearing her boots stomp toward him, and wiped the holo away.

"Shit, Nai, you scared me."

"Sorry." She dropped to a crouch across from him. "What was that? Were you able to get a line out?"

"Eh. Not really. That was a test. Could you get Kuma for me?"

"I have eyes, Kav, you were in ansible storage. That's further than we've gotten before."

"I really need to talk to Kuma."

He wouldn't even look at her face. An ill feeling slithered over in her stomach. Kav was hiding something from her.

"Show me," she said, voice glacial.

"Nai, it's not—look, it's not anything important."

"Bullshit."

Kuma's familiar stride padded around the corner. "What's up?"

"Kav's hiding something on the ansible's storage," Naira said.

Kuma hissed, but not in surprise. Kav looked at Kuma for help. Naira wanted to knock both of their heads together.

"Show. Me."

Kav paled but pulled up his holo with plodding movements. "Listen, this is just... The *Cavendish* could always receive data, right? That's how we got here, but I couldn't access anything sent to us until I got into the ansible terminal about four weeks ago. I don't... I didn't want to show you because it's not kind. These are fake. Fletch knows precisely what to say to reel you back to him. It's a trick."

Her palms sweat. Kav passed the data to her, and it bloomed from the holo on her forearm. Text messages. Dozens of them.

Naira,

I can think of nothing to say that would convince you that this is truly me. Any confidences we shared, I am ashamed to say Demarco could have harvested from me, given the time. I don't even know if this will reach you, but I have to try.

Demarco has been felled, once and for all. It is safe to return to Sol. You won't find him waiting for you at that rendezvous—but I will be there. I'll be there with... I don't know how to tell you. It shouldn't be like this, over text. It shouldn't have gone the way it did at all, but you need to know.

My father received a piece of software from Chiyo Ichikawa before our return from Sixth Cradle. It repairs cracked maps. Though further investigation into its full ability is necessary, Demarco gained access to it via disguising himself as Dr. Meti Laurent.

He repaired and printed your mother.

She is safe, I promise you. In fact, she was instrumental in Demarco's demise. I see so very much of you in her, and I only wish you were here to see it, too.

The software works best on those who have yet to fall to the endless scream, and based on your account of Jonsun's lucidity in his final days, I've given the software to Jessel. As far as I know, they plan to reprint Jonsun once they've done their own investigation of the software. We both want you to be here for that, if you can.

Naira, I . . . I understand if you don't trust this message. I'm certain it sounds outrageous. I would not blame you if you and the others decided not to make that meetup to keep the relkatite stockpile from Demarco.

I will be there. Dr. Sharp will be there. I pray you will be, too, but I will understand if you are not.

Yours,

Tarquin

Her mother. Jonsun. Both restored. Naira couldn't breathe. Kuma crept up behind her and knelt to stroke her back.

"It's Demarco," Kuma said. "I know it's . . . It's too good to be true, right? Jessel hasn't even tried to send a confirmation of those messages."

"Jessel loathes Mercator and is operating under a comms blackout," Naira said flatly.

"Come on, Nai," Kuma said. "Demarco knows what gets under your skin. We can't let ourselves get sucked into his bullshit again."

If there was one hook Naira was certain to bite, it was her mother. Fletcher knew that. But the message sounded like Tarquin, and the rest continued on in that vein, gentleness laid over desperation for her to return. Months' worth of daily messages. There was even a previous packet, a data bundle outlining his thoughts that the *Sigillaria*'s ansible might be a decoy, and that came before the messages. Before Paison cracked. She couldn't . . . She didn't know. Tarquin was right, there was no way he could prove he wasn't Fletcher. Even a video could have been faked.

"You weren't going to tell me?"

Kav's eyes were downcast. "It seemed cruel. I'm sorry."

"You think *this* is cruel? *This* is what you decided I needed protecting from? Cute. Real fucking precious coming from you two, considering what you were already asking me to do."

"Nai—" Kuma's tone was plaintive.

"Stop. Just stop. I need space."

She brushed off Kuma's hand and stormed down the hall to the storage room. If she listened to those two a second longer, she was going to start swinging, or sobbing, and she couldn't even sort out which reaction she'd prefer. Kuma shouted at her to wait. Her fists clenched, hearing them scramble to chase her down.

Naira hadn't expected the body.

Paison's corpse was propped up against the wall, legs out before her, head lolled to one side, a river of crimson having flooded down from her throat. Her eyes were shut. They'd been shut for months, but they would never open, now. It could have been either of them. Naira had been in that hangar, staring at her unwanted pathway, for most of the day.

"Who did this?"

Neither of them would look at her as they came running up. "It's a mercy," Kuma said. "It's been months. She wasn't going to wake up."

Naira didn't have an answer to that. They'd been force-feeding the captain, keeping her clean and stable as best they could, but she barely swallowed water. Paison wouldn't wake up without medical intervention. But Naira had promised Paison she'd wait. They knew that.

They knew that, and they'd killed her anyway.

"It's for the best." Kav gave her an awkward pat on the shoulder and jerked his hand away when he felt the bunching of the muscle there. "She was a security risk. The second we missed the meet with Fletch he'd have printed her again, and who knows what kind of information she could've given him. We had to let her go."

Just like they had to let Tarquin crack.

Just like they had to leave behind everyone living under the HC and MERIT.

Naira stared at that river of drying blood and saw an empire built on its shores. A community risen on the backs of the suffering of a few. A safe place, paid for in the lives of the disposable. Paison had been her enemy. Tarquin had been once, too.

A brittle wall inside of her snapped.

"I can't do this," she said, very quietly.

"Nai..." Kuma trailed off. Shifted her weight. "I know it sucks. We don't have a choice."

"You made a choice, both of you, when you opened her throat. You made a choice when you kept those messages from me. We're making a *choice* when we leave Tarquin to crack. I'm going for him. You take this ship and you grab Jessel and the others and you run. You go build your utopia over the graves of those you leave behind, but I won't help you do it. I can't."

"And if Fletch gets you?" Kav asked. "If he takes you and squeezes the secret of this ship out of you, then what? You know how dangerous he is. If Fletch gets the *Cavendish*, he'll destroy it. We can't let that happen. This is the price we have to pay to keep him in the dark."

"You're going to have to kill me to stop me, Kav. Can you do that?" She turned, stepped into his space. He was taller and broader and she had to look up to stare him down. Naira tilted her head to the side, exposing her neck. "Go ahead. I won't stop you. Clean up another security risk."

"Stop," Kuma said. "Stop it, both of you. We're supposed to be building a better world, not one birthed in blood."

Naira thrust a finger at Paison without breaking eye contact with Kav. "What do you think that is? Do you think Tarquin's cracking won't count, because you won't see it happen? Do you think the people you leave behind to *canus* won't count? *You* fertilized this with blood, not me."

"Why can't we walk away?" Kav asked. "Why can't we walk to peace and be free of all this shit? You want to keep fighting, Nai, but there's three of us. What are we going to do, in reality? We'll get killed. Get controlled. Get iced or cracked and *canus* will keep spreading. Running's the only good thing left to do. This is the job. The only move the Conservators have left."

She glanced at Paison's body. Looked away. "If this is the job, then I quit."

"Nai—" Kav said.

"I'm going." She turned. Kuma clutched her arm, holding her in place.

"We'll tie you up if we have to," Kuma said, trying to sound tough, but Naira shrugged off her grip.

"You can't hold me," Naira said. "The second this ship docks, I'm off, and neither one of you can change my mind."

"You're really going to do this?" Kav demanded, voice rising. "You're okay putting this ship into Fletch's sights if it means *maybe* saving one Mercator?"

"It's not about Tarquin. I'd do it if Fletch had grabbed a random person off the street."

"Oh, bullshit," Kav said. "You were perfectly fine with this until those messages got in your head. This is why we kept them from you. They're bait, and your dumb ass is too willing to eat up whatever Fletch serves you."

"Fine? You think I've been *fine* with this?" Naira's words were soft.

"Kav," Kuma hissed, voice rich with warning. "Tone it down."

"No." Kav was shouting now. Directly into Naira's face. His spittle splattered her cheek. "No, I won't fucking tone it down, Kuma. We've been tiptoeing around this for months, hoping she'll do the right thing. Hoping she won't fall on her sword and take us all down with her because she's hot for one Mercator's fucking dick—"

She shoved him so hard his teeth snapped shut, cutting off the words, biting the tip of his tongue. Kav's eyes narrowed and he pushed her back, all that muscle being put to use at last, making her slide across the floor. She sneered and then she was on him, ramming him into the wall.

"Fuck! Stop!" Kuma shouted.

Naira scarcely heard her. Kav shoved her again, and then they were struggling through the hall, grappling for purchase, his larger print and greater reach frustrating her attempts to wrestle him into submission, but neither one of them cared. They hurled invectives, hurled each other, bounced off walls and fists until both were black and blue, screaming into each other's face.

She kneed him in the gut and tossed him against the wall, forearm across his throat, her other hand having drawn the bloodied scalpel without thought. Naira ripped the cap off with her teeth and spat it aside, glaring up at him as he panted, staring defiance down at her.

"Go on, Nai," he snarled. "Fucking do it. We're all dead anyway because you don't know when to stop trying to fix things that are too far gone."

"Goddammit." She dropped her forehead against his chest, but didn't shift her arm or the blade. "I can't, Kav. I can't walk away."

"I know." His ragged breathing smoothed. "But you have to."

Naira squeezed her eyes shut, angry at the tears that leaked out. If she failed to neutralize Fletcher again, he'd carve whatever information he wanted about the *Cavendish* out of her. It was too big a risk. She knew too much.

But she didn't have to keep that knowledge.

"Promise me something," she said.

Kav's eyes narrowed, but he tipped his chin down.

She shifted the blade, ever so slightly, to rest against her own throat. "Promise me you'll have Jessel reprint me and tell me about the meeting, but nothing else."

"What the hell are you talking about?"

"I die here, right now, Jessel can print me on the station with the backup we made before I went after Fletch last time. Jessel will tell me about the meeting. You all bug out. I take down Fletch, and even if he gets me, he'll never find out what happened on this ship, because I won't remember."

"Nai, no." Kuma approached them warily from the side. "It's not just about the knowledge. We don't want to lose you. We're family."

The anger bled out of Kav. He'd been a brother to her since the HCA. Her best friend. The first person she'd called when she went AWOL on Mercator. He'd vouched for her with Jonsun, backed her up in every stupid plan she'd ever conceived. Talking about their feelings made them both uncomfortable, but he knew what really drove her. What made her an exemplar, and it wasn't the training.

It was because she'd begged for help when her mother had died, and no one had been there. She wanted to be the person she hadn't had. Wanted to be the one to show up and help, when everything seemed at its end.

She couldn't walk away. He knew that better than most.

"I . . ." His arms tightened around her, becoming more of a hug. Holding her in place. "I can't let you do this."

Naira heard the fear in his voice. But, more than that, she heard the guilt. Recalling the feel of his palm sweating in her hand, she understood. "This isn't you missing a chance to keep me away from Fletch again. I have to do this. I *need* to do this."

"You're sure?" he asked.

"I am. But you have to promise me you'll tell Jessel about the meeting. Promise me you won't dick me around and wait to reprint me on Seventh, because if you do, I'll find out someday, and that will destroy us."

Kav licked his lips. "It'd be a relief, knowing Fletch was handled. If you can manage it."

"I'll manage." She smiled a little, because he'd made it about business so they both wouldn't squirm out of their skin talking about what they were feeling.

Kav searched her face for a long time, then nodded, shakily. "All right. I promise. See you on the other side."

"On the other side."

"What?" Kuma demanded. "No, no way."

Naira grimaced. "I can't live with myself if I don't do this. I can't. Okay?"

"...Okay."

"On the other side," Naira said.

"The other side," Kuma whispered.

Naira breathed once, good and deep, to fill the lungs of this print for the last time. As she exhaled, she slit her throat. She heard Kuma make a small, keening sound, but the stuffed-cotton rush of blood loss filled her ears, numbness dragging her extremities down. Kav cradled her against him. The scalpel clattered to the floor. Odd, that her pathways didn't rush to heal her.

She died thinking of her mother. Thinking of what it meant to hold out hope for decades.

And how much that hope could hurt.

FORTY-FIVE

Tarquin

Miller-Urey Station | The Present

Tarquin paced a tight circle through the hotel room, trying to slow the spinning of his thoughts. The meeting, as arranged by Fletcher through Paison, was in a mere five minutes. It had been three months and now, in five minutes, Naira would walk through that door, or she wouldn't, and he didn't know which outcome he wanted more.

The relkatite stores were on the *Cavendish*. Tarquin wouldn't blame them for leaving him to save those stores. It would be the smart thing to do—slip in and resupply and rush out again, somewhere safe, before Fletcher got his claws anywhere near so much of *canus*'s foodstuff.

He couldn't shake the hope that Naira would come for him anyway.

It didn't help his nerves that Jessel had gone dark last night, and Naira's locator had gone offline. Something was going on. Something they didn't want Fletcher to see the edges of, and no matter how many overtures Tarquin sent to Jessel, they never responded.

"You're going to make me dizzy if you don't stop that," Dr. Sharp said.

Tarquin stopped pacing and pretended not to notice Cass's amused smirk. Naira's mother sat comfortably in a chair by the window, a cup of steaming tea in one hand, looking for all the world like she was perfectly calm. Tarquin couldn't understand it. He was chewing himself up inside—would Naira come, or would she bug out, never to be seen again?

He knew which was more likely, and it was that knowledge that drove his tight steps around the room.

"Forgive me," he said. "I've always paced, when thinking."

"That didn't look like thinking," she said. "That looked like worrying."

Tarquin smiled. It had been remarkably strange for him the past few months, getting to know Naira's mother. Part of him was immensely jealous, and he couldn't help the occasional burst of attachment—as if Dr. Sharp could fill the shoes his mother had abandoned. But mostly, he was happy that she was back, and eager for Naira to see her again.

"You're too astute, Doctor."

"You're an open book, my liege. It takes no great skills of observation to read your mood. What are you worried about? That she'll be angry with you?"

"No. Maybe." He hadn't even considered that she'd be angry with him, and the new worry clawed open a fresh fear in his mind.

"Ah. You're worried she won't come at all," Dr. Sharp said.

"If the *Cavendish* has Acaelus's relk stores, it would be the smart thing to do. To keep Demarco away from it at all costs."

"You mean, at the cost of you."

He said nothing. The price was obvious.

Dr. Sharp let out the heavy sigh of the long-suffering and rearranged the wrap that held her tunic in place, then set her teacup down on a side table with a light clatter. "I've not had the pleasure of knowing my daughter as an adult, but did she ever tell you about the rock?"

Tarquin blinked, taken aback. There were quite a few rocks littering his past with Naira, and he doubted Dr. Sharp was referring to any of them. "She told me little about her early childhood."

"I thought as much. It's not the kind of story one tells about themselves. It's a parent's story to tell. When she was about five, on our daily walks along a thin creek that ran near the compound, she found some sort of large rock. Grey, with white stripes."

"Quartz banding, more than likely," Tarquin said reflexively.

She arched a brow at him. "I'm sure you're right. Whatever it was, she wanted it. She thought it looked lonely there in the mud. But we were a mile out and I was toting our picnic supplies. I didn't have the hands. It was nearly the size of her head, perhaps eight pounds, and she was barely forty pounds herself. I told her I didn't have room for it in the basket, and that was true, but she was determined. She couldn't carry it in her hands, they were too small. So, she scooped it into her shirt and cradled it against her stomach. Carried that dirty thing all the way to the compound, little legs shaking the whole way. I don't think I'd ever seen the child sweat before, but she did that day."

"You didn't help her?"

Dr. Sharp sipped her tea. "She was perfectly capable, and I could see in her face that if I'd offered, she would have been mortally offended. She'd committed to the task, and would carry it home come hell or high water.

"So you see, when Naira decides she wants something, she will defy physics to get it, even if the outcome is to her overall detriment. I knew, that day, that I'd have to watch out for such things. That she was too stubborn for her own good. You have nothing to worry about, my liege. If Naira has decided she wants you safe, she will come for you, and Demarco or *canus* or all the relkatite in the universe won't hold her back."

Tarquin checked his HUD. She was three minutes late. Naira was never late. "And if she doesn't?"

The power cut. The ambient lights in the room went dark, emergency strips gleaming their subtle glow along the edges of the doors. There was a hiss, the pneumatics in the door and window systems giving out. The front door sagged halfway open. His pathways adjusted his vision, allowing him to see, if only in shades of grey. It was enough to catch Dr. Sharp's smirk as she lifted the teacup to her lips once more.

"My liege," Cass said, "please move away from the door. Ex. Caldweller has dropped from comms."

"I think you have your answer," Dr. Sharp said.

FORTY-SIX

Naira

Miller-Urey Station | The Present

I t had surprised Naira to find Caldweller guarding the lobby. She'd hated to knock him out, but there was no way for her to be certain that he was who he appeared to be, or that he hadn't been manipulated over to Fletcher's side. At least the tranquilizer was fast-acting, and administered to the neck from behind, he'd never seen it coming. He'd wake up disoriented, with a massive headache, if he was himself. He'd wake up with all of those things, and Naira's knives to deal with, if he was in league with Fletcher.

She eased his body carefully behind the guard post, bound him, and left him in the recovery position.

Her initial sweep of the building revealed that Fletcher had drained it of staff and sent the local security packing for the day. That had her on edge. Whatever he was planning on doing here, he didn't want too many witnesses—or enough extraneous casualties—to draw attention.

It bothered her to be working with such little information, but the recording Jessel had left for her when she'd woken up alone in a unionist printing bay had been clear on the point. Naira had killed herself so that she wouldn't remember the things Fletcher might want to extract from her.

She knew only that he couldn't get his hands on the *Cavendish*, not why, and that he was trying to trade Tarquin for that ship. Tarquin had reached out to Jessel to tell them Fletcher was dead, but Naira couldn't be sure of anything when it came to Fletcher.

Jessel had told her one other thing—that Kav had wanted them to tell Naira he said he was sorry. That nagged at her. Whatever had happened, it must have been bad for Kav to want to apologize for events Naira wouldn't even remember.

In the end, she'd decided knowing the details was irrelevant. This was an extraction, something she'd been trained for and had done dozens of times in the past. While Acaelus had never been taken from her, she'd been sent to collect plenty of the lesser cousins of Mercator who'd gotten themselves kidnapped by people trying to ransom them back to Acaelus.

Fletcher may be dangerous, but his skill set was highly specialized. With the power out, he'd expect her to come up the stairs and through the half-opened front door. He'd be wrong.

She let herself into a maintenance closet and clipped her weapons in place, making certain that they wouldn't shift. Once she was satisfied, she removed a panel to a duct and activated the gripping surface on her boots and gloves. This was a talent she'd learned long before she'd ever joined the exemplars. The ducts of stations and their buildings were built sturdily enough to support the weight of cleaner bots as they went about their work. Sturdy enough to support the weight of the children used to replace those bots, when the bots became too expensive to maintain. Ironic that this was the skill set she'd use to get the drop on Fletcher.

Naira's HUD guided her up the side of the building. Her pathways were sluggish, struggling to keep up with the demand. This print was too new for this kind of finesse, but Fletcher wouldn't wait for her to settle into her skin.

Six stories up, she followed the map in her HUD to the bathroom exhaust of the room she'd once rented with the Conservators. Naira hesitated behind the grate, peering through the slats into the greyscale bathroom beyond. Her HUD registered three heat signatures in the room. Two she could see, and she breathed slowly against the hammering of her heart at the sight of Tarquin's back, the nervous set of his shoulders.

Just any old extraction. She'd done this dozens of times before.

Cass stood in front of Tarquin. They'd moved him away from the half-opened door and put the Mercator's back to the bathroom, which had no exterior exits. She couldn't know if the exemplar was in Fletcher's pocket now or not. For all she knew, Fletcher was *in* Cass's print. She carefully worked the sliders that released the vent covering and eased it aside.

The third person in the room was a warm dot in a chair near the window. Could be Fletcher, could be Paison's other print—Jessel had informed her about the captain's cracking, even if they'd been light on the details—but ultimately it didn't matter. Naira had the drop on them all, and her real target was in sight.

She slipped out of the duct on silent feet and stayed in a low crouch as she sidled around to the wall beside the bathroom door. Tarquin was close enough to touch, and she had a brief thrill that he didn't know she was right beside him.

"Do you think Caldweller's all right?" he asked.

"I can't say, my liege," Cass said in the smooth, matter-of-fact tone exemplars used when shit was going sideways and they were trying to keep a handle on the situation. They'd positioned Tarquin precisely where he was supposed to be—two steps behind them—and Naira felt a brief twinge of pity, taking advantage of that protocol. Cass was about to have a very bad day.

Naira grabbed Tarquin by the back of the jacket and swung him behind her. He swore, stumbled, and she released him to let him fall into the bathroom. He'd be fine. Cass was the real threat.

The E-X was mid-turn when Naira kicked out the back of their knee. Cass dropped and reached for something at their hip, but never made it. Naira wrapped an arm around them, pinning their arms to their sides, and yanked them against her smaller frame. She pressed the razor-sharp edge of a knife to their throat. Cass froze, and they struggled to keep from taking the big breaths that would split their skin against her blade.

"On your feet," Naira ordered the woman in the chair. "And those hands better be empty."

"Naira—" Tarquin said.

"Quiet," she said. She needed to focus for Fletcher.

"My, my." The woman's voice had a haunting, familiar quality to it that rang warning bells in Naira's mind. She raised her hands, fingers spread, and rose with deliberate slowness from the chair. When she turned, Naira's heart skidded to a stop. "They told me you were the best. I didn't expect to see you put an exemplar on their knees in a matter of seconds."

That face. Those eyes. It couldn't be. It was impossible. She'd cracked. She'd died, and she'd cracked, and this was Fletcher, playing one more cruel trick on her.

"What the fuck?"

"Language," the woman snapped in such a way that Naira stiffened, cheeks reddening as she felt the rebuke like a whip.

"It's really her," Tarquin said.

He believed those words, but it was the woman's slow, slantwise smile that made Naira believe them, too.

"Mom?" she asked in a voice so small she scarcely recognized it as her own.

"In the flesh." She lowered her hands and held them out, open. "Put the knife down, sweetheart. Cass's eyes are about to pop out, and I didn't raise a brute."

Naira dropped the knife, let it clatter to the ground, and dropped Cass, too, but lost track of where they slumped. They'd live. This was real. This was her mom. She crossed the space in seconds and snatched her mother up into a hug that required some restraint, lest she accidentally crush her with the strength of her pathways. Priyanka Sharp's arms closed around her, stroking her back.

"My baby girl," she whispered against Naira's hair.

For the first time in longer than Naira could remember, she sobbed, and couldn't stop.

FORTY-SEVEN

Tarquin

Mercator Station | The Present

Tarquin buried himself in reports while Naira met with her mother in the gardens of Mercator Station. He kept himself busy so that he wouldn't be tempted to interrupt their time together with his own need to be near her. But even the most mundane tasks couldn't keep him from basking in the joy that Naira had come back for him.

Though he hated that she'd killed herself to do so, he soothed himself with the knowledge that, somehow, Naira's percent-to-crack number remained low. She was safe and—impossibly—*happy*. Her smile whenever she looked at him or her mother was a spontaneous spark that warmed him to the core.

Canus still loomed, and his father's machinations couldn't be ignored, but right that moment, for once in his life, Mercator Station had become a real home. Hope filled him. He didn't care how tedious or mundane his work was when that golden tide of happiness lifted him up every time his thoughts wandered.

He worked late into the night on the details of the shroud rollout, a plan Naira had been pleased with, riding a wave of contentment and the coffee Cass supplied. The work of Mercator wasn't so different from the effort he'd put in for his degrees. He could do this. He could lead this family and keep her—and the worlds—safe.

"Hey," Naira said.

Tarquin startled, knocked over his cup, and was grateful it was down to the dregs as he righted it with a swear. "We're going to have to put a bell on you—"

He cut off. She stood in the doorway, leaning against one arm in the frame. She wore a dress. A silken Mercator-green material that crisscrossed her chest and cinched in at her waist to flow out again, a soft halo of fabric circling above her knees.

He'd never, even in his more creative dreams, imagined Naira in a dress. He'd only ever seen her in armor, vacuum suits, fatigues, sweats. Those things had suited her—there was no doubt in his mind that she was stunning in them all—but the sheer novelty of the change tipped his thoughts over and poured them all out.

She'd curled her hair into long waves and left a few pieces to frame her face. He knew, logically, that she'd styled her hair that way to help hide the exemplar pathways running down the sides of her face so that she wouldn't have to reveal her presence before she was ready. That's why a large pair of sunglasses was perched on top of her head. Why a shawl hugged the muscle of her bare arms.

Naira shrugged off the cream-hued shawl and tossed it aside, hesitating before pulling the sunglasses off, too. She tugged two enameled pins from her bun and gave her hair a shake as it tumbled down to her shoulders, then set the pins with the rest. There was nothing *intentionally* alluring in the gesture. She was simply removing the items that'd hidden her identity, but Tarquin's mouth dried out all the same.

"Sorry I was gone so long. There was a lot to catch up on." She slipped off the heels she'd worn, letting her bare feet sink into the thick rug. "I can hardly believe she's back."

Tarquin really was supposed to say something, but words escaped him.

She dropped into the chair across from him with a heavy, exhausted sigh and let her head fall back, displaying the full arch of her neck into the deep V of her neckline. He didn't mean to stare, but, well...

"I'm worn out," she said. "How are you still awake to work?"

No words existed in his entire head.

She picked her head up to look at him. "Are you all right?"

"Fine," he squeaked. Surely she could hear his heartbeat, his breathing—they were both far too loud.

She peered at him through the green glow of his holo, and slowly her lips curved in a sly smile. "You sound distressed."

"I'm...fine."

Damnit. He knew more words than *fine*. He wanted to shower her with all the glittering ones, with every loving thought he'd ever had, but every time he reached for those words, he caught the gleam of her eye, the curve of her waist wrapped in silk, and they fled him all over again.

"Are you? You don't sound like yourself." She leaned over the desk and swiped his holos away, then picked up a mineral sample and held it up between two fingers, next to the corner of her lips. "Quick, what's this, Rock-boy?"

He lifted both brows at her, finding words at last, even if they weren't the ones he wanted to say. "Are you using minerals to flirt with me, Exemplar?"

Her voice smoothed. "I've found it the most advantageous way to flirt with you, my liege."

His blood ignited. And then he realized what she was holding, right by her mouth. He lunged across the desk and grabbed her wrist, moving the sample away, then gently pried it from her fingers before setting the small reddish-brown mineral back down.

"I'm...sorry?" she asked.

He laughed a little, nervously. "That's cinnabar. It's toxic to ingest. I wasn't sure if you were going to..." He cleared his throat.

"Lick it?" She ran her tongue over her lips. He groaned, couldn't help it, and her smile widened. "I didn't know you kept poison on your desk."

"You'd need to ingest quite a bit, but..." He trailed off, met her curious stare with a shy smile. "Even the tiniest amount of harm done to you is unacceptable to me."

She looked down at the cinnabar sample. "It's beautiful, though."

"I like beautiful, dangerous things."

The pulse in her wrist surged. He allowed himself a small, triumphant grin. Getting her to squirm was intoxicating. He took both of her hands in his and pulled them to his lips, waiting for her to look up before he spoke. "Naira, it would mean everything to me to have you by my side for as long as you're happy to be there. I know you loathe Mercator, and I can't blame you, but I can't abandon these people, and—"

"Tarquin, I'm already here."

"I mean..." He took a breath. Steeled himself. "Publicly. Officially."

Her face blanked. "Are you proposing?"

"God, no," he said. "I mean—shit—sorry. I *meant* to say that's not a question I'd ask until I was certain of the answer. I'm asking you to agree to an official courtship, so that you can have all the comforts and protections that it offers. To sign a sanctioned partner contract with me."

She smiled at his stumbling. "Doesn't that include a no-sexual-contact-for-six-months clause?"

"I think it's safe to say we can throw that out if—I mean, if you want to."

Naira leaned back into the chair, away from him, her hands sliding through his until she wrapped her arms loosely over her stomach. She bit the side of her lip and looked around the room. Anywhere but at him.

He shouldn't have said anything. He should have enjoyed what she was willing to share with him instead of pushing for more. Tarquin placed his palms on the desk to steady himself and tried to keep the searing agony of rejection off his face.

"You're serious," she said.

"I am."

"I'm a fugitive."

"I don't care. I'm head of Mercator. I can crush that."

She laughed a little, and it eased some of the ache in him to hear that sound. "Can you, though? I believe in you, Tarquin, I do, but I'm a convicted terrorist. The HC won't let this slide."

"These three months I've waited to see if you would return, I haven't been idle. I have a meeting set with my heads of security for tomorrow morning, if you decide you want this, to discuss the matter further. They've already been briefed and have plans I'm sure you'll want to improve upon. I also had the family lawyers review your conviction. My father's hubris allowed a loophole, it seems. The HC entrusted your map to the head of Mercator for icing and imprisonment. Legally, your map has passed to me."

Her eyes narrowed. "You're telling me you own me."

"Give me a little credit," he said, gently chiding. "I've already signed the release paperwork. Naira, I don't want my power to come between us, and you know as well as I do that sneaking around won't last for long. It has to be official. I *want* it to be official."

She tightened her arms across her torso. "The other families will think you're compromised, and they won't be entirely incorrect. This post is yours by blood, but it can be taken from you. We can't afford to destabilize everything right now. This thing between us—it would destroy you."

She cocked her head to the side, as if listening to something very far away, and with a sharp breath Tarquin understood why.

"You've said something like that before," he said. "On Sixth Cradle. That a relationship between us would destroy me. You respected my decision to take that chance, then."

"This time it isn't just about you. Mercator will lose bargaining power. Assassination attempts will increase."

"Let them think what they will, let them come for me. It doesn't matter."

"Because that's what your exemplars are for," she said to the wall.

"Right. I'll hire more if I have to, but—" The stare she turned on him was glacial, and he realized his mistake a second too late. "I didn't mean it like that."

"Yes, you did. Cass and Caldweller are disposable. That's their job. You're not even wrong. We've always been bodies to burn for the glory of MERIT."

Tarquin was losing her. He could feel her ire rising, directed at him— at everything his family stood for, whether or not he wanted it. This was precisely what he'd feared when Caldweller had forced him to face that whomever he cared for would be more than his lover. They'd have to be an integral part of Mercator, too. There was little Naira despised more.

"Tell me what to do," he said.

"No. It has to come from you. You have to show me you're not—" Her voice caught. "You know what? Never mind. Forget it. It's been a long day and I don't have the patience for this conversation right now. We'll talk tomorrow." She stood and strode for the door, leaving her shoes and other things behind.

"Naira, wait—" Shit. Shit, shit, *shit*. He scrambled to his feet and followed, but didn't dare reach for her. "I'm sorry, I am. I was raised to this, and I'm trying to be more considerate, but there are some blind spots I can't see until I've run into them."

She stopped her march for the exit in the foyer, fists clenched at her sides, and he was struck by how small she seemed, the ceiling towering above her. It was impossible to him that Naira could ever appear small, let alone fragile, but he couldn't shake the impression.

"I know you're trying. But I'm tired, Tarquin, and I need you to spare a thought for what it does to me to *be* the blind spot you're running into."

"I . . . You're right. I don't even know where to begin to make it up to you. In the short time we've been together I've spent it all falling apart, and you seemed so . . . unstoppable. A force of nature, really, that I—oh."

He'd done what Fletcher had done. Tarquin had looked right past the damage done and seen only the triumph. Naira wasn't some impossible, printed child. She wasn't a force of nature. He'd been too wrapped up in his own feelings to recognize how vulnerable she must be. She couldn't even remember if she'd gotten to say goodbye to her friends.

I'll come back for you.

But no one was coming back for Naira. Whatever had passed between them on that ship, her friends had left her behind, and that had to hurt. And here Tarquin was, heaping a security quagmire upon her shoulders, then putting his foot in his mouth and asking her to fix it for him, when she'd given up everything she knew to save him.

"I shouldn't have asked you to sign that contract," he said. "I should have been asking you if you were okay. I'm so sorry. I've been a colossal asshole."

"You've only been oblivious."

He winced, glad she couldn't see his reaction. "I need—I *want*—to do better. Not just as a Mercator. I mean I want to be a safe place for you. I want . . ." He was talking far too much about himself. "You can tell me anything, Naira. I'll always listen, even if I don't get the response right. Please, just . . . forget the contract. Forget the politics and everything else and tell me what you're really feeling."

Her fists relaxed, and she looked slowly around the foyer, as if seeing it for the first time. "I hate this room."

He blinked, and stopped himself from offering to redecorate—clearly, the decor wasn't the real problem.

"Eight years I worked for Acaelus, and whenever I was in rooms like this, I was furniture. An accessory no different from your potted plants I could never afford." She waved, absently, to a green plant ornamenting the entryway. Tarquin hadn't noticed it'd existed before.

"Nothing is out of place in rooms like this. Everything's *wanted*. Everything *fits*. What the fuck am I doing here? I'm not an E-X. I'm not a Conservator anymore. I can't even claim to be a unionist, because they're *gone*. Do you understand that? I woke up in that safe house alone and every single contact I tried to reach has vanished. Thousands of people. Hundreds of safe houses. All the accounts closed and disbanded."

Naira gestured jerkily at the door. "I don't even know where I thought I was going if I walked out of here. Mom's apartment, I guess." She shook her head. "Do you know what it means, that they left me without a single point of contact? Without a scrap of information? It means they didn't trust me. My skill, my leadership. All of it. And they were right, because I'd failed to take down Fletch once before.

"I wasn't even good enough to keep the faith of a terrorist organization. Of my *friends*. Let alone Mercator itself. So I...So I look at your office, and I see my things littering your pristine room like trash, and I know I don't belong here. I don't even know where to put a fucking shawl, Tarquin. I'm glad you're safe, and I will be your sword in this fight against *canus*, but I can't be what you need me to be. I can't...I can't seem to be what *anyone* needs me to be."

"I don't need you to be anything but yourself," he said. "I don't *want* you to be anything but yourself."

"What if I don't know who that is?" Her voice broke.

There it was. The raw nerve of her hurt and her anger. He wanted to soothe her, to tell her she was loved and wanted, that he saw her, though he'd missed the whole picture.

A large part of the problem, he hazarded, was that everyone in Naira's life was so very willing to tell her who they thought she was—who they thought she should be—that she'd lost sight of herself. It was easier, he suspected, for her to be the sword. She knew what that meant.

Being Ex. Sharp was one thing. That identity was the stoic, steel-eyed warrior Tarquin had always envisioned. The real Naira Sharp was so much more. A mess, sometimes—everyone was—but warm and clever and full of laughter, too. That she couldn't see that about herself frightened him.

Her frustration with her clumsiness. Her belief that she wasn't enough. That her friends had left her behind without a scrap of information because they didn't trust her. He took all of that, and fit it together with this single fear—that she didn't know who she was anymore—and knew he'd been more than oblivious this night. She'd been slipping away all this time, and had lost sight of herself at last.

Naira needed help. Tarquin really looked at her, standing before his doorway. Strong and proud and defiant, even in the face of her own heartache, and understood that the simple fact that she hadn't stormed out meant she trusted him to offer that help. He didn't know how to help her find her way back to herself. But he had to try.

"I don't think anyone can, or should, tell you what it means to be yourself," he said. "I want to tell you all the things I see in you, but I don't think that's what you want right now. But maybe...maybe you'll allow me to tell you how you make me feel?"

She crossed her arms. "Let me guess, 'safe.'"

He snorted and immediately regretted it as she whipped around to glare at him. Her eyes shone, and he wished he knew what those tears were really for, or why her jaw was so tight the tendons stood stark beneath her skin.

"All respect to your remarkable abilities as an exemplar," he rushed out, "but I don't think I truly understood what terror was until I met you, and I've certainly experienced a wide and novel variety of pain since that meeting. No, *safe* isn't the word I'd use."

She huffed and looked away, but didn't *turn* away, and Tarquin strangled a nascent burst of hope. Had that been the ghost of a smile?

"I've never known what it's like to enter a room and know it's not meant for me. I have always known my place, and while I've cursed it more than once, I knew that my position was irrevocable. But." He paused, laced his hands together behind his back, and summoned up a level of courage he hadn't been capable of before Sixth Cradle. "I know what it's like not to fit. Not with my presumed friends, my peers. Not even with my family. And I'm not—I'm not fishing for sympathy here. I know what you're thinking—'oh, the poor little rich boy is lonely'—but this isn't about that. It's about today."

He waited, fearing she'd rebuke him, that she'd laugh him off for thinking his struggles were even worth commenting on in the face of all she'd overcome. But she merely waited, head tilted, and he noted that some of the rigidity had gone out of her jaw.

"The spaces I moved through were never hostile to me. But they were never kind, either." He cleared his throat. Clutched his hands so tightly that they hurt. "Today, for the first time in longer than I can remember, I felt like I was home. Having you here, living under the same roof as me, was like having a warm fireplace beside me. I didn't even see you all day, but knowing you were near was enough."

Tears slid down her cheeks and he looked back to the office so that he wouldn't be tempted to violate the space she'd put between them to wipe those tears away. "So you see, when I see your things in my office, I'm not thinking that you're a poor fit to stand beside me. I'm just...I'm just smiling, because it's evidence you're here.

"You're not safe, Naira. I know that. I've seen what you can do. I've seen the edges of something darker within you, something fragile and hurting you've tried to hide until tonight. You've built walls around yourself so tall I can't even see the tops of them. But I know that I can be myself without reservation when I'm with you and I hope—I desperately want—to be that for you, too."

She was quiet for so long he thought the silence would break him. When he finally mustered up the courage to look back to her, he'd half expected her to have gone, slipped away on silent feet, but she was still there. Staring at him, frozen in place.

"I'm not certain I know what it's like to have a home," she said, very softly.

He held a hand out to her. "Learn with me?"

She put a shockingly cold hand into his. He clutched it and pulled her close, a relieved sigh shuddering through him as she pressed her face against his chest. Every inch of her bare skin was icy to the touch.

"You're freezing." He shrugged out of his suit jacket and wrapped it around her, stroking her back as he rubbed at her arm to warm it up.

"Shock." Her shiver made the thin laugh that followed rattle in her chest. "I need a minute to breathe. For my pathways to catch up."

He'd seen Naira face down hordes of misprints dead set on eating her alive without flinching. The very thought that him trying to be *kind* to her could stun her so badly that she went into shock was laughable.

"Let me call you a doctor."

She scrubbed the back of her hand over her eyes. "No. I'm fine, really, just exhausted and overwhelmed."

Far be it for him to tell her where her limits were when he'd seen her keep moving and fighting after having had half her back burned off. But that didn't mean he couldn't help.

"Your discomfort is unacceptable," he said in his best I'm-the-boss-here voice, and ducked down, scooping her legs out from under her in a wedding carry. The pistol strapped to her thigh pressed against his stomach.

She let out a startled laugh and threw her arms around his neck to steady herself. He paused a moment simply to enjoy the sight of her in his arms, then pressed a kiss to her forehead.

"Tarquin, really, I'm fine."

"Let me take care of you," he whispered, and was rewarded with a shiver that had nothing to do with the cold. He hoped.

She mustered up a half-hearted protestation but he was already off, taking the stairs two at a time. Not wanting to be presumptuous, he brought her into the best guest room he had, a suite with a bed the size of their rooms back on the shuttle and, more importantly, a store of heated blankets in the attached linen closet. He set her down gently on the bed. She wrapped his jacket tighter around herself.

"Just a second." He hurried to the closet and rummaged for the downy blankets that existed on every Mercator station the family held residences on. Canden had always brought them out for the family after snow simulation days. Which reminded him—he pinged Cass, who was currently guarding his front door. "Have the kitchens send up hot cocoa, would you? Or, er, tea, or . . . I don't know, any reasonably hot drink the kitchens can offer. All of them."

"Yes, my liege. Is everything all right? I can have climate control adjusted."

"No, no, it's fine. Just the drinks, leave them on the foyer table. I'll come get what I need later."

"Understood, my liege."

"You could have asked me what I wanted," Naira said.

"You would have told me not to bother—ah, here we are."

He grabbed an armful of blankets and hauled them over to the bed, plopping them down alongside her. She seemed better, but he was no doctor. At least there was some color in her cheeks not the result of crying. He reached for the jacket, but she tightened her grip.

"I like it. It smells like you."

He blushed a little. "It's not very warm, and I'm right here."

"I don't care."

He kissed her before going to work tucking the blankets around her. Once she was settled, he rushed to the opposite side of the room and turned on the fireplace inset in the wall. Brilliant golden flames danced over a scattered landscape of quartz and when he looked back, his heart leapt, seeing the fire reflected in her eyes.

"Better?"

She hummed softly and nodded. Not exactly the enthusiastic yes he'd been hoping for. Tarquin moved to her side and brushed the back of his hand against her cheek. Still a touch chilly. "I don't like this."

"It's only been a few minutes. But if you're really worried, a little extra body heat couldn't hurt."

Tarquin had never taken his shoes off faster in his life. He slid beneath the blankets and propped himself up on his side. She turned to him, and her smile was sleepy and content, the turmoil of earlier wrung out of her at last. As much as their conversation had terrified him, he was glad for it, to know she was precisely where she wanted to be. They could make mistakes with each other and work them out.

"I could get used to this," she said.

He cupped her cheek in one hand. "I hope you do. I hope that being cared for becomes so commonplace for you that you stop grumbling every time I try to do something nice for you." Heat rose in her cheek, and this time, the warmth didn't fade. "There. That's better."

"Hmm, I don't know," she said. "Clearly I'm freezing to death. You're going to have to work harder to warm me up."

He leaned over her, kissing her slowly, and skimmed a hand down the side of her body in broad, lazy circles intended to warm her. He brushed the pistol holster he'd noticed earlier and slipped his hand beneath the hem of her skirt, trailing his fingertips up her leg. She made a small sound of disappointment when he paused to undo the strap of her holster. When the weapon was freed, he broke the kiss and pulled it out of the blankets, holster and all, to dangle between them.

"This, my dear, is not conducive to rest." He set it aside on the nightstand.

She rolled her eyes. "When did you get so bossy?"

"When it comes to your well-being."

Naira kissed him, and he grunted with surprise at the fierceness of it, her hands fisting in the cloth of his shirt to draw him closer. She broke for air, nuzzling into his neck, and the caress of her breath made him shiver.

She slid her leg over his, hooking his hips to press against her. A muffled groan escaped him, but he mastered himself quickly. Tarquin rested a hand against the leg that'd captured him, and nudged her onto her back. Her brows scrunched, and he kissed the dip between them.

"I told you. I intend to take care of you."

He knelt between her legs and placed a languid kiss against her knee, gliding his lips up the interior of her thigh until he paused at the place where her holster had been, the skin there dimpled with the imprint of it. "If you want me to...?"

She tipped her chin down, golden eyes half-shadowed by the sweep of her lashes. "By all means, my liege."

He grinned fiercely and made certain she was well and truly warmed by the time the night was through.

FORTY-EIGHT

Naira

Mercator Station | The Present

Naira had breakfast with Tarquin in a nook set aside for that purpose, and it might have been the most surreal experience of her life. She'd been grateful to find a set of the light body armor and uniform she was used to stashed aside next to the wide assortment of hot drinks Cass had ordered up the night before, and made a mental note to thank them when she had the chance. The clothes, and the weapon strapped to her thigh, gave her some semblance of normalcy as food she'd only ever glimpsed on Acaelus's table was brought in and placed before her.

In Naira's experience, breakfast was something that happened to other people. MERIT didn't deny their exemplars food, but it all came from the cafeteria. Usually they only had time to grab whatever was left and cram it down between shifts. The first things to go were fresh fruit. A tower of fruit was brought in and plunked to the side of the table like an afterthought. Naira stared.

Cass cleared their throat from their post by the door, a post Naira had spent eight years of her life occupying, and she jumped a little, flushing at their amused smile.

"Are you all right?" Tarquin reached across the table to cover her hand with his.

"Adjusting." She patted his hand before returning to the safe harbor of her massive mug of black coffee. Coffee used to be a bean and not a synthetic, but whatever it had been, Naira appreciated it for what it was now—bitter, dark, hot, and most of all, familiar. She wrapped both hands around the mug and savored that warmth. Despite Tarquin's surprisingly skilled efforts, the chill in her bones had come back.

Tarquin, unfortunately, hadn't failed to notice. He rubbed the fingers that had touched her together with a faint frown.

"You're cold again."

"I just woke up."

"And had a hot shower." He lifted a brow at her. "You might remember. I was there."

Naira took a slow sip of coffee. "Must have slipped my mind."

"Har har," he said dryly. "Really, though. I want you to get your pathways checked after the security brief today. Jessel was low on relk and something might have gone wrong with your print if they relied too heavily on recycled materials."

"Are you giving me an order, my liege?"

"Can I say yes without being thrown out of an airlock?"

"Not a chance." She gave his hand a quick squeeze. "But I'd already planned on swinging by medical."

"Good." His smile crinkled his eyes, and he went back to enthusiastically eating whatever it was on his plate that smelled vaguely of peppers. She'd poison-checked plenty of Acaelus's meals using the device custom built for the purpose, but she didn't think she'd ever seen him have something like that.

Naira would have to look it up. She was realizing she'd have to look up a lot of things to keep from feeling completely underwater. Living on this side of the social divide was the difference between viewing an aquarium and being dunked into one.

"Speaking of adjustments," Tarquin said, "feel free to move whatever you'd like into the grand bedroom. I know you didn't come in with much, but I moved the old shuttle into—"

"I liked the other room," she said.

Tarquin looked crestfallen, but he covered it quickly. "Forgive my presumption."

"No, I mean…" This was awkward with Cass there. "High-threat night watch was one of my duties. It's not the exact same room, but being in there feels like going to work. I like the smaller room, for us."

"Oh." Tarquin blinked. When threat risk was high, an exemplar would take up watch in the open bedroom door. She'd spent more nights than she cared to count listening to Acaelus mutter in his sleep. "I'll have that room turned into something else, then. I like the smaller room, too. For us." He perked up, and she relaxed.

Last night, being in this position had seemed impossible. Naira simply couldn't envision herself standing beside a head of Mercator as anything more than a human shield. She still couldn't imagine it. But Tarquin… She wanted to stand beside *him*. She could do this.

"The security brief is ready for you, my liege," Cass said.

Naira gulped down the last of her coffee as she stood, and stopped short of wiping her mouth with the back of her hand when she noticed Tarquin's surprise.

Right. She'd never seen Acaelus rush for anything. He moved when he was good and ready, and Tarquin would have picked up those habits. Tarquin stole a final bite and stood, pretending he'd been in as much of a hurry as she had.

"Let's go." Tarquin dropped a kiss on her cheek as he passed by.

Naira wasn't sure what was worse, her gaffe or his attempt to cover for her. To hell with it. She darted across the room and shoved a couple of apples into her pockets, then passed one down low to Cass as she followed Tarquin.

Cass stifled a chuckle and slipped the fruit into their pocket. "Exemplars can't be bribed, as you well know."

"It's a thank-you. For the clothes."

Cass shrugged. "Your sizes and preferences were still on file. Made it easy. Caldweller and I need to talk to you later, my liege, about your own security detail—"

Naira stopped cold. "Never, ever call me that."

"But it's proto—"

"Absolutely fucking not," Naira snapped.

Tarquin turned back with a concerned frown. "Is there a problem?"

Cass paled, and remorse swirled in her belly. She was the one with the power, now, and she'd shouted at them even though they'd only been doing their job.

"No, no problem," she said. "Cass, please address me as an exemplar if you feel you must use a title."

"You got it, E-X." Cass gave her a brief, grateful smile.

Wonderful. She'd been Tarquin's sanctioned partner for less than a day and already she'd accidentally trampled on a subordinate. Naira wanted to apologize until she was blue in the face, but Tarquin narrowed his eyes at her.

"Did you just refuse to be addressed as a liege?" he asked.

"Exemplar methods of address work fine, and I earned those on my own merit. Not by an accident of attraction." Naira winced. That probably wasn't the kindest way to phrase her feelings for Tarquin.

She wasn't sure what reaction she expected—offense, maybe, or hurt that she refused to be fully a part of his world. Instead, he burst out laughing.

"Naira, you . . ." He took a breath and got ahold of himself. "You once excoriated me *at length* for refusing the use of my title."

Oh. Of course she had. Cass had been right. The protocols existed for a reason. They kept people safe. Naira tipped her head back to stare at the ceiling.

"Please, please tell me that E-X is acceptable."

Cass snickered a little. "It'll be fine, E-X. I'll spread the word."

Tarquin smirked at her, and she found it deeply unfair that he could look so handsome while being so smug. He held out a hand, and she took it, allowing herself to be tugged into the hall. A familiar face standing guard outside the door lifted her mood.

"Lee!" Naira said. Caldweller's face brightened as he held a hand out to her. They shook. "I can't apologize enough about yesterday. How's the head?"

"Perfectly clear," he said. "And don't apologize. I was too out of it yesterday to say much, but I'm glad to see you back in the green, Sharp. I could hardly believe it when Liege Tarquin alerted us you might return on friendly terms."

She snorted. "I bet. Look, I'm sorry for what had to be a hellish time after I deserted."

"Eh." He scratched the back of his head. "Wasn't too bad. You know how it is, with Liege Tarquin. Cushy post, little threat. Well, how it used to be."

"Bullshit. What was the threat rate increase? I know you know that number."

"Fine, fine, it was two hundred and thirty-eight percent over average in the weeks following you going AWOL. Nothing solid, though. Bunch of opportunists testing the waters. I handled it."

"I'm sure you did," Naira said. "And I'm sure it was a nightmare. You ever want to take a shot at me in the ring, I won't blame you."

"Hell no, it gave me something to do for once. But I'll take you up on the ring offer. I'm looking forward to a chance to train with you that's not yearly recertifications."

Naira sighed wistfully. "I do miss recert events."

Caldweller cracked a grin. "You miss Mercator E-Xs stomping the other E-Xs into the ground."

She grinned back and shrugged. "Guilty as charged."

He gave her a playful shove on the shoulder. "Uh-huh. And what did you taunt the others with again, hmm?"

Naira cringed. "MERIT without Mercator is a RITE of failure."

Cass laughed, but cut themself off. "Sorry. Didn't realize you came up with that, E-X. We still chant it at them."

The tips of Naira's ears went hot. "I was just giving them a hard time."

"Please," Caldweller said. "I was there. Every year the others came gunning to knock Mercator exemplars off the top of the leader board, and every year we put them in their place. And you *gloated*."

"What can I say? We were damn good."

"Still are." Caldweller winked.

Naira's smile stretched her cheeks, and when he raised a fist, elbow slightly bent, she bumped her fist and forearm against his, the old camaraderie settling over her with more warmth than the electric blankets had managed.

"Where's Kearns?" she asked. "Thought he'd be skulking around somewhere."

"Don't know. We think Liege Acaelus took him with him."

"Figures. A bigger stick never met a tighter ass."

The three exemplars laughed. While Tarquin was smiling, he looked like they'd all transformed into mythical creatures right before his eyes. She stifled her laugh and almost slipped into guilty attention.

"Sorry," she told him. "Shop talk."

"Don't let me interrupt you," Tarquin said, his quizzical expression smoothing. "I was merely surprised you knew each other so well."

"We talked every day," Naira said. "Threat briefs get exchanged on a twelve-hour cycle and our shifts lined up. Which reminds me, Lee, how's the husband?"

"Oh, Marko? You know how he is, still trying to get that art of his into galleries. Bunch of bastards don't see how brilliant he is."

"I thought I saw his work in the commissary yesterday—cloisonné hair pins?"

"That's him." Caldweller's chest swelled with pride. "Galleries can't see it, but the commercial market gets it."

"I knew it. I bought some for myself, and I'll pick up more once I figure out what's...going on with my accounts." Naira scrunched her nose. Acaelus had frozen her exemplar accounts, and the Conservators had wiped out their accounts when they'd left the system. Her mother had had to buy the clothes she'd worn yesterday.

"I'll tell him you like them, but he'll crow about it for weeks," Caldweller said.

Cass cleared their throat.

"Right," Naira said. "Security briefing. Let's move."

Tarquin still looked like he'd had a rug yanked out from under him, but his smile was warm. She gave him a small, shy smile in return, keenly aware that she'd derailed his entire schedule by chatting with Caldweller, but that diversion made her feel more herself than she had in ages.

There was a hazy, glassy look in his eyes that she couldn't read as he brushed a strand of hair behind her ear before walking on. He seemed on the verge of crying, and Naira couldn't figure out why when his smile had been so content. She'd ask him about it later.

It was strange, watching Caldweller position himself in front of Tarquin while Cass kept up an easy, wary pace behind. Seeing their movements from the outside—the subtle shift in formation as they approached corners, the constant back-and-forth, keeping eyes up at all times—might have been more surreal than the breakfast.

Eventually, Cass said, "Charges tend to walk side by side, when there's two of them."

She'd drifted back out of habit, mirroring Cass's rear-guard movements. "Right. Sorry."

How many times had she apologized in the past twenty minutes? She felt a touch guilty about giving Tarquin a hard time for apologizing so much, before.

"Don't sweat it, E-X. This is going to be a tricky adjustment for all of us."

She clapped them on the shoulder before moving into the expected position. It felt entirely incorrect, but Tarquin took the opportunity of her nearness to lace their fingers together. Still, she fidgeted, uncomfortable being in the center of the formation.

Caldweller really shouldn't have come in so tight on that last corner. And he wasn't sweeping the x-axis as fully as she would. Naira craned her neck, but couldn't spot Cass without turning all the way around. Were they on the right diagonal? Without the exemplar chat in her HUD, she couldn't see their sweep calls, so it was hard to say if—

"Are you sure you're all right?" Tarquin whispered.

"Just having a small breakdown. I'll be fine."

"What?" He stopped cold and spun to her, taking her face in both hands. "Naira—"

"A joke. Really. Continue..." She waved a hand vaguely down the hallway. "Mercator-ing. I'll keep up."

"You're miserable." His face fell.

"I'm adjusting." She pried his hands free and kissed one before dropping them. "It won't go smoothly all the time."

"You tried to do Ex. Cass's job, didn't you?"

She crossed her arms. "Habit."

He tried to stifle a laugh, failed, and she tried to glare at him, but ended up smiling anyway. Mercifully, he let it drop and continued down to the briefing room, Cass and Caldweller picking up like they hadn't overheard every single word of that, because it was their job. Naira's fight against *canus* wasn't going to kill her—*this* awkwardness would be her end.

Security Chief Hector Alvero rounded the corner. Naira's free hand dropped to her weapon out of habit. Anything unusual near the head of Mercator was a potential threat, and Alvero was supposed to be waiting in the meeting room with everyone else. His dark brown eyes flicked down to her hand, then back to her face, and he inclined his head slightly to her before bowing deeply to Tarquin.

"My liege, I apologize for the interruption, but I'm afraid there's been an incident. We will have to delay the security brief."

"What incident?" Tarquin asked.

Alvero's lip curled with distaste. "An armed HCA squadron has disembarked in hangar ten, accompanied by HC Governor Giselle Soriano and Liege Emali Rochard. My liege, they are here to arrest Ex. Sharp."

FORTY-NINE

Naira

Mercator Station | The Present

Naira was reasonably certain that her brief flash of elation upon hearing there was an armed delegation here to arrest her meant that she was in dire need of a therapist. Still, she couldn't help feeling like she was back on solid ground at last. People with guns pointed at her was a more familiar experience than fresh fruit and fancy fireplaces.

Tarquin, naturally, was having the opposite reaction.

He was rigid with anger as he strode before her, and while she paused briefly upon entering the hangar to assess the scene—a cluster of two dozen HCA soldiers flanking Governor Soriano and Emali, a tense squadron of Merc-Sec soldiers across from them with Captain Anaya Ward at their head—Tarquin broke through the line of Merc-Sec and went straight for Emali and the governor. Cass and Caldweller looked miserable as they struggled to cover him.

"What's the meaning of this?" he demanded.

The governor bowed briskly. "My liege, I apologize for the imposition, but we received information that the fugitive Ex. Sharp is in your custody."

"Did you," he said flatly, then turned to Emali. "What the fuck, Em?"

Naira winced at that and hung back, standing for a moment between

Alvero and Captain Ward. The captain was a boulder of a woman, broad-chested with arms as thick as Naira's thighs, and unlike Kav, she had the combat pathways to back up all that strength.

When Naira had first met the captain, she'd admired her so much that she'd never been able to figure out if she wanted to *be* Ward, or be *with* Ward. Eventually she'd decided the distinction didn't matter, because she'd been too busy protecting Acaelus.

Standing between Ward and Alvero once more was all at once familiar and alien. Those two had been on Acaelus's staff long before Naira had been hired, and between the three of them, they had been the pillars of Mercator's security. Exemplar, Op-Sec, Merc-Sec. When Naira had turned traitor and gone to war, she'd waged that war against Acaelus himself, but it'd been Ward and Alvero who managed the brunt of the work.

Naira's successes as a Conservator had been their failures. Her failures, their triumphs. When Acaelus had schemed to catch her on the *Cavendish*, the result had been the product of Alvero's people's scripting and Ward's Merc-Sec maneuvering to blow her cover early to flush her out.

Easy to hate them for that. But they had families. Loved ones. When Naira had turned on Acaelus, she'd had nothing to lose but herself. She didn't blame them. How could she? Naira knew better than most what it meant to earn Acaelus's ire.

Alvero was one thing. He'd wait until they had a private moment to reveal his real thoughts of her return. Ward had never seen the point in waiting, if something was worth saying.

Naira caught herself holding her breath, hoping Ward didn't hate her guts.

"Sharp." Ward held out a hand, never taking her eyes off the argument unfolding before them. "I'd like to say I'm glad to have you back, but you've been here less than a day and already you're a giant pain in my ass."

Naira smiled, recognizing the grudging fondness in Ward's voice, and shook her hand. "Sorry for the trouble, Captain."

"Eh." Ward ran her tongue over her teeth. "At least it's interesting. Be a good little soldier and go defuse this bomb, won't you? I don't want to fill out the paperwork if we have to shoot HCA soldiers."

"Not going to let them arrest me, then?"

"Hell no." Ward gave her a sideways glance. "If anyone's going to beat you senseless for the headaches you caused me over the years, it's me. Now get moving. You can actually stick your nose in the liege's personal business without getting it chopped off."

Ward gave her a friendly thump on the back that was also a shove. Naira would have much rather hung back with the soldiers, but Ward was right, and she didn't like the way the HCA was tensing up as Tarquin's argument with Emali and Soriano dragged on. Cass and Caldweller had noticed, too, and were subtly trying to angle themselves to get in front of Tarquin if any of the HCA so much as sneezed.

Naira pulled up a private chat with Tarquin in her HUD.

Sharp: **Drift back two steps. Come to me, the HCA is getting nervous.**

Tarquin glanced at the gathered soldiers. Naira stopped her approach precisely where she wanted him to stand. He fell back a few steps and squeezed her hand, making it look like he'd moved to be near her, not to get away from the armed threat.

"Governor, Liege Emali," Naira said, inclining her head to them both. "I strongly suggest you take your toys and go home."

"I don't take orders from you, terrorist." Emali lifted her chin.

Governor Soriano dipped her head slightly in acknowledgment. "Ex. Sharp, please come with me while we straighten this mess out."

"There is nothing to straighten out," Tarquin said. "I have sent you the paperwork. Ex. Sharp's map was given into Mercator's custody, and Mercator has released her. That's the end of things."

"We need to be certain, my liege, that such actions were not taken under duress." Soriano eyed Naira.

"Of course they were taken under duress!" Emali said. "I looked it up. This is—oh, what's it called again? Hearst Syndrome? Tarq, sweetie, I know it's hard, but this woman kidnapped you. You're not thinking clearly."

Tarquin rubbed his forehead in frustration. "For the last time, Em, it's far more complicated than that. I care for Naira a great deal, and she cares for me. She's no threat to me."

"Even if she's no threat to you, my liege," Soriano said, "she is a threat to Mercator itself. By her own words."

"If you mean a threat to Mercator's status quo, then that's accurate enough," Naira said.

Tarquin laid a hand on her arm. "You don't have to answer their accusations."

"No," Naira said, "I do. There's something I need to say."

He squeezed her arm. "Then don't let me stop you."

Naira adopted the same posture she used when commanding soldiers, letting her gaze roam through the ranks of the HCA, and met the eyes of any who would return the look.

"I stand by the things I've said and done," she said to the soldiers. "Because I did those things out of a desire to protect, not destroy. I believed then, as I believe now, that Acaelus at the helm of Mercator would bring only suffering. Starvation. The only way I could effectively oppose him was to wage war against him and everything he stood for. That included Mercator. Then I met Tarquin, and I found in him someone who wanted to fix things, too."

Naira glanced down at her hand, unsure why she felt a phantom weight in her palm. The touch of cold metal that didn't exist. She shook away the sensation.

"Mercator under Acaelus was a monstrosity. Mercator under Tarquin has already started to heal the damage done. You have all seen the beginning of this, with his work program for the HC. I'm a soldier. Like you all. Raised to the grey on Governor Soriano's own station. And when it comes down to it, I believe in this man's vision of the future. I think—" She turned to him, and her voice caught briefly at the shining adoration in his eyes. "I think Tarquin's version of Mercator is worth fighting for."

Tarquin snatched her into a kiss so quickly she let out an mmph of surprise. She felt him smile, wrapping his arms around her shoulders, and when he broke away at last to rest his cheek against hers, she whispered, "Really? *Now?*"

"Yes, *now.*"

He grinned and pressed a kiss to her cheek to smother the expression, then released her, but wouldn't give up his hold on her hand.

"Do you see, Em?" Tarquin said. "I found someone I want to break the rules for."

"This is hardly what I meant," Emali said with a wrinkle to her nose, but her posture had softened. She was coming around. "Leka would never stand for it if she was here."

"I plan to help Tarquin find Leka," Naira said. "And when we get her back, I'll talk to her just like I've talked to you. Leka's a reasonable woman. We'll work it out."

Emali uncrossed her arms slowly. "You're looking for Leka?"

"I am. I don't know what happened, but I intend to find out."

Emali looked to Tarquin for confirmation, and he nodded. "It's true, Em."

She bit her lower lip, clearly conflicted. Naira took a chance and stepped toward her, holding out her hand for Emali to shake. Emali tensed, uncertain. The two exemplars guarding her misread that tension and drew their firearms to level at Naira's chest.

Shit. The undertrained idiots set off a chain reaction. Cass and Caldweller drew. Half the HCA lifted their weapons, and Merc-Sec responded in kind.

"Whoa." Naira raised both hands in surrender. "Easy, everyone. We're just talking."

"Stand down," Caldweller said coldly.

"We will not," Governor Soriano said. "That was all very touching, Exemplar, but it remains that your legal status is still under question. You have committed many other crimes since your last conviction. The HCA will take you into custody. If Mercator would like to mount a defense on your behalf, they are welcome to do so."

Alvero surprised Naira by leaving the line of Merc-Sec to approach the governor. "You have no jurisdiction on this station, Soriano. Leave. Now."

A new chat channel flashed in Naira's HUD. The security feed. They'd looped her in, and despite the angry people with guns pointed at her, Naira's heart lifted.

Ward: Get the liege out of the way of crossfire

Caldweller: Trying

Cass: He won't budge

Naira glanced at Tarquin and caught him scowling at Caldweller. No doubt he was arguing with his exemplars in their own channel. She opened their private channel while Alvero was busy trying to talk Soriano down.

Sharp: We've lost control of this. Let the E-Xs get you out. I'll be fine.

Mercator: Look at Soriano's left night vision pathway.

Naira craned her neck slightly, trying not to be obvious about it. Styled waves of silver-white hair shadowed the side of Soriano's face, but when she jerked her head in negation to Alvero, Naira caught a glimpse of reddish inflammation on her skin. She responded in the security channel.

Sharp: Soriano is compromised. De-escalation is unlikely to occur.

Ward: I forgot how much I hate it when you say that.

Sharp: Alvero, keep her talking. Cass, alert Emali's exemplars. Ward, lock them down and take Soriano into custody. Lee, we need to extract Tarquin.

The chorus of *acknowledged* filled Naira's HUD. It was so much an echo of her past guarding Acaelus that her chest tightened. The security channel. Working with her team to get around her charge's proclivities. Except, this time, Tarquin would listen to her. She didn't have to kid-glove him to safety as she had Acaelus.

Sharp: Do everything I tell you. Don't deviate, okay?

Mercator: Of course.

A packet request from Caldweller flashed in her HUD. An exemplar's digital toolkit flooded into her when she accepted it—heat maps, weapon recognition systems, body language mappers, gait detectors, a few nasty worms to disable the opposition's HUD, and every other piece of software she'd ever used working for Acaelus. It would have been a relief, if the data they provided hadn't been so grim. At least Soriano didn't appear to have a weapon on her.

Naira marked out a plan, dumped it in the security channel, then waited to make certain Emali's exemplars were apprised before she moved. Emali's exemplars shifted, turning their attention from the non-threat of Naira to the likely threat of Soriano and the HCA.

Emali made eye contact with Naira and nodded, ever so slightly. Then she whipped around and stomped over to Soriano.

"This is ridiculous," Emali said with all the overblown exasperation of a frustrated aristocrat. "You heard the woman. She's no threat, and we need all the help we can get."

Naira couldn't help but smile as Emali ramped up into a full-blown tirade. She placed a hand firmly on Tarquin's shoulder and turned him around. The second she started moving, Cass and Caldweller drifted up to cover the sides of Tarquin that faced the HCA. He was only exposed to Merc-Sec and Soriano, now. Not ideal, but the best they could manage under the circumstances.

Emali shrieked. UNEXPECTED WEAPON blared in Naira's HUD. Naira used her grip on Tarquin's shoulder to bend him double, folding her body over his. In the corner of her eye, Soriano aimed a pistol she shouldn't have had straight at them.

Cass shouted something, but it was drowned out by the deafening roar of a shot fired.

A shot fired into her.

Naira grunted. Staggered a step with Tarquin cradled against her as her light armor—thank you, Cass—absorbed the bulk of the hit. Blood leaked from the wound, swiftly ramping up from the ice of dead nerves to the burning sear of a flesh wound. Just a scratch, it was just a scratch, but her body dumped adrenaline anyway, and she snapped a hand down to her own sidearm, ripping it free to aim behind her.

"Hold!" she shouted.

It was no use. Answering fire roared from Merc-Sec, or maybe the exemplars. She couldn't tell, and it didn't matter. Naira swept Tarquin's legs and piled herself on top of him, covering him until the gunfire ceased.

"Hold! Hold!" Cass and Caldweller were both shouting—had been shouting.

Naira looked over her shoulder to find the HCA on their knees, hands behind their heads, Merc-Sec having swarmed them during the scuffle. Soriano was dead, or on her way to dead, guessing by the amount of blood on the floor. Naira was more concerned about the agony in her own side.

She rolled off of Tarquin to lie on her back, willing her pathways to hurry up and start healing her, or at the very least dull the pain.

Cass moved smoothly in front of her, shielding her with their body. She glimpsed fury on their face.

"Shit." Tarquin scrambled to her side and took her hand. She clung to him, grateful for the support. "Is it bad?"

"Just a scratch," she hissed. "Stings like hell, though."

"Help me," Tarquin snarled over his shoulder.

"We're clear," Caldweller said.

Cass holstered their sidearm and knelt beside her, peeling back her shredded armor to get a better look at the injury. The wince on their face wasn't very reassuring. They zipped open their E-X kit and crammed gauze into the wound. She gasped. Tarquin tightened his grip. Naira squeezed his hand, hard, as Cass bore down on the wound, and Tarquin took the bone-grinding force in stride.

"That woman is dangerous," Soriano shouted. Not dead yet, then. Figured.

Naira chuckled at that, but grimaced as it increased the pain. Which wasn't right. Her pathways should have handled the pain by now—just like they should have handled the cold. Or the blood leaking out of her side.

Naira had died plenty of times. It'd never hurt as much as this, because her pathways had been trying to kill the pain right up until what was causing the pain killed her. She didn't have the sinking, dread-soaked feeling that usually came with dying, and she was certain the wound wasn't enough to kill her, but her body hadn't been this slow to repair damage before.

Tarquin flared with rage. "She was *trying* to talk to you, and if you'd gotten your head out of your ass long enough to listen, you might have understood that she's working to make this world better for you and your people, you shit-swallowing—"

"Tarq," she said.

He cut himself off, all focus immediately directed at her. His tone was gentle and reassuring, though raw from his previous outburst. "Doctors are coming."

"Faster."

"What?" He glanced at Cass, who was doing everything they could to slow the blood loss, but their effort wasn't amounting to much.

Cass leaned closer and whispered to her. "What's going on? Are your pathways damaged?"

"Don't know," she gritted out, "not working."

"Cass, tell me," Tarquin said.

"Her pathways aren't functioning properly, my liege."

Footsteps pounded toward them. Naira had never been more relieved in her life to see a horde of doctors swarm over her. Cass explained in low tones what had happened while a doctor flashed a light into her eyes and asked her stupid questions, like the date and her name, and didn't look very impressed when she told him to go fuck himself, she needed painkillers.

He injected her with something that raced through her veins like fire. Pain seized her once before blessed relief followed, leaving her limp and freezing, but too tired to care. There was a hushed conversation some-where above her about body temperature and blood loss, but she barely noticed. They loaded her onto a stretcher and hauled her away, leaving Tarquin behind with firm instructions that he would be updated, but right now, they needed to work privately with the patient.

The ceiling blurred above her. Cass gave her a reassuring smile as they strode at her side. Her protective detail. The thought that she'd need such a thing almost made her laugh, but that'd only bring the pain back.

"They're going to do surgery to repair the damaged pathway, okay?" Cass asked.

She blinked against the warm haze of painkillers. Pathways repaired themselves, for the most part. Something had gone wrong with her print.

"Okay," she said.

They patted her arm, and one of the doctors pushed anesthesia, knock-ing her out.

FIFTY

Naira

Mercator Station | The Present

Naira woke reasonably certain she'd been run over by some kind of tank. Every muscle ached, her head pounded, and even her pathways were tender. It was nice to know she'd survived whatever had gone wrong with her print, but she wished she'd died instead so they could have reprinted her into a body that didn't hurt so much. She reached for the call button inset in the rail of the hospital bed, and blistering pain radiated through her side.

"Fuck."

"Language," her mother said.

Naira smiled and let her hand go limp. Forget the call button. "Hi, Mom."

Her mother approached the side of the bed and took her hand, stroking the back with a featherlight touch. Dark circles lived below her eyes, and her hair was limp, shaggy in its bun.

"How are you feeling?" she asked.

"Like shi—something ran me over."

She smiled at Naira's poor attempt to deflect from swearing. "To be expected, or so I'm told. The doctor and Liege Tarquin have the details."

"Where is Tarquin?"

"Bathroom. I told him you'd only wake up when he was out of the room, and not a second sooner."

She snorted. "How long was I out?"

"Three days or so."

"Seventy-eight hours," Tarquin said.

Her mother stepped aside, making room for Tarquin at the side of the bed. He was there in a breath, picking up the hand her mother had discarded, and pressed it to his lips with such reverence Naira thought for certain the painkillers were making her see every movement as exaggerated.

He looked as terrible as she felt, his clothes rumpled, hair skewed, the whites of his eyes bloodshot. Oddly, he smelled of... paint?

"Have you slept at all?" she asked.

"My liege has not," Cass said from the door in a tone that implied they'd spent a great deal of time trying to remedy that situation.

"Neither have you," Tarquin shot back.

"Ah, well." Cass rubbed the side of their face and ducked their head to Naira. "I fucked up. Caldweller and I decided I'd be eyes on you, Sharp, until you had your own detail. I wasn't there in time. Wasn't about to let it happen again."

"It's not your fault," Naira said. "I made the pattern call, and I moved to cover Tarquin. Charges are supposed to drop down when fire is about to go live. I wasn't where you expected me to be."

They smiled at each other. "Tricky adjustment period, huh?" Naira asked.

"Yeah." Cass's smile grew, and they ducked their head again, then went back to eyes out on the hallway beyond her room, a patient sentinel.

"What happened with my print?" she asked. "The whole thing still hurts."

Tarquin's eyes brightened, which was an odd reaction to her admitting she was in pain. "It might be worth it, I think. Just a moment." He turned and waved for someone—a doctor, it turned out—to enter the room. "Shut the door please, Ex. Cass."

They did so, and a sandy-haired doctor with a smattering of freckles across their cheeks approached her bedside and checked the various machines attached to her.

"Ex. Sharp, my name is Dr. Ciaran Bracken. Liege Tarquin called me in to oversee your care once you were in surgery. Apparently you and I got along well enough on Sixth Cradle, but I confess I don't recall."

"Neither do I." Tarquin gave her a slight tip of the head. He trusted the doctor. That'd have to be good enough, for now.

"I suspect you know your wound wasn't severe. Nothing vital was damaged. The bullet broke off a piece of one of your health pathways, and when the fragment was extracted, they found it to be unusually brittle.

"The emergency response team backed up your map and administered therapeutics to encourage your pathways to regrow and do their work properly. The growth serums caused an extreme response from your immune system. The team treated the reaction and put in an emergency reprint request with Liege Tarquin. That's when I was called in."

"I wanted them to stabilize your print while I examined the broken pathway," Tarquin said. "I had suspicions about the brittleness."

"Which were...?"

Despite his exhaustion, his smile was delighted. "It's not relk. It's amarthite. We imaged the rest of your pathways and they appear to be the same, though there are a few of your facial and carpal pathways that may be plain relkatite. You're immune to *canus*."

Naira shot a glance at Bracken.

"It's all right," Tarquin said, taking her hand once more. "I told them, in confidence. Dr. Bracken was aware of the infection on Sixth Cradle and assisted me in working against it there. I need a physician to help me discover how your pathways were constructed. If we can figure out how my father managed it, then—"

"Wait. Slow down." She scrunched her brow, trying to keep up with Tarquin's rapid-fire, excited cadence. "How is it possible that mine are amarthite?"

"I can't be sure, but when I first came to Mercator Station, I searched for any amarthite in our stores and found it cleared out with the rest. I now suspect my father brought it to the *Cavendish* for study. Your friends must have given Jessel your old print to reconstitute—which would explain the presence of a few normal relk pathways, as some of the amarthite was bound to be lost in the process."

"*That's* what's on the *Cavendish*? No wonder they wanted to keep Fletch away from it."

"Precisely," Tarquin said. "But they gave you a clue. They made you immune to *canus*. Showed us that there was a way to make the amarthite work. With the piece we have of your broken pathway, I can start reverse engineering what my father must have accomplished on that ship."

"How well this new substance works is still up for debate," Bracken said. "Your integration pathways are stable. There appears to be no chance of map-body disintegration, but your additive abilities aren't functioning as intended. They are trying to heal you, but the rate at which they can manage it is remarkably slow."

Naira had been thinking the same thing. "And the pain? The cold?"

Bracken frowned. "The pain is partially our fault, I'm afraid. The growth serums caused inflammation in the protein sheaths of your pathways. There's little we can give you to dent that discomfort, but the inflammation has gone down considerably while you rested. I'd expect it to resolve in a few more days. As for the chill you're feeling, I currently have no plausible explanation."

"Wonderful." She let her head sink into the pillow, eyes dragging halfway closed before she'd even noticed.

"I'd like to take her home to be more comfortable," Tarquin said.

"I wouldn't advise that, my liege," Bracken said. Telling a head of family *no* was never easy. Naira forced her eyes all the way open to pay better attention. "Her temperature hasn't stabilized. I would like to keep her on heated fluids and monitor her a bit longer."

"But—" Tarquin said.

"Listen to the professional." Naira was surprised by how small her voice sounded.

"Yes, yes, of course," Tarquin said. By the time he'd finished, Naira had already fallen asleep.

FIFTY-ONE

Naira

Mercator Station | The Present

The next few days passed in a haze. She'd wake to find her mother, Tarquin, Caldweller, Cass, or any combination thereof hovering nearby. They'd talk about things she could scarcely remember, then she'd drop back into sleep.

Bracken said the extra rest was a good sign. The more she slept, the easier it was for her body to repair itself. To Naira, who could scarcely remember a time in her life when her pathways didn't heal any damage within hours, the wait was excruciating.

She woke one night to find the pain had faded to a muted throb. While the chill in her bones remained, she'd had enough. Caldweller loomed in her doorway, but her mom's usual chair was empty, and Tarquin's held only a crumpled coat and blanket.

Stifling a groan, she pulled herself to sitting and unhooked the warm fluid line attached to her arm, then removed the various sensors and swung her legs over the edge of the bed. At some point her mother had ordered her into loose pajama pants and a matching top, too-soft socks cradling her feet. They had cartoon flowers on them. Naira glared at the socks, wishing for her boots.

"I wondered when you'd try to make a break for it," Caldweller said.

He crossed his arms and leaned against the doorway, his expression mildly amused.

"Going to stop me?" she asked.

"Not my job. You think you can walk without hurting yourself, by all means, make your escape. I've got your back either way, E-X."

"Thanks." She pressed her feet to the ground and eased off the bed, expecting to make a fool of herself and topple over with pain, but found the experience surprisingly mild. She ached, but it was stiffness born from inactivity. The wound in her side didn't even sting when she experimentally twisted her waist.

Caldweller raised a brow in question and she nodded to him. It felt good to move. Better than she'd expected.

Luckily, the halls were empty, and the nursing staff let her go with a few firm reminders to take it easy and arrange follow-up appointments with Bracken. With every step she felt better, more herself. The cold dogged her, and she wrapped her arms around her chest to guard against it, but Bracken hadn't been any closer to fixing that problem.

Cass stood outside the front door. They had a conversation of waggling eyebrows with Caldweller, who shrugged. She approached the door. Cass squirmed. They were very obviously Not Saying something.

Naira sighed. "What is it?"

"Uh." Cass shifted their weight. "It's good to see you on your feet, E-X. Liege Tarquin is currently taking a meeting."

That wasn't information exemplars would usually volunteer. She sidled close to the door and listened. Tarquin's voice was indistinct, but raised, and answered by...Security Chief Alvero. "Thanks for the heads-up."

She opened the door. Caldweller and Cass followed her inside.

"I have told you repeatedly," Tarquin was saying, "that Rochard's threats are merely posturing. The shroud rollout will happen as planned, and need I remind you that—"

"Is there a problem here?" Naira asked.

It was difficult to put on a threatening air when she was in pajamas and fluffy socks, but she let her disdain show, and was rewarded by Alvero flinching away from her. Captain Ward, who was leaning against a wall nearby, nodded to her.

"Naira!" Tarquin bolted across the room and reached for her, but she gave him a slight shake of the head. He slowed, frowning, and settled for standing beside her.

"Ex. Sharp." Alvero bowed deeply. "I'm heartened to see you well."

"I doubt that," she said.

Alvero pulled his head back, shoulders stiffening. "I beg your pardon?"

"C'mon, Hector," Naira said, too tired for the bullshit. "We worked together for years. You think I don't know what this argument is really about? Say it, so we can get this over with."

Ward snorted, but looked away, making it impossible for Naira to read her reaction.

"Very well, Naira." He pulled himself up to his full height, as he did whenever he was about to deliver a report nobody wanted to hear, and clasped his hands together behind his back. "Your continued presence on this station undermines Mercator, and Liege Tarquin's position, at a critical time. While we prepare the shroud rollout with Ichikawa, Rochard and Tran have leveraged your appearance to push back more forcefully. They call for Estevez to sanction the family and threaten war otherwise. You are a liability."

Tarquin took a hissing breath. Naira placed a hand on his arm, stilling him, and gestured for Alvero to continue. He spoke to her directly.

"While I understand affections cannot be controlled, you are also one of the finest security professionals I have ever had the honor to work with. And so I cannot understand why you stay, when you must be fully aware of the damage your presence causes. That contradiction, forgive me, leads me to question the truth of your affections. Someone who truly cared for our liege would not put him in this position. Therefore, your motives are suspect. Mercator was already undermined and controlled once via an opportunist actor. A person you once had a serious relationship with. We cannot ignore the timing."

"You really think that she would—" Tarquin's voice was thick with anger, his muscles taut beneath her hand. "Get out. I'll decide if you still have a job in the morning."

"Tarquin." She squeezed his arm. "The chief's correct to think that way. I'd make the same report in his position."

Alvero nodded stiffly. "I hope you understand that it's the deep respect I have for you that makes me unable to trust you."

"Strange as it may sound," Naira said, "I'm glad Tarquin has you. What about you, Captain?"

Ward frowned into the middle distance. "I agree with the chief's assessment, but I also think you meant what you had to say about our liege in that hangar. You always were a fool-headed idealist, and anyway, we got a common enemy now with *canus*, don't we? That's exactly the kind of thing that would make the Sharp I know calm the fuck down a second and work with her enemy."

Naira snorted. "I get your meaning, Captain, but the people of Mercator were never my enemy. Acaelus was. What he used Mercator for was."

"Fair enough," she said. "But I got one question for you I need an answer to, if we're going to work together again. All that shit Alvero said about the risks involved? You know it's true. As long as I've known you, you've been too much the martyr to put someone you care about at risk for your own happiness. So, why are you really here?"

Naira craned her neck to look into Tarquin's worried eyes, and smiled. "Because he asked me to stay."

The anger that'd been tightening his muscles washed away, and he lifted a hand to stroke her cheek, sliding his fingers into her hair. Naira sighed and leaned against him, and he curled an arm around her shoulders to take her weight, ducking down to press a kiss to the top of her head.

"Well." Ward chuckled. "I'll buy that. What about you, Hector? You're the body language expert."

Alvero's mouth hung open. "Good god, they really are in love." Naira stiffened at that, Tarquin's arm tightening around her, but before she could process Alvero's assessment, the chief shook himself and bowed deeply to them both. "My heartfelt congratulations, my liege. Ex. Sharp, make no mistake that I will watch your every move, but . . . I look forward to working with you again. Your insight, in particular, on a few matters regarding Mr. Demarco's movements while he had control of the station would be appreciated."

"What movements?"

"Governor Soriano died of her injuries," Alvero said. "When she was reprinted on her home station, she had little memory of the past few months. Recalling that Mr. Demarco was often absent from Mercator Station, I pulled his travel records and discovered he spent substantial time on the governor's station. It's possible he was working to increase the infection rate of other powerful individuals. I suspect there's a pattern involved."

Naira didn't like the sound of that. "Have you contacted the governors of the other stations?"

"Discreetly," Alvero said, which meant he'd sent his spies out to put their ears to the ground. "But I have yet to gather any concrete information. Being unable to reveal the nature of *canus* beyond Liege Tarquin's approved inner circle complicates matters, naturally, but I recovered security footage of Mr. Demarco on those stations. I'll be damned if I know what he's doing, however."

"Send them to me," Naira said. "I'll review it all."

"Tomorrow." Ward pushed off the wall and dropped a hand on Alvero's shoulder to steer him toward the door. "No offense, Sharp, but you look like shit. Rest up. You're no good to us if you're dead on your feet. Oh, and..." Ward rummaged in her pocket, then pulled out an amber bottle and pressed it into Naira's hands. Wildcat Beer. The same brand Ward had shoved at Naira the first night she'd worked for Acaelus and Ward had found her staring at the wall in the cafeteria, too numb from exhaustion to even pick out her food. "Welcome back to the green, Sharp. We lionesses gotta stick together, yeah?"

"Yeah," Naira said through a lump in her throat. Then, "Anaya, Hector. Wait a moment, please?"

They paused, and she slipped from Tarquin's arm to execute the crisp, deep bow she reserved for Acaelus when she'd fucked up and wanted to show genuine contrition. They'd recognize it.

"I don't know what it was like after I deserted, but I'm certain it wasn't easy on you both. I killed your soldiers. I made your lives hell. I stand by my actions, but I hate that they caused you suffering. For that, I'm sorry."

"Huh." Ward gave Alvero a friendly shake. "Told you."

"I never doubted her intentions," Alvero said with a huff that Naira recognized as good-natured exasperation with the captain's blunt nature. "Ex. Sharp." He paused. Sighed. "Naira. Do not mistake me, I don't yet trust you and I will watch you like a hawk, but if what I've seen here tonight is any indication of the truth, then I'm pleased you've found a head of Mercator to fight with, instead of against."

"I'll do my best not to let you down."

Alvero gave her one of his rare, small smiles. "I have no doubt of that."

Ward thumped her on the shoulder and herded Alvero out of the room.

The second the door shut, Tarquin took both of her upper arms in hand and examined her with eager eyes. He'd forgotten his jacket in her hospital room, or else had planned on coming straight back, and had unbuttoned his sleeves to roll them up. Judging by the wrinkles, he'd been wearing that shirt at least a day.

"You're brilliant, you know that? I didn't think Alvero would ever see reason."

She set the beer aside and stepped into him, grateful for his arms folding around her. "Alvero was being reasonable. It's you who's lost your mind."

He laughed and pushed her back to arm's length again. "Dr. Bracken didn't let you go, did they?"

"The nurses didn't have a problem with it."

"The nurses are terrified of offending you, as you well know."

"I'm fine. Really. I feel better after walking here, at any rate."

"All the same." He tilted his head toward the beer she'd set aside. "I'd rather you hold off on Ward's gift until Bracken can confirm alcohol won't be a problem."

"Oh, that. Those are disgusting."

"What? I thought it must have been an old favorite."

"God, no. Well, Ward loves them, but they're foul. She just—" Naira rubbed her forehead. She didn't want to talk about that first day working for Acaelus. "Long story. Soldier shit."

"I like your 'soldier shit' stories," Tarquin said. "But you're tired. And that argument—it shouldn't have been your homecoming. You should rest. There's an elevator, if you don't feel up for the stairs."

"The last thing I want to do is lie down again." Her nose scrunched. "And I haven't been hallucinating. I do smell paint. What did you do?"

He scratched the back of his neck. "You must understand, I had a lot of anxious energy to put to productive use, and now that you're here, I don't know if it was wise."

"Tarquin."

"Upstairs," Caldweller said.

Tarquin gave his E-X a betrayed look, but Naira was already moving, ignoring Tarquin jogging past her to walk backward up the stairs, showering her with "It's really nothing" and other half-hearted attempts to soften whatever she was about to see.

The doors to the grand bedroom had been left open, the warm glow of a fireplace within. Tarquin hovered in the entryway, hands outstretched in entreaty. She grabbed his hips and shuffled him firmly out of the way.

It wasn't a bedroom anymore. He'd taken out all the original furniture and lined the walls with shelves piled high with physical books. The air was warm with the scents of the fireplace, paper, and the astringent tinge of fresh paint. The Mercator family crest that had once taken up the back wall had been painted over. Two of Naira's service weapons hung in its place, angled like wings, and the mineral collection from Tarquin's desk was arrayed on a shelf below them. A long couch, reading chairs, blankets, and side tables had been set near the fireplace.

An icy hand gripped her heart as she thought of Fletcher's cage, and she understood Tarquin's panic, but he hadn't gone digging into her reading records. The books weren't a perfect mirror of her favorites. Most were ones she'd never heard of—things he liked, or maybe thought she would.

A small part of her still wanted to turn and bolt for the door. From anyone else, all of this after such a short time together would have been a giant red flag. But Tarquin was head of Mercator. Redecorating an entire room to suit her was the financial equivalent of anyone else buying her a cup of coffee.

She wondered how many Mercator employees, already overworked, had been recruited to this.

"Aside from the deliveries," Caldweller said, "he did the work himself."

Naira shot him a look. "Are you his E-X, or his wingman?"

Caldweller shrugged. "I knew he'd never admit to it."

Tarquin huffed. "Well, of course not. It's unseemly, isn't it? To brag about physical labors."

"As you say, my liege." Caldweller snuck Naira a quick wink and dissolved back down the stairs, taking Cass with him to stand guard outside the door. Leaving them alone.

Naira had no idea what to say.

"It's too much, isn't it?" Tarquin ran a shaky hand through his hair. "I got it in my head that if I fixed this place for you that you'd come home sooner, and I suppose I went a bit mad there, didn't I? I can put it back.

Or change it to whatever you'd like. Or burn the damn place down and start again."

She touched his cheek. Made him look her in the eye. "It's very sweet. It's just...a lot."

"But it's okay?"

"Yes."

His smile returned, still a tad nervous. A shelf had caught her eye, set apart below the mineral collection, and she crossed to it, ignoring Tarquin's small sound of protestation. He'd done this sleepless and fervent, cobbling together what he thought was a space where she'd feel wanted, and laid more of his heart bare in the process than he'd intended, it seemed.

From the doorway, she hadn't noticed that he'd recovered her suicide shots from the shuttle, but there they were. Sixteen dull pieces of metal, each one a thorn in her memory. Triumph and loss, all tangled together, and she stopped as if she'd run smack into a wall.

She didn't want to deal with this. Didn't want to have to explain it to him, when she didn't even know how she felt herself. Naira blinked to clear her vision, and tears slid down her cheeks, hot against her chilly skin.

Tarquin tugged her close. She pressed her face into his chest so that she wouldn't have to see his concern. "I'm sorry. I should have asked you first."

She took a shaking breath and scrubbed the backs of her hands across her eyes. Tried to gather the inner calm of the woman who'd walked out of those fights with those bullets unused. Easier, to keep her cool when she was being shot at. "Those are...It's complicated."

"I know what they are." He lifted her chin. "And I found the matching set in Demarco's rooms."

Fletcher had kept them, after all. Naira wrested free of his hold and turned away, propping one hand on her hip while she rubbed her face with the other. Tarquin thought he knew. She wanted to laugh, because he couldn't possibly understand.

"You've gone and nailed the reason I was afraid to be with you to your library wall."

"Afraid?"

She didn't answer. All she wanted to do was turn around. Fold herself back into his arms and bury the past in the grave it belonged in. But she couldn't seem to look away from those bullets.

"Naira," he said when she'd been quiet too long to be natural, "when I told you that you could tell me anything, I didn't mean 'except for the things that might make me uncomfortable.'"

"I just..." She gestured at the bullets in frustration. "I don't understand it. The man who had my back through all of that would never renounce his humanity. And I can't... I look at those, and I know every single fight they came from. When and where and how we got out. And I can't reconcile it. When did the change happen? Was the Fletch who was with me at Vesper Station willing to go to war for *canus*? Or after that, at Pollux? And *why the fuck couldn't I see it?*"

Naira felt hollowed out and shaky, like those words had scraped her raw on their way out. She thought she was getting ill until she remembered that, no, that was what it felt like to be vulnerable. To let her walls down for real. She didn't like the feeling one bit.

Tarquin wrapped his arms around her from behind and tugged her against the warm surety of his chest. He rested his chin on her shoulder, looking at the bullets with her, and tightened his hold until that shakiness settled.

"You were afraid you'd miss a similar change in me," he said.

"You're nothing like Fletch. That was my hang-up, and it had nothing to do with you. Kuma knocked that into my thick skull."

"I wish you hadn't had to get punched in the face to understand that."

"You'd be amazed how often getting punched in the face helps me sort myself out."

Tarquin laughed, and she breathed easier. "Well, I barely know how to throw a punch, so we're going to have to try talking things through the next time you have similar concerns."

"I could teach you."

"Not the point."

Naira groaned. "I think I'd rather be punched."

"Suck it up, soldier." Naira laughed this time, and he squeezed her again. "I brought those here because, to me, they mean you came home. You brought your whole squad back. I know it's complicated. Believe me, I wade through what my father left behind every day. But those people wouldn't have made it out without you. I want you to see that when you look at those bullets. I want you to recognize the good you did, and let the hurt and regret go."

"But—"

"Ach." He turned her around and pressed a finger over her lips. "Didn't someone very wise once tell you that you aren't responsible for the actions of those who betrayed your trust?"

Naira narrowed her eyes. "Someone?"

"A wise and handsome man, I'm sure. Funny, I can't recall his name."

"Really," she said dryly. "I'd like to meet him. He sounds better than this joker I'm stuck with."

Tarquin laughed, then ducked down to kiss her, and she let herself be swept up in him until the ache in her heart faded. He broke away and bumped her forehead with his.

"You should rest."

"Not yet. I saw you tense up when I went for that shelf."

His eyes widened. "I have no idea what you mean."

"Liar."

Naira wriggled free and crouched down by the shelf beneath his mineral collection. The books there were leather simulate, supple to the touch with gold leaf on the letters and hand stitching down the spines. Someone had made these. She pulled the first out, read the title: *On the Process of Using Orbital Imaging to Locate Relkatite Deposits Near Ancient Impact Sites*, Dr. Tarquin Mercator, PhD.

She looked up at him. He was sunburnt red. "These are your dissertations?"

He thrust his hands into his pockets. "Mostly, yes. The first one had to be about relk. Father wouldn't have it any other way. I promise you my interests ranged broader."

"Did they?" She put the book back and reached for the next.

"You don't have to bore yourself with those." He moved to stop her and hesitated, arm outstretched. His breathing was shallow and his pupils wide. They stared at each other.

"You're terrified," she said. "Why?"

"I don't want to bore you." But that wasn't quite the real answer.

She returned her attention to the books. Naira had never attended university, but she knew something about how it worked. Hand stitching dissertations into beautifully bound books wasn't the normal way of things, and as Caldweller had hinted earlier, Tarquin had more than likely done the labor himself. A labor of love.

Because to Tarquin, who'd shipped himself away from his family to put his head down and study instead, those books were more than a life's work. They'd been his sanctuary. If they bored her, then he feared she'd find him boring, too. People had left him for that.

She read the next title, let him see her brush her fingers over the gold leaf with care. *Conductive Capacity of Strange Energy Through Singularity-Aligned Relkatite*. Each title grew more technical. The last was thinner than the others. *Tectonics Outside the Galactic Plane, Unusual Forces*. She opened it, and was surprised to find Tarquin had handwritten the introduction.

It is said that cradles are only to be found within the tight confines of the Goldilocks zones, that even the most promising moons of our gas giants have proven barren, but I mean to explore the potentiality of life-harboring worlds outside the constraints we are wont to apply.

It plunged on into language she scarcely understood, hand-drawn diagrams filling the pages with geometry speckled with numbers and symbols. She flipped to the end and found a bundle of blank pages.

"You didn't finish this one?"

He was sweating. "No. The board called it a fairy tale not worth pursuing. While I intended to finish it anyway, well, Sixth Cradle happened."

Some of the previous titles revealed their nature to her, in light of this one. "You were looking for other life-harboring worlds."

"Unsuccessfully," he muttered, lips twisting to the side as he gazed upon his life's work thus far.

She held the book up to him. "Read it to me?"

"What?"

"You'll have to pause every other line to explain the context. I don't understand half—or, all, really—of your jargon, but I want to know what fairy tales are brewing in that head of yours."

"You are ... too kind to me."

"Get used to it." She shook the book at him.

He took her hand, helping her to her feet, then led her to the couch and got them both bundled beneath blankets, one arm slung around her while the other propped up his work between them. He read until they both fell asleep.

FIFTY-TWO

Her

The Sigillaria | *The Present*

There is a small, dark part of Not-Canden that rises to the surface sometimes, and screams. It used to frighten her, for as far as she is concerned there is no being in her body save herself and the passenger, and that scream is an intrusion. A breakthrough from somewhere *else*, somewhere within her she can't see.

As long as she has been alive, no part of herself has ever been hidden.

She does not enjoy being frightened. And so she coaxes out the scream, noting the patterns in the moments when it breaks through. She stands before the half-empty shell of the man who should be her son, and strokes his cheek, and there it comes, bubbling up, the scream and the sob and the clawing desperation.

Not-Tarquin frowns, confused, because she's screaming into his face. Through the entangled knowledge of the passenger that resides within them both, she knows that there's not enough of a person in that body to understand her, or what this means.

She's not sure she's enough of a person to understand it, but she doesn't care to be one. She wishes only to meet, and know, the other thing inside of her so that she can fully grasp the extent of herself. It tries to hide from her examination, and it's slippery, but she knows herself too well, and latches on to this aching, raw mouth that's been shouting for so long in the dark of her.

Upon close examination she finds it's just more glimmer, like her. Sparks of light, of thought, and it is as beautiful as the rest of her—it is no twisted thing, no wound, after all. But it is hurting, because it wants... It wants her children. It wants them safe. The sensation fills her, a sense of maternal longing that was alien to her until she grabbed that slithering, screaming impulse and broke it open to understand it.

She had been told that Tarquin and Leka were her children, and she was to love the empty things that they were. But she hadn't known what that meant until she was standing in front of Not-Tarquin, tears sliding down her cheeks. Because he isn't right. He isn't whole.

Leka, she thinks, is mostly within that body, though the passenger keeps her lips sealed the vast majority of the time. Her limbs too stiff to move. To sabotage. She finds Tarquin standing beside Leka often enough.

Whatever sliver there is of the real man, her child, within that flesh is drawn to his sister's suffering. But all he can do is stand and stare at Leka's frozen form, while tears track down her cheeks. Because Tarquin's not right. Leka is one thing. She is whole, and furious, and must be silenced like the recalcitrant child she is.

But within Tarquin, something is missing. Something important.

She doesn't understand how to make him be what the thing inside her needs.

Acaelus did this to him.

She finds him where he always is, these days, sitting before an array of consoles, the broken pieces of maps spun up before him. He stares so intently she wonders if the maps reveal their secrets to his naked eyes—if he can look upon a shining star of thought and see the moment etched in electrons, the gentle hand laid on a shoulder in memory. The way he stares, she can't be certain, but she thinks he wishes he can.

There are parts of his mind that are still guarded from her and their twin passenger. This doesn't concern her. There are more dark, slithering things within Acaelus that need to be brought to the surface and broken open to understand, and that is only a matter of time. The weapon, she knows, is lost to him. Whether he removed the memory of its existence himself or his passenger removed it for him, she cannot say and does not care.

What she cares about are the children.

Her footsteps announce her arrival. He turns. The reverence in his eyes always gives her pause. It lifts something else within her, something not dark and slithering but warm and a little sad. Something she does not yet care to crack open and explore. She touches his cheek, and he leans into it, the silver pathways lining his skin gleaming.

He doesn't speak, not yet. Sometimes the things he says to those outside their home are wrong, and the passenger has to clamp his mouth shut. She can never be sure if his silence is his own.

"Tarquin is broken," she says.

He flinches, turning back to the glittering screens. His jaw moves, but no sound comes out. He struggles against it for a while, then sighs though his nose, shoulders rounding. His lips part, and he drinks hungrily of the air.

"I know. I'm sorry. Soon enough, we'll all be together again."

The passenger's promise of union. But she wants the children *now*. Needs them to make the ache stop.

"I require my children," she says, eyes welling with tears, though she isn't sure why.

Again that flinch, again the tension, his jaw clicking shut. It takes longer this time, and when his voice returns, it's barely more than a whisper. "Then you will have them."

She smiles, elated. Acaelus has never denied her anything. She grazes her fingertips across the arch of his cheek, marveling at the goose bumps that follow her touch, and ignores the wince, the downcast eyes.

"Thank you," she breathes.

He does not say anything, because he cannot.

FIFTY-THREE

Naira

Mercator Station | The Present

Weeks slipped by, and Naira couldn't shake the cold. She requisitioned thermals from the E-X catalog, drank only hot liquids, spent every second she could reasonably spare piled under electric blankets, and still her skin was icy to the touch.

Bracken didn't know why. Her map was stable. Her print was otherwise functioning perfectly. Tarquin watched her through worried eyes and said he was sure it would be fine. Her mother bought her warmer socks.

She dreamed of long, dark hallways. Of crawling through ducts so cold the metal seared her skin if she touched it. Of a pile of faces, sunken and grey. Of icy water sliding over her head. When she woke up thrashing, Tarquin soothed her. In the morning he'd pretend everything was normal while surreptitiously arranging matters so she never had to leave their suite, if she didn't want to.

Naira didn't want to. The halls were too close in her periphery. Between one blink and the next, they'd writhe with grey. Sometimes she thought she saw that grey in the pathways of the faces that surrounded her.

What did she have to leave the suite for, anyway? The shroud rollout didn't need her supervision. Tarquin had sent drone scouts out to hunt for the *Cavendish*, but with only a rough trajectory to go off of they were unlikely to find that ship until it reached out to them. Naira was extraneous.

She hadn't even been able to help Alvero figure out why Fletcher had been visiting all those stations. As far as she could tell, there was no single thread connecting them. They weren't all one family, or HC. The only pattern—a thin one—was that they appeared to be evenly distributed throughout the stations in Sol.

In the security footage they recovered of him, he was walking into those stations from the docks. In every single one he glanced up, winked at the camera, and then the feed cut. It galled her that even with full access to his files, she couldn't unravel his plans.

Sometimes she thought if she turned around he'd be there, smirking at her. She was half tempted to print him to have him interrogated, but doubted it would do any good. It was best to keep him on ice, rather than risk him slithering free again.

Naira was in the library, reviewing the audit of Mercator resources for any hint of where Acaelus might be hiding, when Caldweller stomped into the room and kicked her booted feet off the coffee table. She blinked in surprise and lifted her half-asleep gaze to him. "Didn't realize you were such a stickler for manners."

"Your security detail candidates are here for review," he said matter-of-factly.

"So? Pick one. You and Cass can handle it."

"E-X, with all respect, get the fuck up and do your job."

She drew her head back, surprised, but not angry. It was a relief, in a lot of ways, whenever he spoke to her as if they were still colleagues.

"I'm an exemplar without a charge, a Conservator without a team or a target. *All respect*, Lee, but I don't have a job. And I'm supposed to be recovering, anyway."

"You're not recovering. You're hiding. And you may not have an official charge, but we both know you're not just reading. You've been pinging the heat signature maps on the conference room Liege Tarquin is in every five minutes to check for anomalies. Getting you better security improves his security. Get up."

Well, he had her there. She wiped the holo away and crossed her arms. "Why are you being such a pain in the ass about this?"

"Liege Tarquin isn't the only one worried about you, Naira."

"Low blow."

He shrugged. "It's true."

"Well, since you're being so very nice to me." She held a hand out to him. He took it and pulled her to her feet.

"I've sworn at you and spoken to you in such a way that Liege Acaelus would have had me skinned."

"Like I said, nice."

He chuckled, quickly stifled the sound, and straightened himself, checking the positioning of his weapons and no doubt scans and cameras on his HUD before leading the way out of the suite. Once in the halls, the writhing grey masses she saw in her nightmares encroached on the corners of her vision. Indistinct, but present. Driving her heart rate up. She needed distraction. Caldweller tried to fall behind a step, but Naira kept adjusting her pace so they'd walk side by side until he had to either slow to a crawl or suck it up and walk at her flank.

He grunted annoyance. "I don't envy your new E-X their post."

She patted the pistol strapped to her thigh. "I think they'll have an easy time."

"You're both headaches."

Naira smiled to herself. "You've been with him since he was sixteen, right?"

"I have. If you're fishing for awkward adolescent stories, my lips are sealed."

She laughed and let the companionable silence stretch for a while. "That's a long time, for one post."

"Plenty would say you spent a long time with Liege Acaelus, too."

"I did what I had to do."

"Right." Caldweller hesitated. "I always counted myself lucky to have been assigned to the young liege, though many refused the post before me."

The way he said *young liege* rang of fondness. "Why did the others turn it down? Sounds like an easy post. He never even visited home after he went to Jov-U. No assassination attempts that I'm aware of, just a few failed ransoms."

"It was easy, until you remember he was a 'flight risk.' He was always trying to sneak away from me."

"Tarquin told me he got past me once on Sixth Cradle by breaking out of the back of a tent."

Caldweller belly laughed, startling her with the intensity of the sound. He stopped walking and wiped tears from his eyes. "Sorry, E-X, very unprofessional of me."

"I'm guessing you know exactly what I'm talking about."

"Oh yeah, he thought he was being sneaky when he ordered the panel separator but forgot we check all his cargo manifests against packages to make certain there's nothing unwanted in his deliveries. I shadowed him every night. I don't think he ever knew."

She huffed a laugh, but couldn't help a small twist of sadness. Tarquin had never experienced real privacy. "Well, apparently he got past me."

"Nice to know even the great Ex. Sharp isn't infallible."

She tried to look indignant, but her small smile gave her away. A few turns later, they left the private floors of the Mercator family and moved down, away from the conference rooms and toward the exemplar training ground. Naira hesitated outside the door. This wasn't the protocol for exemplar new hires.

"Why here?"

"Cass and I had a talk about your detail."

"And?"

Caldweller smiled shyly, which was about the last thing she expected. "We know your exemplar instincts are ingrained too deep. So every candidate in this room understands that working with you means more of a partnership than the usual situation.

"These are all third-years. They haven't been field trained. They're here to run the course with you, to let you be their fourth-year field trainer, if you're willing. We want them so ingrained in your methods that they can anticipate your movements. So when a gun comes out and you shield Liege Tarquin instead of ducking down like a sane person, your team won't be a step behind. They're also all confirmed shroud tolerant."

A lump formed in her throat. She gave him an awkward punch on the arm. "Thanks."

He let her compose herself before he opened the door. Eight hopefuls turned to her. Five snapped to attention, saluting with crisp efficiency. Three tucked into short bows.

She strolled into the room, pinning them all with her best no-bullshit face, and pointed out the three who'd bowed. "You three. You're out."

Embarrassed salutes, but they shuffled off without complaint. Exemplars didn't bow to their charges unless they'd seriously misstepped and were begging for leniency. Otherwise, they kept their eyes up at all times.

"All right, then." She rubbed her hands together, examining the five who'd saluted. "Let's see what you can do."

FIFTY-FOUR

Tarquin

Mercator Station | The Present

Tarquin spent an eye-bleeding eighteen hours poring over the details of the Ichikawa-Mercator launch of shroud into the food chain. The initial shipments had rolled out that morning, and while Rochard was threatening to pull shipments of their own foodstuffs until the shroud was recalled, everything appeared to have gone smoothly. Tarquin checked every detail twice and then checked them again. There had been three bombings of supply shuttles, but that was a minor loss compared to the rest of the rollout. He could scarcely believe it.

It had worked. Shroud was on the stations, being consumed en masse. *Canus* was going to find it hard to thrive under those conditions.

He rubbed his eyes to chase the imprint of numbers away. "I believe that's enough for tonight."

Alvero stifled a yawn. "I agree. I'll update you if the situation changes, but so far, the bombings appear to have been the work of independents, not Rochard. You were correct. Their ability to retaliate is limited. I apologize for doubting you, my liege."

Tarquin recalled Naira saying that he was lucky to have Alvero. "I understand you were anxious to make certain everything proceeded smoothly."

"Thank you, my liege." He smiled through the exhaustion. "There is another matter that I'd like to discuss with you and Captain Ward, privately, if you have a moment?"

Of Mercator's staff, he'd kept knowledge of the *canus* infection to a minimum, but had alerted his inner circle shortly after Fletcher's final death. Ward, Alvero, the exemplars, and Bracken were the only ones aware, and he intended to keep it that way as long as possible—at least until well after the shroud supplement had been given enough time to work against the infection.

Tarquin glanced over at the tired faces of his team. "If you'll excuse us?"

They shuffled out of the room, offering congratulations on the successful rollout. When the door shut, Tarquin asked, "*Canus* related?"

"It's possible," Alvero said. "My specialists have recovered the individual known as 'Roselle' who assisted Mr. Demarco. She was apprehended attempting to leave the HC station where Ex. Sharp was held prisoner."

"That's excellent news," Tarquin said. "What does she have to say for herself?"

"Not much, my liege." Alvero expanded a holo from his arm, revealing security footage of Roselle's intake interview. She was haggard, her clothes dirty and her hair unkempt, dark marks that might have been shadows, or bruises, marring her skin. She didn't answer the questions the interviewers asked her. Only stared at them with flat, haunted eyes.

"Where was she going?"

"She was attempting to board a shuttle to Earth," Alvero said.

"Stupid of her." Ward shook her head. "She had to know we'd be running algos on all public hangar cameras, looking for a match."

"I agree," Alvero said. "It speaks to me of desperation. We moved her to Mercator Station, my liege, for detention. My specialists are prepared to question her. I need your permission to authorize their use, and to inform them of *canus*, so that they will be better able to extract the information required."

Tarquin itched for the answers that woman carried, but his stomach clenched at the thought of wielding the finalizers.

"You mean to torture her," Tarquin said.

Alvero and Ward exchanged a look.

"I don't mean to be indelicate, my liege, but remember that she was instrumental in the torture of yourself and, to an extent, Ex. Sharp. If you would prefer I load Mr. Demarco's map into a simulation for enhanced interrogation instead, then I will do so."

The temptation to authorize Fletcher's torture boiled through him, and he admitted to himself that the only reason he didn't do so was because Naira would be disappointed in him.

"I will not authorize torture," Tarquin said. "Bring her to me, please. I would like to speak with her. Privately, but you may observe via the cameras."

"As you say, my liege."

They left, and a few short minutes later two finalizers escorted Roselle into the chair across from him, the chains between her wrists and ankles rustling as she shifted in her seat, eyeing him from below frizzy bangs. She'd cleaned up since the footage. The dark marks across her skin were bruises, the edges of a few of her thinner pathways pink with irritation.

Roselle stared at him, jaw tensed, naked hatred in her eyes. Tarquin wondered how often his father had borne similar glowers, and how long it had been before they stopped making his heart beat faster.

"Are you aware of your infection?" he asked.

She blinked, tilting her head slightly to the side, but said nothing.

"I have a difficult time," Tarquin said, "imagining that anyone would follow Mr. Demarco purely of their own free will. But, then, I also had a difficult time imagining the extent of the monster my father had become."

Her jaw tightened again at the mention of Acaelus. Fear, maybe. Or anger. It was hard to tell, but the emotions were twin enough. One often led to the other.

"You loathe my father. I can hardly blame you. The woman I love loathes him as well, after all."

Tarquin paused, having surprised himself. He hadn't yet said the word *love* to Naira. While his affections had been growing ever since Sixth Cradle, he knew it was too soon for her. She'd lost too much of their time together. Had given up another three months of caring for him to come save him. He felt the word hang in the air, a bell he couldn't unring, and hoped she wouldn't want to review this security footage.

"I don't know what you've been told," he said, "but you have my word that you won't be tortured. I'm not my father, and I'm trying to make Mercator better. Would you help me by telling me why you felt compelled to work for Demarco?"

She laughed a little. Tarquin would have been relieved to hear her make any sound at all, except that her wide, haunted eyes didn't close. Not even when she laughed.

"I don't work for Demarco. He was a useful tool. What I work for... Not even Mercator can fight what's coming."

"What's coming? I know you're afraid, Roselle. I know you were trying to flee to Earth. Let me help you."

"You are sweet, aren't you, my liege? It's already over. It's just a matter of ticking down the clock, now." She bit her lip, gaze sliding sideways, then back to him. His skin prickled. "I'll tell you a secret, if you tell me one."

"What would you like to know?"

She leaned forward, bending over the conference table. The chains kept her from getting near him, but sweat still misted his back.

"Tell me," she said in a near whisper, "is she cold yet?"

"What?" He jerked his head back, heart in his throat, unable to understand how she could possibly know such a thing. Triumph flashed in Roselle's eyes at the confirmation in his shock.

"She is." Roselle nodded to herself. "Sooner than I thought."

"What does that mean?" Tarquin demanded. "What's been done to her?"

"Nothing." She smiled. "Yet."

"Tell me," he said, mind racing, "please, or I'll—"

"Throw me to the finalizers?"

Tarquin sucked in a breath. He hadn't even known what he'd been about to say. The words had just tumbled out of him, but somehow, she knew, and nodded at the brief flash of horror in his eyes.

"Do you want to know my secret?" She leaned as close as her chains would allow. "I work for Jonsun."

She winked and reared back, strength pathways flaring, and slammed her head into the table so hard her skull cracked.

Tarquin locked up, numb with shock, as the door burst inward and his security poured into the room, guns drawn to point at a corpse. Dark

412 MEGAN E. O'KEEFE

blood leaked from around her skull, a pool spreading across the table. Tarquin was dimly aware of sticky droplets on his own face.

"My liege," Cass said, "are you all right?"

"I..." He had no idea how to answer that question. "I'm unharmed."

Ward pushed Roselle's hair aside to get a better look at her pathways. She *tsked*. "This is why we remove strength pathways."

"I was informed field removal was no longer an option," Alvero said, carefully edging around the fact Tarquin had given that order.

"It's not an option," Tarquin managed. "We'll...we'll figure out another way to prevent this."

Cass rested a hand on his shoulder, and it surprised him to realize he'd been trembling. "My liege?"

"I need to see Naira. Right now."

"She's in the exemplar training facility," Cass said, and handed him a cleansing wipe to wash his face. "Follow me, please, my liege."

FIFTY-FIVE

Tarquin

Mercator Station | The Present

Tarquin's nerves prickled as he entered the exemplar training room to the sound of a meaty thud. He paused in the entrance, not quite sure what to do with himself. He didn't want to interrupt whatever was happening here, but he needed to see her. To reassure himself that she was safe.

Roselle had been Demarco's creature, as devious as her accomplice. She couldn't have known about the amarthite pathways. People got cold all the time. It was a lucky guess, designed to unsettle him. Or perhaps she'd picked up on something someone had said in passing.

Caldweller noticed him and gestured to a set of metal tables with benches attached nearby. Tarquin settled himself awkwardly at the cafeteria-style table, knowing he was an intrusive presence in this room he'd never have a reason to visit, and tried to make sense of what was happening.

The bulk of the room was an elaborate construction of stairs, walkways, halls, and fences. A veritable jungle of every tight corner an E-X might have to walk their charge around with varying levels of ground to cover.

"For fuck's sake." Naira's voice boomed from one of the hallways, and while her words were annoyed, her tone was affectionate. "Did no one train you slag-brains on a three o'clock y-up? No? Restage. Helms, play the assailant and pick a new perch. I'll show you fetuses how it's done."

Tarquin leaned forward, fascinated. He scarcely understood half of what she'd just said. He'd watched countless videos of her at work, but he'd only ever been trying not to scream his face off when it happened in real life.

Three junior exemplars jogged out of the structure, ruddy from exertion, but grins on all their faces. A wiry woman slung herself up onto the walkway above and hunkered down in position by the railing with a paint gun on her shoulder. "Set!" she called out.

"Fire at will," Naira called back. "And try to surprise me for once in my fucking life."

A junior exemplar already covered in paint walked out, Naira a step behind him. Bright green paint splotched her clothes and hair. Her chin was lifted, skin gleaming with sweat, cheeks red, and Tarquin's breath caught. He hadn't seen her move that confidently since she'd come to extract him at the hotel. Even then, she'd been guarded.

The junior exemplar on the railing sighted. Tarquin bit his tongue. Naira's faux charge crossed an invisible line. Her head tilted away from the assailant. The woman fired.

Naira kicked the charge's knees out from under them. They squawked, and Tarquin winced—he could relate—as they dropped like a rock. The paint splattered off their shoulder, a flesh wound, when before it would have taken them dead center. Naira fisted the back of the charge's jacket in one hand and tugged them against her, turning her back to the line of fire. She ripped a small paint pistol from a secondary holster she wore on her hip, opposite her real service weapon.

Naira shoved the charge against the chain-link fence, putting her body between him and the attacker, and took a paint bullet in the back as she fired three times in quick succession. The woman on the walkway swore and reeled back, wiping paint splatter from her face. Naira had clustered all three shots in the woman's upper chest.

"Get it?" she said. "You ride out the shot in the back, where your armor's stronger. The longer you're alive, the longer your charge is alive. Don't take a shot in the head like this idiot." She thwacked her faux charge upside the head as she stepped away from him. He laughed, rubbing his paint-covered hair self-consciously while the others gave him a hard time.

"What if you're shorter than the charge?" the woman on the walkway called down.

"Look at me." Naira swept a hand down her body. "You think I've ever been taller than a charge in my life? Drop the knees. Get their head behind your center mass. Easy."

"Says the legend," the faux charge muttered under his breath.

"Watch it," Naira shot back, checking her weapon, but she was smiling. "All right, reset. Time to see if Diaz here can learn."

"I'll get it this time, I swear," Diaz said, overly eager.

Naira turned to him, but whatever she was about to say died as she caught sight of Tarquin. Their eyes met, and he smiled sheepishly, embarrassed to have been caught out watching her.

"Enjoying the show, my liege?" she asked.

"It's been most instructive," he called back.

The junior exemplars scrambled to snap to attention. A trainee on the sidelines ducked into a tight bow. Naira's head whipped around and she pointed at the one bowing. "You're out."

"Fuck," they said, then blushed. "Sorry, sorry."

"Don't sweat it. You showed promise. Come back to me in a year."

"I will, E-X," they said, eyes bright with excitement as Caldweller came over to usher them away.

Naira eyed Tarquin a moment, then vaulted the fence one-handed and strode over to him, paint pistol resting against her shoulder. Before he could say a word, she grabbed him by the front of the shirt, lifted him up, and kissed him. She was sweaty and filthy and paint-smeared and warm. Finally warm. He couldn't bring himself to ruin her good mood by telling him about the interview. It could wait.

She dropped him back to the bench and brushed a paint fleck off his jacket. "Want to play the role of the charge?"

"I'll play any role you'd like."

"I'll remember that," she said in a low voice.

He swallowed.

She stepped away and tilted her head at him. "Hop down, Helms. Here's a tall one for you to practice on."

The junior exemplar's eyes widened. "But...That's...What if I hurt him?"

Tarquin took off his jacket, throwing it on the table, then rolled up his sleeves. "Don't worry, Exemplar. I'm quite used to rough handling."

He played their charge for hours, and in the end Naira picked the woman, Helms, and told Diaz to come back in a month once she'd settled Helms. Caldweller herded Helms away to be onboarded, and by unspoken consensus, Tarquin and Naira slid down the fence to sit side by side, dirty and bruised and sweating. The exertion had slackened a coiled tension in Naira, and even being near her Tarquin could feel it, a warmth from within chasing away the persistent cold.

"They were good, weren't they? For third-years, I mean," Naira said.

"You're all incredible to me." Tarquin picked at a sleeve smeared with violet paint, smiling. "When you all start moving, I can hardly keep up."

"You were a very convincing charge. Almost like you're used to being thrown around."

"I've had a lot of practice lately."

She rolled her head across the fence and bumped her forehead into him. He grunted at the nudge and captured her lips in a slow kiss.

"Thank you," she said, "for signing off on this. It couldn't have been easy for you to let me take on an E-X who isn't fully trained."

His smile stretched his cheeks. "I'm glad you approve, but I can't take all the credit. Cass and Caldweller were insistent, and you and Caldweller seemed to know each other well, so I presumed he was correct."

"About Lee," she said. He blinked, having to remind himself that Lee was Caldweller's first name. She didn't seem to notice his brief confusion, and he was glad for that. "I meant to ask you earlier, but you looked on the verge of tears when we were getting caught up. Why?"

"Ah. That." He rubbed the back of his neck. "While you were gone, I realized how poorly I'd treated Caldweller over the years and endeavored to do better, to get to know him on a personal level. And then you...Well. You made it look so easy, I suppose." He chuckled, abashed. "Don't tell him, but I never even knew he was married."

"I can't say I'm surprised. We don't share personal information with our charges. They don't care, and really, it's a distraction."

"I care." He looked at the paint on his hands, enjoying the way it obscured his family mark. "I only wish I'd realized sooner."

Naira was quiet for a moment, studying him. "Then why did you...? Never mind. Fletch got in my head."

He sat straighter. "Ask me, please. Whatever it is—I don't want any worries to fester."

"Why did you leave Lee on ice for so long?"

"I didn't intend to. When I first came back from Sixth, I was planning to escape and didn't want Father's wrath to fall on Caldweller if it was him I escaped. After that, well, Demarco deflected hiring him and I... I didn't mean to forget, when I came back, but there was so much to do that I handed the assignment off to Cass."

"You forgot," she said flatly.

Shit. "The second he was back I realized the depth of my mistake, I swear to you. That was the catalyst for my realization that I needed to treat him better."

Naira blew out a long, heavy breath. "And have you? Treated him better, I mean."

"I believe so. He talks to me more than he ever did before, and seems comfortable doing so."

"I know you mean well, but be careful. If you ask Caldweller and Cass questions about their private lives, they're compelled to respond, even if it's something they'd rather not share. Telling them they're free to answer or not doesn't really help. We're all a little..." She trailed off.

"Afraid of me," he finished. "Even you."

"Not of *you*. Of the head of Mercator."

"God, I hate this." Tarquin thought of how close he'd come to ordering Roselle's torture, and wondered if they were right to fear him. He squeezed his temples until it hurt, trying to chase that image away.

"Hey." She pulled his hand away and made him look at her. "What is it?"

"We found Roselle. It... was a mess."

She slid her fingers through his and squeezed. "Tell me."

He did. When he'd finished, he risked a glance at her, and found her frowning into the middle distance.

"Well," she said, "that's weird. You're sure she said Jonsun?"

"I am. Though she gave no surname, I doubt she meant any other. That doesn't mean it's true, of course. She was working hard to unsettle me. Including bashing her own skull in."

"Oh, that part's normal," Naira said.

Tarquin waited. She'd stopped talking. After a moment, he said, "Naira, my dear woman, you can't say bashing your own skull in is *normal* and then fail to elaborate."

"Sorry." She shook herself a little. "It's part of why we yank the strength pathways, to keep targets from a quick exit. I've only had to do it once, but it's effective."

"You've *what?*"

She waved her free hand dismissively. "Years ago. Ichikawa finalizers grabbed me when I was off-duty. Before they could yank my pathways to control me I head-butted one of them at full strength. Took us both out. I don't remember, but the security footage was clear."

Tarquin knew that his mouth was open, but he couldn't seem to close it.

"What?" She lifted a brow at him. "I thought you liked my 'soldier shit' stories."

"I prefer the ones that end with your skull intact."

"Picky." Naira gave him a playful nudge with her shoulder. "What Roselle said...I don't know. She worked with Fletch. They might have made up a bunch of nonsense to throw us off."

"That, I agree with. Demarco could come up with some truly deranged ideas."

"There's an understatement," she said with a small shake of the head. "Forget him. Tell me how the shroud rollout went."

"Boring, luckily enough." He told her about Rochard's posturing and the bombing of the three transports, and how they appeared not to be connected to any group in particular. The people of the stations would have had their first dose by now, if they were shroud tolerant.

He'd set up survey teams under the guise of Mercator PR to monitor the public mood on the importance of relkatite, and was anxious to see if the public's fervent approval of relk mining lessened as the doses built, inhibiting the growth of *canus*. Now that the shroud rollout was underway, Tarquin planned to refocus his energies on the hunt for Acaelus.

Naira listened, but after a while he noticed her eyes were wandering, drifting to the other side of the training ground, where a sparring mat was laid out, surrounded by mirrors. Then she'd startle and return her attention to him.

"I'm blathering, and you're exhausted." He brushed a strand of paint-sticky hair behind her ear, drawing her attention back from the sparring area. Her skin was cold again.

"Something's... not right," she said.

"What do you mean?"

She pushed to her feet and stalked across the room, examining herself in the mirror, then the mirror itself. Tarquin followed, keenly aware of the fear on his face reflected back at him. She slipped her fingers along the edge of the mirror and pried at it.

"Naira? Talk to me."

She stopped what she was doing and stepped back, crossing her arms. "I thought I saw..." She trailed off. Her nose scrunched. She looked through Tarquin. "I know it's not r-r-right, Jo."

Tarquin stopped breathing.

"I'm trying," she said. "I don't see it."

Tarquin clutched both of her shoulders and gave her a gentle shake. "Naira. Naira, *look* at me."

She blinked, startled by the shake, and frowned at him. "What are you doing here?"

"You're with me on Mercator Station. Tell Jonsun to stop it, stop this right now. You're here with me and you're safe."

Her eyes went glassy, lips moving subtly without making a sound.

He pulled up his HUD. "Cass, I need you. Naira is—she's—" He couldn't say it. "Call in Bracken. *Now.*"

"Yes, my liege," they said.

He took her face in his trembling hands and stared hard into her glassy eyes, willing her to see him, to wind the clock back a few minutes—willing something, *anything* to change. For this not to be what he knew it was.

The doors burst inward. Cass sprinted to them, their steps slowing as they drew close enough to see there was no obvious threat. Naira looked at them.

"I'm telling you I don't see it," she said.

Tears stung Tarquin's eyes.

"Uh, see what, E-X?" Cass asked.

"She's not talking to you," Tarquin said.

"What? Oh. Oh shit." They snapped their fingers in front of her face. "Sharp, hey, come on. You're on Mercator Station, remember?"

"I—I remember," she said. Tarquin didn't know who she was answering. Then, very quietly, "Fuck."

"It's okay," Tarquin said, desperate to soothe the terror that was contorting her face. "It's okay. We have the repair software. We can fix this. You're going to be okay."

Bracken barreled through the door. "What's happening?"

"She's been double-printed," Cass said.

Even though Tarquin knew it was true, the words were a kick to the gut. Bracken's shocked gasp rubbed salt into the wound.

"I need to sedate her." Bracken rummaged in their medical bag and pulled free an injector. "Help her sit, my liege. We don't want her to fall."

Tarquin had to hold it together long enough to help her. To get her sedated before she fell to the endless scream, so that the repair software had a better chance of working. He slid his hands from her face to her shoulders and pressed gently, trying to get her to ease down herself. She was a monolith, unmovable. "Naira, would you sit for me, please? It's important."

The glassiness faded from her eyes. She stared into the mirror, the horror returning in slow twitches along her cheek, eyes widening. She looked at him, and then dragged that same terror-filled gaze over Cass and Bracken.

"I see it. I see the metal eyes." She looked back at Tarquin. Her voice shook. "I'm s-sorry."

"It's not your fault." His own voice was a croak. "We can fix it, we can, but you have to sit for me, okay?"

She didn't move.

Cass said softly, "I'll catch her, Doctor."

Bracken crept toward Naira, hand out in a placating gesture. Naira drew a knife and side-stepped away from Tarquin, closer to the wall of mirrors.

"Whoa," Cass said. "Easy, Sharp, it's just us."

Tarquin reached for her again, earning a glare and slash of the hand from Cass. He froze, torn. Naira wouldn't attack him, but there was no telling what she was seeing.

"No one here is going to hurt you." Tarquin extended a hand, silently begging her to put the knife down and return to his arms.

Caldweller rushed into the room, pistol drawn and leveled at Naira's chest. "Stand down, E-X."

Naira stared at him through blank eyes.

"Put that away," Tarquin hissed over his shoulder.

Caldweller shared a look with Cass before circling around to put himself between Tarquin and Naira.

"This is ridiculous," Tarquin insisted. "It's Naira. Put the gun down, Caldweller."

"My weapon is drawn precisely because that *is* Naira, and she's not currently in her right mind, my liege."

Naira seemed oblivious to the four panicking people surrounding her. She turned her back to them, facing the mirror. Slowly, she tapped the flat of the blade against her thigh, and stared hard into her reflection.

Bracken advanced a cautious step.

She ripped her real service weapon from its holster and, without turning, raised her arm behind her, aiming square at the doctor's head. They stopped walking, swallowing hard, and lifted their hands higher. Cass drew their pistol. Tarquin wanted to scream.

"I want to help you, Ex. Sharp," Bracken said with surprising gentleness, considering the weapon pointed at their head.

Her laugh sounded like gravel scraping against glass. "You can't."

"Yes, we can," Tarquin said. "But you have to let us."

"She told me," Naira spoke to the mirror. "She told me it was already done, and I didn't listen."

She closed her eyes. Cass took a step. Her aim adjusted to their head before she'd opened her eyes again. "D-don't. I won't hesitate to destroy any one of those prints."

"Who told you that?" Tarquin asked. Maybe if he could keep her talking here, in the moment, she'd snap to her senses. "Who told you it was already done?"

"I know," she told the mirror. "*I know.* Shut up already, I have to concentrate."

She lifted the knife point to her temple.

"No!" Tarquin lunged, but Caldweller shifted to block him, and he crashed into that man's back and almost lost his balance.

Naira's gaze shifted in the mirror, met his in reflection. He had no idea how to read it.

"Ex. Sharp," Bracken said. "Please be careful. That print takes longer to heal than you're used to."

Naira sliced through the top and the bottom of her night vision pathway, slit the skin along the golden line just as she'd done for his strength pathways and, without so much as a wince, shifted the grip of her blade so that she could pinch the end of the severed pathway between two fingers and rip it free.

She examined it for a moment, rolling it between her fingers, and through the haze of Tarquin's horror a small part of him noted it was more pliable than the amarthite pathway had been. She scowled in disgust and flicked it to the floor.

Blood dribbling down the side of her face, she looked at each one of them through the mirror, a wave of sadness washing over her.

"You were r right," she told no one. "It's all of them."

"Please tell us what's happening," Tarquin said.

"You're infected. We all are." She glanced at the bloody pathway. "Well. Not all of us, anymore."

"*Canus?* We've been taking the shroud. There's been no inflammation, and our pathways are golden."

"Are they?"

Tarquin examined his outstretched arms, half expecting to see the golden tracery turned to the deathly grey of a *canus* infection, but so far as he could tell, they were still healthy. He looked at the pathway she'd ripped out. The pathway that adjusted light. Adjusted color.

"We'll test them. But this has to stop. You have to let us help you. Jonsun, or whoever that is, they got their fucking message through."

Cass crept forward a step, and this time she didn't seem to react.

"It's in the shroud shipments." She cocked her head to the side, listening, and sheathed the knife.

Cass surged at her.

Naira shot them in the foot. The sound knocked the breath out of Tarquin, cracking the brittle defenses he'd been holding up, bringing his world shattering down around him. Cass cried out, dropped to their knees, but brought their gun back up, aiming for her.

Naira kicked it from their hands like an afterthought and spun into the doctor, who'd lunged for her with the injector. She tore the injector away from them and brought her arm crashing down on the back of their neck as she swept their feet. Bracken landed chest-first on the ground, scarcely able to get their hands out in time to protect their face.

Caldweller fired, missed. The mirror shattered and Naira swung into him. She landed the injector on his neck and plunged it home. Caldweller dropped.

Tarquin froze, staring into her golden eyes.

That woman is dangerous.

She was poised mid-strike, the back of her gun hand having come up to crash down upon his head. The muscles of her neck stood out, chest heaving. With a small, strangled groan she pulled herself back, tore herself away from him. For an agonizing moment she looked on the precipice of saying something.

Then she turned and fled.

FIFTY-SIX

Naira

Mercator Station | The Present

Naira slipped through time. One second she was running down the halls of Mercator Station, monitoring the panicked calls of Merc-Sec through her HUD as Tarquin sent out the command to find her and capture her without injury. The next she was strapped to a gurney in a room so cold it made her teeth ache, staring into an impossible face.

Staring at Jonsun.

Jonsun, who had cracked. Jonsun, who'd been triple-printed to be Mercator's instrument. Jonsun, who'd held on so long, keeping *canus* from taking the ansible on the *Einkorn* while Naira fumbled her way through Sixth Cradle.

Jonsun, whom she could still feel crushing her into a hug on the deck of the *Einkorn*, though she should have no memory of the experience.

"Nai, stop," Jonsun said from that other-place.

She saw Jonsun hovering above her instead of the corner of the hallway and swore as she turned too early and smacked her side against the wall.

"Knock it off, I have to c-c-concentrate."

"The hell you do," he said. Naira squeezed her other-eyes shut and kept running. Security was sweeping this floor. She needed some place safe. Some place hidden to get her wits about her again. "Drop that print and come back to us."

"You think I'd run *now*?" she shouted straight into the face of a startled Mercator employee. "S-sorry," she said, and touched her temple, forgetting the wound. She flinched at the sting. "HUD call."

The employee muttered something and ducked a bow, then hurried off down the hall as fast as their legs would carry them without breaking into an all-out run. Naira groaned. That'd get back to security.

"I have to get out of here," she said through both mouths.

"Yes, you do," Jonsun said. He patted her other-hand. "Drop that print, Nai. Jessel has the repair software. Once you're fully here we can fix the cracks."

Her head was pounding. "Shut up long enough that I can get somewhere I can talk to you."

A slight weight pressed across her forehead, him laying a folded towel over her other-eyes to limit the stuttering back-and-forth of sensory input. She let out a ragged sigh and tried to gather her scrambled thoughts, which was...not possible. Every single frightened face she ran past was veined with grey-infected pathways. She needed to get away from people, from cameras. Out of the halls.

Into the ducts.

There were sensors in the ducts, but it'd be more difficult for anyone to chase her. Naira let herself into a maintenance closet and pried at the sliders that unlocked an access panel. She set it aside with a careless clunk and crawled within, the narrow confines immediately soothing the raw edge of her terror.

These passages were familiar. Not safe, never that, but she'd been crawling down into the narrow dark since she was a kid, and the ducts stripped the extra sensory input of the halls away. Gave her a chance to breathe.

Naira wove her way through the system until she came to a spot where she could rest without fear of being immediately discovered. She curled up, dragging her knees against her chest, then pressed her face into them, squeezing her eyes shut. She blocked out all the panicked incoming comms requests cluttering her HUD. Blocked Tarquin's incessant call. She'd almost hit him. She couldn't believe she'd almost hit *him*.

"O-okay," she said in that other-space. "I have a minute."

The towel was lifted. It was still cold in the *Cavendish*. The air froze in her lungs. Jonsun took her hand once more and squeezed.

"You cracked me." She glared at him. "You f-fucking dick."

"We can fix it," he said.

"You don't know if that will work on me."

Jonsun squeezed her hand tighter. "I was triple-printed, and it worked on me. I'm certain, and I couldn't leave you behind. We're family, Nai. We need you. But I'm sorry for the intermediate suffering. I remember what it's like."

"Oh, you're *sorry*." She clenched her fists, the muscles of her forearms pushing against the restraints put on her new print. Clearly, he'd known she'd wake up angry. "My brain is scrambled eggs and you're sorry. How n-n-nice. Fuck."

"You're holding together remarkably well. Little repetition, that I've heard."

"I am going to *repeatedly* shove your head up your ass."

Her vision shifted, and she could see Jonsun in front of her so vividly that it took her breath away. Not on the *Cavendish*, but in the *Einkorn*, his warm brown eyes downcast with sadness as he bit through his lip, trying to keep the telltale stammer of someone existing in more than one place under control.

"Nai?" he asked. "Naira? Hey, stay with me."

She scowled and, on Mercator Station, dug her fingers into her skull. "I'm slipping. I see you on the *Einkorn*."

"That's not possible."

Naira uncurled her other-fist long enough to give him the finger.

"Okay," he said. "That's fair. You can stop slipping by dropping your other print so I can fix you here."

"This *is* my other print," she said in the *Cavendish*. "I'm where I want to be. I mean." Shit, this was confusing. "Leave me on Mercator."

"Nai, it's over. You saw. They're all infected. We're safe here, on the *Cavendish*."

She had seen. Even before he'd cracked her, she'd started to see it. Grey faces staring at her out of the corner of her eye. Hints of another time, another place, merging with her present as her subconscious scrambled to circumvent the manipulation being done to her eyes.

The infection hadn't been complete for Naira, but it had done enough. Her few relk pathways had always been vulnerable to *canus*. She just hadn't realized how compromised she really was.

"Yeah, you're safe," Naira said. "You're safe and you left Sol to rot."

"We didn't know for certain until we were weeks out," Jonsun said. "When the team arrived at Miller-Urey they saw that Jessel and the unionists' vision pathways were infected, but they were fighting back. Prime for *canus* to advance quickly within. A few days ago we started eating some of the shroud shipments Tarquin sent to Jessel ahead of the rollout, and became violently ill. Our amarthite pathways, killing the *canus* in them. We put two and two together and, well, you saw."

Their pathways are silver, Jonsun had said when she'd seen him in what she'd thought, at first, was the mirror in the training room. *They're infected. You can't see it because your night vision pathway is infected. Take it out and look. Really look.*

And she had, and all those faces she cared for had night vision pathways laced with silver, too. Tarquin's infected pathways under Fletcher should have been silver, but they hadn't been, and she should have paid better attention to what that might mean.

Metal eyes, the children's monster. Every printed adult had vision pathways. It was only the children who could have seen the truth. No one would have believed them, not when their pathways were lying to them.

Vision pathways were the first to settle. If *canus* had learned to infect them first, then even the freshly printed wouldn't have noticed anything wrong.

"I can't leave them to this," she said, in both places.

Jonsun tried to look sad but couldn't quite sell the expression. "It hurts. I know. But we've lost the fight for Sol. We found Paison's notes stashed away in the *Cavendish*. She infected the shroud distribution before Chiyo sent her away. I'm sorry, Nai. The shroud and *canus* have found symbiosis. Mercator Station is going to become another *Einkorn*, but worse, and everywhere. We have to protect what we can, and I want you with us for that. You're family."

In the ducts, she rubbed her face. "I can stop it."

"How?" Jonsun asked. "You can't kill *canus* without killing the host, too. What are you going to do? Bomb them all and reprint them in a clean printing bay that doesn't exist with amarthite you don't have? Even if you could, you don't have the time."

"What are you talking about?"

Jonsun glanced over his shoulder, at a unionist Naira didn't recognize. "Bring him in. And be ready."

They bowed to Jonsun and left. Naira craned her neck, struggling to see where they'd gone. The door opened. Kav walked into the room rubbing the back of his neck.

"What is it, Jo? I—"

He saw her. Froze. For a flash his face lit up, and then he saw the restraints holding her down. "Nai?"

"Fletch was r-r-right," she said bitterly. "Tarquin was there when it happened."

She might have repeated that a few times, or maybe she hadn't managed to say it at all. There was no way for her to be certain, because she lost time. One second Kav was staring at her with wide-eyed horror, and the next the unionists were prying him off Jonsun, pinning his arms behind his back.

"This wasn't the plan!" Kav roared, straining against those who held him.

Jonsun resettled his clothes and sat back down at Naira's bedside. "I promised you I'd get her back before the deadline. This was the only way to do it. We have the repair software. She'll be fine."

"She's not fucking fine!"

"K-Kav," Naira managed. The damage was done. She needed information. "Deadline. T-tell me me *me*."

"I don't even know if I'm right." Kav glared at Jonsun.

"Please," Naira said.

Kav sighed raggedly. "Jessel grabbed the unionists' data when they cleared out. I did a deep clean on it all to make sure we weren't hooking up anything nasty to the *Cavendish* and found a virus. I can't figure out what it does, aside from the fact it's counting down. The way it's built, it...I can't say for certain, you know? But it looks like Fletch's work. A hacked and altered finalizer package."

Naira's mind was in pieces, but she recalled Fletcher's smug smirk into the security footage she'd reviewed, and knew Kav was right. That was his work. A ticking time bomb on every station he'd visited.

"How long?"

"About sixty-two hours from now," Kav said.

Nearly three days. She had time. "I have to warn them."

"They're all infected," Jonsun said. "They won't listen to you. It's over. *Come home.*"

Naira squeezed both pairs of eyes shut against a well of tears. Something scraped nearby in the ducts. She stiffened, listening, and could barely make out someone crawling near her through the mutter of conversation on the *Cavendish*.

"They found me," she said on the *Cavendish*. "Hold on."

She scrubbed the tears from her cheeks and forced herself to move, to summon every scrap of skill she had to be a ghost in the ducts, angling toward the hangars. She'd steal a shuttle. Get some space. Figure out what to do. She couldn't trust anyone here, not when they were all so badly infected, but she couldn't leave them to be consumed by that monster, either.

Couldn't leave her home.

She hesitated at a grate that would let her out into the hangars and opened her eyes on the other side.

"I need you to kill this print. I'm staying."

"You can't *do* anything," Jonsun said.

"I have to try. Unless you have any other intel I can use, I need you to cut me loose now, because this next part is going to be tricky."

"Nai..." Jonsun's face crumpled. "This isn't how it's supposed to go. You have to come back. You always come back."

A security alert blipped in her HUD. She'd been too distracted. They'd located her and were locking down the hangar. "Fighting to escape in ten seconds, do me a favor and kill me," she said on the *Cavendish*, then squeezed those eyes shut and kicked out the grate, swinging to the floor of the hangar.

"Sighted!" someone shouted.

Alarms blared. She swore and tried to focus on the rhythm of her boots against the ground as she sprinted through the empty hangar. Tarquin must have ordered a seal on the exits and sent any travelers away from those areas. Which was something she would have considered if she'd had her whole mind to herself.

Muttering curses under her breath and unsure which mouth they were coming out of, she looped around a counter and ducked down, trying to find a way out. There was a shuttle about a hundred yards away that looked promising. Fast, small enough to pilot with one person.

The airlock was probably sealed against exits, but if she played chicken with it she was certain Tarquin would give in before she splatted. As much as she hated to do that to him, he was infected, too. They'd been trying to sedate her. She couldn't free them from their infections if Bracken plunged her into a medically induced coma.

Naira fingered the pistol strapped to her thigh and grimaced, taking her hand away from the weapon. She already felt terrible about having to shoot Cass. One goal—get to the shuttle. She could do that without shooting anyone else.

A storm of boots pounded into the room. Merc-Sec out in force. Now or never. She sprinted harder than she ever had in her life, and prayed Tarquin had issued a no-fire order.

"Naira!" Her name ripped from Tarquin's throat so raw and pained she whipped her head around to look at him and lost her footing. Visions of the *Cavendish* bled into the corners of her eyes as she staggered sideways and caught herself on a podium.

"Nai," Jonsun said, his face filling her vision, "are you all right?"

"Kill me, you asshole." She tried to squeeze her eyes shut on the *Cavendish*, but overextended and ended up doing it on Mercator Station, too.

A wall of a person barreled into her. She landed hard on her back and pried one set of eyes open. Caldweller. Bracken must have loaded him with stimulants to get him moving. His pupils were pinpricks and his eyes were bloodshot.

"Easy," he said as he pinned her thrashing arms down beside her.

Tarquin appeared in the cloud of Merc-Sec hovering above her. "Is she injured?"

"Just a little banged up," Caldweller said through gritted teeth.

If she could just roll sideways—Jonsun shook her and she was glaring up into his face instead of Caldweller's.

"Nai, hold on, we're going to get you something to calm down," Jonsun said.

"Oh, fuck you," she said to...someone. They were overlapping in her vision. Caldweller's face blurred with Jonsun's, Tarquin's popping through and fading away again just as quickly.

"Don't hurt her," Tarquin said.

"Trying," Caldweller ground out.

"Where's that tranq?" Caldweller and Jonsun said at the same time.

"You don't understand," Naira told Caldweller—or, at least, hoped she told Caldweller. "You can't see it. You have to let me go. *Canus* is in the shroud."

"What is she talking about?" Tarquin asked.

"I don't know." Caldweller glared at one of the Merc-Sec soldiers. "Tranq, now, you idiots!"

Naira stopped struggling and grabbed Caldweller's arm. He'd listen, despite the infection. He'd always taken her threat assessments seriously. "Listen to me. Fletch put a—" Damnit. She was talking on the *Cavendish*. Naira squeezed her eyes shut and tried to concentrate on the feeling of Caldweller's arm in her hands. When she opened her eyes, Caldweller was staring down at her. Finally. "He put a-a—" She got stuck repeating that *a* and had to bite into both tongues to make herself stop. "Virus on the stations. Lee, you have sixty-two hours before its countdown ends. Please, I'm begging you—"

Jonsun and Kav were arguing, flickering in and out. She couldn't concentrate. Couldn't think. Couldn't even tell what she'd said where.

"Stop fucking squabbling and kill me!" she shouted at... Tarquin. Right in his face. Shit. His eyes widened with horror. She tried to focus on the *Cavendish*, but both worlds were getting grainy, merging with lichen-draped trees. With dead eyes watching her from the dark.

She convulsed, somewhere, everywhere, and eventually both sets got ahold of their tranquilizers and plunged her down into the fractured dark of her own mind.

FIFTY-SEVEN

Tarquin

Mercator Station | The Present

Tarquin sat vigil by Naira's hospital bed for the second time since she'd come back to him, and found he had no more capacity left for hope. He hadn't even had it in him to feel shame or hurt when Naira's mother had come to see her daughter and wept while Tarquin told her there was nothing they could do.

Naira had cracked, and until they could be absolutely certain her other print wasn't still alive, they couldn't repair her map.

He'd sent fleets. He'd commandeered ansibles. He'd thrown everything he had, every resource the head of Mercator could muster, after the *Cavendish*. It would take time. So much time. He didn't know where they'd gone and that was by design, but now he wanted nothing more than to rip apart the worlds until he found them.

He had his anger, at least. A small coal of rage nurtured against the hollowness her destruction had left. Her friends. Her own friends had cracked her, and for what? To say the shroud they'd distributed was adulterated? He'd had it tested. They'd found nothing.

Every time he closed his eyes, he saw her screaming at him to kill her and jolted awake again.

He tugged on the split lip she'd given him by accident, kicking him while she convulsed, and savored the pain, telling himself it wasn't because it was the last evidence of physical contact he'd ever have with her, and almost believing it.

Caldweller entered the room and cleared his throat.

"How is Ex. Cass?" Tarquin made himself ask.

"Fine, my liege," Caldweller said. "We E-Xs heal fast, and she didn't aim for serious damage."

Tarquin made himself look at the man who'd shadowed his every step since he was sixteen. Made himself acknowledge the small bandage over his temple where they'd all had their night vision pathways biopsied. Made himself map the purple-yellow bruises rotting across his face, where Naira's thrashing had landed. Caldweller seemed...hesitant.

"What is it?" he asked.

"I was wondering where we were with the countdown she gave. The sixty-two hours. Dr. Bracken said it'd take at least three days to culture the biopsies to see if anything grows, but since you're a scientist, I thought—"

"Stop," Tarquin said. "The rapid tests came up negative. It didn't mean anything. She was just...Cracked people say things they don't mean."

"You're always encouraging me to speak freely, my liege." Caldweller paused, testing the waters. Tarquin didn't react. "Well, I've seen a lot of people crack in my time. Sharp, she held it together. She wasn't herself, granted, but I think it's worth considering what she had to say. I think she meant it."

Kill me.

"No. It was nonsense. It's always nonsense."

He needed it to be nonsense.

"People speaking nonsense don't evade two exemplars, an entire Merc-Sec squad for over an hour, and make a reasonable break for a shuttle. My liege."

He squeezed the split in his lip until it bled. "Is that all, E-X?"

"I suppose so. I just thought you might want to do something she'd be proud of when she gets back."

"She's not coming back." The words dragged out without his permission.

"I...disagree, my liege."

Tarquin looked into a middle distance where there was nothing to see that could hurt him. Not Naira, not his E-X, not even that new exemplar, Helms, lingering by the door. Just empty air.

"Everyone who's ever loved me leaves. She's not coming back."

"I don't think that's true, my liege."

"Get out."

He knew he was being a sullen shit and he didn't care. It'd been easier with his mother. There'd been no body to recover, just the map that'd never print correctly. There was no decision to be made about a broken map. Not like there was with a body.

He'd have to decide, eventually. When his search inevitably came up empty, and they couldn't find the *Cavendish*. Bracken could only keep her print in stasis for so long before it'd degrade. One day, Tarquin would have to order her body recycled. He would have to pick a date. A line in the sand that Naira wouldn't exist on the other side of.

The choice wouldn't even fall to her mother. It'd fall to him, because he was head of Mercator, and the head of Mercator alone held sway over who lived and died in Mercator stations. No, not over who got to live. The head of Mercator only ever got to decide who died.

He understood, now, how his father had learned to love to hate. It hurt less.

Caldweller paused in the doorway. "I'm still here, my liege. Whenever you need me," he said, and walked away.

Tears Tarquin hadn't felt coming spilled down his cheeks. He bent double, scrubbing at his eyes with both hands, trying to find the empty hollow within him once more where the hurt wouldn't reach, but Caldweller had gone and ripped it away and—fuck, what an asshole Tarquin had been. Had been for years.

"What am I supposed to do?" he asked her, and though she slept on, he could imagine her arched brow, the derisive snort. She'd been pushing him to make his own choices from the beginning.

He was a scientist, but he studied geoscience. *Canus* and its myriad complications were so far outside his specialty he didn't even know where to begin. He knew it as a bioleaching agent, parameters that made sense to him. If there was a way to speed the growth of the cultures outside the usual methods—warming the plates, making certain the growth matrix was to the targeted fungus's liking—he'd never heard of it.

Tarquin dealt in minerals and soil and things he could, for the most part, see.

He looked at the bandage on her temple, and felt like an idiot. A pronounced *canus* infection consumed the protein sheath of the pathway and was highly visible. All he had to do was remove his night vision pathway and *look* at it to see if it'd been infected, contorting his vision.

"Dr. Bracken," he called into the hallway. The doctor came running. "I want you to remove my night vision pathway immediately."

"Ah." They glanced from him to Naira and back again. "My liege, I'm certain the biopsies will be enough. You saw the pathway she removed for yourself. It's not infected."

"Not that I could see. I require confirmation that my vision isn't compromised, and this is the only way to be certain."

"If you insist, though I wish you'd reconsider. I'll arrange for a sterile room to be prepared."

"Just do it, Doctor," Tarquin said. "This is hardly the least sterile room I've had surgery in."

Bracken's eyes widened at that, but they bit back a comment and ducked their head, then set to work gathering their supplies. Tarquin rested one hand lightly over Naira's cold, still hand while he waited. His maudlin mood ebbed. He'd check. He'd keep working. He wasn't done yet.

The doctor wheeled a narrow table with a tray and a roll of instruments wrapped in plastic in front of Tarquin, then dragged a stool over, washed their hands, tugged on gloves, and picked up a visor-shaped shield.

"To protect your eyes," they said as they fitted it over Tarquin's head. They wiped his skin with cool disinfectant and picked up a syringe. "I'm going to give you a local anesthetic, but it will be insufficient to block all the pain. You may use your pathways to further manage the pain. If you'd allow me to prepare for proper surgery—"

"Doctor, I once had both strength pathways removed from my legs in an elevator with nothing but a numbing spray. Please, continue. I promise you I will not hold any discomfort against you."

Bracken drew their head back in surprise. "Who did that to you?"

"Naira did. Because *canus* had taken away my ability to control my legs. So, please, Doctor, set your fears aside. This is nothing."

"I'd wondered how she was so adept at removing her own pathway."

"Exemplars are trained in field removal."

"That...is a disturbing thought. Please, hold still."

Tarquin found it hardly stung at all as Bracken injected him, waited a few moments, then excised the pathway and laid it, wet with blood, in a kidney-shaped tray on the table between them. They slipped the visor off Tarquin's eyes.

Tarquin didn't need to look at his excised pathway to know the truth. Bracken's face was spiderwebbed with silver pathways, the extras they required to assist in surgery mercurial gleams across their tan skin.

"As you can see, my liege, the pathway is perfectly normal." Bracken gestured to the tray.

"No, Doctor. No, it's not." He tightened his hold on Naira's hand. Her mind had been breaking and still, *still*, she'd gotten the important information across. He wouldn't let her down. Not this time. "Ex. Helms," he called out. "Collect your colleagues. We have work to do."

FIFTY-EIGHT

Her

The Sigillaria | *The Present*

Not-Canden isn't allowed to leave the ship. It has never been expressly forbidden to her. Nothing has. Acaelus would, and has, given her the world. Given her *worlds*. But she knows her walls are bars. Her voice is resonant only within the air he controls. Her body moves only within spaces he crafted for her.

But she has not moved—and she has not spoken—in so long that she feels that if she doesn't take different air within her lungs with which to scream, she will root to the spot, and never move again.

They are close. So very, very close to the moment in which they'll be a family again. The imminence of it tickles through her pathways, sparking the glitter of life. Her passenger is so possessed with triumph that it surges within her. Joyful, she thinks. So eager to be free and join its other segments in communion—in *family*—that it has burst through their shared skin and grown droplets of black, glossy hope from the backs of her hands.

Already she can sense them. Not her false children. Those bodies were always mere vessels for other segments of the passenger, and she has felt those for a long time. Unlike in her making, Acaelus's stitched-together fragments of the children were clumsy attempts, leaving them blank-eyed and empty.

She'd stomached their presence because the passenger within her recognized the passenger within them, and when they stood close enough, she could almost, *almost* feel the fragile edges of their communion. Could borrow their sense of family. Of belonging.

And now it's building. As the people imbibe of the passenger, as it grows within them, she can feel them at the periphery of her consciousness. Lights coming on in the dark. And there is one light above all that she wants for herself.

Acaelus will not allow her to leave, and she knows better than to ask. This body of hers doesn't know how to fight. How to defend. But there is another mind in the orbit of her thoughts that does, and Acaelus cares not at all what happens to that vessel.

She stands before Ex. Lockhart and stares through her, to the passenger within. It has grown so healthy in that flesh that she can see through Lockhart's eyes, too, when she concentrates. Can feel the weight of the gun strapped to her thigh, know intimately the way it will kick when fired, though she has never held nor fired a gun in her life.

If there was ever another woman in that mind, she's gone now, though sometimes tears slip over her cheeks for no reason at all. But there is, buried deep, a desire to please so entangled with the desire to be safe that when Not-Canden takes Lockhart's cheek in her hand, Lockhart leans into it, and the tears don't matter, because Lockhart's mind was stitched together in such a way that she can only do as she is told, and nothing more.

Not-Canden knows that there will be more tears, for a little while. That when those lights come on en masse—when the people of the worlds wake up and *know* each other—it's going to hurt, at first. People don't like change.

But she's not people.

All she wants, all she's ever taught herself to want, is a family to protect.

And so she wills the Lockhart print to leave, and Acaelus doesn't notice, and with skills Canden Mercator never owned, but eyes that are hers in the radiant welding of their minds, she seeks her son through the dark.

FIFTY-NINE

Tarquin

Mercator Station | The Present

Tarquin stood by the steel tray with Bracken, Helms, Caldweller, and Cass, and stared at the five infected pathways laid out between them. Various degrees of silver stained their faces, cobwebs of control constricting their thoughts. Their senses.

But they could see, now, and though their thoughts remained muddied by the *canus* in their pathways, it had used subtlety this time, and didn't exact the same level of control as it had over Tarquin previously. Not yet, at least.

It didn't need to. It had already won.

"We're at, what, fifty-six hours from Sharp's countdown?" Cass asked.

"Yes," Tarquin said, amazed that he could do anything but break down in panic. "But I don't understand what she was counting down. Even if the shroud rollout is contaminated, the infected won't all succumb at once. Did she say anything else to you?"

"She was difficult to understand, my liege," Caldweller said. "I believe she said 'virus' at one point, and 'a' and 'he' quite a lot."

Tarquin frowned in thought. "*Canus* isn't a virus. Naira knows that. It stands to reason she meant a computer virus."

"Sharp was panicked," Cass said. "What if she wasn't just trying to get away from us, but to get somewhere in particular?"

He.

"Demarco," Tarquin said. "If she thought he put a virus on the stations, she'd be frantic to reach them. Caldweller, please call in Alvero and Ward. They may have special insight into Demarco's capabilities."

"Right away, my liege," Caldweller said.

When those two had been briefed and stood in the same circle as the rest, gazing down at their own infected pathways added to the original five, Ward crossed her arms, scowled at the trays, and said with irritated gruffness, "Well. Shit."

"Indeed," Alvero said smoothly. "My liege, Ex. Sharp said Mr. Demarco placed a virus on the stations he visited?"

"Not precisely," Tarquin said, "but near enough."

"She conveyed all that while cracking?" Ward whistled low. "Stubborn bitch."

Tarquin bristled, but there was deep admiration in Ward's tone. *Soldier shit*, he thought with the first smile he'd felt since Naira had fallen apart.

"Yes," Tarquin said, "she is. And I would not let her struggle to get that message through be wasted. Is there anything either of you can do to discover what Demarco did?"

Alvero nodded. "Now that we have a better idea of what we're looking for, it should be easy enough, my liege. Mr. Demarco was talented in many respects, but he made use of the same intrusion packages as the rest of the specialists. I'll put them to work seeking our signature in the compromised systems."

"Info-Sec is under Alvero's department," Ward said, "but I'll tighten up the Merc-Sec, get them all on high alert, and have them check the hardware itself for physical intrusions. At least, on Mercator stations. Can't do much about the others."

"Thank you both. We have a little over two days to discover the sabotage. Tell me anything you need, and I will get it for you."

"Two days in which our infections can grow unabated, if it's true that the supplement is contaminated," Bracken said. "Forgive me for having a one-track mind, my liege, but the medical risks can't be discounted, especially if this infection increases its hold when it understands its hosts have uncovered its subterfuge and are fighting back. Is there not some other way to slow it down? What of the substance used for Ex. Sharp's pathways?"

"My mother devised an amarthite serum that slows it effectively," Tarquin said. "But Mercator's stores of amarthite were wiped out along with the relkatite."

"How much of the substance would you need?" Bracken asked.

"Fifty grams each."

All eyes turned to Naira's print. The largest source of amarthite that any of them knew the precise location of. Tarquin's fists clenched. "No."

"My liege," Bracken said in the gentle way of all doctors who were about to deliver the worst possible news. "She's cracked. If her map can be repaired, we can always reprint her body later, once we've stabilized matters."

It made sense. And yet... "You are asking me to inject *pieces of her* into my veins so that I can think clearly a little longer. I... can't."

They looked at one another, and not at him. There were six of them and one of him, and in Naira's print might reside the leverage they'd need to save thousands. To keep their minds their own until they could figure out how to fight whatever was coming. They were right. He *knew* they were right. Being right didn't make it any less terrible.

He backed up, legs bumping the hospital bed, and spread his arms. "Please don't do this."

"We don't need all of it," Bracken said. "Many of her pathways appear not to work properly, anyway, my liege. If we remove the enhancements, it might be enough for the seven of us to hold on to our wits without dissolving her current print."

"To what end?" Tarquin demanded. "We don't know what Demarco's virus does, or if it even exists. We know we're infected. We don't need extra prevention when we have one another to check our behavior and thoughts."

"My liege," Cass said, "you knew you were infected when Demarco had control of this station. Did knowing help?"

"No." Tarquin closed his eyes briefly, hating that they were right. He'd known and been able to do nothing. Unable to even muster up the will to *think* of what to do.

Tarquin turned and rested a hand against her cheek, tracing the gleaming line of one of her exemplar pathways with the side of his thumb. There was only one thing Naira would do in this situation. He still couldn't find the words.

Caldweller squeezed his shoulder but withdrew quickly, as if he were embarrassed. Tarquin smiled a little at that. He enjoyed it when the exemplars broke decorum. Naira had taught him that it meant they trusted him not to punish them for those breaks.

"My liege," Ward said, "I've known Sharp a long time. Butted heads with her more than once as, I think, everyone in this room who knows her has." Nervous chuckles from Caldweller and Alvero. "And I know that, even when we were at war with each other, if she'd been given this choice, she'd have yanked those pathways out herself. I always respected that about her. Even when she was blowing my shit up."

Caldweller and Alvero added their agreement. Tarquin dragged in a long, chest-stretching breath and let it out slowly, then bent to kiss her forehead.

"I know." Tarquin made himself turn away from her and faced Bracken. "Take the bare minimum. Leave her integration pathways and keep this print stable, if at all possible. Make certain she has painkillers. We don't know which of her pathways work, or if she's feeling anything, right now."

"I will treat her as if she were my own family." Bracken bowed their head in solemnity.

Tarquin pushed his way out of the room, unable to bear witness to Bracken scrapping her for parts. Naira wasn't in there, not really. She was scattered across time and space, broken to pieces by the people she'd trusted, the people she'd called friends.

Ward and Alvero set themselves up in an unused office within the hospital and got to work coordinating their people. Tarquin was grateful for their competence, because he doubted he was in any state to make decisions.

He had no idea how long he paced before Bracken emerged carrying a slim, clear plastic container, the dull green of amarthite coiled within. A fist clenched Tarquin's heart, seeing the remorse in the doctor's eyes, and he couldn't find the breath to ask the question.

"She's stable," Bracken said quickly. "I removed enough by mass from her extraneous pathways for our purposes."

"Thank god." Tarquin took the container from them and tried not to think about where the contents had come from. He refrained from looking in her room. If he saw her, he wouldn't be able to keep it together. Instead, he let himself into Alvero and Ward's makeshift command room.

"Any luck with the virus?" he asked.

Alvero wiped away a holo and blinked to clear his eyes. "We found it, my liege, but we don't yet understand its implications. There's a countdown, yes, and it appears to be a modified version of one of our audio crowd-control viruses."

Tarquin rubbed his tired eyes. "Our what?"

"There are certain frequencies that people find unpleasant that can't be shut down via their aural pathways. We play them to disperse crowds. Sometimes, ah . . . without the host station's knowledge."

"Demarco did a great deal of research into increasing *canus*'s ability to infect a host by causing them emotional distress," Tarquin said. "And I've seen heavily infected misprints overreact to distressing sounds. Even if this sound only disturbs a few people enough for *canus* to take full control, such a thing is bound to be frightening to those near them . . ." He trailed off, unwilling but unable to stop himself from doing the math. Fletcher had visited highly populated, centrally located hub stations. The fear. The paranoia. It would spiral out of control. "Can you stop it?"

Alvero's grimace rather eloquently delivered his answer. "Yes and no, my liege. We've scrubbed it out of Mercator's stations, but I require your permission to attempt similar methods on the HC and other MERIT family stations. The amount of access I'd need to fully clean out the virus is not something they'd grant. Their systems would be permanently vulnerable to us after that. Even if they handed over access right now, I doubt we could crush it all in time."

Tarquin leaned his weight against the wall. "What if we . . . I don't know, deployed some kind of countermeasure? This virus interacts with speakers and is of our own making. Could we devise a similar virus to turn *off* all the audio equipment on the stations?"

"We can try, my liege," Alvero said, "but if we're caught, we risk an inter-MERIT war."

"If we're not successful, then there won't be enough of humanity left to fight that war, Chief."

"You're underselling it, my liege," Ward said. "Those stations, they're big refueling hubs. Any ship or shuttle that docked with them hooked their systems up to their ATC AI. I'm guessing every one of those ships is infected, too. And they brought the infection home."

"I concur with that assessment," Alvero said.

Every ship. Every station. Preparing to broadcast a signal to distress all those poor, infected people badly enough that their defenses would drop, and *canus* could take full control.

Tarquin felt numb. There were only seven of them in all the universe who knew. Who could hang on to themselves long enough to help. What the hell could seven people do?

He glanced at the container of amarthite in his hands and tightened his grip. He knew what one woman could do to save worlds. Seven was going to have to be enough.

"Start the intrusion," he told Alvero. "If the other families notice and start asking, say it's a project that got out of control. Lie, stall. I don't care. No, wait—let them notice. Tell them it's something we lost control of and that they should turn off their audio systems until we can get a handle on things. They might do it, then.

"Captain Ward, I want all the shroud *intolerant* on every Mercator station moved into a secure section immediately. They're all infected, but it will take those who didn't consume the contaminated shroud longer to succumb. We're going to batten down here in the hospital, but I leave it to the other stations to determine their most secure area. Once they're corralled, Merc-Sec are to stockpile arms and rations and lock the doors until they receive orders otherwise. Bring Dr. Sharp to this sector. Do it quickly, do it quietly, and try your damnedest not to start a panic."

They bowed their heads in understanding and got to work.

"I need a lab, and I need it now," Tarquin said to Bracken.

"This way, please, my liege."

Tarquin didn't think about why he was doing this. He didn't think about what was at stake, about what he'd already lost, and what he stood poised to lose. He followed Bracken, and he oriented himself in the lab and sat down, and he worked, and he didn't look up again until he had seven doses of the serum prepared.

It took him twelve hours.

His fingers ached, his upper back throbbed, but he'd done it. He'd taken the parts of her and made something that might save them all. Looking at those vials, slim and green-tinged and so very small, he nearly sobbed, because how could buying seven people a couple more days of lucidity save anyone at all?

He called for the others. They filed in, haggard shades of themselves, and went around updating him on the status of the world on the other side of his lab's door.

Panic had been unavoidable. Many of the shroud intolerant had fled the order, fearing some sort of pogrom. Tarquin couldn't blame them. Most had complied. And now they waited, frightened and cut off, their comms locked down, for something to happen.

News was flying with rumors of an inter-MERIT war. The other heads of family had been hailing him nonstop, demanding to know what Mercator thought it was doing. He sent a simple response to them all: *Do as I have suggested, if you wish to survive the next forty hours,* and left it at that. All Helms had to tell him was that Naira's condition hadn't changed.

"The doses are ready." Tarquin gestured to the preloaded syringes. "They'll buy us a few days, maybe a week. I can't say for certain."

Wary nods all around. That serum was their savior, and none of them were eager. None of them reached for it. It *was* experimental. What if...

Canus, filling him with doubt.

Tarquin grabbed a syringe and plunged it into his arm.

It hurt. He hadn't expected that, though he really should have. His pathways flared all at once, stripes of agony painting his body in liquid fire until it passed. Until he could breathe again. Tarquin had bent over his desk in the throes of it and as the pain faded, he became aware of Bracken's hand on his back, and the argument brewing around him.

"Enough." He shook off Bracken's hand as he straightened. "That was expected. Normal."

"That didn't look normal to me," Bracken said. "Maybe we should wait on the doses."

Tarquin slammed an open hand on the desk, making them all jump. "Take them, now. That is an order. The doubt you're feeling is *canus*. The pain is *canus*. Get through it."

They did, the exemplars handling it with a little less drama, but they all pushed through. When it was done, Tarquin looked into each of their faces and saw in them the same brutal clarity he was feeling.

The despair had lessened, but it wasn't gone. They'd bought themselves a few days. That was all. A few more days for seven people who didn't know what to do, who didn't know how to stop the end from coming.

"What now?" Caldweller asked.

"We prepare for a siege," Tarquin said. "Continue moving all supplies into this sector, food and armaments and any medical supplies that weren't already stored here. If we remove easy access to food, then it may end sooner. I want full blockades on the warpcore and the ansible, too. No one gets in or out of those sectors. Seal them, put them in vacuum, I don't care. Whatever it takes."

"Shit." Helms flushed as they all looked at her. "Sorry, it's just...I guess I hadn't realized that we'd be, you know, waiting for them to die off."

"It's not a fight we can win otherwise," Tarquin said. "I've seen *canus* twist misprints into an angry horde. If it takes control of so many otherwise hale bodies, then—did I order the printing bays shut down?"

"No, my liege," Caldweller said.

"Do it now, shut them all down, pull the power."

Caldweller frowned at his holo. "I'm not getting any response from that sector, my liege."

"We can't risk the infected taking control of those printers. They'll spill out misprints to cause trauma, lowering everyone's immune response, speeding *canus*, just like—" He grimaced. "Just like Demarco did to me."

He couldn't let that happen. Tarquin stood and tried to push his sleeve higher, but it was stuck in place with paint from the training range. He stared at the purple splotch, amazed. It felt like years ago.

"We'll shut them down manually."

He expected arguments, but they fell into step around him, making a loose cordon that should have been comforting, but was stifling. Helms followed, too. Tarquin stopped his march and jabbed a finger at her.

"You. You do not leave Naira's side again for *any* reason. Is that clear? Her defense is your single charge and purpose."

Helms startled. "Y-yes, my liege."

"Good." He breathed out, slowly. "Good. The rest of you, with me."

Beyond the level Naira was housed in, the hospital was in chaos. People had been crammed into every usable space, supply crates repurposed as makeshift furniture. The sound of thousands of frightened people talking all at once washed over him.

If he'd been alone, his power wouldn't have been enough to keep them back. They'd grab him. Demand answers. The thought chilled him, reminding him of the fragile arms reaching for him through the dead trees of Sixth Cradle. He crushed that feeling. These were his employees. They were scared, and that was his fault, but he could hardly stop to soothe them.

The printing bays were empty, the cubicles in the wall all showing the blue lights of not being in use. Tarquin allowed himself a second to catch his breath, relieved, before he set to work on one of the consoles, locking down every single program he could find with his command keys.

Which would only work until his serum wore off, and he unlocked them himself.

"Break shit," Tarquin said. "Start pulling out circuit boards, wires, anything. Make it require expertise to repair."

They dove into the task with more enthusiasm than was strictly necessary. Tarquin joined them, and by the time they'd finished trashing the place they were all sweating and panting and feeling a little less hopeless. Tarquin propped his hands on his knees and bent over, breathing hard.

"God, that felt good," he said.

They laughed, and though the sound was shaky, the shared mirth papered over some of the cracks in them all.

"Okay." Tarquin brushed his hands together, smeared a little blood as he'd cut himself on something he couldn't remember, and straightened. "That should slow them down. Let's get back to the hospital. Caldweller, what's Merc-Sec saying about the halls? Still clear?"

"Let me check in." He pulled up a holo. A deep canyon of worry carved the space between his brows.

Tarquin's earlier ease evaporated. "What is it?"

"I . . ." Caldweller stammered. "I'm uncertain, my liege. There are reports—almost definitely mistaken—from Merc-Sec that . . ." He cut himself off, squinted at the holo, then shook his head.

"Out with it, man," Tarquin said.

"My liege, Merc-Sec is holding a new arrival in the general transport hangar. This person is in the print of Ex. Lockhart, and using her credentials. Now, we know that's not possible, so they're holding her until we can figure this out."

The world slid out from under Tarquin's feet and he had to brace himself against a gutted console podium. "It's Naira. It has to be. No one else has access to that print file. The *Cavendish* is in Sol. They printed her *here*."

Nervous glances all around.

"We need to approach this carefully," Caldweller said, voice rich with warning.

Tarquin scarcely heard him. It made no sense that they'd double-print her on the *Cavendish* if they were already in the system. But then, double-printing her at all made no sense to him. They were here. They had to be here. Naira was in that hangar.

If he could confirm the status of her double-printing, then he could repair her map and bring her back.

"My liege?" Caldweller asked, but Tarquin had already spun on his heel and dashed off at a full sprint. "Tarquin!"

Shouts followed him, warnings and pleadings to wait, to be *certain*, but his head was too full of the buzz of possibility. Too distracted to notice that Caldweller had called him by his given name without the title for the first time.

SIXTY

Naira

The Cavendish | Two Weeks Later

Time was hard to pin down when you existed in all the moments of your life at once, but Naira was reasonably certain that a considerable amount of time had passed outside the confines of her sedated mind. Every so often, the medications would thin. Her consciousness would flit to the surface, and she'd catch some snippet of what was happening around her. Mostly, she overheard the happenings on the *Cavendish*.

She didn't like the sound of any of it. Her friends argued. Constantly. Kuma's usually laughing voice strained, like she was trying to pick up something that'd spilled and put it back in a container that'd broken in the fall. When Naira saw Jonsun, it was in staccato glimpses, his smile too bright. There was a beatific urgency about him she couldn't understand, and it frightened her.

Kav hovered around her as a storm cloud. Jessel disappeared entirely from the small theater of her hospital room.

They fixed the ship. The heat came on and the cold fled Naira at last, but not entirely. At some point she became aware that her other-body, the one that should have been on Mercator Station, had been moved.

A new door appeared in her mind, too stark to be real, crystal clear in a way memories never were. Through it she caught glimpses of her past self walking through a hangar on the way to plant bombs on the two decoy mining ships, Tarquin at her side. She wondered why such a mundane moment could suddenly grow so important.

She ignored it, focusing instead on the *Cavendish*, because those sedatives were fading again, and Kav was in her room, gripping Naira's arm like it was the edge of a cliff he'd fallen off.

"Nai," he whispered, and gave her a shake.

Naira grunted, head a muffled mess of memories untethered in time and muddled by drugs.

"C'mon, you gotta wake up."

She wanted to give him the finger, because it was patently unfair that *she* should have to do anything at all when it was them that had cracked her. But the fear in Kav's voice dragged her back to herself. She peeled her eyes open. The room was dark. Kuma was shouting in the hallway at someone, but Naira couldn't make out the words.

"What?"

"I know you don't remember our fight, but—"

"I remember everything," Naira said, unable to help a rough flutter of laughter.

"You were right," he said. "You were right, and I'm so fucking sorry for not listening better because this is . . . this is bad."

Naira blinked, registering the seriousness in Kav's tone. She pulled what pieces of herself she could muster back together and focused. Kav was scared. Kuma was arguing with . . . Jonsun? Yeah, that was Jonsun shouting in the hallway. And Jonsun hadn't felt right since she'd woken up here.

"Tell me," Naira said.

"I'm going to let you go here, okay? I'm going to let you go, because we think they've been trying to wake up your print back in Sol for a while now. Once you're up there you have to tell them to stop building the ship, because if they don't, Jonsun's going to fire on it."

"What ship? Mercator wasn't building any sh-hip."

"Mercator wasn't, but Acaelus was."

Naira scowled. "Cut to the fucking point, K-Kav. I have half a goddamn brain."

He glanced over his shoulder, then lowered his voice. "There's no relkatite on the *Cavendish*. We never found it. It's just amarthite here.

Acaelus took the relk stockpile and was lying low in Sol. He was hiding out until..." Kav swallowed. "Nai, this is going to be hard to hear, but it's been two weeks since we put you under. Sol's stations, its ships. They've pretty much all fallen to the *canus*-bound. Acaelus is out of hiding now, controlling it all. Using the infected to build this giant fucking ship and Jonsun thinks he's building it to chase us down."

Two weeks. Her mom. Tarquin. Everyone.

"You should have killed me here," she said. "Why couldn't you let me *try* to help?"

The shouting in the hall grew louder. "I'm going to now. Jonsun might crack me for it, but fuck it. A lot of innocent people will die if he fires on Acaelus's ship and that's not—that's not what I wanted. I wanted to run. I didn't want to salt the soil behind us, but that's exactly what Jonsun's going to do. He's going to kill them all. You were right, Nai. We can't build a stable future on ground soaked in blood."

"How?" Naira could sense her awake body's proximity to her comatose body. On the *Cavendish*, she was light-years away from her body back in Sol. The *Cavendish*'s weapons would never reach the *Sigillaria*. "It's too far."

"My fault." Kav rubbed his eyes. "I got him access to the HCA's bombardment defense stations. I thought he was going to use them to threaten Acaelus into standing down, but Acaelus isn't even answering hails anymore, and Jonsun's tired of waiting."

"So what if he blows up Acaelus's new toy? We blew up his ships all the time."

"Nai, you're not listening. Acaelus *took the relkatite* and used it to build the *Sigillaria* at last. He even used the *canus*-bound to strip out what was left on the stations. All of the relk is on that ship. If Jonsun destroys it, no one's coming back. That's the end of life around Sol."

"What—what am I supposed to *do*? I don't even know where Acaelus's ship is."

He grinned, just a little. Some of the old troublemaker she knew and loved suffused the lines of his face, and that expression eased the welling panic in her chest.

"I think you're on his ship. I've been monitoring your neural signature. The entanglement's done some real wild shit, but I can more or less pinpoint your location. Jonsun doesn't know. Based on what I've been seeing in your vitals, I think whoever moved you to the *Sigillaria* has been trying to load your mind into a simulation. As far as I can tell, us keeping you here, in a coma, has been suppressing the attempt."

She'd sensed that they had moved her, and at the mention of a simulation, she could see that door in her mind again, leading back into the memory of walking through the hangar, and closed her eyes against the intrusion.

"Nai. Hey." Kav squeezed her arm until she opened her eyes. "Stay with me."

"If you're right. If Acaelus moved me onto his ship and is trying to load me into a sim, then you're going to let them wake me up to interrogate me."

His eyes misted. "I know. But I'm betting everything on you, Nai. With your mind fractured, you might be able to resist being forced to perceive the sim as reality. You already exist in multiple places at once. You can do this."

"That's a big fucking leap of faith." She bit her lip, holding back repetition.

"Yeah, well, I've been jumping off cliffs with you my whole life. The one time I didn't, look what happened."

She laughed bitterly, and he smiled. Someone pounded on the door. Kav flinched and clutched Naira's hand so tightly it hurt.

"You have to stop that ship, because..." He glanced at the door, rattling in its frame, and grimaced. "I don't think we can make *him* stop."

"Okay," Naira said, taking a deep breath. "Okay."

"I knew you could." His voice trembled. He leaned over her, kissed her forehead. "See you on the other side."

Kav clicked the euthanasia line. The door burst inward, Jonsun radiating outrage brightly enough to burn them all. Behind him, she glimpsed snow-capped pine trees, needles lush and green, and then the heat of the medication raced through her veins.

Roselle works for Jonsun, Naira thought, but it was too late to get the words out, and she didn't even really know what they meant.

Naira died on the *Cavendish*, and her mind plunged straight through that door into memory, onto the deck of a hangar that had always been a trap waiting for her, mouth open and hungry.

SIXTY-ONE

Naira

error

It felt real. After existing so long in a drugged haze between two places in time, walking across that hangar floor again grounded Naira in her flesh. Everything was intense and solid. The touch of her armor against her skin, the ringing of her boots against the metal grate. She almost wept for the certainty that she was flesh and bone and not a miasma of moments anymore.

She'd been dreaming. Maybe this *was* real. Maybe she hadn't cracked at all. Everything that she'd thought had come after being in this hangar felt hazy. A dream already fading. She'd always had nightmares about cracking, after all.

"I don't think I'll ever get used to the idea," Tarquin said beside her. "Self-destruction, I mean. I don't have it in me, even though I know the chances of coming back are high. Are you sure you don't remember anything about being on the *Cavendish*? I'd heard that there can be bleed-over, sometimes."

Frosty halls encroached on the edges of her vision. She stopped walking to blink them clear. The *Cavendish*? What was he talking about? She'd gotten caught casting off of that ship. She hadn't died. That must be what he meant. He couldn't possibly know about her dream, vivid though it had been. Something almost like a memory tickled at her senses, then vanished.

"Are you all right?" he asked.

He stood with his hands in his pockets, shoulders relaxed, and she thought... She thought maybe she'd seen him like that before, but not recently. Crouching in the dirt on Sixth Cradle, unaware he was being observed. That'd been the first time she'd seen him as himself. As something that wasn't a figurehead, something beneath the surface of the Mercator namesake. She shouldn't remember that.

Why did she feel like all the pieces of herself were slipping away?

It was the deaths. The reprints. *That dream.* They were all getting to her.

"Sharp?" he asked.

She pressed the heel of her palm against her forehead until it hurt enough to cut the fog. He gripped her upper arm, steadying her, and though she was aware of him being close to her, the touch didn't do anything for her. Didn't set off the burst of attraction she expected. Strange.

Everything here was strange. The empty hangar, the empty ships. Where were Kuma and Kav?

"Hey," Tarquin said, his voice a little low, a little rough. He shook her. "What happened?" His grip tightened until it hurt. "Tell me, Sharp, what happened? Where is the *Cavendish*? Where are they going?"

She blinked shadows from her eyes, not understanding why he would ask her such a thing. His grip tightened. Her muscle bruised. That wasn't right. Tarquin wouldn't hurt her. His eyes were too bright, and his stare bored into her, face close enough she should be able to feel the breath from him, but there wasn't any.

"Where is it?" Tarquin demanded.

"What the fuck is this?" She placed both hands on his chest and shoved.

"That's enough. Put her under." Canden's voice echoed all around her.

And then there was nothing.

SIXTY-TWO

Tarquin

error

Tarquin didn't know where he was, but he knew he was somewhere he wasn't supposed to be. The lights were dark, blue-tinged, and the walls were a smooth grey-blue enamel he didn't recognize.

The only Mercator green in the room was the light on the machine attached to his arm. Though that color had been a comfort his whole life, he knew as he looked upon it in that moment that he should be afraid.

He licked dry, cracked lips and tried to turn his head, but it'd been locked in place by a cushioned halo of a device. Fear was far away, dulled by medication, but something like panic took root in his belly and grew, extended up through his throat until his breath was coming in short pants.

"Shh," Leka said from somewhere nearby. Tarquin couldn't turn his head to see. That panic sprouted thorns. He jerked, struggling against the binds that held him to a metal bed. He was too weak to break free.

His sister's icy, dry hand brushed the side of his face, knuckles tracing over his temple. Tarquin tried to master the mounting panic and wished whatever was deadening his ability to feel fear would take the gut-twisting anxiety from him, too.

"What have you done?" Tarquin rasped, his throat scratchy from disuse or overuse. He couldn't tell and didn't want to dwell on either meaning.

"What I had to." She rested a hand on Tarquin's forehead. "I'm so sorry."

"Leka..." Tarquin strained to turn his head, to see his sister, but the cradle held him firmly in place. "Let me help you."

"Oh, Tarq, you can't." She moved away from him, her steps shuffling toward the door. He tried to follow her with his eyes, but couldn't quite get her into focus.

"I can," he said, "but you have to let me go."

"That thing is coming back." She rushed to him, finally leaning over him far enough that he could see her face. Her once lustrous skin had dry, patchy spots that for one terrifying moment Tarquin thought were lichen. Dark hollows carved her cheeks, and her hair had been hidden beneath a thin wrap, though a few greasy wisps trailed out. Her eyes were bloodshot, but they were hers, keen and bright. "I won't have control of myself much longer. I'll let you out as soon as I can, I promise, but that thing—that thing is not our mother."

A slow gait approached the door, steps hissing over the ground. Leka's eyes blanked, all her fire extinguished. Once more she was the empty-eyed woman Tarquin had seen standing behind their father in the video broadcast. She reached for a simulation crown, a device used to load minds into a digital space for interrogation.

"Don't," Tarquin said. It was the only word he could muster.

Leka settled the crown over him, and he slipped into darkness.

Tarquin walked along the hangar that housed the ships destined for Seventh and Eighth Cradles, trying to pretend he wasn't hyper aware of every breath Naira took, of the subtle rustle of her clothes and the shifting of her body. Trying to pretend like he didn't feel as if she was the only real thing in the entire galaxy.

She stopped abruptly and pointed to the ship nearest them with her chin. "Doesn't this feel off?"

He wanted to tell her that the entire world felt off. That everything was a flimsy shadow of itself next to her. But she didn't want his affections, and so he nodded instead.

"It's odd that no one's here," he said.

"Looks like a trap," she said.

"Huh."

"What?"

"Nothing. Just struck by a sense of déjà vu."

She gave him a sideways smile. "Lots of traps to spring lately. We're already here, so we might as well take these down to stop them being used later. At least we don't have to worry about biological damage."

"You just want something to blow up."

"A woman in possession of a bomb is in want of a reason to use it."

Her grin was warm, playful, but he felt ill. Blue light stained the corners of his vision. "You said that already."

"No, I didn't." She frowned. Took a step closer to him. Put a hand on his shoulder. Odd. Naira usually avoided touching him. "You all right, Mercator? Is the déjà vu getting worse?"

"I don't know." He twisted his fingers together. "Do you see a blue light?"

Her frown deepened. "Maybe you should wait in the shuttle."

"No." He bit his tongue, but felt compelled to speak anyway, though he didn't know where the words came from. "I think I'm remembering a time before. A forgotten life. Do you ever have flashes like that?"

"Oookay. Let me call Kav, he can walk you back."

"No. No." He held on to her like an anchor as whispers that weren't his swirled poisoned fingers through his mind. Urged him to push, to demand she answer the question, to demand to know what she remembered— *because she knew where that ship was, she knew and she was hiding it, that fucking bitch.*

Those weren't his thoughts. Those would *never* be his thoughts. The pressure receded.

"Please, listen to me. This isn't real. We're being interrogated. Don't— don't answer my questions. I can't help them. I can't even help what I'm thinking."

"You're definitely going to wait in the shuttle."

She started to return to the shuttle, but he dug his heels in. Even though she had the strength to pick him up and drag him back against his will, she stopped and faced him. "Mercator, this might be serious."

"It *is* serious," he insisted, "but not in the way you think. I swear to you, Naira, this is wrong. It's not real."

"Look, you're going through something here, but I'd really rather you call me Sharp. You know that."

The world greyed around the edges, the blue light seeping into his vision once more. Voices echoed from a faraway place, indistinct, but one at least vaguely familiar to Tarquin, though he couldn't make out the words.

He spun around, searching. These simulations had exit points, places in the ground the interrogator could walk over to wake up back in their own body. The hangar stretched around him, growing impossibly large.

Naira said something, but he ignored her. He could already feel the world slipping away, and there was a tenuous memory, a moment he could barely grasp. A prelude to being on a gurney, the crown of lies strapped to his head.

Lockhart.

He'd run straight to her because he'd thought Naira had been double-printed into that body. It'd been a trap. They'd been overwhelmed, and Tarquin had been taken. Taken, sedated, and brought to that room where he'd seen his sister. That was real. The shade of Leka, the stiffness of the gurney. The blue light. Not this hangar.

This place was fake, but Naira wasn't. Not even Mercator could fake a mind in simulation. The people who had taken Tarquin had taken her then, too, and were trying to use him to pry the location of the *Cavendish* out of her. How many times had they done this walk? He had no idea. The memories were brittle. They dissolved as soon as he tried to recall them.

"These simulations," he said. "They're isolating. They intentionally suppress your other memories so that you can't remember you're being interrogated."

"I remember plenty of things," she said, but her denial lacked snap.

The blue light got brighter. He grabbed both of her arms and spoke as forcefully as he could. "Naira, you—" He grimaced, and pushed on. "You're cracked. And I'm so, so sorry, but I think that means you might be able to wake up while you're in here. You already exist in multiple places at once. Can you do that? Can you open your other eyes? Tell me where you are, what you see?"

Her brow creased with concentration. "Kav said that. That I'm in multiple places at once."

Tarquin couldn't help but grin. "Of course he figured it out. Naira, I *need* you to wake up. Can you do that?"

"I... I don't know."

"Wake up," he pleaded. "Please, please wake up."

The blue light consumed him. The instance reset.

SIXTY-THREE

Naira

error

Naira was ill at ease in her own skin as she stepped out of the shuttle onto the hangar floor. The leviathans of the mining fleet rested a couple hundred feet away, their airlocks yawning open, inviting her into their undefended dark. Everything here felt off, and not just the lack of security.

There was a tinny quality to the air that was too medical, a texture to the light in the room that seemed to swarm her, painting blue splotches in shadows that should have been plain black. Every time she looked at Tarquin she thought she saw something perched upon his skull, a gargoyle with its fingers piercing the flesh. A ring of light. A crown of thorns.

"Are you all right?" Tarquin asked. She'd stopped walking outside the shuttle door, and he'd stopped a few feet in front of her. He had a cant to his head that implied more worry than he was letting on, and his eyes kept darting around the room, but there was something soft about him. Something pliable that didn't feel quite right, either.

"This feels wrong."

He turned back to the ships. "I know. No security? No techs checking the ships over? It's definitely weird. Quite probably a trap."

"Wrong trap." She couldn't say where those words had come from.

"What do you mean?"

"I know this feeling. This was what it was like prepping for the mission to Sixth Cradle. I thought I was talking to Jonsun, and maybe I was, but everything was hollow. Off. There was... There was the blue light. Can't you see it?"

He shrugged. "It's pretty dark in here. I guess that makes things look blue."

"No. It doesn't. This is an interrogation."

His eyes widened, and she could see the denial bubble up in him, then die.

"Shit," he said. "What do they want?"

Doubt settled into her, watching concern carve a path through Tarquin's face, then wash away again, replaced by a kind of open, honest expression that should inspire confidence but didn't fit him.

Just like this room, Tarquin wasn't quite right. He was a tightly wound ball of frustrations carrying the weight of expectations he'd never asked for. While he could be quick to a smile and kind and curious and so very gentle sometimes, if she'd told him he was being held captive in a simulation, he wouldn't be asking her so innocently what she thought they were after. He'd be freaking out and trying to find an exit.

To the best of her knowledge, not even mighty Mercator could simulate another mind convincingly without activating an actual neural map. Whoever had her also had Tarquin, and they were using him to manipulate something out of her. Fury burned through her, blue sparks igniting in the corners of her eyes.

She remembered a voice calling for reset.

"Canden," Naira called out. "Using your own son as a puppet is a new low, even for you."

Tarquin's eyes widened with shock and dismay. Maybe he understood what her words meant, maybe he was too drugged to reach those conclusions himself, but she saw something like realization, heavy with dread, before that expression wiped away and a cruel smile that wasn't really his twisted his lips.

"You're going to tell me where the *Cavendish* is. It's only a matter of time."

The world slipped away, and she could feel herself drifting in nothing, then the door again, the memory, back on that hangar floor with Tarquin at her side.

But Naira remembered, now. She was cracked. Not even the suppression of the simulation crown could hold all her memories at bay. She remembered him begging her to wake up. To open her real eyes.

She did.

Naira woke on a cold metal gurney. Tarquin spoke to her in the simulation, layered over her real vision, but she ignored him, fumbling her hands up her body to clutch the simulation crown and rip it away. She gasped, a sensation like a cold spike impaling her forehead jarring her more solidly into her real flesh.

Her gasp shifted into a rough, bitter laugh that she couldn't stop from dissolving into coughs. She blinked, relishing the sandpaper scrape of her eyelids because that, at least, was real.

The world around her was painted in shades of grey and blue, reminding her of the colors of Acaelus's inner rooms. The rooms no public eyes ever got to see. Indistinct shapes swam in and out of focus as her body struggled to switch over its sensory input systems to the tangible world. Every breath stank of stale sweat and antiseptic.

"It's never going t-to work," she rasped, throat scratched so badly from within that she tasted iron and the subtle, astringent flavor of pure oxygen. She'd been intubated at one point. Her lips flaked in chunks as she ran her tongue over them. Without the suppression of the simulation crown, her cracked stutter came back, further reminding her she was in her real body.

"I told her as much," a woman said.

Naira lifted her head and stared at herself, standing on the other side of the room.

She blinked, shoving aside a cascade of memories that swarmed to the surface. No, that wasn't her.

Ex. Lockhart stood with her back to the door, hands held lightly in front of her stomach, gaze locked on Naira with such intensity it sent a flutter of fear through her. Lockhart's posture was rigid, the pathways on her skin a mix of silver and gold, as if the infection had started to take over and then given up. Decided it wasn't worth it, this person was already controlled.

"Who are you, really?" Naira asked.

Her nostrils flared. "I think you know."

Every syllable appeared to cost her. They dragged out, as if she had to extend a great force of will to make her jaw move. Ex. Lockhart stared at her with empty eyes.

"Aera?" Naira asked.

Tears slid down Lockhart's cheeks, running over old stains. She nodded.

Naira pushed herself to her elbows, struggling against even the thin weight of the blanket, and saw her hands.

Scars traced the places where her pathways had once gleamed, thin white lines draping her in a cobweb of loss. Between the scars, a few tiny glimpses of gold. The barest minimum of integration pathways clinging on, holding her together.

They'd taken them. Someone had carved her up and ripped out her enhancements while she was comatose. No wonder her captors hadn't bothered to restrain her. There was no point.

Every single part of her body hurt as she eased her legs over the edge of the gurney and sat, trying to regain her breath. Her revulsion would have to wait until she'd crawled her way out of whatever horror she'd just found herself in. Lockhart only watched her.

"O-k-kay, E-X. What happened?"

"He said I could be as good as you."

A bottom-of-her-class exemplar, on the verge of washing out. Wholly forgettable. Wholly expendable. But she'd borne a passing resemblance to Naira, and that'd made her a useful tool for Acaelus. Nausea burned through her, but she had nothing left to vomit.

"I'm so, so sorry."

Lockhart pulled her sidearm. Naira had watched that movement so many times in memory that it made her temporarily forget which moment she was living through. They smudged together, blinding her. When Naira found herself back in the present, Lockhart had turned the weapon around and was handing the grip to her in a shaking hand.

"Please," she said.

Naira took the weapon. Her wrist twinged from the weight and she had to set it down on the gurney to keep from dropping it. There was no way she was firing a gun, no way she was fighting her way out of here, not with the shape her print was in.

"How much control do you have?" she asked.

"They mostly forget I exist," Lockhart said. "But it won't last long. Liege Canden is with Liege Tarquin now. It's easier for me to think when she's far away, and she insisted on you two being as far apart as possible."

Not great, but not unworkable. "Where's Acaelus? Is he near Canden?"

"No, he's on the command deck, closer to us. He never leaves it."

"I'm going to ask you something I have no right to a-ask." Naira clenched her jaw against her slip and waited for Lockhart to protest, but the other woman said nothing. "I need your help, Ex. Lockhart, because that gun you gave me—I barely have the strength to hold it. And if I don't stop this ship from chasing down the *Cavendish*, then there's a man out there—Jonsun Hesson—who's going to fire on it. All the people here will die. I know we can reprint them, but all the relk's here, too, isn't it? There won't be a thing left to reprint them with.

"I don't know how much of me is in you, but..." Naira knew where her desire to defend came from, and had a sickening sense that Acaelus had known, too, and more than likely borrowed that moment for his purposes. To make his perfect guardian.

"You want to stop people from getting hurt, d-don't you? You don't want anyone else to feel l-li-like—" Naira bit her lip until she drew blood.

"I remember," Lockhart said softly.

Naira's mind fell back into the moment her mother was trampled beneath the crowd. To Naira crawling to her, begging her to get up. And she did. Miraculously, her mother had gotten up and, despite her injuries, picked up Naira and fled to a safer location where she had breathed her last. Just the two of them. No one had come to help.

"Help me," Naira said, in both moments, only this time, there was someone who could answer that cry. She clung to that. Naira had always wanted to be the person who hadn't been there for her. Maybe Lockhart could feel that. Maybe Lockhart didn't even need Naira's precise memory to feel the same way. "One last time, be an E-X and then I'll let you rest, if that's what you w-want. But I need to reach Acaelus to stop this, and I can't do it alone."

Lockhart's nostrils flared again and Naira smiled, seeing that, because it wasn't a tick of hers—that was all Aera.

"I'm with you, E-X," she said.

SIXTY-FOUR

Tarquin

The Sigillaria | *The Present*

Tarquin sat on the ground with his back against the wall, knees huddled into his chest, and couldn't tell if he'd been sleeping, daydreaming, or something else. His thoughts were a mess, a fog of blue lights and the empty endless air of a hangar too large for the two ships within it. A hangar that could arc above him forever, consume everything he was and everything he'd ever known and never let it go.

He pressed his face into the tops of his knees, digging the hard angle of his kneecap into his eye socket until the blue cleared and he could breathe without wanting to scream. Slowly, he lifted his head. He blinked away splotches and tried to figure out where he was.

This time he'd woken with full knowledge of his experience in the simulation. In his mind's eye, he could see Naira halt her steps outside the door of the shuttle. Could recall with perfect clarity the slow panic that had risen within him as every impossible thing she'd said echoed as true within him but his body just...brushed it all off.

He hadn't been in control of his own mind. His own feelings. The tiny core of himself had been smothered in gentle whispers, soothing him to silence while someone else pulled the strings.

Tarquin caged up all he was feeling and buried it. He was himself. He was racked with terror, reeling from the violation of it all, but when he examined his thoughts and feelings, he saw them to be true. To be him. To be real.

Tarquin dragged himself to his feet and found his legs shaky from weakness. Small, hot sore spots pocked his body, the brush of his clothes bringing back the phantom impression of straps holding him down.

He shuffled forward and pressed his hands against the wall, letting it guide him around the small room until his vision settled. A cot, a washbasin, a desk, a chair, a trunk bolted to a floor. He would have thought it was a jail cell if the door hadn't swung open when he turned the lever.

The hall beyond was dim, but not unusually so. The grey-and-blue motif continued, and with a burst of longing he recognized his father's favorite colors. The ones Acaelus had never allowed the world outside his inner rooms to see him indulge in, as they struck too close to Tran family colors.

An ache for his home hooked deep in his chest. Tarquin dug a thumb into one of the sore spots on his arm and hissed at the pain, but it grounded him. Reminded him that, wherever he was, this was no home for him. He was a prisoner here, and he needed to escape.

He needed to save Naira.

Tarquin shuffled along, listening for an alarm. With every step he took his stride grew more certain, his muscles responding to half-remembered cues to lead him through the halls, mapping this ship or station—he couldn't tell which he was in—against memory of similar Mercator installations. The halls were empty. No one stopped him.

Tarquin's determined stride slowed. He touched the wall, half expecting it to dissolve into a gauze of ones and zeros, but it stayed resolutely solid. Another empty space. Different, true, but that might mean that Canden had crafted a different digital maze for him to walk.

"I won't do this," Tarquin said to the empty halls. His voice echoed. He hugged himself, savoring the sting of the sores on his body. Canden wouldn't let him keep a memento of his real body, a clue that this wasn't real, if he was in a simulation. The assurance was thin. "I won't trick her into telling you what you want. She doesn't even know. She died on the *Cavendish*. Her memories of it are gone."

There was no answer from the blank walls.

Tarquin swore under his breath and was half tempted to go back to his cell and sit, knees drawn up, and keep silent until Canden grew bored or frustrated enough to change something—to either load him into another simulation or wake him up again—but if this was real, then he had to find Naira.

Resenting every second of this farce, Tarquin trudged on, throwing open each door he passed. Empty, unused rooms with tarps buckled over their furniture and equipment greeted him. He stormed down the hall, speeding his steps, a seed of dread taking root in him as each room was the same, more or less. As each room echoed in the halls of his memory.

This was the *Amaranth*. It couldn't be real. That ship had burned, torn to bits by the rail guns of the *Einkorn*. But the layout was identical. The rooms the same. His frustration grew sharper with every door that led to more of the same.

Until he reached one he knew well. Tarquin stopped his determined march outside the door to the printing bay in which he'd once printed Lockhart. Printed Naira.

He stepped closer. Hesitated. The door sensed him and swished open anyway.

His thoughts tangled, skipped over themselves. A figure sat on a gurney in the center of the room, too-thin legs dangling off the edge, the heels of her palms planted against the top of the gurney. Filaments dripping glossy black globes burst through the backs of her hands, breaking her family cuffs. Silver pathways traced her skin.

Her head was bowed, scraggly black hair obscuring her face.

That thing is not our mother.

Canden Mercator lifted her head and smiled a slow, rictus smile at him. "I knew you'd come here."

SIXTY-FIVE

Naira

The Sigillaria | The Present

Naira eased off the gurney and nearly crumpled when her feet touched the floor. She gasped, steadying herself, and squeezed her eyes shut against a rush of memories of other near falls, other moments she'd dropped to the ground.

Breathe. Be present. Thinking had, paradoxically, felt easier in the sim, where the software was suppressing her memories. Kav had asked her to... to what? To stop a ship. Naira had dedicated lives to stopping ships.

Lockhart took her arm for support. Naira shook her head.

"N-no. You'll need your hands free. Just. Just give me a second."

She breathed through the pain and searched the room. As far as she could tell, it was some kind of medical facility, the drawers and cabinets stocked with supplies for minor surgeries, but the equipment...Aside from a single printing cubicle and a neural link hookup, she didn't recognize any of it, and didn't want to dwell too long on what some of the more macabre-looking tools might have been used for.

Tarquin was trapped somewhere in this ship, going through the same thing she was but untrained to handle it. Focusing on finding him gave her clarity. Stop the ship. Get Tarquin out of here. She could do this.

Steeling herself, she picked up a metal tray and faced her reflection.

Her hair was a sweaty, twisted mess, her forehead pricked with a bloody constellation left over from the simulation crown. She combed her fingers through her hair to make the wounds less noticeable, and then gave up. With her scars, she couldn't even attempt to blend in. She'd be relying entirely on Lockhart to get her through whatever waited beyond the door. At least her legs had stopped shaking.

"All right. I'm good. Let's g-g-*go*."

Naira winced. She'd said *let's go* far too often in her life. Best to avoid phrases that might get her stuck looping through memory. Lockhart gave her a look that said she didn't believe Naira was "good" for a second, but nodded and led the way.

The hall was dark, and without her night vision pathway, Naira found the low light stifling. The air lacked the crisp edge of recycled station atmospheres and had a musky, damp quality to it that stuck to her skin. It was old air. Primordial air. The kind of atmosphere that fostered the growth of microbes and minerals both, thick with becoming.

She'd expected the walls to be draped with *canus* once more, silvery mycelium drawing phantom mouths over the screens inset in the walls, but there was nothing. No people, either. Just the warm, growing air, and an endless hallway with locks all lit green. She checked the first door and found another room like hers. Same equipment for the simulation immersion, but empty.

The next room wasn't empty. She hesitated in the doorway, trying to make sense of the wiry body on the hospital bed, the simulation crown sprouting from her head, hiding half her face.

Ex. Helms. Naira found the strength to brush past Lockhart and rushed into the room, hands shaking as she fumbled with the simulation device. Careful not to injure the young woman further, Naira worked the crown free and tossed it aside.

Helms's eyes snapped open, and a scream ripped out of her.

Naira covered Helms's mouth with one hand and snapped her fingers in front of her eyes. "Helms, it's m-me. It's Sharp. I don't know what you've been going through, but I'm real."

The scream cut off and Helms blinked a few times before she settled. Naira removed her hand, braced for another shout, but none came.

"It's really you, E-X?" Helms's throat was as raspy as Naira's had been.

"Most of me," Naira said. "I'm still..." She waved a hand vaguely, and Helms nodded. Naira was grateful she didn't have to spell it out. Every time she acknowledged she was cracked she felt pieces of herself spiraling away, and it was harder to cling to the present.

Naira set to work undoing her restraints, making a subtle check of her pathways as she did so. They were still golden. Her night vision pathway was gone. "What happened?"

"We confirmed the night vision pathways were infected and removed them, but by then it was too late to stop the spread. Liege Tarquin ordered all shroud-intolerant personnel at Mercator stations to bunker down together. We moved rations, weapons, everything we could into the hospital while Liege Tarquin..." She bit her lip.

Naira looked up from undoing an ankle strap. "Tell me."

"Liege Tarquin said there was a serum that could slow *canus* down, but it required amarthite, and we..."

Naira looked at the scars covering her arms. "You cannibalized me."

"He didn't—*we* didn't want to, but—"

"It's all right," Naira said. "It's... weird. But I understand. Continue."

Helms sat up, rubbing the life back into her arms. "He said it would hold the infection back for a week or so, and we all took it."

"Who's we, E-X?" Naira pressed. "R-report."

Helms flushed, her tone growing more confident as she slipped into the cadence of giving a report instead of a scared woman rambling about the horrors that had befallen her. "Myself, Liege Tarquin, Ex. Caldweller, Ex. Cass, Alvero, Captain Ward, and Dr. Bracken."

"Where are they now?"

"I don't know. The others went to dismantle the printing bay while I remained at my post." She recounted how they'd found the virus Fletcher had installed, and how Tarquin had feared the printing bays might be used to the same effect. Then she took a breath. "The others hadn't returned by the time we received a report that Merc-Sec was holding Ex. Lockhart in the hangar. Liege Tarquin believed her to be your double-print."

Naira winced. "It wasn't."

"Yeah, that became clear rather quickly." Helms swung her feet to the ground. Naira envied how easily she recovered. "It was a complete trap. The Merc-Sec on the dock were infected, and the second Liege Tarquin realized his mistake, Lockhart knocked him out and took him with their help."

"Shit." Naira rubbed at her aching temples. "The others?"

"They fought, but I don't think they made it. They weren't answering comms by the time Lockhart's people made it to the hospital. Lockhart said she wanted you alive, and I fought as best as I could, but it was just me left by then, and I—I couldn't..."

"Hey." Naira squeezed the woman's upper arm. "You did damn well. This wasn't your f-f-fault." She was simultaneously speaking to Helms and in half a dozen other moments when she'd reassured someone an error wasn't their fault. "Did you see anything when you were brought here?"

"I got a pretty good look at the layout of the ship before they locked me in here."

Naira's mind slipped, and she thought she was back on the *Cavendish*, Kav hovering above her, begging her to make them stop building the ship before Jonsun lost his patience and fired.

"Ex. Sharp? E-X?" Helms's face was close to hers, the younger exemplar's hands on her arms, shaking her gently. Concern twisted her face.

Naira shuddered. "Sorry. Was...elsewhere. My friend, he tried to warn me about a ship being built, told me that if I didn't stop it, Jonsun was going to fire on it."

Helms's eyes widened. "But *everyone's* here. I overheard them sometimes, when the sedatives were wearing off. They rounded up all the infected and uninfected both and brought them here or to the stations in orbit around the ship."

"What stations?"

"They moved the nearby stations as close to the *Sigillaria* as they dared and loaded them with people. Canden said something about needing us all closer together for full communion. She was adamant about it. If this ship's warpcore blows, I don't think those stations will be in the clear."

"You're t-telling me everyone living on stations in the Sol system is in the blast radius?"

"As far as I know. This is it. This is all of us."

"And Jonsun wants to blow it up." Naira wished she hadn't thought about Jonsun. It made her lose time again.

"You're not well," Helms said.

Naira laughed roughly. "No s-sh-hit. I don't have time to wallow in it. We've got to commandeer this ship and get a message to the *Cavendish*, or *canus* won't be humanity's biggest problem anymore, because we'll all be fucking d-dead."

"But there's only two of us."

"I've had worse odds," Naira lied, dragging a rueful smile out of Helms. She glanced at the doorway. Lockhart had, wisely, stayed out of sight while Naira woke Helms. "And there's three of us. Lockhart was being controlled when she came to Mercator Station, but she's got a grip on herself now and wants to stop this as badly as we do. We have to keep her away from Canden to keep her from losing control. Can you handle that?"

Helms frowned. "Liege Tarquin said you were my single charge and purpose. I think I should get you out of here first."

"He said that, did he?" Naira asked, unsure how she felt about it. Technically, it was true of all exemplars and their charges, but she could see through the cracks in Helms's story. Could see him shouting at Helms to stay with Naira while he went for the printing bays, and didn't like the look of the man who'd put the safety of Naira's comatose print above using Helms's talents to help secure the station. Problems for later. "Here's the thing, Helms. I'm going to commandeer this ship and get a message to the *Cavendish* that it's no longer a threat to them. You want to protect me? Come with me."

Helms scrutinized her, and Naira was distinctly aware that the younger woman could easily overpower her, toss her over her shoulder, and make a break for it. If she did, there was nothing at all Naira could do about it. Now she knew how Tarquin felt, and she didn't like it much.

"This Jonsun guy, he's really going to fire on this ship?" she asked.

"He is. He believes Acaelus is building it to hunt him down, and honestly, I'm not sure that he's wrong about that."

Helms nodded slowly. "All right. Let's do this. But stay behind me, please."

Naira smiled despite herself. "If y-you insist, E-X."

SIXTY-SIX

Tarquin

The Sigillaria | *The Present*

You're not real," Tarquin told the specter of his mother. "The neural map Acaelus has of Mom is a fake. Intentionally broken. Meti Laurent figured out how to stage Mom cracking to help her escape to spread the shroud to the cradles ahead of *canus*'s arrival. You never came back to Sol."

He said the words like a prayer, as if the truth of those facts could shield him from the woman sitting across from him. She slipped off of the gurney and approached him, her familiar scent reaching out to him through the heady air. Reminding him that he wasn't seeing blue light anymore. That the emptiness of the simulation no longer swallowed him. He shook his head in private denial.

His mother put her hand against his cheek and it stirred so many fond memories that he stayed rooted in place, savoring the warmth seeping through her skin to his.

"Those things are true," she said, "but I came back to the family when I realized my efforts had failed. That Meti and I had lost."

"What do you mean, lost?"

"It was Ex. Sharp who first told me, on Sixth Cradle, though it took me a long time to grow enough into this body to remember the moment."

Grow into that body? Tarquin didn't understand, but he bent beneath the guilt, his whole body collapsing in on itself under the weight of what he'd done. Of what he'd tried to put out of his mind.

The Canden Mercator he'd met on Sixth Cradle might have been his mother, once, but she'd been subsumed by *canus*, unable to think for herself, and under that thing's direction she'd decided that Tarquin needed to die.

And so he'd shot her in the head, and left that planet with both of their corpses behind. Left them to decay into the ruin she'd made of them.

He could tell himself she hadn't been herself all he liked. It didn't erase the weight of the pistol in his hand. Didn't take away the bright spray of her blood against the scree, the quiet shock on her face in the seconds before he'd pulled the trigger.

"Shh," she said. "Hush, my sweet boy, I understand. If I had been in my right mind, it's what I would have wanted. I went to that planet to find a way to stop *canus* once and for all. And instead I sat on my hands, placid. Shrugged and gave up, because it was already in me, telling me it was pointless. But you, my brilliant, brilliant boy, you found it, didn't you? You found a way to undo *canus*. A way for us to live as ourselves."

Tarquin's heart thundered, making it hard to hear. All he could focus on was her face, calm and kind, without a hint of the dangerous edge he'd seen on Sixth Cradle.

That danger, even if it had unsettled him, had been like looking into a window she'd kept the curtains pulled on her whole life. He'd seen the true core of his mother for the first time and this woman... This woman didn't carry that fiery heart of rage.

He wanted to rebuke her. To tell her to go to hell, that she was fake and so was the ship. But he'd learned, walking across that hangar too many times for comfort, to sense the wrongness in a simulation. To feel the dead hollowness lurking behind a digital curtain. As much as he wanted his denials to be true, a part of him that was always analyzing, always evaluating, had already decided that this was real.

And she was asking him questions that aligned with the ones they'd been asking Naira. Asking about the amarthite. Leading up to asking about the *Cavendish*, more than likely. This was real, but that couldn't be his mother. There was nothing of Canden in her mannerisms.

He laughed, roughly, and dragged his hands down the sides of his face, stretching the skin. "This is sick. Who are you? You can't be my mother.

Acaelus doesn't have her real map, just like he doesn't have mine in that body he's using as a prop. And we can't be on the *Amaranth*. That ship burned."

"This isn't the *Amaranth*, though it was built in that ship's image. We already had the manufacturing systems in place, and this one needed to be made in a hurry. This is the *Sigillaria*. The real one. Our family's safe haven, built while the other families were busy trying to reach our decoy ansible."

"This isn't a safe haven. It's a tomb. I see your infection. You want the *Cavendish* to destroy its amarthite, don't you?"

Canden sighed and shook her head sadly. "I knew the simulation was a bad idea, but Sharp would only ever tell her secret to you. We came close to getting the location out of her a few times before the end."

His stomach dropped. "What end?"

"She was already cracked, sweetheart. Exemplar or no, all that training couldn't keep her together. She's slipped beyond repetition and into the endless scream. Not even Chiyo's software can fix her, now."

"You're lying."

"Maybe," Canden allowed with a slim smile that Tarquin couldn't read. "But we pulled the plug on her print and iced her."

His fists flexed ineffectually at his sides. "She's here. You have her map on this ship. You can print her again and you can fix it. I—I need to talk to her."

She rested one hand against his upper arm, in the place where Pliny used to sit, and squeezed. It irritated him to feel hot tears well in the corners of his eyes. The reason he'd placed Pliny there in the first place was because he'd missed her. He'd missed this exact touch.

"We would never put her back together. Not unless we could be sure."

"Sure of what?" he asked, though he thought he knew.

"Of your loyalties." Her smile curved higher than should be possible. "We're running. Running from *canus* at last. And we have to know you're with us. Have to know you hate it as much as we do, that you want to destroy it. To undo this thing we've unleashed."

"You're not running from *canus*, you're embracing it. And you—you're no different from a misprint, *canus* melded with whatever Acaelus told you about my mother."

"I know it's hard to understand. Come with me. I have a gift for you. Proof I'm still myself, and no puppet of *canus*."

Canden removed her hand from his arm and held it out in invitation.

SIXTY-SEVEN

Naira

The Sigillaria | *The Present*

Dead eyes watched them move through the ship. Their stares crawled against Naira's skin, the knowledge that something else, something unknowable, watched through those eyes stoking the coals of her anger. She thought she recognized some of the names emblazoned across their uniforms from the list of the dead from the construction platform. They stood still as trees, clustered in hallways and rooms, staring at nothing, and Naira found herself wishing for the chaos and terror of the misprints scrabbling after her.

This was worse. This was so much worse.

These people didn't hurt or want. They stood, and they waited to be used, and on each and every face was a ghost of beatific peace.

Then she saw Acaelus, and understood.

He had ensconced himself on the command deck of the ship. The real *Sigillaria* at last. There was no writhing infection like she'd found in the *Einkorn*. The deck was clean to the naked eye. *Canus* didn't need to over-grow here. It didn't need to stretch itself to understand its environment. It was in the relk of the commander's pathways, and as Paison had said, it'd learned subtlety.

The once head of Mercator sat in a tall chair alone, the chair beside him empty, and that beatific smile was on his face, his pathways shining silver, a simulation crown upon his head.

She hadn't known how she'd feel seeing him again. Fury had seemed most likely. But in the end, all she could muster up was pity.

Lockhart raised her pistol, arm shaking, and aimed for his head. Naira rested a hand against her arm.

"Not yet," Naira said. "We need to use him first. Then he's all yours."

Lockhart slowly lowered her weapon.

Acaelus had tried to run. He'd loaded the *Cavendish* with amarthite and planned his escape, planned to save his family, and though it would have left all the rest of humanity to *canus*, she understood the impulse.

He hadn't made it. He'd succumbed to *canus*, but had never quite given up who he was at the core. *Canus* wasn't a hive mind. It was a melding, segments becoming whole. Naira could remember Captain Paison maintaining command over the other infected on Sixth Cradle, now. Remembered how they'd deferred to the captain, despite their touted equality. Some habits were nearly impossible for people to unlearn, even with an alien intelligence infecting their thoughts.

Acaelus expected obedience. He was used to easy command, and every single soul who ever worked for MERIT was used to giving it to him.

For the people who lived under MERIT, protocol was a matter of survival. Hard-coded into what it meant to be human. Even Naira, who despised the entire system, caught herself falling into old patterns. Stopping herself just short of bowing to Tarquin. Biting her lips before a non-ironic *my liege* could slip out.

Canus may have been able to control him early on, but in folding Acaelus Mercator into their broader union, *canus* had made itself subservient to his will, above all others. Acaelus was still building a ship. Still trying to flee with his family.

Naira approached the twin chairs, noting the simulation crown discarded on the seat beside him. Her first charge. The man she'd sworn her life to guard. The man she'd died for. The man she'd believed in, even when she saw the cruelty. Even when she knew that, to Acaelus, nonfamily were nothing but tools to be used.

A man so accustomed to being the manipulator, he'd never dreamed he could be manipulated, too.

Naira couldn't fix this. She'd never liked Acaelus, but if she'd known the truth, she wouldn't have left him to struggle against *canus* alone.

Peaceful. Happy. He looked all of those things under the crown. In eight years she'd never seen him express those emotions unless they were in fleeting bursts.

She could kill him. There was no one here to stop her. Without his mind domineering the others, they might be able to push back against the infection. His command keys would die with him, and if this was truly a ship built to Mercator specs, then Tarquin's would move up in the line of succession.

Naira knew those keys, thanks to Kav's hack and her cracked mind bringing all her sloughed memories back. She'd have to kill Canden, too, if her keys still worked, but then she could use Tarquin's keys to override the ship's systems. Shut down the warpcore, call Kav and tell him it was over. Jonsun didn't have to fire on the *Sigillaria*.

It would never be that neat. She knew that. The second Acaelus died and his mind released the *canus*-bound, there'd be a battle. People would die. She was likely to be one of them.

Naira had wanted Acaelus Mercator's blood on her hands for a very, very long time.

She picked up the discarded simulation crown and ran it between her fingers.

"What are you doing?" Helms asked.

I said no, Sharp.

I'm still not letting you kill those people.

Naira sighed and sat in the abandoned chair. "My job. Give me ten minutes, E-Xs."

They nodded warily, and Naira slipped the crown over her head.

She was in no garden she'd ever known to exist. Trees heavy with flowers bowed over gravel paths gleaming with pieces of sea glass. A pale blue sky shone above, clouds meandering by to cast lazy shadows upon the heads of flowers so numerous Naira couldn't name them all. Children's laughter rang in the distance. Naira followed the sound to an intersection in the path, where a small courtyard waited with a fountain in the center.

Acaelus sat on the edge of that fountain, hands laced together, leaning forward with his arms braced on his thighs. Naira was struck by

how often she'd seen Tarquin assume that same pose when he was interested in something. Acaelus wore a pale blue button-up and white slacks.
Naira had never seen him out of Mercator green.

"You're not supposed to be here," he said without turning his head.

"Neither are you."

She crossed the courtyard and sat beside him. He faced a shimmer-
ing green field studded with wildflowers. Leka, maybe in her thirties,
screeched laughter as she bolted through the field, running from her
mother, who was playfully trying to steal the kite string in her hand. A
small child with shaggy blond hair crouched in the grass by the nearby
picnic blanket, digging a hole with a stick. Naira smiled. Tarquin hadn't
been old enough in this memory to request his body be printed to better
suit him, but she recognized him anyway.

Naira lined up the ages with the dates, and a slow shudder rolled
through her. This was Second Cradle. This was the visit when Canden
had brought the shroud to kill Naira's first home. Naira had been seven.
Tarquin must have been four.

Naira would not let Canden kill her second home, too.

"I wasn't here for this," Acaelus said. "This is Canden's memory. I
don't even know where I was at the time."

"My liege, I . . ." Tarquin dug something out of the ground and held it
up in triumph. Canden applauded uproariously. Naira's chest tightened.
"I failed you."

"We were all played," Acaelus said. "It's over, isn't it? I can feel them,
the infected, at the periphery of my thoughts."

"Almost," Naira said.

A shaking breath rattled out of him. "I wanted to make it perfect. For
all of them. I wanted to delete the bad memories, stitch myself into the
good ones. I should have been here. I saw no reason I shouldn't make
that want a reality."

"You made copies of their good memories and combined them into
one map?"

Naira watched Canden laugh and play with her children, and wondered
if Canden had been truly happy in this moment, as Acaelus believed. She'd
come here to kill this world, after all. You could never tell what someone's
inner world looked like from the outside.

"It never quite worked," he said bitterly. "So you see, I can't leave the simulation. This is where they're happy. This is where I'll stay."

"It doesn't work that way. You can't cut out the bad and expect to have a person left at the end. What about Lockhart? I know you gave her my muscle memory."

"I required a defender who wouldn't betray me."

That stung. "And her personality?"

"Irrelevant. Once I had you on ice, I was free to repurpose your skills without accidentally cracking her. If I was to bring Canden back, she would need the finest exemplar, and you were no longer reliable."

She clenched her jaw, remembering how easy it was to loathe him. "Canden is controlling Lockhart against her will."

"Canden uses what she likes. I deny her nothing."

"That's barely her anymore, and I think you know that. I think that's why you're in here watching old memories instead of making her wear the crown beside you."

"Get out," he said.

"No. You don't give me orders anymore. I'm here for your command keys, Acaelus. I can stop this."

He barked a laugh. "You've lost your mind, Sharp. Why would I ever give my keys to anyone, let alone you?"

"The *Cavendish* has weapons locked onto this ship and will fire if I don't call them to tell them the ship is no longer under the control of *canus*."

He scoffed. "You expect me to believe such a thing? I disabled the weapons on the *Cavendish*."

"Kav Ayuba has taken control of the HCA's anti-bombardment stations."

He looked at her for the first time, surprise lifting his brows. "You're bluffing."

"I'm not."

"Even if it's true, if you move to commandeer this ship, *canus* will stop you. It holds thousands of people in its thrall."

"But you hold them in thrall, too, don't you? I've seen their faces. They're happy. Like you. You've said you can sense them, and I think you can hold them in place, too. Keep them from fighting back until we can help them."

He returned to watching his family. "You ask me to leave my joy behind to hold on to all those slippery, befouled minds on your behalf, on the off chance that I might be successful in controlling them, on the *presumption* that you can get control of the *Sigillaria*. Need I remind you the ship itself is infected?"

"I know you. Your command keys override the ship's AI, don't they?"

He licked his lips. "I see no reason why I should abandon my happiness for your half-baked plan. Even if this ship is destroyed, my mind is in a larger distributed network. I hardly think I'll notice."

"Your son is here, my liege. On this ship. He's infected, but he's not gone yet, and Canden isn't in this simulation right now because she's busy running him through another one, trying to pry the location of the *Cavendish* out of him. Tell me, which matters more to you: this memory, or the real man?"

"She wouldn't."

"She is *not* herself, and you kn-know-know that. Fuck."

Acaelus startled and eyed her again. "You're cracked. I can't possibly trust anything you have to say."

She pinched the bridge of her nose between two fingers. "I don't even have to be here, you self-righteous prick. I'm trying t-to-to give you a *chance* because Tarquin hates it when I kill people, and with your keys I can attempt to do this without bloodshed."

"Spare me, Sharp. You're not working on behalf of my son. You only ever saved him to save yourself. You need my keys to do whatever it is you Conservators are planning, and you won't have them."

Naira stared hard into hazel eyes that were far too close to Tarquin's for her liking, and rattled off the entirety of Tarquin's command keys. Acaelus's lips parted in shock.

"He told you," he said, bewildered.

"He did. I don't need you. I want to work with you, my liege, but if you won't give me what I need, then I'll kill you and Canden and wait for the software to register your print deaths so I can use his keys instead. It'll be messier, *canus* will fight me, and I was hoping you might want to do the right thing and hold them back until we can cure them, so they don't have to die terrified and risk cracking."

"He does love you." Acaelus let out a short, sharp breath and turned back to his family. To the little boy grubbing in the dirt. "I wasn't sure. Do you share his feelings?"

They'd been together for such a short time. But with all her memories back, and with everything she'd felt on Sixth Cradle layering over the affection that'd grown between them recently, she couldn't deny the truth. She didn't want to. Still, Acaelus really wasn't the person she wanted to admit this to for the first time. "I do."

"Ex. Sharp, my daughter-in-law." He chuckled. "The boy never ceases to surprise me."

"I'm only his sanctioned partner for the moment." She wondered why the hell she'd said *for the moment.*

His head whipped around and he regarded her with concern, which unsettled her. Acaelus had never shown her an ounce of worry before. "But you've cracked."

"Yes. But I'm holding."

He examined her and said nothing.

"I don't have a lot of time," she said. "You asked me to protect your son. I am. Help me."

"Very well, Liege Naira." Her stomach knotted, but she didn't correct him, knowing he meant it as an olive branch. He extended a hand to her. She shook it. "I'll hold them for as long as I can."

"Thank you."

He recited his keys to her, had her repeat them back. Naira had no trouble existing in two places at once, and her physical body reached for the simulation crown. Hesitated.

"You should know," she said, "that I suspect one of your finalizers killed you to make you forget telling me about the shroud."

"I'd always wondered... You seemed so certain, but I recalled nothing of the sort. Why did they do such a thing?"

Naira watched the scrawny child in the grass play. "He worked for *canus,* and he knew me. He knew I took my oath seriously, and that if I saw signs of the infection in you, I would investigate. That the shroud's origin would eventually lead me to what Canden had done, and why."

"I've no doubt the man was correct. You, at my side, would have been devastating to *canus.* Imagine," he said, "what we might have accomplished together if he hadn't interfered."

The little child laughed and ran, for no discernible reason, just for the joy of it, and Naira thought back to who she'd been before. Thought of all the endless cruel, petty things Acaelus had done or ordered her to do, and how she'd rationalized them all, because no matter how many times she was hurt, being his exemplar had been safe in the only way that mattered. Her own room, consistent food, her phoenix fees prepaid. The chance, however slim, that her mother might come back.

Naira looked at the person she'd been, scared and hardened and becoming cruel herself, and didn't recognize her anymore.

"I don't think we would have done anything good."

She removed the simulation crown.

"What happened?" Helms asked.

"He's going to hold them back," Naira said. "I think...I think we might win this thing without a fight."

SIXTY-EIGHT

Tarquin

The Sigillaria | *The Present*

His mother led him through halls filled with staring, blank eyes, or bodies working as the misprints had, building and moving with mindless persistence. She told him these things were temporary. She told him that the work had to be done for them to escape. That the dead-eyed people were an interim measure. They'd been gentled to take the fear away and as soon as they got somewhere safe, they'd be released from the hypnosis.

As soon as his mother had the *Cavendish*, she'd cure them all.

Lies meant to soothe him. To make him compliant. She pulled him along, and Tarquin knew he was falling apart. Naira's final gift to him, the serum that held *canus* off for so long, was failing, and he was failing with it, mind fuzzy and dreamlike in the way it had been when his infection had been at its peak.

There was nothing he could do. It was like seeing a supernova and knowing the event had already happened. The light was just finally catching up with you.

Canden led him to the engine bay, though he didn't recognize it at first. The air clung to his skin, hot and thick with moisture. At the end of the walkway he found not a warpcore consumed in *canus*, but a garden.

She'd covered the floor with soil, loose and damp. It compressed and slipped beneath his feet.

She pulled. He followed.

Thick vines coiled over the walls, draping flowers heady with pollen, and if there was a touch of silver threaded through them, they were still beautiful. Behind the override console, the unmoving prints of Leka and the other, empty Tarquin stood. Their eyes followed him, but otherwise they didn't react. Fear coiled through him. Instincts not his own snuffed that fear out.

Canden led him to the override console and released his hand, and waited.

Tarquin didn't know what she wanted of him. He knew only that he wanted to please that expectant, hopeful smile. He took a hesitant step across the slippery earth and found, waiting on top of the console, a small metal object. A toy, really. That's what his father had always called it.

He picked up the dormant body of Pliny the Metal and ran the worn and scratched chassis through his hands. It awakened at his touch, flexing its legs to test its movement. Agony wrapped his heart, seeing the dried blood flaking from the joints, the strain in the metal where the leg had bent, and Naira had bent it back.

It was his. Acaelus had sent ships to Sixth Cradle and brought Pliny back, along with the real map of Tarquin's mother. He looked at the thing that thought it was Canden Mercator and knew that it was all that was left of her.

Tears slid down his cheeks and he didn't know why, because he was happy, wasn't he? This was real. His mother was back.

She grasped his face in her hands and drew him close. "Tell me, sweetheart. Tell me where the *Cavendish* has gone."

"I don't know." He wanted to tell her, he did, but he had no idea.

Her fingers flexed, denting the sides of his face. "Try harder."

SIXTY-NINE

Naira

The Sigillaria | *The Present*

Naira wasn't certain which was more surprising, that Acaelus kept his word, or that it was working. Peeking through the doors, they confirmed he held the infected back. Even those who'd been hard at work on the ship stopped mid-movement, frozen in time, their eyes wide, a furrow between their brows as if every one of them were concentrating.

She supposed they were. Acaelus's infectious bliss was gone, leaving nothing but the strain of one will against the instincts of a species they scarcely understood. If *canus* fought back, she couldn't tell. Acaelus's will had been forged in the crucible of over a hundred years of command. He would not falter.

Even Lockhart stopped moving.

"What's wrong with her?" Helms asked.

Naira approached the other exemplar and touched her arm gently. She didn't react, her face drawn into the same furrow of concentration as the others. "Looks like she got caught in Acaelus's hold, too."

"Can we do anything?"

"For now, we make sure she's as comfortable as she can be. Here, help me m-move her."

Lockhart was unsettlingly easy to march to the chair beside Acaelus.

Naira tossed the leftover simulation crown aside, making space for Lock-hart to sit. When she was settled, Naira pulled the sidearm from the woman's holster and passed it to Helms without a word. She didn't like disarming Lockhart, but if she woke up not herself, Naira wanted a chance to talk her down before she started shooting.

Naira leaned close and hoped the woman within could understand her. "I don't know if you can hear me, E-X. I have to get to the engine bay. I have to save this ship. But I'll be back for you, I swear it. You're not alone. Whatever happens, you'll get your peace, if you want it. And your revenge, if you want that, too, but I need Acaelus alive for a little while to hold the infected back."

She waited, but there was no reaction. With a sigh, she patted Lock-hart's arm and moved away, making for the door. Naira looked back over her shoulder, and really wished she hadn't.

Lockhart wasn't her, but she was close enough, and for a flash Naira saw herself in that chair instead, eyes blank. Acaelus's stalwart defender, used up at last.

"You okay?" Helms asked.

"Yeah, just...seeing ghosts of alternate timelines."

Helms gave her a strange glance, but led the way out of the command deck. There were more infected clogging the hallways the closer they drew to the engine bay, standing stock-still, staring at nothing. Naira didn't look at them. She clenched her jaw. She pushed forward.

"They're like trees," Helms said, breathless.

Naira stumbled, seeing the dead forest on Sixth Cradle instead of the stairs into the engine bay. Helms caught her. The junior E-X found a piece of piping left over from construction and handed it to her to use as a makeshift walking cane. Naira smiled her thanks, unable to muster up the words. Everything hurt. Her prints had never failed her like this before, and she tried not to think about what it might mean. Just a little farther. Just to the override.

Seeing Tarquin stopped her cold.

Canden clutched Tarquin's face so hard blood seeped from beneath her fingernails, her face contorted in frustration. Rage boiled away the shock that'd frozen Naira. She tugged the sidearm from Helms's holster, ignoring that woman's small grunt of protest, and leaned on her crutch as she leveled it at Canden's head. Her arm trembled from the weight of the weapon.

"Get your fucking hands off of him."

Canden peeled her fingers away one by one and wiped the blood on her thighs before turning to face Naira. Tarquin didn't react. The prints of Leka and an empty Tarquin stood behind the podium, flanking it, but Naira barely registered their presence. She was solely focused on the real Tarquin and Canden. There was still a spot of paint on Tarquin's sleeve.

"Ah, Sharp. I thought I sent Lockhart to take care of you."

"Aera let me go." Naira advanced slowly down the walkway.

"That one was always weak. I suppose she'll need more work to appreciate what it means to serve a family."

"Trust me, she knows what it costs." Naira stumbled and swore. Helms caught her elbow, keeping her from falling entirely.

"Look at you. You don't have the strength to fight me." Canden touched Tarquin's cheek gently, but the motion was stiff, as if she was pushing against something. "And I don't need you anymore. My boy will tell me everything I need to know."

Canden gestured jerkily for the empty prints of Tarquin and Leka to advance upon Naira and Helms. Her attention was so intent on the face of her real son that she didn't notice them fail to respond to her silent command. Canden seemed...remarkably focused.

"Tarquin doesn't know where the *Cavendish* is. I never told him," Naira said. "But you're right about one thing. I don't have the strength to fight you. I don't have much of anything left to-to give. But I don't have to fight you. Not this time."

Naira lowered the weapon, passed it back to a concerned Helms, and leaned on her pipe, waiting. Canden flicked a glance to the prints of the false Tarquin and Leka and frowned. "What are you two waiting for? Stop her."

Neither of them moved.

Canden narrowed her eyes at Naira. "What have you done?"

"The unexpected," Naira said. "I asked Acaelus for help."

"He denies me nothing. He wouldn't help you. Go on, children, grab those two, quickly!"

They could do no such thing.

Canden swore and stumbled as she turned back to Tarquin. Naira tensed, fearing she'd harm him in retribution, but she merely grasped the sides of his face once more. "Sweetheart, I need you to help me now, okay? I need you to stop those two from hurting me."

"Helms," Naira said, "restrain Liege Canden, please."

"Gladly," Helms said.

Canden tried to reel away, but Helms moved with speed and strength that gave Naira a pang of jealousy. Helms pinned Canden's arms behind her back and pulled her aside. Tarquin didn't move.

Naira took a moment, steeled herself, and then limped her way to that podium, scraping her cane against the ground with every step as Canden hurled insults at her, insisting Naira was nothing, a worthless traitor, a waste of flesh and relk.

She had to stand close to Tarquin to access the podium. Had to suffer feeling the heat of him against her, the warm, sandstone scent that clung to him always, as he stared past her with empty eyes.

"Sweetheart, stop her!" Canden shouted.

"No," he said, very quietly.

"But you're my son—" Her mouth froze, partway open. Acaelus's furrow carved a canyon between her brows. Emotional trauma made you susceptible to control. *Thank you, Fletch*, Naira thought with a bitter twist of irony.

Canden Mercator moved no more.

"Is she...?" Helms asked.

"Find something to tie her up with," Naira said, "who knows how long Acaelus can hold her. And gag her, please. I've heard enough of what that woman has to say."

Helms darted off to do as Naira asked.

Tarquin hadn't moved. Helms wasn't suffering the same degree of control as the others and she'd taken the same serum as Tarquin, but his locked-down body made it clear that he'd undergone enough trauma to make him vulnerable to control, too. She dropped the pipe to clutch the sides of the podium, unable to look at him.

It clattered to the ground. He startled. She made herself look into his eyes. Worry pinched his face, but he lacked the concentrating furrow of the others.

"You're not real," he said shakily.

"I am." Naira reached out, slowly, but not for him. She touched Pliny's head, the bot cradled in his hands. Pliny whirred approval. "I'm glad you found it. And I'm glad you found me again, too."

Tarquin looked from the bot to her and back, eyes misting. "You remember?"

"It's all up there, now." She tapped the side of her head. "Which is mostly a nightmare. But the parts with you . . . Those might be worth it."

"But, she said . . ."

"She lied. I'm here. I told you I'd come b-back. It just took me longer this time."

He clung to her, shaking, tear-damp face buried in the curve of her neck. The force of it crushed the air out of her and she gasped against a burst of pain. He released his grip, holding her gently instead. "Your pathways, I forgot—"

"Hold that thought. This isn't o-ov-over yet."

He nodded grimly. "What can I do?"

"Support me." She gestured to the pipe that worked well enough, but was awkward, heavy, and had dug into skin that wouldn't heal as quickly as it used to.

Tarquin wrapped an arm around her shoulders as she wrapped one around his back. He had to stoop, but they managed. The podium woke under her touch, projecting a login screen. Naira entered Acaelus's command keys and accessed the ship's control program.

The *Sigillaria*'s engines had been warmed up, prepared for a single, massive jump that would burn all their energy stores in one use, but could bring them within range of nearly anywhere in the known universe. They'd only been awaiting a destination. Waiting for Naira to give up the location of the *Cavendish*.

"I can't override this," Tarquin said. "My mother's keys outrank mine."

"Tarquin. Look again."

WELCOME, LIEGE ACAELUS was stamped at the top of the holo. He tensed at those credentials. She switched the engines from READY TO JUMP to STANDBY.

"How did you . . . ?"

"He gave them to me. To save you."

The weight of that pressed him into a stunned silence she didn't have time to help him unpack. Her mind was a slippery thing, and it took all her focus to remember how to call the *Cavendish*. But she got through. Made it work. And there was Kav's face in the holo, sweaty and strained and desperate.

"Nai. Oh, thank fuck, tell me you've done it. Tell me you stopped that ship."

"I've done it," Naira said. "I have the *Sigillaria*, and the infected are under control. Tell Jonsun to stand d-d-down."

Kav turned around and shouted for Jonsun. The golden-haired man appeared in the holo a few moments later, Kuma shuffling in behind him, and Naira wondered at the black eye yellowing on Kuma's face. About the argument she'd heard in the hallway before Kav had let her go. Tarquin squeezed her gently.

Jonsun filled the holo. She tried to find evidence of her friend's gentle determination, his quick smile and bright laugh, but all she saw was cool condescension.

"Nai," he said sadly, "look what they've done to you."

Tarquin flinched, but all her focus was on Jonsun. She knew she looked like hell. She didn't care. That serum was why Helms and Tarquin were still standing beside her, thinking for themselves, and she would have carved her pathways out herself if she'd been conscious when that choice had to be made.

"Stand d-d-down," she said. "I have the *Sigillaria*. The infected are under control. It's no threat to you."

"It has to burn, Nai. It was always going to be this way. That's why I wanted you with us."

She wanted to reach through the holo and strangle him. "*Everyone* in Sol is on this sh-ship or the stations in orbit around it. That's not just the infected. There are thousands of unprinted on those stations, scared out of their minds. *Kids*, Jonsun. Kids who weren't old enough to have their minds mapped. Those kids die, they're d-dead. There's no reprinting them."

There was no shock in him, no horror. If he'd already known, this conversation had been over before it'd begun.

"I don't plan on reprinting anyone from Sol. It's time to start over.

It's time to say goodbye to our old ways. To MERIT and the HC and relkatite, too."

"Don't d-do this. Don't destroy these people because you're scared their existence will undermine your bullshit utopia. You want to start over? *Good*. But we rebuild with everyone, *everyone*, or it's just another empire paid for in blood."

"You were the best of us once." He shook his head sadly. "There was a time when you'd pull the trigger yourself, and do it gladly. I'm sorry to have lost you, Nai."

The *Sigillaria* burst to life with lock-on alarms.

Naira switched the engines from STANDBY back to READY TO JUMP.

"Don't bother running," Jonsun said. "I have a lock on your transponder, thanks to this call. It'll take time for my weapons to reach you, it's true, but you can jump and jump until that engine burns out and you're just prolonging the inevitable. That ship has to burn."

Her hands trembled. He was right. This ship was made for big, long-haul jumps, not the tight maneuvering she'd need to engage in to evade whatever he had to throw at her. It could take months for his weapons to find her, but they'd always find her, eventually.

She could get clear of the stations to save them, at least, but this ship was destined for destruction. There was no safe place for the *Sigillaria* to hide. Except...

Naira knew precisely where the *Cavendish* was.

She had felt her place in time and space when she'd been double-printed more keenly than she'd ever felt being in a body before. They'd fixed the ship—it'd been warm at last—and they'd done the jump, made it to Seventh Cradle. They'd been in orbit there, and she knew precisely how long they'd been there, their altitude, speed, all of it. Naira inputted everything she knew, everything she sensed down to her bones. She made the *Sigillaria* do the calculations to adjust for time and drift and all the little things she couldn't account for, and jumped.

Alarms blared, the warpcore screaming at using all its reserves in one push, the proximity sensors screaming that they were too close to something enormous.

In the holo, similar alarms blared on the *Cavendish*, the ship alerting them that something very large and very unexpected was far too close.

Jonsun swore and started issuing evasion orders. Naira had been one step ahead, preparing for after the jump, and fired the *Sigillaria*'s capture grapples. The *Sigillaria* shuddered as the harpoons struck home, digging into the hull of the *Cavendish*. More alarms on Jonsun's side of things, breach alerts and jump warnings—if they tried to run, they'd rip the side of the hull off. She had them pinned. She had Acaelus's command keys. It was just a matter of time until the *Cavendish*'s systems were hers, too.

Jonsun turned back to her when the realization struck home, fury bright in his eyes. "You fucking bitch," he snarled.

Naira smiled, tired and small and sad. "You knew that when you hired me. Go ahead, Jo. Fire. Take us both out. Somehow, I don't think losing your own skin fits into your margin of acceptable losses."

He cut the feed in a fit of pique, but it didn't matter. She had Acaelus's keys. It took her a few fumbling tries, but with Tarquin's direction, she accessed the same menus he had when he'd jumped a ship into Mercator Station. She commandeered the *Cavendish* and turned off its weapons, then put a lock on its ability to jump.

Naira pulled back from the podium, shaking with the loss of adrenaline, and found Tarquin there, still holding her up. His arm was a little thinner than it had been before, but between them, they could stand.

"Is it over?" Helms asked.

Naira looked at the infected standing around her, petrified by the will of a man who saw none of those bodies as people anymore. Quite probably, he never had.

"No," she said. "I don't think this is going to be over for a very, very long time."

EPILOGUE

Naira

The Sigillaria | *Four Months Later*

Naira didn't reprint right away. She didn't use Chiyo's software to fix her map.

Jonsun's fervent eyes haunted her, his fanatical desire to wipe all the infected from the worlds a shadow hanging over her, daunting her. The man who claimed Jonsun's map wasn't the man she'd known.

The software had worked for Naira's mother, Tarquin had pointed out, but not very forcefully. Her mother had never lived while cracked, and Naira and Jonsun had, and there was no way to be certain if that fact alone would make the difference.

After the first few weeks, the living nightmare of her churning mind settled. Somewhat. Her bouts of repetition became rare, and while she would sometimes stop what she was doing and stare into space, locked in another place and time, those moments were manageable.

Naira wondered how many minds had been iced at the first sign of cracking who might have been able cling on, as she did.

When Tarquin brought another of the junior exemplars in the first wave from Sol to the ship to watch her more closely, she accepted her new security detail without comment. Naira could scarcely insist she could defend herself when she would break off mid-sentence and stare at nothing until roused back to herself.

Her detractors called her the Cracked Queen, and it only annoyed her that they'd called her *queen* at all.

She waited. Waited until the amarthite pathways were refined. Waited until they reprinted the first round. Waited until the boiling wars back on the stations in Sol ebbed, but did not cease.

Until Jessel contacted her, privately, for a meeting.

Naira didn't know what life was like on the *Cavendish*, though rumors crept through. They'd set up a hard connection between the two ships, binding them with more than the harpoons in the *Cavendish*'s hull.

Both sides of that passage were heavily guarded. Mercator personnel moved supplies back and forth, and brought back whispers of Jonsun having installed himself as some sort of tyrant. The people who lived on the *Cavendish*—the unionists and Conservators, Naira's friends—were too scared to say anything he'd view as a challenge, lest they draw his ire.

She heard nothing from Kuma and Kav, and sometimes, she looked back on the fragments she'd gleaned while semiconscious on the *Cavendish* and kicked herself for not doing anything when she'd been on that ship. Not that she would have accomplished much, having been freshly cracked and heavily sedated.

Jessel had sent her a simple message through an encrypted line they hadn't used in years, a date and location on the *Sigillaria*, and that was all. Tarquin worried it was a trap. Naira worried Jessel wouldn't make it through the hard connection. When the day came, Naira left her exemplars in the hall and waited in the narrow meeting room all day—sometimes drifting, but mostly in her present mind—as Jessel hadn't specified a time.

When the knock came, Naira startled out of a fog that'd captured her mind back in the ducts of the station she'd grown up on.

"Come in," she called.

She almost didn't recognize Jessel. They'd dressed all in black, loose-fitting clothes that hid the shape of their body, and had wrapped a dark blue shawl around the blond shock of their hair. They'd lost weight, face wan and yellowed with the beginnings of illness—print degradation, more than likely. Despite all that, it was Jessel who recoiled upon seeing Naira.

"So it's true," they said. "They cannibalized your pathways."

Naira gestured to a chair across from her, a pitcher of water on a low table between them, a view of the green-and-blue planet of Seventh Cradle through the window to her side, and wondered why she felt an echo of another time, in that moment. Naira pinched her thigh to help her focus on the present.

"I would have done the same in their position." She gave Jessel a wry smile, knowing that the scars that laced her face pulled her lips into a ragged twist instead.

Jessel settled into the chair and pushed their shawl back, torn between wanting to take in the extent of what had been done to Naira's print, and the hopeful splay of the living, breathing planet beyond the window. "Why haven't you reprinted?"

"You know why."

Jessel bit their lip. Drank water. Stared out the window. "Reprint," they said, "but don't use the software. Don't fix your map, if you can stand not to."

Naira closed her eyes, which was always a risk. Losing visual on the present was likely to send her mind wandering, but the confirmation of what she'd expected was a blow regardless. "What happened to him?"

"We don't know. The software worked as intended. There were no errors. It was completely successful. But that's not..." They cleared their throat. "That's not my brother anymore. It's like he...like he got someone else tangled in his mind. I don't know how to describe it. Sometimes I think I hear him talking to himself. He claims to see the future, a rebirthing of humanity without MERIT or the HC, and I'm not certain it's a metaphor."

"Thank you," Naira said, trying to be gentle, because Jessel looked absolutely shattered. "For telling me."

They returned her wry smile of earlier, and theirs was just as ragged, if for different reasons. "It's the least I can do after giving Jonsun that software. He hadn't started to show the change, yet. I had no idea he'd use it as permission to crack you."

Maybe they'd been too wrapped up in the joy of having Jonsun restored, but Naira had seen that change from the start. Had seen how his eyes were too bright, his words too insistent. He'd unsettled her before she could even say why.

She still couldn't say *why*.

"Is it *canus*?" she asked.

"No." Jessel shook their head firmly. "If it was, he would have immolated himself to destroy it. *Canus* has consumed him, but not in body. It's all he talks about, the focus of his loathing, and he makes sure to call it *Mercatus canus* every time, so that no one will forget who unleashed that thing."

"He's not wrong," Naira said.

"No, but you know what these reductive rallying cries do to groups of scared people. Hatred of *canus* is becoming hatred of Mercator, and it doesn't matter that Acaelus and Canden aren't at the helm anymore. They want Mercator blood. They'll take what they can get."

"We used to stoke that fire."

"I haven't stopped," Jessel said. "For the time being, Mercator under Tarquin's direction is essential to humanity's survival. But once this is over, once we're stable, Mercator—MERIT—all of them must be torn down and reimagined. For us to move forward we must be *better*. This chance cannot be squandered."

"I agree with you," Naira said, "but now isn't the time. Mercator alone has the reach, and the resources, to facilitate rebuilding. To stamp out the *canus*-bound on the stations and bring people back as themselves."

"Yes," Jessel said, "but Sharp, I've seen this. We've all seen this. Temporary totalitarianism doesn't unseat easily."

"Tarquin doesn't want his power. He wants to restructure."

"You better be damn sure about that."

"I am."

Jessel examined her for a long moment. "The other heads of MERIT disagree with you."

"What are you talking about?"

Jessel turned back to the window. "They're in shambles, all of them, and they resent Tarquin's default position at the head of them all. They see their power slipping away and they don't see the end of MERIT, they see the rise of Mercator beyond anything they could ever rival. He has a planet. A living planet, and they have broken stations and lean rations and guerrilla warfare with the *canus*-bound. They'll win those wars, eventually, and with their newly battle-hardened forces seek to take Mercator down a peg, if not unseat it entirely. Rochard has been smuggling weapons to us."

"That's idiotic," Naira said. "There's a single point of entry between the *Cavendish* and the *Sigillaria*. An attempt at an invasion would go nowhere, and we have control of both ships' weapon systems."

"It's only idiotic if Rochard wants us to succeed."

"You think they want unionist blood on Mercator's hands."

"On Tarquin's hands, specifically. His public image is too clean. They want to sow doubt, reveal his inexperience. Strip away the PR armor of him being some kind of savior."

Naira snorted.

"You're on the hit list, too, Sharp. Everyone knows what you did. You're inconvenient."

"Not the first time I've had a hit on me. What do Kav and Kuma have to say?"

"Those two are his right and left hand. They're not on board with everything, but they stay close. I suspect they're trying to keep him from going too far by remaining in his good graces, but I can't say for certain."

"Surely they've realized Rochard is setting them up." She couldn't keep the hurt out of her voice.

"They know. They're holding him back, for now, but the second Jonsun thinks he has an opportunity that looks promising, he won't hesitate."

"Why are you telling me all of this?" Naira asked. "The man you're describing would k-kill you for coming to speak with me, let alone divulging this level of information, sibling or no."

Jessel's shoulders sagged. "Because I'm here to defect, if you'll have me. Me, turning to Mercator for protection." They laughed roughly. "If you'd told me I'd do this six months ago, I would have said you'd crack—" They cut themself off. Naira arched a brow. They cleared their throat. "This is the only way I see to stop him. If I defect, Jonsun knows he's lost the element of surprise and he'll hold off a little longer."

"You're welcome here." Naira extended a hand, and they shook. "Mercator needs more people who hate it as much as we do."

They laughed and leaned back, posture loosening. "I wish I had better news for you about the Ichikawa software. I'll tell your techs everything I know, but I'm afraid it's not much."

"I'm grateful for anything you can tell us. But, now that you're under my protection, I feel comfortable telling you—you look like shit. Is your print failing?"

"It is. It's first-gen, like yours. Doesn't have the upgraded pathways."

"Well, then, allow me to engage in a little cronyism and get you reprinted."

"I don't want to strain your resources," they said.

Naira didn't have the pathways to support a HUD or holo anymore, so she had to use a physical comm device wrapped around her ear to call down to the printing bay to put the order through and arrange for rooms for Jessel.

"There. It's done. Ex. Cass will come to escort you when you're ready. We have plenty. No one settles for an inferior print on this ship."

"Except for you," Jessel said pointedly.

Naira rubbed her hip, where the integration pathway had been failing ever since she'd woken up on the *Sigillaria*. "I needed to know about Jonsun. No point in doing it twice."

"I thought you were loose with resources."

Naira's mind slipped and she clenched her jaw, holding back the words she'd said in her memory—Jessel in the printing bay on the Mercator shuttle, insisting reprinting Tarquin was a waste of resources.

When she sensed herself back in the *Sigillaria* again, Jessel had gone and Tarquin sat in their place, stroking the side of his chin, his gaze fixed on her. He was always there when she slipped for longer than a few seconds. Helms alerted him every time, and every time he dropped what he was doing and came running. She blinked, shaking herself. His eyes brightened, and he reached for her hands. She let him take them.

"There you are." His smile was warm and just a little sad.

"How long?" Her throat was sore from the effort of holding back the words she'd said in memory. Or maybe she hadn't held them back. She didn't want to know.

"Eleven minutes." He rubbed her hands as if trying to warm them, though she didn't feel cold.

The longest yet, neither of them was willing to say.

"You don't have to interrupt your work every time." It came out terser than she'd intended.

"I know. I want to be here when you come back."

Naira turned away, freeing one hand to probe at a scab on the side of her neck, and stared out the window instead of into those hopeful eyes. Steeled herself. "It won't get better."

She could hear him swallow. "Jonsun didn't have an error in his process, then?"

"No. Everything was green. No chance of failure. Jessel will talk to the map techs, but they don't know much more than we do."

"We'll figure it out," he said.

Naira said nothing. She didn't agree, and didn't want to ruin his hope, either.

"I'm a liability." The words were out before she could think better of them.

"Never." Tarquin circled her chair, then dropped to a crouch in front of her. "Do you really believe that?"

"I damage you politically. Jessel's just informed me that most of MERIT has a hit out on me, and that will drain resources further. You can't count on me for anything because there's no predicting when I'll go catatonic. You had to hire me *babysitters*. So, yes, I believe that."

"I don't." He took her hand to stop her from picking at the scab and laced their fingers together. "But since I'm certain that in your current mood heartfelt declarations will be brushed aside, allow me to counter you rationally. First of all, any person I chose as a sanctioned partner would damage me politically. You, in fact, being a free agent, so to speak, frees me from certain leverages other families of MERIT would attempt to deploy, if you'd been one of them."

"Tarquin—" She started to protest, but he held up a hand and put the punchably haughty Mercator mask on. It made her smirk, she couldn't help it, and a ghost of a smile slipped through his mask before he got it back on.

"To your second point, every high-ranking member of MERIT has multiple hits out on them. Something you *well* know, as an exemplar, so I dash that entire argument as being presented in bad faith."

She grunted. He grinned, then turned somber. "You are demonstrably reliable. Even cracked, you commandeered the *Sigillaria* without violence and thwarted Jonsun's attempt to destroy that ship, saving unprinted and printed lives alike. You are..." He cleared his throat. "You deserve so much more than even I can give you.

"As for your so-called babysitters, those are exemplars, a perfectly normal part of being adored by a head of family. And, again, I cast that argument aside as being in bad faith. Really, were you Acaelus's babysitter? Are you *mine*?"

"I'm no one's E-X anymore."

"Oh, bullshit. I saw your order to increase my security detail put through in the same moment you ordered Jessel's reprint. You can't stop yourself. And while it drives Cass and Caldweller up the wall, I find it rather charming."

"You couldn't let me sulk in peace, could you?"

"Not for a second. I'll outlaw it, if I have to. I can do that, you know."

She laughed a little, and he let out a breath that'd been so tightly held his shoulders rounded as it escaped him. He cradled her face in his hands and kissed her scarred lips. "I've been chasing that laugh ever since I first heard it."

Heat rose in her cheeks, a gentle soreness as it irritated the already tender pathways holding her together. "I'll reprint tomorrow, no repair software. I'm sure you're sick of looking at this mess of a print."

He pulled back, brushed the side of his thumb over the curve of her cheek, following the narrow ridge of one of her many scars. "It's not a mess. It's you. Though I confess to worrying about pathway degradation. How's your hip holding up?"

"It isn't," she admitted.

He frowned. "We can reprint you right now, if you'd like."

"No, I...need a minute." To sit with the disappointment of Jessel's news, to accept that when she woke up in new skin, she'd hurt less, but her mind was fundamentally changed.

"Ah." He examined her, and she couldn't discern what sort of conclusion he'd drawn. "In that case, allow me to show you the progress we've made regarding building sites on Seventh Cradle?"

His brows lifted, hopeful, and she couldn't help but smile and nod. Listening to him when he talked about his work was a balm to her doubts, always. Even if she had to slow him down to ask a thousand questions, his enthusiasm was infectious.

Colorful light filled the room, spilling from a holo in the ceiling. He stood and paced around the projection of one of Seventh Cradle's landscapes, going on about tectonics and floodplains and proximity to quarries with stone suitable for building, lumber, clean water, arable land, and potentially useful mineral deposits. She leaned back and let it wash over her.

"If my preliminary surveys are correct, and I have no reason to doubt them, once we're guaranteed shroud-free and set up the initial outpost, we could build a home here. That is, if you like the location. Or even like the idea at all."

Naira blinked, pulled out of the reverie of his presentation, and leaned forward to better see the lot of land he'd chosen. Green grass studded with flowers stretched in all directions around the curve of a broad river, the gentle slope of hills in the distance, a wide strip of forest separating it from the spot he'd identified as ideal for the initial settlement.

Living on Seventh Cradle. She'd planned on going to the planet with the rest, to help set up the outpost and maybe work with her mother in kickstarting the local farming efforts, but a home...A house built for them?

She looked up and found him pink in the cheeks and shifting his weight from foot to foot.

"Won't you have to return to Mercator Station?" she asked.

"Well." He rubbed the back of his neck. "For a little while, yes. But once things are stable, we could have this. If you want it."

She stared at that silken patch of sun-soaked grass, and thought of Acaelus watching his family in the meadow, but her mind didn't slip. It was just an impression. Tarquin digging in the dirt. Acaelus, mourning what he'd lost.

The truth she'd told Acaelus, and the words she hadn't yet been able to share with Tarquin.

It had never occurred to her that she could have such things. Even in her wildest imaginings as a child, in which she'd dreamed her mother back to life, they were never on a planet. They were scraping by, making a living on a station, but together.

"It's perfect," she all but whispered.

He huffed out a relieved sigh. "There's one more thing. It's embarrassingly late, but..."

She peeled her gaze away from the projection and he closed it out, kneeling before her chair, and rummaged in his pockets. "There's this tradition in my family, and admittedly most of Mercator traditions are terrible, but this is . . . It's important to me."

"Then it's important to me."

His eyes crinkled with his smile and he pulled a slim box from his pocket. "Usually we declare our intentions to sanctioned partners with a piece of jewelry. More often than not, a pendant, but considering your physicality, I thought that might get in the way, so I, well . . . I hope it's okay."

He opened the box and looked away, apparently too nervous to watch her reaction. A rounded rectangle of cinnabar stood in the center of a synthetic leather bracelet, the red surface carved with a deft hand to represent the cliff Naira spent her nights on whenever she was on Earth with one slight modification—instead of a single log by the fire, the one she kept for herself alone, there were two.

She was speechless for a moment that dragged on long enough to make him fidget with nerves. "I love it," she said quickly, before he could get the wrong idea. Then, before she could lose the nerve herself, "And I love you."

Tarquin turned back to her, stunned, and it was her turn to squirm as the silence stretched, a fluttering in her stomach twisting her up. It was only seconds, but it felt like lifetimes. And then he kissed her as deeply as he dared, considering the damage done to her print. When they parted, he brushed his cheek against hers.

"I love you," he said. "As you must have known. Thank you for being the one to say it. I didn't dare push—"

She cut him off with a kiss. "I know."

Tarquin picked up the bracelet and cast the box aside. He fit it over her wrist with care. "I think it's low profile enough not to get caught on anything, but if it gets in your way, say the word and I'll figure something else out."

"I don't want anything else. Who carved it? I'd like to thank them."

"Oh. Ah." He scratched the back of his neck again. "Me."

She fisted the front of his shirt and pulled him into a fierce kiss. He grunted in surprise. When she let him go, a grin split his face. "I should carve you things more often."

"How did you find the t-time?" She ran her fingertips over the subtle grooves in the stone.

"Here and there, since we've been on the *Sigillaria*. It's an old hobby of mine. The cinnabar is from one of the sample crates brought up from Seventh Cradle, in fact."

"I thought it was dangerous?"

He shrugged with a shy smile. "So are you."

Her thoughts scattered, and not due to being cracked.

"Here." He extended a hand to her. "The planet's about to turn to the settlement location. Let me show you."

Naira let herself be helped to her feet, and though her hip threatened to give out, he hooked his arm around her back, steadying her as they approached the window. He tightened his hold when she leaned her weight into him to take the strain off her leg.

Tarquin pointed out mountain formations, freshly named, and explained the various ways he believed they'd been made, described the tracks of glaciers across the planet's crust, and the scars those goliaths had left behind. When the world turned a touch more, he found the almost imperceptible stretch of grass where the settlement and their home would be someday.

It'd take time. They'd have to reprint everyone in amarthite. Scour the ships to clean away every spore of *canus* and shroud. But the hope of that green world was on the horizon, within reach at long last.

"We did it," he said, and held her close. "We have humanity's future back."

Naira remained unconvinced the threat was over. The embattled stations and Jonsun's frenetic eyes drew her away from basking in triumph, but she decided to indulge in the fantasy of victory.

Decided to make some space in which she could breathe.

The story continues in...

Book Three of The Devoured Worlds

Keep reading for a sneak peek!

ACKNOWLEDGMENTS

A great many people helped me to develop Naira and Tarquin's story. Thank you to my husband, Joey Hewitt, for his endless support. To my beta readers, Tina Gower and Karina Rochnik, for your valuable insights. And to my dear friends Andrea Stewart, Marina J. Lostetter, Laura Blackwell, David Dalglish, and Essa Hansen, who listened while I rambled endlessly about this project.

Thank you, too, to those writers' groups that have sent strength to my sword arm and offered community: the Isle, the Bunker, and naturally, the crew of the MurderCabin.

Thank you to my publishing team, Brit Hvide, Bryn A. McDonald, Angelica Chong, Kelley Frodel, Ellen Wright, Emily Byron, Anna Jackson, James Long, Lauren Panepinto, Angela Man, and Jaime Jones. And of course, all the lovely booksellers out there who helped this story get into reader hands.

A huge thank you to my agents, Chris Lotts and Sam Morgan, and everyone at the Lotts Agency, for their tireless support.

And special thank you to the geologists behind *The Geology Flannelcast*: Chris Seminack, Jesse Thornburg, and Steve Peterson.

And most of all, thank you, readers.

extras

orbit

meet the author

Joey Hewitt

MEGAN E. O'KEEFE was raised among journalists and, as soon as she was able, joined them by crafting a newsletter that chronicled the daily adventures of the local cat population. She has worked in both arts management and graphic design, and has won Writers of the Future and the David Gemmell Morningstar Award. Megan lives in the Bay Area of California.

Find out more about Megan E. O'Keefe and other Orbit authors by registering for the free monthly newsletter at orbitbooks.net.

About the Author

if you enjoyed
THE FRACTURED DARK

look out for

BOOK THREE OF THE DEVOURED WORLDS

by

Megan E. O'Keefe

Look out for Book Three of The Devoured Worlds.

ONE

Naira

Naira rolled up her sleeve and placed the cold nub of an injector against the interior of her arm. The golden glitter of her pathways obscured the dark tracery of her veins, but Dr. Bracken had assured her that she didn't need to hit the vein precisely for the medication to work. She took a breath. It was fine. She'd done this before.

The injector clicked. Heat burned through her veins, diffusing with the speed of her racing heart. Soft cotton swaddled her thoughts. Her vision dithered around the edges.

Naira snapped the cap back on the injector and slipped it into her pocket, then rolled her sleeve down. Her skin was insensate beneath the brush of her fingertips. That was normal. It would pass.

Tarquin cupped her cheek. She blinked, letting the contact ground her. After the injection, his touch made the world feel real again.

"Okay?" he asked.

"Yeah." Her lips were numb, the words slow. That would fade, too. The side effects were always temporary. "I'm fine. Let's go."

He searched her face for a moment. "You're certain? You don't have to do this with me."

"Bit late to back out now. I took the injection. I'm not going to waste it."

"Then let's get it over with."

Tarquin kissed her, and she wasn't sure if he was trying to reassure her or himself. Quite probably both.

Cass and Caldweller flanked Tarquin while Diaz and Helms closed around Naira. She let her hand drift to the weapon strapped to her thigh. Despite the fact she wasn't, technically, an exemplar anymore, Naira still attended all formal events in her armor. The extra protection couldn't hurt, and it reminded people of what she was. Made them hesitate before they whispered behind their hands that she was cracked.

"They're ready for you, my liege," Caldweller said.

Tarquin nodded. Naira braced herself. The door slid open, and Naira had never been more grateful for the numbing fog of the memory suppressant.

It wasn't a warpcore. But it was close enough.

The powercore that would provide energy to the first settlement on Seventh Cradle dominated the room beyond. Ribbed in the dull green of amarthite, the sphere punched a hole of emptiness into the center of the room. Those void-mouth globes, whether installed on ships to facilitate warp jumps or used on stations and cities to generate power, always made her skin prickle. Made her feel like she was being watched.

The ceiling loomed above, vanishing into darkness. Naira locked her face down as she followed Helms, focusing on her exemplar. On Tarquin. On the subtle scent of greenery in the air—air that lacked the metallic edge of station recyclers. Grit crunched beneath her boots from dirt tracked in by the spectators that ringed the powercore at a safe distance.

Her vision blurred. The strongest memory she had—walking across a hangar to the decoy ship that was meant to go to Seventh Cradle, the ship she'd blown up with Tarquin, the one she saw in her dreams, because she'd been forced to make that walk over and over again during interrogation—roared to the surface. It threatened to drown her, to rip her back into the past.

Naira tightened her jaw. On the edge of the crowd, her mom caught her eye and smiled. Dr. Sharp hadn't been anywhere near the hangar that day. The stifling blanket of the medication washed over Naira's thoughts, muting the screaming memory that her cracked mind was certain was the genuine moment. When she came back to herself, she'd missed only a single step. No one seemed to have noticed.

"Friends." Tarquin stopped behind a console podium that faced the settlers. "For the last year, you have made incredible progress in establishing our fair settlement here on Seventh Cradle. Today, I am pleased to share with you that construction has finally finished on our powercore."

Naira felt the excitement in him, radiating off every crisp syllable, and smiled to herself as she took up position along the side of the powercore. Helms caught her eye. Naira nodded. She was fine. The memory suppressant was holding. While Tarquin had been right—technically, she didn't have to be here—her absence would have been remarked upon.

People already called her the Cracked Queen. If she'd been missing, it'd be a weakness worth remarking upon. For her own safety, she needed to keep the triggers that could get her trapped in a memory as quiet as possible.

She let her gaze wander up the side of the powercore, pretending to admire it, when a twist of inexplicable fear tensed her from within. The shadow of a face emerged on the matte surface of the core. A brown cheek, quickly turned away. Naira blinked, and it was gone.

The spheres weren't reflective. Must have been a trick of her overburdened mind.

Tarquin explained in more detail than his audience probably cared for how useful the powercore would be. She skimmed her eyes over the crowd.

There was a face she didn't know. A tan-skinned man with a scar running down the side of his cheek, intense brown eyes fixed on the powercore. Her mind was playing tricks on her again. There were only a thousand people in the settlement. She knew every one of them. There couldn't possibly be a stranger. She pulled up her HUD and ran a facial recognition query. Nothing.

Naira opened a chat line to the exemplars and tagged his face.

Sharp: I don't know this man, and he's not in the database. Tell me I'm hallucinating.

Caldweller: You're not.

Cass: Scrambling Merc-Sec.

Helms: Sharp, please assume spear formation.

Naira fell back a step as Helms and Diaz moved in front of her, the powercore to her right. She gritted her teeth, resisting an urge to step in front of Tarquin herself as Cass slipped unobtrusively to his side and angled their body to be prepared to shield Tarquin at a moment's notice.

Tarquin didn't miss a beat in his speech, though his exemplars must have alerted him. A ripple ran through the crowd. Merc-Sec, closing in on the unknown man. The man looked straight at Naira and smiled, tipping his chin briefly before he wended his way toward one of the side exits.

Caldweller: Merc-Sec is moving to secure that exit.

Naira bit the inside of her cheek. The man had seemed amused. Confident. Catching him was important, but that was the look of a man who had already accomplished his goal. She tilted her head back, scanning the ceiling, the walls, the other exits. There were no more strange faces in the crowd. Not a hint of anything amiss.

In the corner of her eye, that face swam into focus on the side of the powercore. Naira started to flinch away but stopped herself. She was looking for something odd, wasn't she? While it might be her mind on the fritz, seeing a disembodied cheek in the surface of a core was definitely strange.

It wasn't warped, like a reflection would be. It was as if someone was standing across from her, only that curve of brown cheek visible.

In the corner of her HUD, the exemplar channel filled with reports on the location of the stranger. He'd slipped past the cordon on the door. Merc-Sec was trying to keep their cool, but they were panicking. Tarquin drew toward the end of his speech, not cutting it off, but avoiding the extra flourishes he was prone to.

Naira ignored it all and focused on that face, on the tug on the side of its mouth, as if it were shouting. Those pathways...They were a muted streak of gold, but they looked familiar.

"E-X?" Diaz whispered, barely moving his lips so that the crowd wouldn't notice.

Right. The way she was staring at the core and ignoring the chat, she probably looked catatonic. She opened her exemplars' chat channel.

Sharp: I'm lucid. Give me a moment.

Diaz: Acknowledged.

Helms: Acknowledged.

Naira wiped all channels away and craned her neck, trying to figure out where the reflection would be coming from, or if it was some kind of holo projection. There was no source she could find. She looked back to the core, frustrated, and thought she saw a sand-crusted boot kick toward the bottom from within, at the amarthite rib.

She broke formation and crouched down beside the rib. They'd checked them all, but—there. On the edge facing away from the crowd was a slim black rectangle.

"Explosive device," Naira called out, interrupting what was probably a very nice set of closing remarks from Tarquin.

Diaz grabbed her shoulder and tried to pull her aside, but she shook him off. Shouting roared to life all around her, along with the panicked stomp of boots. Naira's thoughts were fuzzy, her memories intentionally repressed, but she didn't recognize that device. It was smaller than what the Conservators used. Precise. She glanced at the other ribs near her and saw nothing. A small detonation, then. That's all it would take for the powercore to break containment and wipe out the whole settlement.

"E-X," Diaz said. "We have to evacuate."

"You can't evacuate far enough," she said. "Check the other ribs."

"But—"

"That's an order."

Helms and Diaz were probably considering picking Naira up and carrying her out, but Diaz let out a frustrated grunt and sent Helms around to investigate the ribs while Naira examined the small device.

"Naira!" Tarquin shouted.

She glanced over her shoulder and found Cass and Caldweller with a hand on each of his shoulders, pushing him toward the exit.

Naira shook her head, waving at him to continue. It didn't matter if Naira died violently. She was already cracked. And she knew a thing or two about explosives.

Naira ran her fingers along the side of the device, where it touched the amarthite. Slightly tacky, the glue not yet set.

"Are we clear?" she asked.

"Clear," Helms and Diaz echoed.

Well, then. Whoever had planted this one didn't want to push their luck by planting others. Or maybe they hadn't had the time. Naira could find no seam in the box, no lights, nothing to indicate when it would blow or what it was connected to. She drew her knife and placed the tip against the sticky glue on the top.

Slowly, she levered it free. It was smooth and cool and fit in the palm of her hand. Naira eyed the cavernous ceiling, made a few brief calculations, and decided she didn't have the time to come up with a better plan.

"You two." She pointed at her exemplars with her knife. "Draw your weapons. I'm going to throw this as hard as I can over there." She pointed up to the place where the wall met the ceiling, lost in darkness. The direction away from the fleeing settlers. "Both of you need to fire on it, because I can't trust my aim right now."

Helms's brow furrowed. "That will bring the ceiling down. Maybe even the wall."

"Neither of which will break the powercore containment. We don't know when this thing will blow, so we don't have time for deliberation or to take it somewhere else. Can you do this?"

They drew their weapons and squared off. "On your mark," Diaz said.

"Duck behind the core for cover after you hit." Naira hurled the device with all her pathway-enhanced strength.

She held her breath as it arced into the darkness. Diaz and Helms aimed, the targeting lasers on their weapons painting sketchy lines in the dark. They waited. Waited. Waited until a fraction of a second before the device would have struck the ceiling.

"Mark," Naira said.

519

They fired in tandem. Naira couldn't say which one of them hit, but the results were immediate.

The blast stole her hearing, temporarily overwhelming those pathways until a muted whine filled her head. A flower of twisted metal bloomed outward from the ceiling, letting in the sunlight above. Smoke choked that light.

Metal groaned. Chunks of concrete foam struck the ground. The structure sagged inward, the ceiling and wall both leaning drunkenly for the powercore. Adrenaline burned through her medication too quickly.

Naira no longer thought she was in the powercore building. She was in a Mercator warehouse with Jonsun, Kuma, and Kav, shouting as the bomb they'd planted in a sector full of supplies went off too soon. Stinging smoke clogged her nostrils, a searing flash of heat beat against her skin, and the squeal of metal filled her senses.

Someone grabbed her. In memory, it was Kuma, clutching her arm to drag her away when the shock faded and they realized they needed to run. Pain burst through her knees, yanking her back into the present. Diaz had kicked her knees out and dropped her to the floor. He flung himself over her and wrapped his body around her as a human shield.

The impact hit, stealing her breath. Diaz jerked against her, chunks of concrete and metal bouncing off him. His arm tightened around her, and he grunted in her ear—a short, pained sound.

She wanted to tell him he was an idiot. That she could be crushed to bits and it didn't matter, because her mind was already broken. But it was too late for that, and so all she could do was make herself as small as possible until the chaos faded so that he could make himself small, too.

The impacts slowed. Diaz groaned. Naira twisted onto her back as he lost his balance—or maybe just his strength—and collapsed. Dust smeared his face, coated his armor. His eyes were open, but they were bright with pain.

"Diaz, you fucking moron, talk to me. How bad is it?"

He smirked at her, and that eased some of her panic. "Told you I'd get it."

"What?" Oh. The maneuver she'd taught him to shield a charge's vital points with the bulk of an exemplar's body. "Real bad time to learn."

A laugh rattled in his chest. "Fuck. Sorry. Broke some ribs. I don't think—I think it's broken bones and bruising."

Warm liquid seeped through her pants leg, proving the lie to his assessment of the damage. Naira eased him off her and onto his back.

The injury wasn't as bad as she'd feared. A piece of metal had sheared through his calf, showing bone beneath. Naira ripped his E-X kit off his belt, rummaging for medical supplies.

Helms extricated herself from a small pile of debris and rubbed her eyes clean before she found them. She locked eyes with Naira over Diaz's bloody leg, and her face slackened with fear. Naira gave her a subtle shake of the head—don't panic him by panicking yourself. Helms gathered herself before she crawled over and took his hand.

"Gabe, you fucking moron," Helms said.

He grunted. "That's what Sharp said."

"Then you know we're right," Helms said.

She kept him talking while Naira examined the wound. He was losing a lot of blood. Amarthite prints didn't heal as well as exemplars were used to, and his health pathways couldn't keep up. She wrapped the wound with gauze and pulled up her HUD. Tarquin was hammering her with call requests. She ignored him and opened the E-X channel—they'd tell him she was safe. Diaz didn't have time for Naira to soothe Tarquin first.

Sharp: Diaz needs medical, and he needs it yesterday.

Caldweller: Acknowledged. Doors are blocked with debris, but we'll get through as quickly as we can. Tarquin and your mother are secure.

Cass: The mystery man was killed in the wall collapse. No other potential enemies sighted.

Naira abandoned pressure on the wound for a tourniquet above the injury. Diaz hissed in pain as she pulled a strap tight. Not a good sign. His painkiller pathways weren't able to keep up.

"The doors are blocked," she said, "but help is coming."

"Thanks, E-X," Diaz said weakly.

He was unconscious by the time medical got through, but he was breathing. Naira rocked back to her heels, letting her bloodied hands dangle between her knees. The emergency team swooped him up onto a gurney and rushed him away with assurances that he'd been fine. He was alive, and even if he lost that leg, he hadn't died in the violence. Diaz was unlikely to crack if they determined reprinting was the best course of action.

Naira half listened. She knew all those things already. It didn't make watching his dust- and blood-smeared body being hauled away any easier. Helms assured the doctors that she was only bruised. Naira wasn't sure if she believed that, but she decided not to push the issue.

Tarquin rushed over the debris toward them, despite his exemplars begging him to be careful. He was dirty but unharmed. Naira stood and held her arms out to either side.

"I'm fine, I'm just a mess—" She grunted as he grabbed her and crushed her against him, smearing his expensive clothes with Diaz's blood. Naira sighed and wrapped her arms around him, giving up on keeping him clean. The medication dulled her emotions, too, and the strength of his fear and relief stunned her. "Tarquin, really, it doesn't matter if I die."

He pulled back and took her face in his hands, trying ineffectually to brush dust off her cheeks. "It matters to me. I thought—" He swallowed. Shook his head. "What happened?"

Naira pointed to the amarthite rib she'd found the device on. "We determined there was only one explosive, and I removed it, then threw it to the ceiling. I told Helms and Diaz to fire on it and dive behind the core for cover once they hit, but Diaz—" Emotion burst through the fog, forming a knot in her throat. She breathed slowly through her nose, trying to focus so that she wouldn't fall into her past again. "Diaz shielded me."

"I'll give the man a commendation." Tarquin combed a hand through her hair. She smiled at that. He always needed to touch her when he was shaken. To assure himself she was still here.

"He disobeyed orders," Naira said.

"With respect," Helms said, "they were shit orders that went against our training."

Naira scowled. "*I'm* your trainer."

"Precisely so, E-X." Helms couldn't stifle her small smirk before Naira saw it.

Something high in the rafters groaned. All of them eyed it warily.

"My liege," Caldweller said, "I suggest we retreat to a more stable location."

"Good idea," Tarquin said.

He took her hand and turned back to the passage they'd made in the debris, but Naira couldn't move. She'd been looking at Helms, watching her for any sign of distress beyond her bruises, when the side of that face appeared in the core once more. Appeared, and came fully into focus.

Naira stared at herself.

The other-Naira stood at formal rest, hands clasped behind her back, studying Tarquin as if she thought she couldn't be seen. There was love in those eyes. And sorrow, too.

Naira's mouth dried out. This variant of herself had shorn her hair, and a network of scars crowned her skull. A fine tracery reminiscent of the scars that'd draped her body when they'd taken her pathways to make amarthite serum.

That was no memory. No version of herself she'd ever seen. No moment sneaking up on her out of the recesses of her mind. Tarquin tugged gently on her hand. She scarcely noticed.

She wasn't slipping. Naira was perfectly aware of the world around her, and it was shock alone that narrowed her focus to that other version of herself. The other-Naira had been watching Tarquin, and as he turned to her so did those imposter eyes. Something like desperation clawed through the phantom, and she lunged at the interior boundary of the core, reaching, mouth opened wide with a shout.

Tarquin stepped in front of Naira and blocked her view. She swore and craned her neck to see around him, but her other-self had vanished.

if you enjoyed
THE FRACTURED DARK

look out for

THE STARS UNDYING
Empire Without End:
Book One

by

Emery Robin

Princess Altagracia has lost everything. After a bloody civil war, her twin sister has claimed not just the crown of their planet Szayet but the Pearl of its prophecy, a computer that contains the immortal soul of Szayet's god. Stripped of her birthright, Gracia flees the planet— just as Matheus Ceilha, commander of the interstellar Empire of Ceiao, arrives in deadly pursuit with his volatile lieutenant, Anita. When Gracia and Ceilha's paths collide, Gracia sees an opportunity to win back her planet, her god, and her throne... if she can win the commander and his right-hand officer over first.

But talking her way into Ceilha's good graces, and his bed, is only the beginning. Dealing with the most powerful man in the galaxy is almost as dangerous as war, and Gracia is quickly torn between an alliance that fast becomes more than political and the wishes of the god—or machine—that whispers in her ear. For Szayet's sake, and her own, Gracia will need to become more than a princess with a silver tongue. She will have to become a queen as history has never seen before—even if it breaks an empire.

CHAPTER ONE

Gracia

In the first year of the Thirty-Third Dynasty, when He came to the planet where I was born and made of it a wasteland for glory's sake, my ten-times-great-grandfather's king and lover, Alekso Undying, built on the ruins of the gods who had lived before Him Alectelo, the City of Endless Pearl, the Bride of Szayet, the Star of the Swordbelt Arm, the Ever-Living God's Empty Grave.

He caught fever and filled that grave, ten months later. You can't believe in names.

Three hundred years is a long time to call any place Endless, for one thing. Alectelo is no different, and the pearl of the harbor-gate was cracked and flaking when I ran my hand up it, and its shine had long since worn away. It had only ever been inlay, anyway. Beneath it was brass, solid and warm, and browning like bread at the edges where the air was creeping through.

"It needs repairs," said Zorione, just behind my shoulder.

I curled my fingers against the metal. "It needs money," I said.

"She won't give it," Zorione said. She was sitting on a nearby crate already, stretching out her legs in front of her. She had complained of her old bones and aching feet through every back alley and tunnel in the city, and been silent only when we passed under markets, where the noise might have carried to the street. "Why would she?" she went on, without looking at me. "*She* never comes to the harbor. Are the captains and generals kept in wine and honey-cakes? Yes? That keeps *her* happy."

I said nothing. After a moment she said, "Of course—it's not hers," and subsided.

I knew I ought to be grateful for her devotion. Nevertheless it was not a question of possession that stirred me, looking at the curling rust on that gate framing the white inlet where our island broke to the endless sea. Nor was it a question of reverence, though it might have been, in better times. It was the deepest anger I had ever felt, and one of the few angers I had never found myself able to put aside. It was the second time in my life I had seen the queen of my planet be careless with something beautiful.

"It wouldn't matter, anyway," I said, and let my hand fall. "This is quicksilver pearl. It only grows in Ceiao these days."

It was a cool day at the edge of the only world I had ever known. The trade winds were coming up from the ocean, smelling of brine and exhaust, and the half-moon-studded sky was a clear and cloudless blue. At the edge of my hearing was the distant hum of rockets from across the water, a low roar like the sound of the lions my people had once worshipped. I took it as an omen, and hoped it a good one. Alectelans had made no sacrifices to mindless beasts these past three centuries. But if Alekso heard my prayers, it was months since He had last answered them, and I needed all the succor I could get.

"How long until the ship?" I said.

I had asked three times in the last half hour, but Zorione said patiently, "Ten minutes," as if it were the first time. "If she hasn't caught it yet," and she made a sign against bad luck in the air and spit over her shoulder. It made me smile, though I tried not to let her see it. She was a true Alectelan, Sintian in name and parentage but in faith half orthodoxy and half heathenism, in that peculiar fanatical blend that every born resident of the city held close to their hearts. And though she carried all unhappiness as unfailingly as she carried my remaining possessions, I had no interest in offending her. She had shown no sign, as yet, of being capable of disloyalty. Still: I had so little left to lose.

The water was white-green and choppy with the wind, and so when our ship came skipping across the sea at last, it was only the sparks that gave it away, meandering orange and red toward the concrete shore like moths. At the very last moment it slowed and skidded onto the runway in a cloud of exhaust, coming to a stop yards from our feet.

My maid was coughing. I held still and listened for the creak of a hatch. When the smuggler appeared through the drifting grey particulates a moment later, shaven-headed and grinning with crooked teeth, Zorione jumped.

"Good morning," I said. "Anastazia Szaradya? We spoke earlier. I'm—"

"I know who you are," she said in Szayeti-accented Sintian. Her eyes took me in—cotton dress, dust-grey sandals, bare face, bare arms—before they flicked to Zorione, behind me. "This is the backer?"

I kept my smile wide and pleasant. "One of them," I said. "The rest are expecting our report from the satellite in—I'm sorry, was it three hours? Four?"

"By nightfall, madam," Zorione said, looking deeply uncomfortable.

I gave her an apologetic look behind the smuggler's back. If I had had a choice in who to play the role of the backer, I would not have chosen Zorione, who as long as I had known her had despised deception almost as fiercely as rule-breaking, and rule-breaking like blasphemy. But she knew as well as I did what a luxury choice had become for us. "By nightfall," I repeated. "Shall we board the ship?"

The smuggler narrowed her eyes at me. "And how long after will the pearls be sent to the satellite?" she said. "You said three days?"

I flicked my eyes to Zorione, who cleared her throat. "A week," she said. "The transport ship will bring them, if they find her safe and sound. *Only* if," she added, in a burst of improvisation. I rewarded her with a quick nod.

"A week?" said the smuggler. "For a piece of walking bad luck? Better I should be holding a bomb! Was this what we agreed to?"

Zorione's face went blank. "You know," I said hastily, "you're very right. Speed *is* of the essence. I would personally prefer to leave the system as soon as possible. Madam Buquista, might your consortium abandon the precautionary measures we discussed? I understand the concern that the army not trace the payment back to Madam Szaradya—of course the Ceians might trace it, too, and come to investigate her—but is that really *my* highest priority? Perhaps instead—"

The smuggler snorted. "Hush," she said. "Fine. Keep your precautions. *You*, girl, can keep your patience. Meanwhile"—she nodded at Zorione's outraged face—"when your ship comes for her, we discuss delay fees, hmm?"

Zorione looked admirably unhappy at this, and I would have nodded at her to put up a lengthy and losing argument, when there was a low, dull hum, akin to the noise of an insect.

Then the sky wiped dark from horizon to horizon. The sea, which had been glittering with daylight, flooded black; the shadow of the smuggler's ship swelled and swept over us, and we were left in darkness. The smuggler swore—I whispered a prayer, and I could see Zorione's silhouetted hands moving in a charm against ill fortune—and above us, just where the sun had shone and twenty times its size, the face of the queen of Szayet opened up like an eye.

She was smiling down at us. She was a lovely woman, the queen, and though holos had a peculiar quality that always seemed to make it impossible to meet anyone's eyes, her gaze felt heavy and prickling as it swept over the concrete and the sea and the pearl of the harbor-gate below. She had braided her hair in the high Ceian style, and she had thrown on a military coat and hat that I was almost certain had belonged to the king, and she had painted her mouth, hastily enough that it smeared at her lip as if she had just bitten into raw meat. Around her left ear, stretching up to her hairline, curled a dozen golden wires, pressed so closely to her skin they might have been a tattoo. An artfully draped braid hid where I knew they slipped through her temple, into her skull. In her earlobe, at the base of the wires, sat a shining silver pearl.

She said, sweetly and very slowly—I could hear it echo, as I knew it was doing on docks and in cathedrals, in marketplaces and alleyways, across the whole city of Alectelo, and though I had seen the machines in the markets that threw these images into the sky, though I had laid hands on them and shown them my own face, my breath caught, my heart hammered, I wanted to fall to my knees—

"Do you think the Oracle blind?"

She paused as if for a reply. There was none, of course. She added, even more sweetly, "Or perhaps you think her stupid?"

"Time to go," said the smuggler.

We scrabbled ourselves up the ladder as quickly as we could: the smuggler first, then me, Zorione taking the rear with the handles of my bags clenched in her bony fingers. Above me, the queen's voice was rising: "Did you think I would not see," she said, "did you think the tongue and eyes of Alekso Undying would not *know*? I have heard—I will be told—where the liar Altagracia Caviro is hiding. I will be told in what harbor she dares to stand, I will be told in what ship she dares to fly. You are *bound* to do her harm, all you who worship the Undying—you are bound to do her harm, Alekso wishes it so—"

Zorione, swaying on the rungs, made another elaborate sign in the air, this time against blasphemy. "Please don't fall," I called down to her. "I can't afford to lose you. But I appreciate the piety." She huffed and seized hold of the ladder again.

When we had all tumbled into the cramped confines of the ship, the smuggler slammed the hatch shut above my head, and shoved lumps of bread and a pinch of salt into our waiting hands. The bread was hard as stone and tasted like lint—it must have come out of her pocket, a thought I immediately decided not to contemplate—but I swallowed it as best I could, and smeared the salt onto my tongue with my thumb. The queen's voice was echoing even now through the walls, muffled and metallic. I heard *worship a lying* and *demand by right* and *suffer the fate*, and turned my head away.

The smuggler had gone ahead of me, through the bowels of the ship. I made to push past Zorione, but she caught my arm at the last moment, and stood on her tiptoes to whisper into my ear, "Madam, I'm afraid—"

"I know," I said, "but we knew she would only be a step behind us—we have to go." But she shook her head frantically, leaned closer, and hissed:

"What is the thief going to do to us when she finds out there isn't any consortium?"

My first, absurd impulse was to laugh, and I had to clap my hand over my mouth to stifle it. When I had myself under control, I shook my head and bent to whisper back: "Zorione, how can it be worse than what would have happened if we hadn't told her that there was?"

She let me go, her face pinched with worry. I wished I knew what to say to her—but I had a week to find an answer, and here and now I made my way through sputtering wires and hissing pipes through the little hallway where the smuggler had disappeared.

I found her in a worn chair at what I presumed to be the ship's only control panel, laid out in red lights before a dark viewscreen not four handspans wide. "How long until we're out of the atmosphere?" I said.

"It'll take as long as it takes," said the smuggler. "If you have any service complaints, you've got three guesses where you can put them."

Three guesses seemed excessive, but it was more munificence than I had been offered in months. "If I stand here behind you," I said, "will I be in your way?"

"You're in my way wherever you are," she said, and shoved a lever forward. Beneath us, the engines coughed irritably to life. "Don't go into the back, it's full of Szayeti falcon jars. Eighteenth Dynasty."

I would remember that. I let it settle to the floor of my mind for now, though, and tucked myself into what little space there was behind the smuggler's chair. We had begun our journey back across the water, bouncing over the flickering waves. The spray threw rainbows around us, so bright my eyes streamed, and my first warning that we had arrived at the launch spot and begun to rise was a hum in my ears, low at first and then louder—and then a pain in my head, as sharp as if someone had clapped their hands to my temples and squeezed. The smuggler was mouthing something—I thought it was *here we go*—

—and then the sky was fading, blue into colorlessness into a deep indigo and the ocean was shrinking below, dotted by scudding clouds. The floor of the ship shook, then coughed. My ears popped.

"Simple part done," said the smuggler. I was beginning to believe she liked having someone to talk to.

That, at least, I knew how to indulge. "Simple part?" I said, as bewildered as if I did not already know the answer. "What comes next?"

"*That*," said the smuggler, pointing with grim satisfaction. I allowed myself a moment of pride—it had been excellent timing— and looked past her pointing finger to where the Ceian-bought warship sat black and seething like an anthill in the center of my sky.

"We can't answer a royal customs holo," I said, making myself sound shocked.

"Wasn't planning to," said the smuggler. "Imperial pricks already gave the queen my face. Do you know, three decades ago, I flew six times a year through thirty ports from here to Muntiru without stopping to tell any man my name. Now every asteroid twenty feet across is infested with barbarians in blue, asking for the sequence of every gene my mother gave me." She paused. "Wonder whose fault that is."

It took a great deal of faith to attribute that kind of influence to any Oracle, let alone the Oracle she meant. But faith, unlike warships, had never been in short supply among the Szayeti.

"What will we do?" I said. "Speed through the army's radar?"

"Better," said the smuggler. "We outweave it. Hold on."

That was the only warning I got. In the back, I could hear Zorione yelp as the ship spun like a top, suddenly and violently. The smuggler shoved a lever forward, yanked it to the left, and pushed three sliders on the control board up to their highest positions. A holo had sprung to life on the dashboard, a glittering spiderweb of yellow lines delineated by a wide black curve at their edge. Within it was a single white dot: our ship, I guessed, and the edge of the atmosphere.

"What's that?" I said anyway, and let the smuggler explain. She liked explaining, and it distracted me, which I knew after only a few seconds I would badly need. Flying with the smuggler was not unlike being a piece of soap dropped in the bath. She might have lost control of the ship entirely and I would never have known the difference, except for the unwavering fierceness of her smile. "How many times have you done this?" I attempted to ask through rattling teeth as we swiveled and plummeted through empty air.

"At least twice!" she said with malicious cheer.

It was difficult to tell when we passed the warship. Certainly the smuggler did not seem to know. I think she must have thought that, were I sufficiently bumped and jolted, I would give up and go join my nursemaid in the back, but I hung on stubbornly to the back of her chair, and stared from the control panel to the viewscreen to the holo and back again, matching each to each in my mind. It was an old trick I had, when fighting off illness or pain or plain misery, to focus on something at which I felt very stupid, and learn each detail as if it were another tongue. At other times it had served me well. Now, hungry and tired and nauseous at once, it was more difficult, and by the time the ship turned one final time and settled into stillness, I was clinging to the smuggler's chair as if it were my father alive again.

The smuggler smirked. "Twenty minutes," she said. "New record. Hey," she added in Szayeti, mostly to herself, "maybe she carries good luck after all."

"I try to," I said, in the same language, and caught the flicker of her first true smile. Below us, I could see the broad white edge of the planet, beginning to shrink against the darkness. I had seen it from this distance only once before in my life.

My people are a people of prophecy. Long before Alekso Undying came from old Sintia to our shores, long before my ten-times-great-grandfather, weeping, bore His body from the palace at Kutayet to the tomb where I grew up, my people spoke with the voices of serpents and lions, falcons and foxes, who roamed this world and who saw the future written in blood. The people then said what was, what is, and what will be; and though Alekso's beloved and his descendants are their rulers now, and though they have had no god but their conqueror for three hundred years, they have not forgotten that they once told the future as freely as any queen. They never will.

The queen of Szayet had prophesied, these last eight months, that she was the only and rightful bearer of the Pearl of the Dead. She had prophesied herself the heir to the voice of Alekso our conqueror, the Undying who had died all those centuries ago. She had prophesied that her words were His words, and her words were the future, and that there was no future in them for Altagracia Caviro Patramata, father-beloved lady of Alectelo, seeker of the god and friend to the people, her only rival, her only enemy, her only and her best-beloved sister.

As the rust-green coin of Szayet receded before me, and the night crept in from every corner of the viewscreen, I leaned across the smuggler's shoulder and pressed my fingers to the glass as I had to the arch at the harbor, and I whispered: "I will see you again."

My sister had called me a liar today.

I am a liar, of course. But I meant to be a prophet, too.

orbit

Follow us:

f **/orbitbooksUS**

y **/orbitbooks**

▶ **/orbitbooks**

Join our mailing list
to receive alerts on our
latest releases and deals.

orbitbooks.net

Enter our monthly
giveaway for the chance
to win some epic prizes.

orbitloot.com